RB:
The Enchantress

by

C. C. Colee

AmErica House
Baltimore

ISBN: 1-59129-065-1
PUBLISHED BY AMERICA HOUSE BOOK PUBLISHERS
www.publishamerica.com
Baltimore

Printed in the United States of America

Chapter 1

Morgan awakened to the ship bell announcing the hour for the beginning of the first watch. With a yawn, he sat up and ran his fingers through his sandy-blond hair. It seemed he had just fallen asleep and now it was time for his watch. He got up from his bunk and lit the lantern, turning it down low. Looking over at his new roommate, he noted that she was on her side, facing away from him.

Quietly, he prepared himself for the day. As he picked up a clean shirt, Aubrey began to whimper in her sleep. He turned to look at her as she drew in a sharp breath and rolled over onto her back with a mournful sob. In her sleep the top of the shirt that she wore had come open, slightly exposing her. In the dim light Morgan caught sight of something on her skin and he moved closer for a better look. He clenched his teeth as the top portion of the mark on her upper left breast was visible. The loops for the R and the B were unmistakable and he knew immediately what he was seeing. His blue eyes shifted to his cabin door as though he could see through the wooden planks of the ship to Mala in her cabin. Now he understood Aubrey's comment from the previous day about there not being enough time in the world for Mala to accept her.

He was brought out of his thoughts when Aubrey began to whimper again. He reached out and lightly stroked her hair. "Shh, Miss Aubrey...it will be fine." He found himself saying quietly.

She let out a long mournful sigh then seemed to drift off to sleep. He sat gently stroking her auburn hair when a soft knock was heard at his door. Frowning at who could be summoning him at this hour of the morning, Morgan got up, pulled his shirt on over his head then opened the door.

Willie stood in the corridor, looking from side to side. When the door opened, the old man gave him a sheepish look and said, "Beggin' yer pardon, Mr. Alcott, but I need yer help in the galley."

Willie took a step back as Morgan stepped into the corridor and quietly closed the cabin door. "What is it, Willie?" Morgan asked as the two walked through the dimly lit corridor.

"Tis the Cap'n. She is, well..." The old man began hesitantly.

Morgan nodded in understanding and said with a sigh, "The *Widow Maker* is at the bottom of the cove with the captain and the crew."

"Aye, and she is worse this time 'cause of it, I be thinkin.'" Willie told him.

"I can imagine she would be." Morgan muttered.

They entered the galley to find Mala passed out from her drinking. One arm was stretched out across the table with her head resting on it, the long black masses of her hair cascaded over the side of the table. Her other hand was still holding a nearly empty tankard. Morgan could smell the rum as he looked down at his captain and sighed with understanding. Mala had been following the *Widow Maker* for as long as he had been a member of her crew. But now with Rene Black dead, what would she do? Though she had never admitted it, Morgan knew that Black was an important part of Mala's life. Why they were no longer together was a mystery to him but then Black was never too far ahead of Mala for them to really be apart from each other.

"Let us put her in her cabin before the crew sees her in this condition." Morgan said glancing at Willie who nodded in agreement.

Willie gently moved the tankard from her slackened grasp while Morgan looked at her other hand. Entwined through her fingers was a gold chain with a medallion dangling over the edge of the table. With slow and gentle movements, Morgan untangled the chain then stuffed the necklace into the pocket of his britches.

"Go ahead of me, will you Willie?" Morgan asked as he carefully lifted the slender form in his arms.

The old cook hurried ahead as the two walked stealthily through the corridor towards the great cabin. Morgan glanced down at the feathery weight in his arms to look at her face. The serenity he saw now was so very different from the woman he knew.

"What happened in your past for you to be so hard-hearted and cruel, Mala?" He mumbled to the unconscious woman. His blue eyes drifted over her face noting the long dark lashes covering the brown eyes that could be cold and menacing.

Willie was lighting the lantern as Morgan slipped through the opened cabin door. The old man turned the flame down low then hurried to throw back the covers of Mala's bunk. Morgan smiled his thanks then gently laid their captain upon her bunk.

Reaching for her boots, Morgan glanced at Willie and whispered, "I will take of her from here. You go back to your duties. Thank you, Willie."

"Aye, sir. I will prepare her brew for when she awakens."

Morgan grinned and nodded as Willie backed out of the cabin and softly closed the door. As Morgan slipped off her boots, Mala mumbled incoherently in her drunken stupor. Looking down at her, Morgan reached into his pocket and pulled out her necklace. He stopped to look closer at the medallion that was no bigger than a piece-of-eight coin. Within the circle that outlined the edge, two letters were ornately scripted—RB. His gaze shifted to looked sympathetically at Mala. Even in death Rene Black had a strong hold on her.

Looking to the door, he thought of the mark he saw on Aubrey and wondered if Mala knew of the mark. The mark meant that Aubrey had been with Captain Black and if that were true, would Mala have taken in the girl?

With a sigh, Morgan bent down and carefully slipped the gold chain over Mala's head. He gently placed the medallion on Mala's red shirt then straightened up. His gaze shifted to her left breast where he knew Mala had a similar mark from her time with Black on the *Widow Maker*.

Shaking his head, he reached for the covers and gently placed them over the sleeping woman. "Sleep well, Captain." He whispered and headed for the door.

His shirt fluttered lightly in the breeze created from his strides as he reached for the latch then stepped out into the corridor. Letting out a long sigh and, with one last look at the closed door to the captain's cabin, he headed for the starboard aft companionway steps leading to the main deck as he tucked the tails of his shirt into the waistband of his britches.

From the other companionway leading to the main deck, Deats watched the first mate. The Scotsman had turned when he heard a door open and was surprised to see Morgan step out of Mala's cabin still in the process of dressing. Anger seethed in the quartermaster as he glared at the sandy-haired man. Mala was his, damn it! Deats thought to himself, and soon she would truly be his. With a growl in his throat at the thought of Morgan Alcott spending the night with Mala, Deats took the companionway two steps at a time.

Morgan was leaning on the railing, looking through the still dark night sky at the sea when Deats saw him. With slow steps, the Scotsman let the breeze attempt to cool his burning desire to toss the man overboard.

Taking deep breaths of the sea air, Morgan was thinking of his new roommate and her time on the *Widow Maker*, wondering what she had to endure while she was with Black. With his mind still tumbling with the possibilities, he turned from the railing and came face to face with Deats.

"How did Miss Malone fair last eve?" The Scotsman asked with a hint of sarcasm in his voice.

"Fine, although she had a nightmare." Morgan replied.

Deats merely nodded as he scanned the horizon. The lyin' bastard! How would ye know since ye dinna sleep in yer own cabin last night? The Scotsman thought. His brown eyes shifted to Morgan who did not notice the intense hatred in the baleful glare.

"I am going to the galley for a bit of breakfast before my watch." Morgan said then turned away from him.

In the galley, Morgan got a plate from Willie, then very nearly threw himself onto a bench at a table across from Robert. He stabbed at the food with his fork, his mind lost in deep thought.

"Mornin' Morgan." Robert said when no greeting was spoken. Morgan's gaze shot up to look into the eyes of his best friend.

"Mornin' Robert." Shoving a forkful of ham into his mouth, Morgan looked back down at his plate, brooding. Robert poked at the food on his plate in silence for a while before finally drawing a deep breath.

"Had a bad night?" He asked, looking Morgan over objectively. "I see no bruises or black eyes so I take it that your new bunkmate was calm and passed a quiet restful evening."

The comment was meant to torment—a jest between friends. But Morgan's mind was still reeling with the discovery he had made. Blue eyes lifted slowly to bear on Robert as Morgan clasped his hands over his plate, still holding his fork.

"My 'bunkmate' is fine but I saw something this morning that disturbs me deeply."

"What?" Robert asked curiously.

"Well I think that this is best left in confidence between the two of us because if Mala ever finds out all hell will break loose on this ship." Morgan began as his eyes darted to the tables around. The galley was nearly full, but no one was paying them any mind.

Robert filled his fork and, not looking up, said quietly, "She already knows."

Morgan looked at him in surprise, "What?"

"She already knows that Miss Malone has the mark of Black on her breast." Robert reported.

Morgan sat back heavily and wiped his mouth with his hand. He frowned at Robert and asked suspiciously, "And how would you know?"

Eyeing his friend, Robert shrugged and replied firmly, "Now lower your hackles, Morgan. I was on the beach with the Captain, remember? I pulled the girl out of the surf the second time when she broke away from Willie and went back in screaming at the top of her lungs at the *Widow Maker*. When I finally caught hold of her, her clothing was nearly half off her from the tow of the waves." Then with some hesitation, Robert added, "Deats saw it too."

"So Deats knows too?" Morgan said almost to himself.

"Aye, he does. But my question is how did you see it? You know Captain Mala will have your…" Robert began.

Morgan threw up his hand in defense, pointing his finger in Robert's questioning face, "I never touched her. I am as innocent as you are in seeing it. The shirt she wears came open in her sleep and I only caught a glimpse but it was enough for me to know what I was seeing."

"Aye, well say nothing that you know. To her or to Mala." Robert said as he resumed his breakfast.

"Thank you for your vote of confidence, Robert. I would like to think that I am a bit more discreet than that!" Morgan growled. Robert grunted in reply before the two sat in silence finishing their meals.

Leaving the galley, Morgan turned to Robert and asked, "Did you see any other survivors?"

"None, the British took good care to clean them all up." He reported shaking his head.

Stepping onto the main deck and almost in unison, they breathed deeply of the sea air. Looking around, they saw Mala on the quarterdeck and Aubrey at the starboard railing, staring out to sea. Clapping Robert on the back, Morgan gave a small smile and said, "See ya later, Robert."

"Aye." Robert nodded and went in the opposite direction.

Standing on the deck of the *Enchantress*, Aubrey let the wind and the spray caress her face. She watched as the heavily overcast clouds blocked the reddest hue of the sun over the horizon. Hearing the bells toll four times for 6am, she looked down at the water that capped white tops and thought of Jean Luc and the sinking of the *Widow Maker*. She inhaled deeply the salty air hoping that would stop the tears but they fell despite her efforts.

"Oh Jean Luc, what am I to do without you now?" She whispered to the water below.

Sensing someone standing beside her, she glanced up to find Morgan leaning back on his elbows against the deck railing. He was looking up at the sky beyond the tall masts. She smiled thinking that he may be trying to guard her privacy.

"Looks like rain." He said conversationally. Aware that he had gained her attention, he added, "Of course, it may be late today if we get anything. Depends on which way the captain takes us."

Thinking of this new captain, Aubrey looked to the quarterdeck and found the dark haired woman in conversation with the helmsman. They were looking to the skies and, every now and then, the woman captain looked to the water before gazing to the horizon ahead.

"Aye, we are headed straight for it, I think." Morgan said following her gaze to watch Mala. "Guess we should get you some breakfast while we can. With this motley crew, you get what you can while you can."

Aubrey could not help but smile then followed Morgan off the main deck towards the galley. Mala watched them leave without expression on her face as Deats came across the main deck. He caught sight of the two and smiled. Morgan would have that one in his bunk soon enough, orders or no orders from the Captain. Thinking of his own cold bunk, he looked up and found the object of his desire on the quarterdeck. Mala had kept herself from him, because of a memory and so far nothing had worked to erase that memory.

Thinking back, Deats remembered how he had found her to be the sole survivor of a massacre on an island and was busy burying the dead. He thought her to be the most beautiful creature he had ever seen. He had helped her with the morbid task, then he took her away from the island, and inadvertently helped her to become captain of her own ship. He thought that she would have warmed up to him. But even though she was friendly with him and the crew, she never allowed him to be any closer.

Then one evening, his need for her was overwhelming so he thought he would get her drunk and entice her to bed with him. He knew of her violent nature, having been witness to it many times, but he thought that in a drunken state, she would be more receptive. Deats had never been so wrong and the miscalculation nearly cost him his life. During his time sailing with her, Deats had never been able to predict her thoughts or actions. The only thing he knew for certain about Mala was that she was no fool.

As Deats stood watching Mala on the quarterdeck, he could feel his need rise. Somehow he must break her hold of the past with Black and put himself in her life. With Black's death, he knew what he could do to break down that wall Mala had built around herself. His gaze dropped to where Aubrey and Morgan had disappeared down the companionway.

With a smile and a plan churning in his mind, Deats moved to stand next to his captain. After a moment, he said nonchalantly, "Ach, she is a pretty one. But then Morgan wouldna have offered ta share his cabin unless he thought he could ...well ye did mention ta him that he..."

"He knows, Deats." Mala interrupted curtly.

The Scotsman caught her tone and added as if speaking to himself and with a look of sympathy he did not feel, "I just wonder how much she misses her ...ah...life on the other ship."

He glanced at Mala for her reaction but was not sure she was even listening to him now. She seemed engrossed with the approaching storm.

"Morgan tells me the poor lass cried out during the night with nightmares." He fairly purred. Mala looked to the waves then the horizon again. Deats wanted her attention so he tried again. "Do ye suppose she cried for someone in particular?"

"Possibly." Mala replied. She was listening and he almost smiled. "Since you are so concerned over the welfare of this 'poor lass,' perhaps you should see to her." Mala added turning to him.

Deats was taken by surprise with her suggestion. "Well Mr. Alcott seems ta have taken her under his wing."

He felt as if Mala's intense brown eyes bore into him and could read what he really meant. She caught the tone in his voice and turned her attention back to the weather, "A moment ago, you were concerned with Morgan's..." She paused for effect. "...care."

"As ye say, Captain, he knows how far ye will allow him ta go with this care."

"He does, Mr. Deats." Mala retorted looking him in the eye. "I also recall stating that she is now with us. Whatever she may have endured on the *Widow* is of no concern now. Our rules are different just as I am different."

"Aye Captain, I do remember. But..."

"Good!" She said, cutting him off. "She is Morgan's charge and therefore, you have nothing to concern yourself with. I have seen nothing that would be deemed inappropriate or adverse by her attitude. If you have, then I expect a full report."

Deats remained silent as he glanced away from Mala and caught Timmons covertly watching them. His attention was drawn to Mala and found that she turned to him waiting for a reply. "Nay Captain, I hadna heard nor seen anything out of place."

"Well then leave her to Morgan. We are closed on the matter."

"Aye Captain." Deats replied calmly though inwardly he was furious. He knew that Mala disliked the young woman only because she was on the *Widow Maker* with Black.

Mala turned her attention back to storm ahead, dismissing him. She moved closer to Timmons and said, "Judging by the caps on the waves and the clouds ahead, the storm is a fast one and will be very bad." She pointed to an island off their starboard bow. "Go there. We will use the island as cover. Find a cove where we can drop anchor and wait it out."

"Aye Captain." Timmons replied.

"I am going below. Have you had breakfast?" She asked Timmons.

"Not yet, I will wait."

"Nonsense, you will go when I return and I will take over the wheel."

"Aye, aye." Timmons replied.

"Deats, will you join me?" Mala asked her quartermaster as she headed for the steps. She added over her shoulder before Deats made a reply, "Or do you have other plans?"

"No other plans, Captain." Deats answered.

Mala waved for him to come along as Timmons watched them leave. He liked this captain even though she was a woman. She outsmarted many warships and many other pirate ships that thought to board hers. But what he liked most about her was how she was always conscientious of his time at the wheel and the time the rest of the crew put in their work. She would allow extended shore leave whenever possible and made sure no one was left behind. But he could not say the same for Angus Deats. He knew that Deats grew impatient when men did not return on time for departure. If not for Captain Mala's standing order that all men were to be accounted for, Deats would leave them behind.

Timmons remembered that many times the Captain would don her lavender dress and rich looking cloak to pay whatever fines her men may have incurred after a night of rowdiness. Or she would merely strap on her cutlass and carry several pistols to retrieve her men from a town that was a bit too rowdy itself. Of course, such actions of paying their fines did not go without due punishment. Captain Mala's idea of punishment would be to assign the chores that the particular man would consider being the nightmare of all chores. No man would voice his objections about the added chores because everyone knew the alternative by the Captain's way of thinking would be a trip overboard regardless of where the ship happened be. Yet Deats would have just left them to rot. Yes, this captain certainly took care of her crew. Timmons knew as well that, in return, the crew would always protect their captain, even die for her.

The helmsman smiled thinking that Captain Mala would not be in the galley for long. She would practically swallow her meal whole so that she could relieve him at the helm. Even if he finished his breakfast before they reached the cove, Timmons knew that the Captain would most likely see to the mooring herself. Remembering the storm, he put his attention to getting the *Enchantress* close to the island before the storm was upon them.

Mala and Deats entered the galley talking about the storm ahead and the plan to wait it out. Her crew raised their cups as she passed their tables. Mala made a point to speak to each man who spoke or she clapped him on the back in greeting. Her interaction with the crew angered Deats and he followed her impatiently until he was able to squeeze by towards the captain's table.

Willie was sitting with Aubrey and Morgan at a table near the wall in idle chatter. Seeing him, Deats growled low in his throat and walked over to them.

"The Captain is here, old man. Go aboot your duties." Deats ordered sternly. "And see that she is fed properly this time."

"The Cap'n eats what she wants ter eats." Willie replied with a shrug as he stood up.

His tone showed that Deats' gruffness did not perturb him in the least. Deats pursed his lips in irritation that the old cook would not take him seriously. He would have to talk to Mala yet again about replacing that old man. He turned his attention to their new guest as Mala stepped up and greeted them.

"Good morning, Morgan, Miss Malone."

"Morning, Captain." Morgan returned as he stood up in the presence of his captain.

"Good morning, Captain." Aubrey said timidly, catching the coldness in those dark eyes.

Mala glanced at her briefly before turning to her first mate. "Morgan, there is a storm ahead and I am planning to use a nearby island as cover. Check below for possible weak areas and let me know. Pull any man you need to do quick repairs. I do not want to take in any more water than necessary."

"Aye Captain, I will get right on it."

Mala turned to her new guest and eyed her closely. Aubrey had been watching her as she spoke with Morgan and could hear the command in her voice even though she was not rough or demanding in her tone. The cold dark eyes were now on her and Aubrey felt as if she were laid bare for all the world to see.

"I trust that all is to your liking, Miss Malone. I am sure Mr. Alcott is seeing to your total comfort."

"Aye Captain, Mr. Alcott has been quite refreshing considering what I had been subjected to." The young woman stated thinking of Thomas Beaufort. Noticing Deats' eyeing Mala, Aubrey turned to find Morgan watching his captain with a concerned look. Meeting Mala's cold look, Aubrey thought that the dark eyes had now turned deadly. Now what was wrong? Aubrey wondered.

Willie seemed to have appeared from nowhere to stand beside Mala. In his hands were two plates of cured smoked ham, eggs seasoned with peppers and some hardtack.

"Here ya go, Cap'n, Mr. Deats." Willie said standing next to Mala.

Without another word, Mala turned away and headed for her table in the back of the galley followed by Willie carrying the two plates of food. Deats briefly nodded to Aubrey and Morgan before turning to follow. A small, evil smile crept upon his face as he followed Mala to the table. Without even knowing it, Miss Malone was about to become his little helper, Deats thought as his gaze roamed over his captain's slender form.

Mala took her seat that faced the galley as Deats sat in a chair next to her facing Morgan and Aubrey. He saw that their heads were close together and he glanced to Mala to find her watching them as well.

"Sorry, Captain, but twas ta be expected after all this time. Although tis unfortunate that she bears his mark, it does let a man know the extent of their relationship."

"Do be quiet, Deats." Mala growled in annoyance, glancing at him briefly.

Willie appeared with two tankards and a bottle of rum. When he left, Mala pushed her plate aside and poured a tankard full of rum. She threw herself back in her seat angrily as she swallowed a good portion of the rum. As she had poured more rum, Deats watched while he idly picked at his food and smiled inwardly. This young lass was definitely going to aid him in breaking down Mala's resistance. This was much better than he had hoped. Perhaps the captain would warm his bunk within the week.

Deats looked over at Aubrey but found Morgan watching. The Scotsman could not resist a small smile toward the Englishman whom Mala trusted above all others on this ship. Morgan caught his smile and his jaw set in disapproval for he knew what Deats wanted.

Smugly, Deats took a bite of his eggs—then nearly choked. The seasonings were too much for his taste and his eyes began to water. He grabbed his tankard and, realizing that it was still empty, quickly grabbed the rum and poured the liquid in his cup. After he drank down a good portion to quench the fire in his mouth, he wiped his eyes and cleared his throat several times, drinking intermittently to put out the small fires still simmering inside his mouth. He looked up to find Mala watching him.

"The bastard!" He croaked. His voice was hoarse because his throat was scorched by the hot red peppers. Deats took another swallow of his rum. "Christ, Mala! How much more are we made ta endure? That old man has ta go. Put him off at the next port and..."

"Forget it, Deats." Mala interrupted.

His mouth dropped as he stared at her in disbelief. "Mala, he damned near killed me with this..." Deats quietly argued, then leaning on his arm to get closer to her, "He canna even fix these eggs..."

"Nonsense, Deats, he is not poisoning you." Mala said, then paused thinking of the right words. "They are just highly seasoned."

Deats stared wanting her to take a bite of her eggs knowing she had not even touched her food. He decided to pointedly look at her plate instead. Mala caught his look at her plate and looked down at it before lifting her gaze to meet his. With a raised brow, she slid her plate towards him and silently ordered him to try hers. Deats took a bite to find that hers were seasoned just fine. He took a drink of his rum then took another bite of her eggs to confirm his first findings.

Mala's eyes moved to the front of the galley to find Willie peeking around the corner from the cooking area. She had to take a sip of her rum to keep the smile to herself as she watched Deats take another bite of her eggs. She wanted to ask Deats about the ham but refrained, knowing that she would not be able to maintain her composure. Taking a slab of ham and a biscuit, Mala stood up. "Enjoy it, Mr. Deats. I will be topside."

Deats looked up at her then back to her plate to find he had eaten nearly all of her eggs. He gave an apologetic look but Mala waved it off and left him to her meal. Deats pushed his plate aside disdainfully and put Mala's plate before him.

As she headed out of the galley, Mala turned to Willie instead. He stood just within the doorway and watched shamefaced as she approached.

"I know he can be quite bothersome, Willie, but please refrain from overly spicing his food."

"Aye Cap'n." The old man said meekly with a slight bow of his wizened head.

Mala put a hand on his shoulder. "Just a little spicy to shut him up and enough for me to eat a little."

Willie looked up to see her smiling at him. He nodded returning the smile. As she turned away, he grabbed her arm, "Ah, Cap'n?" When she faced him, Willie reached over and handed her another plate full of ham, eggs and biscuits. "Fixed just right fer ya, Cap'n." He said with conspiratorial smile.

Mala nodded her thanks then walked out the galley, sneaking the plate out as well, hoping she would not be stopped.

Chapter 2

After hurriedly eating her breakfast in her cabin because of the way the ship pitched and rocked, and making a note in her log about the storm, Mala went to relieve Timmons at the helm. As she had feared while eating her breakfast, the storm was faster than first thought and she wondered if they would make it to the island for cover in time. The swells were growing bigger and the wheel was becoming harder to hold.

Morgan and Aubrey came up on the main deck and were as surprised as Mala was to find the storm so close. They looked to find Mala fighting to hold the ship on course.

"I have got to help her!" Morgan told Aubrey.

"What can I do to help?" Aubrey asked.

Morgan noticed Robert approaching as they talked. Summoning him to them, Morgan told him, "Miss Aubrey wants to help and I do not want her to be alone. Take her and go below to check for leaks then report to me. I hope to God you find absolutely nothing."

Robert and Aubrey headed for the lower deck area being tossed from one side to other as they made their way down through the *Enchantress*. Robert stopped only to light a lantern before continuing down the corridor and helped Aubrey through the decks checking the areas.

After some time, Aubrey and Robert emerged to the main deck to find the storm fully upon them. Immediately the two of them were thoroughly soaked. They looked to the helm to find Mala and Timmons together fighting to maintain their course against the onslaught of the storm. Aubrey noticed that Mala kept looking up and following her gaze, she found Morgan up on the main mast with several men trying to furl the sails. The ship dipped violently and the men grabbed for something to keep from falling. The ship then bucked upward and Aubrey lost her balance. Robert could not reach her and she fell hard against the bulkhead of the quarterdeck. For an instant, memories of another storm came to her mind.

"Are you hurt?" Robert asked concerned as he helped her up.

Aubrey shook her head then gasped as she saw one man drop from the mast. He had caught a rope and swung in the air.

"Sweet Mary!" She exclaimed when she realized the man was Morgan.

Robert turned back to her, shouting above the storm, "Stay here!" She nodded as he left her to help Morgan.

Aubrey noticed a movement and found Mala headed for Morgan as well. Seeing the captain on the deck, Aubrey knew that only one person was at the helm. She carefully made her way across the deck by clinging to the wall until she made it to the steps. When she made it to the quarterdeck, she grabbed the wheel with all her strength to help hold their course.

"Ye should not be here! The Cap'n will not like it!" Timmons yelled over the storm.

"I want to help you! You cannot hold this alone!" Aubrey argued.

Timmons knew the truth of that statement and the captain had to help Mr. Alcott. Lashing her to the wheel with him, he let her add her strength. The two fought the wheel in silence and watched breathlessly as Mala easily climbed up the ratlines to the main topsail. Deats joined her from the opposite direction and the two pulled up the rope that Morgan held. On the fighting top, Morgan had steadied himself with Deats and Mala as they all tried to catch their breath from the exertion. Suddenly the ship dipped then bucked again, making Mala lose her balance. With a curse, Mala felt herself falling.

"Captain!" Timmons yelled as he watched her topple over onto the ratlines. Aubrey watched in horror as Deats and Morgan made to grab for her but each barely had a hold and lost it just as quickly. Mala slid down the ratlines then grabbed at the ropes just as she was tossed to the side and nearly off the lines. She swung in the air holding onto the edges of the ratlines. Glancing up, she saw Deats and Morgan about to come down after her.

"No, I can make it down!" Mala yelled up at them and shook her head furiously.

They remained as they were watching her. Her arms grew tired quickly after the work she put them through at the wheel. She needed to get a foothold on something fast before her arms gave out. She glanced over her shoulder and saw the ship dip sideways, leaving nothing but ocean beneath her. Why was she still here? What was she waiting for? Mala thought fleetingly. To die now after all that had happened and all that had been lost, but it was as if some invisible force made her search for footing and tighten her grasp instead of letting go and dropping into the ocean below.

Her crew watched anxiously as she swung to get her legs looped on the edge of lines. The ship appeared to sense how close she would be to getting a foothold and it would sway, buck, or dip to impede her efforts. Mala could feel her arms tremble now as the last bits of strength began to ebb away. Taking a deep breath, she tried several more times until finally getting a leg hold to pull herself up.

Timmons and Aubrey tried to desperately hold the wheel steady as they watched Mala attempting to catch hold of the lines with her legs.

"Come on me dear." Timmons was saying. Aubrey looked at him questioningly, thinking that he was speaking to her, then he added, "Yer captain has been good to ya and ya know it. Now be good and help her out this time."

Aubrey smiled as she finally realized that Timmons was talking to the *Enchantress*. When they saw that the captain had a leg hold, the entire crew on the main deck seemed to breathe a collective sigh of relief. Mala willed her aching arms to keep on working as she hauled herself over the edge of the ratlines then lay facing the main deck below resting her aching body. Her head pounded from the exertion and her body screamed for rest but she still had the task of climbing down to the deck. Her weakened arms shook from the ordeal as she made her way slowly down the lines. When she neared the bottom, Morgan and Deats were there to help her down.

With her feet on the deck once more, Mala nodded in thanks to her quartermaster and first mate as she held on to the ropes and leaned her head against her arm in momentary relief.

"I need to help Timmons at the helm." She gasped against the onslaught of rain in her face.

"But Captain..." Deats started.

"Captain, we will see to the course and the mooring. You barely have enough strength to stand much less fight the wheel." Morgan said to her with much concern.

"I am fine! I will see to my ship first, then I will rest!" She told them as she headed for the quarterdeck.

"Aye, Captain." They replied.

Mala looked to the wheel and found Aubrey with Timmons. She turned to Morgan and angrily growled, "What in the hell is she doing up there, get her below! I am not going to get into the habit of constantly saving her from the waters!"

On the quarterdeck, Aubrey and Timmons looked on with concern before Timmons asked, "Are you all right, Cap'n?"

Mala looked at him and replied, "I am fine, Mr. Timmons." Casting a condescending look at Aubrey, and grabbing a handful of Aubrey's shirt to pass her off to Morgan, Mala snapped, "Morgan!"

"Aye Captain, I will take her down now!" He shouted above the din. Realizing that she was being dismissed, Aubrey turned away with Morgan to head back to the cabin they shared. She looked at Morgan as he smiled and winked at her while they made their way off the slippery main deck.

Once in the shelter of the corridor, Morgan lowered his head toward Aubrey, to speak over the sound of the raging storm, "Thank you very much for your help. That was very brave of you."

Aubrey smiled weakly in reply. When she was up on the deck, every fiber of her being had been charged with energy. Now as the sensation was subsiding, Aubrey felt weak and hoped that she would not collapse in the corridor as he ushered her along.

Smiling, Morgan added, "Really, Aubrey. With your help, Timmons was able to hold the ship and we did not lose our captain."

Aubrey's smile was stronger now as she looked up at Morgan. Then a mischievous look appeared as she confided to him, "That man, Timmons, talks to the ship, you know. He told the ship to be good and help the captain."

Morgan smiled handsomely and with a twinkle in his eye, he replied, "And I will bet the ship listened and obeyed." Aubrey giggled and nodded in agreement as the two continued on their journey.

Timmons found a cove in the dim light of overcast day and pointed it out to his captain. She nodded and the two navigated the *Enchantress* into it. The storm was as ferocious as Mala had expected but the cove provided some relief from its onslaught. After seeing the ship was well anchored, Mala ordered another of her crew, Slate, to take over the helm to give Timmons a much-needed rest.

Only then did Mala go to her cabin knowing that her ship was a bit safer in the cove. With an exhausted sigh, Mala slumped into a chair at the long table and put her head down onto folded arms. Within seconds, her rest was disturbed by a knock upon her cabin door.

"Come in." Mala called out reluctantly. As she had expected, it was Deats.

"Thought we lost ye up there, Captain." He said as he closed the door. He noticed that Mala was still in her wet clothes and was getting up from the chair. He had hoped to find her in some state of undress. In Deats' imagination, he saw her naked from the waist up and droplets of water cascaded down her bare back from her long dark hair. The very thought of the sight left his mouth dry and a burning need in his loins.

Mala's tired reply brought him out of his lustful thoughts, "Timmons is a good man, Mr. Deats. He can coax the *Enchantress* into anything."

"Aye, Captain and Miss Malone's help was an added bonus." He added, feeling the need to bring up the young woman in hopes to accentuate her anger at finding Aubrey at the helm in the first place.

Mala went to her logbook and idly thumbed through it. She appeared to be in deep thought as Deats poured out a tankard of rum for each of them and waited patiently for her to acknowledge him again. As he poured the libation, his eyes wandered over the front of her wet shirt. Even in the meager light of the quarter gallery windows from the heavily overcast skies, Deats could see her hardened nipples protruding from her wet clinging shirt.

When Mala stepped away from her desk, he offered her a tankard which she happily accepted. With arms still aching from the morning's ordeal, Mala placed the tankard down on the table before she dropped it. Resuming her seat, she looked at Deats who had remained quiet. The Scotsman took a chair to her right and drank from his tankard, the sight of her shirt flashed in his mind. He was thankful that she could not see the desire that it stirred in him now.

Mala sat back in her chair, propping her chin in her hand and stared at Deats, wondering why he was here. "Is something on your mind, Deats?" She finally asked tiredly.

"Captain, ye must be cold. Do ye not want ta change ye clothes?"

"In a moment." She replied shortly.

"Well, actually there is a matter I wish ta discuss with ye." He began.

Mala rolled her eyes wishing now she had not asked. She watched Deats as he repositioned himself into his chair and took a sip from his tankard. Without looking up at her, he stated hesitantly, "About Miss Malone, tis apparent that her presence here will be far ta upsetting ta ye. I must renew my suggestion that we drop her off at the next port and see that she is sent home or wherever she prefers." Mala looked at him tiredly and listened as he rambled on, "But then she probably wishes she was still on the *Widow Maker* with her man. Although I cannot imagine why she would prefer that."

Deats paused, looking up at his captain for a reaction. He expected a look of anger at the reminder of Aubrey's obvious position on the *Widow Maker* but he did not see it. Instead he saw a look of amusement in her eyes and Deats frowned. What would Mala find amusing about this thought? Still frowning, he added, "After all ye had been avoiding meeting up with him in the first place. Whenever we entered a port and that ship was in, ye would go around ta the other side of the island and go ta some nearby cove. Ye had even steered clear of him out at sea."

"You know my reasons for that." She snapped.

"Aye, Captain but ye knew that one day ye would have ta meet up with the *Widow Maker* and her captain." Deats' voice trailed off and met her eyes. In a quieter tone of voice, he asked, "What would ye have done then, out at sea?"

Mala stared at Deats and knew he was right. She had been able to avoid meeting up with the *Widow Maker* and her crew at sea. Well, there was that one time when she crossed his bow on the way to Bimini. Mala had plans for the *Widow Maker* that day but then she had changed her mind.

Now the *Widow Maker* was at the bottom of the sea along with her captain and crew. Although she had not wanted to be near the ship or her crew, she could not shake the empty feeling she had since she watched the *Widow Maker* go under the day before. How could anyone have survived that? But yet now she had someone on board her ship who had survived.

Mala remembered another time when she had come close to the *Widow Maker*. It was when she dropped off Jean Luc in Charlestowne after a careening of the *Enchantress*. She could even make out members of the crew on the deck that morning through her eyeglass. She had seen him and Jean Luc knew she saw him. That was what had started the argument all over again but Mala was firm with Jean Luc. She reminded Jean Luc of the deal they struck when he had run into her in that town and had asked for her assistance. All she asked in return was that Jean Luc conveniently forget that he saw her – ever! He did not like the terms but when she walked away and he still needed her help, he agreed with the greatest and loudest reluctance she had ever heard from him.

"It no longer matters now, Deats." Mala replied with a shrug.

"Knowing she has the mark and what it means?" He pressed on.

"Deats, must we discuss this now? I am tired and would like to rest a bit before I see what damage we have sustained."

He took a deep breath and stood up. He had hoped to get further into this conversation but he did not dare counter her. He swallowed the last of his rum and turned to leave.

"Deats? Miss Malone was not the only subject you wished to discuss with me, was it?" Mala asked.

"No Captain, but I will hold all my other topics for later. As ye say, ye need some rest."

She nodded but stopped him again when he reached the door, "Send for Morgan."

Deats nodded and exited the cabin. As he pulled the door closed behind him, he clenched his teeth in anger at having been dismissed because she was too tired yet she would call for Alcott. Why was she callin' for him? I could have takin' care of anything she needed, Deats thought angrily to himself.

Mala sat at her table sipping her rum. The warmth of the liquor reminded her that she was still in wet clothes but she did not care. She sat listening to her ship as it rocked with the storm. She listened to the thunder in the distance and could see lightening flashes now and then. The rain poured hard outside and she made a mental note to tell Morgan that only the barest of crew needed to be on duty topside in this storm.

As she stared at her mug, Mala soon drifted back to a time when she felt that Fate had finally dealt her a fair blow. She remembered the laughter and the fun and Rene Black.

She was so deep into her memories, she did not hear the knock nor did she hear Morgan step in. He stood quietly watching in concern as he leaned against the closed door just inside the cabin. He knew that look. She was in the past again. He felt a deep sympathy for her but knew he could not help her because Mala would not allow it.

Morgan stayed against the door and softly called out to her. After several attempts, she finally noticed him. She waved him in and offered a chair, "Sorry, Morgan. The life of a captain is wrought with decisions." She said ruefully.

He smiled knowing that she would have never admitted to drifting back in time. He saw the second tankard on the table, and following his gaze, Mala offered, "Care for some warmth to wash away the chill?"

"No thank you, Captain."

Mala took her tankard and drained the last of her rum then placed the tankard away from her. Sitting back and resting her elbow on the arm of her chair with her cheek in her hand, she looked to Morgan, "Any problems below deck that needed tending?"

"No, Captain. I sent Robert to check on that while I helped out on the deck and they found nothing out of the ordinary."

"They?" Mala echoed.

"Aubrey wanted to help so I sent her with Robert." Morgan shrugged.

"She knows about ships?" Mala asked curiously.

"Apparently so. I sought out Robert on my way here to see what he thought. He was quite impressed with her knowledge."

"Robert would be." Mala said with a small smile. "Any woman who bothers to learn about ships is ranked high in his mind."

"Aye Captain, especially if that woman makes captain." Morgan added with a smile and a twinkle of mischief in his blue eyes.

"I am not sure that was what impressed him. He may have been afraid to oppose me, you know." Mala pointed out.

Morgan laughed. "Possible but I doubt it. You have proven yourself."

"As I recall, Mr. Alcott, you were in the midst of disbelief yourself when you found out."

Morgan smiled at the memory. Disbelief was definitely an understatement. To find that Mala was the elected captain of this bunch of ruffians was a shock but the real surprise was hearing how she had been elected. If he had not already witnessed her powers of 'persuasion,' he would never have believed it from a beautiful woman.

"Aye, but then you are not some ordinary wench neither, Mala." He said with a smile.

As expected, a brow rose and she retorted playfully, "Wench? Who are you calling a wench? The last wench I saw you with had left you panting after her for more of whatever she fed you the night before!"

"A true gentleman does not kiss then tell." Morgan told her with a chuckle.

It was quiet for a moment before Mala asked, "How did our guest fare her first night?"

"She was tired but she showed signs of being frightened."

"Frightened?"

"Aye, she tried to become a part of the bulkhead whenever I came near her." Seeing her arched brow, Morgan added quickly, "She had a nightmare. I tried to comfort her."

"Careful Morgan. I will not tolerate…" Mala began.

"I know, Mala. And although I find her quite attractive, my senses tell me she has already given away her heart." Mala looked away and Morgan hurried to add, "I will find out who he was and settle the matter in both our minds."

"It does not matter, he is dead now." She said quietly. Mala and Morgan shared a sadness that showed on both their faces. She gave him a sad smile, "But then I would guess they are both gone."

"I will still try to find out who he was, just as I said to settle the matter in both our minds."

There was a long silence before Mala finally said, "Morgan, make sure that only a few men are out on the deck. With this storm and the deserted cove, I am not expecting to meet up with undesirables."

Morgan smiled knowing that Mala hated the thought of her men out in the weather and would rather be out there as well. "Aye Captain. I will see to it."

Chapter 3

Mala continued to be standoffish with Aubrey in the days that followed. On this, her fourth day of being on the *Enchantress*, Aubrey sat alone in the corner of the galley near Willie's little cookstove. She watched as Mala sat with Deats and Morgan at her table in the back of the galley, sharing a jovial conversation.

She was alarmed when Mala's dark eyes drifted across the room to fall upon her. Bravely, Aubrey returned the stare but the scrutiny was more than she could stand and Aubrey exited from the room. Standing in the passageway, she pondered her rescue by these pirates. Captain Mala seemed to be the female epitome of Rene Black! And when those dark eyes stared unblinkingly, it was more foreboding than any look from Black or Uncle Jonathan. Tears began to well in Aubrey's eyes as she hurried to the cabin and shut the door fiercely behind her giving into them.

She had no idea how long she had barred herself away before there was a tapping at the door. Aubrey pressed her forehead against the door and asked, "Who is it?"

Willie's kind voice came from the other side, "Lass, would ya be a darlin' and take this up and throw it out fer a poor old man? Me bones is aching today and a trip up the steps would just set 'em to hurtin' more."

"Yes sir, I will help you." Wiping the tears, Aubrey smiled and opened the door. She was glad to have something worthwhile to do for a change. She took the bucket of dirty water from the man and carried it up the companionway steps making small distasteful faces at the smell of it. Fish heads and the insides of fish floated in the bloody water but she tried to keep her eyes adverted.

After dumping the nasty mess over the side rail, Aubrey stood with the empty pail in her hand and looked out at the ocean. It laid relatively flat and calm. Looking up into the sails she noted that they were being gently buffeted by a wind in those higher places. She was surprised when she noticed that Mala was high in the sails, working with the men. Aubrey watched in fascination as the other woman worked. She moved sure-footed and graceful along the yardarms. Her long dark hair fluttered in the breeze as Mala called to and laughed with the men while they worked.

A sadness fell over Aubrey once more and tears came as she dropped her gaze to the deck. Suddenly, she became aware of someone nearby. Looking up, she saw that Deats was standing not far away, looking quizzically at her. She quickly left the deck and returned the pail to the old cook who thanked her graciously before returning to the cabin and burying her face in the pillow.

It was nearly dark when Morgan's watch was finally over and he wandered to his cabin tiredly. With an amused smile, he stopped in front of the door. It was not just his cabin anymore. He knocked on the door lightly, respecting her privacy. There was no reply from the other side, so he carefully opened the door and poked his head in to find the cabin dark and quiet. A small sigh was the only indication to him that Aubrey was even in the room. He lit the lantern, turned the wick down low then proceeded to pull off his jacket, shirt and boots before lowering himself into his bunk and closing his eyes.

It seemed like he had only been asleep for a few minutes when he was awakened by a group of men going past in the corridor to the galley and talking loudly about the evening meal. He stared up at the ceiling and stretched sleepily. With a slight frown, he turned his eyes to look in the direction of the bunk across from his. His blue eyes came to rest on the intent gaze of Aubrey's hazel eyes.

How old had she told him she was? Ten and nine was it? She seemed so childlike in some ways to him. She was six years younger than he was. At her age, most young women were worldlier—at least the ones he knew. He wondered how she had survived the time she had been on the *Widow Maker* with Rene Black. He had spent long hours over the past several days just trying to get a few pieces of her personal information from her.

She laid on her stomach, staring at him quietly as he crunched his pillow up under his head while turning toward her. Staring at her for a few more moments he smiled in mischief but she remained undaunted. Morgan winked at her and she buried her face into her pillow with a delightful giggle. Laughing lazily aloud, he sat up in his bunk, "Did you have a good day?"

"I suppose." She shrugged. This was another game he had to play every night. He would try and get her to talk and share her experiences and feelings of the day.

"I saw you were helping Willie. The old man likes you a lot you know."

"Yes, you have already told me so." She said with a nod.

"Are you ready for dinner?"

"I am not hungry." She said flatly as she suddenly turned her head away from him.

Morgan's shoulders slumped and he stood up to pull on his shirt, "Well, I am starved."

"Bon appetit." She said without looking around at him. Knowing by now not to press the issue, he winced at her use of the French language as he left the cabin to go to the galley. The moment the door shut, Aubrey's stomach growled loudly in protest of being very empty.

"Thank you for waiting until he was gone." She said sitting up.

In the galley, Morgan took his plate to sit with Mala and Deats. The Scotsman eyed him objectively, "Where is yer young charge?"

"In the cabin." Morgan said crisply as he began his meal.

"Do ye not allow her ta eat?" Deats asked.

"She said she was not hungry. I suppose that since she was helping Willie today, he fed her." Morgan shrugged.

"I think that ye keep her prisoner in the cabin—she barely ever comes out and about." Deats pressed on as he shot a glance at Mala then he sneered at Morgan over his plate, "One has ta wonder why Miss Malone will hardly look at anyone else on board or speak ta them. She acts as if she has been frightened inta being quiet. I think that perhaps ye may have placed some stringent rules on her behavior Mr. Alcott, in yer efforts ta—protect her." Deats looked to Mala again but she ate in silence as if the two of them were not even there.

Morgan's eyes narrowed. "That is your opinion. She is not a prisoner—she comes and goes as she pleases. I do not put rules on her behavior. She only shares a space in that cabin and no more. I am tired of your lewd suggestions that state otherwise." With his retort, Morgan put down his fork and slammed his fist down upon the table.

The force of the pounding fist was enough to set Mala's tankard rocking. Three pair of hands shot out to try and steady the drink from spilling. Mala won out grabbing for the tankard and she took it calmly to her lips, casting her dark eyes at the pair of them over the rim. After taking a drink, she set the tankard down firmly and growled, "That will be enough—both of you."

The two men glared at one another then looked at Mala, wondering which of them would be the recipient of her reprimand. She merely resumed her meal in silence.

After a swallow, Mala began quietly, "Mr. Alcott." Deats smiled evilly that Morgan was going to be reprimanded for the confrontation. "Miss Malone may do whatever she pleases on this ship within reason—so long as it does not jeopardize herself or any member of my crew." Mala said then put a forkfull of food into her mouth.

After swallowing again, she added, "Miss Malone answers to no man on this ship, unless she chooses to do so." There was another stretch of extended silence as both men waited patiently for they knew she still had more to say. Mala pushed her plate away and sat back, throwing her napkin onto her plate, "Take her a plate anyway, Morgan. I do not want her getting sick."

27

"Aye Captain." Morgan said as he pushed away his own empty plate. Deats turned his head slowly in her direction, unable to believe that she was actually showing some small degree of care for the girl. Mala shot him a look of question, "Do you have something to say on the matter?"

"Nay." He said stiffly then looked at Morgan with seething anger in his brown eyes.

As if he possessed an uncanny ability to read minds, Willie appeared on the scene like a little old elf in his stained and soiled apron. "Where is my helper?"

"In the cabin, Willie." Morgan said with a small smile as he noted that Willie held a heaping plate of food in his hand.

"Ye take this to her, Mr. Alcott—and ye tell that lil miss to eat every bite or I be tanning her hide but good." Willie said as he thrust the plate at Morgan.

Taking it with a slight chuckle, Morgan glanced at Mala, "I thought you said that Aubrey did not have to answer to any man on this ship?"

"Willie does not count." Mala said with a slight smile.

Deats was glaring at the pair of them and finally he got up from the table with a huff. Mala and Morgan exchanged glances as the Scotsman went storming away and Willie returned to his cookstove. Mala rolled her eyes in reaction to Deats' hasty retreat.

Seeing the look, Morgan snorted a short laugh and leaned close to Mala, "Tell me again why he is the quartermaster?" Dodging the hand that shot out, Morgan chuckled and stood up saying, "I think I will just take this to Aubrey."

"First name basis now, is it?" Mala asked mocking Aubrey's Irish drawl.

"Aye." Morgan nodded, his smile growing bigger.

"She does not want you, Morgan."

"I know that she pines for someone else." He nodded. Mala's dark eyes shot up to look into his face and he could see the warning there.

"But Mala, I am certain that she does not pine for the man you have on your mind. There was another but I cannot get out of her who he was." Morgan said in sad explanation.

"And you probably never will." Mala said stiffly as she stood up. "And you will probably never have her."

"By your order, it will only be on her terms, Captain." He said as he stepped aside to let her pass before him.

"Goodnight, Morgan." She said casting him one last glance.

"Goodnight, Mala." He replied as he stood with the plate in hand and watched her leave the galley. Her posture suggested sadness to his knowing eyes. With a sigh, he left the galley and headed for his cabin.

Aubrey was still in the bunk, on her back now with bare feet propped up on the bulkhead as she stared up to the ceiling planking.

"You have been like that all this time?" Morgan asked as he tossed his hat aside and sat down.

"Yes." Came the quiet reply.

"I was directed to bring this to you with the implicit order that you eat all of it or Willie will tan your hide. Can I watch?" Morgan said with a hint of mischief in his blue eyes.

Aubrey was forced to smile at him, "Watch me eat?"

"Oh hell, are you gonna eat now? I wanted to see Willie tan your hide." He tormented on.

Aubrey sat up and took the plate, saying, "Not bloody likely." Then she smiled a polite 'thank you.'

Morgan nodded and sat back in his bunk, "I guess you shared a cabin on the *Widow Maker*."

"Yes." Came the curt reply through a mouthful of food then after swallowing, she added, "But not by my choice."

"I suppose not." He said easily.

"What are you suggesting?" She asked, looking up at him.

"I am not suggesting anything. I just do not get the feeling that you were happy." He shrugged.

Aubrey ate in silence for a while before she finally put the plate aside, "Willie has given me too much again." Silence fell between them before she finally broke it with one small bit of information for him to chew on, "Sometimes I was happy."

Morgan thought well to leave that alone for now. He stretched his lean frame and said, "Well, you know, I think that there is a full moon tonight—I do not pay much attention to the sky at night, not being the navigator and all. But..." He paused in his small speech to look at her in puzzlement when she choked on her water. "Are you all right?" He asked in concern.

"Yes, yes, I am fine. What were you saying about the moon?" She asked quickly.

"I was going to ask you if you would like to go up on deck for some air." He said easily.

"Really?" She asked in new interest.

"Certainly, come on." He said extending his hand to her. She looked at the offered hand. "It is dark in the corridor and the companionway." He suggested.

She tentatively slipped her hand into his and got up from the bunk. Morgan smiled into the darkness and squeezed her hand ever so slightly as he led her along.

Once on deck, she pulled her hand free and walked out further into the openness of the dark deck. Her head was tilted back to look up at the night sky. To be out on deck after dark was always an awesome experience for her when she was on the *Gull* and the few times while on the *Widow Maker*. The sky was peppered with stars and the moon was large and full, just as he had told her. A shooting star streaked across the sky and she yelped in delight, "Did you see that?"

He chuckled at her and leaned back against the railing with his arms folded over his chest, "Yes, I have seen them many times."

"But—they are beautiful! Look at it, Morgan!" She went on. He watched her in her delight. It made him happy to have found something that seemed to pull her out of her constant state of depression.

Finally as she had turned full circle looking at the sky and had come to lean against the railing next to him, he asked, "Were you ever out on deck at night?"

The delight quickly disappeared and in a quiet tone of voice, she said stiffly, "No."

Morgan pursed his lips and mentally chastised himself for having thrown her back into sadness. When he thought that all was lost she said quietly, "Well, I did once and I got caught in a rain storm. It was very cold and I—got into trouble for it."

"For being in the rain?" He asked with a puzzled frown.

"No, for disobeying orders." She said quietly again.

Morgan chuckled and patted her on the back, "A woman after my own heart. I am always in trouble for disobeying orders!"

"Captain Mala likes you. I doubt that you could ever get into any real trouble with her and make her angry." She said with a small smile.

"Well I have gotten into a little trouble." Morgan said with a mischievous grin.

They stood in silence for a while as she gazed still in awe of the heavens above. So this was how Jean Luc made their charts for which way to go. How she would have loved to be up on the deck with him like this…with him close by. Aubrey shivered and rubbed her arms suddenly.

Morgan noticed and straightened from the railing, "Are you cold? Would you like me to warm you?" The words had spilled out of his mouth before he could check them. After they were out, he could have slapped his own mouth. She drew back and looked at him in mild alarm, remembering the day that Black had caught her up on the deck with the same sentence.

"I mean, I could go fetch you a jacket—or—here, you can put this one on if you like." He said as he quickly shrugged out of his jacket. Aubrey stared at him for a moment as he held it up for her. "You would be warm, and you could stay out longer." He suggested easily.

Morgan reminded her of Jean Luc. Would every kindly man she met the rest of her life remind her of him? She turned her back to him and let him slip the jacket up over her arms. Pulling it closed about herself, she turned back to him with a small smile, "Thank you, Morgan."

"Let us fix those sleeves. You look like a little lost urchin." He smiled as he turned up the cuffs on the sleeves. Aubrey smiled back up at him. He was a nice man and she felt safe in his company.

There was a loud splash very close to the side of the ship that broke the encounter and Aubrey fairly leapt into his arms. "What was that?" She whispered.

Morgan, always playful, said in a serious tone, "A sea monster."

"What?" Aubrey asked in alarm as she craned her neck to peer into the darkness. There was another splash, this time off the starboard side. Aubrey's head turned to look in that direction as she clutched at the sleeves of Morgan's shirt.

"Sweet Mary, they are all around us!" Morgan was hard-pressed to keep from laughing at her as she dug her fingers into his arms, "We must go below. They will not sink the ship, will they?"

"No." He said stifling a laugh. Another splash came, much closer this time. Aubrey's fingers pinched into his skin and he yelped in pain. "Aubrey, relax, I was only playing with you. They are animals of the sea. Here, look." He said as he pulled her to the railing.

She fought to get free, "No!"

"Hush, look. See there? As the light of the moon lies on the water?" He soothed close to her ear.

"Yes." She said quietly, a bit fearfully and still clutching at his arms. A sleek gray and shining creature broke the surface of the water then slipped back into the dark water with the same splashing sound. Aubrey's mouth dropped open again.

"Men have told tales of how they were lost at sea or shipwrecked and those creatures came to help them." He told her quietly as they watched several of them playing in the moonlit waves now. "Wait till you see them in the day. They seem to always have a smile on their faces."

Aubrey's stomach let out a low growl and she shot her head to look at Morgan in embarrassment. He pushed her gently out to arms length, "I heard that and it was no sea monster. You are still hungry and we are going below for you to finish your dinner."

"I hate to go." She whined as she looked back to the light on the water and the stars above.

"We will come out another time." He promised.

From his place at his station on the quarterdeck, Deats watched the scene on the main deck by the portside railing. Neither Aubrey nor Morgan saw him as he stood in the shadows with a smile across his face. Alcott was working on the girl, he thought with a sneer. She had on his jacket now but she would be down to the skin with him before the week was out. Deats decided to save this observation for a more opportune time—a confirmation to Mala that the girl had most certainly been with Black. Aside from the obvious mark that bore the fact, she apparently was game for any man who came by with a smile and a show of interest in her.

In the cabin, Morgan pulled off his shirt in preparation of bed as Aubrey ate the food left on her plate. "Thank you again for taking me up, Morgan." She said easily.

"Anytime, love." He smiled as he pulled off his boots. To be totally undressed before her did not bother him in the least, yet he always waited until lights out. "You are not tired of sleeping in your clothes? You can borrow one of my shirts." Morgan suggested.

"No thank you. I will be fine." She said quickly. Never again would she wear a man's shirt as her nightclothes.

The next day, the *Enchantress* moored in Santiago de Cuba. The main order of business was to allow the crew time for shore leave. For two days, they would be moored in a cove away from the main harbor. There was a rotation that half of the crew was ashore and were to report back to the ship by the next morning watch for the other half to go ashore. Mala was back on board before nightfall the first day and did not leave her ship again.

Aubrey noticed that everyone reported back as ordered. She also noted that there were few supplies brought on board. Willie had told her that their next stop, Bermuda, would be where they would buy a storeroom full of supplies.

It was mid-morning of the second day that Mala had Morgan broach a serious offer to Aubrey. "We could leave you here and you could book passage to anywhere you like." He was saying.

"Morgan, please understand. I have no money, no jewels, nothing to trade for passage. Besides, I have nowhere to go." Aubrey answered.

"You wanted to go to Africa once."

"I know but I have no one there." Aubrey replied sadly.

Morgan smiled and patted her hand. He was glad she was refusing but wondered what he would tell Mala. He knew that the captain wanted to be rid of her and the reminder of Aubrey's stay on the *Widow Maker*. "Then I

will just let Captain Mala know that we have a new crew member on board."
Morgan said with his winning smile. Aubrey smiled up at him a bit more
hesitantly. She doubted that Captain Mala would be pleased.

In the next few days, Aubrey's suspicions proved right. The dark haired
woman seemed to avoid her whenever possible. Unfortunately, Aubrey saw
more of the Scotsman than the captain. Whenever Deats looked at her,
Aubrey had the urge to scream. Sometimes, the man reminded her of
Beaufort in his silent tormenting and his very presence unnerved her. At least
Deats showed no interest in her as Beaufort had. Aubrey had noticed that the
Scotsman's attentions seemed to focus on the captain but the woman was not
returning any of his attentions.

Although Captain Mala barely spoke to her directly, Aubrey noticed that
the woman definitely had a commanding quality and that the men on this ship
did exactly as they were told. Aubrey also noticed that Mala did have a
humorous side. Well at least with her men anyway. Was it yesterday or the
day before that one of men caught a large fish nearly as long as a tall man?
Mala had walked up to him and slapped him on the back saying, "At least this
time we can share in your good fortune. The last time the large fish nearly
had you on the other end of his hook."

The man was slightly embarrassed but laughed with everyone on deck.
Aubrey found out later from Morgan that this man had caught a large fish but
was unable to pull it in and ended up overboard.

Aubrey longed to be friendly with Mala but her bravery often failed her.
Going up on deck, she noticed storm clouds on the horizon of the portside of
the ship. She found Mala on the quarterdeck talking with Deats and
Timmons. Taking a deep breath and gathering up her courage, Aubrey
headed for the quarterdeck. Glancing at the storm again, Aubrey saw
lightening and stopped at the rail to watch for a while.

"Here she comes, Captain." Deats said, catching sight of Aubrey. Mala
made a disgusted sound and looked to the storm.

Aubrey was climbing up the steps to the quarterdeck when she heard the
captain order, "Deats, drop the sails and turn our backs to the storm.
Timmons, use the wind to our advantage. Maybe the storm will blow us all
the way to Bermuda."

The men acknowledged and Deats moved to the deck. He greeted Aubrey
with a subtle nod as he passed her at the foot of the steps. Aubrey watched
as did everyone else when the sails were dropped then flapped and swayed.
Finally the wind caught them just right and they bellowed open. The men
flew into securing lines.

Trying to ignore the younger woman, Mala turned to look at the storm.
She had found out that Aubrey's time at sea had been confined to the *Gull*

and then the *Widow Maker*, being constantly informed by Morgan and Robert who had somehow managed to get some part of her recent history out of her. The thought of Rene Black and this woman together on board his ship made Mala think of the mark she had seen on Aubrey's chest. Knowing how a woman would receive such a mark and what it represented made Mala seethe inwardly with jealousy.

Aubrey stepped up onto the quarterdeck. Not sure of how to talk to the captain, Aubrey opened her mouth and the words tumbled out in her nervousness. "It is unusual to see a woman pirate and probably not one that would be a captain who would order a crew of men. How did you come to be captain?"

Mala turned and looked Aubrey unblinkingly for a long moment. If Aubrey thought Black was menacing, then this Captain Mala was the epitome of impending doom. Suddenly wishing that she had asked Morgan the question instead, Aubrey was surprised when Mala answered the question in a dry tone.

"I walked up to a British officer and shot him in the face, at close range, on a busy city street, in the middle of day, on a dare. Then I walked away." The dark haired woman said with her unwavering stare.

When Aubrey's mouth dropped open and Mala's unsmiling visage did not change, Timmons had to look at the storm again before getting caught in a smile. Neither woman noticed his shoulders moving slightly with the chuckle that he tried to hide.

Aubrey regained her senses and asked incredulously, "You just walked away?"

Mala nodded and when Aubrey continued to stare at her, she added, "You see Miss Malone, human nature cannot escape the shock effect which may last only a few seconds. With it, I was able to just walk away. By the time the shock effect wore off, I was already across the street and about to disappear in the back alleys."

Mala paused a few seconds, then shrugged and turned to look at the storm. Over her shoulder, she continued to explain, "No matter how schooled one may be in self-control, the shock effect is the best defense we have. If you do not think quickly, you are either dead or caught and soon be dead. Thieves and robbers know this to be true. So as pirates who are both thieves and robbers..." Mala trailed off with another shrug.

"But a British officer in the middle of the day?" Aubrey whispered in disbelief.

"As a pirate, I have no use for the British Navy or any of those who play hero. To me, it was just one less British officer." Mala said undaunted by the younger woman's stunned expression.

Deats had returned having heard most of the conversation. "Captain, one of the men mentioned that the cargo hold is showing signs of water."

Mala rolled her eyes and reminded Timmons to watch the storm before leaving the quarterdeck. Aubrey watched her leave still unbelieving. "Mr. Deats, did she really?"

"Rally what?"

"Do that? Kill a man on a dare?"

"Aye, Miss Malone."

"My God! Who would dare someone to kill another person for no reason?" Aubrey repeated still unbelieving that someone could be so cold.

"I did." Deats answered simply.

Aubrey stared at him speechless. *What kind of people are these?* She thought. Deats shrugged and continued in his heavy Scottish accent, "The deal was if Mala did it and returned ta the ship unscathed, the men agreed that she would be their captain."

"Why?"

"Ye see, Miss Malone, the men figured that if someone was that cruel as ta kill a man in that fashion, in broad daylight and with so many witnesses aboot, then they would have a captain who would show no fear and who wouldna give up in a fight. Thus far, Mala has no' shown fear and has no' walked away from a fight."

"That I can believe."

"Good, ye would stay alive longer then. Dinna make her angry and dinna question her in front of the men again. She is the captain. Her word is law."

Aubrey left the quarterdeck still in mild shock over Mala's cruelty. When she entered the cabin, Morgan looked up, "Oh good, I was about to..." His words trailed as he noticed the expression on her face. "What is the matter?"

"I just found out how Mala became captain."

"Humph! Deats likes to..." Morgan began but Aubrey was shaking her head.

"No, not from Deats. From the Captain herself!" She said sitting down heavily on her bunk.

"She told you about that? Why would she even bring it up? She..." He was cut off by Aubrey's impatient reply.

"I asked her!"

Morgan burst out into laughter. "You asked her? I told you not to ask a question before checking with me first."

"My God, Morgan, she just walked up and killed a man on a dare! Do not lecture me..." She began.

"You mean two men." Morgan corrected.

Aubrey stared at him. "Two British officers? In broad daylight?" Morgan nodded chuckling at her expression as she whispered, "But the witnesses..."

Still chuckling, Morgan said, "Now there was the best part. The witnesses could not agree. Some witnesses said that the killer was tall and skinny, others said short and plump." Then with a shake of his head, he finished, "But they all agreed that the killer or rather assassin was a man!"

Aubrey shook her head and mumbled, "The shock effect."

"Aye that. Mala loves the shock effect as she calls it. She loves to see how people react." Morgan stated. Aubrey made a face and shook her head that he had such admiration for Mala.

Chapter 4

Captain John Alexander could do no more than look on as Captain Rene Black and about twenty members of *Widow Maker* crew were led into the courtroom. Alexander was a strikingly handsome man nearly a score and ten with blond hair and blue eyes. His tall and lean build along with a face rugged and lined from the sun and the sea made him irresistible to women, especially in his uniformed attire. His eyes turned to cold blue steel and his jaw set angrily as he looked at the prisoners.

Such a farce, he thought to himself. These men would have never made it this far had it not been for Lord Admiral Sir Walter Rothschild II and his ridiculous ideas of justice. Although the fate of Black and the *Widow Maker* would have been a watery grave, Alexander would have gladly celebrated the demise of this pirate and his crew as it would have been by his hand. Instead he was made to endure this idiocy of a tribunal for the sake of appearances.

This ordeal had taken a long time to come about. After the sinking of the *Widow Maker* and on the return to Charlestowne, Lord Admiral Rothschild had taken ill and they were forced to stop at Fort Caroline for medicines. For the last week, the Lord Admiral had been recuperating in his home south of Charlestowne. These entire proceedings had waited on the Lord Admiral as he regained his strength for the journey to Charlestowne.

Alexander's thoughts were interrupted as his eyes met Rene Black's. That one should not even be on this earth—walking and breathing! Alexander could barely control the rage of injustice he felt at that moment. His inner rage only heightened when Black gave him the barest hint of a smile before facing forward to watch the proceedings from the front of the pack as the trial began.

A smile! Alexander knew that if he stayed in the room any longer, he would end up destroying everything in his life because he would kill Black with his bare hands or at the very least, shoot the man. Turning to his aide, Alexander said calmly, "I am going out for some air. There is a stench in the room that is becoming unbearable."

Alexander gave a brief glance to the pirates as if to identify the smell he mentioned. The aide smiled at his commander's remark and nodded, "I will find you should they call you soon."

Alexander nodded his approval and stood up. Some eyes turned in his direction including Rene Black's. The women in the room fluttered their fans in hopes of attracting his attention so they could lower their eyelashes in a coquettish fashion. Men in uniform were considered a fine catch for marriage and Alexander normally would have played his part well but his mind was on the blasted Captain Rene Black.

As he stepped out of the building, he was hit by the humidity of the South's late summer. The heat of the day hung heavy in the air and the rains from the early morning hours only intensified the haze and humidity the South had become known for. He hated the Colonies, hated this weather and its unbearable heat, and adding to his frustration, hated the waste of time this trial was about to embark. Although trials for known pirates were only a formality because the pirates were always found guilty and were punished by hanging, the next few days were going to be a painful reminder to Alexander that he must remain careful with his own pleasures. If the Crown was to ever find out what he and his crew of the *Majestic* considered as a pleasurable sport, Alexander knew that he and his own men would be standing where the pirates now stood and face the same fate. For that reason, he always made sure that no one lived to tell any tales.

Alexander lit a cheroot and inhaled deeply the aromatic smoke. His mind drifted to those islanders who were simple, uneducated, and highly superstitious and who made the sport so enjoyable. How many times had he eased himself on a young island girl barely a woman, struggling beneath him? His officers certainly had enjoyed the fringe benefits just for being the elite of his crew. He smiled thinking that he certainly liked the fear that flowed from the women and more so when they fought him as he took his pleasure. Their fear made the taking of their innocence all the better. Their tears and screams only made him laugh as he 'plundered' the depths of their womanly being. God, he wanted to be at sea, to find another village filled with the young and untouched!

He shook his head in disbelief as he thought of these simple people and how they believed in unseen powers that controlled their lives then guided their spirits when the body ceased to function. He remembered one old woman who wore clothes of vivid colors along with a necklace of many strange decorations. She held a short staff with feathers and strange carvings embedded along its length. The old woman had made him laugh at the time, but he wondered why he would now remember her words?

With a bony crooked finger pointed at him, she had told him in a singsong voice, '*You will be the last! You will watch as your men slowly die away then you will face Revenge alone! You will find Revenge and she will repay you by taking your last breath! You cannot escape her for she will always be around. Her beauty hides well an inner wickedness and evil and you would not be able to resist the temptation she will offer! You will die!*'

The old woman had managed to scare one of his officers and Alexander remembered well what happened after that day. The officer was new to his crew but he enjoyed the added benefits. The old woman's words stayed with him for days, making him complain incessantly over equal shares while the officers met in the great cabin. Alexander was getting tired of the man's complaints. As it was the next island they came to had been the man's downfall. These islanders had an incredible disregard for what was valuable. Some of these islands had a wealth of gemstones just lying around.

As they gathered these gems and other goods that would bring a price, the new officer stated his complaints again, "There is no equal division in the shares. You and some of the better officers take more of a share than the rest of us and the crew. We should be equal in our take."

Alexander seemed to ponder this as he strode away from the man. His thoughtful gaze touched briefly on his 'better' officers as he looked in their direction. There were four of his officers who had been with him since the beginning, never requesting to be transferred to another command or be promoted to captain of their own vessel. They stayed with him and were loyal to him. Others had left for their own commands with his recommendations but met with accidents.

Alexander walked up to a pile of spears leaning against a hut. He picked up one idly and heaved it, testing the feel of such primitive weaponry. Some of the men around him glanced at one other in uncertainty as they watched him with the weapon.

"Well, Mr. Thompson, as I have said before, I do acknowledge your point and will take it under advisory."

Suddenly Alexander lunged forward with the spear in hand. The man, Thompson, was surprised at his sudden movement and did not react quickly. The spear was embedded into his chest, the point finding an exit through his back. Thompson fell dead on the ground near several of the dead natives. Some of the officers looked at Alexander warily as he took a step toward the dead body. His four friends merely smiled or chuckled, looking unconcerned.

"However, I find that I disagree with you." Then looking around at the other officers, he smiled handsomely and in a flippant tone, added, "Sorry to see this happen, men. One of the natives managed to surprise one of our own. Most unfortunate, do you not agree?"

Laughter came from his 'better' officers while the others smiled, somewhat taken aback. Alexander chuckled evilly and said, "Well the only good thing to this misfortune is that Thompson has relinquished his part of the take. We will divide his share among ourselves. The crew need not know, what say all of you?"

"That sounds like an excellent plan, Captain." One man said as he stepped over Thompson's body and around the spear protruding from it.

"Aye, Captain. He was always complaining anyway. If you had not killed him, then I would have." Said another man as he took hold of the spear and moved it from side to side. Alexander chuckled at their disregard for the dead.

Still chuckling, he and his 'better' officers turned away from the dead body, preparing to leave. A man stood looking down at the dead body and asked, "Captain Alexander? Are we to leave the body here? Should we not take it home for burial?"

His answer was a hearty laugh from the five officers. "Certainly not! We leave it. The fewer questions asked the less we must answer. As far as anyone is concerned, Thompson was swept away during a storm." Alexander told him then turned away to gather some of the goods that could be traded or bring a nice price.

"And the crew back on the ship?" The man continued to question.

"Damn! They will believe what you tell them! You have a brain, do you not? Must I always put the words in your bloody mouth!" Alexander exploded.

Alexander slowly became aware of the covert glances he was getting from the women who walked passed him. His smile and nod caused many women to hide their smiles behind lacy fans. As he watched a pair of attractive women pass him, Alexander realized that the Carolinas were not so bad after all. Perhaps some good will come to help him to salvage an otherwise wasted court vigil.

His aide appeared at his side and with a nod of acknowledgment, Alexander tossed down the remains of his cheroot onto the dusty road then followed the younger man back into the building. Black watched as Alexander and his aide returned. Not taking his seat but continuing on, Alexander faced the magistrate.

Standing before the pirates in the witness box, the accuser introduced himself to the court, "I am Captain John Samuel Alexander of the *HMS Majestic*. My present assignment is to control the waters off the coast of the Colonies and due south to the Windward Islands from marauders and pirates. I have tracked the before-elusive pirate, Captain Rene Black and his crew of the *Widow Maker*, for the last two years. While escorting the Lord Admiral Rothschild and his ship, the *Lady Elizabeth*, we were finally able to engage the captain and his crew off the coast of Bimini, a small island in the Caribbean."

"What say you of the charges against these men?" The magistrate asked.

"Your Honor, these men are dangerous to humanity. They have killed passengers of innocent ships all for the jewelry and small fortune they may have possessed. These passengers were men and their families, women and children, who..." Alexander was saying in a horrified tone for the full effect of the women present. Murmurs from the crowd greeted his statement. He lowered his head as if in sorrow for the innocents lives lost and played on the sympathy.

The magistrate was calling for silence as Black watched Alexander with a smile. What a performance! Black thought to himself. His dark eye turned to the crowd where many women waved their fans and shook their heads in disbelief.

"Continue when you are able, Captain."

"Yes, Your Honor." Alexander replied then paused as if to remember what he was saying. Raising his head, he presented a sad and grief-stricken face, "Men and their families desiring to make the Colonies their new home. Instead their lives were snuffed like a candle at the hands of these devils before you." Alexander flung his arm out in the direction of the pirates.

Again there were murmurs and raised voices. Again the magistrate quieted the crowd.

"Do you, Captain, have proof of such dastardly deeds by these men particularly?" The magistrate asked.

"Indeed!" Pulling from a pocket within his uniform, Alexander unfolded a posting. The magistrate held out his hand for the paper as Alexander stepped from the witness box and presented it to him. Stepping back to the witness box, the British captain waited for the magistrate's attention.

"This is a notice concerning the disappearance of a young woman by the name of Miss Aubrey Malone. She is the niece of Jonathan Hacker, a prominent man from London."

There was a rumbling not from the crowd but from the pirates themselves. Beaufort's bellowing voice could be heard over the muted chatter of the men, " ...so the little Irish bitch had an uncle! So what!"

Several of the pirates jabbed Beaufort in the ribs to silence him but the magistrate had heard his words. "You know of her?"

"Aye, we ...what the hell...!" A cuff to the ear stopped Beaufort. The magistrate looked to Black who gave a slight nod of his dark head to the magistrate.

"And her whereabouts at this moment?"

"Who gives a bloody hell about her!" Beaufort said angrily, turning to his right to dare Boulet to cuff him again. This time the cuff came from behind given by his other pal, LaVoie. Beaufort gave an angry retort in rapid French.

"Curb your tongue!" The bailiff said menacingly as he stepped towards them.

Black lifted a hand to stop the bailiff and the magistrate spoke up, "Never mind, Lieutenant."

When the pirates quieted themselves, the magistrate asked again looking at Black, "Her whereabouts?"

"In hell!" Beaufort replied loudly. This time the cuff came from Rene Black.

"Be quiet, you idiot!" He growled in French and turned an angry glare on Beaufort. Seen by all in the room, Black's angry look only reinforced in the minds of the gathered crowd that pirates were ruthless and hell-bent.

"Captain, can you explain the whereabouts of Miss Malone?" The magistrate asked pointedly.

Black looked at Alexander then back to the magistrate before answering calmly, "At the moment, I have no idea where she is."

A murmur ran through the crowd as Black caught the knowing smile of Alexander. With pure mischievous intent, Black added, "She was on board my ship when the *Majestic* bombarded it with cannon fire and caused it to sink. I believe that Miss Malone could not swim and had a fear of the water."

A hush filled the room as all eyes then turned to Alexander who looked around and said defensively, "I had no idea that she was aboard that pirate ship. How could I possibly know that?"

"You are accusing me of taking her. Where else would she have been?" Black asked quietly as if presenting a child a thoughtful question.

"Dead! But not before you took her innocence!" Alexander exclaimed, pounding his fist angrily on the smooth wood railing. His outburst caused the courtroom to once again fill with shocked tones. The magistrate called for silence again while Alexander and Black held hateful glares on the other from across the room.

"Do you have any other proof, Captain?" The magistrate asked the blonde Captain.

Alexander did not twitch as he continued to glare at Black and the magistrate was made to call on him several times before getting an acknowledgment.

"Yes, Your Honor. On one occasion, I spoke with a Captain Rosset of the *Artemis* who told me that Captain Black approached him with the intent of selling a young woman as a slave. That young woman was identified by Captain Black as one Miss Aubrey Malone."

A deathly silence filled the courtroom and all eyes turned to Black. Seeing the expressions and noting the reactions of those in the room, Alexander decided to further discredit Rene Black in the eyes of the court, "This young woman was only ten and nine years when she was taken from the safety of the *Gull*. This by the word of Captain Rosset who had confirmation that Captain Black orchestrated the attack on the *Gull*. Black told Rosset himself."

Slowly closing his eye, Black realized that in a moment of rage and humiliation, he had signed his own death warrant by bragging to Rosset about the *Gull*. Alexander paused again for effect and looked at Black.

Seeing the pirate captain's reaction, a small smile of victory stole across Alexander's face. Making a quick decision, Alexander added, "I have also spoken with several merchant captains that tell of a ship answering to the description of this pirate's vessel raiding and burning villages in the Caribbean. When my crew would investigate, we would find entire villages burned and the inhabitants slaughtered."

Many of the pirates angrily bellowed in French. Black, however, stared intently at Alexander. So intense was the stare that Alexander felt as though Black sensed or knew the truth. Impossible! There was no one left behind to tell tales!

But Black was guessing at the truth. He remembered a burned village, many graves, and a heavy heart. Was it possible that Alexander was responsible? Did Mala survive because Alexander had taken her prisoner, the spoils of war? Mala hated the British and Black knew that. Could she be blaming him for Alexander's appearance and her captivity by him because she had been left on that cursed island? Suddenly Black felt an insatiable urge to kill the man. What must she have endured at Alexander's hand?

The magistrate gestured for Alexander to step down. The bailiff approached the magistrate and spoke in low tones. When the bailiff stepped away, the magistrate announced, "His Lord Admiral Rothschild has experienced some difficulty in his arrival. We will reconvene in the morning."

The magistrate stood up and left the room. The bailiff and his guards escorted the pirates from the room. Black was the last to leave as he watched Alexander with new interest. He would have been just as surprised as his men at the accusation of the burned villages had he not witnessed one himself.

Alexander eyed Black as the pirate was escorted from the room. The look he received from Black left him disturbed and very uncomfortable. What did the man know? Alexander was certain there were no survivors of the *Majestic*'s excursions in the Caribbean.

It was late in the afternoon when Alexander appeared in the holding area where Black and his men were jailed. Alexander found that Black had a cell to himself and was sitting on the floor with one arm draped over a raised knee while gazing up at a window high on the wall.

The jeers and disparaging remarks to his family lineage gave Alexander's

43

presence away. Black looked around to find him approaching his cell.

"Wishing to be out there?" Alexander asked in gloating fashion.

"No, just wondering where someone is right now." Black replied, smiling reflectively.

"I am sure Miss Malone drowned by your carelessness, Captain. From her description on the notice, I imagine that she was quite fetching."

Black merely shrugged. His mind was not her but on another woman. In answer to Alexander, Black said with a smile, "I suppose she was pretty in her way."

Alexander chuckled at the remark, "Most women are pretty in their own way. Some radiate while others merely twinkle."

Black smiled as his mind drifted again to Mala. Alexander looked hard at the man then with his own smile, he said, "You are not thinking of Miss Malone. Someone else more lovely, perhaps?"

Black pondered for a moment before replying, "More dangerous, I think. No, deadly." With a nod as if to confirm his own musings, Black said a bit quieter, "Oui, deadly."

Alexander was intrigued as he glanced up at the small window. A dangerous yet deadly woman was out there somewhere. A woman who had captured the thoughts of this pirate captain.

"I think I would like to meet this one." Alexander said as he looked back at Black.

"You may have already, Captain." Black replied with a strange look.

"I am sure, Captain, that I would have remembered such an encounter." Alexander responded with a smile.

Black looked at him and decided not to venture any further. He did not like the idea of Mala in the hands of Alexander and at the moment he was certain he did not want it confirmed either.

A silence prevailed for a few moments before Alexander said conversationally, "We both know that these trials are for the benefit of the magistrates. It merely feeds their self-worth." Adding a shrug, he put in, "You should consider yourself lucky that you are here and having to endure the proceedings. Most pirates die at sea and not always going down with their ships as the stories are told."

Black knew Alexander would have killed him when he was taken from the *Widow Maker* had it not been for Lord Admiral Rothschild. After Alexander had struck Black in front of the Lord Admiral without cause, the Lord Admiral had guessed at his junior officer's intent. So by Rothschild's order, the pirates were imprisoned on the *Lady Elizabeth* and not the *Majestic*. That ship under the command of Alexander merely continued with their duty of escorting the Lord Admiral.

"How many islands am I responsible for destroying?" Black asked, looking at the blond-haired man.

The question took Alexander by surprise. Black had cut straight into the heart of the matter. Alexander eyed him and, after a few seconds of deliberating, he replied, "One could never really keep count of such misfortunes."

"Interesting word you use, misfortunes. I wonder if the villagers had thought of that in their final moments." Black mocked as he stood up and turned casually to face Alexander. "But then misfortunes do occur far too often and at the most inopportune times." Black said, thinking of all the obstacles that had gotten in his way and caused his delay in getting back to Mala during that fateful journey.

"Indeed, Captain. Such is an example of poor Miss Malone. It was her misfortune to be on the *Gull* when you decided to raid it. It was her misfortune to be young and beautiful that you could not resist taking her along with you. It was also her misfortune that you did not ask her opinion in the affair, you just kidnaped and ravished yet another young life." Alexander said smugly.

Black smiled at the man. He never had Aubrey. Beneath his very nose, his own quartermaster dared to take his woman. Black turned away from Alexander still smiling. By his own choice and in memory of a lost love, Aubrey was never really his woman. Finding that Mala was still alive, Black could not have been more pleased with the outcome of his relationship with Aubrey. He could honesty tell Mala that nothing ever happened. Taking a deep breath, Black realized that he might never see Mala again to tell her any of this. Once again, prison bars had come between them.

"Tis a pity though that Miss Malone is no longer with us. I am sure she would substantiate all that I say is true. Fortunately, the courts consider officers as fine witnesses and, if no other witnesses are available, our word is enough." Alexander continued in his self-importance.

"Yes, fortunate for you. What I do not understand is why you say you were tracking me for nearly two years. I do not recall encountering you at sea." Black said.

"You are responsible for the death of my uncle. He helped me throughout my military training, his influence helped my quick rise to the rank of Captain, and obtaining my first command of a British warship, the *Majestic*. According to some of your pirate acquaintances who had not been as fortunate as yourself the benefit to undergo a trial, I was told of your boasting in the demise of a certain ship." Alexander refrained to mention that his uncle was also the one who had taught him the pleasures found among the Caribbean islands and its inhabitants.

"Captain, I am responsible for the sinking of many ships. After all, this was what you have implied in the courtroom today." Black said with an air of boredom. "So which ship had I encountered that earned me your wrath?"

"As you say, Captain, you are responsible for destroying many ships. You may not even remember but my uncle was the captain of a ship named the *Dodger*."

Black's entire body tensed at the name. He did remember that ship and very well. It had been the ship that changed his life forever. Turning slowly to face Alexander, Black took a step closer to him. Through clenched teeth of barely controlled anger, he said quietly, "Oh, I do remember that one, Captain, and if I could have then, I would have killed the man a thousand times over for what I found in his hold."

Alexander was taken aback again, this time by the fierceness of Black's rage. But ignoring common sense, he too took a step closer to Black and snarled, "Slaves are a matter of business, Captain. There is nothing wrong with that."

Without warning, Black's hand shot through the bars and had Alexander by the throat. The other pirates had been watching the encounter and now made noises to encourage their captain.

"Aye, kill him!"

"Kill the bastard, Captain!"

"Break his bloody neck, Captain!" They yelled out.

The ruckus attracted the attention of the guards who came running to Alexander's aid. Before they reached him, Black shoved him away and moved to the center of the cell out of reach of the guards' truncheons.

Alexander laid in a huddled heap gasping and coughing for air. One guard was helping Alexander to his feet while the others collected around the cell door waiting for another guard to unlock it. Black, so enraged with the reminder of the *Dodger*, was ready for a fight. He needed the outlet even if it meant that he would be beaten to death by the guards.

The lock clicked and the guards prepared to overtake Black when Alexander managed to order in a pitiful croak, "Wait!"

The guards looked at him in disappointment that they could not handle the prisoner their way. Alexander shakily stepped into the cell with Black. It was Black's turn to be taken aback. The man would dare to take the chance. But Black did not care and took a step toward Alexander. He stopped suddenly as Alexander pulled out his pistol and pointed it directly at Black's forehead.

The remaining crew of the *Widow Maker* quieted in an instant. Time seemed to stand still as all were motionless until Black's deep resonating voice finally broke the silence, "Shoot me and you will miss seeing me hang."

Alexander understood the double meaning to that statement. Although he could plead innocence in the entire episode, this particular magistrate was not known for patience of mishandling prisoners. Even the guards would have received stiff punishments for what was seemingly justified. Alexander was becoming disillusioned with the entire justice process. Shooting Black would have been a pleasure at sea where no one would know the truth. But here, after one day of trial, the act would be considered irrational and excessive.

Alexander lowered his pistol and turned his back on Black as if daring him to strike now with the guards present. Then, turning at the opened door, Alexander said, "I will make sure to be present for your hanging, Captain. I will want to ensure that nothing goes wrong on that day."

Glaring at Alexander, Black felt the urge to break the man's neck but had already decided as the guards fumbled with the lock that he would escape from this prison instead. Somehow he would escape to find Alexander and put him through the same punishment Mala had to endure at the hands of his uncle. If possible, he would also find Mala and let her be witness to the slow and agonizing death of the nephew.

Chapter 5

The next day, the trial proceedings had continued with the appearance of the Lord Admiral. If the magistrate knew of the incident in the prison, he made no mention of it. But Alexander felt uncomfortable throughout the day, wondering if he was going to be called to explain his actions in the prison. He had made his testimony already and, therefore, his contact with the prisoners was no longer necessary, nor warranted.

After the Lord Admiral made his testimony, the magistrate called for a break to partake of the noon meal. Once again, Black and his men were escorted back to their holding cells.

"How long do you suppose we have before they hang us, Captain?" One of the men asked.

Black shrugged indifferently, "Depends on whether they want us to hang all at once or one at a time, I suppose. I figure we have at least a week."

"A week?" One man said weakly.

That afternoon they found out they had nearly a month. A platform to hold four at a time was to be constructed and when the magistrate returned from his appointed court circuit of the Carolinas, which he speculated would be one month from that date, the hangings would take place.

Alexander smiled at the verdict. As was expected, he had thought. Now Black had a month to think about all that had happened and that 'dangerous and deadly' woman. In the meantime, Alexander would set sail to find this elusive creature. Black's description intrigued him as Alexander imagined such a woman in his bed.

Alexander chuckled quietly as the magistrate asked the prisoners if they had any last comments for their defense. The loud one named Beaufort spoke up, "I will see you all in Hell!"

As the courtroom emptied, Alexander raised a hand to stay the guard who was about to take Black away. When there was no one within earshot, Alexander stepped up closely to Black and looking the pirate in the eye, said softly, "I was so intrigued with that description of the dangerous and deadly woman that I made inquiries in the local taverns." Alexander watched an unblinking Black for a reaction and received none. "In those inquiries, I was fortunate enough to get a name."

Still, getting the same lazy stare from the pirate, Alexander said softly with a crooked smile crossing his lips. "Mala."

With a nod of his head, he signaled for the guard to take Black away. The pirate craned his neck to continue to stare at the British captain as he was being taken from the courtroom. That subtle reaction was the confirmation Alexander needed to tell him that he was right.

Standing outside of the building, Alexander lit a cheroot and began to make plans to set sail. He had been cooped up in this port too long and he was ready for some sport. He was sure his men were ready to leave as well. A woman who strolled ever so slowly on the boardwalk across from him caught his attention. Her blonde curls bounced as she walked and her parasol twirled to attract his attention. Having gotten it, she smiled shyly and looked at him from beneath her darkly painted lashes. Returning the smile, Alexander decided that the next morning would be a good time to leave instead as he made his way towards the young woman.

Since she had decided to stay on the *Enchantress*, Aubrey helped out where she could. Most days she was in the galley with Willie. But other days, she was able to work alongside the crew when Morgan and Robert would assign her duties such as mending or helping with the sails. She learned to keep time with the men she was working with, matching every pull as they hoisted the sails, even though the men were doing most of the muscle work. On those days she was assigned to that duty, she would wear a shirt with the sleeves cut out at the shoulder. From working the sheets and lines, her upper arms were becoming firm and strong and being on the deck in the sun for long periods of time, her once fair skin turned a light golden brown. The sun had intensified her auburn hair that hung just at her shoulders, and she almost always wore it pulled back with a ribbon or loosely braided.

The *Enchantress* was on a course to Bermuda and the long warm days gave way to idle lazy hours for the crew. All duties aside for the day for the both of them, Morgan decided that it would be a good day for Aubrey to practice her hand at using a weapon, the rapier.

Aubrey was in the cabin, lying on her bunk looking at a book that she had borrowed from Mala's large library with Morgan's help. She had not had the courage to approach Mala since the day she asked about how she became captain. Her loose auburn hair was fanned out on the bunk under her head and her booted feet were propped up against the wall. She glanced up at him as he entered the cabin then went back to her reading without a word.

"It is lovely on deck this afternoon. Mala has us drifting so the men could do a bit of fishing. Are you up to some practice?" He began then saluted her with his rapier. She closed the book and sat up, watching him with a small twinkle in her eye.

To her, he was nothing more than a teacher, a friend, and a roommate, although she knew he wished for more as his conversations had sometimes suggested of late. But she did love fencing with him. Morgan had been teaching her the basic skills but Aubrey was ready to try her hand at actually using the weapon in a mock battle.

"Very well." She replied.

He sheathed his weapon and opened the door for her, "After you, Miss...and by the way, the winner today has to serve the other's dinner."

"Pardon me?" She asked as they went down the corridor.

"Well, we certainly are not intending to kill one another, so there has to be some kind of stakes or reward in this battle..." He shrugged. Dinner being served to him was the one thing he could honorably ask for after a victory against her.

She was pulling on her gloves as they walked along but now she stopped suddenly turned and offered a hand to him, "A deal then sir... and a duel." He shook her hand and they went topside.

Deats was on the quarterdeck and watched them questioningly as they came out into the sunshine, "And what are ye up ta?" He called down to them from the railing.

"A bit o' practice for the lass." Morgan said with an exaggerated Irish accent for her benefit making her roll her eyes.

Deats regarded him then replied, "Well, dinna kill anyone, and whatever mess ye make, ye will be responsible for cleaning it up."

"Aye sir..." They replied in unison with fake Scottish accents to torment him as well. He exhaled and walked away from the railing. Mala came up to the quarterdeck from another set of steps.

"Morgan is giving her lessons in fencing." Deats informed before she asked.

"The children must play." She said with half a smile.

Morgan was standing close to Aubrey, obviously explaining something to her and demonstrating moves and thrusts as she was watching and listening intently. Then he was behind her, with his arms around her, showing her how to hold the weapon for certain thrust techniques. Aubrey was beginning to not like his closeness as she tried to shrug Morgan off, "Are we going to practice or shall I go back to my book?"

"If you are ready." He said stepping back easily.

"I have been ready since we came up on deck." She replied in a matter of fact tone of voice.

"Very well then, on your guard, Miss." He said taking the initial stance himself. He nodded to her left hand, "Remember, always good form, even in battle."

She promptly tucked her left hand to the small of her back, "Unless I have a dirk in that hand."

"You are correct." He agreed as he suddenly thrust toward her.

51

Aubrey put everything into the practice and soon felt the thrill of it. As she parried and thrust at Morgan, a vision of Jean Luc crossed her mind's eye. Would he have taught her this? She wondered.

Morgan noted a smile on her lips, "Battle is serious business, Miss Malone..." He taunted as he made his attacks a bit stronger. She was good, he had to admit, and it had not taken her long to get this good. He had no doubt that she would be able to easily defend herself against any man if need be now. That was his goal because he knew that this was what his captain would want as well. He saw Mala from over Aubrey's shoulder as she stood with Deats on the quarterdeck watching them.

After several maneuvers, he backed Aubrey against the gunwale as she continued to fend him off. At one point he was pushing his blade against hers and she was bent slightly backward, but holding her own against him. He made certain not to use his full strength against her, mindful that this was a woman. But she was incredibly strong for a young woman, a strength gained from her duties on deck. She pushed against his blade with hers and she held his wrist with her free hand. He was very close again, his lower body against hers.

She started to bring up her knee and he backed off with a smile. Looking down at her leg, he said, "Let us not get personal, Aubrey."

"Would that not be the correct move if this were a real battle?" She asked in mock innocence.

"You have a point, but we will not need that move today." He nodded with a slight smile. She shrugged and brought her weapon back into the initial position. "Just practicing." He reminded her.

At the sight of the struggle by the gunwale, Deats winced and muttered, "Ach, that is close." He glanced at Mala but her face was void of expression. The two made another round about the deck below. Some of the men had stopped to watch and could be heard cheering Aubrey on. She was against the gunwale again and Morgan sensed that she was tiring. He pressed in hard again and disarmed her with one quick swirl of his blade against hers, her weapon clattering to the deck behind them. The men announced their unhappiness with 'boos' and 'hisses' and calls of 'bad form against the lady, Mr. Alcott' toward him.

He still leaned in against her with his blade close to her throat, his face just inches from hers. As she brought up her hands to push against his chest, she felt the hilt of his dirk. Seizing the dirk in a swift move, Aubrey swung her arm out to the side.

Morgan felt the move and at the same time felt her knee come up again. He chuckled and grabbed the back of her knee. Feeling herself falling overboard brought back an old fear and she dropped the small blade to grab him by the front of his shirt with both hands. The momentum of her falling backward, holding onto him, and his being bent over so close to her was all that was needed to assist gravity in pulling him over the side with her.

They hit the water almost at the same time. Morgan came up first and shook his head to clear the water from his face and hair. He looked around for Aubrey who surfaced seconds later near him and was sputtering water and gasping while she thrashed frantically in the water. He grasped her by the shoulder of her shirt and smiled, pulling her towards him.

"I guess I won." He told her.

She grabbed for his arm that held her and sputtered in horror, "I...I cannot swim."

When the two went over, Deats cursed quietly as the lookout was heard to call out with much humor in his voice, "Man overboard!"

A broad smile spread across Mala's face when they popped back up out of the blue water. With a chuckle, she turned to Timmons and said quietly, "Woman too." Timmons laughed as Deats grunted in disapproval.

"Mr. Alcott, do get back on the ship before you become shark bait." Robert called down from the railing amid his chuckles.

"I have you." Morgan soothed as Aubrey still had a death grip on his arm while he was treading water.

"Sharks?" Aubrey fretted.

"There are no sharks, we are fine." He laughed.

Aubrey's face turned suddenly serious and she pulled herself closer to him. "Morgan, what is that?" She asked pointing behind him.

"Damn!" Robert spat out the word as he saw what she was pointing to. Several of the men were leaning over the sides pointing excitedly. Morgan turned to see a gray fin had surfaced behind them some distance away. He put his arm around her chest and took her in tow as he easily swam toward the ship. One of the men dropped down a rope ladder for them and Morgan helped Aubrey to get her footing.

"Relax, he will only nibble you a little bit...just as I might do." He muttered softly. She snapped her head around to look at him but he only smiled and went back to helping her. "Be still, thrashing around will only heighten our...uh...his interest." He finished with a small smile.

"Get out of the water now, Mr. Alcott!" Robert was calling with some urgency from above.

Aubrey was up the ladder first. With the shark just a few feet away, Morgan pulled himself up out of the water. Out of the corner of his eye, he saw a flash and turned to see a long pike embedded into the shark's thick-skinned side. The shark thrashed noisily then finally turned belly up in a pool of blood. Aubrey looked down at Morgan who was close behind her on the ladder.

"See what happens to animals that bite people?" She told him. All he could do was smile and shrug at her quick wit.

Robert hoisted a very wet Aubrey onto the deck and she thanked him. As she twisted water out of her sleeves and the tail of her now loose shirt, Aubrey's face turned serious. Mala had approached them, eyeing her then looking at Morgan who was just climbing on deck. Impressed that Aubrey thought to use her opponent's weapon against him, Mala smiled and purposefully clapped her on the back so hard that the younger woman stumbled forward.

"Thanks to you Aubrey, the men will eat well tonight." Aubrey turned in surprise to Mala, unable to believe that the captain spoke to her pleasantly.

"I beg your pardon?"

"You proved to be very good bait." Mala said with a smile.

Morgan and the crew on deck roared with laughter with the exception of Deats who found nothing amusing from the episode. Aubrey smiled at the remark as Mala turned and walked away.

"Shall we shed these wet clothes." Morgan began. She turned on him and he put out his hands in surrender, "Discreetly! Discreetly!"

She followed him below deck and once in the corridor she grumbled, "The deal was that one of us would serve the other dinner, not serve as bait for dinner!"

Morgan laughed again and opened the door to their cabin, "You first, loser. Call me when I can come in."

"Keep that attitude up and you might find yourself standing out here in wet clothes all night." She said sweetly then closed the door firmly.

When the *Enchantress* reached Bermuda, Mala and some of the crew were going to shore to the marketplace located in townsquare. Morgan had asked Mala for permission to allow Aubrey to go to shore as well. Granting the request, Mala ordered that the younger woman dress up like a cabin boy to hide her gender and prevent unwanted attention. Now while she waited on deck for Morgan, Aubrey tugged and pulled at her clothes, muttering to herself.

"Stop that." Morgan admonished as he and Mala walked up behind her.

With a startled gasp, Aubrey turned and said disgustedly, "Look at me! I look like a boy!"

"Not quite, put this hat on." He told her.

Aubrey stared at the tricorn then, with a loud sigh, she piled her auburn hair on the top of her head and stuffed it under the hat. She rolled her eyes as Morgan looked her over with humor twinkling in his blue eyes and said with a smile, "And now you are convincing boy."

He slapped at her hands as she tugged on the waistband of her britches. Aubrey let out a low growl as they headed for the rope ladder leading down to the longboat. Neither of them noticed Mala's smile of amusement.

Chapter 6

The small market was found in the center of the townsquare and Aubrey looked at the unusual foods on display. Mala had called them fruits but Aubrey did not care for those called mangos. The texture felt strange on her tongue. That word 'strange' kept coming to Aubrey's mind as it seemed to summarize a great deal of what she was seeing.

Watching as Mala conversed easily with a merchant in a language she never heard before, Aubrey looked at the basket of fruits the man handed the captain when she laid down the money. As Mala started away, the man called her back by name for her change but she waved it aside with a smile.

At the same moment, not far away, John Alexander heard the name carried on the wind. He turned in time to see Mala step back up to the stand in response. Alexander watched with intense interest while this dark haired beauty completed her transaction then turned away with a smile. He smiled to himself as he thought of how fortuitous it was that he decided to come ashore. He had done so only out boredom and yet here was the very person he had been looking for since that conversation with Rene Black in the prison.

His eyes roamed over her, noting each line and curve of her body. She wore a red silk shirt and black britches with black knee-high cuffed boots. Tucked into the gold sash she wore around her slim waist, she carried two pistols, a cutlass and a dirk. His smile widened as he muttered aloud and nodded in agreement, "Indeed, dangerous and deadly. But you left out one very important detail, Captain Black, she is also very beautiful."

Stepping away from a table covered with an unusual aroma of prepared foods, Aubrey bumped into someone. Turning to apologize, she knocked over a basket of eggs that broke over the man's once-highly polished boots. All words stuck in her throat when she saw the British uniform.

With a vicious curse, the man exclaimed, "Son of a bitch! Look at what you did to my boots! What have you to say for yourself?" When Aubrey only stared wide-eyed, the man growled at her again, "Well, do you have a tongue, boy?"

The commotion attracted the attention of several people, among them were Mala and Alexander from their respective places. Before she could say anything, Robert stepped up and scooped Aubrey behind him as he faced the officer with an apologetic smile, saying, "Sorry, matey. This one is a clumsy little fish. Ain't worth picking on since there ain't much there to pick."

The officer snorted in reply and, glaring in Aubrey's direction, he reached around Robert trying to catch a hold of her sleeve and grumbled, "The boy needs to learn to clean up the messes he makes."

At that moment, Mala caught Morgan's eye and, with a slight jerk of her head, gave Morgan the command to step in. As he headed in their direction, the officer grabbed Robert by the front of his shirt and threw him aside with another curse. Robert crashed onto a nearby table leaving Aubrey exposed to the officer's assault.

"Ame damne!" Mala exclaimed under her breath as she too headed in their direction.

As Morgan approached, the officer had a struggling Aubrey by the arm. Seeing another man coming to him, the officer gave a mighty shove and Morgan soon found himself on the ground. When the officer turned his attention back to the boy, Mala interjected herself between the man and Aubrey. With a sweep of her arm, she broke his hold on Aubrey who fell to the ground. Now out of the officer's clutches, Aubrey scampered under a nearby table.

"All this for a pair of dirty boots." Mala stated calmly as she faced the officer.

Startled, he stepped back and noted the woman's attire. Seeing the surprise etched on the officer's face, Mala took the opportunity to bring her fisted hand up to squarely meet the man's chin. The officer's teeth met with a loud 'clomp' then he fell backwards in a graceful drop as Mala knocked him unconscious.

Alexander was amused to see his lieutenant knocked out cold by a woman. He watched as his men advanced on Mala who then drew her cutlass. Noting that several other men, including the two that his lieutenant had thrown aside, were preparing for battle, Alexander folded his arms across his chest and leaned against a nearby post to watch the show with amusement. This trip into the market was getting more interesting by the minute, he thought to himself as he watched Mala fight off his men.

The marketplace turned into chaos as townsfolk ran to get out of the way of the fight. Contents from tables were ripped or strewn around as the tables gave away under falling bodies. From her hiding place under a table, Aubrey scanned the area for Mala and Morgan. She found them fighting with their backs together.

With bodies falling and tables crashing around her, Aubrey looked for another safe haven. She noticed one man in a British uniform standing aside and watching the fight. Her curiosity peaked because the man stood with arms crossed and did not look like he was going to intervene.

A table crashing nearby brought Aubrey back to the matter at hand. Seeing no shiny boots nearby, she crept out from under the table. Just as she was about to stand, she was grabbed and lifted up from behind by unseen hands.

"Oh, what have we here?" Said a man from behind her.

Aubrey could see some of the men, pirates and British alike, stop fighting to look in her direction. Suddenly, her hat was swept off her head and sent sailing away from her. As the hat was swept away, the wind caught it and it landed at Alexander's feet. He stared at it idly then bent to retrieve it as his officer exclaimed, "Look, Captain! They were hiding this girl!"

Her auburn hair had spilled over her shoulders. As the man had caught her up, Aubrey knew he had felt the curve of her breast against his arm. He hoisted her as if to get a better hold but it was only to adjust his hold so that his arm still encircled her but now his hand covered a breast.

"And she feels mighty good to me!"

One of Mala's men was close enough to grab for Aubrey. His yank loosened the officer's hold on her and Aubrey found herself jerked away from the soldier.

"Hey, what the..." The man started to say but the point of Morgan's sword found its mark as he swiftly jabbed his sword into the man's chest.

The fight was about to resume when a report of a pistol was heard. Mala had her arm in the air and her pistol in hand. Looking into the mass of uniforms, Mala found one with the rank of Captain standing a short distance away. Meeting eyes with the man, she found herself staring into a face from the past. Images filled her mind as she looked at John Alexander then her blood ran cold and her stare turned deadly.

"You!" She spat full of hate. Standing next to her, Morgan glanced at her in surprise then followed her gaze to see the British captain.

Alexander was surprised to see the look of recognition in Mala's eyes. He had never met this beauty before yet she obviously recognized him. He was so intrigued with her expression that he did not miss the cold and cruel gaze. The woman absolutely fascinated him. His attention was drawn to one of his men who was about to strike the unsuspecting Mala.

"No!" He ordered. Hearing the authoritative voice, all eyes turned to Alexander. Face to face with the very man she had sought out for the past year, Mala felt the burning desire to kill him. Instead, she let out a shrill whistle and almost instantly the captain and crew of the *Enchantress* disappeared into the throngs of townsfolk who had gathered to watch the confrontation.

Seeing his quarry getting away, Alexander gave the order for his men to pursue but it seemed the whole town had taken the side of the pirates. They were blocking his men's pursuit and allowing the pirates to get away. Alexander cursed violently. Throwing down Aubrey's hat, he crushed it under his polished boot.

Deats was at the docks overseeing the loading of supplies when he heard the pistol shot and then the shrill whistle. By the time Mala, Aubrey, Morgan, and Robert appeared, he had the *Witch* prepared to cast off. In the longboat, Mala could see that her crew was being ferried back to the ship by some of the townsfolk. Then her eye caught sight of the *Majestic* moored nearby and her mouth dropped open as she stared at the ship.

Deats saw the look and knew where her thoughts were going. Aloud, Mala muttered, "All the better."

"We dinna have the time, Mala!" He shouted. Aubrey and Morgan followed Mala's gaze.

"Sweet Mary!" Aubrey exclaimed as she saw the warship up close.

Mala turned to Morgan and said in a tone that brooked no argument, "Man the cannons the moment we are on board!" Morgan nodded in agreement as Deats tried to reason with her.

"No Mala! We are ta close! When their magazines explode, we will go as well!"

"I will get my ship out of range, Deats! Morgan, you hit her until there is nothing left!" Mala ordered.

"Nothing will miss her!" Morgan replied firmly.

Aubrey felt the tension in the longboat as Deats held his tongue, glaring at the warship, while Morgan and Mala practically tasted the excitement of what was about to happen next. Not waiting for the longboat to settle beside her ship, Mala jumped for the rope ladder and raced up leaving the longboat to rock slightly. Aubrey sucked in a breath as the water sloshed over the sides, getting her legs wet. Morgan took her arm to soothe her as Deats helped with the longboat.

"I will be fine, Morgan. You go. She is expecting you." Aubrey whispered.

Morgan nodded and was up the rope ladder in an instant. Deats did not wait to ensure Aubrey's safety as he took the ladder next. As Robert went up next, the oarsman, Coleman, helped a shaky Aubrey to the ladder and said softly, "Ye best hurry up, Miss Aubrey. Ye want to be on board when she lets loose her cannons."

Aubrey nodded in understanding. The *Enchantress* would buck and rock with each blast of the cannons. Taking each step tentatively but hurriedly, Aubrey reached the railing and was aided on board by Robert who was watching and waiting for her.

"There you are, Miss Aubrey. Now find a safe place and hold on." He was saying as Mala bellowed orders to get the *Enchantress* out of range from return fire and the final explosion. The sails dropped and men ran about their duties to get the ship underway.

Aubrey sank down beside the bulkhead of the forecastle. From this vantage point, she could see the slow retreating shoreline as the *Enchantress* moved away from Bermuda. The warship looked grand and powerful as the *Enchantress* passed by. She could hear Morgan's voice yelling orders as he manned the cannons then there was the sound of the port doors dropping and the heavy cannons rolling into place.

Boom! The *Enchantress* pitched and rocked at the first blast. Boom! The second blast came quick on the heels of the first. Morgan's aim was remarkable. They hit the warship's broadside and Aubrey watched it shudder and roll slightly sideways. She covered her ears from the report of the deck cannons. As if in slow motion, the *Majestic* rolled to its side exposing its hull, then two more blasts came from the *Enchantress*, crashing into the hull of the big warship at the water line.

Aubrey looked up to see the sails of the *Enchantress* full of the wind. She could feel the ship pick up speed but the island seemed to be the same distance while the *Majestic* moved further away. She remembered that the *Enchantress* was anchored with her starboard side facing the island and realized that Mala was not heading for open sea but sailing along the shoreline of the island. She looked around for Mala and found her at the stern helping Timmons to navigate the ship while glancing over her shoulder to judge the distance.

After a moment, the sound of the cannons rolling back and the port doors closing could be heard. Moments later, Morgan appeared on deck and looked out at his handy work.

"Only four blasts?" Aubrey asked, moving to stand beside him.

"Tis all it will take today. I do not want to waste firepower. Hitting in the right places will get my desired results in short order." He replied confidently.

"Are we far enough away?" She asked squinting her eyes to look at the floundering warship.

At that moment, the *Majestic* turned into a fireball and Aubrey involuntarily ducked at the explosion. The magazine had ignited and now the ship was engulfed in flames. Splinters and other debris rained upon the port and docks while some had managed to land on the deck of the *Enchantress*. Men were ready with buckets of water to douse the burning timber.

One sail caught a burning timber and the winds fanned the heat to flames. Deats jumped into action by cutting the sail's stay lines and the stiff breeze swept the sail into the air, away from the ship.

Morgan smiled at Aubrey, "I guess that answers that."

Aubrey looked around for Mala and found her standing at the stern of the ship watching the black bellowing smoke of the *Majestic*.

As the *Enchantress* sailed safely away from Bermuda heading for their next destination, Mala stood rigid watching the *Majestic* burn and sink into the sea. Her fingers caressed the gold medallion that was hidden just inside her shirt. "For you, Rene …and you, Baccus." She muttered to herself. No one saw the sadness in the dark eyes.

Back on shore, Alexander bellowed orders to his men to get to the ship. Cursing and pushing aside anyone who got in his way, he finally fought his way through the masses of people in the market. As he cleared the crowd, he heard the first cannon fire in the harbor. He stopped in his tracks and waited, listening as his eyes darted wildly. He heard the report of deck cannons then there was the sound of a second large cannon. Breaking into a dead run, he headed for the docks.

As he rounded the corner of a building, the last between him and the water, he came to a sliding stop on the cobblestone street and looked out to the harbor. Looking towards the pirate ship, he noted that smoke wafted from her cannon port doors.

"That dark haired bitch is firing on my ship!" He growled to himself. His blue eyes widened with rage as he watched the *Majestic* roll up and present her belly to the pirate ship. "Christ!" He spat as he stepped forward unconsciously while two more blasts broke his ship at the waterline.

The *Majestic* was going down quickly. There seemed to be a surreal calm over the harbor and things seemed to be happening in slow motion for him. Suddenly, the silence was broken by the sound of a massive explosion and John Alexander watched as his mighty warship disintegrated before his eyes. The percussion and sound of the explosion caused him to involuntarily duck. With a deep intake of breath, he slowly drew himself to his full height and straightened his waistcoat from the wrinkles it had encountered during his run to the docks. Smoothing his blonde hair carefully, his teeth clenched tightly, he looked at the *Enchantress* as she sailed, nearly unscathed from the harbor. One of her sails was ablaze and he smiled evilly, "Fire on me, will you?"

But the smile faded quickly as he saw the sail flutter away from the ship and land in the debris-strewn waters between him and the *Enchantress*. "You are mine, Captain Mala." He said in a low growl. "I found you once, I will find you again and you will pay."

Turning back toward the town, he saw members of his crew standing in shocked silence at the sight. With a sudden inhuman growl, Alexander vented out some of his anger by smashing his fist into the jaw of the man standing nearest him. The man fell like a rock into the street. Blind rage masked the British captain's face as he advanced several steps toward the still gaping men. They scattered like crows, unwilling to be the next victim of his volatile anger. Turning back to the harbor, Alexander looked at the mess of floating, burning debris that was once his ship then looking down at the unconscious man at his feet, he drew back a booted foot and kicked the man savagely in the ribs.

Chapter 7

Days later as darkness was falling, Mala took up her mug and drained the remainder of the contents in it. Morgan was in her cabin with a chart spread out before him and he was talking quite adamantly. She really did not feel like entertaining him in any fashion, whether in conversation or business, but he was full of energy that it could not be contained. All she really wanted to do was go to her bunk and sleep until the blasted monthly curse was over.

"Well?" He asked as he sat perched on the corner of the table next to her chair.

Mala's dark eyes scanned the chart of the Colonies again. "Morgan, as I recall, the last time you were there, you got into a pack of trouble and I had to get you out of it." She began with a deep sigh.

He laughed lightly and pointed a finger at her, "You had help."

"I know." She replied, her tone hinting of a sadness. Morgan's demeanor reflected the solemn attitude of his captain for a moment. Each of them drifted back in their minds to that time and the comrade who had been her helper.

"Come on, Mala. We are nearly there—think of the possibilities. Merchant ships go up through there all the time on the way to the cities on the Chesapeake. We might catch one off guard—take a good haul." His voice was laced with excitement.

"They are hanging pirates like leaves from the trees up there, you simpleton. Not to mention that it will take us nearly two to three days to careen, if we are to have a good job done." She growled.

"No, we will not get caught off guard. It is well sheltered. You can see everything, but you cannot be seen." He fussed as he ran his finger along the chart to show her. He had chosen a small back bay off the northeastern shore of the Chesapeake. She pondered her first mate's selection as he drummed his fingers on the chart.

"Be still Morgan, you have far too much energy this evening." She said as she easily put her hand over his to stop the drumming that was beginning to irritate her. He looked at her for a moment and then leaned forward.

In a cooing voice he smiled, "You are tired, Captain, and you need a rest. While I, on the other hand, need to go ashore."

Mala removed her hand from his and sat back in her chair. She stretched her legs out, propping them on the other corner of the table opposite him, "So you plan to go ashore. To that town?" She paused and ran her fingers through her long dark hair. She watched him nod with a smile. "Morgan, do you want to die?" Her voice rose a bit in sarcasm as each word came out of her mouth.

"Hell no, Mala, I just need to go to shore." He told her smiling sheepishly and giving her a shrug.

"Oh." Mala stated simply as she sat up a bit straighter, catching his hidden meaning.

Morgan sat quietly and watched her in great anticipation. In an effort to sway her decision, he said suddenly, "I can take Aubrey then she will be out of the way. You know she will want to help with the careening and Deats would not be pleased over that prospect."

Mala watched his blue eyes as they sparkled in the candlelight. Even for her malady, she tried diligently to suppress the mirth that built in her but to no avail, it erupted with great gusto. He threw up his hands and got up from his seat on the table, "Ah, now what is so damned funny, Mala?"

Then her amusement erupted into real laughter, a welcomed, yet very rarely heard sound from the dark haired beauty that he called his captain and his friend. She was surprised to find that his comedy was actually making her feel better.

"You are, Morgan." She said stabbing a finger at him.

"Me?" He asked in perturbed puzzlement. He watched her dark eyes dance and he was forced to let the mood in him subside and a lazy chuckle slipped out. "I am funny? Why?"

"Yes, you. You should hear yourself. While I have no doubt that you have the funds to go to town, I do not think that you have used your head in this grand plan." She began.

"I was not going to ask to borrow any money from you, and why do you think that I have not thought about this?" He asked firmly. Leaning towards his captain, he added, "Believe me when I say that I have thought a great deal about this!"

"Aye Morgan, I am quite certain that the thought of all this has consumed your very soul. You are correct in thinking that I would not give you money for what you plan to use it on!" She continued to laugh.

Morgan crossed his arms over his chest and looked at her with a sideways glance, "Well then, will you just please get on with your real concern on this issue?"

She stood and leaned her palms on the table before her, her mouth still turned upwards as she tried to stifle her laughter, "Morgan, were you planning on taking Aubrey into the bordello with you or did you just plan to tie her to the hitching post outside?"

Morgan's handsome face fell into a blank expression as he looked at the dark haired woman. She nodded with another soft laugh building in her voice. "Like I said, you have not thought this grand plan through."

"Well..." He began thoughtfully and unfolded his arms. Mala watched him in anticipation as his mind worked diligently on a reply. "I will, ah, see that she is taken care of and that she stays out of the way."

"Hmm, you will just tie her to a tree when we get there?" She further tormented.

"No, damn it! I will think of something." Morgan said as he slumped into a chair.

"Go topside and tell Timmons to steer us in a northwesterly course for the Chesapeake. And tell Deats to come here." She said with a smile as she resumed her seat.

"Thank you!" Morgan said happily as he literally leapt from the chair. The chair rocked slightly from his hasty departure when he left the cabin.

"Praise be, one man made happy this eve. Now if they would all just leave me alone for a few hours." She sighed as she poured herself another mug full of water then leaned her head back against the tall back of the chair and closed her eyes.

Sooner than she wanted, Deats came rapping on her door, "Ye sent for me?" He asked as he entered the cabin.

Mala stood up and moved to her desk. "I did. On the chart there you will see that I have marked the place where we will be careening the ship. Give Timmons the directions plotted out." She said as she pointed to the chart that was still spread out on the table.

Deats looked at the chart and studied it. "Ach, Mala, no' there." He moaned his Scottish accent revealed his disagreement.

"Do you question my decisions?" She asked curtly as she poured water into her mug. Deats rolled his eyes and cast a look into the mug.

"Nay, Captain." No sooner had he said the words that he suddenly flew into a fluster with his Scottish temper up. He strode around her cabin in a heightened state of aggravation. "Ach! Ya know that the bloody British are literally crawlin' all over the damned place there. I heard tell that they had some executions up in Urbana on the Rappahannock. Then too in Yorktown on the York River. They hung some men in Williamsburg..."

Mala watched him in his tirade and asked when he seemed to take a breath, "What are you, Deats? The town crier?"

"Dinna ya understand, Mala? We hafta sail by all those places ta get ta that blessed place!"

"Well, that will just keep us on the alert." She growled back from her chair. As she watched him, she found herself wishing she had Morgan back here again with his simple antics as opposed to Deats.

"Let us no' forget that ye had ta rescue Morgan from a hangin'." When Mala made no comment, Deats finally looked at her in question and with true concern in his lowered tone, he asked, "Captain, are ye all right then?"

Mala sighed loudly and said in a tone denoting her tiredness, "I am just incredibly tired, Deats. Now if you will excuse me, I would dearly love some privacy. Please have Willie send me four big buckets of hot water for my bath and I am not to be disturbed for the remainder of the night unless the ship is under attack, sinking, or on fire."

After sending Deats to the captain, Morgan had made his way to his cabin. Aubrey laid in her bunk on her stomach, a book spread out before her. He put aside his weapons and shrugged out of his jacket as he informed her, "We will be sailing into a small bay to careen in a few days."

"Careen? What is that?" She asked in interest as she looked up from the book. She cast a suspicious hazel eye at him as he sat on the edge of her bunk.

"Well, that is when we take the ship ashore and we tip her on her side then we clean off the hull and make repairs. It has been a while since we careened so we need to take a good look at this beauty." He told her as he demonstrated the procedure with his hands. When he spoke of the ship as '*this beauty*' he patted the wall of the cabin in emphasis.

Morgan stopped in his demonstration and pulled his shirt from the waistband of his britches. This movement drew more serious and suspicious attention from Aubrey who lowered her head but kept her eyes on him when he peeled out of the shirt. He tossed the shirt onto his own bunk as he continued with his narrative, "You see, besides damage from cannons and shot, there are these worms that...."

"Worms? Morgan, I do not want to hear about worms!" Aubrey squealed with a face as she swatted at him with the book.

He shook his head and went on, "They get into the wood and they eat little holes, then we get leaks and with hurricane season upon us, we want to make sure we are in good seaworthy condition. So we scrape them off and replace the damaged wood." Aubrey cast her hazel eyes over his bare back, watching the muscles ripple as he leaned down to pull off his boots.

"Tip the ship on her side? What about us?" She asked in all sincerity as she sat up, making distance between them. Why is he undressing on my bunk? She thought to herself. He noted a mild look of distress on her pretty face as he turned to her but thinking her distress was wrought from the prospect of the ship being tipped on her side, he chuckled at her expression.

"We will be fine. We stay on shore while the ship is careened." She looked at him for a moment then, casting a wary eye over him again, she picked up the book. "We would be vulnerable to attack though." He said in a conversational tone of voice, completely unaware of her discomfort.

"Attack?" Aubrey echoed, distress still building in her.

"There may be British soldiers in the town, sometimes other pirates." He began as she watched his face when he talked, his countenance serious. She shrugged, trying to maintain her composure.

"Well I am sure that Captain Mala will have us protected."

"I will be the one in charge of that." Morgan said proudly.

"Forgive me then, Master Gunner Mr. Alcott will make sure we are protected. Now get off my bunk." She corrected.

He watched her for a few moments as she resumed her reading. A small mischievous smile spread across his face as he finally realized what really distressed her. In torment, he stretched his arms up into the air and arched his back, "Whew! What a day, I cannot wait to get some sleep."

"Then get off my bunk and get into your own." She said as she scooted a few inches more away from him. The space only offered him more room to torment and she had succeeded in plastering herself against the wall. He leaned down on his elbow, lying on his side, his head and shoulders just inches from her face further trapping her as she tried to concentrate on her book. "What are ya reading there?"

Up until now, he had remained within the confines of his own space in the room and she remained within hers. Now he was invading her space in a serious way, barely clothed, and she wanted him to stop. In her distress, she did not recognize it as playful torment. "You would not be interested, Morgan. Get off my bunk." She said easily.

Then he looked down the length of her body and his eye came to rest on the booted feet that had been swinging idly up in the air when he had first come in. He had never noticed the scabbard made into the right boot before now.

A thoughtful look crossed his face before he sat up and leaned forward to reach into a drawer under his own bunk. With his movement to sit up, she let out a breath in relief. Morgan ignored her loud sigh of relief as he continued to search through his clothing in the drawer.

Finally, with much courage, she used her shoulder against his lower back and said firmly, "Get off my bunk, Morgan. Ya know the rules, this is my space, that is yours."

He continued to dig in the drawer, "Stop that." He growled as she pushed at him again, a bit harder.

"Get off my bunk, how many times do I have to tell ya?"

Smiling, he turned to her with a small bladed knife in his hand. She scrambled back away from him, slamming herself into the bulkhead with an alarmed yelp. "Good God, Morgan, what are ya goin' do with that?" She gasped.

He was full of mischief tonight, and lowering his voice to sound ominous, he turned the blade in his hand and said, "There is one thing we really have to worry about." Looking up to see her worried expression, he went on to say, "Well, since we will be along a secluded shoreline, and far out from the civilized town, we will have to be on the lookout for Indians."

She looked at him for a moment, finally realizing that he was being notoriously mischievous tonight. She pushed at his arm. "You are lyin'. Get off my bunk, Morgan Alcott. Put that thing away before someone gets hurt, it looks awfully sharp."

"Oh it is sharp, I would not have them any other way," He began as he looked at her with a feigned insane glimmer in his blue eyes. She began to get nervous again as her mouth dropped open and she stared at him. "And neither should you. Now come here and listen." He said as he suddenly threw an arm over her shoulders and pulled her close to him, still holding the knife in his hand up in front of their faces. A mild panic began to rise in her and she felt a scream of alarm building in her throat.

"Morgan, let me go." Her voice was small and frightened as she pushed against his chest.

"I would not lie about something like possible attacks of any kind." He said then felt her try to shrug off his arm.

"Morgan, get off me."

"Be still and listen. Indians are real. They will capture you and take you back to their village, and one of their braves will make you his own, his woman." He began as he held her in place and turned the blade in his hand. Letting the light of the lantern gleam off the sharp steel, he watched the blade.

"Stop it, Morgan! Get off my bunk." She said in a strained but frightened voice as she managed to push him onto the small space of floor between the bunks.

He dropped to the floor on his knees, laughing at her, and turning toward her with the blade still in his hand. Instinctively she scrambled back toward the wall and kicked out at him with her right foot. Anticipating the move, he dodged the foot and smiled. His hand shot out and he caught her by her right ankle.

"I want you to have this." He began as he held her ankle firmly. She drew up her other foot in defense ready to strike when he slipped the blade into the boot sheath. He was surprised by her reaction as a light of recognition shone in her hazel eyes when she looked into his blue ones.

Aubrey closed her eyes as a flash of goose bumps ran over her body and she had to clench her teeth to keep from crying out Jean Luc's name. Her mind was snapped back to the night she was with him in his quarters and he had given her a small blade for protection then she had lost it in her battle

70

with Black the very next day. When she opened her eyes, she was back in the present and Morgan was still on his knees before her, holding her ankle and looking at her puzzled.

"Are you all right? I was only playing with you. I just wanted you to have this for your protection. It might come in handy in just such a situation. I meant you no harm, Aubrey. Just think of this as another lesson." He tried to soothe as he released her ankle. Finally, struggling to suppress the sob that was building, she merely nodded at him. He frowned at her. "What is the matter?"

Aubrey bit her lip and pulled her legs under herself. Leaning forward, she embraced him around his neck in a friendly hug, "Thank you, Morgan." She said, her voice thick with emotion.

He slowly put his arms up to return the embrace. "Hell if I had known that a small blade would cause you such distress then I never would have—but I was only playing with you. You know I would not hurt you in any manner." He began apologetically.

"No, I am fine—really—I just overreacted. I am tired I guess and I just never would have dreamed that anyone else would…" Realizing their close proximity, she immediately pushed herself out of his returned embrace. "Thank you Morgan, I will take good care of it—and only use it if necessary."

He eased himself up onto his own bunk and watched her worriedly. Sighing deeply, he realized that she had thrown up the barrier again. God how he wished she would let him get closer. She did not deserve to torture herself like this and force herself to be so lonely.

He turned her previous comment over and over in his mind. She had almost slipped out a part of her secret that she had carried on board from the *Widow Maker*. Anyone else would …what? Care enough about her to arm her for her own protection? He shook his head at his own thoughts. What man who cared for her would not arm her for her own protection?

She had gone back to her book, but it was obvious to him that she was not reading as he watched the book tremble in her hands. She appeared to just be staring at the pages, her mind lost in deep thoughts of her own. He frowned at the sight. How many times had he seen that same look on Mala's face?

Damn it, he mouthed silently and made a face. He had never meant for his playful torment to upset her so. He ran his fingers through his sandy colored hair and said breaking the silence, "You are welcome. I am going to give you a cutlass and dirk as well when we go ashore to make camp. You will be protected."

The comment brought a nervous giggle from her, although she did not look around at him right away. "I will have a hard enough time walking on land as it is, Morgan, now you propose to weigh me down with weaponry?"

"We all have to be armed and prepared to protect ourselves. You know how to use them—you have been doing well with our practices." He said in stern firmness.

"If you say so. But I will not be straying off. I will stay close to the shore and the ship. I do not want any weapons." She said quietly.

"I say so and, as the head gunner and man in charge of the distribution of arms, I order it." He nodded. She burst into another louder giggle, finally turning her head to look at him.

"Oh yes sir, Mr. Alcott, sir. By your order, sir!"

Morgan's face broke into a smile and he laughed aloud at her foolishness, smacking at her arm as she made saluting gestures with her hand. Aubrey swung her legs back around and put her feet on the floor. She pulled off her boots then sat looking at Morgan. "Do you delight in scaring me? Telling me stories about sea monsters and Indians."

He leaned down close, his nose almost touching hers, and grinned. "I tell you those things so that maybe you will—stand a little closer when we are out or sit a little closer at meals, or..." She held up a finger in his face as he opened his mouth to continue.

"Goodnight, Morgan." She replied.

"Goodnight, Aubrey." He chuckled as he straightened and moved to put out the lantern.

Morgan returned to his bunk and removed his britches. Lying in the dark of the now quiet cabin, he smiled. His older brother used to torment him on how he had the ability to win a young girl's heart and affections with just his smile. But all the smiles and torments he had tried so far had been completely useless against Aubrey's resolve.

Just moments before, Deats had been passing by the cabin on his way to his duty of having water brought to the captain. He had heard Aubrey's voice and Morgan's laughter. A thin smile stole over his lips as he moved back to the great cabin and he was called to enter by Mala's tired voice.

"Yer water is on the way, Captain. Is there anything that I could do for ye?" He asked hopefully.

"No thank you, Mr. Deats. That will be all." She replied without looking up as she made a few entries into the log while she waited for her water.

He wandered idly around the room, looking at the various knickknacks on the quarter gallery window. He missed Mala's quizzical glance as she wondered what the hell he wanted now. Besides… She cut that thought short then rolled her eyes as she turned her attention back to the log. Finally stopping at the desk, he faced her saying conversationally, "The girl is causing unrest among the men. They are beginning ta grumble, wondering why Morgan has been quite literally given a woman..." Deats began carefully.

"She has been with us for some time and I have heard no such grumbling except from you, Deats. Now, back to your post." She said quickly cutting him off.

"Aye Captain." He nodded with an air of dejection.

Chapter 8

The next morning, Aubrey was tidying her area of the cabin and she thought about her time thus far on the *Enchantress*. The crew was far more polite to her than that of Black's ship. Captain Mala certainly ran a tight ship. The only one of the crew that seemed to resent her presence was Deats. He did not seem to trust her and seemed to be watching her constantly.

She had just finished and was looking over her area for anything left undone when Morgan entered. He smiled at her and asked, "Had breakfast yet?"

"No, I was about to go now."

"Good, I will go with you. Unless you were meeting someone else…" He let the statement trail off as Aubrey giggled.

"No, I am afraid not. My escort is nowhere to be found, sir."

"Ah well then, his loss is my gain." Morgan said with a smile and offered her his arm.

"Morgan, is it my imagination or does Mr. Deats… I mean, he is always watching me." She began as they headed for the door.

"Oh, pay him no mind." Morgan told her with a shrug. "He is just looking out for himself and worries too much that everyone else is trying to make him look like the fool."

Then he had looked around as if someone could overhear making Aubrey giggle. Whispering as if it was a secret, Morgan confided, "The problem the poor louse just cannot seem to understand is…" Morgan looked around again and Aubrey slapped at his arm, giggling. He ignored her as he continued on in mocking Scottish accent, "He rally does no' need our help in making him look like the fool. He is doon a foin job all on his own."

Aubrey roared with laughter as Morgan moved about the room in a mockery imitation of Deats ordering men about. He finally stopped and sat on his bunk while Aubrey tried to gather herself from her gaiety. When she had calmed herself, he stood up presenting his arm to her again.

"Thank you, Morgan."

"Anytime, love." He smiled down at her.

Now sitting at breakfast with Mala, Deats, and Morgan, Aubrey could not suppress a grin as she looked at Deats and remembered Morgan's mockery. Morgan and Aubrey looked at each other but neither of them missed the surprised look from Deats when Mala practically ordered them to join her and Deats for breakfast. Then with a shrug, Morgan and Aubrey sat down.

Willie brought over plates of eggs, cured ham, and biscuits. After a few moments, Willie returned with tankards filled to the brim, some of the ale splashing over as he set them on the table.

"Just water today." Mala replied as she moved her tankard away from her. Deats gave her a sideways glance as Willie and Morgan exchanged looks but made no comment. "We should see the coastline this afternoon, correct?" She asked ignoring the looks.

"Aye, Captain." Morgan and Deats replied in unison.

"Good, I want to go up the river under the cover of darkness. Towns are building up along the coast and I do not want anyone seeing us."

"Aye Captain, we could fly..."

"We will just fly the Union Jack." Mala ordered interrupting Deats.

There was a long and awkward silence at the table and Aubrey kept her eyes to her plate. She did not see that Deats merely pushed his food around his plate or that Morgan was having a hard time restraining a smile.

Willie brought the mug of water then leaned close to Mala's ear, "Care for another hot bath?" Mala nodded and Willie left to take care of the matter. At that moment, two men approached the captain's table somewhat shyly. They stood before the table glancing at one another waiting for the other to speak first.

"What is it?" Mala asked quietly as she took a sip of her water.

One man looked at the other and then began, "Cap'n, I had this idea about our..."

"Ye what?" The other man interrupted. "We both had the idea."

"Aye, but it was me that thought we ought to tell the Cap'n!" The first one defended.

"Blast ye! I thought of it!" The second growled.

"By God, ye mangy mongrel!"

The two men faced each other in anger as they argued over the point. Mala, who was about to take another sip, held her tankard just off of her lips and looked at the men over the rim. Deats and Morgan stared at them, convinced that they had lost their minds. Aubrey was watching for Mala's reaction since her back was to the two men.

With an impatient sigh, Mala gave them a dark look as she slammed her tankard to the table. The resounding bang halted all conversation in the galley. In a very quiet voice that denoted her anger, Mala asked the men, "Must I be present for this?"

Both men stumbled over their apologies as each eyed the other as if it was that one's fault the captain was angry. Halting the apologies and pointing to one man for a reply, Mala asked, "What is it?"

Swallowing hard, he gave one last baleful look at his companion then said,

"Beggin' your pardon, Cap'n, but we was wonderin' if it would be all right to go huntin' in the mornin' once the careenin' gets started."

"Hunting?" Mala repeated, somewhat surprised.

Their heads bobbed up and down. Before Mala could reply, Deats interjected perturbed that these two would even suggest such a thing. "We need all hands in the careening, gentlemen. Our stay here is no' for relaxation."

"Aye sir, but our hands ain't gonna be needed 'til later in the morn. So we thought..."

"Ye are no' here ta think..." Deats started but now Mala interrupted as she spoke to Morgan.

"As I recall, there are plenty of animals in the area."

Morgan nodded his agreement, "Aye Captain, and I do believe that Willie is low on meat. Some venison would be good and be welcome change from salted pork."

Grinning at Morgan's comment, she looked back at the two men and replied, "Before first light, you two take three other men and hunt the game. I do not plan to make any other stops on our way to Charlestowne so we will need the meat. But do not over do it that we end up wasting it."

With broad smiles, the men nodded and said as they backed away, "Aye Cap'n. Thank ye, Cap'n."

When the men had left, Deats said without looking up, "Why do ye coddle the men like that? We do no' have the time ta spare."

"Deats, the men need to stretch their legs and use up their energy in other sport beside women. They thought of the distraction and I see no reason why five men cannot go out hunting the game that would fill Willie's storeroom. Tis a simple task for you, all you need to do in the morning is make sure only five men go hunting."

Deats looked at his captain and said grudgingly, "Aye, Captain. I shall see that only five men leave the ship in the morning."

"Good! Now if you will excuse me," Mala said as she stood up. "I will be in my cabin but see that I am not disturbed for at least an hour." Without waiting for acknowledgments, Mala left the galley. Aubrey watched her leave and wondered why she had invited them to her table. The captain seemed preoccupied and very quiet. Deats grumbled and made a departure from the galley as well.

"Well that was interesting." Morgan said with a smile.

"Interesting?" Aubrey asked.

"Aye, the captain is definitely not feeling well. She does not normally go back to the cabin like that." Morgan whispered to her, not wishing to be overheard.

"Do you really think so?" Aubrey asked.

"Just a guess, m'lady." Morgan replied with a smile.

"Morgan, why do you suppose she insisted that we join her for breakfast then she does not even speak to us?"

"Hmm, another piece of the puzzle." Morgan said. Then in a conspirator's voice, he added, "But if I were a betting man, and I am, I would say that the captain did not want to listen to Deats this morning and thought that company would hold him at bay."

"Morgan, be serious." Aubrey laughed.

"Oh, I am, my dear Aubrey, I am. Deats is usually quite a bore and can be tedious in his sermon of who is worthy and who is not from the night's watch. If I had to listen to that dribble every morning, I am afraid I would have shot the man long ago."

Aubrey looked aghast at the first mate who laughed at her expression then added, "Of course, that is not to say that someday, our esteemed Captain Mala may find that alternative the best one to take."

"Morgan! You are talking about the quartermaster." Aubrey scolded him. She was thinking of Jean Luc and how she last saw him, the quartermaster being taken care of by the captain. The thought scared her that she would witness such a scene again.

Morgan merely shrugged not realizing her inner turmoil. She grew quiet and reserved that Morgan looked at her askance.

"Ah, I would not worry about that, Aubrey. The Captain at times has a short fuse on her temper." Morgan smiled as Aubrey gave a disbelieving look. "But if she were to shoot the blasted man, I would say she would do it over something more substantial than a night watch report."

Shaking her head, Aubrey quickly finished her breakfast then stood up, saying, "Well, I am done. I suppose I should find something to do or Deats' next report will include me, more often than it does now."

Morgan chuckled and downed the last of his drink as he stood up, saying loudly, "Then let us be off for the day's chores. The smell of the sea, the rock of the ship under foot, and the cry of seagulls to be our song and dance for the day."

There were chuckles throughout the galley as the men heard Morgan's words. Aubrey hit him on the arm and scolded, "Why must you make such a spectacle of yourself?"

Morgan rubbed the arm as the roar of laughter rent the air, "Wounded, I am! And by a lass so fair!"

The men clapped at the man's idiocy and as Morgan bowed to his audience, Aubrey could be heard to say as she left the galley, "Sweet Mary, preserve us!"

It was nearly dawn as the *Enchantress* sailed almost majestically into a cove of the northern shores of the Chesapeake Bay. Timmons showed his skill of maneuvering the twin-masted brigantine up the river with only the light of the moon. Wisps of fog lay over the water, giving the area a surreal appearance. Mala, Aubrey and Morgan stood at the starboard railing of the quarterdeck. Somewhere in the darkness, a flock of geese proclaimed the presence of the sleek ship with a chorus of loud honking.

"This is beautiful." Aubrey breathed to Morgan.

"Aye." Morgan nodded.

"Are we armed in the event of nosy townsmen or an Indian raid?" Deats asked as he approached them.

"We are." Morgan replied. Aubrey shot a look at the Scotsman, but did not make a sound. Mala saw a glimmer of smile in Deats' eye and rolled her own eyes heavenward. Damn him, she growled in her mind, was he trying to frighten the young girl?

Morgan drew Aubrey off the quarterdeck by her elbow, nearly making her stumble as they went down the steps to the main deck. "Good Lord Morgan, let me go." She complained.

"I want to ask you something." He began, standing close to her.

She drew back from him slightly. "Well you do not have to stand on top of me."

Mala was tightening the buckle straps on her boot as Deats leaned toward her. "Will ye be going inta town?" He asked.

"Aye." She answered, unconcerned as she pointed her toe and inspected the buckles from the reflection of the moon.

"Will ye be gettin' a room?" Deats' voice sounded odd, almost husky.

Mala lifted her gaze to meet his. "You know, I will not leave my ship for that long a period of time when she is so vulnerable. She will be out of the water, Deats, remember? We are not merely moored somewhere that we could return swiftly, weigh anchor, drop the sails and be gone." Her tone was almost condescending. Deats did not hear the tone as he concentrated on the face that was so close. He could feel the warmth of her breath in his face as she spoke causing a stirring in his loins.

"Morgan is going ta town?" He asked as he cast his brown eyes down toward the other man, trying to fight the urge to pull Mala up into his arms and press his mouth on her full lips.

"I think that he has business to tend to, yes." Mala replied with an air of nonchalant.

"A whore ta lay." Deats said under his breath.

"I think that that would be his business, Mr. Deats." Mala said sharply as she glared up at him.

"Why does he waste his money in town ta buy a whore when he has her in the cabin with him?" Deats asked in a low voice.

He watched Mala's reaction out of the corner of his eye. She had set her jaw and looked down over the decks at the young woman. Her keen eyes could see very well in the moonlight. Aubrey was smiling up at Morgan as he hovered over her brandishing his most winning smile. They could not hear the conversation between the two on the lower deck, but Aubrey suddenly giggled loudly and pushed at Morgan.

Mala closed her eyes and the muscles at her jaw went taut. In her mind's eye, she saw a picture of the young woman with Black, smiling up at him in very much the same way. Mala inhaled deeply as the scene changed to show the young woman under the lean form of Black and he was delivering the young woman gentle kisses—touches that she herself remembered so well from times long past. Seething anger began to rise as Mala slowly opened her eyes.

Deats could read the look on Mala's face, and to fuel the temper and jealousy that he saw was taking over, he ventured to say quietly, leaning a bit closer to her, "Do ye honestly believe, Mala, that he had her on board for anything less? Ye know why she was on the *Widow Maker*, she was his whore."

"Be quiet, Deats." Mala finally spat, cold chills ravaging her body that had nothing to do with the early morning mist.

Aubrey emitted a giggle over Morgan's silliness and pushed him away saying, "Morgan, what is the matter with you?"

"When we put in, how about we go for a little walk?" He asked.

"In the dark?" She exclaimed.

"No, during the day of course." He said with a sigh.

"Do you have to help with the ship?" She asked.

"No, I am the gunner, remember? Weapons? Guards?" He said firmly.

Aubrey pondered the offer for a while and then she nodded. "All right then. Just so long as ya do none of your foolishness and try to scare me. If ya do Morgan, I swear, I will hurt you." She warned flashing a small fist in his face in the semi-darkness and using her Irish accent to its fullest for effect.

"Hmm, I love it when you threaten to get physical with me." He tormented close to her ear. She shoved at him again and moved away to watch the night-shrouded shorelines. He chucked and propped a booted foot up on the carriage of a nearby cannon.

Tipped on her side at the shoreline, the *Enchantress* looked like a beached whale. Having taken a better part of the day to tip the brigantine, men set to work immediately on the hull, scraping and patching bad spots. Aubrey sat along the edge of the encampment watching the scene with interest while Morgan was off making sure that sentries were posted for their protection and everyone was well armed in the event of an attack.

Looking in the direction of the shoreline nearest the ship, Aubrey spotted Mala dressed in a lavender gown and adjusting an expensive looking cloak over her shoulders. The captain was speaking with Deats at great lengths. Frowning, Aubrey cast her eyes down to the sand and stones beneath her booted feet. Mala had scarcely said a word to her today. The dark haired woman seemed to be angry with her again. Mala seemed to be mad at her all the time, although Aubrey could not figure out why. Looking back at her, Aubrey wondered if there would ever be any friendship between them.

In these quiet moments as she sat alone, her mind drifted to Jean Luc. A lump was forming in her throat as she mourned his demise. She tried not to think of him being trapped in the hold as the *Widow Maker* went down.

It was late in the morning before Morgan was able to pull himself from his duties. He had seen Aubrey sitting and watching the men work on the ship. He smiled as he came up behind her and tapped her on the shoulder. His sudden presence made her jump.

"What?" She asked as she made a half turn to look at him, wiping a lone tear that had slipped out. He frowned down at her and dropped to one knee beside her.

"Why the long face? The *Enchantress* will be back up in no time—good as new." She exhaled hard and shrugged at him. Her eyes wandered back out across the water now and she watched a flock of seagulls bobbing in the water.

"Ready for our walk?" He asked as he adjusted his cutlass in its scabbard as he knelt there beside her.

"Oh Morgan it is late now and I do not think that I could..." She began in a small voice. She just wanted to be left alone today.

"Yes, you can." He said as he pulled her to her feet. He walked along backwards for a few feet, gently pulling her toward him, smiling. "Look, see there you are, a little shaky, but you will get used to the land soon enough, and get your land legs under you. Come on now, you promised." He coaxed.

"No, I did not promise." She argued as he pulled her along. Her feet and legs felt like lead.

"You said, 'all right' when I asked you and that is as good as a promise to me." He told her.

"Well then, I shall be careful to what I tell you is all right from now on since you are so tricky." She smiled as she finally gave in to his gentle persuasion.

"Where is Morgan?" Mala asked Deats as she scanned the encampment and the work area.

"I saw him take Miss Aubrey up yon hill." Deats replied. Mala seemed to be pondering this information before she looked at Deats.

"I will take York and Johnston into town with me. You possess the knowledge of a master carpenter and since we have no other carpenter that is so skilled and qualified, you are in charge here." Mala said as she nodded toward the ship. "We will be fine here. Morgan has placed his men around the perimeter but it will be your responsibility to get the job done quickly so we can be on our way. I long for the sea, Deats, and I wish to be back out in open waters." She said firmly as she moved away.

He watched her go, taking in every move of her body in the dress. She looked the epitome of a prominent townswoman in all her womanly glory—and he could not have her. She longed for the sea—hell, he longed to strip off that damned dress, hold her in his arms and make love to her. Making a face, he realized that she would get her wish much sooner than he would get his.

When she was well out of sight, Deats summoned Robert and left him in charge. Then he stepped into the woods to follow the path that he had seen Morgan take. He fumed over having been left by Mala and the thought that she had wanted Morgan to go with her. Maybe he would catch the man at something and that would help to discredit him in her eyes.

Halfway up the hill, he managed to spot Morgan and Aubrey in their assent. He smiled at the near breakneck speed with which the man seemed to be pulling her along. Deats decided that this would work out for him very well. Perhaps she was not giving in to Morgan as easily on board, so now he was obviously taking the girl far up out of sight and earshot to force himself upon her, knowing that if he attempted to do so on the ship, he would be found out. That would be disobeying Mala's orders from the very beginning since she had told the man that he was to be on his best behavior with her. Unless, he was right about Morgan and the little whore being already acquainted with one another. It did not matter to him which way it was as long as he could build his case against her with any type of intimate contact between them.

Smiling, Deats came closer to the area where they had stopped. He would witness the act, and then in a gallant effort to save the girl from Morgan's 'attack,' he would shoot Morgan. But of course he would be too late for the girl, because Morgan would have already killed her. Deats smiled as he decided that he would use Morgan's pistol to bludgeon her to death. That would surely make it look like Morgan had done the awful deed. Satisfied with the story he would tell Mala, Deats moved in closer, fingering his pistol in his sash.

Chapter 9

Morgan was pulling Aubrey by the hand through the trees. She tried her best to keep up with him, but his stride and pace proved too much for her and she stumbled, almost falling. Catching herself, she continued to follow but soon she was stumbling again and her hand slipped from his. She went down on her hands and knees with a grunt. He stopped and came down on his haunches to help her to her feet.

"Morgan, take me back. This is too tiring." She gasped as she struggled to her feet.

"It is only a little further, then you can rest."

"Why could we not just walk along the shoreline? It is flat down there." She asked breathlessly as she looked back down the trail from where they had come. The trail was winding upward in a gentle yet clearly visible slope.

"Too open. Besides, we cannot get there from the shoreline." He said pulling her up a slightly steeper incline. Her booted feet slipped on the fallen leaves and woodland debris. Catching her easily again, he righted her and pulled her on their way.

"Get where? Morgan, I do not like it up here in these woods." She said as she shielded her face with her free hand from overhanging branches.

"Relax, you are fine, here we are." He told her as they came out into a small clearing. She looked around to find that they were standing on a grassy cliff overlooking the bay and the shoreline below. Putting an arm around her shoulders, he pulled her close to the edge, "Look."

She clutched at his jacket, gasping in fear. "Oh, Morgan, this is too close! Did you bring me up here to throw me off?"

"No, love, you are all right, I will not let you fall. Now, look." He soothed as he held her and brought her nearer the edge. She dragged her feet in the grass, making him chuckle lightly at her reaction.

"Relax." He cooed in her ear as they stood a few feet from the edge of the cliff.

Aubrey peered over the edge, still fiercely holding onto him. Her breath came in heavy gasps from the exertion and fear as she saw the *Enchantress* below them. With another gasp, she clamped her eyes shut and staggered against him, clutching at his jacket.

"Oh, please, Morgan, this is very nice, but very high."

He smiled at her and gently pulled her away from the edge and down with him onto the soft grass, "There, you are away from the edge. Sit here and rest."

Her breathing had reduced to panting now and he smiled at her as he pulled off his gloves and tucked them away. "I do not feel well, Morgan. I think that I might be sick." She gasped with her eyes still closed and she pushed sweat-dampened hair from her forehead.

"I had no idea that you were so afraid of heights." He said, leaning back on one elbow beside her.

"Well, you did not ask me." She said.

She pondered the remark as she pulled her hair up into her hand to get it off the back of her neck, fanning herself frantically. The thought of going up into high places had never frightened her before. She had climbed trees as a child and that had never bothered her in the least. This fear of heights had come only when she had reached the fighting top that day on the *Widow Maker* and was confronted by the man up there who had brought her back down to Black.

"Do you not think that it is hot here?" She asked, finally opening her eyes and looking at him.

"Hmm…no, there is a nice breeze, just calm down. Here, lay back and close your eyes." He coaxed as he tugged at her sleeve.

She laid in the soft grass and closed her eyes but her heart was still pounding. After a few quiet moments she said, "It feels funny."

"The breeze?" He chuckled. She swatted in his direction, keeping her eyes closed all the while.

"No you idiot, the ground, I mean underneath us. It feels funny. I am used to the rocking motion of a ship."

"Hmm, I had not noticed." He said, his voice seemed strangely quiet to her. Silence fell between them and the wind rustling through the trees overhead was the only sound.

After a few moments she asked, "How do you know of this place?"

"I saw it from the ship as we sailed in." He said as he idly split a blade of grass.

"You have a very good eye, Morgan—to find and remember such landmarks. You should be the navigator, not the gunner." Aubrey said. She was beginning to calm down and cool off, but she kept her eyes closed, fearful that if she opened them she would catch sight of how high they were.

He snorted at the thought and the response made her angry. "What is wrong with being a navigator? You act like being the gunner is great fun."

"Oh it is." He said, smiling down over her. She opened one eye to look at him with a slight frown then up into the trees. They were a dizzying height and she clapped her eye back shut.

He broke the silence, a hint of smile in his voice, "You should look at this view, we are really not that high up."

"Do not talk about high up." She scolded, closing her eyes all the more tightly.

He laughed lightly at her. "You will never be able to climb the ratlines with this fear." His comment took her back again to that day on the *Widow Maker* and she shuddered visibly.

"I tried that once and I do not want to climb the ratlines anymore." She said stiffly.

"When did you do that?" He scoffed.

"If you must know, I did it on the *Widow Maker* to get away from the captain." She snapped.

Morgan considered this information. She must really have been afraid to go to that extent, especially since she was not seaworthy. Then he asked quietly, "I take it that you were not happy in the presence of the Captain on the *Widow Maker*?" He asked quietly.

She remained silent and threw her left arm over her eyes to shield them from the sunlight that filtered through the trees.

"What is this?" He asked as he took a hold of her left wrist, pulling her arm out away from her face. There were bloodstains on her sleeve. Pulling open the tie on her cuff, he pushed up the sleeve to reveal a long scratch on her inner forearm, "Ah, you must have done this when you fell."

She looked at the scratch and then much to her surprise, he pulled her arm to his lips and kissed the injury saying, "I am sorry. That would have been my fault that you were hurt."

She drew her arm away in alarm. He made a face and then looked out over the bay. He slipped an arm behind her shoulders and pulled her into a sitting position closer to him, before she had a chance to protest. "Look out there. You can see the whole bay from up here."

Just looking over the bay as he had suggested gave her a dizzy feeling. She grasped at his jacket again as if she thought she might be drawn off the edge by the sight. She closed her eyes to the frightening feeling, shivering in his grasp. "I do not want to look at the whole bay from up here. Can we go back down now? Then I will look at it all day from the shoreline," she answered.

"In a while." He said quietly.

"I am sorry, Morgan, that I do not enjoy the view as you do. It is just too high up for me. We are sitting really close to the edge. We should back up a bit." She gasped trying to scoot back with her eyes tightly shut.

Morgan held her in place and laid his free hand along the side of her face then turned her head toward him. "You are doing fine, Aubrey. Relax, you are not going to fall. Open your eyes and look at me."

With great hesitation, she slowly opened her eyes and found that her face was just inches from his. She drew her head back a bit, looking at him warily. He held her gaze for a moment with tenderness in his blue eyes then he slipped his hand behind her neck and pulled her head towards his. He touched his lips to hers then pulled back to measure her response, still holding her. She dropped her head almost shamefully and pushed at him.

"Morgan, what are you doing?" Her voice was quiet but her resistance was so slight that he decided to try again.

Slipping his hand to her chin and raising her face to his, he said quietly, "I just want a kiss, tis all." He pulled her in and pressed his lips a bit more firmly on hers. This kiss made her dizzier than the height did and she went limp in his arms for the moment. Lost in that moment and responding to feelings she remembered, she found herself returning the kiss. Morgan pulled her closer against him and pressed the kiss deeper as he gently laid her back down on the soft grass. His hand slipped along her jaw and down her throat. Suddenly she was pushing at him insistently, breaking from the kiss and gasping, "Morgan, please."

When Deats came upon them, they were both on the ground. He watched from behind a tree as Morgan drew her into the kiss. Smiling as he saw Morgan's hand wander down her throat, Deats thought, oh yes, sweet submission. Someday that would be Mala under his gentle embrace.

Aubrey did appear to be willing. All the better, this would prove that she was the little whore that he had proclaimed her to be. If she would come up here willingly with Morgan for this encounter, then she most definitely had laid willingly with Black as well. Mala would be livid at the thought. Suddenly Deats frowned slightly as he watched Aubrey push out of Morgan's embrace. Shrugging uncaringly, Deats took out his pistol. He would just have to go with his first plan.

Morgan sighed deeply and sat up, running his fingers through his sandy-colored hair. Aubrey was looking away from him with her knees drawn up and her arms holding them close to her body as she rocked slightly. He recognized the stance she had taken for he had seen it many times in the cabin.

"I am sorry Morgan, I do not intend to tease." She said quietly, not looking at him.

"You did not tease me, love." He smiled as he touched her arm gently. She merely nodded, but did not look at him. "Who was he? Please tell me."

Aubrey looked at him thinking, perhaps it was time to open her soul and talk to someone. Morgan did always seem to have her best interest at heart. Taking a deep breath, she turned to face him. "His name was…"

Suddenly in the quietness of the woods, a shot rang out and Morgan's body lurched forward. His movement pushed her down flat onto the ground under him and they both grunted with the impact. Bark from a nearby tree showered over them, then the area fell still and silent, devoid of the sounds of birds and insects. Holding her down with his body draped fully over hers, Morgan reached between them to draw his pistol. He raised his head slightly to peer into the woods beyond them. Aubrey clutched at his arms and craned her head back to look in that direction as well.

"Someone is shooting at us." She breathed fearfully against his throat.

"Shh!" He scolded, not taking his eyes off the woods.

After his shot, Deats turned in alarm. Another shot from behind him had been fired just a split second before he pulled off his. The sound had startled him, making him miss his mark. There was a jubilant cry from the woods below, apparently some of the men were hunting nearby. He looked back at his intended target and cursed when he saw Morgan pull himself up off of a shaken Aubrey.

"Someone is shooting at us." She said in fear again as her head turned, looking around in all directions. She continued to cling to his shirt, holding herself close against him as he got up.

"No, the men must be hunting…listen." He soothed as he pulled her to her feet. They heard the gleeful shouts of successful hunters below. "Remember, they asked the captain if they could go hunting when we came to shore?" He reminded. Aubrey nodded her head hesitantly.

"They are fine marksmen. They can pick a man off the helm of a ship with one shot or bring down a big deer for our dinner. Why would they shoot at us?" He said easily. His eye caught sight of the tree just beyond them. It was apparent that a ball had lodged there. He listened intently to the sounds in the forest but heard only the men below them, talking loudly in their excitement. Looking back at the tree, a frown crossed his brow. A chill ran through him as he realized that there was no way that one of the hunters, his men could have fired that shot in a miss at a deer.

"Morgan, can we go back down now?" She asked in a small voice as she dusted her clothing off nervously still looking around them.

"Aye." He nodded, scanning the area with narrowed eyes of cold blue steel. He did not want to alarm her but all signs pointed to the blatant fact that someone had been shooting at them.

Morgan continued to scan the encampment as he and Aubrey entered the area. He noticed Deats coming from the bushes at one end of the encampment, adjusting his clothing. Taking care of Mother Nature's call, Morgan thought wryly. He waited until Deats came closer before asking, "Have you seen the captain?"

"In town." Deats replied as he looked down at Aubrey noting that she looked no worse for wear.

"In town? Alone?" Morgan snapped.

"She took York and Johnston." Deats growled in reply as he reached out to pluck a dead leaf from Aubrey's hair. He deliberately held it up for Morgan to see then dropped it. The leaf fluttered to the ground on the gentle breeze. "Been enjoying nature, Mr. Alcott?" The Scotsman sneered.

"Mala went to town and did not take one of us?" The lewd comment had gone by without comment from Morgan and the Scotsman frowned when he did not get the reaction he had hoped for.

"Well that would have been damned difficult seein' how she left me in charge of the work and you went disappearing off on your little foray." Deats said angrily as he glared at Aubrey once more. She drew back away from him and behind Morgan. Deats was beginning to remind her more and more of Rene Black every day.

"Well damn it, it is going to be dark soon, and I am going into town for her!" Morgan spat as he started away.

Aubrey grabbed his arm and pleaded, "Morgan, take me. Please do not leave me."

"I am sorry, love, but you cannot go with me, it is too dangerous. You stay here." He said soothingly as he stroked her arms. She cast a glance at Deats then looked back at Morgan in the waning light of day. She drew back out of his grasp and stared at him. The scenario was all too familiar as she felt she was to be left again. But this time there would be no Jojoba and no Jean Luc to watch over her.

"Aubrey?" Morgan called in concern trying to gain her attention. Ignoring him, she turned her back to the pair of them, walking away without another word.

Deats snickered, "Ach, now ye gone and put her inta one of them little temper tantrums she throws so well. If ye ask me I think that the little bitch needs ta grow up."

Morgan whirled on the man in anger and pointed his finger in Deats' face, "No one asked you for your opinion."

"Are ye forgetting who I am? Perhaps I should report this ta the captain?" Deats sneered, never flinching.

"Tell Mala if you like, you tell her everything else unimportant!" Morgan growled. With that, he called for two of his men to follow and left the encampment to go to a waiting longboat.

Aubrey sat on a log by the shoreline. This was beginning to feel more and more like the *Widow Maker* every minute—even if it was on land. Aware of a presence behind her, she turned quickly then drew in a sharp breath. Deats was standing over her and she leapt to her feet. The night seemed to fall more quickly with the woods surrounding them. The darkness made it hard to see his face and had she not known it was the Scotsman, she could have sworn that Rene Black was towering over her. Deats was wearing all dark clothing, something that she had noticed that he had taken to doing of late. When she had first come on board, he had usually been dressed in tan britches and a white shirt.

"Stop yer poutin' and get over here by the fire." He demanded reaching for her.

"I am fine, Mr. Deats, thank you." She said backing away and easily avoiding his grasp. Her backward movement caused her to step into the gently lapping water and she looked down in alarm.

"That was no' a request, but an order, Miss Malone." He said firmly. She reluctantly obeyed and, following him, she sat down on a log near the large fire that had been built.

The day's kill, a large deer was being turned on a spit over the fire. Beyond, at another smaller fire, Willie had set up a makeshift galley. There was an extended silence between her and Deats while Aubrey watched the men moving about in the camp. She shivered involuntarily thinking she was alone again. Deats seated himself near her on the ground, making sure he brushed up against her in the process. He noted her unease with an evil smile as she moved a bit farther from him and she stared into the fire. In an attempt to soothe herself, she finally decided to speak to him.

"Mr. Deats, are you not fearful that this big fire might be seen by someone from the town across the river or by Indians in the area?" She finally asked quietly.

Deats snorted as he took up a mug and held it under the tap of a nearby rum keg. "It kinna be seen. If anyone comes near the camp that does no' belong, they will be shot."

"Oh." She said as she drew a ragged breath. He handed her a mug and she took it. Raising it to her lips, she caught the smell of the contents and handed it back, "No, thank you."

"Too good ta drink with the likes of me, lass?" Deats snorted regarding her with dark brown eyes.

"No, I just do not drink rum." She replied quickly.

"It could be a chilly night, lass. Would ya take a bit of wine then—ta warm ye?" His tone seemed a bit nicer now. She looked at him warily. "Or

91

would ye prefer the arms of a man ta warm ye tonight?" He mocked.

Aubrey closed her eyes to the comment, wondering if it had been an offer. He laughed at her reaction and waved to one of the men who was pouring wine from an onion bottle.

"Here." He said handing her the mug of wine. She looked at it and then at him, wondering that if she took the offering would it perhaps warrant some type of payment. He pushed it toward her again. As she took the mug, she noticed a strap under his arm and a small knife tucked away. Aubrey frowned thinking that it was strange place to keep a knife. "Thank you, Mr. Deats, this will do fine to keep me warm."

Laying slightly on his side and leaning on one elbow, he took a long draught from his mug and then exhaled deeply, looking up into the sky at the stars. Aubrey took a drink of her wine and resumed staring at the fire. "How long were ye on the *Widow Maker*?" He asked suddenly.

She looked down at him in alarm. After a moment she said quietly, "I was taken aboard her in late spring."

"Prize of the captain, I would wager." He nodded with a snort.

"I was rescued by the captain from a burning, sinking ship." She said thickly.

"Why was she burnin' and sinkin'?" He went on to ask with a thin smile. Aubrey looked down at her nervously working fingers entwined around her mug.

"The pirates, I mean, the captain and his crew boarded her and took all they wanted before they did away with her."

A delightful guttural chuckle emitted from him as he set down his mug, "Merchant ship with passengers? Folks with money and jewels? Anyone else taken?"

"Yes sir, it was a merchant ship with passengers but no one else was taken."

He regarded her with brown eyes for a moment. "No other women on the ship?" He pressed on.

"There were two old women but they perished." She replied.

"Any men taken?"

"Two men—one who could read charts and a sailor."

"Ah, so Black's men impressed them ta be members of his crew." He nodded. Aubrey frowned, not understanding what he meant by 'impressed.' The Scotsman rolled his brown eyes and explained impatiently, "Black forced them ta be crewmembers."

"The two that were taken aboard besides myself were pirates from the *Widow Maker* who were planted on board the *Gull* back in London."

"Clever ruse. A very ingenious man that Rene Black." He watched her covertly as she shuddered at the mention of the man's name. Cocking his head, he asked, "And where did ye stay on the *Widow Maker*?" He knew full well what the next answer would be.

"In the great cabin." She said quieter still.

"Did he treat ye well? Teach ye all manner of ways ta please a man? Present ye with fine pretty things? Pretty clothes and jewels from plundered ships?" Deats continued on. She set down the mug and looked at him in anger as he went on, "If I was the captain of a ship and had me a fine woman, I would."

"I do not care to know what you would do, sir, and I do not care to discuss this anymore. I think that I will retire." She said coming bravely to her feet.

"Sleep where ye like lass, I am sure any of the men would gladly lay ye doon." He shrugged with a slight smile as he raised his mug to his lips.

She put her hands on her hips and anger flashed in the hazel eyes. "Mr. Deats, kindly tell me why you insist on attacking my dignity with such remarks." Her voice had caught the attention of the men at the spit as they looked up in interest. The Scotsman came to his feet as she continued in her tirade, "I will be havin' a word with the captain when she returns about your attacks and nasty accusations of me, sir."

Deats towered over her, his dark eyes flashing in the firelight. He stood so closely to her that the soft breeze that buffeted the shoreline blew his long brown hair against her cheek. Aubrey backed up a step, her bravery wavering in the presence of his intimidation.

"Ye listen here lassie, ye willna be threatenin' me. Only an idiot would believe that ye are pure and chaste. Ye warmed the bunk of Rene Black that much is evident with the mark upon ye."

Aubrey's mouth dropped open in shock at his comment and her hand went to her breast. His tone was low and ominous as he pointed to her chest. "Aye, girl, me own eyes saw it that day on the beach. Branded ye are, right there on that left breast so dinna ye go actin' a saint with me. Captain Mala willna put up with ye hoppin' from one bunk ta another on her ship and she wouldna believe a word from ye either. Tell her if ye like, but ye be earnin' her wrath, not I!"

Aubrey remained silent staring at him. Finally she looked down and said, "If you are quite finished, Mr. Deats, I would like to retire now." He gave her no reply as he cast his dark eyes over her then jerked his head sideways, a signal for her to move on.

Aubrey found a sheltered spot near Willie's cook fire, a place where she felt safe. The old man fussed over her for a time, trying to get her to eat but with no luck. He gave her a blanket then stroking her hair with a weathered hand he bid her goodnight. She curled up under the blanket and soon drifted off to sleep listening to the sounds of the men as they moved about the encampment.

Chapter 10

Morgan was startled awake by a strange tapping noise at the window. Slipping easily from under the arm of the young woman who slept draped over him, he got out of the bed and pulled on his britches. The tapping sound persisted as he crossed to the window. He swung the window open easily and was pelted with several small stones.

"Son of a bitch." He cursed in a low voice as he leaned out the window to look to the street below.

"Oh, sorry Morgan." Came a chuckle from under the window.

"York, what in the hell are you doing?" Morgan hissed harshly to the man below the window.

"Cap'n says that you are to get dressed and come on. We gotta get back." The man called quietly.

Casting his blue eyes to the bed, he watched as the young woman stirred and rolled onto her back, covers pushed down to her waist. A groan escaped him as he gazed upon the naked beauty there.

"Morgan! Come on!" York pressed from below the window.

"Christ." Morgan growled as he looked longingly at the bed. The cool air from the window brought goose bumps to his bare chest and arms. It wafted past him and across her bared breasts, making the nipples stand pert and inviting. He wanted to crawl back in the bed and wake her with caressing kisses.

"Morgan!"

"Aye!" He finally hissed out the window.

Shutting the window, he crossed to the bed, picking up his shirt and pulling it on along the way. He sat on the edge of the bed where the young woman exhaled sleepily and cuddled up to his waist as he began to pull on his boots. "It is chilly in here. Why are you up so early? Come back to bed." She murmured.

He turned to recline halfway over her and kissed her deeply, "I gotta go, love." He said forlornly as he caressed her arms.

"Will you be back?" She asked.

"Not for a while I think." He replied.

He had been fortunate this trip—coming to town and finding this young woman again. She had been an acquaintance from a time long past in this same town. She caught him around the neck and pulled him down for another kiss. "I was glad you got away the last time. I have missed you."

"Aye, just remember not to tell anyone you saw me." He smiled as he buried his face in her ample young breasts. He began working his lips over her and she purred under his caresses. The tapping sound came at the window again.

"Damn it." He cursed quietly against her skin as he reluctantly pushed himself up from the bed. "You take care." He said with a wink as he picked up his scabbard and pistol then easily slipped out the door.

In the alley below, York met him. "Come on, Morgan, the captain is getting restless."

Following York's gaze to the end of the alley, Morgan found Mala standing against the wall of a building, her arms folded over her chest, and was looking down as she kicked a booted foot idly. He noticed that she had changed from her lavender dress into her usual attire of black and red. As they neared her, she turned and began walking ahead of them. Walking a bit faster to catch up with her, Morgan left York behind to watch their backs.

After a few moments of silence, they came to the edge of the town. Mala glanced at Morgan and asked, "Did you take care of your business and expel that extra energy you had?"

"I could have taken care of more business…expelled more energy." He muttered.

"Sorry, Morgan, but I did not fancy leaving you here in the town alone to come out in the light of day." She replied slapping at him with her gloves. She pulled them on as they made their way through the woods along the banks of a broad creek.

Morgan nodded, "Aye, I suppose I must thank you for that."

"I do not have the time nor do I have the help to liberate you from the gallows again." She told him as they came to the shoreline.

Johnston and another man who waited with the longboat met them. Mala climbed into the boat and sat down as York and Morgan pushed the boat off into the water and hopped in soundlessly.

"What in the hell is all that?" Morgan asked as he settled himself across from Mala and looked at a pile of packages on the floor between them.

"Unlike you and these others, I made wise use of my time in town. I have been shopping for needed items." Mala said smugly.

"My time was well used." Morgan defended.

"Mine too." York nodded.

"And mine." Johnston smiled.

Mala rolled her eyes but smiled at her men. Morgan leaned forward and grasped something white that stuck out from one of the packages. "Needed items? Needed by whom?" He asked quietly of her as he held up an embroidered camisole.

"Damn it, Morgan, stay out of that." She scolded, snatching the piece of undergarment from his hand as he chuckled.

"Who is that for? Will ya be givin' it to Deats? To wear with his little skirt?" Morgan joked, referring to the Scotsman's kilt that was worn on occasion. The other men chuckled and Mala could not help but smile at Morgan's foolishness.

"No." She said through a soft laugh.

"Well, why in the hell do you spend your money on the likes of this, Mala? We can get these things from any merchant ship that carries passengers." Morgan said.

"It is not for me, you idiot. I have what I need." She replied flatly. "I got them for Aubrey."

"Aubrey! Oh Christ!" He quietly exclaimed. With the sudden remembrance, he slapped his forehead with a hand.

Mala raised a brow and tormented amid the other men's chuckles, "Have you forgotten her already?"

"No, I left her at the camp. I left in a hurry when I found out that you had gone to town." He replied.

"Then it is a good thing you did not tie her to the hitching post." Mala whispered teasingly.

Morgan grunted and rolled his eyes at the reminder. His gaze drifted back to the fine ladies unmentionables and wondered it were a ploy to pry information out of Aubrey about her association with Black on the *Widow Maker*. He had to admire Mala for her methods. She never ceased to amaze him in how she was able to make people talk, divulging needed and necessary information. He was just glad that she was not taking the violent route with Aubrey, considering the circumstances.

Soon they were at the encampment and were met by two of Morgan's guards. "We made a place for ye over here, Cap'n." One of them said as he waved her toward a lean-to they had erected in some trees.

"Thank you, Wallace." She replied with a tired smile.

"Where is Miss Aubrey sleeping?" Morgan asked quietly.

"I think she bedded down up by Willie's cook fire. The old boy has a soft spot in his heart for the young lass." The sentry told him.

"Do you need anything, Captain?" Morgan asked a bit more formally now.

"No, go find yourself a spot, Morgan, and go back to sleep. Sleep well." She smiled as she sat down heavily on the blankets the men had laid out for her to sleep on in the small sheltered space.

"Well, not quite the same, but thanks." He said as she began to pull off her boots.

Morgan went to the cook fire, squinting into the darkened recesses beyond. He saw Aubrey lying curled under a blanket, sleeping peacefully. He helped himself to a bowl of stew from the pot Willie had hanging there and sat down near her to eat.

Aubrey sighed deeply and turned onto her back. Staring at her, he thought about the young woman he had left in town. Casting his eye over her, he frowned almost with pity at Aubrey. She was no match for the girl in town as far as breasts were concerned. But aside from those attributes, Aubrey was attractive in her own way.

Morgan watched her sleeping face in the firelight as a small smile stole across her lips and she murmured quietly. He wondered once more about the other man who had stolen her heart that she would not allow any other man in. He had almost found out today, had they not been interrupted. Finishing his bowl of stew, he moved away from the fire to bed down among the rest of the men. The thought of someone firing upon them worried him again and, despite his fatigue, he laid looking at the stars for a long time pondering the incident.

Eventually, the encampment fell quiet, with only the sounds of snoring men, mingled with the crackling and popping of the fires. Around the encampment, night insects sang their songs and the water lapped gently at the shore. Mala turned in her slumber and a smile crossed her beautiful sleeping countenance. In her dreams, she was in the arms of Rene Black again and passion ran high in both of them.

Very early the next morning, just as the dawn's light was turning the clouds pink, Aubrey stirred awake. She frowned at first, wondering where she was before she heard the sounds of the men as they began to rise as well and stop by Willie's fire to get a bite to eat before beginning their day's work. She sat up and combed her hair into place with her fingers, looking around with sleepy eyes. Some of the men spoke to her quietly in passing, bidding her good morning.

"Mornin', luv. Here ye go. Yer gonna eat today now or I will turn ye over me knee and paddle yer britches!" Willie said immediately putting a bowl of stew into her hands nestled in a piece of leather. She smiled at him knowing his threats were innocent.

"Thank you, Willie, I think that I will eat today. It has been a long time since I have had my britches paddled!"

"Ah now, who would give such a sweet child a whippin'?" Willie scoffed.

"My mama, when my little temper would get the best of me." She said smiling over her bowl.

"Hmm, you have a temper? I would ne'er have guessed." He tormented as he busied himself about his makeshift galley.

Aubrey sat cross-legged on her bedroll and ate the stew. She looked over the encampment but did not see Mala or Morgan. Deats was wandering about, speaking with the men along the way. He came to the cook fire and accepted a bowl. As he dished himself some stew, he glanced at her.

"Mornin' Miss Aubrey." He drawled with his thick Scottish brogue and seated himself near her again.

"Mornin' Mr. Deats." She drawled back in her own accent, wondering why he was taken to sitting so close. He took off his hat and laid it aside then stirred the contents of his bowl.

"Did ya sleep well then?" He asked.

"Yes, I did." She replied quietly as she continued to eat her meal.

Deats watched her intensely as she ate. She pretended not to notice but hastened her meal so she could move away. Gracing him with an apologetic smile, she stood up and excused herself. He watched her as she moved away from the fire and down to the shoreline.

Aubrey dropped to her knees at the water's edge. After a couple of moments, she cupped water in her hands and washed her face and neck then she wet her hair and smoothed the dripping tresses into place with her hands. She sat with her legs folded under her looking out toward the bay that Morgan had tried to show her the day before. Her eyes drifted up to that high place above the encampment where he had taken her. From down on the shoreline, it looked even higher up. She bit her bottom lip and her eyes clouded with tears. "I am sorry, Jean Luc, I did not mean to kiss him. For a moment, I thought that I was with you. I wish that I was with you." She whispered to the trees on the hill before she dropped her head in shameful remorse.

From his bedroll in the main body of the camp, Morgan had awakened almost at the same time as Aubrey. For a while he laid watching the sky change colors. The ground certainly was not the comfortable bed that he had left in town. He smiled to himself and thought about how the men who snored around him last night were a far cry from the soft woman who had nestled herself beside him. Yawning, he wandered to the cook fire for his breakfast. Before he could inquire from Deats on Aubrey's whereabouts, Mala stepped up beside him.

"Good morning, gentlemen." She said briskly.

"Morning, Captain." Morgan nodded.

"Mornin,'" Deats echoed as he stood in respect for her, though he was still infinitely angry at the decision that she had made the day before. "Well, I got a careening to tend to." He said, using the excuse to remove himself from her presence. She cast a cursory glance at him as she sat down in his place.

"Here ye go, Cap'n." Willie said as he handed her a bowl of the steaming liquid shrouded in leather. She smiled in reply as he turned to hand Morgan a bowl as well.

"Son of a bitch!" Morgan roared as he juggled the bowl from one hand to the other and finally set it on the ground before him. It was only then that they noticed Willie had on gloves. Mala watched in amusement as Morgan pulled on one of his gloves and picked the bowl up in the gloved hand.

"Why does he take pains to make sure you are not burned by yours?" Morgan pouted as he painfully licked a sore thumb.

"Because I am the captain, you idiot." She replied flippantly. Morgan frowned at his burned thumb. They ate in silence for a time before Mala finally said quietly, "Please allow me to apologize again for drawing you away from your whore last night."

Morgan blew over the spoonful of stew that he was about to put into his mouth. His tone sounded annoyed and disapproving, "She is not a whore, Mala." Her dark eyes looked at him intently as he continued, "She is an acquaintance from when I was here before. Mary is a young woman who lives in the town."

"Morgan, please tell me that you have not taken to wife-stealing. Moreover, please tell me that you do not leave a wife here!" Mala chided as she ate.

"No, she is unattached as am I. Mary makes a very honorable living." He said.

"There are some who believe that whoring is an honorable living." Mala said over a spoonful of stew.

"She is not a whore." He said with much emphasis. "She works in the bakery."

Mala nodded and, with a mischievous smile that only he would appreciate, she said in a hushed voice, "Well then, I would wager that she is experienced at handling hot things—that rise."

Morgan rolled his blue eyes at her as she chuckled wickedly and he smiled at her with a shake of his head. Mala kicked a booted foot at him playfully and took another spoonful of her breakfast. Looking around the encampment, her eyes came to rest on the bedroll that Aubrey had used the night before, "Have you seen Aubrey this morning?"

"No, I have not seen her since yesterday. I stopped by here last night to talk to her but she was sleeping so I left her be." He replied as he ate.

"You talked to her last when you took her up to yon hill?" Mala asked, never looking up from her bowl.

Morgan stopped eating and lifted his eyes to look at her. Mala waited, letting him ponder on her knowledge. She was nearly bursting inside to make her next comment at just the right moment. Watching him covertly from under lowered eyelashes, she saw him put a spoonful of stew in his mouth.

"You had to kiss her." The comment came so nonchalantly that Morgan spit out the mouth full of stew and began to cough. Wiping the back of his sleeve over his mouth, he looked at her in surprise through watery blue eyes.

"How in the hell do you know that?" He hissed as his eyes darted about the camp to make sure they were not being overheard. Mala regarded him with dark brown eyes.

"I am the captain of this ship and this crew. I make it my business to know what is going on." She told him with a shrug.

"I suppose I am in trouble now?" He said as he rolled his eyes. He set down his bowl and spread his hands out in surrender, "Mala, I do not know her as you may have been led to believe. She still pines very deeply for whomever it was on the *Widow Maker* that she loved and I know for certain that it was not Rene Black. She guards her virtue well and you know that I would not..."

"I know, Morgan." Mala soothed as she met his gaze but in her mind his words seemed to echo, *'I know for certain that it was not Rene Black.'* Getting to her feet, Mala said with sigh, "Never mind, Morgan. Finish your breakfast and go find her before she wanders off and gets lost."

Chapter 11

Morgan searched the camp, making inquiries and finally came upon Aubrey as she was still sitting at the water's edge. "I am sorry that I left you alone here so abruptly yesterday evening." He said stepping up from behind her.

Glancing around, Aubrey smiled at him and said, "You have your duties and responsibilities. You do not have to explain yourself to me or answer to me." She shrugged with an air of indifference as she looked out over the water. "Mr. Deats said that you and Mala would not be back last night. Did you just get in this morning then?"

"No, ah we got back late last night. I stopped by to check on you but you were sleeping. I guess Willie took good care of you." Morgan replied as she smiled and nodded her head. He watched her pull her wet hair up from the back of her neck then began to braid it.

"How much longer will we be here?" She asked quietly.

"A couple of days perhaps." He replied looking at her carefully. "Did you sleep well?"

"I do not like sleeping on the ground, I miss my bunk." She complained as she moved away from the water's edge and sat on a nearby tree trunk. There was no room on the trunk for him to sit, so he sat on the grass beside her. "It is very hot here. I mean I like heat, but I do not like the sticky air. It is much cooler at sea."

"I believe that there is a mill nearby here with a pond where we could go swimming to escape the heat of the day." He suggested.

"I do not think that I want to cool off in the pond only to walk around in wet clothing all day long, Morgan."

He lowered his voice and kept his gaze on the water before them while his arm slipped around behind her hips on the log. "Who said anything about swimming in our clothes?" He glanced up at her and watched a blush flood over her cheeks. She looked down at his hand on the other side of her and moved slightly forward so that his arm was not touching her.

"If you will recall, I cannot swim anyway."

"I could teach you." He offered quietly.

"With no clothing on." She replied flippantly. He gave her a mischievous wink.

They both started when Deats spoke up behind them, "Mr. Alcott, do ye have duties ta tend ta?"

"My duties are taken care of, Mr. Deats. My men are in their places around the camp." Morgan replied stiffly nodding to the men down the shoreline as he came to his feet slowly and faced the Scotsman.

Aubrey glanced over her shoulder at the quartermaster then back to Morgan. His handsome features were a mask of controlled anger. They always seemed to be at odds with one another, she thought as she watched them.

"Find something constructive ta do then." Deats growled.

Morgan rolled his eyes and clapped his hat against his thigh, "Aye sir."

After Morgan was out of earshot, Deats stepped closer behind Aubrey and said sarcastically, "Ye look mighty pretty and clean today, lass, but I do not think the men will have time ta notice ye."

Aubrey bit her lip. The urge to jump up and spit a reply at him was strong, but she just did not have the courage. He reminded her too much of Black. She heard him chuckle as he moved back toward the camp.

"Will you leave her alone, Deats? It is far too hot to start any foolishness this early in the day and there is too much work to be done." Mala said sternly when he neared the center of the camp.

"I dinna bother her. I went over ta send Morgan on his duties. He would sit by her and pet her all day if we left him ta do so." Deats said defensively.

Mala raised a brow. "Pet her, Mr. Deats? It sounds like you are becoming jealous of Morgan. Perhaps you are interested in Miss Malone yourself?"

"Nay Captain, I am neither jealous of Morgan nor interested in Miss Malone." He replied stiffly as his mind raced. The woman Deats wanted was standing right before him. There was no man in her way, only a damned memory.

"Carry on with your duties then." She told him as she swept past.

"Aye Captain." He muttered with a scowl. He glared at her back as she walked toward the shoreline.

"Is Mr. Deats causing you some distress?" Mala asked as she approached Aubrey.

"No." Came the small reply.

"You do not sound very convincing." Mala said easily as she knelt to cup water into her hands and splash it over her face and throat.

"He just puts me in mind of someone." Aubrey said looking out at the ship.

Mala frowned down at the water and pondered the reply. Now that Aubrey had mentioned it, Deats had seemed to put on a persona of someone else. The dark haired captain glanced back and found Deats in conversation with some of the men. She noted his dark clothing and merely grunted.

"So, what were you and Mr. Alcott discussing that has caused Mr. Deats to froth at the mouth?" Mala asked suddenly as she turned back towards

Aubrey. The younger woman's mouth dropped open that the captain would joke with her or even venture to engage her in conversation.

"Nothing, we were just talking. Mr. Deats does not like it when we talk. I am not sure why but we do not seem to bother anyone else." Aubrey said. Mala's eyes regarded her keenly.

Aubrey had the strange feeling that the woman knew more of what was going than she let others believe. Looking back at her, Aubrey licked her lips nervously. This strong woman captain seemed to possess an ability to read a person's thoughts.

"Morgan invited me for a swim—to cool off." Aubrey finally confessed. "He says there is a mill nearby with a pond, but I cannot swim."

"I am quite certain that he would gladly teach you." Mala said as she smoothed back her long dark hair.

"He offered to do so." Aubrey said with a blush of embarrassment crossing her cheeks.

"He has become quite fond of you. Did you enjoy your walk yesterday up to yon hill?" Mala asked with a devilish grin.

The question caused very much the same reaction in Aubrey as it had in Morgan. Aubrey shot her head around to look at Mala, "How…"

"Morgan is decidedly the best catch on the ship. I feel certain that he would take care of you. Surely he would administer much more affection than the mere kiss he gave you yesterday." Mala went on to say as she idly poked at the sand with a stick.

Aubrey shot to her feet and exclaimed in a low voice. "How do you know of that?" Then she glanced toward the encampment, a couple of the men nearest them had looked up in interest at her sudden movement. "I did not lead him into that incident, Captain."

"No one said that you led him to anything. In fact, no one has to lead Morgan into anything. He generally goes there himself." Mala replied with a shrug. Aubrey was staring down at the ground now as she easily lowered herself back down to the log. "You cannot pine forever, Aubrey. Someday you are going to get—lonely." Mala said easily.

Aubrey looked at her and wondered if she detected a hint of that loneliness in Mala's voice. Suddenly, the captain was changing the subject again as she stood up. "I have some things for you, come back to the camp with me." Her voice held a commanding tone and, without thinking, Aubrey obediently followed her. "I thought you might like these." Mala said, indicating a pile of packages inside the lean-to.

Aubrey looked at her in amazement as Mala stared at her indifferently and asked, "Well, will you insult me by ignoring my offer?"

"No, of course not, Captain." Aubrey stammered as she dropped to her knees in mild fear. With shaking hands, she picked up a package and tore open the brown papers that wrapped it. Pulling out three finely made camisoles, she looked up at Mala who merely shrugged.

The dark haired woman dropped to her knees as well, replying in a low tone, "I suppose that perhaps someone such as yourself misses the added comfort of such undergarments. Since we sail with one hundred or more men, dresses on a daily basis are not practical. White gauze and cotton shirts do not offer much discretion, especially on wet days."

"Someone such as me?" Aubrey echoed carefully.

"A refined young woman." Mala corrected.

Aubrey frowned at her and looked down at the cotton garment she held in her lap, "My refinement was left in London, Captain. I am changed now."

Mala gave her a narrowed-eyed stare as she was reminded of the mark that the auburn haired woman bore. "Indeed."

Seeing the icy stare, Aubrey looked down again. A stare just like Captain Black when he was angry, she thought and almost shivered. "Thank you for the gifts." Aubrey said quietly.

"Not gifts. It is not this captain's practice to bestow gifts. You have been working on the ship, helping Willie, so consider them payment for your work." Mala corrected stiffly. Aubrey had no problem catching the undertones of the comment.

"There are some britches and shirts as well, ones that fit you." Mala told her. The girl was nearly a twig of a person. That would have to be addressed with Morgan. Perhaps he could coax Aubrey into better eating habits. Mala found herself remembering the grand spreads of meals that she had dined on in another time—on another ship.

She inhaled deeply, pushing the memory back into the recesses of her mind, "Gather your clothing, we will go find this pond of Morgan's. I could use a swim and a cool bath. I hate this damned heat here in the Colonies."

Aubrey quietly obeyed, opening up packages and extracting a shirt and britches, "Would it be dangerous? Morgan says there are Indians."

"Morgan likes to play the joker. There are no Indians to bother us here." Mala scoffed.

"But will the men see us?"

"Not if we do not tell them that we are going." Mala replied as she gathered up some clothing of her own.

An hour later, they were relishing the refreshing coolness of the pond. It was not very deep as the water level was only to their shoulders. Aubrey had gone into the bushes, slipping out of her shirt and putting on a camisole. Mala frowned at her as she emerged and stepped into the water in britches, camisole and bare feet. Alarmed that Mala stripped off her own clothing at the pond edge, Aubrey averted her eyes and blushed in embarrassment before turning her back to the woman. Mala seemed undaunted by her nakedness before the other woman as she slipped into the pond's cool water and sighed.

Aubrey finally turned, knowing that the water would cover Mala now. The island woman ignored her as she splashed water over her head, wetting her long dark hair thoroughly. Aubrey's eye came to rest on the scars on Mala's back when the captain turned away from her and the younger woman had to squelch a gasp at the sight of them marking the otherwise smooth light bronze skin. Shivering, Aubrey remembered the day that Black had offered to have Jean Luc beaten. Mala had been on the *Widow Maker* with Black. Had the man put her under the whip?

Mala submerged herself and came back with a slight gasp at the coldness of the water, bringing Aubrey out of her musings. Now Mala faced her, busy with scrubbing her arms with the coarse soap that they had brought with them. Stealing a glance, Aubrey saw that she wore a medallion around her neck on a chain. The sun glinted off of it so that Aubrey was unable to see what the markings were on it but it was then that she saw the edges of Black's mark. Sighing deeply, Aubrey set about to her own bath. With some degree of hesitation, she unfastened the britches and slipped out of them as well as the camisole. She tossed the clothes up onto the small wall that surrounded the pond on three sides. Taking the offered soap after Mala was finished, Aubrey began to scrub herself vigorously.

Baths completed and dressed in clean clothes, she and Mala sat on the wall pulling on boots and brushing back their wet hair.

"What do you think of Morgan?" Mala asked easily.

"He is—nice." Aubrey stammered.

Mala nodded as she buckled the straps on her boots. "Did he give you that blade?"

"Yes, he did."

"Morgan takes weapons very seriously." Mala said with a small smile.

"So I have noticed." Aubrey giggled, a bit more relaxed now. "Why does Deats carry his knife under his arm? Is that not uncomfortable? It surely cannot be unsheathed quickly."

Mala smiled at her. "Did it have a black handle about this long and the blade of about the same length?" She held up her index finger and thumb to Aubrey with a space of several inches. Aubrey knitted her brows in thought then nodded.

"Tis a bonnie little blade as Deats would say." Mala replied with a hint of the Scottish accent then smiled at her own jest. "It is called a Sgian Dhu and is traditionally worn under the arm. It is quite a handy little tool for those close quarters battles and can be just as deadly as a dirk or stiletto when hitting an opponent in the right place."

"But it seems uncomfortable." Aubrey said.

Mala shrugged and leaned back on her hands to look up at the clear blue sky. "He is used to it there."

Their conversation was broken by the sound of snapping twigs in the forest before them. They both looked up at the sound and then exchanged glances.

"Deer?" Aubrey asked quietly as Mala straightened up slowly. The wary look in the captain's dark eyes as she peered into the bushes before them, unnerved the younger woman. Her question was answered as three men stepped from the trees. Mala and Aubrey exchanged glances again as they came easily to their feet. Watching Mala lay her hand on the hilt of her cutlass, Aubrey realized with great dismay that she was unarmed except for the small blade.

"Your men?" Aubrey whispered hopefully barely moving her lips.

"No." Mala replied.

"Well, what 'ave we 'ere?" One man drawled as they came forward a step. "Been usin' my pond eh?"

"Gonna make 'em pay fer it, Pa?" The youngest of the small group asked.

Mala pursed her lips and watched him guardedly. Aubrey thought that the boy looked no older than Henri.

"So Will, 'ow do ye reckon they should pay?" The second man chuckled as he eyed the two women before them. The older man cast a glance to the boy, looking for his reply. The boy's eyes shone with a lustful gaze of a young man in the throes of puberty.

"Got a fire in yer britches, boy?" The older man laughed, making the boy blush. "Well, I tell ye what, the dark 'aired one, now she looks experienced. That one there is fer yer ol' Pa 'ere. That little one, ye boys can fight over 'er. But William me lad, best to let yer big brother 'ave at 'er first, 'e can teach ye 'ow to lay a woman." The three men chuckled.

"There will be no laying of either of us." Mala said menacingly as she glared at them.

The older man sneered then suddenly lunged at Mala. Her cutlass was up in a flash and she slashed him across the forearm. He roared in pain and stepped back as her dark eyes shifted quickly to the other two.

"Bitch!" He spat as he grabbed for her again. Mala slashed at him again. The man's sons stood in shocked surprise of the spectacle before them, "Well what are ye waitin' for? Get that damned thing away from 'er!" He roared as he backed off again, holding another bleeding place on his arm.

"Be glad that you were not closer or you would be holding a bloody stump." Mala said smugly as she pointed her bloody cutlass at his injured arm.

The older of the two sons made a lunge for her and she jumped back with a warning, "Are you certain you want this fight?"

He drew a cutlass of his own, smiling at her, "I know what I want."

Mala stood to defend herself against him as he approached her while sweeping Aubrey behind her with her free hand growling, "Find something to protect yourself with, damn it." Mala then emitted a shrill whistle through her teeth that made Aubrey's ears ring. A chord of familiarity flashed across Aubrey's mind as she looked around for a weapon of some kind and saw nothing but rocks and sticks. Her eye came to rest on pile of old discarded boards nearby, remnants of repairs to the nearby mill.

"Yer on my land, woman. Anything on my land is mine." The injured man growled at Mala as she took her stance against his son.

"I think not." She growled back at him as she slashed out at the second man. Much to the surprise of all of them, Aubrey came up with a small length of board studded with nails.

"Then I suppose that this belongs to you." She said as she smacked the leader soundly with it in his already injured arm.

The nails stabbed deeply into his arm and he roared in pain again, drawing the second man's attention for a split second. Mala took the advantage and slashed out at him with her cutlass. Her attack did just as she had hoped, lying open his shirt and his chest. He fell backward, clutching at his chest, blood spurting like a tiny geyser with every beat of his heart. The older man pulled himself up to his full height despite his wounds, "Bitch! Look what ye did to my son!"

Mala shrugged indifferently as she stood on her guard. Staring at the gaping wound in the man's chest, Aubrey was taken off guard. The leader grabbed the board from her hand and swatted at her with the back of it. The wood connected with her shoulder, knocking her down.

"Get 'er, boy! She is on the ground just where ye want 'er. Christ, do I gotta lay 'er fer ye too? Mind ye though, the dark 'aired one is mine. She just killed yer brother and she is gonna pay for that." The man finally managed to draw his sword and stood against Mala, "Ye fight like a man. Well, once I have ye down we will see what is under them manly clothes."

"Over my dead body." Mala hissed.

"Alive or dead—it matters not to me now." He said then lunged at her but she parried him off. Steel clashed against steel as they fought and Mala was holding on skillfully.

William had finally pulled himself from his fog of shock at the sight of his older brother bleeding to death before him. With a curse, he charged Aubrey. Scrambling to her feet as he ran forward, Aubrey ran to grab another board.

The gangly young man was on her in an instant, all arms and legs. Both of them went down and they tumbled on the ground fighting for possession of the board.

The leader dealt Mala blow after ringing blow with his weapon. Defensively she backed herself toward the low stonewall. She emitted the shrill whistle again as he bore down on her. Suddenly, Mala was surprised when the bleeding man reached out a bloody hand and tripped her. She fell backwards against the wall, losing her cutlass. It clattered over the wall to land with a splash into the pond below. A look of surprise then anger crossed her face as her attacker grabbed at the front of her shirt. He smiled at her. "I got ye now, ye black 'aired bitch."

Aubrey was on the ground on her back, the young man straddled over her. Thankfully, the boy seemed more intent on fighting over the piece of nail-studded board than his first interest. She looked around frantically and noticed a palm-sized rock lying nearby. Fighting still with one hand, she reached with frantic clawing motions to reach the rock. Finally, in an act of sheer desperation, she let go of the wood. The force of him pulling against her for the makeshift weapon caused him to tumble backward when she let go.

In the next instant, he saw the blur of a hand and felt the pain as the rock slammed into the side of his face. Gasping, he released the board and put both hands to his paining face as he fell forward over her, blood oozing from the split in his skin at the cheekbone. Aubrey shoved at him savagely, screaming in his face before she scrambled out from under him.

Mala kicked a booted foot at the older man, connecting soundly with his right knee. The leg buckled under him and he went down with another roar of pain. She pushed him aside, freeing herself from the pinned position between the wall and him. Aubrey had come to her feet and Mala grabbed her by the shoulder of her shirt, pulling her as she began to run, "Come on!"

With Aubrey in front, the two women sprinted off into the trees, leaping over fallen trees and exposed roots. Aubrey ran like she had never run before. With a quick glance behind them, she realized that the two men were on their feet and in close pursuit. Limbs and thorns shot out to block their way and catch their clothing, but they both ignored them, jerking free, then continued to run.

Winded, Aubrey was dropping behind Mala. Her young attacker was leaping through the brush like a deer, coming between her and Mala to separate them. Glancing back to see Aubrey beginning to turn, just as the boy was directing, Mala shouted and reached out for Aubrey's arm, "No, stay with me!"

Lungs burning like fire and fear spurring her on, Aubrey turned toward

Mala, tightening the distance between them as they broke out into an open meadow. Mala managed to let out another shrill whistle, hoping that her alarm had been heard and that she and Aubrey could make it. The men who chased them were close, but they had no idea that they were being led into a pirate encampment.

The terrain was better for Aubrey when suddenly she tripped and went down with a cry of alarm. Looking over her shoulder, Mala saw that she had regained her footing, but like an attacking cat, the boy lunged and dragged her down once more. There was a blur of arms and bone-chilling screams.

Mala's attacker was on her heels and she had no time to help Aubrey. Looking ahead toward the trees, Mala saw Morgan and Deats emerge at a full run into the sunlit meadow. She saw Deats stop and raise his pistol. Seeing the glint of sunlight on the barrel of the pistol, Mala threw herself sideways onto the ground just as he pulled off the shot. The man fell with a crash behind her, disappearing into the tall grass. She laid gasping to fill her burning lungs with air.

Morgan and Deats scanned the field as they neared Mala at a dead run. "Aubrey! Where is she?" Morgan was shouting as he frantically looked over the tall grass of the meadow.

At that instant, they heard a shrill scream and the meadow suddenly fell silent. Morgan ran toward the sound, his heart clutched in fear. Suddenly, Aubrey stood quickly, almost right in front of him. He stepped back in alarm at her sudden appearance and saw her shirt was splattered with blood. She was looking down into the grass, the small blade he had given her was clasped tightly in her right hand and the shiny steel was dulled with blood.

"What happened?" Deats asked as Mala got to her feet.

"Get my ship back in the water." Mala ordered.

"But we just started..." Deats began.

Mala whirled around and said angrily, "We leave, finished or not! Those dead bodies are going to be missed, Deats. Get the men together and get my ship to rights, now."

Mala headed for the encampment followed by her men who had joined Deats and Morgan in the rescue. The Scotsman glanced toward Aubrey and Morgan then walked away quickly to catch up with Mala.

Morgan stepped a bit closer as Aubrey continued to stare down at the younger man lying face down, unmoving. Grasping the boy by the arm and turning him over onto his back, Morgan cast a questioning glance at Aubrey. There was a long gash across the boy's stomach. Aubrey looked at Morgan blankly, still holding the dripping blade tightly.

"Give me the knife." He said quietly.

"No, this is mine." She replied firmly, looking at the man on the ground.

"I know, I will give it back, I promise. Now drop it." He insisted as he gently took her by the wrist and shook her hand easily. She finally relaxed her fingers and he took the weapon.

"Come back to camp." He said as he took her gently by the arm.

The camp was bustling with activity when Morgan and Aubrey entered the site. Mala was barking out orders and men were heading back to the ship. Realizing that they were preparing to leave, Morgan decided to take care of Aubrey first then help Mala.

"You come with me." He demanded as he took Aubrey by the arm and pulled her toward the shoreline. "Wash off this blood." He said easily as he took her hands and dipped them into the lapping water. "Why do you go off by yourself?"

"I was not alone." She replied.

"Very well then, you obviously were with the captain. But what in the hell were the two of you doing?" He asked firmly.

"We went to the mill to bathe in private."

"To the mill? To bathe? Without an escort or protection?" His tone was sharp with disapproval.

"Did ya not hear me then? I said we went to bathe. Do ya think we wanted a bunch of ya watchin' us?" The Irish brogue was heavy with anger. Morgan looked at her and some of his anger subsided.

"So there were only two of them?" He asked a bit calmer.

"Three." She corrected.

"Three? I saw only two." He said looking up and taking note of the activity around them.

"Mala killed one of them back at the mill. Sweet Mary, we left the clothes!" Aubrey exclaimed.

"Never mind about that. Those clothes are not the usual attire for women anyway." He told her. Cleaning the small blade, Morgan asked carefully, "How do you feel? I mean, you just killed a man."

"He is not the first person I have had to kill." She muttered, looking at the water lapping near their feet. Morgan looked up in surprise. "On the *Widow Maker*, there was a man who tried to, I mean I thought it was Captain Black returning but I suddenly…" Aubrey began to explain.

Morgan interrupted her and said soothingly, "Just do not wander off without me or Robert with you. Mala can take care of herself, she has had a lot of practice but you are still learning. The next time, you may not be so lucky." When she remained quiet, Morgan bumped his shoulders against hers and added conspiratorially, "I suppose you are more of a pirate than I had first thought. You are a thief, a liar and now a murderess…all ya need now is a ship."

He was glad to hear a soft lazy giggle emit from her as she looked up at him. "Lie down here and rest for a while." He told her gently.

Aubrey sighed and laid down on the soft grass turning onto her side. Morgan looked at the activity of the camp and happened to catch Deats' glare. With a sigh, he leaned over her and realized that she had fallen into an exhausted sleep.

Slipping her knife back into her boot, he stood and waved one of his guards over. "I want you to watch over Miss Aubrey here, she is taking a bit of a nap."

"Would she not be more comfortable on a bedroll?" The man asked as he looked down on her.

"Does she look uncomfortable to you?" Morgan asked curtly as he pointed at her.

"Well, no."

"Then leave her be and just watch over her." Morgan ordered as he moved away. "And take care not to get too close. She has been known to kill men who tend to get too close." He called over his shoulder with a grin.

Morgan looked back to see the man looked down at Aubrey with some surprise on his face. "A bit like the Cap'n, ain't she?" The man called after Morgan in a hushed tone of voice as not to disturb Aubrey. Morgan chuckled as he moved into the midst of the encampment.

Chapter 12

After they were well on their way from the isolated cove of the Chesapeake Bay's northern shores and were out to sea on their way to Charlestowne, Mala and Aubrey had recounted their adventure to Morgan and Deats over dinner that night in the great cabin. The men had looked at them sternly but both knew better than to voice their real opinions on the matter in the presence of Mala.

The next morning while Morgan shaved, Aubrey finished making up her bunk and moved soundlessly to the door. "Goin' to breakfast? Wait for me and I will join you." He chirped as he turned and picked up his shirt.

She stopped mid-stride, her hand resting on the latch, her back to him, "No thank you Morgan, I am not hungry this morning." The voice from her came small and quiet.

"Why not? Where are you going then?" He asked with a frown. Flashing her an impish grin, he added, "Old Willie will tan your hide if you do not show up for breakfast."

He eyed her curiously and noted that she was wearing some of the new clothing Mala had purchased for her. They fit her much better than the ones she had been wearing which had been nothing more than hand-me-downs from various members of the crew.

"Aubrey, you need to eat. What is the matter today?" He asked as he wiped his face with a small towel.

"Nothing, nothing is wrong. I am just not hungry."

"You had those bad dreams last night again." He said gently placing his hands on her shoulders. "Aubrey, you have to let him go." She pushed at him with both hands wanting to get away but he remained unaffected by her discomfort. "You are not alone. Is that what is troubling you today?" Morgan asked softly.

She stared into his eyes. Those piercing, yet caring blue eyes. The sound of caring in his voice. The feelings that she had known with Jean Luc came flooding back. Her pause gave Morgan a spark of hope. Lowering his head towards hers, he took the opportunity to try and kiss her. For a few fleeting moments it looked as if he might succeed but when his lips were just inches from hers, she suddenly pushed at him with all her might then slipped past him. Turning, she threw open the door at the same instant and flew from the small cabin.

He let out an exclamation of pain when the edge of the door caught him squarely in the center of his face. The pain was excruciating as he turned to blink bleary-eyed at himself in the mirror. Moving his hand from his face, he noticed that his nose was bleeding.

Only after she was out in the corridor and heard his exclamation of pain did Aubrey realize that she had hit him with the door. Panicking at the thought of him being angry and coming after her, Aubrey flew up the companionway steps. She flew past Robert on the main deck, nearly running him over as well.

"Who in the hell is chasing you, Miss Aubrey?" Robert asked but she gave him no reply as she hurried toward the stern of the ship. Aubrey came to a sliding stop at the stern railing leaning halfway over it, looking at the water.

"Oh my God, Morgan is going to kill me." She gasped to the water and looking fearfully over her shoulder to see if he was coming. Robert stood where she had passed him, looking puzzled. As she looked at Robert, one of the men approached him and spoke close to his ear. He nodded and when the man moved on, Robert approached her.

"Miss Aubrey? Are you all right? Are you sick?" He queried. He had seen many a stout man in his day race for the railing to empty the contents of his stomach overboard.

"No, I am fine, Robert." She managed to say as hazel eyes darted past him.

He looked at her still puzzled for a few moments before saying, "Well, Captain Mala wants to see you in the galley."

She began to wonder if she might have knocked Morgan out before Robert's words finally registered in her mind, "The captain wants to see me?" She echoed worriedly.

"Aye, and you better hurry now." He said with a small smile.

Aubrey smiled nervously in reply as he turned away and she moved slowly back toward the companionway. Seeing the captain at her table, Aubrey had already decided to tell her what she had done before the woman found out from Morgan or some other source. Laying her hands flat on the table, Aubrey took a deep breath. "Captain, I..." She began looking at the dark-haired woman.

Mala's eyes were averted from her to something behind her and a puzzled frown crossed the beautiful face. Carefully, Aubrey lowered her own eyes and glanced down at the floor to see a familiar pair of boots beside her. A sick feeling rushed over her and she closed her eyes.

"Morgan, what in the hell happened to you?" Mala exclaimed with a suppressed laugh. Aubrey slowly opened her eyes and turned a hesitant gaze upon Morgan. He was looking at her sternly and deliberately bumped against her as he sat down.

"You know the rules about fighting on board this ship." Mala began but Morgan interrupted.

"Aye Captain, I know. It is only a difference of opinion." He muttered as he shot a glance at Aubrey.

Mala pursed her lips and scanned the pair of them with a knowing look in her brown eyes. "Aubrey, please sit down."

Aubrey stole a glance at Morgan while taking a seat opposite him. It had not taken long for his eyes to go black from the hit. Mala had to suppress the urge to laugh at the scene. By now, her intuitiveness told her that Aubrey was somehow responsible for the two black eyes that Morgan now sported.

"Captain, we have some bad weather ahead." Reported one of the men who had approached the table.

Mala looked up at him in all seriousness now and set down her mug. Aubrey watched in alarm as Mala rose smoothly from the table and started away, leaving her alone with Morgan. "Settle your, ah, difference of opinion, Morgan. Duty calls, Aubrey but I am sure Morgan will keep you company." Mala said over her shoulder as she left them. Only Willie saw the grin on the captain's face as she exited the galley.

Morgan turned a blank stare on Aubrey and watched as her face wrinkled in distress. "I, ah, think I will go and see if Willie needs any help to fasten things down." She said nervously as she made to stand. Morgan stood up as well making Aubrey pause. The hesitation gave him time to move around to her side of the table. She cringed away and tried to take a step back and nearly stumbled.

Morgan reached out to steady her and said with a smile, "Careful there, we would not want you to bump your head."

Worried hazel eyes searched his face. His nose still bled slightly and there was a small knot in the center of his forehead between his eyes. Swallowing hard, she turned her gaze to the men who were quickly leaving the galley to go topside to their posts. They appeared disinterested in them as the room was becoming empty very fast.

"You know…" Morgan began, his voice startling her. "Since you are my responsibility, and we have this bad weather coming, I think that I will just escort you back to the cabin and tuck you away there."

"That will be fine, Morgan, I can take care of myself."

"No, you are coming with me." He said clamped a hand over her wrist. Ignoring her protests, he pulled her out of the galley and along the corridor to their cabin.

At the door to the cabin, Morgan pulled Aubrey inside. When she tried to dart back out, he squeezed her wrist painfully and said sweetly, "Get away from the door, love. I would not want to hit you with it when I close it."

Aubrey's face paled as she stepped away from the door and tried to make some distance between them. But as soon as the door was closed, she flew into nervous chatter. "Oh God Morgan, I did not mean to hit you, I am so sorry that I hurt you. Please do not be angry with me. I did not mean to hurt you. Are you really angry with me?"

"Aubrey—Aubrey." He managed to interject as she finally hesitated to draw a nervous breath. "Be quiet."

"I…" She began then clamped her mouth when he raised a brow.

"Now, sit down there, we need to talk." He said as he pointed to her bunk. She slowly lowered herself onto the end of the bunk and looked up at him innocently.

"It is a wonder you did not break my nose. How am I going to explain this? We have had no battle, no boarding, we have not been to shore for a tavern brawl or street fight." He told her as he gingerly touched the tender spot.

"Tell them the truth!" She said innocently.

"The truth! I would be the laughing stock of the ship!" He exclaimed.

The cabin was quiet for long agonizing moments as Aubrey stared past Morgan and bit her bottom lip nervously. Unable to contain himself any longer, Morgan grinned then immediately winced. Pointing a finger at her, he said with a hint of laughter in his voice, "Christ girl, I never took a hit from a man as hard as that!"

"You are not angry with me?" She asked in surprise.

"Of course, I am." He told her amid a chuckle.

"Really?" Her timid response made him burst into laughter. At the realization that she was not in trouble, Aubrey began to giggle as she leaned toward him and took his face gently in her hands to inspect the injury. "It looks like I gave you a bit of a nose bleed as well. Sit still here."

Aubrey got up and went to the basin to wet a rag from the pitcher. Returning to stand before him, she slipped a small hand behind his neck and began to gently dab at the dried blood under his nose. He tilted his head back in submission as she worked gently to clean his paining face. Letting his eyes drift down over her, Morgan thought about how he would gladly submit to any touch she might bestow upon him if she wanted to. Then he began to think about the touches that he might bestow upon her in return.

Sudden pain from her pressing the rag on his face brought him out of his lustful musings and back to reality. He caught her by the wrist and waved her away with his other hand, growling, "Stop fussin' over me, damn it, that hurts."

"Well, I was only trying to make amends for what I did." She told him as she took the rag back to the basin and rinsed it out.

"Well if ya feel that badly about it, a little kiss might help." He tormented mischievously.

"Now is that not what got you the knot on your head in the first place?" She asked raising a brow. They looked at one another for a few quiet moments before they both burst into laughter.

"I must get topside now. I need to make sure we do not have any cannons rolling around on deck during the storm." Morgan said and pulled on his hat then left the cabin, shutting the door behind him.

Sitting down on her bunk her thoughts drifted back to Jean Luc. She cocked her head to one side and wondered if she had ever struck him. Smiling, she recalled the morning she had slapped him soundly in the doorway of the galley. A loud clap of thunder overhead sent Aubrey into other memories of Jean Luc ...and storms.

Mala was on the main deck, overseeing the preparations being made for the storm. Deats stood nearby, shouting out orders. The dark haired woman turned toward Morgan as he approached. Catching her long hair in her hand against the onslaught of the wind, she asked, "Did you settle that fight?"

Morgan smiled sheepishly. "Aubrey accidentally hit me with the door as she was leaving the cabin this mornin.'" He confessed close to her face to keep from being overheard by Deats.

"Do tell?" She said smiling. He nodded in reply and started to walk away. A look of surprise crossed his face as he felt himself being drawn back. He glanced over his shoulder to find that Mala had him by the baldric and was pulling him back. "Following her a wee bit close, were we, Mr. Alcott?" She asked with a mischievous twinkle in her dark eyes.

"Well..." He began.

"It was for another kiss." Mala finished for him and smiled. She released her hold on him as he stared in surprise while shrugging the baldric back into place.

"How in the hell do you know these things?" He grumbled.

"Morgan, I have told you a hundred times, I am the captain of this ship, it is my job to know what goes on." She replied with a sigh.

Lightening lit the sky and thunder cracked over them. They both ducked involuntarily at the sound and looked up. Morgan brought his gaze back down to meet hers and his tone was low and full of mischief, "Even to knowing the thoughts of every man on board?"

"Aye." She smiled playfully.

Morgan frowned and exhaled deeply, rolling his blue eyes. "Then I guess I better be careful how I think about you."

Mala pursed her lips and looked at him, reaching for her pistol in a playful gesture of drawing it on him, she said easily, "To your post, Mr. Alcott."

Morgan eyed her hand on the butt of the weapon and he tapped the brim of his hat, "Aye, Captain."

Of all her crew, Morgan was her favorite. Their tie of friendship ran deep, even deeper than her friendship with Deats. The Scotsman had helped her once when she was in trouble and although he protected her far more diligently than any other quartermaster did any other captain, she still looked on him as nothing more than a good friend. Mala shook her head with a small smile crossing her lips as she watched Morgan stride away.

"All is secure, Captain, as soon as Mr. Alcott gets his cannons tied down." Came the Scottish accent from beside her.

"Thank you, Mr. Deats." She nodded.

"What in the bloody hell happened ta him?" Deats growled as he nodded toward Morgan who was now calling out orders.

"It has been settled." Mala said flippantly as she started away from her quartermaster.

He followed hot on her heels as a cold rain began to pour from the heavens. "Well I am the quartermaster of this ship, he is one of the crew. If there is a problem, I need ta know aboot it and it will be dealt with. A sound lashing should cool their tempers." Deats droned on in his Scottish accent.

Mala turned on him angrily. "There will be no lashing of anyone on my ship and well you know that, Mr. Deats. Might I remind you that first and foremost, I am the captain of this vessel? If there is any punishment to be administered, I will be the judge and name that punishment."

"Who was he fightin' with?" Deats ventured to question despite her apparent anger.

Mala blinked her eyes at him in disbelief then turned away to go up the quarterdeck steps, saying, "It has been taken care of, Mr. Deats."

"If ye ask me, I think that he gets away with just a tad bit more than he should be allowed." Deats continued to argue.

Mala had finally had enough and she turned on him slowly as she topped the steps. Since he stood below her, two steps down, she looked down at him and said in a low tone, "Mr. Deats, since you are so concerned about the welfare of the men on this ship, you will remain on deck to make sure that all stays secure during the storm."

A flash of lightening illuminated her face and thunder clapped above them, but this time, Mala did not flinch. A retort was on his lips but seeing the steady gaze, he wisely replied more calmly, "Aye, Captain." To argue with her further from his present position would surely earn him a quick trip backward onto the deck. Mala was not beyond striking any man for his impertinence.

"Very good." She replied as sheets of cold rain assaulted them. "I am going to my quarters now and get out of this terrible weather." She added turning from him.

Deats pulled his hat down over his eyes a bit more. Mala brushed past him and went down the steps without a look back at him. The brush against him was meant to intimidate, but it only inflamed his desire for her all the more. He watched her disappear down the companionway steps and he exhaled hard. His breath came out of him in a vaporous cloud with the coolness in the air from the storm. Taking the remaining steps up to the quarterdeck to lean on the railing, he realized that perhaps she let him get away with a great deal as well. A curse had been on his lips, but he had known better than to express it. He had seen many men take a ball from her pistol between their eyes for far less.

Later in the day when the worst of the storm had passed, Morgan's entrance into the galley behind Aubrey drew a chorus of guffaws and catcalls from the men in the room. He eyed them with a crooked smile and waved her to a bench at a nearby table. As he eased himself down beside her, Willie was there almost immediately with a plate of turtle meat and hard-boiled egg that he set before Aubrey.

"I expect ye to eat all of it, luv." He told her as Riley and York sat down across from them. Aubrey nodded to him as she eyed the amount of food on the plate.

When Willie turned away, Morgan grabbed his arm and asked, "How come you did not bring me a plate as soon as I got in here?"

"Aye Willie, we were the ones up on the deck in the cold and rain fighting them sails and keepin' the ship afloat." York agreed as Riley nodded his agreement.

Willie regarded them with twinkling eyes and carefully put his callused hands on each side of Aubrey's face as he stood behind her. She remained undaunted and merely looked from one man to the other at the table as she chewed a piece of the turtle meat she had taken from her plate.

"Ye ask me why I bring her a plate and not ye three ruffians?" Willie began. The three men nodded and smiled.

"Do you see this face?" Willie drawled as he turned Aubrey's head toward them as if to display her. More nods and smiles. "I gave her a plate 'cause she is little and purdy and yer not. Now get up off yer big lazy arses an' get yer own damn plate." He growled at them.

After a few moments of silence, the three men erupted into chuckles. Willie released Aubrey and moved away grumbling to himself. York turned an inspecting eye on Morgan and asked, "Did you get them black eyes out on deck in the storm?"

"Nope." Morgan replied as he poured himself a mug of rum from the bottle that York had set down on the table.

"I hear that he came out of his cabin like that this mornin'" Riley offered.

"Well, what happened then?" York asked with a grin directed at Aubrey.

"If you must know, York, I got a bit cheeky with Miss Aubrey here and she punched me soundly on the nose. I would be careful what you say to her. She packs quite a punch for the little bit that she is." Morgan said bluntly.

Aubrey rolled her eyes at his lie as the two men burst into laughter. Morgan offered her his most winning smile and plucked a piece of meat from her plate.

"Well, ya know what I always heard." Riley began with a wink at Morgan.

"What is that?" He asked as he popped the morsel into his mouth.

"The tougher the battle, the sweeter the conquest." The man replied with a nod. The table erupted with laughter again and Aubrey's face crimsoned. Emitting a deep sigh, she stood and picked up her plate.

"Where are ya goin'?" Morgan asked as he tried to get another morsel from her plate.

She held it from his reach and said, "Somewhere else and leave you three to your amusements alone. And get your own damned plate like Willie told you. You are always hollerin' at me to eat and now you go eatin' my meal." As she moved away, the two men continued to chide Morgan over his black eyes and she could not help but smile as well as she moved away from them.

Chapter 13

Morning dawned clear with calm seas. Aubrey was making her bunk when a voice from the open doorway startled her out of her own thoughts, "Clobbered him pretty good, huh?"

Mala was leaning with her arms folded over her chest against the doorjamb with a solemn look on her face. The look of alarm on the other young woman's face almost made her smile.

"Captain Mala." Aubrey breathed as she straightened almost to attention.

"You gave Morgan two real nice-looking black eyes." Mala informed.

"It was an accident, Captain." Aubrey defended almost fearfully.

"Well, you could have just let him have the kiss." Mala said with a small grin as she stepped further into the cabin.

Aubrey's mouth dropped open in surprise before her gaze lowered to the floor. Mala saw the beginnings of a slight frown and smiled at the thought that the young woman was wondering how she would know of the encounter.

"But the truth of it is, you were afraid that he would not stop at just the kiss." Mala stated informatively. Aubrey remained silent and would not look up at Mala. The silence was confirmation enough for the dark haired woman. "Morgan is different, Aubrey. He is not like the men that you encountered on the *Widow Maker*. He has a far more caring nature and he would not do anything to hurt you. You can trust him." Mala offered easily to the silence. Aubrey finally raised hazel eyes to meet the captain's dark brown ones.

"I knew a man like that once. He was on the *Widow Maker*." Aubrey's voice was small and hinted of deep sadness.

Mala's steady gaze seemed to bore into her for a moment before she said firmly, "I think that we need to have a long chat someday."

"Really?" Aubrey asked with a mixture of doubt and surprise.

Mala looked around the cabin. It was the first time she had come to the cabin since Morgan had taken in his new roommate. Aubrey followed the dark eyes as they surveyed the room. It clearly reflected the young woman's strong attempt to keep herself apart from her male roommate, despite the closeness of the quarters. All of Aubrey's meager belongings were neatly confined and tucked in the space of her bunk.

Attempting to put the conversation back on a lighter note, Mala said, "Well, he will wear his battle scars for a while." Her tone held a hint of laughter and Aubrey suddenly felt a giggle rise.

"He said he had never been hit that hard by even a man but he is such a storyteller. I really did not hit him though, he ran into the door as I opened

123

it." Aubrey told her.

Mala smiled with dark eyes twinkling in humor. Aubrey felt a weight lift from her shoulders at the sight of the smile.

"Tell no one, let him keep his pride." Mala said and Aubrey nodded in agreement. Looking about the cabin once again, the captain added, "We will have that talk someday when I am sure the time is right. In the meantime, keep Morgan in line. He tends to get a bit unruly sometimes—not dangerously so, but more like a bad little boy."

"I will, Captain." Aubrey replied with a nod as Mala turned and left as quickly as she had appeared.

Halfway along the corridor to her cabin, Mala stopped and took a deep breath. Her mind tumbled in thought about the other young woman. Deats had been saying a great number of things about her of late and Mala could not help but feel a twinge of jealousy at his comments. Morgan had contradicted everything she had said about Aubrey and the doubts that Deats had managed to place in her mind. Looking up as she pulled herself out of her own thoughts, she saw Morgan as he mounted the companionway steps on his way topside.

"Morgan, a moment if you please."

"Certainly, Captain." He said with a nod.

"In my quarters." She ordered easily as she walked past him.

Mala walked to the quarter gallery windows with her hands clasped behind her back as Morgan stood patiently waiting for her to speak. Turning to face him, she said, "I think that one kiss has thrown you into an infatuation, Morgan. You should resign yourself to the fact that you will probably never get so close as you did on that hill again. I have noticed that although you do try to maintain a distance with her, you are not playing by your own rules. I charge you, do not force yourself or you will answer to me."

Her comments made him angry as he stated tightly, "You have known me for a long time, Mala, I would not do that. I know she is in love, but the man she loves is gone…" Morgan replied. Mala watched as his blue eyes drifted down to the front of her shirt and he continued as he flipped a thumb towards the closed door. "She cannot mourn forever. In my opinion, it is beyond all reason that you two should put yourselves through this personal hell. I know that you cared for him, Mala. But he is gone now and you are not."

His blood warmed from the frustration of not being able to get closer to Aubrey. The rarely seen temper that he possessed was slipping out. Even in battle his demeanor did not always reflect this side of him. But Mala knew Morgan and, while he did well to keep his temper in check, he could be very cruel when he was pushed or provoked. They remained staring at one another for an extended period of time.

"Thank you for sharing your thoughts and opinions on the matter, Morgan." Mala said trying hard to put her own temper in check.

Morgan looked at her pointedly, "Anytime Captain. I have duties to tend to."

"Carry on, Mr. Alcott." She said tightly. Morgan turned on his heel but as he reached for the door latch, she reminded him. "Take care that you do not change your demeanor with her just to prove a point, Mr. Alcott. My first order still stands."

Morgan batted angry blue eyes at her and clapped his hat on his head, "Aye Captain, I remember your order."

With that, he opened the door and exited the cabin, shutting the door soundly in his retreat. Mala shook her head and exhaled deeply. What in the hell was going on here? She wondered. And why were she and Morgan suddenly at one another's throats? She never really put much stock into Deats statements before, so why did she attack Morgan like that? She trusted Morgan more than anyone else on the ship. She knew he would always watch her back, would never go against her. So what was happening?

The late morning sun had warmed the day but the sea breeze kept much of the heat from being felt. The *Enchantress* was now back in open sea but still close enough to land to have seagulls hover overhead. Aubrey watched the gulls as she broke a pieces of hardtack and tossed them in the air for them. She laughed at those who missed and dove into the water for the tidbit.

"Ye shouldna feed them, Miss Malone." Deats stated as he approached her. His voice startled her from her play and she nearly dropped the biscuit into the water.

"I like the sounds they make." She said conversationally.

She heard something like a snort but ignored him. She tossed more into the air for the birds. Deats did not leave but instead rested his arms on the railing and leaned forward. She glanced at him wondering what was on his mind.

At that moment a gull landed on the railing beside her and gave a loud screech. Aubrey backed away from it warily and bumped into Deats. The bird looked at her before giving another loud screech. She tossed it a few crumbs, which was caught expertly with its pointed beak. Then with wings flapping and more screeching, the bird moved towards her. She gave a short cry of alarm before she saw Deats' arm wave beside her and the startled bird flew away. Aubrey watched it then looked at Deats who was also watching the bird ascend into the air.

"Thank you." She whispered.

Deats turned to look at her as she smiled timidly in her thanks. He grunted as he straightened himself. Then giving the sky one last baleful look for the offending bird, he said, "Rodents with wings. Pests, they all be." Facing her, Deats looked pointedly at the crumbs in her hand. "Ye shouldna fed them. Tis a shameful waste of food." With that, he left her as abruptly as he had approached her.

Aubrey watched him leave then looked dumbly at the crumbs in her hands. The screeching caught her attention as she looked up to find several birds flying around them. She tossed the remaining crumbs over the railing then slapped her hands together to get rid of the crumbs clinging to her palms.

Turning away from the railing, she found Morgan walking towards her. Seeing the swords he carried, she let out a long sigh. "I do not feel like practicing right now, Morgan." She told him as he neared her.

"Ah, you do not feel like it." Morgan said with a speculative look on his face. "Then I suppose when a worthy opponent approaches, you can hold up your pretty little hand and tell him, *'I do not feel like it right now.'* The poor lad will oblige, I am sure, and look elsewhere for a fight."

"Oh do be quiet, Morgan!" Aubrey replied a little of her accent showing her irritation.

He did close his mouth but she saw the small smile on his lips. He stood with his arms crossed and each sword stuck out from each side. He looked so ridiculous that Aubrey fought to keep from smiling. She did not have to fight over the smile too long, for at that moment, Mala approached them. Clapping Morgan hard on the back, making him nearly lose his balance as he did not notice her approach, Mala easily maneuvered around the swords sticking out from beside him.

"So, what are you two about?" The captain asked.

Morgan regained himself and, pointing at Aubrey with the hilt of a sword, he replied in a mocking tone, "Does not feel like practicing right now. Wants to play with birds instead."

Aubrey had the urge to stick out her tongue at him, but with Mala present, she decided against it. Mala looked up to watch the birds in flight for a few moments. Then briefly glanced at Aubrey before turning her attention to the sea. "It is not wise to feed them. They will follow us out to sea and they can be troublesome."

Aubrey now wished she did not feed them. It was bad enough that Deats' few civil conversations with her had to be about not feeding the gulls but now Mala was disappointed in her as well. Her dejection was evident in her sigh and showed on her face as Mala and Morgan looked at her when she sighed aloud.

Morgan opened his mouth to soothe her but Mala spoke instead, "Then again I have been caught feeding the blasted things myself before even realizing it."

As she spoke, the captain looked up at the gulls and studied their flight for a few seconds before looking at Aubrey who seemed to have brightened a small measure. Morgan was smiling at her as well but Mala gave him a stern look that only broadened that smile. Deciding to change the subject, Mala tapped the sword that was held downward with her booted foot and asked Morgan, "So what moves have you taught her?"

"You know what moves, Mala. I see you watching us while I make her practice." Morgan said still smiling.

Mala gave him another annoying look. "Well then, what else have you taught her? Pistols?"

"Only in the loading of them. Too much powder and it can blow up in her face."

As he spoke, Mala crossed her arms over her chest and looked at Aubrey as if appraising her worth. Aubrey felt uncomfortable under the unwavering dark-eyed stare. "What else?" Mala asked.

"We have not done too much other than that. We do have our chores to tend to as well." Aubrey looked at Morgan in surprise still startled that he would be so bold as to use certain tones when speaking with Mala. "You have something in mind that I should teach her?" Morgan asked.

Without answering him, Mala asked Aubrey, "How much climbing have you done?"

Morgan's mouth dropped open and his head tipped back to look up at the ratlines. Stepping closer to Mala, transferring both weapons to one hand, he whispered, "Mala, it would not fair."

She ignored him as she looked at Aubrey for an answer. The dialogue confused Aubrey but she answered, "I climbed trees when I was a child."

Mala smiled still watching her with piercing dark eyes. "Of course, young ladies do not climb trees."

Aubrey smiled weakly and nodded. She noticed Morgan step closer to Mala again and whisper in his captain's ear. Mala still paid no attention as she continued to give Aubrey that appraising look. Growing apprehensive under Mala's continued stare and, with the look on Morgan's face, Aubrey knew that whatever thought the captain had, it did not sit well with Morgan.

"Would there be a reason for me to climb?" Aubrey asked, remembering her fright as she climbed the ratlines on the *Widow Maker* that day to escape from Black.

Still close to Mala, Morgan whispered again, "This would not be fair. Give me time to teach her." Again Mala ignored him as Morgan could see her determination.

"A reason to climb?" The captain repeated. "One never knows when a situation would arise that involves climbing, shooting, sword fighting, and …swimming." Mala added the last knowing that Aubrey could not swim. Her brief glance to the water surrounding the ship emphasized the last item on the list.

Aubrey turned and looked over the vast sea surrounding them. Swimming! She thought. The idea of learning of how swim was frightening and to actually learn it would be long and embarrassing. Aubrey released a long sigh as she stared at the water.

She was brought back to the present as Mala said, "First things first. Let us see what you do know and we will go from there."

"What I know about what? Climbing?" Aubrey asked as she looked overhead. "How high?"

Mala pointed and Aubrey asked, "To the crow's nest?"

"Not that one. The other one." Mala said smiling.

Aubrey's mouth dropped open as she looked at Mala as if she had lost her mind. Then her head tilted back as her gaze moved from the lower crow's nest to the fighting top. She had climbed it to escape from Black but now Mala was about to have her climb the height again, for fun!

"Mala! This is really not fair!" Morgan protested loudly. "Give me a chance to show her the..."

"Hush Morgan! Time is never on our side and well you know it!" Mala admonished. "One never knows what awaits us at the next turn."

Mala studied Aubrey's blanched face as the younger woman continued to stare high above her. Morgan had told her about Aubrey's climb to escape Black on the *Widow Maker*. After a few agonizing seconds for both Morgan and Aubrey, Mala relented and said with a smile, "But I suppose since she has not climbed in some time, we could go to the mid-mast."

Morgan breathed a sigh of relief but Aubrey felt no relief at all. Even the well-used crow's nest was too high for her comfort.

"In a battle, would climbing merely trap me?" Aubrey asked, trying to reason the captain out of the idea.

"True." Mala replied. "But if confronted by a worthy opponent, you could always dive into the sea. The height would give you an excellent advantage for spotting an area unmanned."

Ignoring Aubrey's slack-jawed expression, Mala walked over to the railing and jumped onto it holding the ratlines for support. Then with an impish grin, the captain crooked her finger for Aubrey to join her on the railing.

Aubrey stared at her then felt Morgan's hand on her arm guiding her to the railing. Fear gripped her heart as she tried to slow Morgan's pace by the slow movements of her legs. Her auburn hair undulated in the slight breeze as she shook her head and whispered frantically, "Morgan, I cannot do this!"

"You will do fine. Stay close to the captain and nothing will happen." Morgan whispered trying to give her courage.

"Why would she help me? She does not care about me." Aubrey whispered back.

"Of course she does, silly. Why would you say that?" Morgan asked.

"Because I was on the *Widow Maker*."

"So was she once."

"Exactly!" Aubrey exclaimed yanking her arm from his grip.

Morgan laughed before he continued to guide her to Mala who was waiting patiently and seemingly not paying any attention to their conversation. When Aubrey reached the railing, Mala held out her hand to help the younger woman up. With a boost, Morgan and Mala helped an uncontrollably shaking Aubrey onto the railing.

"Hold here." Mala instructed. Aubrey clutched the rope tightly and looked down. "No, do not look down! Look up to where you want to go!" Mala ordered. Aubrey lifted her head but could only look straight ahead then she shut her eyes tightly.

"Now, place your foot on the rope." Aubrey was startled when Morgan took hold of her foot. Looking down at him, she kicked at him but he only laughed as he grabbed her foot to place it on the rope.

"Good, now place your other foot one step higher." Aubrey faced Mala, her breathing ragged and her face white with fear, silently pleading to stop. "Come on, move your foot." Mala ordered sternly, ignoring the look on her face.

"I cannot." Aubrey whispered.

"Yes, you can! Your life depends on it!"

With eyes tightly shut, Aubrey slowly moved the foot and finally reached the next rope. Cheers and shouts of encouragement met Aubrey's small victory but did nothing to her lacking courage.

"Very good!" Mala praised her. Looking down, she called out, "Morgan, help her down!"

Aubrey's eyes flew open and met Mala's grinning face. "Lessons are easiest one step at a time. In your case, you need to take one more in order to get back down." The captain said encouragingly.

Aubrey felt Morgan's hand on her lower foot as he softly spoke for her to step down. Mala had moved back down to the railing and was also helping Aubrey down with a steady hand. Once on the safety of the deck, Aubrey took a deep breath and leaned against the railing, feeling light-headed and still very shaky. Mala clapped her shoulder and said loudly, "We will make a sailor out of you yet, Miss Aubrey Malone!"

The comment was met with laughter as members of the crew, who stood nearby, offered their congratulations as well. Aubrey smiled weakly as they praised her. She saw Morgan had stepped away and to allow room for the others to approach her. Mala was walking away, heading for the quarterdeck where an unsmiling Deats and broadly grinning Timmons awaited.

Later in the day, with arms folded over her chest, Mala leaned easily against the portside rail of the main deck with her back to the sea. She was watching her crew throw daggers to a target on the forecastle bulkhead. Aubrey sat on the deck near the quarterdeck bulkhead, cross-legged, watching the fun as Morgan stepped up for his turn at the target.

His throw nearly hit the center and knocked off the contending champion from his perch. The loser bowed his head and laughed as his friends playfully jeered him for losing. Aubrey found the camaraderie on this ship so much different from the other one. Even Mala laughed with her crew and had joined in at times. Aubrey thought of Black and how he rarely joined in the fun. He always seemed to separate himself from the crew as a king among the peasants. But here was Mala, leaning against the railing and laughing at some antic someone would do to distract the thrower.

"Who dares to toss me from my win!" Morgan challenged.

A couple of men rose to the challenge but did not throw well. Finally, someone shouted, "Come on, Cap'n! You cannot let him get away with that! You be the best of 'em of all!"

"Thank you, but I will save my throws for the enemy!" Mala replied laughing.

"Then teach Miss Aubrey. Gawd, do not leave that to Mr. Alcott!" Another shouted bringing a roar of laughter around the deck.

Mala looked to Aubrey and shouted over the din, "Care to learn!"

"I never threw anything at anyone ever in my life!" Aubrey whined.

Morgan hooted as he bowed to Mala. "Tis a lesson only you could administer, my dear captain. I beseech your wisdom in teaching this poor and unsuspecting student of your vast knowledge in expertly throwing a dagger at the enemy!" His playfulness caused another roar of laughter around the deck as he made a show of his gentleman's bow. Even Aubrey laughed until the words sunk in and her mouth dropped open. Mala stepped away from the railing and approached the stunned Aubrey.

"You must stop that, Miss Malone, or the enemy will mistake you for a codfish and snare you in their net."

Those nearby laughed as Mala beckoned Aubrey forward. Slowly getting to her feet, Aubrey pleaded, "I really..."

"Nonsense! Now watch what I do and you do the same thing."

Mala took an offered dagger but as quickly as it was in Mala's hand, it was gone. Aubrey looked at the target and the dagger was still vibrating from the impact—and in the center of the target. Mala handed her a dagger but Aubrey stared at it, not taking it.

"Do the same thing? I did not even see you throw it!" Aubrey exclaimed.

Mala smiled as others laughed, "Then pay attention. Watch me again." This time Mala moved slower and the dagger ended up so close to the first one they both vibrated. Holding out another dagger, Mala offered it Aubrey. When Aubrey did not take it, Mala clicked her tongue then took Aubrey's hand and slapped the dagger into it.

"Now, hold the tip. Good! Throw your arm back and..."

As Aubrey threw her arm back, she released it too soon and the dagger flew behind her instead of to the target. Shouts of surprise and sounds of men scrambling could be heard over Mala's laughter. Others laughed as they realized what happened. The men on deck looked over to find the dagger embedded on a step leading up to the quarterdeck.

"Sweet Mary!" Aubrey exclaimed. She turned to apologize to Mala but found her doubled over with laughter. "I told you I never did this before!"

Mala straightened, her face streaked with tears for having laughed so hard. Still trying to catch her breath, the captain replied, "And that is good, Aubrey! I do not have to break any old habits."

Aubrey was surprised that Mala was laughing at her misdeed. She could have seriously harmed someone. Behind her, Deats stood stone-faced on the quarterdeck. He found no amusement that Mala would teach the girl anything. First climbing and now daggers. What could possibly be next? Deats thought to himself in disgust. As he stared at Aubrey's back while she tried more successfully at throwing the dagger, he knew he had to come up with more images of Miss Malone on the *Widow Maker* with Captain Black.

Chapter 14

The next morning, Aubrey and Morgan joined Mala and Deats for breakfast at the captain's table in the galley. Willie was hovering about filling tankards as Mala sat back after the last bite of her breakfast, "Willie, as always, it was very good."

The old man beamed with pride. Morgan could not resist saying, "Ah c'mon, Willie. Show us that for once you are gracious of the compliment." Then adding with a smile, "We at least have to eat this stuff."

Willie sniffed loudly then replied indignantly, "Compliment? Tis a matter of survival. If it were not good, the captain and crew would have strung me up long ago." Mala watched her cook with a slight smile as Morgan took his drink before the old man added, "I ain't stupid, you know."

Willie got the desired effect. Morgan choked in his cup as some liquid dribbled down his chin and the front of his shirt. Still coughing, Morgan turned watery eyes to the old man who smiled and, with a tip of his hat to the captain, he turned away to saunter merrily back to the cooking area. It was not often when Willie could get in the last word, even if it meant drowning his opponent. With his accomplishment, Willie whistled a happy tune.

Mala smiled as she watched her cook then turned to Morgan who was also watching him. "You asked for it so you can forget about doing him in." When she gained Morgan's attention, she added pointedly, "As a matter of fact, should anything happen to Willie, guess who the new cook would be?"

Aubrey could hardly maintain a passive face as the captain was doing. How does she do that? Looking at Deats, Aubrey found the Scotsman seemingly perturbed over the whole scene. Her day-to-day activities with Morgan brought out the mischievous child within the young Irish woman at this very moment.

"Mr. Deats, you are not in good spirits today?" Just as Aubrey suspected, Mala turned her head to look at her quartermaster.

Giving Aubrey a small smile as Mala and Morgan looked to him, Deats replied, "Actually, Miss Malone, my mind was on other matters. I am afraid I was no' payin' attention."

Aubrey smiled but gave him an innocent look.

Mala, of course, had to know. "What other matters?"

At that moment, a crewmember ran into the galley and looked over to the captain's table saving Deats from making some sort of excuse. Mala caught the movement and was immediately alert.

"Beggin' yer pardon, Cap'n." He started as he tried to catch his breath.

Then with a loud gulp of air, he added, "Another ship approaches. A pirate ship."

"Hold our course, Mr. Givens, and let them pass."

"Should we not give them a wide berth, Cap'n?" The man asked.

"Just watch her and see..." Mala stopped abruptly as they heard a distant boom.

"Are they firing on us?" Aubrey asked incredulously.

A splash some distance from the *Enchantress* and a curse from the ship's captain could be heard. Mala emptied the contents of her tankard as she stood and set it down with a resounding bang. With a look of pure venom, similar to one that Aubrey had seen on the face of another captain, Mala hissed in the quietness of the galley, "Sink her."

The room burst with activity as men ran out in anticipation of battle. Deats and Givens hurried out with the men as Morgan grabbed Aubrey's arm. She was nearly running as she kept the fast pace of Morgan and Mala.

Topside, the pirate ship was closer than Mala had thought. It was so close that the cannonball they had just heard could easily have hit her ship. Mala's intense anger erupted into a volley of curses that surprised Aubrey then Mala ran up to the quarterdeck, yelling as another cannon was fired, "Turn her about, Mr. Timmons, and give her our portside."

Timmons and those around her looked surprised that she would put the *Enchantress* in the other's path.

"Mala, wait!" Deats yelled as he ran across the deck.

"Cannons, ready!" She yelled.

"Captain!" Deats yelled as they were sprayed with water from a cannonball as it landed beside the *Enchantress*.

Mala grabbed his shirtfront and snarled, "Help get the damned cannons ready, Mr. Deats. Now!" She threw him off balance as she shoved him from her.

"Cannons ready?" Deats yelled down to Robert.

"Ready, sir." He answered, his arm raised for the signal.

"Morgan, prepare the swordsman and riflemen!" As Morgan turned to run off, he stopped at Mala's sharp command, "Morgan! Get Aubrey below!"

Everyone froze as another cannon fired and they watched as the cannonball flew high and over. "Stay here and keep your head down!" Morgan yelled as he left Aubrey on the deck near the companionway. He would probably be in trouble for not obeying orders, but he had a job to do and Aubrey would be safe enough there.

"Thank God the damned bastards cannot aim!" Mala grumbled in annoyance. Leaning over the quarterdeck railing, she yelled down, "Let us show them how to hit a damn target! Fire!"

Aubrey was slammed against the wall of the companionway as the *Enchantress* bucked with cannonfire.

"Again!" Mala roared. Two more cannons rang out and the ship rocked. Aubrey caught her balance and peered out to see where they hit. She could hear the other ship fire again and watched as their shots fell short of the *Enchantress'* bow, spraying water over the forecastle and the deck.

The *Enchantress'* volley hit their marks. One fell on the bow, blowing away a good portion of the ship's forecastle. Another sailed over but clipped the top of the main mast, which sent sails and wood crashing down on the deck. Another shot fell short of the ship's deck but it hit below the waterline making the ship rock from the impact. The last shot clipped the quarterdeck.

Cheers rang out from the *Enchantress* as they watched the other crew run about in chaos. Aubrey looked to the other ship and could tell that it was taking on water in quick order. In no time, the ship would be gone. Aubrey looked to Mala and found her still angry, judging from the unsmiling face as she spoke with Timmons. Turning her attention back to the other ship, Aubrey could see men jumping into the water and the front end of the ship was completely submerged. The stern looked strange as it was very low along the water surface.

Mala stepped down to the main deck and motioned to Morgan, "Put them away!"

As he began collecting rifles and cutlasses, he noticed the men were distracted and turned in time to see Mala shoot Givens in the chest at close range just as the man turned to face her. The man flew backwards from the shot but Mala turned away with her pistol at her side, still in her hand. The deck was silent, the only sound heard were of the men of the other ship in water.

"Get back on course!" Mala yelled up to Timmons who nodded and turned the ship about.

Morgan caught sight of Aubrey who stood against the bulkhead of the quarterdeck, her mouth open in shock. She watched as Mala walked past without even noticing her. She looked to Deats who was merely gazing down at the dead man and shaking his head.

Running across the deck to Morgan, Aubrey heard Deats order in the strange silence, "Throw him overboard."

"My God, Morgan. Why did she do that?" She asked, her face white.

"I will find out." He replied calmly.

"She just shot him. Sweet Mary, she is worse than..." Morgan noticed Aubrey's abrupt stop and knew she spoke of Black. He merely shrugged, taking more arms and leaning them against the bulkhead, "She killed him. She just walked up to him and killed him! My God..."

"You do not understand, Aubrey." He began.

"Understand!" Aubrey threw her arms out in exasperation.

Suddenly she found her arms seized in a vise grip and looked up as Morgan spoke quietly and with a hint of irritation, "She is a pirate. We are all pirates. Tis best you remember that because she allows no room for mistakes. One mistake could be all our lives."

At that moment, screams could be heard from the men in the water. All eyes turned to find gray fins and some of the men disappearing from view. Aubrey's fingers grabbed Morgan's arms and squeezed.

"Sharks." He said flatly. Turning her to face him again, he grabbed a couple of rifles and thrust them in her arms, "Here, take these. We need to get these below."

Aubrey cringed with each terrifying scream until they were below and could no longer hear them. "She just left them!" Aubrey croaked in horror.

Putting a finger to her lips as she was about to speak again, he said gently, "Consider this. If we had gone back and saved even one, who is to say that we would be alive come sun up. Remember that they just tried to sink us, but instead, they sank. What fitting revenge that crewman would bestow upon us. He would cut our throats while we slept all in the name of revenge." Morgan could see that Aubrey was following him, "On the other hand, even if the captain went back, the sharks are faster. Do not think about it, just keep to your work."

Aubrey nodded hesitantly and he led the way as they went up to the deck for more arms. When she was finished helping Morgan, she went to the galley to help Willie.

Mala sat listening and drinking at the long table in her cabin as she stared out the window. Sometime later, there was a knocking upon her door and she called for the person to enter. Morgan stepped in and took off his hat.

"Would you mind telling me what that was all about?" He asked pointedly as he waved his hat at the door and obviously indicating the recent altercation.

Mala picked up the rum bottle and offered it to him, "Drink with me."

Morgan sat in a chair near her, taking the bottle she offered. He tipped it and took a long swallow before setting it down between them. He eyed her as she followed suit before answering his question. "Timmons called my attention to the problem." Mala told him.

"Problem? What problem?" Morgan asked.

"That bastard, Givens, let the other ship get close to us before he ever came down to alert us."

"And that is why you shot him." Morgan said in understanding.

"Aye, for all I know, the bloody bastard was planted on my ship at the last port in hopes of aiding his captain to board and take the *Enchantress*." Mala said as she slouched slightly in her chair, then added ominously. "Nobody takes my ship."

Morgan watched her as she took a drink. The look of determination was etched on her beautiful face. She protected what was hers with such a fierce intensity that Morgan sometimes forgot that she was a woman. He remembered that on the *Widow Maker* after she had recovered from her wounds, Captain Black had showed a keen interest in her, even beyond the fact that she was his woman. He had taught her how to shoot, to throw daggers, even to fight. Morgan covered his smile with a drink as he took the bottle to his mouth for a swallow. Now Mala was teaching Aubrey! Even though he was skilled with the weapons, the only person he knew that could do better was sitting before him.

Mala stood and went her cupboard to retrieve another bottle of rum. Setting the bottle roughly on the table, she resumed her seat as Morgan looked at her closely. She was not drunk but the look in her eye told him that she was doing some remembering of her own. Mala looked at him and was about to speak when there was a knock at the door. Her look turned into one of disgust and annoyance as she glared at the offending portal.

"I will wager a gold piece that would be Deats." She grumbled making Morgan chuckle.

"I will lose for sure if I bet against you. The man seems to sniff you out."

Mala grunted in agreement and, with a smile, she leaned close to Morgan as if to tell a secret, "Make a note that the next time we are in port, I will order him to find a whore."

Morgan chuckled again and leaned close to her as well, "He wants you."

"But I am no whore." She stated with a raised brow and still smiling as the knock was heard again.

Mala's smile was beautiful, Morgan thought. How could Black have let her go? His thoughts were broken into when Mala called for entry as she sat back in her chair. Turning slightly, Morgan found Deats entering the cabin. Mala and Morgan glanced at one other and smiled as she reached for the bottle to take another drink.

Deats did not miss the exchange between the two of them and felt the rage within him. Not only was Mala not alone but Morgan, the bloody bastard, was in here with her drinking.

"Sorry ta interrupt, Mala." His use of her name instead of her title raised her brow as she looked up at him but said nothing. "I was wonderin' what Givens had done."

"He did not report the other ship until she was upon us." Deats opened his mouth to speak but the sound of someone running and the frantic knocking at the door stopped him. With a nod from Mala, Deats opened the door to find York.

"Sorry, Cap'n, but lookout spotted another ship on the horizon. We lowered the flag until we could identify it but he is sure that it flies the Union Jack."

Without a word, Mala stood up and left the cabin with Deats, Morgan, and York on her heels. She headed directly to the quarterdeck and looked through her eyepiece that she always wore hanging from her sash. Not able to make out anything, she looked to the crow's nest. She could see Edison peering through his eyepiece, leaning slightly over to get a closer look.

"What do ye see?" Deats called up from the quarterdeck. Morgan craned his neck looking over the horizon but could not make out anything.

"She is flyin' the Union Jack all right!" The man called back down then put the eyepiece back to his eye.

"Damn! Those idiot pirates attracted their attention." Mala muttered as she looked at Morgan and Deats. Taking in their surroundings, Mala spotted several small islands nearby but none could provide cover for a tall-masted ship.

"Shouldna we leave the area, Captain?" Deats asked.

"I want to see who this is." Mala replied as she looked over the islands. Morgan, Deats and Timmons looked her in surprise.

"Why? Let us just leave while we can. They may not have seen us yet." Morgan was saying.

Having decided on an island, Mala faced them and said, "Because I am looking for another one. Go there, Mr. Timmons."

"Looking for another one? Which one? The *Majestic* is gone!" Deats replied.

Seeing the questioning looks, Mala replied softly, "The *Lady Elizabeth*." Morgan and Deats exchanged worried looks.

"We are going back? That island will not cover us." Morgan stated in amazement.

"No, but it will give us enough cover until we can identify it." Mala explained.

"Then what? Ye want ta attack a British warship?" Deats asked in disbelief.

"I have done so before, Mr. Deats." Mala replied calmly.

"But the *Lady Elizabeth* dinna fire on the *Widow Maker*. The *Majestic* sank her and ye took care of that one." He continued to argue.

"Deats, we are just going take a look." Mala said becoming impatient with the Scotsman.

Timmons guided the *Enchantress* to the island as instructed. Sails down and the anchor lowered, the crew of the *Enchantress* waited. Aubrey stood with Morgan and was looking up along with other members of the crew on the deck. Mala was at the fighting top along with her lookout, Edison, peering through a long glass.

"Gawd, look at 'er, Cap'n. She is a beauty!" Edison was saying as the warship glided by to inspect the debris left from the now sunken pirate ship.

Mala saw none of the beauty as she noticed the name on the ship's bow, *HMS Lady Elizabeth.* An evil and malicious smile appeared on her face as she started down. She looked up when Edison said nervously, "I think they noticed us, Cap'n."

"Get in the crow's nest and stay hidden until the signal is given."

"Aye, Cap'n." Edison said as he started his climb down to the crow's nest. Mala made quick order of climbing down and called out orders as she went. Men prepared and assumed their places as planned. Aubrey joined Willie in the galley, her eyes wide.

"I cannot believe she is going to attack a warship."

"Now ye need not worry, lass, we have done this before. The Cap'n knows what to do."

Aubrey smiled at the old man whose faith in Mala was unshakable. As she sat with Willie waiting to hear the first sounds of battle, she knew the waiting was going to be the worst part.

Chapter 15

The *Enchantress* hoisted anchor and was let to drift in the current. The sails flapped loudly as the stay lines were released. No one could be seen on the deck, even Timmons abandoned the helm, giving the *Enchantress* the illusion of a deserted ship dead in the water.

Mala stood with Morgan on the cannon deck. With arms crossed over her chest, she peered out at the approaching warship through a peephole near the bow of the cannon deck. Jordan peered through the peephole near the stern. He looked at his captain then at the men manning the cannons. Everyone seemed ready and waited for the order. The port doors were still closed but men stood by ready to drop at the first command. All eyes were on Mala.

Morgan stood behind Mala trying to peer through the hole. The *Enchantress* had drifted in the strong current and was now clear of the island. He could make out the warship as it rounded the island and was moving in alongside their ship.

"Are you sure you want to do this?" Morgan asked, knowing that they were already committed.

"Aye." Mala replied still watching the warship. She glanced back at Morgan and added firmly, "Very sure."

He watched her as she faced the peephole again. He could tell from her profile that she was sure indeed. The *Lady Elizabeth* may not have fired on the *Widow Maker* but her presence there was enough in Mala's mind. She might have gone in to aid Rene Black in the attack but against two warships, that would have been disastrous.

Morgan stepped away from her and took his position behind the cannons, his gaze never leaving the dark-haired woman. Mala raised her arm for readiness and everyone tensed for the drop. When her arm dropped, the port doors fell open and the cannons rolled into place almost simultaneously.

"Fire!" Mala yelled not taking her eyes from the warship. The cannonballs flew and her crew quickly reloaded.

"Again!" Morgan ordered as the deck area filled with the smoke and smelled of the gunpowder.

Mala closed the peephole and headed to the stern of the ship. As she passed behind Morgan, she stopped and said loud enough for him to hear, "You keep hitting them until there is nothing left."

"Aye!" Morgan acknowledged as another volley of cannonfire blasted away at the unsuspecting warship. His gaze turned to follow Mala as she left the cannon deck area. Wherever you are in Hell, Rene Black, you better be smiling! All this, she is doing for you! Morgan thought, shaking his head at Mala's determination.

Coming up the companionway steps to the main deck, Mala could hear the rifle shots as her men picked off the British on the warship's deck. As she stepped onto the main deck, she looked to find all the sails furled, stay lines tied down, and the wind carrying them with the current. She looked over at the warship and saw that Morgan's shots were hitting their marks. Taking the quarterdeck steps two at a time, she hurried to Timmons and helped him steer the ship clear before the magazine of the warship exploded.

"We are still ta close!" Deats hollered from the main deck. He aimed his rifle to a man on the other ship and fired.

"Let us take advantage of this strong current, Timmons." Mala said as she turned the wheel to straighten out the ship.

Deats reloaded his rifle then joined them on the quarterdeck. Looking over at the warship that turned in pursuit, the Scotsman blurted out in amazement. "Ach, now will ye look at that." Mala and Timmons turned at his words. "There is a Lord Admiral on board their vessel."

Stepping over to stand next to him, Mala looked over at the warship. She found the Lord Admiral easily as he waved his arms and shouted orders to his men. He was in command and by his command, the *Widow Maker* was blasted by the *Majestic* and sunk. With a look of pure malice and seeing the sinking of the *Widow Maker* in her mind, Mala took Deats' rifle from his grasp and aimed. Her shot hit the Lord Admiral squarely in the chest and the man clutched at his wound then staggered. He hit against the railing and fell over the side of the *Lady Elizabeth* into the water below.

"Not anymore." She growled in her deathly quiet voice that held her hatred in check. Mala handed Deats back his rifle then headed back for the wheel and Timmons.

The *Enchantress* tacked away easily with the current and her sails were filled with the wind. With the warship behind them and no longer a target, Morgan appeared on the quarterdeck, his face was blackened from the gunpowder. "Well now, that was fun." He said with a grin as he joined Mala.

"We are still ta close." Deats stated still watching the warship. As if to emphasize his concern, the warship suddenly exploded. Everyone ducked involuntarily as the *Enchantress* was showered with burning debris and hit with a soft gust of heat. There was the sound of glass shattering and wood splintering within the bowels of the *Enchantress*. Mala looked at Morgan, the concern on his face mirroring that of her own.

"Check below." She ordered but Morgan was already heading towards the quarterdeck steps.

Mala headed for her cabin through the rarely used doorway from the quarterdeck. Opening the door and stepping down into her cabin, she noticed that the quarter gallery windows were blown in and that pieces of jagged wood were swinging at places still connected to the stern of the ship. The contents of her desk, windows and shelves were strewn about the cabin. She looked around her cabin searching for any unbroken objects. On her bunk laid several broken and unbroken jars, pieces of glass, and splinters of wood, big and small. Her logbook laid on the floor, the opened pages flapping in the breeze. Near the logbook laid the inkwell, the spilled ink leaving a dark blotch.

Mala stepped further into her cabin and moved towards the bunk. The crunching of glass denoted her passage. Deats stepped in behind her and looked about the room.

"Aye, we were still ta close. Look at this mess."

Mala looked at the jars on her bunk. She gingerly picked up one and examined it. A smile crept over her face as she replied to Deats' statement, "Aye, but it was well worth it, Deats. Well worth it."

Deats shook his head as he straightened up from picking up her logbook from the floor. He glared at her back. Always so mysterious in her message but Alcott would most likely understand! As if on queue, the sandy-haired man appeared in the door from the corridor.

"Christ!" He exclaimed as he stepped into the cabin, crunching glass under foot. His gaze tried to take in everything at once. Turning to York who was behind him, he ordered, "Get some men in here and get this mess cleaned up."

As Morgan stepped carefully into the cabin, the sound of running feet was heard in the corridor and soon Aubrey and Willie appeared in the doorway. News of the damage was quickly making its rounds on board the ship and the men hurried to try and help clean up. Some looked in through the door from the corridor while others peered in from the quarterdeck.

"Morgan, are there any other damages?" Mala asked.

"Minimal, Captain." He replied as he joined Mala near her bunk. Seeing him next to her by the bunk, Deats felt the anger rise up in him. He slammed the logbook onto the desk and headed towards them.

"We will need ta pull inta port and make repairs, Captain." Deats stated as he moved between Morgan and Mala. Morgan turned an icy stare on the man who turned a smile on him, daring him to say anything. Mala was not paying attention to them or anyone in her cabin as she searched the other undamaged items. Many of her herbs and spices jars were unbroken and lying on her bunk. One jar, in particular, was placed carefully on the table.

"Make do with what we have for now." Mala said as she placed more saved items on her table. She glanced at the large opening where windows once were.

"The nights will be too cold for you with the windows gone like that." Morgan said, following her gaze.

"Aye Captain. Ye will need ta sleep elsewhere until the repairs are made." Deats said looking at the large opening as well as he contained a smile.

"I will stay here, Mr. Deats."

"But ye will..." Deats started to protest.

Morgan turned on Deats in Mala's defense. "Then we make the repairs so she does not catch a chill."

"Back ta yer post, Mr. Alcott." Deats growled.

"My post is wherever the captain is, Mr. Deats." Morgan countered.

The men in the cabin took a step back as the quartermaster and the first mate face off each other. Their captain seemed to ignore the two men as they glared at one another. York had appeared with brooms to begin the clean up but, seeing the two men facing each other, he stopped to wait for entry.

Noticing York's hesitancy out of the corner of her eye, Mala turned to her two officers and said tiredly, "That is enough from the both of you. Let us get this place cleaned up and repairs started. Deats, when we reach the Cape, we will get supplies for the windows and make those repairs on our way to Charlestowne."

Deats and Morgan faced her in unison as she spoke. Deats nodded and took several men with him to find what they needed while Morgan stepped aside for York to pass him. As Aubrey, Willie and some of the men carefully swept the floor of glass and debris, Mala looked for any other items that may have been on the floor and was salvageable.

"Tell me again why he is still quartermaster?" Morgan asked as he moved to stand next to his captain.

"Morgan." Mala replied with a tone of admonishment.

"I am telling you, Mala. That Scotsman cannot be trusted." He whispered in a low tone.

Mala looked up at him as he stood so close to her. His blue eyes met her dark ones as she said, "And you know, I can take of myself."

Morgan gave her a slow smile that she did not return. "Sometimes I forget who I am talking to."

"Obviously." Mala replied, though not as perturbed as she wanted it to sound. Morgan did not take the reprimand to heart if his smile was any indication. He turned his attention to the cleaning as Mala began to straighten up some of the shelves.

A few days later, Mala ordered the *Enchantress* to be moored further down the coast from Charlestowne near a small island. Her longboats could go near the city, but the big ship would be tucked out of sight from other pirate vessels or the bothersome British Navy while they made the finishing repairs to the ship.

The constant hammering and sawing in her cabin to repair the quarter gallery windows finally was taking its toll on her nerves. Mala closed her eyes to calm herself but the pounding seemed to intensify. With a glare to the men working diligently in their task, Mala stood up and made a quick retreat topside. Her exit went unnoticed by her men.

Approaching Aubrey who was leaning on the gunwale looking at the island, the dark haired woman said quietly, almost sadly, "It reminds me of home." Aubrey straightened slowly as Mala continued, "I am taking a boat ashore, I need to feel sand beneath my feet." Then tossing a sideways look towards the companionway where the sounds of the repairs drifted up, Mala added, "And some peace and quiet for a while. Would you like to come along?"

Blinking in surprise, Aubrey asked, "Are you serious?"

"Yes, I am. Come on, we will just sit and chat." Mala shrugged.

Nearly an hour later, Mala and Aubrey, accompanied by four of Mala's crew were rowed to the island. Aubrey saw Deats looking down from the quarterdeck and he did not look pleased at their leaving. Standing near the forecastle, Morgan watched the men pull powerfully on the oars, taking the boat closer and closer to the island.

Chapter 16

Before they touched the beach, Mala was out of her boots and out of the boat, slowly wading through the surf. The four men leapt from the boat to pull it onto the beach with Aubrey still inside. She pulled off her boots and looked up to find Robert approaching her. He easily plucked her out of the boat like a child and carried her further up onto the beach. He gently set her upon her feet and steadied her there until she could stand on her own. She stumbled slightly against him but he caught her easily.

"Thank you, Robert. This is very difficult." She apologized.

"There now, Miss Aubrey. Just take it slow, you will get your land legs back directly." He said smiling at her.

"Gentlemen, Miss Aubrey and I will be resting and perhaps walking here for a time. Keep a lookout for us if you please." Mala ordered.

"Aye, Captain." The four men replied as they moved away to their respective positions, allowing the women some privacy.

Aubrey eased herself down onto the warm sand and looked out to sea at the *Enchantress*. From this viewpoint, it was still a beautiful ship. She sat on the beach with her knees drawn up under her chin, hugging her legs with her arms. Tears welled in her eyes as she thought about Jean Luc and watched the big ship. Mala was further down the beach, just walking, in a world of her own.

When Mala returned to Aubrey's side, she sat down in the sand. "Will you tell me who he was?" She asked quietly. "Was he Rene Black?"

Aubrey's facial features tightened and she brushed away a tear. "No." Was the firm reply.

"No? No to the question of will you tell me who he was, or no to the question if it was Rene Black?" Mala asked.

"No, it was not Rene Black." Aubrey said curtly.

Mala pursed her lips and looked out at the surf, "Very well, will you tell me who he was?" Aubrey did not look up as she hesitated to answer so the dark haired woman negotiated instead. "Tell me your story first then I will tell you mine."

Aubrey smiled weakly and asked, "Where shall I begin?"

"At the beginning, of course." Mala replied.

Aubrey painstakingly recounted her history that led up to the time she had come to live with her uncle in London to booking passage on the *Gull* and finally to the battle at Bimini.

"Rene would never have allowed them to board his ship without a fight.

147

He would die first and take the *Widow Maker* with him." Mala said, her voice quiet. Aubrey could barely hear her next words as Mala spoke them so softly, "So he is gone and the *Widow* with him."

"There was a fight but the last I saw of him was the night before. Forgive me for what I am about to say, but I am glad that Rene is dead. I would have liked to kill him myself. The worst of it all is that he took Jean Luc with him."

Mala heard the hatred in Aubrey's voice and she understood. She had some hatred in her for him as well. "You loved Jean Luc very much." She said to Aubrey.

"I still love him, I will always love him, and there will never be another man for me." Aubrey retorted.

"It was very resourceful of Jean Luc." It was quiet for a few moments before Mala said reflectively, "The way that he tricked Rene into thinking that he had bedded you."

"I did not care for the pain he had to cause to make the mark." Aubrey said softly, remembering the suddenness of it.

"What pain?" Mala asked with a frown.

"Jean Luc had to bite me to make the spot where Rene put his mark…" Aubrey did not finish. She hated the mark on her left breast—a mark that would never go away.

"Bite you?" Mala asked somewhat confused. Aubrey looked at her in her own confusion.

"Yes, Jean Luc said that Rene bites there then…" Aubrey stopped because Mala started laughing. "What?" Aubrey asked when Mala's laughter died down.

"Rene does not bite to initiate the mark." Mala said chuckling at Aubrey's slack-jawed expression.

"But Jean Luc said that the mark was…"

"Jean Luc only knows that Rene makes a mark then places the tattoo over the spot."

"Well yes but…"

"It is not a bite. Rene does not sink his teeth into you." Mala said trying to calm down in her laughter.

"Well then what is it?" Aubrey asked, her innocence all too evident. Mala missed it as she looked out at the *Enchantress*. As she opened her mouth to speak, Aubrey interrupted, "Never mind. I really do not want to know."

Mala could not help but smile at that. After a long pause, the captain asked seriously, "And he never had you after the ruse?"

Aubrey looked up from tracing her finger through the sand, "Captain

Black?"

"Aye." Mala nodded.

"No, it never happened." Aubrey said firmly.

"A lie to forget?" Mala asked. There was the coldness in her eyes.

"No Mala, never. It is the truth as I live and breathe. Rene never had me." Aubrey told her, imploring the dark haired woman to believe her.

"But he tried." Mala stated. Aubrey looked back at the sand, thinking of the times he had pinned her down.

"A few times but when I think of Jean Luc's advances and compare them to Rene's, it was as though Rene had changed his mind and no longer wanted me. Only once when he drank too much did he think to—but then Jean Luc came up with the ruse." Aubrey explained. She looked up at Mala and saw the look of sadness, "But you loved Rene?"

"Yes I did." Mala said quietly. Then taking a deep breath, she added softly, "I hated him, Aubrey, but I loved him more, I still do which was why I could not kill him in Bimini."

"You tried to kill Rene?" Aubrey asked in surprise but Mala stared out at sea and there was a silence for a time. "Will you tell me now?" Aubrey coaxed.

Mala laughed lightly, "Mine is a far longer story than yours."

"But you agreed to tell me." Aubrey reminded easily.

Mala nodded and sat silently for a time while Aubrey watched her. The other woman appeared to be going back in time in her mind right before her eyes. Coming out of the silent revere, she said, "What I am about to tell you must stay between us. Though Morgan and Deats know of some, they do not know all of it."

"I promise to keep all this a secret." Aubrey said honestly.

"I was kidnaped from my home on the isle of St. Lucia by the captain of slave trader..." She began and Aubrey gasped in shock and surprise. Glancing at her, Mala gave a small smile then continued, "This captain was old and ugly but he prided himself as a lady's man. He would take one of the women from our holding area and make her spend a night or two with him." Mala looked up at Aubrey who was listening intently.

"You can well imagine the rest. Then the day came for me to join the captain. I would not submit to the man and he became furious. When I changed from speaking English to my own language, he stopped his yelling. At some point I decided to upset him by reciting simple rhymes we were told as children. Well he did get upset, but my simple rhymes also frightened him. He started calling me a witch and I was locked up away from my people and was to be put off at the next port. In the meantime, I was avoided at all costs. I had little to nothing to eat or drink. It was as if I was forgotten. A terrible storm came and some of the crew was washed away. The captain thought I was bringing them bad luck so he ordered that I be punished. I was tied to the main mast and given ten lashes, one for each day we had been at sea. The next day, several men came down with a sickness and the captain thought I had placed a curse on them. He ordered me to be hanged."

Aubrey gasped at this treatment and remembered the scars on Mala's back. The dark haired woman looked out to the open sea and the *Enchantress*. Her voice hardening with the memory, "I was dragged up on deck too weak to walk from the lashing, lack of food and water. A rope was placed around my neck and I was being hoisted off the deck when the lookout warned of a ship approaching."

Mala looked at Aubrey and said in a softer tone, "When they saw it was another British ship, I was cut down and put into irons. I vaguely remember the battle above and some men finding places to hide. I found out later that it was Jean Luc who found me and had a man summon Rene. I was taken to the *Widow* where Rene and Jojoba took care of me." Mala stopped in her narrative as Aubrey straightened slightly.

"Jojoba? He was on the *Widow Maker* but not at first. He was not there when they first brought me on board." Aubrey whispered.

"He was always fussing with me to eat so I could regain my strength." Mala added and saw Aubrey's smile. "You too?" She asked.

Aubrey nodded and Mala smiled at her before continuing with her narrative. "I understood French but did not speak. It gave me an advantage. Jean Luc was always asking questions. He could not understand why someone would punish a woman as I had been punished." Mala paused and took a deep breath.

"One day, the *Widow* was attacked and I was alone in the great cabin because everyone was on deck fighting. When Rene and Jean Luc came to my aid, I had already killed two men and yelled at them for leaving me defenseless."

Mala saw Aubrey's smile and paused. With the laughter in her voice, the younger woman said, "Were you really defenseless?"

Mala snickered now understanding the grin. "Actually, the two fools were kind enough to share their weapons with me. I used them as you can well imagine."

Aubrey covered her mouth to try and stifle her giggle when Mala gave her a lopsided grin. Waving away the humor, Mala went on, "In my anger, I forgot my vow to keep silent and they realized that I could and had understood them all along. From that point on, Rene and I became very close. He taught me everything about ships, pirating, and most everything else. We talked of his travels, battles, the treasures they took, and the places he had been. As time wore on, I fell in love with him. While I recovered from my wounds, he had given me his bunk as he slept on the settee. One night I decided to repay him for his care. When he doused the lantern, I went to him and …he taught so much more." Mala's voice was soft and hypnotic as she talked.

Aubrey found herself smiling as she listened in wonder. What could it be like to have a man like him, or any handsome and dashing man love you so much? Jean Luc loved you, you silly fool. She reminded herself. Yes, but Mala had much more time with her lover, so much more. Aubrey continued in her mind. She raised her head out of her own musing when Mala had stopped talking, and sat quietly now, looking at her ship. From the expression on the woman's face, Aubrey could tell that there was far more to the story then that, she waited patiently.

"Did Rene ever take you ashore?" Mala asked, looking at her ship.

The question startled Aubrey. She exhaled hard, "No, I was never allowed off the ship." Much to Aubrey's distress, a smile of victory crossed Mala's face then she nodded and returned to her story.

"One day, Rene told me that we would be coming to a small island where he often stopped to trade with the natives. He said that he let the men go ashore to rest and relax and that the chief there was his friend. He took me to shore with him but when we arrived, the chief was very ill. I examined him from head to toe and I told Rene that the man was dying."

"I went outside to find some herbs. I made a tea and had the women help me to get it into the chief. After a couple of days he was fine, getting up and around." She paused again, sitting in solemn remembrance.

Mala's voice changed, becoming thick with emotion. Aubrey looked at her in awe for she had never seen the woman like this. "We were on the island for about a week and Rene completed his business with the chief. He told me that the chief had asked that I be left there to use my medicinal knowledge to help them through the upcoming rainy season. They always experienced serious illness during that time of year."

"Rene did not leave you, did he?" Aubrey asked in surprise.

"He held me close that last night, before he set sail. He told me he did not want to leave me but because the chief was his friend and they relied so much on one another for trade, he granted the old man the request. Rene left me, promising he would return for me." Aubrey listened intently. Mala looked out at her ship again, "A month later, I realized I was with child."

A puzzled expression etched Aubrey's face, a baby? Before she could question, Mala was continuing, "I asked the chief if Rene would be back in time for the birth of his child. The chief told me that he was sure Rene was a very resourceful man and that he would return soon after."

151

"Did he return?" Aubrey asked.

"Let me finish." Mala scolded. "They made me feel at home. The chief took me in as if I was his own blood. Almost nine months from the day Rene left the island, I gave birth to his son."

"What did you name him?" Aubrey asked quietly.

"Baccus Rene."

"Baccus? The God of wine and song." Aubrey smiled.

"There was a book..." Mala began.

"Yes, a book in Rene's library, it was my favorite." Aubrey informed as Mala nodded.

"You read from his library?" Mala asked.

"I had nothing else to do." Aubrey explained.

Mala gave her a small mischievous smile, "I found other things to do."

Aubrey blushed knowing her meaning and replied flatly, "I did not." Aubrey stared into the dark eyes of the other woman then turned away as the woman continued to look at her.

"Several months later, a ship was spied in a back cove. I left Baccus with one of the village girls so that I could run to the beach. I knew it was Rene returning." Mala looked pointedly at Aubrey and said, "What I found moored in the cove instead was the *HMS Majestic*. The same warship we destroyed when we were in Bermuda. The captain was a man named John Alexander. I saw him in the marketplace that day, Aubrey. He is, or rather, was still the captain of the *Majestic*."

"Oh my God!" Aubrey whispered in amazement.

"I knew that the warship was there for no good—they never are. Before I reached the village, I could smell smoke and saw the smoke rising in the air from a clearing that was near the village. I hid in the underbrush and could do nothing but watch while the British beat the old chief. I could hear Alexander demanding the chief to hand over the pirate Rene Black or he would kill everyone in the village, starting with the chief. It pained me to do so, but I was unarmed, defenseless and alone. Suddenly Alexander shot the chief. His crew then proceeded to rape the women and kill the men. I knew that no one was going to be left alive so from my hiding place I searched for Baccus and Kohma." Mala's voice was clearly showing signs of sorrow now. Aubrey feared that she might cry herself.

"Then I heard him crying in bushes nearby. Some of the men heard him and dragged Kohma out. I could tell that she was holding Baccus too tightly and that had made him cry out. Baccus was taken from her just as she was thrown down to the ground and several men ripped at her clothes. I had never been so scared in my life. I could not move even as I watched John Alexander take Baccus from his man. He shook Baccus trying to get him to stop crying. He shook him and shook him. Finally Alexander let him go and Baccus fell to the ground. He just let him go. Then he drew his sword and killed him. He killed my son!" Mala stopped. Her voice had cracked several times in this part of narrative and Aubrey saw the tears now as they spilled from the dark eyes that could be so cold and cruel. Tears welled up in her own eyes.

"The whole village was burned to the ground. As the men headed back to the ship, Alexander searched the bodies for any left alive. Twice he circled the bushes I was hiding in and I thought he would find me."

"Oh God!" Aubrey gasped. Mala said no more because no more needed to be said. She sat staring at the sand and the tears were gone now.

"When the warship left, I searched the bodies for anyone left alive but I knew there would be none. I started burying them all. First Baccus, and then the rest. A few days later, another ship arrived, the *Tartan*, whose captain was Angus Deats."

"Deats?" Aubrey asked surprised.

"Aye, he and his men helped me bury the dead. He told me about other villages that were much like that one. When Deats and his crew prepared to leave, I agreed to leave with him because Rene never returned as he promised. It had been over a year and Rene did not come back."

"Something had to have happened? Have you asked him?" Aubrey interjected coming to Black's defense.

"I could not be around Rene long enough to ask him anything. To look at Rene was to see Baccus. I wanted to kill him for what happened at the village, to my son. I almost did in Bimini. I had him in an old tavern and all I had to do was shoot him. Instead I made it look like a robbery. That was the last time I saw him alive. We sailed to Santiago de Cuba because he was supposed to sail there next. When he did not show up, I went back to Bimini. The rest you know. I could not help him without losing my ship and my men in the same manner."

Aubrey saw the tears in Mala's eyes again before the pirate captain closed them.

Chapter 17

There were a few moments of silence between the two women. The only sounds heard were the surf and the gulls flying overhead. Aubrey watched their flight as they swirled about the sky. Her gaze fell onto the big ship and Aubrey speculated, "So that was once called the *Tartan*." Mala followed her gaze to the *Enchantress*.

"No, the *Tartan* was much smaller than my ship. I was sailing with Deats for several weeks when I decided what I needed to do. But my revenge included a ship that for the most part was made for speed. One day, as we were moored for supplies at an island, I watched a ship enter the harbor. She was a beauty. She was bigger than the *Tartan* and very sleek. She was that ship." Mala stated as she pointed to the *Enchantress*.

Turning to Aubrey, she went on, "I told Deats what we could do to take her. He did not agree but I knew it would work. Since he was always trying to seduce me in some way, I invited him to have a drink with me. Plied with the right amount of Scottish whiskey and my herbs, I put him to sleep in short order. Then I put my plan into action with the help of a few crewmen. We waited until most of the crew went ashore before we boarded it. What I did not know was that the captain of yonder ship had a sister ship that was already moored in the harbor. When we set sail, they attacked us. Because the captain wanted his ship back, he fired on the *Tartan*. I used the big ship against him and the sister ship. We found an isolated cove so that we could refurbish the big ship and the *Tartan* was stripped before we sunk her in the cove. Deats was so angry that I duped him, he made the mistake of daring me in front of his men. You see, I told him that I could make them all rich. In his rage, he had said that if I was so confident then I should prove it." Mala looked up at Aubrey and smiled ruefully.

"The thought of having a woman as their pirate captain was not overly accepted. So Deats suggested that if I did something so dangerous, so absolutely impossible yet return alive, would they agree that I become the new captain." Mala chuckled lightly. "It was a dare, Aubrey, and Deats did not expect me to return at all. Do you remember what I told you about how I became their captain?" Mala asked the younger woman. Aubrey remembered it very well.

"Yes, you killed two British officers in the middle of the day."

"No, I told you I killed one officer."

"Well Morgan told me that it was actually two. So was it one or two?" Aubrey asked.

Mala smiled and replied, "It was two. I did not want scare you too soon. But at the time, I was not overly pleased to have you on board my ship knowing that you had been on the *Widow*." Aubrey nodded. Mala took a deep breath to clear her mind of that time. "We were still refurbishing the ship when the deal was struck. What they did not know, and still do not know to this day, was those two officers I was sent to kill had been with Alexander that day. I recognized them immediately. My play for captain was made all the sweeter when the condition of the dare was that I killed them in broad daylight and walk away. When I killed them and returned to the appointed spot, Deats claimed it was all in jest. His crew, however, held him to the bargain."

"Did you fear that he would rise against you?"

"I did at one time but no longer. Most of those you see as the crew of the *Enchantress* were once the crew of the *Tartan*. Timmons was once the cabin boy until I noticed his interest of the helm. I told him to make a go at being a helmsman and you see he did well. Many others do jobs that they were more interested in doing but were not given the chance. When the refurbishing was done, the only task left was to name the new ship. The crew turned to me as their new captain for a name. After some thought, I proposed that they vote on my suggestion. When they agreed, I told them that the name I would like to call her would be one that no one would even suspect that we were pirates unless we flew a jolly roger or gave some other indication of what we really were. I suggested the *Enchantress*. What better name for a ship that has a woman captain? My red flag stands for the blood I had planned to spill from the *HMS Majestic*. In a way, it still stands for British blood, for I have no use for the British Navy."

"Was Morgan one of the crew then?" Aubrey asked after some time of silence.

Mala shook her head, "No, he joined me not long after that though. His only wish was that he had been around to see me act on the dare."

Aubrey giggled as Mala smiled for both knew how Morgan could be ridiculous in his antics. There was silence for a few moments before Aubrey asked quietly, "Did you ever return to your home?"

"No." Mala replied quickly. Aubrey looked at her somewhat surprised at the force the one word was said. As if reading her thoughts, Mala added with a tone of tolerance, "I am from a prominent family, a very prominent family of our village and because of that, I was deemed special." Mala paused and Aubrey saw in her dark eyes that she still hated that special treatment. Before she could question the woman captain, Mala continued, "You see, I was promised to someone that I had no, ah, feelings for. He was the son of the chief and he was, well, not to my liking."

Aubrey nodded understanding fully what Mala was feeling towards marrying someone she did not want. A shadow was cast over them and Aubrey looked up as Mala turned slightly to find Robert close by.

"Captain, we should be getting back soon." He suggested.

Looking at the sun low in the afternoon sky, Mala realized that they had been on the beach for quite some time. "Perhaps you are right, Robert. Thank you." She replied.

Aubrey was in awe over the tale she had just heard. Mala had endured much in her young life and there were men who feared her wrath as well as valued her friendship. Robert moved away as Aubrey stood up when Mala got to her feet and stretched.

Aubrey tugged on Mala's sleeve tentatively and said when she gained her attention, "I would like to help you to avenge the deaths ... if you would have me do so. I will dedicate my life to the seas and piracy for the memory of Jean Luc." Mala looked at her with a slight smile, thinking to herself. Could Jean Luc have made that great of an impression on her? Mala smiled inwardly as she remembered how Black had made an impression on her.

Seeing that Aubrey was looking for an answer, Mala shrugged and replied, "My anger is deep, Aubrey. It can sometimes be very ugly."

"I have seen much ugliness in these past few months." Aubrey argued.

Mala regarded her for a time before giving an imperceptible nod. Aubrey smiled broadly but Mala warned, "Stay close to the crew as you have done. They will teach you much and Morgan is very adept with weapons. His lessons, though tedious at times, will be a saving grace to you someday. And you must also learn our signals, seen or unseen. My whistle tells of immediate danger, for example. My men know that I am in grave danger and need help. For me to use the whistle is rare and well they know it." At that moment, Mala emitted the shrill whistle that made Aubrey's head and ears tingle. Almost immediately, Mala's men, who had been heading for the longboat, turned with swords or pistols drawn. Their eyes searched for the danger before seeking out their captain.

Mala waved at them and yelled out, "Never mind, I was teaching Miss Aubrey." The men put away their weapons but cast furtive glances toward the women. Mala chuckled while Aubrey looked at the men in surprise. Their reaction was swift and immediate.

"Was the whistle another lesson from Rene?" Aubrey asked, remembering now how many times she had heard the same sound while on the *Widow Maker*.

"Yes, and it took quite some time for him to teach me." Mala answered with wry grin. "Although he did not use it as a call for danger."

In the longboat heading to the *Enchantress*, Aubrey looked up to find

Deats standing at the railing, arms crossed and obviously quite put out. She remembered how he lost his captaincy to a woman on a dare. She began to giggle softly as she thought of the fact that the man lost out to a woman. Her giggle grew more loud and noticeable. Mala glanced at Aubrey then following her gaze, realized why she was giggling. Slapping playfully at the younger woman, Mala gave her a stern look through she was hard-pressed to contain a smile. Aubrey lost control then and laughed aloud.

Back on her ship, Mala faced her quartermaster still finding it hard to control her grinning.

"Well, I suppose that ye both had a wonderful time." He growled.

"Quite so, Deats. Is something amiss on board?" Mala asked trying to stay serious.

"No just that we are need of supplies yet ye take the time ta sit on a beach for hours on end." He grumbled in low tones so that the men around them could not hear.

Mala watched as Aubrey came over the railing with the aid of Robert. When she straightened and faced Deats, Aubrey sputtered into more laughter. Robert shook his head at her in reprimand. Mala caught his eye and with the jerk of her head indicated the companionway toward the cabin Aubrey shared with Morgan. With a nod, Robert took Aubrey by the arm and escorted her off the deck. All the while Aubrey laughed, wiping her eyes from the tears her laughter brought.

"How are the repairs coming along?" Mala asked as she headed for the quarterdeck. The hammering and other noises were not so boisterous now.

"They are nearly finished." Deats replied.

"Good. At first light, I plan to sail closer to Charlestowne. The men sent out earlier are back?"

"Aye, they have picked out a spot for us ta moor so that we can be undetected and obscured by any roving eye." Deats replied.

"Very well, have them meet me in my cabin at the change of the watch along with Morgan and yourself then we can plan our day tomorrow. I want to be gone by daybreak the next morning, Mr. Deats."

"Aye, Captain."

"Well Mr. Timmons, how are the repairs to the helm?"

"All is well now, Captain. The rudder was sluggish but that was due to the seaweed and other plant life we picked up from sitting in the marshes waiting on the *Lady Elizabeth*. Nothing more serious."

"Well now, how much longer will our luck hold out, gentlemen? Thus far, we have faired out quite well." Deats and Timmons both nodded as Mala looked at the horizon and the sun setting low in the sky.

"I am going to rest now." Mala stated as she stepped off the quarterdeck and disappeared below deck.

In her cabin, Mala looked at the repairs made. Her men had done a very good job at replacing the rectangle windows within the wooden strips. The men carried out the last of the debris made from the repairs as she made her entry in her logbook.

Once alone, she placed her bottles of herbs and plants on the small ledges her men had re-built for her. After replacing the surviving bottles, jars and plants, Mala sat on the large window ledge and watched the sunset. With her back against the wall and legs stretched out before her, she was surprised at how much she had told Aubrey.

It was Jean Luc and not Black who loved Aubrey. Jean Luc had her. Jean Luc was the man who Aubrey held herself for. But Rene Black....The thought of him made Mala close her eyes. He was gone! How many times had that harsh reality crept upon her when she least expected it?

"Mon Dieu, Rene, I miss you!" She whispered as she looked out the large windows.

Reaching within the collar of her shirt, Mala pulled out the gold chain and slipped it over her head. The medallion that hung from the chain flickered as it caught the fading sun. Staring at the medallion, the sorrow she had felt when talking with Aubrey came over her again. Baccus was gone and now Black was gone. She laid the medallion in the palm of her hand and stared at it as she remembered another time and another place.

It was after the first night she and Black became lovers. During the noon meal and clad only in his black shirt that was long on her, Black explained to her about a tattoo he placed on women he had before. He told her that she would be the last one and her mark would be different from the rest because she was special to him.

A man came to the great cabin and Black held up the medallion before the man and asked, "Can you make this?" The man studied it for a moment and nodded. Black produced a gold chain and pulled it through the small hole on the top of medallion. He then placed the necklace on the table before her. She looked skeptically at the two men who watched her and seemed to wait for her answer. Staring at the man, she finally nodded her head for him to proceed. Black told her that it would hurt and he seemed to watch her with proud admiration as she laid still and quiet for the man while he made the tattoo. Not a scream, not a sound came from her, only a grimace when the pain was more than she could will herself to be numb to. She would look at Black and he would smile handsomely at her. When it was finished, Black gave her a tea to drink that had medicines to prevent her from becoming sick. But how he loved her that night.

Mala pressed the medallion to her lips before putting it back around her neck and within her shirt. How she still loved him, even lost to her now. She had held herself from every man since he had loved her that morning before he had left her on that island. Did he ever come back? He was gone for so long! She wondered yet again. But even if he had returned, would she have listened to his excuses? He did not return soon enough because Baccus, her surprise for him, was gone.

Mala reached up and took a clear bottle from one of the small ledges. She gazed at the dark substance within as she held it, caressing the smooth glass with her fingertips. She inhaled deeply to control the emotions that threatened to overtake her. Vaguely she heard through her reminiscence the bell toll eight times for the change in the watch. Carefully placing the clear bottle back to its place on the quarter gallery window, Mala sat and gazed out at the sea. The sky had darkened a great deal during her musings. Time certainly had a way of slipping by unnoticed.

As expected, she heard the knock at her door and she moved from the window ledge as she bade entry. Morgan stepped in and presented his most winning smile.

"Where are the others?" She asked as she returned a sad smile.

Morgan noticed it and frowned slightly. "They are on their way. How are you?"

"Memories, Morgan, I cannot escape them."

Before he could offer any words of reassurance, a knock foretold the arrival of the others. Deats entered with three other men and after the pleasantries, the small group sat about the long table. Mala had set down tankards and bottles of rum and now the men helped themselves to the treat.

"Any problems in Charlestowne?" Mala asked after everyone settled down with his drink in hand.

"No, Cap'n, but there be a number of British merchants and warships in the harbor." One man informed.

"As it should be, Mr. Brockman. These are the British colonies." Mala stated as she sat with her elbow on the table and her cheek resting on the backs of her fingers. Then with a smile, she added, "Such a bothersome lot."

The men chuckled lightly before one man said, "Well we have found a nice spot to moor that is away from the other ships just the way ye like it, Cap'n. When we load, we can move in a bit closer then move back out of the way of pryin' eyes."

"Good work, Mr. Payne." Mala acknowledged then looked to Deats, and asked, "We have started leave rotation, correct Mr. Deats?"

"Aye, Captain. I have a list here of those no' deservin' ta enjoy the city's treasures this time because they chose ta break some rules." He handed Mala the list and she reviewed it.

As she noted the names and the infractions, the third man spoke up, "Cap'n, ye ought to know that there is somethin' goin' on in the city."

Without looking up from the list, she asked, "What is that, Mr. Nelson?"

"It seems that they be preparin' to 'ang some pirates in a few days. The gallows are ready but they be waitin' on the magistrate to return from 'is rounds." Mala looked up then and eyed each man with concern.

"Anyone we know?" She asked.

"N'er 'eard any names, Cap'n, but it be some cap'n and a part of 'is crew." Nelson informed.

They watched as she contemplated this information. Looking at Morgan and Deats, she said, "Make sure the men are careful while in town. When the first group returns in the morning, I want it absolutely certain that everyone is accounted for. I do not want to leave this city with any of my men to face the gallows along with the prisoners they have now."

"Aye." The quartermaster and first mate agreed.

Mala turned her attention back to her three crewmen. "Do you have any clue who they might be?" She asked. Why could she not shake off the feeling that she needed to do something for the prisoners?

"No Cap'n, only that they were captured in the Caribbean and brought here." Payne informed.

Deats eyed her and saw the thoughtful look in her eyes. "Do ye think ta break them free, Captain? We dinna know who they are? They could be…"

"Just considering, Deats." She cut him off. Then with a sigh and shrug, she added, "Stay out of trouble, gentlemen, while we are on shore tomorrow. If you or any of the other members of the crew hear of who they may be, let me know." She looked directly at Deats and said with purpose, "If they are friends, then we will see what we can do for them. As for pulling into the port, we will sail in just at daybreak. Just enough light to see by and before anyone else wakes up enough to notice us. Then we will leave the next morning the same way." Her gaze took in their nods.

"Well then, enjoy the rum, gentlemen. Mr. Payne, what other sights did you find while performing this menial task for me?" The men laughed as they each told a tale of their fun in the city. Morgan glanced at Mala and the two shared of knowing look that Deats caught. It angered the Scotsman that they could communicate so well without words and yet Mala all but ignored him.

After some time had passed, the men bade their farewells to their captain and nodded in departure to Morgan and Deats who stood to leave.

"Morgan, a word if you please." Mala said as the three men left and Deats turned in question. "Thank you, Mr. Deats." She said and he nodded stiffly, tossing a glare at Morgan before leaving the cabin.

Mala waved to the chair Morgan had sat in and he reseated himself. Pushing the list Deats had provided towards him, she pointed at it and said, "Have these men help out with the loading of wagon in town as well as loading the ship. No sense in them sitting about idle." Morgan looked over the list and laughed aloud.

"How on earth were you able to keep from laughing over these silly violations of the rules. Shoving a mate during the course of oiling the railings? Taking extra liberties beyond his rations of food and water? Discarding bits of twine..." He was saying between chuckles.

"Morgan, be that as it may, they are violations, though very small ones." She smiled at his look of total disbelief and gave into her own laughter. "Very well Morgan, there are very, very small ones. Still I must have them uphold the rules or they become worse." She stated trying to regain herself.

She clicked her tongue at her first mate who was still laughing uncontrollably but her smile belied her scolding, "Oh really, Morgan, please control yourself."

He was now laughing so hard that tears ran down his cheeks. After a while, Morgan was calming down and wiping the tears from his face. He leaned forward and trying to sound very serious, he asked Mala, "Tell me again why he is quartermaster?" He flew back in the chair, nearly toppling over as he avoided the arm that swung out at him.

Chapter 18

Deats and some of the *Enchantress'* crew loaded wagons with provisions as Mala leaned against the post idly watching the townspeople go about their business. So that her attire did not cause attention, Mala draped a cloak over her shoulders and held the front so nothing was revealed. Her pistol was tucked in the waistband of her britches and her dirk at her belt. She relinquished her sword because of the attention it would have drawn from under her cloak. Her hair hung loosely down her back, strands of it caught lazily in the breeze. With arms crossed over her chest and legs crossed at the ankles, Mala looked relaxed as she watched her surroundings.

She watched as women moved in and out of clothiers, jewelers, and milliners looking for the latest fashion. Their male companions were drudging along behind them. Young boys played with sticks as imaginary swords and ran across the street. Getting bored, she turned to look at the progress of the loading.

Deats stepped up to her and asked, "I have two sacks here on the supply list. Do ye suppose we need more?"

Mala straightened from the post and looked over the list then at the supplies. "If we have enough room for another sack, buy one more just in case."

"What do ye think of this?" Deats asked, pointing to another item on the list.

Noticing that he pointed to peppers, she almost chuckled at the reminder of the breakfast Willie presented him. With an air of indifference, she shrugged, "Just the one bunch, Mr. Deats. That should be plenty."

Deats nodded and went back to the wagon, making the changes noted. Morgan smiled as he took one bunch of peppers off the wagon and took it back into the general store. He beckoned for a crewman from the store's doorway and had the man carry the other sack in exchange for the peppers.

Moving to stand next to Mala who had resumed her stance of leaning on the post, Morgan watched the passersby as she was doing for a moment before he stepped down into the dusty street before her. She followed him with her eyes and a smile slowly appeared on her face.

"Now I can imagine you among these townsfolk. Wearing that lavender dress and being all proper." He said in a heavy British accent.

"Your imagination is more active than usual, Mr. Alcott. I only see before me a mindless fool trying to act as though it had a brain." Mala retorted playfully.

Morgan gave her a courtly bow, exaggerated by showing a leg and sweeping his hat. Mala's smile grew wider as he straightened and placed his hat back on his head. He extended his hand out for her as she looked at him suspiciously. "A lady is always aided by a gentleman." He stated as he wiggled his fingers.

Still smiling, Mala straightened from the post, uncrossed her arms and went to place her hand into his extended one. As she took a step down, she passed his hand and placed her hand over his face instead. With a slight shove, she laughingly said to her first mate, "Get back to work, Mr. Alcott."

Morgan chuckled as he bowed once again and Mala resumed her stance yet again. Deats shook his head at their antics and glared at Morgan when he returned to the matter at hand. "We would be leavin' this place in quick order, Mr. Alcott, if ye would kindly remember what needs ta be done."

"I know what needs to done, Mr. Deats, I know."

Mala ignored her two officers and returned to the activity along the busy street. Her smile disappeared as two men in British Navy uniform walking on the boardwalk across the street caught her attention. She watched them for a moment disinterested and even grunted as she heard one man laughing at his companion's remark. Watching them, she thought about a condescending nickname a fellow pirate had once used for the British and a smile appeared as she heard the voice in her head. *'Girlie dressed bastards.'*

The two uniformed men stopped, parted, and then doffed their hats as an attractive woman walked past them. Mala noticed that the two continued to watch the woman even when she was further up the street. One man elbowed the other and made a lewd gesture with his hips. Suddenly Mala straightened and stared at the man who had made the gesture. She studied his face intently and ever so slowly, an evil smile appeared on her beautiful face.

Without looking back, she called out easily, "Deats, see to the loading."

So intent was he on the supervising of the loading Deats barely realized that someone had spoken to him. He turned as Mala stepped down into the street. He followed her gaze as he heard her say over her shoulder, "I am going to visit an old friend." Her tone clued him that this old friend was not going to be pleased to see her.

Deats continued to watch as she paralleled the men on the opposite side of the street. The men entered a tavern and a few moments later Mala followed. Taking a deep breath, he shook his head in disbelief at Mala's determination of vengeance. "Tis all she thinks aboot." He muttered to himself quietly as he went back to his work.

Less than a half an hour later, Mala stepped soundlessly out of the tavern through the back door. She had watched then followed the object of her attention up the stairs and to a room on the second floor. Now back outside, she quietly shut the door then leaned against it, closing her eyes. Straightening up, she walked further into the shadowy back alley and stretched out her arms to unfold her cloak that was draped over one arm. Not hearing a sound or noticing any movement, Mala dropped the cloak in surprise when she was grabbed from behind by the throat and slammed against the wall of the tavern.

For a moment, the wind was knocked out of her and she shut her eyes to the pain that exploded in her head as it hit against the hard surface. She felt a body lean into her and her eyes flew open when she heard a familiar voice whisper in her ear. "Now we are even."

She could feel the color drain from her face as she stared in surprise at Rene Black who now stood before her. "Mon Dieu! You are alive!" She whispered.

"Disappointed, my love?" He sneered still very close to her, leaving her no room to move.

"I am sure I will be." She retorted.

He had watched as her expression changed from shock to her usual blank and unsmiling visage. His fingers tightened around her throat as he glanced up to look at the back wall of the tavern. "And what business would you have had in the tavern, my dear?" The sound of his deep voice gave her shivers that she chose to ignore.

"Not what you think, you arrogant ass!" She hissed through clenched teeth. "And get your fingers from around my throat unless you..." Her sentence was cut short by his tightening them a bit more.

"Do not tempt me, Mala. After Bimini, I am not sure I like you right now." He hissed but he released her a moment later.

Mala's face had been turning red from his hold on her throat, but the color quickly came back as Black watched her intently, knowing her temper. She glared at him as she took a deep breath to fill her lungs once again. Carefully, Black stepped back and retrieved her fallen cloak, keeping her within sight.

"I saw you standing outside the general store up the street and was wondering how I could get your attention when you left your men and walked away. But your attention was on those British officers you followed into the tavern, n'est-ce pas? Who were they, Mala?" He asked daring a glance at the building.

"What bloody difference does it make? I know you do not really care." She stated as she snatched her cloak from his hand. She missed his hurt expression as she stepped away from him then added over her shoulder, "Go find yourself a wench, Rene. Leave me alone."

Black grabbed her arm and turned her to face him, pinning her once more between him and the wall. He expected to see the dirk swing out towards him but he was surprised when she did not draw a weapon. He had seen her pistol and the dirk in its sheath on her sash when she came out of the back door. Instead she looked up into his face undaunted.

With an exasperated sigh, Black asked again in a more forceful tone still holding her arms, "Who were they, Mala? From the vill…"

"Damn it, Rene, you cannot possibly be jealous!" Mala hissed. When he made no reply but only glared at her, she added with narrowed eyes of suspicion, "I saw the *Widow* sink. So how is it that you are here before me?"

"I am no ghost, that is for damned sure!" He growled. "I was taken from my ship along with some of my men when the British boarded it just before dawn. Then they opened fire on it." Suddenly his expression changed to look accusingly at her and asked angrily, "If you saw the *Widow Maker* sink, then why the hell did you not come to my aid?"

"You had two warships on you!" She exclaimed incredulously. "The *Enchantress* is faster than your ship and she has as many guns. Against one warship, I could have helped you but not against two. Mon Dieu, Rene! I am not suicidal! Not even for you! And I sure as hell would not put my ship in danger!" She informed him. Although she tried to remain calm, the anger still caused her to speak sharply to him.

Mala watched him quietly, daring to him refute that logic. She saw his eye narrow in suspicion and smiled at the doubt he was now thinking. "One of these days, Mala, I might have an inkling of how your mind works." He stated as his stern look softened into a small smile.

Suddenly she found herself pulled into his arms and he kissed her with all the passion she remembered they used to share. He felt her put her arms around his neck and she was returning his kiss fully. His arms tightened around her and he felt her body molding easily against his. A groan escaped from him as the emptiness of the past two years melted away.

Unfortunately, the kiss did not last long. From the upper floor of the tavern, a woman's scream pierced the air. Black's head shot up and he looked up the tavern wall, but Mala looked to the ground with a curse.

"Ame damne! They found him too soon." She growled. Black looked at her questioningly as they could hear various sounds of turmoil from inside the tavern.

"What did you do?" He asked tightly.

Mala smiled at him sweetly and answered, "Repaid an old debt." Her smile grew wider as she added, "I would suggest we move away from here or the British will find you and then me."

Black ignored her warning. He now had confirmation of Mala's battles with the British, revenge as a witness of a burned village, being the sole survivor, and all due to John Alexander. He asked her again, "What did you do, Mala?"

"Let us go now, Rene!" She urged as she broke from his grasp and began running up the back alley towards the direction of her crew who were on the opposite side of the street.

"Looks like somethin' happened down there." One of the men said to another nearby. Deats looked up from the loading to see what the man was saying. He saw a crowd forming around the front of a tavern down the street.

"Get back ta work." The Scotsman told the men who stopped to watch. After a few moments, Deats remembered that Mala had headed in that direction. He looked down the street to see if he could catch a glimpse of her in the crowd of onlookers as she was prone to do. He looked to the people on the street to see if she was nonchalantly heading back towards them but he saw no traces of Mala on the street.

Morgan's curse was heard nearby for he too tried to find Mala among the crowd. The men stopped their work waiting and watching when a movement between the buildings across the street caught Deats' eye. It was Mala and he saw that Rene Black was with her. Anger filled him as he thought of the two together again. How long had she been gone? And more importantly, how could the man still be alive?

"The Captain may be in trouble, men." He stated as he nodded for them to see the running figures. "You two stay here." Deats ordered as pointed to two men, one of them being Morgan.

"Oh no, I am going with you." Morgan argued as he pointed at another man and ordered him to stay with the provisions.

At the end of the street, Mala turned towards the woods to get away from the town. Black followed and, when he realized that she leading him away from danger, he took the lead. Reaching a clearing, they stopped to listen for any pursuers. They could hear running and knew that it was more than one person following. Grabbing her arm, Black turned to run away when a shout rang out. "There she is! Captain, wait!"

Mala pulled back from Black's arm when she recognized Morgan's voice. Turning, the two captains waited for the others to approach. "Are you all right?" Morgan yelled out as they drew closer.

"Hold your tongue! Are you trying to draw attention?" Mala angrily whispered.

Morgan smiled then looked at Black and said, "I thought you went down with your ship, Captain."

"It would seem that you are mistaken, Mr. Alcott. For I assure you that I am no ghost." With a thin smile, Black repeated his words he had told to

Mala.

Deats stepped forward and put himself between Black and Mala. Glaring at the darkly clad man, Deats dared him to make a move. But Black ignored the Scotsman and watched Mala as she walked to her men.

"One would think that ye were a specter, for ye appear from thin air when one least expects it." Deats replied in low voice to the dark haired man.

Raising a brow, Black taunted him with a smile. "Afraid I might take your captain away from you? Shall we let her make that choice?"

Morgan smiled as Deats glared at Black. Reaching out a gloved hand to grasp the dark-haired man by the throat, the Scotsman growled, "Over my dead body, ye..."

"Enough!" Mala spat as she slapped Deats' arm away from Black. She waited until she had gained everyone's attention, then she looked to Black. She had known what his reply to her quartermaster would have been. "Is it possible that we can leave you here and we get about our business?" Mala asked tiredly.

His gaze roamed over her beautiful face before he gave her a smile, one he knew would irk her before he replied sweetly, "Of course."

Mala rolled her eyes and ordered the two men standing closest to Black, "Watch him so I can think."

The two men moved to stand on each side of Black as if to detain him. Black's smile grew wider while he continued to watch Mala as she turned her back to him. Her stance reflected her irritation, even down to the tapping boot. But she was fast in her thinking and very thorough for the short period of time it took to work out her plan. Black was always amazed at how her mind worked and the ideas she seemed to formulate. There were countless times when her ideas seemed more fun than his own and he could not wait to hear what she planned to do with him now. As he watched, his gaze followed the sleek outline of her body and remembered well the feel of that body. Memories assaulted him once again of the time when they were together and he wondered how it all went wrong.

Suddenly Mala turned and Black found himself looking into her cold, dark eyes. This was definitely a dangerous woman! "Morgan, escort Captain Black to the outer limits of the town. I expect my first mate to return unharmed, Rene." Mala said.

She caught Black's smile but she was not humored and turned away angrily. Morgan took a few steps toward Black with a smile and touched his arm as the two other men stepped back. Deats looked at Mala, his mouth dropped open in surprise as she seemed to dismiss the whole lot of them. With an air of indifference, she was walking back towards town and the supply wagon.

"Mala, now is yer chance ta be rid of him once and for all." He stated impatiently as he tried to catch up with her.

With a low growling sound that came from deep in her throat, Mala swung around to face the Scotsman, her arm out straight. Deats took a step back as he found himself now face to face with Mala's pistol and her fury. "We are not going to argue over what I will or will not do with Rene Black!" She hissed. With a slight tilt of her head, she asked menacingly, "Are we, Deats?"

Deats swallowed hard as his eyes moved from the barrel of the pistol to Mala's face just above. She had not turned her body to fully face him but her face was turned to him and she was watching him with that unnerving menacing stare. He realized that he had gone too far. "Nay, Captain." He answered. Looking down the pistol barrel again, he added thickly in his Scottish drawl, "Nay, we will no.'"

Still she did not move nor did her eyes leave Deats' face. Her eyes merely narrowed as she studied his face as if she were trying to read his mind. She saw him swallow and knew that look on his face—fear. All the men around them stood unmoving and barely breathing, unwilling to draw Mala's attention away from Deats.

"Shoot him, Mala." Morgan whispered low. Still held by Morgan's firm grasp, Black was the only one to hear the statement and a small smile stole across his lips. "Damn it, shoot him." Came Morgan's quiet command again with more purpose.

After what seemed to be an eternity to everyone, Mala slowly lowered the pistol but her menacing look remained. The tightening of her jaw was the only indication that she was attempting to regain control of her temper. Black recognized the inner struggle the woman was having and he knew that Mala's temper could be an awesome beast to control. He turned his head slightly to look at Morgan when he heard him quietly click his tongue in disappointment.

Morgan was displaying a clear show of animosity toward the Scotsman. At first the sight angered Black, wondering of Morgan's place with Mala. But as he covertly watched the younger man's face, he saw that the actions had nothing to do with Mala. But glancing at Deats, he could not be so easily consoled on the matter.

Mala had lowered her arm until it rested along her side as she continued to control her temper, looking to the ground and closing her eyes for only a second. When she opened them again, she was looking at Black's boots. Her gaze slowly followed the figure of the man until she reached his face. He was watching her and, for a few moments, they stood motionless just looking at each other. The heat of passion coursed through Black's veins as he watched her slow perusal of him.

"Morgan." She stated quietly, her dark eyes not leaving the pirate captain's face.

"Aye, Captain, the outer limits of town." He said with a nod. "Come on, Captain Black." He pulled at Black's elbow to get him moving.

Taking a couple of steps, Black's gaze never left Mala as she had turned her back on them. She was heading back towards the town, tucking her pistol back into the waistband of her britches, her long dark hair fluttering in the breeze. Her fast pace was the only indication that her temper was still trying to get the better of her. Her men followed her quickly, one handing over her cloak that she wrapped around herself to cover her attire as before. Black's mouth very nearly watered as he watched her leave the area.

Deats had not moved either. He too watched Mala as she walked away. He knew that he really should be dead now and wondered why she had not killed him for questioning her. He took a deep breath to relieve the tension in his body as he thought of how often he has seen her kill just as swiftly. However, as the tension washed away, it was replaced by new anger.

Morgan looked to Black when he no longer moved to follow and found him now watching Deats. When Morgan looked to Deats, he did not like the look on the Scotsman's face as he watched Mala. Though the anger was there, Morgan had not noticed it to be as intense before. Apparently, Black noticed it as well because he quietly called to the man in his deep rumbling voice, "Monsieur Deats."

His thoughts broken, Deats faced the man he had grown to hate immensely.

"If anything should happen to Mala, I will hold you responsible. I will hunt you down and I will kill you, slowly and painfully. Do you understand me, Mr. Deats?" Black's words were slow yet cold and there was no misunderstanding his intent.

Morgan was pleased to hear the threat but did not show signs of it except for a slight twinkling of his eyes. Deats merely emitted a laugh and said, "Ye are in no position ta threaten me, Captain." He did not bother to disguise the loathing emphasis to the title.

"Tis no threat, Mr. Deats. I will find you and do just as you have just heard. It is my promise to you." Black stated undaunted by Deats' glare.

Stepping closer to his nemesis, his Scottish accent more prominent, Deats growled, "Mala can take of herself. She does no' need ye ta protect her. She has been doin' foin without ye."

Black bristled from the barb but only smiled cruelly, "That, Mr. Deats, I know very well. But then, truth be known, she does not need you either." Morgan tried to hold Black back when the pirate captain stepped closer to Deats and added, "If anything happens to her, Scotsman, I will enjoy killing

170

you."

Glaring at Black, Deats' smile was equally cruel. "If ye happen ta be around at the time, then we shall see who finds whom, Captain."

Black and Deats glared at one another as Morgan stood in amazement of Deats' threat. Glancing at the first mate, Deats took a few paces back, still smiling evilly in the face of the dark haired man.

Suddenly a knife cut through the air between the three men and came to a vibrating halt, deeply embedded into the trunk of a nearby tree. They turned in unison to find that Mala had soundlessly returned. She was too far away to have heard either man's words but she knew that the close proximity of the three did not bode well.

When she had gained their attention, she turned away and headed back to town as before without a word. One man from her group ran up to the trio and said, "Mr. Deats, the Cap'n says that if ye are not be'ind 'er this time, she will finish what she started with ye." Then clearing his throat, the man looked to Morgan, "She also says that ye 'ave yer orders, Mr. Alcott."

The three men looked to the knife once again as the messenger stepped between them to retrieve it for his captain.

"She can take damn good care of herself. Hell, she does not need us at all." Morgan stated to no one in particular as the three men separated. The comment made Black smile as this time they headed further into the woods.

Watching Morgan escort Captain Black away from town, Deats wondered how much of this conversation would reach Mala. Turning, he quickly followed her as ordered having no doubts that she would finish what she had started to do. He found Mala leaning on the post once again, as if nothing had happened. Her dark eyes watched him as he resumed his position of overseeing the loading.

Chapter 19

Aubrey heard the watch call out the captain's returning. She had spent the day fishing off the portside of the *Enchantress*. She had seen others of the crew do this and thought the idea of standing with a pole in hand waiting for a tug of the line that was dropped into the water seemed ridiculous. She had remained behind on the ship and was seated at the bow watching the action of the dock in the distance.

Willie had stepped up and thrust a pole in her hands and, with a smile on his wizened face, told Aubrey, "Make yourself useful, me darlin', catch us some dinner."

Aubrey looked at the pole in her hand then back up at the old man who had laughed at her wide-eyed expression then walked away. "Certainly you jest!" She yelled at him but that seemed to amuse him more as she could hear him laugh harder. Letting out a deep sigh, she got up and moved to the portside of the ship on the main deck.

"What is this?" Aubrey grimaced as she held up the hook. A putrid-smelling hunk of some type of meat was caught thereon.

"Chicken innards." Johnny informed through his broken teeth.

"Ugh!" Aubrey shivered as she moved to the lowest point of the deck and dropped the line down to the water level. It had also placed her very near the place on the railing where the men had cast over the rope ladder.

It was midday when the creaking sound of hemp rope against the railing drew her attention from her stare at the line as it disappeared into the water below. She turned to see Mala come aboard. Bending down to retrieve her catch of a number of fish and presenting them with a proud grin to Mala, she proudly said, "Look at what I ...have ...been…" Aubrey's voice trailed off when she noticed the dark scowl on Mala's face. "What is the matter?" She asked Mala.

Without a reply, the captain stormed past her as Deats hurried to catch up. "Captain! Captain!" He called out to his ignoring superior.

Just as he caught up with her, Mala suddenly turned with her hands locked together. Swinging out at Deats, she caught him squarely on his chin, knocking him to the deck. As he lay looking up at Mala in surprise she hovered over him. "You will never question me again!" She hissed.

Deats got to his feet as she turned away. Aubrey dropped the fish and the pole when she witnessed Mala striking her quartermaster. The young Irish woman's mouth hung open in surprise, making her look now very much like her catch of fish that lay on the deck at her feet.

"I thought ye wanted him dead!" Deats was saying in his defense.

Mala turned as if to hit him again but he grabbed her by locking her arms with his. Both fell to the deck in her struggle to get loose. Deats hit the deck first and had the wind knocked out of him when Mala landed on him. With quick reflexes, she turned with fists and went to strike. He caught one hand but the other slipped from his grasp and caught him above his right eye. The two rolled and fists flew as Mala was able to land a few more punches to his face before he could grab her wrists and pin her down on the deck on her back. As he straddled her, he could see the full fury on her face.

"Please, Mala." He began to plead breathlessly.

"Get off me." She snarled.

He held her there only for a moment when suddenly he was knocked off. With her unique fighting abilities enhanced by her rage, Mala bucked under him then lifting her right leg she managed to throw him over her head in a somersault. Again with a swiftness of a cat she was suddenly astride him with her dirk at his throat. Deats froze under her hand. Now he panted from the struggle as he looked up into her furious, yet devastatingly beautiful face. He wanted her over him in such a position, but definitely not on deck and under the blade of her knife!

"That is twice you questioned my orders and I will tolerate it no more, Deats!" She was snarling breathlessly, bringing his lustful thoughts back to the present. "It would be to your good health that you heed this warning. The next time, I will cut you up in small pieces and feed you to the sharks, do you understand?" The last statement she had spoken quietly and very calmly, her face just mere inches from his—so close that he could feel her breath on his cheek. Deats could see in her eyes that she meant every single word and he knew that he would not be so lucky next time.

With this in mind now, Deats could only nod. The slight affirmative response gave way to the feel of her sharp blade as it was still laid against his throat. She had cut him there once before, a long time ago and he had no desire to re-open that wound again. Mala was on her feet in a flash looking down at the Scotsman as she sheathed her blade. She then looked around her at the crewmembers who stood watching, slack-jawed. Without another word, she turned on her heels and went to her cabin. The sound of her door slamming seemed to break the spell as everyone moved and talked all at once.

Aubrey looked for Morgan who was standing near the rope ladder and was amazed to see him smiling. He stepped over to Deats and held out his hand to aid the man on his feet. Deats looked up at him and after a few seconds took the proffered hand. When the Scotsman was standing, Morgan noticed the cut over the left eye and stepped closer to whisper, "You or Black? I would wager that you will always be the loser."

With that, Morgan turned away from Deats and moved to Aubrey. The Scotsman threw him a glare before he stormed away to his cabin.

"My God, Morgan. What in the world happened on shore?" Aubrey asked in wide-eyed disbelief.

"I think it would be best to be quiet about this for a time. The captain needs to be alone right now." Morgan told her and he was not smiling as he gazed in the direction of Mala's cabin.

"But Morgan..."

"Heed me on this, Aubrey. For your safety, keep a wide berth from Mala for a time. She is not in any mood to be humored now." Then the smile was back as he saw the small mound of fish on the deck alongside the pole. Bending, he picked her catch and said proudly, "What have we here? Hmm, looks like dinner to me."

Aubrey just stared at him and this habit of his toward mood swings. Morgan looked at her shocked expression and stated still smiling, "That is not to say that I cannot be humored."

Aubrey regained her senses and surroundings. With one last glance toward Mala's cabin, she clicked her tongue and replied in near exasperation, "Good God, Morgan, when are you not humored!" Morgan laughed and escorted her to the galley.

In the early morning hours just before sunrise of the next day, all aboard the *Enchantress* was quiet. The ship rocked gently in the far reaches of the Charlestowne harbor. Morgan was sleeping soundly, lying on his side with his back to the room. A sharp sound invaded his sleep and his eyes snapped open. He remained still and alert as he listened to the sounds of the ship, frowning at the darkness and wondering where the sound had come from.

A small cry pierced the darkness, coming from the bunk next to his. He rolled onto his back and peered toward Aubrey's bunk. She was in the throes of yet another of her nightmares. Clicking his tongue and running his fingers through his sandy hair, Morgan sat up. She was speaking now but in French. She had taken to doing that of late as well, which further frustrated him because he had no idea at all what she was saying.

Morgan generally would lay and listen to her in the darkness until she would finally calm and slip into quiet blissful sleep, then he would slip off to sleep as well. However, this morning, he got up to go to her rescue. Pulling on his britches as she still thrashed and fussed in the foreign language, he lit the lantern and turned the wick down low. In the dimly lit cabin, he eased his lean frame down onto the edge of her bunk.

"Aubrey, wake up. You are just dreaming. Come on now, wake up." He said softly as he gently shook her.

"No Jojoba...I cannot swim...where is..." She cried out in English in a small distressed voice that trailed off before she called out a name.

"Where is who, Aubrey? This is Morgan...you are fine. Wake up now. You are not in the water, you are safe now, love." He went on softly as he pushed the sweat-dampened strands of auburn hair out of her face. The gentle coaxing of his voice began to bring her slowly of out the dream and she stirred. He watched as her eyes fluttered open and she drew a deep breath.

"There you go now, love. It was just a bad dream. You are fine. Nothing is going to harm you, no one will hurt you." He soothed. She shivered and moved back away from him toward the wall at the head of her bunk.

"I...I am sorry I woke you again Morgan, I cannot help having the nightmares, I wish I could." Her voice was apologetic.

"I know, Aubrey, I just wish you would share them with me and maybe they would go away. You speak in French and I cannot understand you. But when you spoke in English, you were fussin' about not being able to swim. Did Jojoba put you overboard?"

"Yes, I dreamed of the day the *Widow Maker* sank. I dream of it all the time." She said sadly. "I suppose you must be sorry for having taken me in as a roommate. You have not slept well since I came on board. You work hard and you need your rest at night. Perhaps it would have been better if Willie and Robert had not pulled me from the surf that day, then I would not be a burden to anyone."

"Christ Aubrey...why would you think such a thing? Of course I am not sorry."

"You did not even know me, what difference would it have made?" She retorted as she frowned back at him. They looked at one another for a few quiet moments and he finally exhaled in exasperation for they were at a stalemate again.

"Lay back down there and go to sleep, maybe now that you have told me what dream troubles you all the time, it will not come back to haunt you anymore." He said as he tossed her blanket over her. She eased herself back down and nestled her head into her pillow as he straightened.

"Thank you Morgan, you are very sweet." She said quietly.

"Aye, I know...sweet-hearted Morgan...kind-hearted Morgan, guardian from the bad dreams Morgan. You ruin my reputation as a pirate." He grumbled. She let out a small giggle as he rolled his eyes at her. He leaned over her suddenly in play, "How about a little kiss for the knight in shining armor?"

She let out a yelp and playfully pulled the covers up over her head. He grunted and started to rise from the bunk as Aubrey lay giggling under the covers.

Suddenly the relaxed atmosphere of the dimly lit cabin was shattered by the sound of splintering wood. Morgan turned and Aubrey sat up in the bunk with a cry of alarm as the door flew open. It banged against the wall and swung back to be stopped by a man who stood now in the threshold with a cutlass in his hand.

"Well what have we here?" The man asked in French-accented English as he stood over them. Morgan started to advance, but his mind was quickly changed as the man pointed the weapon at his chest, "Do not get chivalrous, Monsieur."

Morgan did not see the look of terrified horror on Aubrey's face as she recognized the man's voice. She scrambled to pull herself back up into the corner clutching the covers about her as the man waved Morgan to sit on his own bunk. The intruder then stepped closer to her bunk.

"Bonjour Mademoiselle, you are looking exceptionally lovely this morning." The man sneered at her.

Another man entered behind the first and he turned up the wick on the lamp, casting more light into the tiny cabin. "Hmm, comment allez-vous, Mademoiselle Aubrey." The second man greeted as he turned from the task. Morgan watched the two men smile leeringly at her as she cowered in the corner.

"Beaufort. Boulet." She whispered.

Beaufort reached forward to take her up by the wrist and Morgan sprung to his feet in her defense as she cried out in alarm, trying to pry herself free of his grasp.

"Non Beaufort!" She cried in distress as he dragged her bodily from the bunk with an evil chuckle.

"Take your hands off her, damn you!" Morgan spat. He quickly found himself back on his bunk, having been backhanded by Boulet.

"Be still now Monsieur, unless you want her to see you die right here. We have our orders to bring all able bodied seamen to the captain." Beaufort said as he struggled with Aubrey. Boulet drew his sword to hold on Morgan who now lay in a semi-reclined position on his bunk wiping the blood from his lip.

"Able bodied men." Morgan corrected as he cast his eye at the struggling young woman. Then he frowned at the man, "What captain?"

"Be still now, little one." Beaufort said smiling as he held Aubrey against his body. He looked down over her body in the chemise, "Mm, I do not think that I have ever been offered such a view of you before, Mademoiselle. You certainly meet with my approval. What say you, Boulet?"

"Oui." The other man nodded as his eyes wandered greedily over her.

"Let her go." Morgan warned.

"Oh but Monsieur, we are old friends, she and I. Had we not met with our unfortunate accident, she would be gracing my quarters and warming my bunk right now." Beaufort told him as he stroked his gloved hand down along the side of Aubrey's throat.

"Arrête!" She fussed pushing his hand away as it stroked lower toward her breasts.

"What captain? Mala is the captain of this ship." Morgan argued, trying to draw attention away from her.

Beaufort tipped Aubrey's head back to face him. "She knows what captain. Tell him, ma petite." Beaufort said staring into her eyes as he caressed her chin. Morgan watched as her eyes widened in alarm and she ceased to struggle against Beaufort's hand for a few seconds.

The Frenchman smiled and turned his gray eyes upon Morgan, "See, she knows. Bring him along now, Boulet." Beaufort said as he moved toward the door with Aubrey.

She fought him frantically, legs kicking and arms swinging, speaking to him in a mixture of English and French. "Non Beaufort! Let me dress, s'il vous plait." He regarded her with a wary eye as she continued and started to calm down a bit, "Then I will come along peacefully."

"Make it quick, Mademoiselle. If you are not ready, he will die then I will come back in here for you. When I am finished with you, I will then take you to the captain." He said as he roughly released her. Looking up at Beaufort then to Morgan, she slumped back down onto the bunk and put her head in her hands. Boulet grabbed Morgan by the arm and held the cutlass to his throat.

"Oui, Monsieur Beaufort." She finally said weakly, casting hazel eyes up at him.

The two Frenchmen left the cabin with Morgan in tow and the door was shut firmly. Aubrey dressed as quickly as her shaking hands would allow. She was pulling on her boots when the door flew open again.

"Your time is up." Beaufort said stepping inside. He clicked his tongue at the sight of her fully dressed, "Damn, I was looking forward to that." He spat in a low voice as he advanced on her and took her by the arm.

"Perhaps we should kill him anyway, the captain would never know." He said looking out into the corridor at Morgan and then back at the bunk behind her.

"I will tell him." She said in quiet bravery, following his gaze.

He chuckled at her, "Idle threats, Mademoiselle. You never told him about the night I came into his cabin after you had taken that hit out of the quarter gallery window, did you?"

"Are you sure?" She asked.

"I am still here, n'est-ce pas?" He replied smugly, close to her face as he held up his hand to display a scar. "You have spoiled my fun again. Get on with you. The captain will be surprised to see that you are still alive." He said as he pushed her out the door ahead of him. She exchanged glances with Morgan as they were ushered along to the upper deck.

Chapter 20

The day was just beginning to dawn and a light breeze buffeted the sails. Aubrey and Morgan noticed that a few of Mala's men were rounded up and held by two others of the boarding crew.

"Who are those men?" Morgan whispered, nodding toward their captors as he and Aubrey were made to stand together.

"Thomas Beaufort and Michele Boulet. They are men from the *Widow Maker*." She informed with a returned whisper.

"No more talking to your lover now, Mademoiselle. Your captain has returned." Beaufort advised.

"He is not my lover." She retorted thickly in French.

"Of course not, that is why he hovered over you in the bunk. What was he doing to you, huh? Were you able to finish or did we interrupt?" Beaufort asked with a lascivious chuckle. Aubrey's face had crimsoned deeply and she opened her mouth to retort, but the words froze in her throat as the menacing figure of Rene Black slowly stepped out of the shadows.

Morgan did not pay attention to the exchange as he became aware of the man clad in black. Glancing at Aubrey as Black stepped up to her, Morgan thought that she would faint, her fear was so evident.

"I thought you were dead." Came Black's deep resonating voice in the quietness of the early morning as he towered over her.

She cast her eyes downward and said softly, "I did not see you that morning your ship sank. So how is it that you are still alive?"

Black chuckled and put a gloved hand under her chin to raise her face to look at him. "Oh, I had a savior of sorts that took me off the ship before she was gone. It would appear that you had a guardian angel as well." Black said. She trembled in Beaufort's grasp as the dark eye bore down on her.

"Had you not chosen to meet the *Artemus*, you may not have lost your ship." She said in a half whisper. She struggled a bit to free herself from Beaufort's clutches, but she was hopelessly imprisoned between the two of them.

Black turned his attention away from her, still holding her face in his hand and he looked around the deck at the men from Mala's crew. "Which of these men has been the receptor of your favors for your good fortune?"

"None of them." She said licking her lips nervously.

He looked back at her with raised eyebrow, "None of them? I find that hard to believe. You have been known to lie down for a man other than me before. Would it be this one perhaps?" Black dropped his gloved hand from her chin to wave at Morgan.

"No." She said firmly, glancing at Morgan. Her face burned with embarrassment at Black's comment.

"Is it the quartermaster? Where is he?"

Before Morgan could reply, the Scotsman replied fearlessly, "I am the quartermaster of this ship."

Black turned toward Deats. The memory of their encounter the day before made Black's blood boil. Narrowing his dark eye at him, Black asked, "Are you the man she lies with now?"

"Nay." Deats growled as he looked upon her disdainfully.

Black pursed his lips, "Oh well, too bad for you. She is quite worth it." Aubrey looked at Black in surprise at the remark. How dare he make such a comment, she had never succumbed to his advances. "You will follow me and be my quartermaster now since you already hold the rank and the men on this ship undoubtedly would follow you." Black went on to say.

"I will no.' There has been no election for a new captain on this ship. Mala is the captain, I will follow no other captain save her." The Scotsman said defiantly.

Black nodded and then shrugged with an air of indifference, "Then you will lead all who feel as you do below. Put him in irons. Gather up those others who resist my command and put them below as well." He watched with an air of pleasure as Deats and several of Mala's men were taken below at the points of cutlasses and barrels of pistols.

Turning back to the small group before him, Black smiled. "Now, where were we? Oh yes, we were discussing the association of Monsieur Alcott and Mademoiselle Malone." His dark eye rested on Aubrey again.

"They were found in a cabin together. He was in her bunk." Beaufort reported smugly.

Black looked at Morgan with a thin smile. "So Monsieur Alcott, I see you have helped yourself to my woman."

"She speaks the truth, Black, I do not know her as you suggest." Morgan said calmly. At the realization that the two obviously knew one another, Aubrey's mouth dropped open in surprise.

"Hmm, did you know she was my woman?" Black asked.

"I saw the mark." Morgan calmly confessed with a shrug.

"You lie, Morgan!" Aubrey spat in desperation as she struggled against Beaufort.

Undaunted by her outburst, Morgan reaffirmed, "But as I have said, I do not know her in that way. She speaks the truth, we share a cabin, not a bunk."

Black chuckled and turned to face Aubrey. Using her words and ignoring

Morgan's explanation of their relationship, he said, "Apparently he did lie…in your bunk, or you in his, how else would he have seen my mark on you?" He waved a gloved hand to Beaufort, "Let her go, what can she do?"

Aubrey snatched herself out of Beaufort's grasp so violently that she nearly threw herself into Black before she turned on Morgan as the other man held him. Delivering him a vicious slap to his face she screamed, "You are liar, Morgan Alcott! You have never seen his mark on me. How could you have?"

Blinking at the stinging pain of the little hand, he was otherwise undaunted and his voice came low. "The first morning you had a nightmare. I saw it then."

Aubrey drew back in shock and stared at him in disbelief. From behind her, Beaufort chuckled, "I would have done far more than just look at her."

Aubrey and Morgan stared at each other for a few more seconds before her hand shot up with lighting swiftness to slap him once more. This time Black's gloved hand came up and caught hers, stopping her. "Do not strike my men, my dear, that is for me to do." He said with a small smile. "So I take it that you were undaunted by my mark?" Black went on to say to Morgan as he still held Aubrey's hand.

"It is just a mark." Morgan replied dryly with a shrug. "And you were presumed dead. What harm could it hold?"

"You see then, my dear, it is just as I told you. Men of our like are not concerned with such things on a woman. He was convinced that I was dead and you became free game. Sooner or later he would have taken his favors from you. But it has been a long time and if he has been your savior in the midst of these sea dogs, even though you insist otherwise, he has already made his claim of flesh on you." Black smirked.

Waving at Boulet, who still brandished the cutlass, Black ordered, "Put that damned thing away and release him. He will not stand against us, will you Monsieur Alcott?" Black turned his eye upon the place where Deats had been taken. He recalled Morgan's pleas for Mala to kill the man. With finality, Black nodded toward Morgan and said, "He is one of us."

Morgan's eyes met with Aubrey's yet he kept silent. His silence spoke volumes to her as she looked at Black and echoed, "Your men? One of your men?" Her hurt-filled hazel eyes turned to Morgan.

It was Black who answered her questions. "Oui, Mademoiselle. Did he not tell you that he sailed under my command a few years ago? That is until he decided not to come back on board one night."

A wave of coldness washed over Aubrey as she dropped her gaze to the deck. It had happened to her again. Fate had thrown her into the path of a man who was kind and caring and once more that man was commanded by the devil himself.

Black was speaking again, seemingly reading her mind. "Apparently he is just like someone else you used to know."

His dark eye looked up into the lightening sky and smiled at the absence of a man in the crow's nest. With a chuckle and a quick swipe of his hand along the slack jaw of Aubrey, he said to Morgan, "Merci for thinning out the night crew so that I could come aboard this morning." Aubrey's eyes darted to look in hurtful question at Morgan again.

Suddenly there was a loud commotion on the other side of the deck. Two men emerged from the companionway with Mala between them. She was struggling and speaking with much anger in her own language. Black's attention was now drawn away from Aubrey as he turned toward the beautiful dark-haired woman and, with a deep sigh, he muttered, "And now the fun begins."

Still watching Morgan with a look of disbelief, Aubrey was surprised to see a broad grin spread across his face.

"Mala my dear, what a pleasure it is to see you again." Black droned in his deep voice.

"Who do you think you are boarding my ship?" She spat in English and in a very low tone.

"It is my ship now, m'amour." He smiled, ignoring the warning of her tone.

"Like hell it is." She growled as she managed to jerk herself free of one of the men and she spun on him.

The other man caught her as Black called, "Watch her there! Like the name of her ship, she is an enchantress and will cast a spell on you if given the opportunity."

Black turned his attention back to Beaufort and opened his mouth to give the man an order when a painful sound cut through the air behind him. He turned on his heel to see that one of the men who had held Mala captive was now face down on the deck with a dirk firmly imbedded in the center of his back. Shaking his head and with a smile added to his statement, "Or she will kill you."

Lifting his gaze to Mala who was being brought toward him in the firm grasp of the other man, he shook his head and clicked his tongue. "How in the hell do you do that?" He asked almost admiringly.

"Come closer and I will show you." She spat making him smile. Then in the deadly tone he knew all too well, he heard her say, "I will not let you take my ship."

"Do you think that you could stop me?" Black asked.

The sound of scuffling feet alerted him that Mala's men were gathering courage to fight back. Her words seemed to have motivated them and he knew his own men would be facing them nearly ten to one. Grabbing Mala's arm and pulling out his dirk, Black placed the knife at her throat as he held her in front of him.

"What are you doing?" Mala hissed with eyes wide in disbelief. She did not see Morgan's reaction as he took a step forward before catching himself and stopped. Black saw the move as he met Morgan's angry blue eyes briefly.

In answer to her question, Mala heard Black shout to gain everyone's attention, "Do you see your captain? Do you want to see her dead?"

Everyone froze. Aubrey could not believe what she was witnessing nor could she believe that he would make such a threat. Looking at Mala, Aubrey saw the rage on her face.

Black felt Mala shaking with the rage within his hold and knew that if she ever regained control of her ship, he would have hell to pay for this very moment. Keeping his mind on what needed to be done and realizing that he had gained everyone's attention, Black informed loudly, "Now here are the rules. You will sail under my command. You will not attempt to set your captain free. You will not aid in regaining her command. If you try, your captain will be killed instantly. Is this understood?"

When no replies could be heard, Black raised the dirk higher so that Mala had to lift her chin higher in order to avoid the blade. "Do you understand?" Black shouted each word.

Reluctant 'ayes' were heard and Black lowered the dirk. Turning Mala back over to the man who had held her, Black said, "Bring her to her cabin with me. Take this one and put her below." He said as he jerked a thumb at Aubrey over his shoulder.

A cry of anger emitted from Aubrey behind him and he heard the scuffle of boots on the deck. He turned in time to see Beaufort swing back his hand and cuff Aubrey across the face, sending her sprawling onto the deck. With a guttural growl, Black dealt a backhanded blow to Beaufort causing him to stagger only slightly.

"Did I tell you to strike her?" Black asked angrily. Beaufort shook his head in negative reply. Looking down at Aubrey as she still lay on the deck with blood trickling from the cut at the side of her mouth, Black missed Beaufort's glare. "I suggest you behave yourself or I will give you to him." Black told her menacingly. Beaufort smiled evilly at the suggestion as his gaze met Aubrey's while Morgan emitted a snort of protest.

"Get to the helm, Monsieur Beaufort." Black ordered. Beaufort seemed to tear his gaze from Aubrey before obeying his captain.

Gibbs stepped forward and gingerly reached down to pull Aubrey to her feet, "Come along now, little one, like the captain ordered." He said easily as he looked at Black. The latter merely glared at him, but offered no reply or reprimand. Aubrey glared at Morgan as Gibbs started away with her.

Mala unleashed another string of vicious oaths in her language. Black was exhausted and his temper was short. Before he realized what he was doing, he was on Mala in an instant. The man holding her let go in surprise as Black snatched her by the front of her shirt.

"You bastard! Let me go!" She hissed.

Black's eye wandered over her partially exposed breasts and came to rest on his mark on her. The anger in him quickly gave way to passion and want. Glancing at Beaufort, Black ordered, "Take us away from the mainland and set a course for southern waters." His voice was thick with emotion as he looked into the angry dark eyes of the woman he held.

"Aye Captain." Beaufort said sharply as he mounted the quarterdeck steps, taking them two at a time. "Hoist the anchor!" Beaufort bellowed. Men moved to the capstan with an air of disgruntlement.

Black pulled Mala to him and pressed his lips firmly on hers. She struggled briefly, pounding his chest with her fists in anger as she tried to break from the embrace. He finally broke away and called out in his throaty voice, "This ship is mine, and so is her captain."

Mala went still in his arms and glared at him, her voice barely above a whisper, "I will not be a prisoner on my own ship."

He smiled down at her and in a voice deep with passion, he replied, "Hmm, then you will be the pet of the new captain and you can go wherever you please."

It had been far too easy to take her ship but then Morgan had kept his part of the bargain, Black thought as he shut the door once he and Mala had entered her cabin. He cast his dark eye around the cabin in the early morning sunlight that streamed through the quarter gallery windows. The bed linens were rumpled on the large bunk giving testimony to the abrupt awakening that she must have had from his men that had brought her on deck.

He looked at her as she stood with her arms folded, glaring at him. He wondered if she had been dressed or if she had been naked in the bunk. The thought caused mild stirrings in him as he recalled the countless mornings that he had drawn her naked body close to his. A pang of jealousy coursed through him at the thought of his men having ousted her from her bunk in such a condition.

Moving to the table, his booted foot kicked an empty bottle and it rolled across the floor. Seeing another bottle on the floor near the quarter gallery, Black looked closer at Mala. Her clothes were rumpled as though she had slept in them. More at ease now over her state of dress, he sat in a high-backed chair at the end of the table and propped a booted foot up on the corner of the table. Reaching into a bowl to retrieve an apple, he took a bite of the fruit and glanced at her, "This is a fine ship, Mala. Where did you steal her?"

Mala strode to the opposite end of the table and replied impatiently, "From some British bastard—what are you doing here, Rene?"

He merely looked at her grinning while he waited for her to answer his question. In the silence, she rolled her eyes and replied after a loud exhale, "I took her from some British bastard and had her refitted to better serve my purposes."

"She is a fast one. You have done a fine job. It would appear that you learned your lessons well. I have been hearing a lot about you. The woman pirate captain who gives no quarter to the British." He said with a smile as he took another bite of the apple.

"Who are you that you can come on board and take my ship?" She spat.

"Sit with me." He cooed.

"Like hell I will." She spat again as she rounded the table toward him in anger.

He tossed the apple aside, slammed his foot down on the floor and caught her by the arms. The suddenness of his move surprised her. "I said, sit with me." He repeated firmly as he pulled her into his lap.

She struggled against his strength, "Let go, damn it. You can bully Aubrey, but you cannot bully me!"

"Do not be jealous of her, she is nothing." He continued to drone as he held her and she struggled against him on his lap.

"I am not jealous of her." She argued, still squirming.

"She does bear my mark." He tormented on.

"I know all about that mark on her, Rene." Mala said angrily as she fought him, managing to free an arm from his grasp.

"Pray let us take this action over to the bunk my dear, it has been a long time." He suggested referring to her wriggling in his lap.

"Surely you jest, you do not deprive yourself the pleasures of the flesh." She replied.

Black smiled up into her face as he held her, "True, m'amour, but I would have traded them all for you. My needs were never..."

He was suddenly caught off guard as Mala solidly cracked the palm of her hand across his face. Black slackened his hold on her and she was off his lap in an instant. When he stood to grab her, Mala dashed around the length of the table and made sure to keep it between them.

"Damn you, Mala!" Black exclaimed.

"Damn me? No Rene, damn you to hell! Of all the ships in this blasted harbor, why the hell did you have to take mine?" Mala shouted, pounding her fist on the table.

"Because you are on this one and I…need you." Black said softly.

Mala stopped her circling and stared at him. He saw the glimmer of surprise in her eyes before the mistrust and anger reappeared.

"Need? You bloody bastard! Have you any idea what I have had to endure all this time?" She finally hissed.

"Mala, I thought you were dead." He said ever so softly, his dark eye blinking slowly as he tried to reason her to calmness.

"Mon Dieu, Rene, I was dead!" Mala breathed in reply.

"For two years? Where the hell have you been?" He questioned with puzzlement on his face.

"Surviving! It is what I have learned to do best, you arrogant bastard!" Mala replied through clenched teeth as she swiped a tankard off the table angrily.

"But why have you not tried to find me?' He asked softly, undaunted by her outburst.

Black was surprised to see a look of pure malice shadow over Mala's face and was even more surprised to hear the deadliest tone he had ever heard her use, "Why the hell would I?"

He had been slowly inching his way around the table as Mala faced him off, but the last words stopped him cold. His heart sank and he felt as if he was dealt a staggering blow to his mid-section. The two captains met eyes for an extended moment. He had been so elated to see her, to hold her and now, she looked upon him with such hatred.

Mala began to move, intending to put some distance between them but Black lunged for her. Taking a firm hold of her arm, Black pulled her to him. She hit her hip hard against the corner of the table hard then her upper thigh as she fought to get free. Yanking her to him and then twisting her arm behind her, Black held her against him. He pinned her other arm tightly with his other hand across her mid-section.

"This was not what I had in mind for us, m'amour." Black whispered breathlessly from the battle.

"Go to hell, Rene." She spat as she struggled slightly. She was growing tired and Black knew it.

"If you persist, I will be left with no choice but to have you locked up. I need my rest and do plan to awaken. You, my dear, are very beautiful but very deadly to say the least and I would be a fool to lay down my head in slumber with you in this mood."

"Given the chance, Rene, I will cut out your heart. But then, you do not have one!"

Black closed his eye in defeat. He knew that he could not control her in this state of anger. Taking a deep breath, he whispered in her ear, "Very well, Mala. You have made the choice."

Brushing his lips on her temple, Black let his head rest against hers. Mala's mind and pulse raced. What was he doing?

Suddenly, she found herself moving forward as Black used her twisted arm to make her walk. At the door, he called out and soon the door swung open and a man appeared with pistol in hand.

"Get out of the way!" Black ordered in French. The man stepped aside as Black forced Mala to walk forward then followed them as they went below.

Chapter 21

Aubrey had been moved from the deck and taken below by Gibbs to an area in the hold where the barrels of fresh water were stored.

"This looks like a good place for you." He muttered as he tied her by the wrists with rope to the beams in the bulkhead.

"You be quiet now and do not go anywhere." Gibbs chuckled at her as he tested the ropes. Aubrey merely looked at him with worried hazel eyes.

"Maybe if you be very quiet, no one will know that you are here and we will even forget that you are down here."

She shivered uncontrollably at the thought of Beaufort coming into the area while she was imprisoned like this. The cut on her lip stung as she remembered her other encounters with Beaufort all too well. This was the first time he had ever struck her and it further worried her when she recalled Black's threat to give her to the frightening man.

As if reading her thoughts, Gibbs laughed again. Catching her face in his hand, he leaned close to her and said softly, "But Beaufort will find you when he is ready, he will be able to smell you."

Aubrey opened her mouth to scream and his hand quickly clamped down over her to silence her, "Chut Mademoiselle, I told you to be quiet. I do not want Captain Black coming down here at your cry then I would be punished for touching you."

Gibbs left her in the darkness and she listened as his boot falls went further and further away. Leaning back against the bulkhead, she was both distressed and angry at Morgan's change in attitude and alliance. A few moments before the entrance of Beaufort and Boulet in their cabin, Morgan had been softly proclaiming to protect her and that she was safe. Now, he had taken his place among the ranks of Black's men.

"How could you have been so blind? So stupid?" She whispered to the darkness in chiding to herself. "I thought that he was different. I thought that he was like…Jean Luc."

She heard the sound of boots on the floor coming near her and she held her breath hoping that she would not see Beaufort standing in those boots. She drew back as Morgan stepped into the light from the open hold door above. He held his hat in his hands and she noticed that he was well armed. Such a display of weaponry on him and the fact that another captain had come on board to take the ship was not a good sign.

"What rank do you hold now, Morgan? Was there a vote? Are you the quartermaster in the place of Deats? You never liked Deats anyway so that should make you very happy." She said stiffly.

"You never liked Deats either and you were correct in your feelings toward him. It is a wonder he did not take you against your will." Morgan said calmly. Aubrey regarded him with a wary eye as he turned his hat in his hands and stepped closer to her. "Please do not be frightened of me, Aubrey. I will not hurt you." The statement made her laugh and Morgan took in a slow deep breath.

"I cannot trust you, Morgan."

"Aubrey, you will need protection from his men. Since he already suspects us, I will claim you for your protection." Morgan began in quiet tones.

She reacted the way he suspected that she would. The fiery Irish woman exploded, "What would that prove, Morgan? That I belong to one of his men anyway? And you can do what?"

"I am not going to do anything to you. Christ Aubrey, you cannot presume to protect yourself against them. This is your prison right now and like this, you are at their mercy. No one would even hear you scream down here." He said as he moved closer to her and reached out a gloved hand to touch her face. He was dismayed when she moved to avoid his touch.

Her voice held the Irish brogue he knew well. "Ya will not be puttin' yer hands on me, Morgan Alcott. I am here to tell ya that I will kick ya if ya try. My legs are unbound and ya are dangerously close."

He stepped discreetly back, knowing that she would come through with her threat if given the chance. He wondered why she had not just done so instead of warning him of an impending attack. He took the warning as a ray of hope that she could be swayed to see things his way since she just did not understand what had led him to this point.

"Aubrey, please cooperate with me on this and I will talk to you about it back in the cabin. If you stay here, Black's men will have you for dinner and he will do nothing to stop them."

"Why Morgan? Why? Why have you taken a stand against Mala? You should have stood with Deats…" She argued with tears of anger in her eyes.

"There you go with false hopes of Deats again. Did you not hear what I said about him before? He cannot be trusted, mark my words, Aubrey. You do not know him as well as I do. But you know me! Christ, Aubrey, how many nights did you sleep safely with our bunks so close together? Did I bother you then? Did I try and force myself on you? Did I ever expect anything from you in return?" His tone was a mixture of anger and pleading.

"You did not tell me that you saw Black's mark. Why did you bring it out up there?" She asked. Her voice held hurt and the angry tears had given way to ones of desperation. "Let Black's men come then…perhaps they will kill me. Unless you wish to do so yourself."

"Good God, Aubrey, of course I do not want to kill you. Trust me, Aubrey, I..." He was interrupted by the sound of more boot falls coming toward them.

He turned to see Mala being escorted by two of Black's men. Aubrey saw the surprised look on Morgan's face when Mala was shoved into the hold. Casting a deadly glare at Morgan, she was tied like Aubrey a few feet away as Black strode up.

"Monsieur Alcott, please do not frighten, Irish."

Aubrey glared at him as he referred to her by yet another nickname. Black noted that this one struck a cord and he smiled at her reaction. He glanced away from her as Morgan began to speak in low tones to him. "This woman is mine."

Aubrey brought herself out to the full length of the rope that bound her with an exclamation of anger as she kicked at Morgan from behind. Her small booted foot connected soundly with the back of his upper thigh and he stumbled forward.

"You go to hell, Morgan!" She spat.

"Ouch, damn you!" He said angrily, whirling on her.

"Step closer to me, Morgan, so I can kick you properly." Aubrey growled as she dropped a fleeting glance at his crotch.

"Are you quite certain you still want this little Irish bitch? She means to severely injure you." Black said chuckling.

Mala set forth an angry string of dialogue in her own language, which she directed at Black then turned on Morgan saying in English, "How dare you go against me? I will cut out your heart for this!"

Morgan stepped forward toward the dark-haired woman. "Be careful Mala or I will dress a corpse in your clothing and hide it somewhere on the ship." His voice was so low that only Mala and Aubrey heard him.

Paling, Mala fell immediately silent. In all the time that she had known him, he had never threatened her. Aubrey looked from Mala to Morgan in shocked surprise, forgetting her own anger for a moment.

"Morgan, have you lost your mind?" Aubrey asked him, her voice a hoarse whisper.

"No, but if I do as I just said, she will. It is a superstition of her people." He replied ever so quietly.

Mala collected herself and was gracing him with the coldest and cruelest look he had ever seen from her. Looking directly into Morgan's blue eyes, she replied, "Will you be using your own clothing, Morgan? Because it is a dead man that I see before me now."

Black noticed the looks on the women's faces, but could not hear the words. Mala's look was absolutely venomous and he was pleased that it was directed to someone else for a change. After a moment, Black presented a condescending smile as he pulled at his glove, "Monsieur Alcott, will you accost both of my women?"

"You were gone and we picked her up. She is mine now. Release her to me." He said as he jerked his thumb over his shoulder towards Aubrey who flew into a rage again, kicking out at Morgan for a second time. This time, her boot just grazed off the back of his. He whirled on her again, grabbing her by the front of her shirt with one hand and pinning her against the bulkhead.

"Let me go." She said through clenched teeth as their eyes met.

Black stood and watched the scene in mild amusement. After his battle with Mala, it was good to see another man deal with a hellcat. He found himself somewhat intrigued by Aubrey now seeing her like this instead of the timid little girl he had pulled up into his arms to kiss that first day on the *Widow Maker*. Thinking of that, Black looked at Mala who was still glaring at Morgan. His dark eye took in the face that had haunted him for almost two years.

"Be still." Morgan was hissing into Aubrey's ear. She settled a bit as he hovered over her and he could feel her trembling as he pressed in close to her. "Let this happen and we will talk later, I promise. Please just trust me." He said so low and close to her ear that she barely heard him. He cast his eyes over her as she looked up at him.

"Perhaps I will give her to Beaufort." Black said from behind him in a thoughtful tone of voice. Morgan saw Aubrey blanch.

"I told you that she was mine." Morgan growled as he turned halfway to face Black.

"Just who is the captain here?" Black asked looking at Aubrey as she squirmed to free herself from Morgan's grasp. He did not see the man's eyes dart to look at Mala who met his blue eyes with her angry dark ones.

Aubrey was seeing a side of Morgan that she had never witnessed before. He was like a different man now, not the mischievous and fun-loving man she had come to know as her friend. Suddenly his comment he had made earlier came to light. *'You ruin my reputation as a pirate.'*

"Both women will be safe and unharmed right here for now. But..." Black clapped his gloved hands together twice as if in summons, "Come along Monsieur Alcott, let us go find the new quartermaster and meet in my cabin, we have a ship to run."

Aubrey looked at Mala to see a mask of seething anger, but she had remained quiet through the entire conversation. Without another look at the women, Morgan strode away into the shadowed hold on Black's heels as the new captain gave commands in French to two of his men waiting nearby. It was so quietly administered that neither of the women could hear it. The men looked at Mala and Aubrey then quickly removed themselves from their sight.

"Where did they go?" Aubrey finally asked Mala after extended silence.

"Not far, I am sure. He has probably stationed them between us and the rest of the men." Mala replied.

"What in the world has come over Morgan?" Aubrey asked after another stretch of silence.

"I am sure that Rene will protect me and I know he will not protect you." Mala said avoiding the question. Aubrey detected the note of doubt in Mala's voice.

"You know him far better than I do, what will he do with me?" Aubrey asked quietly.

"You may do well to cater to Morgan's whims...even if he is not the Morgan that you once knew. Let him have you if it will keep you alive and out of the hands of that idiot they call Beaufort. Judging by Rene's constant reference of him and your reaction, you may do well to consider which is the lesser of the two evils?" Mala's tone was flat and uncaring.

"Is that what you would do?" Aubrey asked angrily, glaring at her.

"Of course not."

"Then why do you suggest it of me?" Aubrey spat. Mala looked at the other woman for a moment and the two fell silent. Aubrey cringed at the realization that she had spoken so crossly with Mala.

The dark-haired woman shrugged at her expression, "Make good of Morgan now, Aubrey, because when I get free from here, he will be dead."

"Lovely, and then what will I do?" Aubrey asked sarcastically.

"Perhaps someone else will step forward, Robert maybe."

"Good God Mala, you take this all so...easily." Aubrey huffed.

Mala shrugged as her gaze returned to the empty entrance of the hold, "They are pirates and so am I."

Black slept so soundly that it was late afternoon before he awoke. He looked at the ceiling and saw the wooden timbers of the quarterdeck above. Feeling the subtle rocking of the ship, he listened to the creaking sounds and the water lapping along the hull. Had it all been a dream? The sinking of his ship, the prison, the trial? Black wondered as he sat up. He looked around the cabin, then frowned. The long table, the desk, they were in place but they looked...different. He stood up from the bunk then stared down at it. Mala's bunk. Mala's cabin. This was Mala's ship. Black looked out the quarter gallery window and found nothing but open sea. The new wood caught his eye and he wondered if it was damage from a battle. Was Mala in her cabin at the time? Could she have been killed?

Shaking the thoughts from his mind as she was obviously unharmed, a smile slowly appeared on his face as other thoughts assaulted him. He was on her ship and she was with him. His Mala! His thoughts drifted back to the conversation he and Morgan had as they headed out of town.

As they had walked some distance from town, Black had asked Morgan questions about Mala. How did she become captain? How loyal were these men, her crew? Is she as cruel as the stories are told of her? Morgan answered his questions then told Black of rescuing Aubrey Malone and Mala knowing of his mark on her. Black was amused with the responses. Mala was a surprising woman!

Prodded by Morgan's questions, Black explained his escape from prison with his men. He told Morgan about his plans to stowaway on one of the ships in harbor when he noticed Mala's ship in the distance. Only then did Black see Mala and her men disembarking from the longboat and he followed them to the general store.

"I need to meet my men at the Church Street safe house but I needed to talk to..." Black had paused when Morgan stopped in mid-stride to look at him in surprise and he asked, "What is it? Is someone coming?"

"No, tis the safe house, I heard the talk in the store of the escape and that some of the men were captured and shot on sight." Morgan told him. Black sighed then nodded. There was a silence between them again as they walked through the wooded area before Black broached the subject.

"I need your help, Mr. Alcott." Black said slowly. "Help me board Mala's ship."

Morgan stopped in mid-stride again as Black moved on a few paces before stopping himself and looking back. "Have you lost your mind? Turn against Mala?" Morgan asked incredulously.

"No, Mr. Alcott, just help me get on board."

"Captain..." Morgan began but Black raised his hand for silence.

"You must understand that I cannot let Mala leave here without me. I may not find her again."

"Captain..."

"Mr. Alcott, I am asking you for help. I am not interested in her ship or the crew. I just want Mala. I will board her ship and there would be a fight. Do you think she would give up her ship so easily, even for me? Mala may even be injured or, heaven forbid, killed. Do you want that? I certainly do not." Seeing that Morgan was listening to him, Black pressed on. "All I want is Mala. I have to board her ship to get to her and you can help me by seeing that no one is injured. That is all I ask."

"All? Do you have any idea what she would do to me for helping you?" Morgan asked in amazement.

"I can soothe her, you know that. I can help you but I need you to help me first."

Morgan looked at the man who had once been his captain. "Why did you let her go in the first place?"

Black sighed and looked at the ground. The pain hit hard in his chest at the reminder of the sight that had awaited his return. "I did not let her go. She was gone from the island when I returned for her. I had no idea that she was alive until the day when her ship passed us on the way to Bimini." Black looked up and met Morgan's blue eyes. "Please Morgan. All I want is Mala."

Morgan was surprised to hear the pleading tone in the captain's voice and did not miss the use of his first name as Black made his plea. Blue eyes stared at Black for a long time before Morgan asked, "You swear she will not be harmed?"

Black smiled at him, "What would I gain in that? I want her unharmed as well."

"She will fight you for taking her ship."

Black nodded solemnly. "Aye, that I know but that battle will be mine to overcome."

"Any bruises, any harm comes to her, Captain, and I tell you now, I will kill you myself." Morgan had told him with a deadly gleam in his blue eyes.

Black smiled and nodded. "Fair enough. But as I have said, Mala is all I want. I do not want her ship or her crew but, in the taking of them, I will have to assume the duties as the new captain. In truth, the only thing that interests me on that ship is your captain."

The two men stared at each other for a long time. Finally, Morgan had relented with a nod and Black felt relief wash over him. "Thank you, Mr. Alcott. Leave me here and return to your captain. She is expecting you unharmed and I did agree that you would return just as you are. Prepare for me for I will board before the dawn."

"Aye well, I may say you are welcome if she does not kill me first." Morgan grumbled as he shook Black's hand in agreement.

Black smiled and said, his tone more cheerful than it had been in nearly two years, "I will see what I can do for you there."

Black faced the empty cabin once again and took in everything. She had furnished and arranged the cabin very similar to his on the *Widow Maker*. He looked out at the sea once again then noticed the various jars and plants Mala had in her quarter gallery window. The medicinal herbs reminded him of why he had left her on the island to begin with and he abruptly turned away from the window to move to her desk. He saw a closed logbook on top of the desk and he opened it to the last entry made. He noticed that it was dated the day before. Glancing down the page, he caught his name. Interest peaked his curiosity as he sat at the desk and began to read the entry.

I found another one of those British bastards. I remember this one well. His pleasure was not only in the raping of Kohma but taking her last breath as well. He strangled her as he took her. Using a rope, I strangled the life from him just as he had strangled Kohma. I paid the whore 5 gold pieces to find the rope and tie his hands. Then I paid her another 5 gold pieces to forget she ever saw me or I would come back for her. With my dagger, she understood well. Their face and body is their next meal and I reminded her of that fact. Much like Yvette!

Mon Dieu! Rene is alive! I was so surprised and happy to see him today I nearly forgot my anger towards him. I heard while in the tavern that pirates escaped and that some had been found and killed on sight. I can only assume that Rene was one of those they search for so I had Morgan take him away to safety. Why do I still love him so?! Yet I would give up everything to be with him! Je t'aime, Rene. God's speed, m'amour, wherever you may be. Please Rene, wherever you are, s'il vous plait mon cheri, stay safely hidden!!

Black sat back in the chair and stared at the log entry. If this was how she felt about him, then why was she so enraged with him early this morning? He wondered as his gaze drifted to the bunk. They could have spent hours together as he had wanted, hoped for, then slept within each other's arms. He reread the log entry. Her proclamation thrilled him and now he was here on this ship with her.

Not finding answers there, Black moved away from the desk. He moved around the room, opening cupboards until he found where Mala kept her bottles of rum. Taking one down from the cupboard along with a tankard, Black poured himself a drink. He sat in the high-backed chair that Mala usually sat in and drank from his tankard, pondering over the morning's activities. Taking the remaining ten men he found near the safe house location, Black headed back to the harbor...and Mala's ship. His gaze roamed over the cabin that was very similar to his own. He thought of Mala and her anger. He was about to take another drink from the tankard when he stopped suddenly, the tankard close to his lips. A smile crept over his face as he slowly lowered the tankard to the table.

"If someone boarded my ship in the pre-dawn hours, I would be furious too!" Black muttered with smile into the empty cabin. His laughter filled the room as he rested his head on the tall back of the chair and contemplated his next plan of action with Mala.

Chapter 22

The day wore on and soon the afternoon sun was beating down into the latticework of the hold cover above. Aubrey retreated as far back into the shadows as she could to get out of the sun.

"I thought that you said Black would not leave us here long?" She grumbled.

"Oh, he is angry with me right now. It will take him until at least tonight when he gets lonely before he will change his mind." Mala said undaunted.

Aubrey rolled her hazel eyes, "Is that why you were in the cabin with him at first and now you are here? Why is he mad at you? My God Mala, you gave him the ship."

"I did not give him my ship!" Mala shouted angrily at her.

"You are getting loud." Came a scolding French voice from the direction of their guards.

"Ta gueule!" Mala spat back in reply.

"Do not tell me to shut up you bitch, I will..." He replied in English.

"You will do nothing because Captain Black will put a ball between your eyes." Mala shouted back.

Aubrey listened to the exchange and when both of them had fallen quiet she said easily, "Forgive me, Mala, I am sure there is some divine plan in your mind. There always is."

Aubrey decided that it was the heat that caused them to be at odds with one another and she fell silent, closing her eyes.

"Rene and I chose to disagree on a point—that is why I am here. As I said before, when he crawls into a cold lonely bunk, he will change his mind." Mala said easily.

Aubrey remained still, with her eyes closed. Cold bunk, warm bunk, it made no difference to her. She just wished she were in a bunk and comfortable. Her legs and her back hurt and her arms were numb.

"I am sure you gentlemen must be very thirsty over there in this hot place." Mala said suddenly. Aubrey's eyes snapped open, wondering what the other woman was up to now.

"Oui." One of the men replied from the darkness.

"All of this damned water, is there nothing good to drink on this ship?" The other man growled.

"Certainly there is. If you fix our bounds so that we can sit on the floor I will tell you where you can find an excellent keg of rum." Mala offered.

"Ya would put us on the floor then? What a lovely place to be with the two of them!" Aubrey said suddenly, her Irish accent pronouncing her disapproval.

"Oh be still Aubrey, they would not dare bother us. Remember the divine plan? Hush now and listen, you may learn something." Mala hissed.

Aubrey rolled her eyes and replied, "Oh yes, and then what happens when the dark dragon lord returns? How goes your plan then?"

Mala smiled at her and replied, "Fear not the dark dragon lord, little one. His flame can be easily extinguished."

"Aye verily so, but not by me." Aubrey replied.

"Verily so." Mala nodded. The two women broke into soft laughter.

"What is so funny?" Asked one of the men as he rounded the barrels to step before them.

"Nothing that would interest you." Mala said smiling.

"Where is this keg?" He asked.

"Where is your part of the bargain?" Mala countered.

"No tricks." He warned.

"Certainly not." Mala scoffed, batting her eyes as he adjusted the bindings. He grinned at his companion who approached Aubrey and she drew back in fear.

"Oh relax little one, I do not intend to call down the wrath of Cap'n Black for even a touch of the hair on your head." He growled. She looked at Mala who graced her with a smug look.

"The keg." The first man reminded when they had finished.

"Over there, under those sails." Mala directed with a nod of her head. "It is fine Jamaican rum."

Expressions of approval could be heard from the two as they retrieved the prize. Aubrey slid to the floor as the men left to return to their posts around the corner. The heat was oppressive and exhausting as she yawned and closed her eyes. Mala eased herself down as well now that the small bit of shade was on her side.

Drifting off into a twilight sleep, Aubrey dreamed of Jean Luc. In her dream, he leaned over her semi-reclining figure and whispered in her ear, "Trust me." As he drew even nearer, his body touching her, pressing against her, she heard Morgan in her dream, "Aubrey, please trust me."

Her eyes snapped open and she looked around. Remembering where she was, she looked to find Mala on her feet. It was then that she heard the sounds of someone coming and Aubrey scrambled to her feet as well. The heat of the late afternoon was pressing down on them. How had she managed to doze off? Aubrey wondered. She glanced at Mala and found her no worse for wear. Her thoughts were broken as another of Black's men came toward them with two plates of food.

"Dinnertime." He smiled. He glanced over his shoulder, "Cap'n Black ain't gonna be too happy when he sees them two."

"Why?" Aubrey asked.

"Out cold they are." He grunted as he knelt down to put a plate of food on the floor before her.

"Hmm, not much unlike yourself." Mala said as she drew back a booted foot and kicked the man soundly between his legs.

Aubrey flinched as the kick sent the man sprawling headfirst into the bulkhead near her. On impact, the unfortunate man's head made a sickening cracking sound. Food from the plate flew everywhere.

"Sweet Mary!" Aubrey gasped as she looked down at the man.

"Can you reach his dagger?" Mala asked with some urgency. Aubrey tried, but to no avail. She shook her head in sorrowful reply.

Mala exhaled loudly and said with a smile, "Oh well, it was good for a bit of entertainment."

"Entertainment? Sweet Mary Mother of Jesus, Black will kill the pair of us." Aubrey exclaimed.

"No, I think not." Mala replied as she retrieved a piece of bread from the floor.

"I think that the heat has affected your brain." Aubrey groaned as she slid back down to the floor.

The two of them fell silent, and although their part of the hold was now in the shade, the heat grew even more oppressive. Food was everywhere, the guards around the corner could be heard snoring loudly and the man on the floor drooled in his unconsciousness. Mala began to laugh and soon, despite her stress and fear Aubrey began to laugh also.

"Oh God, Black will kill us." Aubrey giggled in a little whiny voice that prompted Mala into even louder laughter.

In the distance, they heard Black curse in French. They fell suddenly quiet and both stood up from the floor. Black rounded the barrels and, with his hands on his slim hips, stepped into the late afternoon sunlight that was on his side of the hold, "How in the hell do you do that?" He asked Mala.

She smiled at him sweetly and asked with innocent eyes, "Do what, Rene?"

Black waved his hand around the hold, "The guards are dead drunk, and this one is face down in what was to be your dinner. Which I might add will be the last meal of the day."

"I have been hungry before." Mala replied with a nonchalant shrug. Not getting anywhere with her, Black turned a glare on Aubrey and stepped toward her making her draw back in fear.

"Did you contribute to this?" He snapped.

When Aubrey opened her mouth to speak, Mala's voice came out, "You are damn right she did."

"Oh God." Aubrey breathed as Black hovered over her.

"So Rene, why have you come to visit us?" Mala drawled, effectively moving his attention back to her.

"I came for you." He said huskily as he removed his dirk from its scabbard and stepped back to Mala. "Take him out of here, and the others." He commanded of the man who had come in with him.

The man nodded and dragged the guard away as Black reached out to grasp one of Mala's tied wrists. She watched his face as he cut her bonds while Aubrey watched them quietly. When Black was not looking at Mala, the woman allowed her feelings to show on her face. Aubrey saw the love and caring now as Mala caressed his face with her dark eyes. A lump formed in Aubrey's throat as Jean Luc and his love came to mind.

"I sincerely hope that you have settled now." He was saying quietly to Mala without looking into her face as he cut the other wrist free. Taking hold of Mala's arm, he turned his gaze upon Aubrey, "You will stay here tonight. He will be your guard. Rest assured he will not succumb to any little games or tricks. But then, I think I take the trickster with me." He said as he cast his eye upon Mala again. He pulled at her easily and she looked at Aubrey with knowing eyes as they left from her sight.

Aubrey sighed and slid back down to the floor as the man rounded the corner to stand where Black had stood. "I will put up with no foolishness, Mademoiselle." He told her before he moved away to take up his post.

Closing her eyes against the heat, she drifted off into sleep again. Her sleep was tormented by visions of the sinking of the *Gull* and the sinking of the *Widow Maker*. But the sight of Beaufort in her dream as he burst into the cabin caused Aubrey to start awake. The light cotton shirt she wore clung wetly to her sweat drenched body. She looked around in mild confusion, remembering with a sick feeling in the pit of her stomach that Mala was gone and she was alone down here. She closed her eyes again desperately fighting tears.

An eerie feeling fell over her. The feeling was further warranted when her foot struck against an immovable object in her stretching. Opening her eyes, she realized that a man was standing over her. Thinking of Beaufort, Aubrey gasped and tried to clamber to her feet but her aching muscles would not cooperate. She managed only to get to her knees. Strong hands clasped her by the shoulders as the man kneeled down before her.

"Let me go!" She cried out in alarm.

"Aubrey." Came Morgan's soothing voice and she ceased to struggle. "I brought you some water." He said softly. She watched him suspiciously as he produced a cup and poured water for her.

Taking it, she drank greedily. "Easy, you will make yourself sick." He warned taking it from her hands.

"What do you care?" She asked pulling it back.

"I do care." He replied tiredly. Looking around the area, he said, "I spoke to Black about you."

Aubrey exhaled deeply and threw the cup at him, some water left in the cup splashed over him. "What did I tell you?" She spat as she pushed him away and struggled to her feet.

He regained his footing before he fell and pointed a gloved finger at her and said in anger, "And what did I tell you?" She turned her face from him as she stood with her back against the bulkhead.

Morgan watched her for a few moments before he growled, "Damn you! You are so stubborn!" She cut her eyes to glance at him, but did not turn her face toward him as he moved closer to her and said in low tones, "You listen to me Missy, I will make Black release you to me whether you like it or not. Now I do not care if you ever speak to me or look at me again as long as you live, but at least I will be content in knowing that you are safe, and I will continue to keep you as safe as I possibly can."

Silence fell between them before he sighed and left, mumbling to himself. Aubrey slowly slid back down on the floor and sighed, closing her eyes once more.

Black escorted Mala to the great cabin. Opening the door, he allowed her to enter first. She glanced around and found everything as she had left it. Her bunk was rumpled partly from her drunken sleep the night before but she knew Black slept there as well for he looked more rested than when he had boarded her ship. Deciding not to dwell on that matter for now, she concentrated instead on the man with her.

Walking over to the corner of the cabin near the bunk, Black pulled back the dressing screen where behind it Mala kept her ornate tub. Her lips parted in surprise to find that it was filled with streaming water, ready for a bath. He smiled at her as she slowly walked to the tub and dipped her fingers into the hot water. Watching her, he was pleased with her reaction to his surprise gift for her.

"Just the way you like it, if my memory serves me correctly, mon coeur."

Mala lifted her gaze to meet his. Mon coeur, French for my heart. Her gaze filled him with hope and desire. Unable to resist any further, Black took her wrist and pulled her slowly to him. His pulse raced as she moved without resistance. He lowered his face to hers and pressed a soft kiss upon her lips. The kiss was tender and sweet as Mala leaned into him. His arms moved around her as he pressed her closer to him.

Suddenly she pulled away and looked down at the tub. Black frowned at her not sure what to make of the separation. He closed his eye and let out a slow sigh, he needed to cool his heels. When he spoke, his voice was strangely deep with emotion, "I will leave you to your bath and allow you privacy. Do not make any attempts to…"

"I will not." He heard Mala's soft reply when she cut him off before he could make any threats.

He watched her as she looked around to find all she needed on the small table next to the tub. With a nod, Black caressed the length of her arm with his knuckles before he turned and left the cabin. Mala stared at the water-filled tub but did not see it. His touch before he departed caused a ripple of desire within her. She closed her eyes and took a deep breath to control herself. Opening her eyes again, she glanced about the cabin and found she was alone. Quickly undressing, Mala stepped into the welcomed bath.

Aubrey could see that it was getting dark through the latticework of the hold opening above. She pulled herself to her feet out of tedious boredom and silence. With the sun gone, the air was now growing chilled.

"Monsieur?" She called hoarsely.

"Oui?" Her guard called back.

"I am cold and hungry." She said carefully.

He chuckled and stepped into view. "Le Capitaine said no food for you. You wasted your dinner there." She made a face and sat back down on the floor.

"But I did not waste it." She pouted quietly.

A rat scurried out of the darkness to snatch a piece of meat from the fallen tray. She gasped in alarm and stomped her foot to scare it away. The man laughed at her, "When you sleep tonight, they may come and nibble on you. Or perhaps Monsieur Beaufort will." The comment sent chills down her spine.

"Captain Black has ordered him to leave me alone." She retorted.

"For now, Mademoiselle, for now."

She drew a ragged breath as her mind working furiously, "Send for Monsieur Alcott." She said suddenly surprising herself with the request. She chided herself in her mind. Why did she ask for him? He had been unfaithful to Mala. How could she trust him? Then she thought of Beaufort—recalling the look in his eye in the cabin. Morgan was definitely the lesser of the two evils—if his offer had been genuine.

"My orders are for you to stay here the night." He said breaking into her thoughts.

"I want Monsieur Alcott." She ordered. "He is the one who has claimed me." She made a face in the darkness at her own announcement. As much as it pained her to do so, she was going to have to play a ruse again. Also for as angry as she was at Morgan, she prayed that it would not end up like the dangerous game she had played with Jean Luc on the *Widow Maker*.

"I do not care what you want. I have my orders from Capitaine Black. Sit down there and be quiet or I will put a gag in your mouth to silence your whining." The guard replied as he turned back to his post. Aubrey kicked at the food on the floor closest to her, trying to push it as far away from her as she could. She slid back down to the floor and drew her knees up close. Exhausted cold sleep overtook her and the fitful dreams plagued her again.

Chapter 23

In the galley, Black and Mala dined together at the captain's table. She knew that they could have easily dined in the great cabin but what Black was doing was showing his men that he claimed her. Mala could feel his gaze on her as she looked around the galley. She saw many of her men and they were watching covertly. Morgan sat with Robert away from other members of her crew and they were whispering in low tones. Robert seemed adamant about his opinion as Morgan seemed to stress his own.

Black followed her gaze when she continued to stare. Seeing that she was watching Morgan, he smiled as he remembered Morgan's words. *'Aye well, I may say you are welcome if she does not kill me first.'*

"You do not trust Morgan, mon coeur?" Black asked drawing her attention back to him. Her gaze was cold, reminding him of the cold stare she had given Deats as she held the pistol in his face. He smiled at her anger and Mala turned from him to look at Morgan once again.

"You need not fear Morgan's influence. He was just doing his job. He was protecting his captain."

From Mala's profile, Black saw her bottom lip drop slightly in surprise before she turned slowly back to face him. She graced him with an unbelieving look that Black laughed aloud, drawing the attention of those within the galley.

"Absolutely precious." He said as he raised his tankard to his lips, his gaze never leaving Mala's face.

"And exactly which captain would he have been protecting? His former or present one?"

"Depends on which of us is considered the former and which is the present?" He stated as he stood and offered his hand to her. "Well, I am finished here. Shall we depart?"

Mala did not move. She continued to watch him and ignored the extended hand. Black's smile grew as she asked, "So how did you manage to turn him?"

Black did not answer as he turned from her still smiling. His gaze met with Morgan's as he left the galley. Mala stood up and watched Black leave, her eyes narrowing. Ignoring Morgan as she hurried to catch up with Black, she missed the worried looks from both Morgan and Robert.

"Rene?" She called when she saw him heading toward the storeroom. "Rene? Damn it, answer me." Still he did not stop but continued his walk further below deck. "Rene, damn it, where the bloody hell are you going?"

Mala asked nearing the end of her patience. She could not see his smile as he turned the corner.

Turning the corner, Mala met darkness. She was near the smuggling cargo hold she knew but could not see to be sure. Suddenly there was a strike of flint and Mala could see Black light a lantern then turn the flame down low. As a reflex, she was immediately on her guard. Her eyes noted the dead-end of the corridor along with the sight of ropes and old sails strewn about the small area.

Black turned to face her making no other moves. Mon Dieu, but she is so beautiful! He thought as his gaze roamed over her face. After a moment, he held out his hand to her. At first, Mala did not move but watched him suspiciously. This time, however, he did not withdraw his outstretched hand but waited on her decision. Finally, with her heart racing, Mala took his hand and stepped closer. Black pulled her into his arms and placed a feathery light kiss upon her lips.

He frowned slightly as Mala stepped back from him. "Mala?" He questioned but she only moved to wrap her arms around his neck. Stepping closer to him again, he held her tightly and this time the kiss was full of the passion and memories of long ago. Mala breathed his name when he released her lips and smiled as he pulled at the strings of her shirt.

"Here?" She asked looking around. She could see his smile in the dim light.

"Of course, here. Why do you think we are here in the first place?"

"You rascal." She chuckled as she pulled her shirt from the waistband of her britches. Her shirt fell to the floor and she reveled in the feel of his hands on her. Black noticed his mark over her left breast as he lifted the medallion that hung heavily just above the valley between her breasts by a gold chain, gifts he bestowed upon her just over two years before.

"You kept these?" He asked in wonder.

"Of course, reminders of a time now lost."

Black looked up and caught a glimpse of the sadness he had noted in her voice before it quickly disappeared.

"But now is not the time for talking." Mala said softly as she lowered herself to the floor and went to task of removing her boots and britches.

Unable to control the passion engulfing him, Black began to undo his britches. Mala laughed softly and said to him, "You will remove your boots first, you big oaf!" Black chuckled and did as he was told.

Turning to her, Black found Mala standing naked before him in the dimly lit space. The look in her dark eyes was so intense with her desire for him that he thought he could not wait any longer. He had to will himself to be slow. His mouth took hers as their bodies molded together. He could feel her breasts on his bared chest and he moaned. Mala's arms tightened around his neck as she pressed deeper in the kiss. It had been so long for her that she could not hold to herself the emotions she had for this man. She loved him and for that, she could not deny him what she too craved. His moan was her undoing as she broke from the kiss, panting. Black quickly positioned their shirts open over the old sails and turned to her.

"We should do this in the cabin. My bunk is more comfortable." She said with a grin.

His dark eye roamed over her as he smiled and said huskily, "This is where I want us to be."

Her smile was soft and alluring as she lowered herself down and he followed closely over her. She whispered his name as his lips moved over her face and throat. She closed her eyes and reveled in his touch as he touched her everywhere and his lips seemed to follow. She gasped as his mouth took a nipple while he caressed and kneaded the other breast. Her arms held him to her as she moaned with pleasure.

"Oh Rene, must you do this to me." She said breathlessly as she shuddered with desire. His throaty laugh greeted her statement as his lips made a trail from one nipple to the other. With his hand free from caressing her breast, he moved it lower until he touched on the womanly softness of her.

She groaned loudly then called out his name as she arched under his touch. Finally he moved over her and she opened to receive him as he lowered himself over her. His lips found hers again and he drank deep the sweetness of her mouth. Her deep and ragged intake of breath as he entered her made him look at her with concern. But Mala smiled up at him and pulled his head down to hers for another kiss. Mala's meeting of each thrust thrilled him as she took him deep inside her. Faster and faster they moved until she arched her back with the violent shudder of climax. Her cry of pleasure was his undoing and within seconds he whispered her name just before he too roared his pleasure.

Neither moved as they floated back from heaven. Heaven? Closing his eye and tightly holding the naked Mala to him, Black thought, yes this is heaven. No other woman had ever pleased him as this one did. This was the woman his body needed, had craved for. He nuzzled her neck, her ear, her cheek, then kissed her mouth passionately. Still inside her, Black's heart skipped a beat as Mala moved her hips ever so slightly to take him deeper. He lifted his head to gaze lovingly into her eyes.

"You are now mine." He was thinking of Deats on board this ship with Mala all these many months.

Mala's smile was tender and soft as she said quietly, "I have always been

211

yours, Rene."

Black smiled remembering her log entry as Mala lifted her lips for another kiss of which he obliged her. After a time and another meeting in heaven, Mala offered, "Shall we continue this in the comfort of my bunk?"

"Only if you allow me the pleasure of making love to you all night." Black said, smiling down at her.

"But of course, Monsieur Capitaine. I had no intentions of doing anything else." Mala replied in the sweetest French that Black had ever heard her say. He stared at her for a few moments before he took her face in his hands and placed the most tender of kisses upon her lips. Mala ached for more and received it for Black who was not ready to move away from her as yet.

When he lifted his head and looked down into her beautiful face, Mala's eyes were closed. He continued to watch her, taking in every inch of her face, until she slowly opened her eyes. She gave him a soft smile as her gaze roamed over his face. With a heavy sigh, Black stood up then took Mala's hand and helped her to her feet.

As they slipped into their britches and shirts, he shook his head slowly, "Mon Dieu, Mala! You are a witch!"

"No Rene, only an enchantress." She reminded with a smile as she walked away carrying her boots. His deep chuckle made her turn slightly and bestow upon him a most provocative smile. He made to follow but she gestured to the lantern.

"Put out the lantern, you simpleton!" He looked back and chuckled. Glancing back to Mala, he saw her turn the corner. As he doused the lantern, he looked to the door that led into the cargo hold and smiled before he followed her.

Topside, Morgan watched as Black and Mala made their way across the main deck towards the stern. He was surprised to see that each held their boots in one hand and held the other's hand with the free hand. Morgan also noticed with a smile that neither had bothered to tuck in their shirts as he remembered Black's words. *'All I want is Mala.'*

High above, the ship's bell tolled for the dogwatch. Aubrey opened her eyes and peered up sleepily at the hold. A thick fog undulated in the light of the torches on the main deck. She shivered and pulled herself into a tighter ball as she sat with her back against the damp bulkhead. Just as she was drifting off once more, the guard stepped up and grasped her by the arm.

"Debout."

Aubrey struggled to her feet, gasping in fear as he had so abruptly startled her out of napping. She flew into self-defense immediately. Crying out in alarm, she tried to kick at his legs.

"Be still!" He hissed as he cut the ropes that bound her.

"Now, let her go." Came Morgan's stern voice from behind them. The man released her immediately.

Aubrey looked to see Morgan in the faint light reflected on the fog above as he stepped closer to her. He held his pistol in his hand and he jerked the weapon at the man, commanding him silently to move away from her. The man did so obligingly. Then Morgan reached out with his free hand to grasp Aubrey by the wrist and pull her to him forcefully.

"She will be detained here no longer." He growled at the man as he put away his pistol and stroked her hair with his gloved hand. Aubrey was numb of mind and body and could do no more than stand shivering. "How are you?" Morgan asked.

"Tired." She replied weakly.

"Come on." He said as he pulled her away and past the guard.

"Le Capitaine will be angry that you have taken her." The guard warned.

"As I have told him before—she is mine." Morgan replied firmly. He led her to their cabin and opened the door. Easily pushing her inside, he followed her and shut the door.

"I know you are angry but do not argue with me tonight." He said quietly as he pushed her gently to her bunk.

The comment earned him a scowl, but she was too tired and too relieved to be out of her prison to argue with him. She eased herself onto her back then turned on her side, curling into a ball. Morgan sat on her bunk and watched her for a few moments. With eyes closed, Aubrey laid in silence, shivering violently as her teeth chattered.

"Here, drink some more water." He commanded quietly.

Aubrey sat up and took the offered cup, sipping at it slowly and watching him with wary eyes. Once she had emptied the cup, he took it from her and put it aside. She lay back down, drawing herself up once more. Ever so carefully, he caught her by the ankle. She started at the touch and pushed her leg out as if to kick at him.

"I am just taking off your boots. You need to get dry and warm." He told her.

With an uncertain frown, she laid still and allowed him to pull off her boots. Pulling a blanket up over her and tucking it in tightly around her body, he spoke to her softly, "You and Mala do not understand why I have done what I have done. As I said before, I will continue to protect you with the same conditions we have always known unless you choose otherwise. But in the face of these men who have come aboard, you must at least pretend that we have more."

"M-m-mala hates-s-s you, M-morg-g-gan. She is g-o-oing to k-k-kill you-u-u when s-s-she gets the chanc-c-ce." She said through chattering teeth.

"Well, if I must die, I would consider it an honor to die by her hand." Morgan said smiling as he reached out and easily stroked her hair. "I know that this is difficult for you to understand and accept. But I..."

"D-do not t-t-talk to m-m-me. Leave m-m-me alo-o-one." She said tiredly.

Morgan exhaled deeply and ran his fingers through his hair. Much to her surprise, he grabbed her up by the arms and hissed, "Listen to me."

He saw the fright in her eyes as he held her suspended there and he exhaled again, closing his eyes to regain his composure. When Morgan spoke to her again, it was as if to force her to understand. "He was going to come on board anyway, Aubrey. He was coming for Mala. When I took him to the outskirts of town yesterday in Charlestowne, he very nearly begged me to help him get on board. He did not want any bloodshed, he did not want any problems. He—only—wanted—Mala." The last four words were spoken slowly and firmly. Aubrey looked at him in silence as he continued to hold her. She seemed to be thinking over the information he had given her.

"Let me go." She finally said, struggling slightly in his grasp until he put her gently back down upon the bunk.

She curled tightly onto her side facing away from him. Stroking his hand over her shoulder, he sighed deeply again. He remained by her side until she drifted back into exhausted sleep. Looking over her shoulder, he noted that her lips were still blue from the chill of her prison. Carefully he put his own blanket over hers then quietly left the cabin.

It was nearly dawn and Black could see the skies lightening up on the horizon as he gazed out of the quarter galley window. Already dressed and ready for the day, he poured himself a cup of water and sat at the table facing the sleeping figure of Mala. His gaze roamed up and down the body under the covers and a smile slowly appeared upon his face as he remembered how well he had become reacquainted with that body and the woman. Mala had surprised him with her need to touch him. Not that he would ever complain, but she did not let him sleep much and even went so far as to remind him that he was the one who suggested making love all night. Black's gaze fell on her face and the serenity he saw there made him wonder what hardships she had faced since he had left her on that island.

The island? He knew now what happened on the island from Captain Alexander himself. He thought of the stories he had heard of the woman captain of the *Enchantress*. How she would kill on a whim, or boldly run alongside a British naval ship then blast it to the bottom of the sea, or her penchant to kill British officers in broad daylight. He remembered how she followed the one officer into the tavern in Charlestowne and how she flew into a rage with Deats – even to point her pistol at him and in such close range! He thought of his conversation with Morgan about how she became the pirate that she was now. His brows knitted together as he wondered why she had become so deadly.

His reverie was broken to the present as he noticed Mala seemingly having a nightmare. He recognized that she spoke in her native language but he also recognized names from those of the villagers when he had left her behind. She spoke the name of the medicine woman, some of the warriors, and the chief's name. With a frightened tone in her voice, Mala called out softly, "Baccus."

Suddenly Mala sat up in the bunk. The sheet fell from her, exposing her to the waist. Black stood up and moved to the bunk, ignoring the sight of her although quite pleasing. He could tell she was still dazed from the dream as she glanced around her, eyes glistening with unshed tears. He carefully sat on the edge of the bunk but when she focused on him, he noted that she looked at him with what seemed to be hatred.

"Are you all right? You were having a nightmare." He asked as he moved to touch her face. Mala avoided the touch and laid down, turning her back to him.

"I am fine." She answered curtly.

Black stared at her bewildered until he remembered her log entry, *'I was so surprised and happy to see him today I nearly forgot my anger towards him.'* What anger? Why was she angry? Suddenly he knew where he could find some answers and without a word, Black left the cabin.

Mala glanced around and found she was alone. Only then did she allow the tears to fall. "Oh, Baccus." She whispered as she turned on her side to cry in earnest.

Black asked for Morgan's whereabouts but he was referred to a man named Robert Bates. Approaching the quarterdeck where Black awaited him, Robert was wary.

"You asked for me, Captain?" Robert inquired, hesitating on the title. Black noticed the hesitation and smiled knowingly, to be expected from the crew when one takes over another captain's ship.

"You are Mala's…?" Black began, leaving the question open.

"Second Mate, Robert Bates."

"Ah, then Mr. Bates, I was looking for Mr. Alcott this morning and hear that he is sleeping in."

"Aye sir, he asked if I would, ah, cover for him."

"And what time would he make an appearance?" Black asked watching him intently. Robert hesitated looking at the dawn breaking and knowing that it would be several hours yet.

"He said that it would possibly be the next watch."

Black raised a brow and put a gloved hand to his chin in a thoughtful gesture. "Umm, that late?"

Robert stood motionless and watched this man. Morgan had tried to tell him at length about the relationship between this man and his captain. He had not watched them together the evening before because Morgan was prattling about Captain Mala killing him before he could talk to her, a point Robert wholeheartedly agreed. If Captain Mala came anywhere close to Morgan Alcott, he would not see another second of the day or night.

Black broke into Robert's musings, "Very well, have Mr. Alcott see me as soon as he about."

"Aye sir." Robert replied and watched as Black left the quarterdeck. Glancing at the helmsman, Robert noticed that it was someone he did not know, one of Captain Black's men.

Chapter 24

Leaving the quarterdeck, Black headed in the same direction as he had led Mala the night before. Opening the door to the cargo hold and stepping in, he looked to the area where he and Mala had made love. His smile could still be seen as he lit the lantern near Deats.

"Did you enjoy your evening? I certainly did." Black greeted.

He was graced with a glare from the Scotsman who could not answer because his mouth was covered with cloth. Deats had heard the two lovers and had a difficult night knowing that Black had Mala again. How often he had tried to coax his captain into more than a captain/quartermaster relationship. But Mala would have nothing of that.

Black removed the gag from Deats, saying, "A conversation should really be with two talking people, n'est-ce pas?" The Scotsman said nothing. Not displeased with the man's behavior, Black continued, "I think I could successfully rid all memory of you where Mala is concerned. After her response to me, all night..." He paused to smile. "I would say you have not been pleasing your captain at all."

"I told ye before, Mala will no'..." Deats started, his accent thick with anger.

"Spare me." Black said lifting his hand to halt the Scotsman's words. "Mala is a very passionate woman. Please do not tell me again that you had not enjoyed her in my absence. If not you with her in her bunk, then I must assume that Morgan has..."

"Morgan!" Deats growled out and remembered the many times he would go to Mala's cabin to find Morgan Alcott already there.

"Well from what I received last evening, Mala wants more than what you both have been offering." Black gloated. The room was silent as both men stared at one other.

"Did she ask aboot yer late arrival on yer promise?" Deats asked.

Black's smile widened as he replied, "We did not do much talking, actually. We were ...too busy with other things."

Deats' jaw tightened in the face of the man's self-satisfaction and arrogance. Black was definitely going to die for this, the Scotsman thought. Surely he could think of something that would wipe that smile off his face. The hold grew quiet again as neither man spoke.

Finally, Deats spoke up, "Well, tis good that the village was no' brought up. Mala rally hates ta discuss what happened during that dark time in her life. The last man ta mention that villages were burnin' under the hands of renegade British, Mala tossed overboard." Deats was gratified to see that the smile was not as big as before.

The mention of the village brought the pain back. In Black's mind, he saw again what he and Jean Luc had found when they returned for Mala. All those graves, all the destruction. He searched the graves because some had crosses with names on them, looking for Mala's. He looked in the destroyed village for any sign of Mala or her body. Jean Luc had questioned who might have buried the bodies but Black could not think past the reality that Mala could not be found.

For months, Black was a man possessed. His temper flared over the smallest infraction. Jean Luc had to finally ask to speak his mind and he spoke volumes, "Do you think Mala would have wanted this from you?"

Black had exploded in reply. "She probably died thinking I was never coming back for her! Mon Dieu, I could not even find a trace of her! It was as if she was never there!"

Black was brought back from his memory as he vaguely heard the smug Scottish drawl, "She willna hear of it. She will no' even talk aboot it with me anymore and twas I who helped her get off that island." Deats paused slightly before adding with a bowed head, "After we finished buryin' the dead, of course."

"You took her from the island?" Black asked surprised for he had thought John Alexander had taken her away.

"Aye, she grew tired of waitin' on ye. She had enough of death and was ready ta leave with anyone who arrived."

Before Black could comment further, there was a sound at the door. One of his men had shown up to guard the door. As Black turned to leave, Deats reminded him, "Remember, she will no' talk aboot what happened. It upsets her ta much ta think of how the villagers suffered durin' that raid and how she dinna lift a finger to help them."

"She would be dead now if she had." Black said almost to himself.

"True, Captain, but does that lessen the guilt she felt and still feels? Mala is a fighter, a survivor. For her ta just watch and no' do anythin'..." Deats stopped when Black walked away not wanting to hear more.

"Gag him." The captain growled to the guard and left. As the man replaced the cloth, Deats was still smiling.

Mala realized that Black could return any minute and did not want to answer any of his questions, so she dressed and went up to the forecastle to look out at the open sea ahead. She had to clear her head of the disaster that seemed to continuously plague her and leave her drained.

Leaning on the railing of the quarterdeck, Black watched as Mala crossed the deck to the forecastle. When she merely stood and watched the open sea, he wondered aloud, "What is she doing there?"

Timmons had watched his captain as well and answered, "The Captain usually goes up there in the mornings. She says it clears her head."

Black was reminded of her nightmare and wondered if that was what she meant by clearing her head. Suddenly he straightened as he noticed three of his men approaching the forecastle.

Timmons caught his move and said in an effort to calm Black, "The Captain can take care of herself well enough, sir."

"I know but tis my men I am worried about." Black replied as he continued to watch. Fortunately, he did not catch the smile on Timmons' face.

Mala's mind was so far away that she did not hear the three men approach her from behind. She turned to her left as someone tapped hard on her left shoulder and found three of Black's men facing her with smirks on their faces.

"Well, look what we have here, mes amis. What is your name, girl?" The tall one said, looking up and down and circling Mala as if he was appraising his prize. "My name is Thomas Beaufort, this Michele Boulet, and that is Martine LaVoie."

Mala let nothing show on her face as the name, Beaufort, registered in her mind. So this was the one that frightened Aubrey? She stared at him as she contemplated her options.

"Do ye think the Cap'n will let us taste this one, Thomas?" Boulet asked eyeing her greedily.

"Of course, he will." Answered LaVoie, confidently. He even licked his lips as if he could already taste her sweetness.

"I think not." Mala replied with disdain evident on her face as she looked at each man in the eye. She made to step away but the biggest of the three, Beaufort, stepped in her way.

"We are not finished with you, girlie."

"Yes, you are." She replied with a smile that held no warmth at all.

"Oh, if she ain't got high airs about her, Thomas." LaVoie said.

"Tis fine with me. I like them with a little fire." Beaufort replied trying to grab her arm.

Mala easily dodged the gesture and stepped around the big brute. She did not want a confrontation so she went quickly down the forecastle steps. The three big oafs, of course, did not take the hint and came after her.

"Damn it!" Black swore as he made his way to assist Mala.

Timmons smiled and shook his head, "She can handle them." He said aloud but no one was there to hear him.

Beaufort grabbed Mala's shoulder and spun her around. "Here now, girl, we were trying to be friendly but we could be rough if that is what you like."

"But of course you can." Mala stated condescendingly as she turned to leave, dismissing him.

Beaufort grabbed her arm and made to pull her to him when Mala turned to face him, her free arm swung around and caught him across the cheek. The force of the blow and his unawareness of it caused him to drop to the deck. However, for a man of his size, Beaufort was on his feet in an instant and a dagger in his hand. Mala had anticipated the move as Beaufort faced her. The big man slashed out but missed his target as she easily stepped back from his reach.

Glancing briefly to his companions, he saw that their attention was drawn behind her. Looking up, he saw Black taking quick strides to join them. He smiled at the thought of the retribution she would face for her insolence in hitting him.

Mala, who had been watching every move Beaufort made, noted the look behind her and knew who it would be. She spoke softly and calmly to gain the man's attention, "Because you are one of Rene's men, I will not kill you this time. But that is the only reason."

Black heard her as he approached and said to Beaufort, "Put that away." Beaufort looked at him surprised that Black would speak roughly to him when it should have been to this impertinent girl. "This one is mine." Black stated simply as he took Mala's arm to guide her away. Mala's eyes never left Beaufort's face.

Enraged that she would not be punished for her behavior and embarrassed in front of his friends, Beaufort blurted out without thinking, "But you have the other one!"

Black cringed inwardly knowing Mala's jealousy. Instead he was surprised when Mala took a step towards Beaufort. Black pulled at her arm but she asked ominously, "And what concern is that to you?"

Beaufort opened his mouth to reply but halted when Black's hand went to his pistol in a silent threat. His friends took each arm and guided the angry Beaufort away.

"None! He has no concerns!" LaVoie said quickly while Boulet said at the same time,

"Come on, Thomas. We have work to do."

Black looked to Mala and found her watching the three until they disappeared below. She then turned her unfriendly eyes to him. "There is a storm ahead, so do not sink my ship while I am having breakfast."

Black stood dumbfounded as he watched Mala leave for the galley. She was angry that was certain from the look he saw in her eyes but she did not say anything.

"Mon Dieu, I will never understand that one!" He muttered as he went back to the helm, shaking his dark head in confusion. He looked ahead and saw the dark clouds low in the horizon. She was right, there was a storm brewing ahead. Rubbing a hand down the length of his face, Black let out a long sigh and thought to himself, if he did not take care, there would be one hell of a storm here on the ship!

Mala entered the galley and found a good many of her men within. At least some of the routine did not change. When her men saw her, they beckoned her over to their tables.

"Ho, Cap'n!" Jordan bellowed. He stood and offered his seat to his captain as he moved down the bench. "Cap'n, why are you allowin' this on your ship?" He whispered.

"I am allowing this only because I need a holiday." Mala answered with a warm smile and getting some delighted chuckles, in reply, "When I decide to take my ship back, rest assured, you will all know about it."

"To the Captain!" Jordan toasted and the men in the galley raised their cups.

For nearly a half an hour, the galley was filled with cheerful bantering, an unusual display given the circumstances. Mala ate her breakfast in relative peace. Every now and then, someone would slap her on the back over something said and laugh that Mala would have to catch herself before she choked on her food.

It was no wonder that no one bothered to notice the three men who entered the merry galley. Beaufort was still smarting from the embarrassment earlier and his two companions had not been able to soothe his ruffled feathers. Seeing that Black was not in attendance, Beaufort decided to retrieve some of his lost dignity. He walked up to the table where Mala sat followed by his reluctant comrades.

"Do you not have work to do, girl?" He sneered at Mala.

"Not at the moment." Mala replied, not looking from her breakfast.

He made to grab her arm but his friends pulled him back when the crew of the *Enchantress* stood up in unison to defend their captain.

There were several uneasy moments when the men seemed to stare down each other. Willie even appeared at the doorway brandishing a butcher knife stained with the blood of whatever meat he was cutting. Mala let out a loud sigh as she calmly finished her drink, wiped her mouth with her napkin, then stood up to face Beaufort.

"Either have a seat or leave. I will not tolerate your bullying on my ship." She told him calmly.

"This is no longer your ship." He stated with a yellow-toothed grin.

"Oh but you are so very wrong, my friend. This is my ship and it will always be my ship. I am only allowing your captain to play master for a time. But when I tire of the game..." Mala let the words trail off and added a shrug of indifference.

"You are not so bold, little one." Beaufort stated in his effort to maintain his upper hand. "The Captain can toss you aside at any time. Ask the Irish bitch about being put aside."

Mala graced him with a smile and a bored look. "It has been done before."

Looking over at the men of the *Enchantress*, Beaufort sneered, still trying to keep the upper hand, "What kind of men are you? A crew who would choose a woman as their captain? Do you let a woman decide your future? Have you no backbone?"

Mala watched as Beaufort rudely looked her up and down. Undaunted by his lewd perusal, she merely smiled at the brute. Waving his arm in her direction, he bellowed, "Behold, the captain's new whore! Do your men win arguments by their performance in bed?"

Her men were outraged and the grumbling behind her told her so as Mala replied, "Actually, I am very good in bed. Unfortunately, you will never know just how good."

She turned to leave by going around the offensive man but Beaufort stepped into her path and Mala stopped. Still smiling, she said calmly to the man, "As I told you before you thick-headed buffoon, the only reason you live now is because you are one of Rene's men and he only has a few that he can call his."

Beaufort was livid at the name she used for him and heard nothing else beyond that. Ignoring the fast-reddening anger on Beaufort's face, Mala moved to pass the man. He grabbed her wrist to twist it around to her back but with her free hand, Mala punched him in the stomach then she brought her knee up to hit his face as he doubled over. Beaufort released her wrist and steadied himself by placing a hand on a nearby table. Her knee connecting to his chin made Beaufort's mouth close with an audible 'clomp.'

Mala stood her ground as she awaited his next feeble attempt. Touching his face with a shaky hand, Beaufort drew it away to see blood. Now his lip and tongue were bleeding. Beaufort's companions moved to help but he growled, "No, she is mine!"

Morgan stepped into the galley, surveying the room and immediately felt the tension. He saw Mala confronting the big man called Beaufort and he saw the crew of the *Enchantress* standing ready to fight. Stepping between Mala and Beaufort, he found that it was a tight squeeze since the two combatants stood closely together. Morgan took a chance and turned his back on Mala.

"Ah, Morgan." She sneered.

He ignored the tone as he looked up at Beaufort and said, "I do not think Captain Black would appreciate your interference with this one."

"She presumes much." Beaufort growled angrily still watching Mala.

"And she will kill you outright." Came Black's deep voice from the doorway.

"She has no weapons!" Beaufort defended as he continued to eye Mala who had not moved.

"Oui!" Black growled as he grabbed Beaufort's arm and swung him around so the man was facing him. "She had none yesterday when we boarded her ship and she killed a man! Mon Dieu, look at you! Now sit down!" Looking around the galley, Black barked out, "All of you! Sit down!" Everyone sat back down except for Beaufort and Mala as she stood glaring at Black.

"She plans to take back her ship." Beaufort told him.

"Of course she does, I would if I were in her place. Now, better be about your duties, Monsieur Beaufort." Black stated as he watched Mala.

Beaufort stood his ground, glaring at the dark-haired woman. His companions had to once again grab his arms and pull him away. Jerking his arms from their grasps, he turned to Black. "We came in here for breakfast. I suppose the food is worth eatin'."

Seeing Willie from the corner of her eye, Mala stated with a chilling smile, "You should try the eggs with the peppers on it." The crew of the *Enchantress* laughed over the hidden meaning behind her words.

Giving Beaufort one last baleful glare, Black took Mala by the arm and guided her to the back table. When they sat down, she said quietly, "I do not need your help, Rene."

Black saw the controlled anger in her eyes and replied in a tone that denoted his own anger was in check, "Indeed, but you have it anyway."

At the first sound of Black's voice in the doorway, Morgan inwardly groaned. He had hoped to talk to Mala first and get her to understand his part of the boarding. Instead he sat at the table with the rest of the crew of the *Enchantress*.

Mala glared at Black as he seated himself to her left. He watched her as she rolled her eyes then looked around the galley. Of course, she did not need his help. But it irritated him that he was not a part of her life. He studied her face as she continued to look around, refusing to look at him. After being separated for a year on the request of a friend then thinking she was dead for another year, Black could only marvel at the fact that she was beside him this very moment.

Breakfast was unusually quiet while Mala sat watching Black covertly as he stabbed at his meal in anger. Beaufort glared at the dark-haired woman while his companions tried to soothe his hurt feelings yet again. The few men of Mala's crew spoke in muted tones as they eyed Beaufort and his companions as well as watching over their captain.

After his breakfast, Beaufort noisily left the galley, his tankard falling to the floor. The other occupants in the galley watched as Beaufort stormed out followed by his two friends.

"I am going back to the cabin." Mala announced as she made to stand.

Black caught her arm and said quietly, "Do not engage Thomas into a fight, Mala. I do not want to punish you in front of the crew, your own men."

Mala merely stared at him. She pulled her arm free of his grasp, which he released easily, and excused herself graciously. He watched as she left the galley and sighed at the thought of the hot-tempered Beaufort and his Mala confronting each other on a continuous basis. He could let Beaufort off at the next port but he needed him here because his gruff manner could help in keeping Mala's men in line. The other alternative was to... No! Mala was not leaving his side!

Mala stepped out of the galley and when she was out of sight of everyone, she leaned against the wall closing her eyes. This Beaufort was going to be a problem. Aubrey expressed her fear of the man and Mala now understood why. She would have to be on her guard with that loud-mouthed fool roaming about her ship. Anything happens to her ship because of that idiot Beaufort, Mala thought to herself, then she would take it back from Rene Black.

With a tired sigh, she headed down the corridor. Suddenly as she turned a corner, the air was knocked out of her when she was slammed against the wall. A vise-like chokehold was around her throat and, with blurring vision, Mala looked up to find Thomas Beaufort's face close to hers.

"Well, whore, tis time you were taught your place."

"Have a care Monsieur Beaufort, your life may well depend on it." Mala warned despite the chokehold.

Tightening his grip around her throat, Beaufort leaned close to her body so she could not use it against him. Cupping a breast and, with his foul breath nearly suffocating her, he said to her, "He cares nothing for you just as he cared nothing for her."

"If you want to live, I..." She started but his grip tightened even more. She pulled at his arms as she gasped for breath.

"I will live, bitch, but you will not. At least not long after I have had the pleasure of your only use on board this ship."

Mala closed her eyes to focus on what devices she had at hand. Suddenly the grip slackened and she felt herself falling. She opened her eyes to find that Beaufort still had his hand around her throat but his grip was not strong, yet strong enough to bring her down with him. Thinking the man meant to take her here and now, she yanked her head back to be released then felt a hand take her arm. Flinging herself away from the hand, she scrambled off of Beaufort and against the wall, ready for the attack.

Black stood before her, his pistol in hand. He extended his hand to help her up, giving the unconscious Beaufort a sour look. Mala looked at him, the pistol in hand, his extended hand, then at Beaufort. Sighing, Black withdrew his hand and tucked the pistol back in his waistband.

"Are you in the habit of attacking your own men?" Mala asked.

Black grunted in disgust, "Not usually, but he is beginning to irritate me."

"Then be rid of him." Mala said as she stood up.

"As you so eloquently put it earlier, I have only a few men with me." He said mockingly.

Glaring at him, Mala said tightly, "I can take care of myself, Rene."

Stepping over the sprawled Beaufort, Black spun around to face her and snarled, "Of all the things I do know about you, Mala, taking care of yourself is on the top of the list!"

Getting an angry glare from her, Black turned away. Heading down the corridor, he growled over his shoulder, "You could just say thank you."

Mala smiled slightly as she watched him round the next corner heading for the great cabin. In the quietness of the corridor, she said softly, still smiling, "Why just say thank you."

Chapter 25

Mala had returned to the cabin soon after Black had. She watched him pour himself a drink then seat himself at her desk. Leaning against the door and staring at him, she waited to gain his attention. "Merci, Rene." She said softly when he finally looked up.

For a long moment, Black looked at her before he nodded in acknowledgment. "Thomas is rather sadistic in his own aggressive way, Mala, so I would suggest that you stay clear of him. I know you are well armed with or without weapons but I would feel better knowing that you would avoid the man."

"Avoid him. On my own ship." She said with a reproachful laugh.

"Mala..." Black gave her an annoyed look. He knew and hated that tone.

"Then give me my weapons." She said moving from the door to lean against the table, placing her hands on the flat wooden surface.

"No. The urge to use them would be too much for you to resist. To punish you over the death of a crewmember is not something I would like to order."

"Rene..." She started but he held up his hand.

"I am firm on this, Mala." His gaze held hers as he maintained his stand on the matter. Mala looked away first, which surprised him. He raised a brow as he watched her move to look out the window.

"Jean Luc was not among your men..." Mala was saying then looked at him when he emitted a low growl. "What happened to him, Rene?"

"Why do ask about him?" He asked quietly looking at her.

Mala was surprised at the look of suspicion on his face. She turned slightly and asked with concern, "What do you mean why do I ask? He is my friend, your friend..."

Black sat back brusquely in the chair. Mala turned to face him fully and asked, "Rene, where is Jean Luc?" He sighed deeply but did not reply. "I know he replaced Jacques as your quartermaster. So where is he?" She pressed on.

"We had a battle of sorts on the *Widow Maker* and..." Black shrugged not wanting to go into the matter. If Mala knew that the 'battle' was over Aubrey Malone, then what? Her anger and jealousy would flare up and he did not want that. What he wanted was right here standing at the quarter gallery window. He wondered if Aubrey had shared any of her experiences on the *Widow Maker* with Mala and if so, how much information. His gaze shifted from Mala to the top of the desk as he thought of his punishment for Jean

227

Luc, his best friend.

Mala watched Black for a few moments. She was sure that this 'battle' was the part Aubrey had mentioned to her while they sat on the beach outside of Charlestowne. She was not sure of what to make of Black's shrug but decided to wait and see.

When he glanced up, he found that she had perched herself on the ledge of the quarter gallery window, looking out at sea. Now with her eyes closed, she sat quietly with her arms crossed and her legs stretched out before her. Black had to smile for she looked so beautiful at that moment to him. His gaze roamed over her as she sat in the morning sun reminding him of a cat sunning itself.

A knock at the door interrupted the serene moment. Mala turned her head to look at the door then turned her gaze to Black who was still watching her. When she looked at him, he smiled as he bade entry. She was granting him charge for now.

Morgan entered and slowly shut the door. He hesitated slightly as he shut the door when he saw Mala in the cabin. Black watched them with amusement. Mala's dark eyes narrowed when their gaze met then she slowly turned her head back to watch the sea. Morgan's eyes dropped to the floor as he took a deep breath.

"Good morning, Mr. Alcott." Black greeted to gain Morgan's attention.

"Good morning, Captain." Morgan replied. The two men looked at Mala as they heard her mumble something in her language. Black smiled slightly as he faced Morgan once again.

"I understand that you took Irish from…"

"Aubrey." Mala corrected.

"…the hold. My orders were that she stay the night." Black went on, ignoring the correction.

"She is mine, I claimed her." Morgan stated firmly.

"Thomas Beaufort has laid to claim to her as well."

"She is not going to him!" Mala interjected angrily.

Still ignoring her, Black said, "He laid his claim while on the *Widow Maker*. That was before your claim, Mr. Alcott."

"Rene." Mala warned.

"And we all thought you were dead along with your crew, Captain." Morgan said glancing at Mala.

Black placed his elbow on the desk and rested his chin on the back of his hand. He seemed to contemplate this as he watched Morgan who was casting glances at Mala while he awaited the decision. Shifting his gaze to Mala as well, Black found her watching him. When his eye met hers, she rolled her eyes away and looked back out to the sea. Black hid his smile behind his hand. Mon Dieu, but he had missed her!

"Very well, Mr. Alcott. I will consider Irish's position. For now she can remain with you in your cabin." He caught Morgan's smile and added, "However, she does not spend the days idle. She will work the same as the crew for her meals and bunk."

"She had taken up helping Willie, our cook, in the galley as well as helping around the ship with anything where an extra pair of hands was needed." Morgan informed.

Black took in this information and nodded. "Then she continues in the galley. Her duties will be to not only help the cook but to also serve those in the galley. She can be something of a tavern wench." ·

"Rene..." Came Mala's warning voice again and this time, Black looked at her lazily as she added, "She will not..."

"She merely fills tankards, serves the food, and other provisions." He told her.

"Other provisions?" Mala questioned, her eyes narrowing.

"Do you have other duties for her?" Black asked, ignoring her question.

"She will not entertain the men." Mala stated firmly.

Black smiled, a smile that Mala did not like, and with a slow closing of his eye and a slight bow of his head, he said to Morgan still facing Mala, "There are her duties, Mr. Alcott. She begins now."

"Aye Captain." Morgan said as he turned to leave. He cast another quick glance at Mala who was ignoring him again before he left the cabin.

His conversation with Deats left him with many questions and Black wanted to talk in length with Morgan about Mala to know of her nightmares but that would have to wait. Though her presence in the cabin was not expected, it certainly was most welcomed.

As if reading his thoughts, Mala stood up from the window and walked over to him slowly. His smile widened as she slowly closed the book that listed the supplies. Her gaze never left his while she tossed it to the table. His gaze moved to the front of her shirt where he knew his mark would be upon her breast as Mala moved to stand beside him and leaned slightly against her desk. His hand reached out for her, sliding along the gold sash she wore about her waist then to her hip as he pulled her to him.

"Shall we now work on that thank you with more meaning?" Mala asked softly as her hand held the left side of his face, her thumb rubbing the scar on his cheek.

"Hmm, I thought you would never ask." Black said and stood up. Mala smiled and offered her lips to him as he lifted her in his arms to carry her to the bunk.

Morgan found Robert in the corridor on his way back to his cabin. Calling out to him, Morgan hurried to catch up. "Black is allowing Aubrey to stay with me for now but she is to work in the galley like a tavern wench."

Robert whistled low and rolled his eyes. "Wait till she and Captain Mala hears about that."

"Captain Mala already knows. She was in the cabin when I met with Black. She made him agree that Aubrey does not entertain. Having met that Thomas Beaufort though, we have a problem." Morgan told him.

"Aye, Captain Mala can handle him but Miss Aubrey does not stand a chance." Robert said leaning against the wall and looking at the floor.

"Exactly. So we need to make sure she is not alone. Tell some of our men to keep an eye on her. If Aubrey has to be in the galley, I do not want her there alone."

"I will get York, Jacobs, and Riley. Then of course there is ol' Willie and me." Robert said.

"That will be fine. Thank you, Robert."

"She certainly needs protection. They are dogs." Robert grumbled. Morgan nodded as they stopped outside his cabin door.

Stepping into the cabin, Morgan found Aubrey lying on her bunk, reading a book. She looked up as he entered but then returned to her reading. Her mind drifted to their conversation the night before. How could she stay angry with him? He had saved her from certain doom in the hold.

She remembered Morgan's firm words as he had held her face in his hand. *'He only wanted Mala.'* With a sigh, Aubrey laid aside her book. Morgan could not betray Mala. His loyalty to her was too strong.

Sitting on the edge of his bunk and facing her, Morgan explained her duties according to Captain Black. "What?" Aubrey exclaimed, jumping off the bunk.

"Wait, wait! He says that you are to only serve food and drinks. Mala said that there will be no entertaining the men." He said quickly.

"Oh, only? With someone like Beaufort, that would be impossible!"

"Then Beaufort will answer to Black." Morgan said simply as though that would be enough to stop the man.

Aubrey sighed in defeat. "Mala knows of this?" She asked.

Morgan nodded. "Aye and she is not happy with it either. But she made him agree on the no entertaining part before I left."

Aubrey sat on her bunk, miserable. Beaufort was aboard this ship now and her life would be a living hell! She would not feel safe! She should have taken up Mala's offer and gotten off in Santiago de Cuba when she had the chance.

Later in the day as Aubrey worked, she mused on how it had been a relatively quiet day and no one had bothered her. Mala's men were jovial, tormenting her in their regular fashion—as a crewmember—not in the awful way that she had grown to know from Black's men. Morgan had been nowhere around all day, busy with the tasks of making up loads for the cannons and stacking them.

She became distressed at the sight of Beaufort and his two sidekicks when they entered the galley. She had been lucky to be working for the better part of the day without encountering him. But with the last meal of day being served, she knew that he would have to make an appearance. She stuck out her chin and willed herself to approach them with a tray of mugs of ale. Willie had patted her back, drawling softly that she would be all right.

"About time you got here, girl." Beaufort said with a lazy smile at her.

Aubrey sighed inwardly. Girl, his condescending nickname for her. She supposed he could have found a far worse one. She ignored his comment, remembering how Jean Luc had told her in the past to not let the man see that she was deathly frightened of him. As she reached out from the end of the table to set the first tankard down, he caught her by the wrist with lightening swiftness, pulling her down over the rest of the tankards on the tray. She gasped at the pain and surprise but did not cry out. Now she found that her entire upper body was lying on the table, her chest pressing painfully into the heavy pewter tankards filled with ale.

"You got no smile for your customers, bitch?" Beaufort asked close to her face. She stared into the gray eyes and sighed. Well, apparently he had found a new nickname.

"I have no reason to smile, Monsieur Beaufort. Now if you will kindly let me go, I can carry on with my work." She said stiffly. There was pain in her voice, but she was trying desperately to sound brave.

"I rather like you down here." He smiled holding her all the tighter.

"Thomas! Get her off the mugs! Her shirt is soakin' up all of the damn ale." LaVoie complained as he dug his hand under her chest to try and retrieve a mug.

Aubrey slapped at his hand with her free one as she tried to break free from Beaufort's grip. A ripple of chuckles emitted from the three men.

"Relax, there is plenty of ale." Beaufort's eye drifted down into the front of her shirt as Boulet scanned her backside from where he sat.

Aubrey was alarmed to feel Boulet run his hand over her bottom as he said thickly in French, "This is a fine piece you have offered me here, Thomas. I…"

His voice turned to a startled croak as the cold steel of the muzzle of

231

Beaufort's pistol stabbed into the side of his throat. "Never you mind that fine piece, Boulet. You will not be gettin' any of it. She is mine." Beaufort growled.

Boulet dropped his hand and Beaufort lowered the pistol then tucked it back away into his sash. His gray eyes shifted back to Aubrey's chest as she lay over the mugs. From the position he held her in, he had a perfect view of her breasts and she mentally chastised herself for not having worn a camisole.

"That ale on your shirt will only sweeten the taste of those little tits." Beaufort told her.

"Let me go Thomas or I will tell the captain." She warned.

"Which one?" LaVoie asked then laughed as he managed to extract a mug from under her. She grunted with the pain of the mug raking against her ribs.

"She means Captain Black. LaVoie, you are such an ass." Boulet growled in reply.

"Let her up." Came the angry voice of Morgan as he stepped up from behind Beaufort. Merely raising his eyes from looking into her shirt, Beaufort did not release her.

"I said—let her up!" Morgan repeated through clenched teeth as he took hold of her free arm.

Beaufort smiled evilly and let her go. Morgan pulled her up close against his chest as Robert stepped up beside him. Aubrey was beginning to feel like a rag doll being fought over by two children.

Glaring at Beaufort, Morgan jerked his head toward Boulet. "Just as he will not be getting a piece of her nor will you be tasting her tits."

Aubrey frowned at his comment. He had certainly taken on a new persona since Black and his men had come aboard. She was glad to be off the table as she stood against Morgan's chest, rubbing her paining wrist and looking around at all the men in apprehension. It was becoming more and more clear to her that she needed to play the ruse of being Morgan's possession for her own safety.

Looking down over Aubrey as the ale on her shirt had soaked her to the skin, the white material was plastered against her chest and the wetness revealed the subtle darkness of her nipples in contrast to her alabaster skin.

"Your work is finished for today." Morgan ordered her firmly. A twinge of desire coursed through him and his tone of voice denoted it, "Go to the cabin."

"But Morgan, Captain Black said…" She began.

"I said you are finished, damn it! Now get back to the cabin!" He spat.

Aubrey dropped her head in submission and Morgan pushed her toward the door. With a final fleeting look at him, she was caught for a moment in an spellbound stare. The look in his eye and the clenching of his teeth was reminiscent of Jean Luc in his fits of rage on the *Widow Maker*. Robert backed up a step to let her pass, putting out his hand to gently push her along. Crossing her arms over her wet chest, she left the galley.

Robert stepped out of the doorway watching her retreat from the galley to make sure none of Black's other men might choose to follow her. All the other men in the room remained seated, the talking had died down to a low murmur as Beaufort and Morgan continued to glare at one another.

Beaufort took a long draught from his ale and smacked his lips loudly. With a salute to Morgan with the tankard, he said sarcastically, "My compliments to you, Monsieur Alcott, your little Irish whore gave a very sweet taste to my drink."

"You son of a bitch." Morgan began as he stepped forward with outstretched hand toward Beaufort to grab the man by his shirtfront. A subtle glance from Beaufort brought Boulet and LaVoie to their feet.

Robert stepped further into the room and hissed, "Captain Black."

Morgan looked up to see the dark haired man enter with Mala close behind. Beaufort followed their gaze and smiled as he set down his tankard and his men eased themselves back into their seats.

"Leave her alone, Beaufort, or you will answer to me." Morgan warned as he stabbed a finger at the man. With that, he turned on his heel and headed out the door with Robert close behind. Beaufort snorted and glanced over at the captain's table.

Mala had remained standing at the table and was watching the five men keenly with her dark eyes. Black, however, had seated himself and reached up to take her by the wrist to gently pull her into her chair.

"What is Monsieur Beaufort up to?" She asked guardedly.

"He looks like he is just enjoying a drink my dear." Black shrugged. He looked around the room, "Where is Irish?"

"Aubrey." She corrected tightly.

"Oui, where is she?"

"You are not an invalid, Rene, get your own drink." Mala replied.

"Why not get one for me?" He cooed close to her ear.

"Which would you prefer—ale or arsenic?" Mala purred back with a smile.

"Hmm, you did not have this attitude about an hour ago." He said as he ran his hand up her thigh.

"Aye, well it must be the effect that Beaufort has in here." She replied smiling sweetly as she caught his hand before it reached its intended destination. She clapped it firmly down on the table. Black chuckled then got to his feet to get their ale.

Chapter 26

Leaving the galley, Morgan was heading for his cabin to comfort Aubrey when Robert came up behind him.

"Morgan, we…" Robert began but stopped when Morgan spun on his heels to face him.

"What the hell happened?" He hissed angrily. "We agreed damn it. Why was she alone in the galley? Willie cannot handle those three bastards by himself!"

"Morgan, listen!"

"Christ, the son of a bitch had her pinned down on a table."

"Look, I am not sure what happened but I will talk with the others. I will set up a meal schedule and no one leaves until the replacement shows up." Robert told him. "Ah, tell her we are all sorry for that. She will not be alone again, I promise."

Morgan stared at him and ran his fingers through his hair as he tried to calm his angry thoughts. Taking his arm, Robert said, "Perhaps you should not return to your cabin just now. Come with me and cool your heels before you face her."

It was nearly dark before Morgan entered his cabin. Aubrey had changed clothes and was reading a book. The shirt she had worn earlier was washed and hanging on a nail. She looked up as he stepped inside, tossing his hat aside.

"I do not want to go up on deck. Will you please take the basin of dirty water out for me?" She asked sheepishly.

"Yes, I agree. I do not think that it would be wise for you to go up there anyway." He shrugged. Looking her over he asked, "Did he hurt you?"

"My ribs hurt a bit where he pulled me down over the tankards, but I will be fine." She said with a small smile. "You were a bit crude in the galley."

"That is what they understand." Morgan said with a shrug. She made a face at him and turned her head away.

"I know." She acknowledged dismally.

"Do not look so forlorn, Aubrey. I am your friend, remember?" He said seeing her dejected expression.

"I sometimes wonder if I have any friends." She said softly.

"Certainly you do, you have always had friends here on the *Enchantress*. Me, Robert, Willie, Mala, Jacobs, York and Riley…hell you have a lot of friends." He said in joviality. She looked at him and gave a small smile.

"I should never have left London. I should have stayed there and none of this would ever have happened. I should have married that little twit and suffered my lot in life." She fretted. Then looking down at the floor with a sudden anger, she grumbled, "I hate Rene Black. God forgive me, I know Mala loves him but I wish he had died on the *Widow Maker* instead of him." Morgan only nodded for there were only a few people who seemed to understand Black.

"Ah now, I am sure that he would not have wanted that to happen, he certainly would not agree. I do not agree." Morgan told her gently.

"All he ever did was show some caring and love for me." She said quietly. Slamming her book shut, she grumbled, "Ugh! I hate Thomas Beaufort. He is the incarnate of Satan himself."

"Well you are right on that account." He agreed.

Aubrey lifted her gaze to look at Morgan. He was sitting on his bunk, looking at the floor and nodding as if his head was about to fall off his shoulders. A giggle bubbled up making her squeak to contain it. Looking up at her, Morgan frowned as he noticed that she was having a difficult time holding her humor.

"I am fine now. Thank you Morgan." She managed to say amid her giggles.

Smiling and not sure what he did to make her feel better, Morgan stood up and said with a shrug, "Well I will go take out that smelly ale water. Want to play some cards when I get back?"

She nodded and got up to hold the door open for him. When she shut it firmly behind him, she turned and leaned against the wooden door facing the empty room.

"What should I do, Jean Luc? I miss you so much." She whispered. "Mala is right, I am lonely." Tears welled up in her hazel eyes.

Morgan stepped out into the darkness and went to the side of the ship to dump out the water. He held the bowl against his chest as he breathed in the warm humid night air.

"You did not lay her long." Came Beaufort's monotone voice from behind him. Morgan turned slowly to look at the man.

"I did not know that it was your responsibility to keep a tally of things like that." Morgan's voice was laced with hatred.

Beaufort shrugged. "All I can say is, she will have to learn to be down a lot longer than that once she is with me. Like I told her last lover, I am going to introduce her to things..." Beaufort boasted.

"You are a pig, Beaufort. She is not some whore from Port Royale or Nassau. If you want that kind of pleasure, why not get it there?" Morgan spat.

"Why should I have to pay for it when I can have it for free and teach her just what I like?" Beaufort said grinning.

Morgan dropped the bowl. He was reaching for his pistol when they heard Black's voice behind them. "Is there a problem, gentlemen? You both know that any arguments are to be settled on shore. There will be no fighting on my ship."

Morgan glared into Beaufort's gloating stare before Beaufort looked at Black, drawling lazily, "Non Captain, Monsieur Alcott and I were just discussing little Irish and her experience in the bed."

Morgan cast a glance at Black as he slipped his pistol back into place, "As I mentioned to Monsieur Beaufort earlier, Captain, I think that if it is experience that he desires, he needs to get it at port." Black's lips drew into a thin smile as he looked from one man to the other.

"Monsieur Beaufort, I believe that Monsieur Alcott has laid claim to her long before you came on board."

"She belongs to you." Beaufort retorted.

Morgan's eyes shifted to Black again as he spoke ever so calmly, "This is true, but alas she and I have …grown apart in my absence."

"And in light of your dark-haired beauty." Beaufort slipped in pointedly. Black merely looked at the man and inhaled deeply to keep his own temper in check. "But, being as how I outrank him, I should have the grander piece of the prize. When a booty is taken does not the captain and the quartermaster get more shares than the rest of the men?"

"That much is true." Black said with a nod.

Beaufort literally puffed up with an air of victory as Morgan glared at Black and opened his mouth to protest. "For the moment she will stay where she lays." The captain said calmly. Beaufort opened his mouth to protest this time but Black silenced him with a menacing tone. "She does still actually belong to me."

"A fact that distresses Mala I am sure." Beaufort dared to say.

Black stepped closer to him and growled, "Captain Mala will be left out of this discussion, do you understand?"

After a short pause of insolent silence, Beaufort very nearly sneered at Black in the darkness, "Aye sir."

"You are on the dogwatch, are you not?" Black asked Beaufort.

"Oui."

"Then get to your duty." Black spat.

"Well, one thing is for sure…she ain't laying around in the dark right under your nose with him like she did with Pierne." Beaufort chuckled in French as he turned away from Morgan. The wind carried his voice away from Morgan.

Black grabbed Beaufort by the arm and spun him around dealing him a hefty gloved backhand, "That is enough from you. To your post, Monsieur." He growled then shoved him away.

Black turned to Morgan who stood quietly watching and frowning as he tried to figure out what Beaufort had said to cause such a reaction in the dark-haired man. Black met his gaze and asked, "Should you be in your cabin?"

"What did he say? I thought I heard a name." Morgan asked.

"It is none of your concern. Does this belong to you?" Black asked as he pushed at one half of the broken washbowl with the toe of his boot.

"Aye sir." Morgan nodded.

"Get it off my deck before he comes back and uses it to slit your throat and then takes from you what he desires. Thomas' brains drop right between his legs when it comes to women." Black warned then stalked away into the darkness.

When Morgan entered into the cabin and shut the door, Aubrey was on her bunk sitting cross-legged in her bare feet. He held up the two halves of the bowl with a sorrowful look on his face.

"What happened?" She whined.

"I, ah, dropped it. It was wet and slipped out of my hands. Sorry love." He halfway lied.

Aubrey sighed deeply, "Maybe I could go get a pot from Willie for us to use as a wash bowl."

She got up from the bunk and started for the door but he caught her arm and said quietly, "No, Beaufort has the dogwatch." Aubrey nodded in understanding.

She sat back down and curled herself onto her bunk at the head. He took out a deck of cards and indicated the foot of her bunk with a nod of his head. At her nod, he smiled and shuffled the cards, winking at her in torment as he sat down. They chatted quietly and tormented one another as they played cards. Morgan was glad to see her smile as she won her third game in a row.

"I believe you are cheating." He grumbled.

"I am not. You are just a sore loser." She told him smiling.

"Yes, you are, where are you getting all of those aces? Where are you hiding them? You have been sitting cross-legged all the while." He teased as he pulled on her leg and reached his fingers up into the lower cuff of her britches.

She giggled and slapped at his hands, "Morgan, stop!"

Beaufort passed the cabin on his rounds. He took a step back and leaned closer to the door, listening. He could hear Aubrey's giggles as she scolded playfully which was followed by Morgan's own chuckle in reply.

All manner of images jumped into Beaufort's mind as he listened. He felt the stirrings of primal urges for the auburn-haired young woman deep in his loins. Dropping his head with an angry frown, he moved on down the corridor. He would have her soon, even if it meant that Alcott would have to fall victim to some unfortunate accident, he mused.

His tour of the ship took him past the great cabin now. Black's droning tones could be heard from behind this door. The tones sounded subtle and almost purring compared to the way Beaufort was used to hearing the man. Mala's voice came soft in response, calling Black's name in a timbre that denoted pleasure and passion. This only added to Beaufort's anger and frustration. He stomped up the companionway steps, not caring whom he disturbed or what he was disturbing them from.

The deck was shrouded in heavy fog as he walked along the starboard railing, feeling the thick wet air hitting his face like a fine piece of wet gauze.

"Where the hell are we? Damned fog is so thick I can barely see my feet under me." He growled as he approached Timmons at the helm.

"We are on course. May as well take up them sails, there ain't no wind. Save the wear and tear on them." Timmons suggested as he nodded up into the sails above them.

"Are you trying to tell me how to do my job? I am the goddamned quartermaster here." Beaufort growled.

"No sir." Timmons replied with an easy shrug.

"Be damned if you are." Beaufort growled then stomped angrily to the portside railing.

Beaufort's voice had sounded like it was right in her cabin and Mala started in surprise as she lay under Black. His head shot up from delivering kisses to her breasts and growled, "Son of a bitch, it is the middle of the damn night."

"What the hell is all that..." Mala began as she tried to move but he held her in place with his body.

"Be still, you are not going anywhere."

"He is at my helm, Rene." She argued pushing at him.

"Do not be ridiculous. The fool cannot even piss in the wind in the right direction, much less navigate a ship!" Black growled as he buried his face back into the softness of her breasts.

"And you put him in charge of my ship!" She exclaimed pushing him from her.

Black took her hands and held them down on the either side of her head before saying, "I have your man, Timmons, at the wheel. You do trust him?"

Mala could not help but smile at the comment. He chuckled, pleased that she had settled back down. He moved his hips against her and she moaned in reply, giving into his lovemaking.

The card game was over and the cabin dark as Aubrey and Morgan settled down in their bunks for the night.

"Morgan?" She called softly in the darkness.

"Hmm?" He asked sleepily. He waited on her to speak again, listening to her move in the bunk.

"Have you ever been in love?" Her voice sounded close. He turned on his side to face her in the darkness.

"I am in love right now, just listening to your voice way over there in the dark."

"Stop being foolish." She scolded.

Morgan rolled onto his back and stretched out his long lean frame. He pulled his blanket up over his chest, "Cold in here. Are you cold?"

"I am serious, have you ever been in love? Truly in love?" Aubrey asked again.

"Aye." He said quietly. The reply seemed to surprise her.

"What happened? I mean, why are not you married?" Her tone was guarded and quiet as if she had been afraid to ask.

"She died." Morgan replied quietly.

A deep pang of remorse shot thought Aubrey and she bit her lip, "I am sorry, I should not have asked."

"Tis all right, Aubrey. She became sick and did not recover." He said, a hint of sadness in his tone.

"When I was ten and six, I was very sick but I got better. My Mama and Da did not." She replied in small voice. It was quiet for several long moments before she said softly, "I am sorry you lost her. Then you really do know how I feel."

"Aye, I know." Morgan whispered.

"Goodnight Morgan." She whispered softly, a hint of sadness in her voice.

"Goodnight Aubrey." He replied. There was a thickness in his voice as well.

Chapter 27

The next morning, Morgan escorted Aubrey to the galley. Upon entering he found Robert, Riley, and several other men sitting together at a table away from the galley entrance having breakfast. They looked sheepishly at Morgan, having already heard of the incident from the day before.

Aubrey went directly to Willie in the galley to help him wherever needed. Morgan watched her, fearful to leave her for the day. At that moment, Black entered the galley with Mala. Aubrey went to work at bringing utensils along with a pitcher of drink and tankards. She met Morgan's gaze before she set about to her duties. The two did not realize that Mala had caught the exchanged look.

Some of Mala's men slowly dispersed and soon the galley accommodated only the two captains, a few men, and Morgan. Black beckoned Morgan to join him at the captain's table when Mala stepped up to Aubrey.

Leaning back against the wall with one foot flat against it and knee bent, Mala folded her arms across her chest. Looking at the floor and she whispered, "How are you? I heard about that bastard, Beaufort."

"I am fine." Aubrey replied. She glanced up to find the dark eyes watching her intently.

After a short pause, Mala said, "Be careful with Morgan, Aubrey."

Aubrey gave her a confused look, then asked, "Why? He is harmless. "

"He also betrayed us." Mala interrupted quietly.

"I am not so sure now." Seeing her skeptical look, Aubrey added quickly, "You did not see him in our cabin or on the deck when we were boarded. You should have seen him when they put you in irons."

"Aubrey." Mala sighed, shaking her dark head.

"Just promise me that if he tries to talk to you, you will hear him out first." Aubrey pleaded. Mala gave her a sideways glance much like Captain Black.

"Irish, I am waiting." Black interrupted.

Aubrey groaned softly as Mala smiled and said as she straightened, "Buck up, mon amie. He is harmless."

Mala laughed aloud when Aubrey gave her an incredulous look. Her laughter filtered through the galley and all heads looked up. As she made her way to her table, Mala greeted her men as she had always done. Black gave a look of displeasure but Mala merely smiled and returned his look with an innocent one.

Black had been watching the two women as they spoke quietly and still wondered at the time they had spent together. Aubrey could have told Mala much about her stay on the *Widow Maker* and that thought left him very disconcerted especially since Mala did not seem angry or jealous. He did know from his short time with Morgan outside Charlestowne that Mala had not taken to Aubrey at first and that she knew of the mark even when she had allowed Aubrey to board her ship. Black glanced at Mala still wondering. He noted that she was watching Morgan with open hostility as she moved among her crew on her way to the table.

While Mala was talking with Aubrey, Black asked Morgan, "I understand that Deats found Mala on the island and she left with him."

Morgan looked at Black askance and said carefully, "I am afraid I know nothing about that. Whenever I talked to Mala about some of the past, she made certain to pass that part. She does not like talking about the village at all."

"Do you know what happened there?" Black asked.

"No, did something happen?" Morgan questioned with a frown.

Black stared at Mala but he could hear Deats' voice in his mind. "Never mind." The dark haired man replied as he watched Mala and Aubrey. Mala's anger with Morgan would make breakfast difficult. "You may leave to go about your duties, Mr. Alcott." He said and motioned with a nod of his head for Morgan to leave. Nodding, Morgan left the table, giving Mala a wide berth as she came to sit with Black.

"Mala, mon coeur." Black cooed.

Aubrey appeared with two plates of food and placed them before the two captains. She glanced at Black to find him watching her. She quickly glanced away and retreated from the table.

"Stop frightening her, Rene." Mala scolded.

"I did not say a word." He replied innocently.

"Your look intimidates her."

"My look does not intimidate you?" He asked softly as his thumb caressed her arm. Mala gave him a lazy smile as she gazed upon his face so close to hers.

"No." She said simply. Black leaned closer, his lips touching her ear. "Eat your breakfast." Mala continued to scold.

"Breakfast? Hmm, can I have you?" He whispered softly as his lips moved to her throat just below her ear. Her smile widened as she cocked her head slightly to give him room.

"You had me already this morning, remember?"

"Hmm, so I did. I suppose, I am still hungry." Black said as his lips moved to her jaw line.

"Enough, Rene." Mala cooed softly as she moved her head away from him.

Black straightened up a bit and looked into her dark eyes. They were soft and gentle from the passion he had aroused in her. With the lowering of her eyes to his plate then back to his gaze, Mala cajoled, "Now be a good boy and eat your breakfast."

Black smiled as he caught her hand in his and placed a kiss upon the knuckles of her fingers, "And if I finish everything on my plate?"

"Then we shall have dessert."

"Oui, sweet dessert." He agreed, setting his gaze on her mouth as his thumb rubbed the back of her hand. Mala squeezed the hand that held hers in silent agreement.

With Mala and Black occupied in their intimacy, Aubrey went to Morgan quickly and said, "It would be wise of you to find time to talk to Mala and quickly. If not, she will cut you down before you can utter a sound."

"Are you defending me, Miss Malone?" He asked smiling. Aubrey shrugged, leaving him without another word.

It was quite sometime later after Mala and Black had exited the galley that Aubrey saw Beaufort enter along with his two companions. Immediately an uncontrollable trembling began to wrack her body and she nearly dropped the tray she was holding. A tankard did fall to the table and Robert scanned the room to notice the three men as they took seats near the opposite wall.

"That one is a mean one." Jacobs said covertly to the men around him. Aubrey overheard the comment and she shivered again.

Robert laid his hand over hers as Aubrey picked up the fallen tankard, "Not to worry, Miss Aubrey. We are here to watch over you."

She looked at him blankly, her breath coming unsteadily. "I beg your pardon?"

"By Mr. Alcott's orders, our crew will watch over you to keep you safe." Riley informed.

"Hey! You girl!" Beaufort bellowed. Aubrey jerked up and looked at the man who frightened her more than Rene Black. Willie stepped away from the cookstove holding a wooden spoon and watched as Beaufort smiled showing yellowed teeth.

"Get me something to drink, girl and not any of that watered-down stuff. Get me a bottle of the good stuff."

Aubrey went to Willie looking around frantically. "Is something the matter, lass?" Willie asked.

"The good stuff is in the captain's cabin." She said breathlessly.

"Aye, and he gets what everyone else gets." Willie said calmly. Aubrey's shoulders slumped but Willie added, "If he has a problem with that, he takes it up with the captain."

"Which one? Black or Mala?"

Willie smiled and placing a hand on her shoulders, replied, "Does it really matter?"

Aubrey looked into his smiling face and felt a bit calmer. "Aye, he takes it up with the captain."

Willie nodded and ran a hand down her auburn tresses. "Ye will be fine, lass. Ye are not alone out there. We are all watchin' out for ye."

"Remind me to thank Morgan."

Willie chuckled and helped her to fill tankards of ale. Aubrey picked them up and, taking a deep breath, stepped out into the galley's view. She saw Robert and the other crewmen watching her as she stepped out then she faced Beaufort and his friends. On weakening legs, she willed herself to walk proudly toward his table. Trying to keep Beaufort from seeing the fear in her eyes, she looked at the tankards as she carefully placed them on the table before the three men.

Beaufort took a huge swallow then made a show of spewing it out. "Christ, girl! I said the good stuff."

"Those are in the captain's cabin. You need to talk to her." Aubrey said quietly.

"Her?" Beaufort roared. "My captain is Captain Black! Not some whore!"

Robert stood up as did several of Mala's men but Aubrey ran to Robert, yelling at all of them, "No! That is just what he wants!"

Black was in the corridor on his way to visit Deats when he heard the noise in the galley. Slowing his pace, he listened to Beaufort's booming voice and Aubrey's frightened reply. Having just left a very pleasant interlude with Mala, Beaufort's reference to her as a whore did not settle well Black. Stepping into the galley, he stopped and took in the scene. Aubrey was pleading with the crew of the *Enchantress* as Beaufort was reaching out for her from behind.

"Arrête!" His deep voice boomed within the confines of the galley. Everyone turned to face the dark-haired man as Aubrey froze and fell silent then she slid behind Robert's tall form.

"You drink what everyone else drinks when they come in here. You get no special treatment." Black informed an enraged Beaufort. Seeing Beaufort's look as if to challenge him, Black raised a brow.

When nothing more was said, Black's gaze swept over the men in the galley as he spat, "You know the rules of this ship, all fights are taken to shore."

LaVoie and Boulet pulled at the man to sit down. Black glanced around the room and saw that Mala's men were slowly sitting down one or two at a time. He turned his attention back to Beaufort who was just taking his seat. "Eat your meal then leave. Anymore and you will answer to me." Black growled, his deep voice trembling with rage.

Aubrey had cowered behind the crew of the *Enchantress*. Black's rage reminded her of the day she and Jean Luc had been discovered. She stood rooted in her spot, visibly shaking as she stared at Black from behind Robert.

Giving one last glare at each person in the galley, Black was about to leave when the sound of muffled running was heard in the corridor and Mala appeared in the doorway. She had apparently hurried to dress into her shirt and britches. Black noticed that she did not tuck in her shirt, did not have on her boots, and did not wear her sash about her waist.

All eyes turned to her as she steadied herself in the doorway. She took in the scene in an instant with a long look at Aubrey who weakly sagged onto a nearby bench near her crew. The savage look Mala bestowed on Beaufort made Black growl low in his throat as he quickly moved towards her. Knowing her temper, Black grabbed her by the arm and roughly pulled her along with him out of the galley.

"What the hell was that..." She started to say as he dragged her away.

Without a word, Black pulled her along until they turned the corner and he suddenly pressed her against the wall, covering her mouth with his. Mala was surprised at the intensity of the kiss. Knowing that he needed the outlet, she returned the kiss with a force of her own. After a moment, he released her mouth and let his forehead rest on hers. Mala's hands caressed his face with an urgency to soothe his anger.

"It will be all right, Rene." She whispered over and over. His eye closed as he listened to her soft voice.

"Mon Dieu, Mala, I have missed you!" He whispered. He looked into her surprised gaze but as she was about to question him, he said more calmly, "Let us go back to the cabin. You have not finished dressing."

Later in the morning, Willie sent Aubrey back to her cabin since there was not much to do until he needed her again. Enjoying the time to herself, she busily washed her 'frillies' as Morgan had called them. Just as she laid out the last article of clothing to dry, there was a knock at the door. Aubrey tentatively opened the door of the cabin to the light, yet insistent knocking. Placing her body against it to push it shut if need be, and with her hand on the bolt, Aubrey peeped out.

"I have a job for you, little one." Came the quiet and kind voice of Robert. Aubrey let out a sigh of relief.

"A job for me?" She echoed, opening the door wider.

"Yes, I am in charge of the assignments for the deck watch crews and I have an assignment for you." He told her smiling.

"Has Captain Mala taken back her ship?"

"No." He replied stiffly.

"Has Captain Black been killed or fallen overboard?" She queried on like a child. Robert was forced to chuckle at her question.

"No, the last time I saw him, he was on the quarterdeck, very much alive and quite dry."

"Damn." She cursed under her breath.

Robert chuckled again and folded his arms over his chest. "Come along now. Do you want to get out of here and get some air?" He watched her as she moved from the door to retrieve her boots. "You will not be needin' them." He told her.

Still with much hesitation, she followed him along the corridor and up the companionway steps in her bare feet.

"My duty today is the starboard watch. Do you remember how the deck watches rotate?" He asked her as they stepped out into the sunlit deck. Aubrey nodded knowing that the deck crews took turns each day. The two deck crews would switch each day, first being responsible for the port side, then the next day the starboard side.

"Who is the head of the other crew?" She asked quietly as she searched the deck of working men for the other person in charge.

"Boulet." Robert reported tightly.

Aubrey's face went ashen, "Sweet Jesus Robert, I will not have…"

"No, you will always be on my crew and you will change watches with my men when it is safe for you to be working." He assured her as he waved his hand toward the starboard side of the ship. She waited as he spoke to a crewman who had stepped up to him. Taking a deep cleansing breath of the fresh air, Aubrey realized how much she missed being on deck.

"Here." Robert said drawing her attention. He placed a palm-sized flat stone in her hands. "This is called a prayerbook by the men."

Aubrey frowned at the smooth stone and asked, "Would ya be havin' me pray with a rock then, Robert?"

With another chuckle, he said, "Well, I am not sure about the prayin', but I have heard quite a bit of cussin' over that stone! Now pay attention here so that when I leave you alone to your task, you will look like you know what you are doin' and no one will bother you." Pulling at her sleeve, he took her closer to the starboard railing and pointed a gloved finger at a man who was on his hands and knees there.

"See Joseph here?" Robert asked and saw her nod. "After York and Riley put seawater on the deck, they will pull the bigger stone there over the larger spaces of the deck. It is yours and Joseph's duty to scrub all the smaller places smooth. Rub the stone along the lay of the plank until the wood is smooth and white." She nodded and dropped to her knees near Joseph.

"Mornin' to ya, Joseph." She said brightly as she rolled up her sleeves.

"'ello luv." He grinned back as he wiped his forearm across his brow. Joseph was in his mid thirties, a seasoned sailor with a scruffy beard and longish black hair. Blue eyes twinkled out of the lined face that was tanned like leather from his years at sea.

"Tis good ta see ya back, luv." York said in a hushed voice as he bent toward her.

After some time, Aubrey found that she was actually enjoying the job a bit. The sun felt good on her back as she pushed her sleeves up higher and rolled her pant legs up above her knees. Within moments, she was humming a little tune her father had taught her a long time ago.

Joseph chuckled nearby. "Well, glory be, I ain't never heard a body sing at this blessed job!"

"I am just happy to be out again." She replied as she waited for York to slosh water her way.

Aubrey smiled up at him, straightening up to stretch her back a bit. The smile melted as her hazel eyes came to rest on the quarterdeck above them. Black stood staring down at her with his arms folded over his chest. Quickly, she set back to work, praying that her newfound freedom would not be short-lived.

Chapter 28

Morgan had been working in the ammunition stores, taking inventory and overseeing the packing of shot. Not knowing that Aubrey had been summoned for other duties, he entered the cabin, taking off his hat and exhaling tiredly. A pang of fear struck him when he realized that her boots were beside her bunk but the small room was empty.

"Oh Christ." He groaned as he turned quickly to leave the room.

He very nearly burst out onto the deck from the companionway, having already checked the galley. His blue eyes searched the individuals on the deck. Black was standing at the quarterdeck railing with a long glass to his eye. Boulet was with the men of his watch on the port side of the ship. But Beaufort was absent. Where was he? He wondered worriedly.

Morgan's keen eye caught sight of Robert as he chatted freely with one of his crew. En route to speak with Robert, Morgan very nearly fell over a crewmember who was down on the deck scrubbing vigorously. The urge to spit a curse at the person and kick him for being in his way crossed his mind but with a frown he drew back a bit and looked at the mate. He was stepping around the person when Robert strode up him.

"Christ Morgan, you look like you are about to explode like one of your cannons! What in the hell has your hair all up?" Robert greeted with a smile.

"I went to the cabin…it was empty…Aubrey is gone…have you seen that louse Beaufort on deck?" Morgan asked, the words spilling out in hushed tones as he scanned the deck.

Robert continued to smile and said brightly, "No, I have not seen Beaufort all day but…"

Suddenly a large amount of water sloshed up his boots from behind and Morgan turned with a growl. Glaring at York, he fussed, "What the hell!"

"Unless you need a polishing on your boots, Mr. Alcott, you need to get out of the way of my crew." Robert said with a hint of laughter.

Morgan's attention was drawn once more to that crewmember scrubbing diligently in the tiny places just under the gunwale. Obscured by a blue striped scarf, he could not see the face of the person.

Suddenly, Robert took Morgan's arm and was tugging him back. "Get out of the damn way, Morgan."

Stepping back, Morgan's anger was beginning to subside for some unknown reason. Perhaps it was Robert's relaxed attitude. His eye was drawn back to the small body and he wondered when Mala had taken on a young boy as a crewmember. He had not remembered Black coming on board with one.

Unable to contain himself for much longer, Robert finally asked with an air of authority, "Is there something here that interests you?"

Morgan turned his head suddenly toward Robert as if just realizing that he was there, "Robert…who…" He turned his attention back to the person who still scrubbed with much determination in the small place. His blue eyes drifted over the small waist and firm bottom as it rocked gently with the motion of the person's scrubbing.

Robert folded his arms over his chest and then reached out one hand to slap Morgan on the shoulder, "Do you have a problem with my crew, Mr. First Mate?"

Ignoring him, Morgan stepped toward the person who worked quietly. Robert bit his lip to keep from laughing as Morgan leaned down to get a better look at the person's face. With a gasp and a click of his tongue, he snapped the scarf off the person's head with one hand and caught the person up by the forearm with his other hand.

"Aubrey?" Morgan exclaimed in surprise.

Aubrey gasped when she was grabbed. Seeing who had her, she exclaimed as he pulled her to her feet, "Why are ya pullin' at me, Morgan? Ya damned near scared me half to death!"

The stone clattered to the deck, nearly hitting her toes in the process. Joseph chuckled from his place at their feet, "See Miss Aubrey, cussin' over that stone."

The pair of them glared down at him for a moment before Aubrey struggled in Morgan's grasp and reached for her scarf. He held it just out of her reach growling in exasperation, "Scared you half to death? I went to the cabin…it was empty…I could not find you."

"And that was cause to be draggin' on me?" She snapped as she tried to free her arm from his grasp.

"I told you to stay in the cabin." He scolded.

"I was called on to work—and that was what I was doin' before you snatched me up." She fussed back as she shot a look to Robert, asking for some support in the argument.

"I took her out, Morgan." Robert finally said stepping up.

"You? You should have talked with me first." Morgan spat at his friend while still holding fast to Aubrey.

"Do not get angry with me, Mr. Alcott or I will put you on the deck." Robert warned, a sudden flash of anger crossing his countenance as he drew himself up to his full height. A dark blur caught Morgan's attention out of the corner of his eye and he glanced over to the quarterdeck to see Black watching the confrontation with keen interest. Beaufort had appeared and was now with his captain.

Taking a deep relaxing breath, Morgan released Aubrey. "You be careful." He began then looking pointedly at Robert, he said, "Do not put her down on the deck like that. It is too—suggestive."

Aubrey dropped back to her knees to retrieve her stone as Robert stated, "Well, you are the only one who has seen it that way."

"If ya stay in my way, I will clap this stone down on your toe." Aubrey warned from under them. Morgan stepped back, knowing full well that she would come true with her threat.

"Every other man on this deck is too busy to be looking at her and thinking like that." Robert was saying.

"Every man but him." Morgan growled as he shot a look to the quarterdeck.

"He is interested in Captain Mala." Robert soothed.

"Not him you ass, the other one." Morgan hissed through clenched teeth as he indicated Beaufort with a nod.

Robert raised his eyes to look at the man. In fact the gray eyes were taking in the sight of Aubrey on her hands and knees on the deck at their feet.

"I am looking out for her. She is safe I promise you, Morgan." Robert said under his breath as he casually tapped a forefinger on the butt of his pistol. Morgan drew him away from earshot of Joseph and Aubrey who were chatting quietly.

"While I trust you implicitly, Robert, next time, please let me know before you take her out." Morgan implored with concern in his blue eyes.

"I will." Robert nodded. Morgan stood beside Robert in silence for a time as he watched Aubrey working. Robert jabbed him in his ribs with an elbow and asked playfully, "What are you looking at?"

Without taking his eyes off her bottom, Morgan asked covertly, "Robert, do you think you can find a place for her to scrub where that is tucked out of sight?" The two men chuckled lightly before Morgan sauntered away.

"What is going on down there?" Mala asked in interest then caught sight of Aubrey at work. Mon Dieu, whose idea was that? She thought disgustedly. That chore she saved for punishment, that and the crow's nest for an extra watch.

"Nothing m'amour…" Black cooed in reply with the hint of a chuckle in his tone as he watched Robert directing Aubrey to another location to work so that she was now facing the center of the deck.

"Damn, looks like a big wind came in and changed the course of that little boat down there. Now she is not in position for a hit from the stern." Beaufort grumbled in French as he scanned the charts laid out before them.

"What?" Mala snapped.

"Nothing." Black said coolly as he cast a look toward his quartermaster.

"Do you suppose that Robert will leave that little boat out after dark, Captain?" Beaufort went on in French with a lewd chuckle to his tone.

"Decidedly not." Black replied in the same tongue. Mala looked at both men with full annoyance when Black caught her eye.

"Nothing, Mala...nothing." Black replied with a smile before she questioned him again.

"There is an awful lot of 'nothing' going on up here, Rene. And you would do well to leave your eyes and tongue where it will not be my way, Monsieur Beaufort or you may lose them." Mala spat as she glared pointedly at Beaufort.

Black smiled in delighted entertainment as Beaufort looked at Mala in surprise. Her response was spoken in perfect French.

"Well then." Black began as he caught her about the waist with one arm, "Let us go below and go on in another way." She pushed him away making Beaufort snicker. "Do you not have something to do, Monsieur Beaufort?" Black asked in annoyance.

"I am watching your back, Captain." Beaufort reported.

"My back is fine. No one stands against me and there is no threat. Now get below and check things there." Black advised curtly as he stood between Mala and Beaufort.

Mala watched the still chuckling Beaufort leave the quarterdeck. The sound of a flapping sail caught the attention of the two captains. One of the knots holding the stay line to the sail came loose and now a portion of the sail fluttered noisily in the wind. Black turned his gaze back to Mala who followed the line down to the portside where several men were grabbing the wayward line in hopes of securing it better. Boulet was making a fuss over their ineptness. Mala shook her head in disbelief and rolled her dark eyes in annoyance. Her gaze turned to Black and found him watching her with a smile playing on his lips.

"Your men are idiots, Rene." She said with an air of exasperation that made him chuckle deep in his throat.

Black watched as she turned and walked away towards the starboard corner of the ship's stern. Mala leaned against the railing, arms crossed and looked down the full length of her ship. Her gaze shifted slightly as Black slowly walked towards her. He smiled as he took into his arms and kissed her. Grinning, they pulled apart slightly as catcalls and other noises greeted them. Mala slipped a hand between them to caress his chest.

"You would have me make love to you here?" Black asked looking as though he was ready to oblige that request. Smiling, Mala peeked around him to the crew on deck who had stopped their work and was becoming boisterous in their merriment.

"Perhaps we should save this for a dark and moonless night." She said softly.

He grunted as he wrapped his arms around her and held her. "Mon Dieu, woman. What you do to me!" He whispered into her hair as he held her tight.

After their watch and the chores done, Aubrey sat at the table in the galley with York, Riley and Joseph as the men chatted quietly over bowls of turtle soup. She remained quiet, exhausted from a day's work on deck, but feeling safe in their company. Beaufort came into the room and flounced at a table near the back and glared at them. With sharp commands, he ordered Willie to bring him some food and drink. The old man obliged with an air of disgruntlement. Finishing off her meal, Aubrey excused herself and left the galley to quickly return to the cabin while the frightening man was busy and she had the time to get out of his sight.

Just as she was nearing the cabin, she heard Mala call softly from behind her. Aubrey turned with a small smile. "You seemed very happy up on deck today working with the men." Mala said.

"I was." Aubrey said, her hazel eyes twinkling. "I was glad to have something different to do today. I am glad that Robert had the choice of picking me to help him as opposed to Michele Boulet."

"That ass did not know that you were on the list of available crewmembers. I made sure Robert remembered that fact." Mala said grinning, giving the younger woman a sideways glance.

"You did that?" Aubrey giggled in astonishment.

"I thought you would like to be on deck and Boulet never realized that he was duped. Though I cannot imagine why you enjoyed the prayerbook." Mala tittered in reply. Amid their gaiety, Aubrey and Mala spoke quietly until they were interrupted by the droning voice of Beaufort from behind them.

"How is it, Michele, that Monsieur Bates had specific pick of Irish here and you did not know of her availability for duty?"

"He must have privileged information of the roster." Boulet snorted in reply.

Mala turned on the two men smoothly and looked at them with an air of boredom, "She is a member of my crew."

"Oh, she beds Bates as well as that ass Alcott, but alas poor Beaufort, she does not bed you!" LaVoie tormented.

Beaufort turned quickly to shove his friend against the wall but Boulet stopped him and said, "I like the way it turned out, Thomas. It makes the view from my side of the deck much more pleasurable."

"Just keep in mind that she is for the quartermaster." Beaufort reminded his friends.

Mala snorted this time then muttered something before taking Aubrey's arm to pull her away from the men. Beaufort stepped up to block the way and he smiled as Mala opened her mouth to speak.

"Is there a problem here, Thomas?" Black asked from behind the small group.

"Non." Beaufort smiled as he stepped aside to let the women pass.

Mala blatantly bumped into Beaufort on their way past him. He grunted and then snickered at her as he and his friends turned to the companionway.

When Aubrey was inside her cabin, Black caught the island woman by the arm and asked, "Were you and Irish conspiring against me?"

"Aubrey!" She corrected firmly. Then the corners of her mouth turned up in a sweet smile. "And oui, you would be disappointed if we were not."

"Care to let me in on your little secret?" He asked as he ran a gloved hand along the line of her jaw.

"And ruin our plans to take you prisoner and take back my ship? Indeed not." She chided.

"Hmm...take me prisoner? I have been imprisoned several times in my life, but I do not think that I can boast of having been held by such an attractive jailer." He chuckled as he brushed his lips against her cheek.

Suddenly, he covered her mouth with his and pressed her against the wall. His lips trailed to the side of her face and he caught her earlobe in his teeth while his gloved hand came up to gently caress her left breast.

She caught his hand and asked, "Will you make love to me right here on the floor, Rene?"

"It has been done before." He reminded her huskily.

"Not here on this floor. Besides you caught me off guard that time, it will not happen again." She purred in reply.

"Hmm, Captain Mala, are you daring me to disprove you on that count?" Black smiled as his thumb ran down the length of her arm.

"No, I merely thought perhaps a bit of new scenery would be in order." Mala smiled back.

"Aye, the stern railing as I recall. Do you think I could lose myself in you without losing you over the railing?" Black asked softly as he pressed a kiss to her temple. She laughed softly as she lifted a finger to trace his scarred left cheek.

"Perhaps I should tie myself to the ship in order to weather the storm." Mala looked up into his dark eye and saw the lust reflected there. With one last look down the corridor to ensure that Aubrey was safely tucked away in her cabin, the dark-haired woman succumbed to the gentle pull on her hand as Black led her in the opposite direction.

Chapter 29

Aubrey helped Willie as he set the captain's table for dinner the next evening. Black had decided to have Morgan and Beaufort join him and Mala in the great cabin. Aubrey eyed the dark-haired woman who had her elbow on the table, her head propped up by the bent arm and, with the other hand, was drumming her fingers. Mala was obviously perturbed at the idea of having company. Chancing a glance towards Black who sat at the desk making entries in the logbook, Aubrey wondered how long he could ignore Mala. Apparently not long...

"Must you do that, Mala?" Black asked annoyed.

"This discussion can be done in the galley." Mala grumbled.

As she poured rum in the tankards, Aubrey glanced again at Black who continued to write in the logbook. She noticed Willie shaking his head as he placed the utensils in place.

"This discussion is hard to do, Mala, without the charts and I need this table to lay them out." Black was saying.

"I do not like the man, Rene. I do not want him in my cabin."

"I am not pleased with him right now either, mon coeur. But he does a job for me and he does it well."

Mala exhaled loudly then stood up from the table, walking toward the quarter gallery window. The sound was nearly Willie's undoing as the old man nearly choked on his own air. Aubrey noticed Black was also having difficulty maintaining a straight face as the quill faltered in its writing stance. At that moment, there was a knock at the door. As Black bade for entry, Morgan stepped in and he smiled at Aubrey as she looked up. Just as he was shutting the door, it was rudely shoved as Beaufort made an entrance. Looking over his shoulder, Morgan eyed the brute. Beaufort entered the cabin as if it were his own and strode up to Black who looked up at him.

"I appreciate the invitation to your cabin, Captain." Beaufort said loudly.

Aubrey's mouth dropped open as she looked to Mala for a reaction. Willie took Aubrey's arm and led her to a corner away from the impending fray. Black raised a brow at the man as he imagined the thoughts running through Mala's mind. Undoubtedly those thoughts contained swords, daggers, and pistols.

Before Black could reply, Mala turned and smiled at them saying, "Alas, Monsieur Beaufort, your Captain merely takes up space in a cabin that still belongs to me."

Beaufort made to reply but Black stood up and moved between the two,

"Regardless, the invitation was issued and now we dine."

Not moving from where he stood between the two, Black waited until they moved to their places at the table before taking his seat at the head of the table. Beaufort eyed the dark-haired woman whose smile never wavered as she took her seat to Black's right. Eyeing Mala, Morgan took the seat beside Beaufort.

"Smells good, Willie. What surprises have you conjured up for us this night?" Mala asked sweetly.

Willie took his queue and served up the dishes as Aubrey held the various platters. Starting with Black and moving to Mala, Aubrey glanced at Beaufort and found the man watching her as he answered Black's questions. No one noticed, however, that Mala was watching Beaufort.

As the dinner progressed, Mala noticed that Aubrey grew increasingly alarmed each time she noticed Beaufort watching her. But having had dealt with the man on several occasions, Mala's reaction to Beaufort was on the other side of emotional scale. The man had such an arrogance about him and a sense of confidence that annoyed Mala. All the more reason to set the man back on his heels, she thought to herself.

"You need to keep the cups full, girl." Beaufort grumbled as Aubrey poured more rum in Mala's tankard.

She stopped pouring and stared at the man. Satisfied he had everyone's attention, Beaufort leaned back in his chair until it teetered on its back legs. Smiling and showing yellowed teeth, he raised his tankard and tipped it over to show it was empty.

"I am about parched for a drink."

Black and Mala noticed Aubrey's shaky hand as she finished with Mala's tankard. As she moved around Black, he stopped her and had her fill his tankard first. "She is getting to you, mon ami." Black said pleasantly to Beaufort.

"Well, she is slow. Just like before, Captain." He emphasized the title for Mala's benefit who merely smiled at the man. Pushing her plate away, Mala slumped in her seat, tankard in hand. "Never did a day's work while we was on your ship. Had other duties, eh, girl? At least she does more work than what she performed for you before, right Captain?"

"Leave it be, Beaufort." Black warned as he glanced at Mala. He did not like the smile on her face and decided to move on to more comfortable topics, perhaps the weather. "Morgan, I saw a storm on the horizon earlier. Have you monitored its progress?"

"Aye, Captain. It seems to keep to our portside." Morgan replied, standing to retrieve Mala's charts.

Suddenly, Beaufort grabbed Aubrey's arm as she reached for his tankard, eliciting a shriek from her. Morgan protested as he easily extracted her from the man's grasp, "See here, Beaufort..."

"Good for nothin, whore." Beaufort grumbled.

"Thomas, release her." Black ordered.

Glaring at Morgan, Beaufort spoke to Black, "Since I am the new quartermaster and this little one has a penchant for quartermasters, I think she should..."

His statement ended in a yelp as Beaufort suddenly found himself on the floor, his chair having fallen out from under him. Mala's comfortable sitting position allowed her to tip the chair just slightly with her toe so that man and chair flew backwards.

Scrambling to his feet, Beaufort fairly flew across the table at Mala who was now standing, "You black-haired bitch!"

Throwing the remains of her rum into his face, Mala followed up with a blow to his face using her tankard. Black grabbed Beaufort by the front of his shirt and threw him bodily backwards, away from Mala. The shove caused Beaufort to stumble over the toppled chair. Losing his balance, Beaufort landed hard over the chair, breaking it.

Taking one of the legs from the chair, Beaufort moved quickly to face his foe. Mala reached over and easily pulled Black's pistol from his waistband before anyone realized her move. Suddenly Beaufort came face to face with the one-eyed hole of the pistol before him.

"Please allow me the pleasure, Monsieur Beaufort." Mala said quietly. Black swore and made to grab the pistol but Mala swung it out of his reach. Surprised at this, Black swore again. "He leaves her be or next time, I will take great pleasure in teaching him a stronger lesson!"

"Mala!" Black warned in a low tone.

Mala ignored the warning and said firmly, "He leaves her be! And he is not to come into my cabin again!" She surprised everyone, most of all Rene Black as she turned the pistol on him. "Do you understand, Captain!" She stated the title with such disdain that it would have envied any slur Deats may have ever voiced.

Having been pulled away from the fray by Morgan, Aubrey watched the three with wide frightened eyes. She knew Mala had gone too far this time. The dark scowl on Black's face told them all that she was going to answer for her actions. Beaufort, with a smile, and Morgan, with a look of apprehension, watched an angry Black place both hands on the table and lean forward to face an equally angry Mala.

"Give me the pistol and I will not punish you." He said through clenched teeth as he barely kept his rage under control.

Beaufort made a sound and Mala looked evilly at the man. Black made no move though he could have since Mala's attention was drawn away but he knew the woman too well to think that she was totally distracted.

"Mala." Black said quietly to gain her attention again.

Aubrey thought the whole world stood still as they watched and waited. It seemed like long agonizing hours before Mala calmly let the pistol roll on her finger and moved her arm in Black's direction. She handed the pistol back to him in an upside down fashion all the while staring at Beaufort.

"Make no mistake, monsieur. You do anything else..."

"Cela suffit!" Black warned.

Mala ignored him and raised her voice over his, "Anything else that disrupts the running of my ship, I will kill you."

"Merde, Mala! Arrête!" Black yelled, pounding his fist on the table.

"Killing a member of the crew? You know the penalty." Beaufort baited.

"If anyone even bothers to miss you, monsieur, then I will deal with the consequences should there be the need." Mala replied with a sardonic smile.

"Mala, please." This time it was Morgan who spoke.

Glancing at him then at Aubrey who had turned white over the whole ordeal, Mala took a deep breath and faced Black. The dark scowl on his face told her she had much to do tonight to calm him but that was another part of the fun.

Calmly, Mala sat in her chair and raised a questioning brow at Black. "Everyone out!" He growled.

Beaufort smiled thinking she was about to be punished. He followed Morgan who helped Willie escort Aubrey out of the cabin. Deciding to talk to Black alone, Beaufort would broach the subject of the Irish wench later. He wanted to see the outcome of this dark-haired woman in the morning, if she dared to face the world with her bruises.

The next morning the galley was full of both Mala's and Black's men that kept Aubrey busy with her duties. She stayed close to a group of Mala's crew that included Morgan and Robert. As she filled their tankards, the voices of Beaufort and his friends made Aubrey look up from her chore.

She watched as the men sat down at a nearby table, not noticing her presence yet. Suddenly Morgan jumped out of his seat with a yelp. Her attention was drawn back to the table to find that she had overfilled the tankard in hand. The liquid had flowed across the table and into Morgan's lap causing his outburst. With a distressed gasp, Aubrey feverishly tried to clean up the mess on the table with a rag while casting furtive glances toward Beaufort.

Her distress peaked as she found Beaufort watching her intently with a slight smile on his face while his friends continued with their conversation without him. Aubrey nearly jumped out of her skin as she felt a hand cover hers. She looked down to find that Robert had covered her hand and not Beaufort as her imagination had led her to believe. Beaufort's chuckle caught her attention as she heard Robert's calming voice. "It will be all right, Miss Aubrey."

Morgan's attention was now drawn to Robert's words as he absentmindedly dabbed at his wet britches. He followed Aubrey's gaze to Beaufort and did not like the way the man watched her.

"Well I think we should consider ourselves lucky for we are the only ship that sails the seas with our own personal tavern wench on board." Beaufort said in a booming voice that quieted some of the conversation within the galley. Members of Black's crew laughed at the remark.

"Do you suppose she performs other duties?" A voice hollered out.

Morgan looked around for the source of the question as he answered, "No, she does not!"

Beaufort snorted in disapproval then slammed his hand down on the table and said, "She has served you now she needs to serve us."

Aubrey's eyes grew wide in fear at the thought of getting close to the man. His actions the previous night had unnerved her even though Mala had taken care of the situation. When she did not move, Beaufort yelled, "Move, girl! I am thirsty!"

Shakily, Aubrey went about gathering the drinks to serve to Beaufort and his men. As she served the tankards around the table, Mala entered the galley unnoticed. She scanned the area, noticing first Aubrey who was in close vicinity of Beaufort and headed in that direction. As Aubrey set a tankard in front of Boulet, she was within reach of Beaufort. He took this advantage by reaching for her as he lifted his tankard to his lips. Before Beaufort could touch Aubrey, he was bumped from behind and was alarmed to find that the contents of his tankard in his lap. He leapt up from chair with a growl. Now Beaufort's friends looked on him with amusement.

Whirling around to see who had bumped against him, the angry comment froze in his throat as Beaufort realized that he faced Mala. His angry look changed to one of surprise at the fact that she was there and unblemished. From his cabin next door to the great cabin, he had not heard arguing or the sound of a beating after dinner the night before but he was sure Black would have dealt with this one as he had the Irish bitch.

"I apologize, Monsieur, for the mishap." Mala said when she had gained his attention. Her gaze moved pointedly to his wet britches. With a smoothness of a cat, Mala took Aubrey's arm and pushed her towards the cooking area. "Get me a drink."

Without a care and ignoring the Frenchman, Mala turned to go to her table. Beaufort grabbed her arm and pulled her back toward him. At that moment, Black entered the galley. Seeing his captain, Beaufort released her as if he had been burned. Mala turned to see Black then clicked her tongue in disappointment. She had been looking forward to a fight.

With a stern look to Beaufort, Black took Mala by the elbow and escorted her to the table. Aubrey stepped up shortly thereafter to bring Mala's drink. "Willie will be bringing out your breakfast." Aubrey informed Mala. Then looking at Black, Aubrey added, "I will let him know that you are here, Captain."

As if on queue, Willie appeared with two plates and set them before the two captains. When Aubrey left with Willie, Black asked conversationally, "What happened to Beaufort, Mala?"

"What do you mean, Rene?" She replied innocently.

"You know what I mean. It appears that Beaufort has spilled his drink down the front of him." Black replied as he took up a forkful of food.

"Can you believe it? As big as his mouth is, he missed it with his drink and spilled his ale all over himself." Mala answered with a shrug.

A small smile stole over Black's lips at her comment as he put the food into his mouth. Leaning back in her chair and looking around the room, she went on to say in a conversational tone of voice, "How could he miss a mouth that big?"

Black caught himself before choking on his food and muttered through his mouthful, "Mala, have a care." She turned back to him smiling innocently. No more words passed between them as they ate and drank in silence. The atmosphere in the galley returned to the usual camaraderie between friends.

After some time, Mala stood and said to Black, "With the extra mouths to feed, I need to check the inventory of supplies in the hold and in the storeroom. I will see you on deck."

Black nodded as he smiled and watched her leave the galley over the rim of his tankard. His thoughts moved to the night before and the pleasure that they had shared. Though he had been angry with her over her outburst at dinner, Mala had more than made up for the altercation throughout the night and even this morning. With a mental shake of his head to clear his thoughts before his body reacted, Black stood and left the galley for the quarterdeck.

Chapter 30

Mala entered the storeroom first and took note of the supplies. The shelves were full and Mala knew that the hold would be low by now. As she exited the storeroom and turned to the direction of the hold, she was grabbed by the arm and forced against the wall of the corridor. Surprised, Mala found herself facing Beaufort.

"That was not a nice way to say good morning to a crewmember." He snarled close to her face. Beaufort had leaned so close to her that their bodies touched leaving no room for Mala fend him off.

Narrowing her eyes, she snarled back, "I have business to tend to, Monsieur. I would suggest you step back and give me room to pass."

Beaufort smiled down at her as he caressed her face with a thumb. "The captain will tire of you just as he grew tired of the Irish wench. When he does, I will ride you hard and I will ride you well. Make no mistake."

With a raised brow, Mala taunted him, "Do you think yourself man enough to the task?"

"Without a doubt, whore." Beaufort said leering at her.

"Since you boast of Rene tiring of Aubrey and that I would be ridden so soon after he tosses me aside, then am I to assume that you have had Aubrey already?" Mala asked leaving much doubt as to his capabilities.

She felt Beaufort stiffen at the remark and he snapped, "That one prefers quartermasters. I am now quartermaster."

"Aye, Monsieur Beaufort, you are at the moment the quartermaster, but as I recall, the last quartermaster met with a tragic end because of her." Mala looked thoughtful for a moment and before Beaufort could reply, she added smiling sweetly, "Let me see, what was it? Ah I remember, he went down with the *Widow*. Drowned. Be careful you do not follow the same fate."

Beaufort made a bold move and cupped her breast, saying smugly, "The fool was not even on board then. And the captain's ship was called the *Widow Maker*. Since the captain has discarded the Irish wench, I will speak to him for her again today. She will warm my bunk this evening, I swear it."

Feeling his hand on her, a strong loathing for the man engulfed her as he continued his caress. Mala's tone grew ominous as she snarled in Beaufort's face, "I would suggest Monsieur Beaufort that you remove your hand or you will face the same fate as Jean Luc Pierne. To watch you drown would be a great pleasure as I will hold your head under the water myself."

Beaufort's gray eyes turned to steel as he whispered angrily, "The captain will tire of you and I will take great pleasures in putting you in your rightful place, whore. And as for Pierne, he did not drown. We marooned him while the Irish whore was recovering from the wound the captain gave her in anger because of her infidelity."

Mala hid her surprise well as she listened to Beaufort. Instead she clicked her tongue and said with much doubt in her tone, "I was told he drowned."

Beaufort smiled as his eyes locked onto her lips. He lowered his head to kiss her while he whispered, "A lie."

Without warning, Beaufort's hold on her went limp and he slowly sank to the floor. Mala watched his descent in wonder then looked up to find Morgan standing before her, his pistol in his hand, having used the butt of it on the back of Beaufort's head. Her surprise was replaced with anger and Morgan noticed the change.

"Ah now, Mala, please let me explain!" He said quickly holding his hands up.

"Explain what, Morgan? That your loyalty to your captain extends only to the first one?" She asked angrily. "Or could it be that you and Rene planned on taking my ship because he somehow managed to misplace his own?" As she spoke, she stepped closer to Morgan menacingly.

Stepping back to keep the distance, Morgan suddenly found himself slammed against the opposite wall as Mala shoved him angrily. The air rushed out of him in a "whoosh." He caught her wrist in time as she let it fly to meet his face. Her other wrist connected with his midsection.

"Christ!" He swore as he changed positions and pressed her against the wall. "Will you listen to me?" He growled.

"No, you traitorous bastard! Deats was right about you!" She hissed as she fought his hold on her.

"That Scottish bastard cannot think past you!" Morgan hissed back.

"Me? At least he was thinking of me..."

"Mala, Deats wants you in his bed! That is all he thinks about!" Morgan reminded her.

"I know that, you traitor! And he knows my answer to that!" She growled.

Morgan's face moved very close to Mala's as he whispered calmer now, "Captain, when you ordered me to escort Black out of town, he and I talked." Mala gave a derisive snort then mumbled in her language but Morgan ignored it. "He had already planned on boarding the *Enchantress*. He suggested that I aid him so that your men were not injured. Captain, can you not see? I had to do it. I could not let Black's men injure or kill any of our crew, maybe even you. He told me that he was sailing with you when the ship left the harbor, with or without my help, but he assured me that no one would be harmed if I helped him. At any rate, when this ship went out with the tide,

264

he was going to be with you again."

Mala had found out from Robert that there were fewer men on the duty watch that night. When Black boarded, no one was seriously harmed as he had apparently promised Morgan.

"He was not going to let you leave without him." He said quietly in confirmation.

Distant voices drifted down to them as they stood in the silent corridor. They turned to the sounds for a moment before Morgan turned his attention back to his captain. She was remembering her conversation with Black that first night together. *'You need not fear Morgan's influence. He was just doing his job. He was protecting his captain.'*

Looking down at the unconscious Beaufort, she said in a calmer voice, "Get help and take him further below."

"Aye, Captain." Morgan said. Relieved that her anger was gone, he released her and stepped towards the fallen Beaufort.

In a swift and fluid motion, Mala turned and took Morgan's arm to swing him to the wall, the roughness of the wood against his cheek. "You aid in the boarding of my ship again, I will kill you." She warned through clenched teeth.

"Aye Mala, I know." He managed to say.

"Then, we too have an understanding." She hissed as she yanked him from the wall. "Now get his feet." She ordered as she bent to grab Beaufort's hands.

Nearly dragging the man further down the corridor and away from the storeroom, they turned the corner and dropped their burden on the floor.

"We will leave him here." Mala said. She stared down at Beaufort for a moment before she said distractedly, "The man is persistent to the point of boring." Morgan chuckled as the two left the prone body of Thomas Beaufort in the darkened corridor.

As they headed back to the upper levels, Morgan said quietly, "Robert and I know where Deats and the other men are being held." Turning to stand in her way, Morgan added, "Before you demand their release, think on this, Mala. The men would listen to you if you order their cooperation but Deats would not…"

"Morgan…"

"Listen, please. Deats would try to mutiny against Black. We know Black has only a few men, one you killed within minutes of his boarding your ship." He saw her look of anger flash at the mention of the boarding but he went on, "But think of what could happen now. I am not proud of what I did but I had to do it to make sure that no one was hurt or killed, at least from our crew. But would Deats give that a thought? You know he would not. His first target would be Captain Black. Do you want that, Mala?"

Giving him a glare as she made to pass him, Morgan dared to block her way again and her look of surprise made him rush through what he wanted to say next, "I have been watching you, Mala. Ah hell, the whole crew has been watching you. As long as you are well and happy, and you cannot deny that you are happy to be with him, the crew will obey Captain Black. He has only taken over command because it was expected and because you have let him."

She shoved him aside as she walked on with purposeful strides. Morgan watched her and knew she would confront Black. He just hoped that the confrontation did not undo what good had come from this boarding thus far.

Topside, the sea surrounded them, the air was warm in the morning sun and breezy but Mala did not see nor feel any of it. Her mind recounted the few days since she and Aubrey were released from the hold. Fleetingly, she remembered another time when she was in chains. Shaking the thought of that bad memory, Mala thought of what Beaufort had said. *'We marooned him while the Irish whore recovered from her wound.'* She knew from Aubrey that it had been several days before she was up and around. So Black left him on an island near Bimini then returned to Bimini to meet with the slave ship.

Disgusted, Mala pursed her lips at the thought that Black would sell Aubrey to some slave ship captain. He had hated slave traders ever since he had found her in the hold of that ship. What on earth was he thinking of? Again her thoughts went back to the bad memories and again Mala had to shake herself from dwelling on that part of her past.

Focusing her attention on the men on the deck, she noted that most of the Black's men were scattered about. She looked up at the crow's nest and though she could not see his face, she knew that he would also be one of his men.

Out of the corner of her eye, there was a glimmer on the portside horizon. She looked overhead but no warning was called. Looking to the quarterdeck, she found Black watching her.

He had been watching her since she appeared on deck and she did not appear to be happy. Her unsmiling visage had always left him wary as she surveyed the men. He knew that she was keeping track of his men and their whereabouts even to include the crow's nest. He smiled slightly, knowing she would miss nothing and think of everything.

Now she was joining him on the quarterdeck. With a greeting to Timmons, Mala took Black's eyepiece and scanned the portside horizon. He watched in amusement as she scanned the area, looking briefly in the

266

direction she seemed to have focused on but could see nothing. As he turned his head away, there it was. A glimmer far on the horizon. Mala lowered the eyepiece and looked to the crow's nest. Still no alarm sounded.

"Is that one of my men or one of yours?" She asked Black.

"One of mine." He replied taking the long glass and spying a ship in the distance.

"Then he is blind as a bat, Rene." She grumbled. Turning to Timmons, she ordered, "Turn the ship hard to starboard and head due west."

"Aye Captain." He affirmed as he spun the wheel.

Mala watched the horizon as Black watched her. Gently his finger swept her temple to capture a strand of hair and tucked it behind her ear. Unable to resist, Black held her chin between his thumb and forefinger, then lowered his head to place a gentle kiss upon her lips.

When he raised his head and looked into Mala's eyes, he wondered of the many times since he boarded her ship that he would just stare at her. He succumbed to the urge of placing another gentle kiss upon her lips and as he lowered his head to do so, the air fairly crackled with a bellowing rage. Black's head shot up in surprise and found the sound came from Beaufort.

"Beaufort." Mala whispered in tired voice. Black looked down at her as she added, "You really must do something about that one, Rene. He is truly becoming a bore and now it appears he means to be a very loud bore."

Black could not help but smile as he wondered again what happened just before he had entered the galley. Now he had to wonder about what happened when he left the galley.

"There you are, you chein en le diable!" Beaufort yelled, drawing Black's attention.

"Now he has taken to calling you names, Rene." Mala said calmly as Black gave the man an incredulous look.

Black chuckled at her interpretations. Of course the insult was intended for her but she managed to find humor in the fact that Beaufort added the reference to 'the devil' and turned the insult on him.

As Beaufort stepped behind Mala, Black realized that the man meant to strike her while her back was still turned to him. Before he could move her away for protection, Mala spun around and landed her fist under Beaufort's chin. Even Timmons who had turned back to his duty heard the loud 'clomp' as the man's teeth slammed together. Black could see the helmsman's shoulders shake as the man laughed silently.

Beaufort, on the other hand, had a headache from the blow Morgan had dealt him. Now he could feel himself falling backwards. His arms flew for some hold but only caught air and Beaufort was on the deck below, unconscious once again. Looking down at him, Black laughed and encircled

Mala in his arms.

"I must admit, Mala, mon coeur, you could never bore me." Mala was trying to shake the ache from her abused hand when Black took it in his hand and placed a kiss on top of it.

"A kiss to heal the pain." He whispered as he lowered the hand and wrapped his arms around her again, pressing her back against him.

Mala smiled then turned in his arms and whispered, "Ah, but what of the ache, Monsieur Pirate Capitaine?"

With a leering grin and a raised brow, Black whispered back, "What does my lady suggest?"

Mala lifted her hand and, with her forefinger, she traced the scar that ran down his left cheek. Her gaze was so provocative at that moment Black could scarcely breathe as his body reacted immediately. Without a word, he took her hand and led her down the companionway steps to the main deck.

"Find a cove and let whoever that is pass us." Mala ordered up to Timmons.

"Aye Captain." The helmsman acknowledged.

At the bottom of the steps, Mala slowed as they approached Beaufort's prone body with the urge to kick the man. Feeling the tug on his hand as she slowed, Black turned then swept her up in his arms, chuckling at her startled gasp.

Timmons smiled and shook his head as the two captains disappeared below. As long as his captain did not mind the intrusion of the other, he did not mind. There was, of course, the absence of Mr. Deats. Although unfortunate, Timmons could feel an air of relief throughout the entire ship. He shrugged indifferently as he peered ahead for a hiding place.

It was early afternoon while Black and Mala dined in the great cabin when she decided to speak of Deats. She had spent the morning pondering what Morgan had said and knew there was some truth to the matter. But she decided that she was going to ask about Deats and the other men. Black made a show of pouring more wine into the ceramic mugs Mala provided with their meal. He smiled to himself as he remembered her saying that she had been saving them for something special. His gaze lifted to her face as he finished pouring and found her watching him.

"Rene." She whispered.

He smiled at her as he placed the bottle back down on the table. "Oui, mon coeur."

"I wonder what you would say if I tell you that I want the rest of my men released."

His smile slowly disappeared and he became wary. "Non."

"Without a word in their defense from me?"

"Mala." He warned.

"Deats is my quartermaster and you have how many of my men held prisoner?"

"Mala." He warned again getting up from the table.

She watched him as he downed the wine he just poured in a long swallow reflecting his irritation with her. He placed the mug onto the table with such a bang that Mala winced. Not because he was angry, she could get around that, but because he could have broken her mug that she had been saving.

"Why do you bring up this subject when the day has been most—enjoyable." He grumbled trying to find that right word.

"Rene." She said as she stood up and he sat heavily in the chair at the desk, glaring at her. She saw he was not happy but she could get around that too.

He watched her approach him and place her hands on the desk to lean forward. Just as she opened her mouth to speak, Black raised his hand and spoke first, "Mala, consider what this quartermaster would do should I release him? You yourself were not very tolerant of him as we stood in the woods outside of Charlestowne."

"He questioned my orders." Mala told him.

Black ignored her statement as he continued, "It seems to me that he would not only challenge me but you as well. What would you do if he managed to rally the men together and there is a mutiny? How many would die because I bent to your whim and released him? This quartermaster of yours cannot be trusted. I would even wager that once freed, his revolt would be against you."

Mala looked at him as he glared back at her. Damn him for saying the same thing Morgan had said earlier. Of course, Deats would go against her. He knew that she held herself only for Rene Black and that was why Deats was so insisted of her killing the man. And the infuriating Scotsman would use her recent relationship to show her crew that she could not be trusted. After all she had let Black command her ship.

Black sat quietly watching her as she stared at the top of her desk, his gaze roamed to the place where his mark would be on her left breast.

"Then release the men and leave Deats. Let me talk to those men and they will do as you say because I will command it." Mala said still not looking at him. Black watched her but still she did not look at him.

"Mala, are you so certain that these men would obey you now?" Black asked reasonably. Mala looked up then and he saw the flash of doubt before it was gone. "You could have demanded this of me on the first day."

"Let me face them and we shall both see. Unless of course they have been mistreated and…"

Black was shaking his head negatively, "No they have been fed and treated well."

"You could have refused me until now." She said trying to sound innocent.

Black smiled and replied, "And the other men of your crew would tell them what they have seen between the two of us."

Mala gave him an annoyed look for she could not reason around him. He was right that she should have asked about them on the first day. But for the first time since she was made captain and given the responsibility of this ship and crew, she was selfish. She thought of only herself and what she wanted. Rene Black was alive and on her ship. After seeing him in Charlestowne, she was willing to give up everything to be with him again. Her eyes softened as her gaze moved over his face and she was not even aware of the slow smile that appeared on her face. That was exactly what she had done. She had allowed him to take command of her ship and her crew while she spent every minute she could with him, whenever he wanted her.

Black had been watching her and saw the change in her expression. He stood and moved around the desk to stand beside her as her eyes followed him. "Do you wish to see them now?" He whispered.

She shook her head almost imperceptibly and he smiled. Taking another step towards her, Mala lifted her arms and wrapped them around his neck as he whispered in a deep voice thick with desire, "What do you wish to do now?"

Her smile widened as she whispered, "Get back to that enjoyable day."

Later that afternoon, Mala had walked uncaringly across the deck noticing Black on the quarterdeck talking with Timmons. She joined Morgan and Robert near the forecastle and they fell into discussion of the recent release of her men.

No one paid attention to Beaufort and his two ever-present companions as they stood on the forecastle. His gray eyes never left the dark-haired woman as she talked with her men then narrowed to steel slits when she moved to the companionway to wait for Black.

"I am getting very tired of that one. When I have my turn on her, she will pay for each and every time she stood against me." Beaufort muttered when his captain joined her and the two disappeared below deck.

"Now Thomas, that one is not even friendly." Boulet said, thinking that Beaufort needed to start forgetting about having Captain Mala warm his bed. Black was not going to give her up any time soon.

"I like spirit." Beaufort countered.

"I would not exactly call it spirit. I would say that it was more like..." LaVoie began.

"I can handle her. Mon Dieu, she is just a woman." Beaufort interrupted.

Undaunted, LaVoie said through chuckles, "Indeed, like the way you handled her that day on deck or maybe it was in the galley or..."

The man found his throat caught in Beaufort's grasp. Trying to get air, the man's vision was filled with Beaufort's face as he snarled, "You get to know your enemy and then you strike."

LaVoie sucked in great gulps of air when Beaufort released his hold and thrust him away. His companions heard Beaufort grumble as he left them, "Women on board. Tis bad luck anyway."

Chapter 31

The soft hues of pink filled the eastern horizon as the morning began to dawn. As was his habit, Black was already dressed for the day. He stood beside the bunk looking down at the woman still sleeping within. She faced the wall, her dark hair tossed over her pillow and flowed over a small portion of his. In the stillness of the cabin, he could barely hear her soft breathing over the lapping of the waters against the hull of the *Enchantress*.

Turning to the table, Black picked up the bundle he had carefully set down when he began to dress. Sitting in a chair facing the bunk, he quietly rolled out the cloth. Within the wrapping were Mala's pistols and daggers. He lifted each one and admired the ornate carvings on the handles. With a smile, he then lifted his gaze to the woman in the bunk and shook his head as he thought of how adept she was with her weapons.

Although Mala proved her ability to handle herself with or without the use of her weapons, Black found that over the past week Beaufort's persistence was becoming more and more bold. As Mala had said so often in those first few days since he had taken over her ship, he had boarded her ship with only a few men. Beginning with ten men, Mala had easily disposed of one during the boarding and he shook his head over the speed in which she had done the deed. She was certainly the fighter! But even so, Beaufort's advances toward her would need to be dealt with. Though Mala could kill the man without her weapons, Black feared that if things continued one of them would certainly end up dead. He would need to speak to Beaufort about Mala before the man found himself in a watery grave.

Mala stirred in her sleep and rolled over to face Black. He smiled when her eyes fluttered open and his gaze lowered to the top of the sheet that revealed the tops of her breasts. He then followed the sheet down as it outlined the curves of her body it covered. Slowly he followed the curves back up to her face where he met her smile.

"Bonjour, mon coeur." Black greeted.

"Morning comes too soon." Mala said as she rose on one elbow. Her smile widened as she watched Black's gaze drop back to her breasts. The sheet had dropped away and left her breasts exposed. "You have seen them often, Rene. They have not changed in appearance." She said as she got out of the bunk and slipped into his shirt that had been left on the floor from the night before.

"Oui, but never enough." Came his husky reply making her chuckle softly as she moved to his side. Black placed an arm around her waist when she bent forward for a kiss. As he kissed her, he applied more pressure about her waist until she ended up sitting across his lap and felt her silent laughter against his lips. After several moments, he lifted his head to gaze upon her while his hand slipped under the shirt to caress a soft mound. She smiled at him then turned her attention to what she had seen on the table a few moments before.

"What are you doing with my weapons?"

"Admiring them." He said then smiled when she turned to look at him questioningly, "Actually, I want to return them to you." Black was hard-pressed to contain his laughter as Mala blinked at him in disbelief.

"You are giving them back?" She asked looking at the weapons.

"Oui, but there is a condition, Mala." He felt her stiffen as she slowly turned her gaze to him. "I will have a talk with Thomas. Though you have proven quite resourceful thus far fending the man off, I thought that with your weapons, you could use them to give him more stern warnings than just verbal ones. But no more than that, Mala. You must promise me that you will not give into acting as captain and proclaim punishment. As the current captain, I would hate to pass a sentence of death on you."

Mala was on her feet in an instant. With hands on her hips, glaring at him while clad in only his shirt, Black was hard pressed to concentrate on her words instead of the body.

"Do not presume to dictate what punishments I decree! This is still my ship!" Mala growled.

Black stood up and faced her, saying flippantly, "Aye, it is and you have enjoyed your rest from your duties. You seem quite content to play the captain's pet."

Mala was swift as her fist flew but Black anticipated her move and caught her by the wrist. In an instant, Black felt the sting of her hand as she managed to bring up her other hand to slap him. "You bastard!" She hissed as she tried to yank her arm from his grasp and, in a swift jerking move, Black slammed her down on her back over the table. He leaned over her, pinning her legs, and holding both of her wrists over her head.

"Arrête! Cela suffit!" Black growled as she fought against him. When she did not heed his order, he hissed, "Merde! I do not want to see you dead, Mala! Arrête!"

"Damn you, Rene." Mala spat.

Black had a hard time holding her down. The woman knew how to struggle in a fight. His anger was rising and he knew he might end up striking her. With a violence that was building within him, Black jerked Mala to her feet and shoved her away from him. She flew towards the quarter gallery window but stumbled over her boots that had been casually tossed on the floor from the night before. Trying to catch herself, Mala's hand hit the wall. Knowing where she was falling, she tried to avoid landing on the large window's sitting ledge. Somehow, she managed to land on the floor. She looked up at Black to find him storming toward the door. Looking at the objects on her ledge, she picked up an unusually large conch shell and threw it at him.

Black opened the door and slammed it behind him. The sound of a crash on the other side startled him. She threw something at him? He wondered and nearly turned to go back but stopped himself. He stood in indecision for a moment before he forced himself to turn around and go topside. He needed the cool morning air to rein in his own temper before facing her.

Storming angrily to the starboard railing, he tried calming himself by breathing deep gulps of the sea air. The sun was just peeking over the horizon but instead he saw the weapons on the table. He had left them in the cabin with an angry hellcat! Mon Dieu, but she was argumentative at times. Since he had taken over her ship, they had argued much over minor things, more like a battle of wills, but the making up was more than enjoyable with her. To vent out some frustration, he pounded his fist on the railing and turned his back to the sea then came face to face with Morgan who was standing a few feet away.

"Is there a problem, Captain?" He asked slowly.

Black glared at him, saying, "Aye, she has to be the most stubborn woman alive!"

Morgan had been walking towards him and smiled at his reference to Mala. He knew that Aubrey was in the galley with Willie and was not the one Black referred to. "Mala woke up out of sorts this morning?" Morgan asked.

Black grunted and rolled his eye in annoyance but made no reply. Morgan stood next to Black and leaned forward on the railing looking out at the rising sun. "I would swear she just loves to fight." The captain grumbled.

"She would not be captain if she acted like a normal woman." Morgan said. Black looked sharply at him as he touched on the very subject of this recent argument. Missing the look, Morgan moved his gaze down to the ocean and added, "But then I truly believe that she is happiest when she is at odds..." Morgan paused and glanced covertly over to Black who was scuffing a booted foot on the deck. "...with someone who is important to her." He finished.

Black slowly lifted his gaze to meet twinkling blue eyes before Morgan shrugged and looked out at rising sun, adding, "I think she does it on purpose just for the fun of it." Glancing at Black to find the man still watching him, Morgan rolled his eyes and let out a sigh, "Well, hell, what else has she got to do since you are the captain now?"

Black stared hard at Morgan as he continued to smile. Raising his face to the morning sun, Morgan turned away from the railing nonchalantly and began to whistle a tune.

It was a half an hour later when Black returned to the cabin to hear Mala behind the screen taking a bath. Willie had told him that she had requested a bath so he knew to remain quiet. The splashing of the water effectively hid his sounds. He held a tray laden with their breakfast and gently placed it on the end of the table near her weapons. Black noticed her weapons had not moved or even looked like they were touched. Taking his own weapons from his waistband, Black set them quietly down next to Mala's.

Relaxing in the tub, she thought of her weapons on the table. He had surprised her by wanting to give them back to her. Then she ruined the pleasure of his surprise by being so petty in one small request. Small? To not give into her tendencies and kill Beaufort! If she had given into her tendencies, Beaufort would have died that first morning out. Mala sighed as she thought of Black. Damn the blasted man for putting conditions on her.

Sitting on the edge of the table, Black waited patiently. The smell of the food on the tray began to permeate the cabin and he smiled waiting for Mala to catch a whiff of their breakfast. He lifted the covers from the dishes carefully and set them aside. The smells were more pronounced now and he fanned his hand to the direction of the tub as if it would speed the aroma to Mala. Within seconds, a gasp and the sound of water sloshing about could be heard as Black laughed silently.

With a towel held against her breasts, a glistening wet Mala peered around the screen. She found Black perched against the table, a hand covering his mouth as he laughed silently.

"Mon Dieu, Rene!" She exclaimed breathlessly as her eyes looked down at the table and saw the tray of food he brought in. He saw her look of astonishment as her gaze lifted to meet his gaze once again. "You came in here and I did not hear you?"

Stepping around the screen and drying herself off, Black took the other end of towel and pulled her towards him. His lustful gaze met Mala's dark eyes as he slowly rubbed her with the towel. Mala closed her eyes to concentrate on the man and the pleasure. She moaned then his mouth crushed hers as he lifted her and carried her to the bunk, their breakfast forgotten.

It was a while later that Morgan entered the galley and joined Mala at the captain's cabin. "Just saw Captain Black on deck. He is not angry anymore." Then with his most charming smile, added, "What did you do?"

Mala leaned back and smiled at him, "What I always do. I directed his attention to more important matters of business."

Morgan chuckled as Willie approached with his plate of breakfast. "Matters of business? Oh ho, Willie, did you know that I was only born yesterday?"

Willie smiled at the young man then replied, "Well now, that would explain everything! I just thought ye was tryin' to prove yer ignorance!"

"Get away from me, old man." Morgan chuckled.

"With no trouble, you ignorant pirate." Willie bantered back.

Mala and Morgan laughed aloud as the cook returned to the cookstove but not before Willie deftly maneuvered away from a backhanded swing from Morgan. Settling back to his meal, Aubrey stepped into the galley and spotted them at the table. Seating herself with her friends, she reached across the table and picked a piece of ham from Morgan's plate.

"Hey, I was saving that!" Morgan exclaimed trying to snatch it back. Aubrey laughed and held the meat from his reach.

"And I thank you for that." She replied to his smiling face.

"Willie!" Morgan yelled out. When Willie's head appeared from around the corner, Morgan ordered, "Bring Aubrey some breakfast before she eats all of mine!"

Willie chuckled and within seconds, appeared with a plate for Aubrey. "Thank you, Willie but Morgan seems to be missing some ham. Please give him mine." She said pushing her meat away with her fork. Willie looked perplexed for he was sure he had given Morgan some of the cured ham.

"You thief!" Morgan accused playfully then added pointing his fork at Aubrey, "That ragamuffin stole mine from beneath my very nose."

Willie set down the plate and turned away, "Ye two settle this on yer own. I will be at me cookstove where tis safe from thieves and ignorant pirates!"

Aubrey's mouth dropped momentarily before she exclaimed, "Who are you calling an ignorant pirate?"

"Me!" Morgan answered. Pointing at her with his fork, he said, "You are the thief, you thief!"

"Children." Mala interjected with a smile and shook her head.

"So what is the plan for today?" Morgan asked Mala as he reached across the table and stole Aubrey's hardtack with a stab of his fork.

"You can have that." Aubrey whispered. She had not acquired a taste for hardtack and hoped that she never would.

Two of Mala's crew entered the galley and from their excited nature, Mala knew something had happened or was about to happen.

"Mr. Davis, Mr. Stone." She called out to them.

"Sorry Cap'n." Davis was saying as they approached.

"Aye, Cap'n. Thought everyone was preparin' for the raid." Stone told them.

Morgan put down his fork hard and asked, "What raid? Why was I not informed?"

"Well Mr. Beaufort was takin' care of armin' the men, sir. Thought he got the key from ye." Morgan and Mala exchanged a look of irritation. If Beaufort was arming the men, then he had broken into the armory.

"What raid?" Mala repeated Morgan's question.

"There be a merchant ship that looks rich and Cap'n Black means to take 'er." Davis answered.

"Damn it!" Mala exclaimed, slamming the palms of her hands on the table as she stood up quickly to leave. Morgan got up quickly as well and was followed by Aubrey. Davis and Stone stood rooted where they were leery of the look on their captain's face.

"How could Thomas Beaufort get into the armory? You have the only key!" Aubrey asked as she hurried to follow.

Mala stopped and turned to face Morgan and Aubrey who stopped suddenly so they would not run into her. She eyed Aubrey then said, "Get out of sight. Go to your cabin and bolt the door." Mala turned to continue her journey to the deck but turned back to the two, "No, go to my cabin and bolt the door. With the likes of Beaufort roaming my ship, he will dare to force his way into all areas of this ship except my cabin. Should he choose to be so foolish, I will kill him this time. Rene be damned!"

Looking at Morgan, Mala ordered, "Make sure Aubrey gets to my cabin safely then join me on deck."

"Aye!" Morgan confirmed then took Aubrey's arm and led her to the great cabin.

Chapter 32

On deck, men moved quickly about their duties. Mala found Black on the quarterdeck looking through his eyepiece. She moved to the middle of the deck, scanning the horizon before them for the other ship. She found a large merchant ship to her starboard side and the *Enchantress* was changing direction to head straight for her. Mala moved closer to the rail, pulled out her eyepiece and studied the ship as Morgan approached her from behind.

"She is a rather big ship for a merchant and judging by the water level at those portals, she is heavily laden too. She must be loaded with goods."

Mala looked at Morgan who was showing signs of excitement for the raid. Then she turned to see Black talking to Timmons. Morgan's eyes gleamed with anticipation until he saw the look on Mala's face as she watched the ship and his smile vanished quickly.

"What is it?" He asked, his voice betraying the alarm he felt.

"I do not like this." She hissed. Then turning to head for the quarterdeck, she hissed again, "I do not like this one damn bit!"

In quick strides, she mounted the steps to the quarterdeck where she found not only Black and Timmons but Beaufort as well. Ignoring the bully, she attacked Black, "What the hell do you think you are doing with my ship, Rene?"

"Tis no longer your ship." Beaufort sneered.

She ignored him as Black faced her with the excitement of the raid and answered, "Look at her, Mala! She is so full, she... "

"You idiot! You are falling for their ruse! She is loaded with cannons and ammunition not goods to be stolen!" Then like a raging bull, Mala stomped her foot, "Damn it, Rene! You are not going to sink my ship! Timmons, get my ship out of here!"

"You are not..." Beaufort started but Mala stepped away to call down to Morgan.

"Man the cannons and be ready at once! Timmons, turn this ship around! Now!"

Black had the long glass to his good eye, studying the ship and was not aware of Beaufort grabbing Mala's shoulder in a painful grip to face him.

"You are no longer in command of this ship!" Beaufort said harshly. Black lowered the eyepiece in time to see Mala, livid with rage, backhand Beaufort across the face.

"Cela suffit, you arrogant ass!" She yelled as she struck him hard. With his grip loosened on her shoulder, Mala shoved him over the quarterdeck railing where Beaufort landed hard on his back onto the deck below. She whirled on her helmsman and told him menacingly, "Timmons, if you do not turn that whe..."

The sound of cannonfire turned her attention back to the other ship. The shot landed behind them, spraying water over them. The portal doors dropped on the *Enchantress* and the cannons rolled into place, a clear indication that Morgan was prepared to fight back. Timmons spun the wheel until it blurred with the speed.

Leaning over the railing, she yelled to her men, "Prepare for speed! We are leaving!"

Mala ran down to the main deck as Morgan fired the cannons at the other ship. The *Enchantress* rocked and threw her against the bulkhead. Black raced down to the deck behind her as she ran to help position the ship's sails. Beaufort was just getting to his feet when Mala passed him. Pulling out his pistol from his waistband, he took aim but he was thrown back against the bulkhead to face an angry Black.

"Leave her be!" He growled at Beaufort. Pointing to Timmons, he ordered, "Help him steer the ship out of the way!"

The other ship fired again as Black turned to find Mala. She and some of her men were climbing the ratlines. His gaze moved ahead to find that a few of the stays had gotten tangled, hindering the sails from unfurling.

"Captain! They changed flags! Tis the Union Jack!" The lookout yelled out.

Black moved quickly to the railing to see the ship was now at their starboard aft since Timmons changed the direction of the *Enchantress*. The British flag flew high and proud in the stiff breeze as the ship made chase. Looking up, Black found Mala perched on the yardarm of the mast, unmindful of the height and the rocking of the ship as Morgan fired back. He felt a cold grip on his heart as Mala tried to maintain her balance and for a moment, her gaze found his before she turned to aid her men in dropping the sails.

Black swore a blue streak as he whirled around and headed for the quarterdeck. How the hell could she know the difference from a heavily laden merchant ship and the British Navy in disguise? He wondered to himself. "As soon as those sails are freed, this ship better make some distance..." Black was yelling as he mounted the steps to the quarterdeck.

"Aye, sir!" Timmons replied while Black was still speaking. "The *Enchantress* is faster than that heavy bucket of scrapwood, you will see." Timmons added proudly.

Black turned to watch the British and muttered under his breath, "I already have."

Another cannon shot flew over the *Enchantress* and landed in the water. Timmons chuckled, "They were never very good at aimin', eh, Captain?"

Black looked at Timmons then looked around at Mala's crew. Their confidence in her abilities as a fighter, a pirate, and their captain astounded him. The sound of a flap overhead was heard and Black looked up to find the sail freed from the untangled lines. Morgan fired again and the ship rocked then picked up speed.

"Now you will see, Captain. We will be gone long before those British knew what happened." Timmons said proudly.

Mala descended from her high perch by climbing down, jumping or swinging from one perch to another whenever possible. Black felt his heart stop as he watched her descend. When she landed on deck with a final jump from the ratlines, Black did not realize he was holding his breath until he exhaled loudly.

She ran towards the quarterdeck but did not join Black and Timmons. Instead she yelled up, "Now, Mr. Timmons, take us out of here!" Then she disappeared below deck.

Timmons smiled and looked over his shoulder at Black, and even though Mala would not hear, he said, "Aye, Captain."

Beaufort opened the cabin door quickly and found the cabin empty. He could smell her scent in the small area as he checked all the hiding places. The cabin was empty!

"Damn her." He swore, thinking to surprise Aubrey but she had eluded him. Then a smile crept in as he thought of a place where she would be. He made his way through the corridor, passing men who hurried to do their duties. He found the galley was empty as well. Beaufort's sudden appearance in the galley startled Willie who was securing pots and pans and other objects.

"Where is that Irish wench?" Beaufort asked impatiently.

"I have no idea. She left with the Cap'n and Mr. Alcott before the battle." Willie replied as he watched Beaufort storm about looking into corners and other hiding places. Giving Willie one last glare, Beaufort stormed out of the galley and back down the corridor.

"Now that is an ignorant pirate." Willie mumbled as he went back to his work.

Beaufort continued his search for Aubrey. He came out of the storeroom and stood in the corridor looking down one direction then the other.

"She did not jump overboard so where is she?" He growled as he stood in the middle of the corridor. Then his eyes lit up as he had a thought and a smile appeared before he made his way to the captain's cabin.

Aubrey stood at the large window, watching the other ship. She gasped as she saw the changing of the flags but Morgan's shots were doing damage to the British vessel. She turned as she heard footsteps outside the cabin door. Wide-eyed, she watched as the handle was tried before there was a knock. She remained silent while the handle was tried again and another knock. Suddenly the door crashed open as Beaufort laid a heavy foot to the door.

"Ah, there you are, girl." He said entering the cabin. Aubrey backed around the large table and used it to keep the distance between her and Beaufort. "I have been looking everywhere for you so you will be very nice to me for the all trouble I went through." He said then suddenly lunged across the table and nearly caught hold of her shirt at the shoulder. Aubrey squealed in terror and whirled around to escape him.

"Do not make me angry, you Irish bitch, or I will take it out on your lovely hide!" Beaufort yelled as he went after her.

Panic-stricken, Aubrey's eyes looked around for a weapon. She threw anything her hands could grab. The logbook and inkwell from the desk flew past Beaufort's head as he easily dodged the objects. Aubrey raced to the large window for the various knick-knacks Mala had decorating the window seat. Her scream was abruptly cut short as Beaufort grabbed her from behind and covered her mouth. She kicked and squirmed as he picked her up by the waist and moved her to the bunk, laughing at her attempts to get free.

"Oh I do like this! Fight me, girl, yes fight me." He laughed as he placed wet kisses on her throat and shoulder. With her head held tight against his shoulder, Beaufort moved his other hand to cup her breast. "How I have wanted this, girl, and you are finally going to give me my pleasure."

They both froze at the sound of a pistol cocking and Beaufort could feel the barrel pressing at his temple. "Not this time." Mala said in a soft and calm voice. "I will kill you before you have that pleasure, Monsieur Beaufort. But then that would be my pleasure. Now release her but slowly."

Aubrey felt tears brimming at the sound of Mala's voice, her relief so apparent. Beaufort's jaw clenched at the interruption as he moved slightly to look at the dark-haired woman. He released Aubrey then remained still. Aubrey ran past Mala and into the opposite corner of the cabin.

"Now have a seat on the bunk." Mala ordered Beaufort. Turning slowly, he glanced around to see Aubrey cowering in the corner. "Move carefully, Monsieur Beaufort. I have no problem if you care to make it your last."

Beaufort sat slowly down on the bunk facing Mala who was backing up. At the long table, she turned a chair to face Beaufort, the pistol still pointing at him. Once seated, Mala glanced at the door then smiled at Beaufort, "Now what will your captain say to that? I certainly hope you did not make it habit of breaking down his door on the *Widow*." She taunted.

Beaufort looked at the door and the damage he had done. A jagged half circle was taken out of the side of the doorjamb where the lock was fastened to the wall. That piece was still attached to the door with the bolt.

They had no idea how long they sat there. Beaufort on the bunk facing an unwavering pistol, Mala at the table, and Aubrey in a corner behind Mala, it was upon this scene that Rene Black entered into the cabin. He looked at the occupants of the cabin then looked over the damage of the doorjamb.

"What the hell happened in here?" He asked but knowing full well what the answer would be since Beaufort was in the cabin. Mala lowered the pistol but did not put it down as Beaufort kept his eyes on it. He had hoped that she would put it on the table and there would be a race for the weapon.

"Well?" Black asked when no one answered.

Aubrey stood up and replied, "He forced his way in to get to me. Mala thought he would and told me to bolt myself in her cabin instead of mine."

Surprised, Beaufort looked at Mala who was smiling at him. With a shrug, she taunted, "You are too predictable, Monsieur Beaufort. But then most men are."

Black stepped up to them and glared down at Beaufort, saying angrily, "Your orders were to help the helmsman if I recall correctly."

"Humph, and you did not even notice his absence from the quarterdeck or even the main deck, Rene. You are about as observant as the blasted British." Mala chided.

Black turned his glare on her before facing Beaufort again. "Aubrey Malone is not your concern and you are lucky that Mala decided to play with you instead of killing you. Now get out and find something to repair the damage you have done!"

Beaufort stood and headed for the door, glancing at Aubrey before leaving. She did not like that look nor did she like the small smile that appeared on his face.

"How was the raid?" Mala asked conversationally, watching Black pick up the logbook from the floor.

As he stood he gave her an irritated look, "Very well, Mala. You were right and I was wrong. Is that you want to hear?" He walked to the desk and slammed the book down. Aubrey jumped at the noise and glanced at Mala who winked at her.

"Why are you still here? Go on to your own cabin." Black barked as he turned and saw Aubrey still standing in the corner.

"No! Sit down here, Aubrey." Mala countered.

"Mala..."

"No! Beaufort is not going to have her and I will not let you put her in his hands by sending her out into the corridor." Mala said as she stood to face Black. Morgan appeared then and looked at the damage of the doorway, fully perplexed.

"What happened in here?" Morgan asked. Aubrey was relieved to see him as he entered the cabin.

"Ah Morgan, very nice shooting as usual." Mala complimented.

"Thank you, Captain. They are sinking and there should be nothing left of them in a few hours. Cannons were not really meant for that kind of vessel and tis a wonder they did not sink with that weight."

"I would imagine that aside from the cannons and the ammunition, the only other things on that ship were the crew." Mala added.

"How did you know?" Morgan asked.

"Exactly what I would like to know." Black piped in.

"Tis quite simple really, gentlemen. Merchants are wary of other ships that come near, especially if they do not recognize them. They tend to prepare for battle in case something goes awry. Raids are far too common, but on that one," Mala jabbed her thumb to the gallery window where the ship was last seen behind them. "There were no men scurrying about the deck. They were either very foolish or hiding. I do not like it when things do not happen like they should."

Looking pointedly at Aubrey, Mala finished, "Then again, I do not like it when things happen as I predict they would either."

"Arrête, Mala. I do believe you are drawing blood now." Black said with a smile that held no warmth.

As if on queue, Beaufort appeared with supplies to repair the doorway. Morgan felt anger rise up in him as he watched Beaufort prepare his materials.

"Well do not just stand there, help him fix it." Mala said to Black and Morgan who just watched Beaufort.

Black gave her an exasperated look while Morgan rolled his eyes. Without a word, they moved to help Beaufort with the repairs.

"And after you are done with that, fix whatever damage was done to the armory." Mala added. To the men, it sounded like an order. Morgan found it hard to suppress his grin while Black did not even try as his throaty chuckle could be heard. Beaufort was the only one who found nothing amusing with the woman issuing commands and could not understand why Captain Black was even obeying her.

While the men were busy with the door, Mala tapped Aubrey's shoulder and indicated the desk. When they stood behind the desk, Aubrey looked questioningly at Mala. "Next time you need a weapon, remember this." Mala whispered.

Looking up at the men, she put her finger inside the hole for the inkwell. She pointed to the leg of the desk on her left. Aubrey looked down and found the ornate woodwork of the leg fall open slightly revealing an ivory handle pistol that was hidden inside the hollowed leg. Shock and surprise appeared on her face as she looked at Mala who smiled at her.

"What are you two doing?" Morgan asked as he looked over his shoulder while holding a strip of wood for nailing.

"Pay attention to your work, idiot!" Mala scolded. He winked at Aubrey then turned back to his work. Mala used her knee to close the hiding place and whispered, "Remember that in case you need it again."

"I will and thank you." Aubrey whispered back as Mala moved to pick up the dripping inkwell. She cleaned it off with a nearby rag then returned it to its place on the desk, hiding the release button inside the hole.

Chapter 33

Several days later, Black entered the galley and was surprised that Mala had not yet entered for breakfast. Taking a seat at the captain's table, he looked around and found many of Mala's men having breakfast. Morgan and Robert sat apart from the others talking in low tones making Black wonder briefly over that. Morgan had managed to get into Mala's good graces on his own somehow. He did not ponder on the thought for long as he noticed Aubrey stepping into his line of vision with his drink and plate of food. She set them on the table before him but as she stepped away, his deep voice stayed her, "Tell Mr. Alcott that I wish to speak to him."

Aubrey glanced in the direction of Morgan and Robert, seeing them talking in a conspiratorial fashion, then nodded. As she approached, she saw that Morgan stopped talking in mid-sentence. "Captain Black wants to see you, Morgan." The two men shared a look before Morgan stood up.

"Aye, sir?" Morgan asked when he approached Black.

Looking past Morgan, Black noticed Robert leaving the galley after one last glance in their direction then indicated the seat across from him. Looking down at his food and selecting a bite of his eggs, Black asked before placing the food in his mouth, "You are not conspiring against me, are you, Mr. Alcott?"

Morgan smiled then answered, "No sir. We were just talking about the activities of the ship." Chewing his food, Black watched him as he responded. The two looked at each other in silence for a moment as Black took a swallow of his drink then he placed the tankard back down on the table. Meeting the man's dark-eyed stare, Morgan thought of Mala and how she could stare a confession from someone with that same look. She had learned much from this man.

Seeing that some explanation might help the situation, Morgan said, "We were talking about finding a port so that the men can have shore leave. This drifting along has made many rather restless. Thought we should bring it up to you and Captain Mala."

Black nodded. Since the appearance of the British ship a few days before, there had been little breeze to move the ship along. The men were becoming irritable with no activity. "Mala has mentioned that fact already." Black said straightening up a bit. Seeing Morgan's smile, he added, "She has apparently noticed that same reaction with the men. They will stay in line until we reach a port, n'est-ce pas?"

Black remembered that Morgan could not speak French or understand the

287

language. "Is that correct?" He repeated in English.

"Aye sir, they will stay in line." Morgan confirmed.

At that moment, Mala stepped into the galley. Black saw her immediately then heard the greetings of her men as she made the slow procession of greeting with the usual morning flare. Letting Mala greet her crew as she had always done did not sit well with Black but it had helped in keeping the men from rising against him. They could see for themselves that she had no problem with the present situation, Black thought to himself.

Morgan excused himself as Mala seated herself beside Black and Aubrey appeared with her drink and food. "Aubrey…" Mala called then handed her the tankard and pushed her food aside, "Just water."

Mala looked at the food on her plate and made a face as it was not appetizing to her at the moment. Black looked up, chuckling to himself, saying to Mala, "I remember that the only time you drank water was when you…" Suddenly his humor was gone and he gave her look of surprise as she smiled at him, "Mon Dieu, non." He grumbled.

Her smile irritated him all the more because he knew the meaning of the water. "You could have warned me it was coming." Black hissed, thoroughly disappointed.

"Je regrette, Rene, but I am afraid this curse was early. I had not expected it myself." Mala leaned close to him and lifted her hand to caress his cheek. "Fear not, mon cheri, I will still be able to care for you and your needs." Mala fairly purred.

Black looked into her eyes as he felt such a need arise. With a heavy sigh, he whispered, "Tis the closeness with you that I enjoy most, mon coeur."

Mala turned her hand to caress his cheek with her knuckles as she whispered back while his gaze moved to her lips, "That too I shall miss but for a short time." Black could not resist the temptation and pressed a soft kiss upon her lips. When he released her lips, her gaze caressed his face tenderly, "Make a note, mon pirate captaine, that we shall be missing for a time when this curse is over."

Black gave her a look that made Mala's heart melt. It was the same look she had seen many times while they laid in the bunk together. His deep voice was thick with emotion, "As always when this happens."

Everyone in the galley watched the two captains covertly. Mala's men felt more comfortable over the taking of the ship as long as their captain was happy and a willing party to the new captain's attentions. Many had heard the rumor that there had been a past association between the two captains and that Black had been Mala's teacher in many, many things. Many had seen the similarities of the two captains in their facial expressions as well as in many actions. Only then did many have the same opinion of Captain Mala as Aubrey had during her first weeks on the *Enchantress*. Captain Mala was the female epitome of Captain Black.

As Black kissed Mala, Aubrey looked away. Her heart cried out for Jean Luc and the tears came in an instant. Quickly, Aubrey retreated into the cooking area with Willie and found a corner to shield herself from his curious gaze.

"Is something amiss, lass?" Willie asked as she moved past him.

"No all is well."

Hidden from his view now, Aubrey let the tears fall as she tried to control herself. All was not well. Jean Luc was gone but Beaufort and Black were here. Why could it not have been the other way around? Aubrey wondered. She would never have wished that on Mala but Black frightened her and Beaufort terrified her beyond words.

Later in the morning, Mala was on the main deck with Aubrey near the starboard railing for some air. As Aubrey looked out at sea, Mala turned to find Black had set his gaze on them. Leaning back against the railing with elbows bent and hands dangling, she also noticed Beaufort standing next to Black. The man was whispering to his captain while the gray eyes stayed on Aubrey.

Mala looked up at the sails. They were slack in the little breeze they had. Every now and then there would be a good stiff wind to move them along. The sunny clime did little to lift the moods on the *Enchantress*. As if to make the point of her thoughts, Mala heard a grunt nearby as one man nudged another to move away while the men went about their task of rubbing oil on the forecastle railing to protect it from the weather. Mala eyed the men as they began to nudge each other angrily. With a soft whistle, she got their attention and merely shook her head. The men bowed their heads in embarrassment over being caught and worse, caught by the captain.

"We need to get to a port soon. I fear this drifting is playing havoc on my men." Mala said as she looked around the deck and saw other perturbed faces. "Tempers are flaring. The men need an outlet for this energy of theirs and the ship is not getting us anywhere anytime soon." Mala idly kicked with her booted foot looking at the deck. Aubrey looked up at the sails that fluttered slightly but were slack for the most part.

On the quarterdeck, Beaufort watched the women and was saying. "About the Irish wench…"

"Must you continuously badger me over her, Thomas?" Black asked irritably.

"You can ease yourself just fine, Captain, but the rest of us…" Beaufort had dared to say.

Suddenly he found himself being pulled to his captain by the front of his shirt as Black snarled close to his face, "Be careful what you say to me, Thomas. I have not made my final decision as yet."

With a shove, Beaufort had to quickly find his footing as Black turned away from the deck to stare out the stern of the ship. Beaufort looked around to find no one watching but Mala who had looked up just as Black grabbed Beaufort. Seeing the angry glare from the man, Mala escorted Aubrey off the deck.

It was some moments later before Black turned to find the women gone. His dark eye gaze looked about the deck then it came to rest on Beaufort who stood rigid. His dark eye took in the deck again. Was it his imagination or were there more men on deck now than before? Moving to stand next to Timmons, Black watched as more men came topside.

Beaufort turned to look at his captain with a questioning frown as more men gathered. Soon Mala appeared on the quarterdeck and she went directly to Black. Taking his arm, she moved him to the stern rail. She leaned against it, crossed her arms, and faced the main deck. Black stood next to her looking at her profile before she looked up at him and said, "We need to go into a port. There is one nearby that if we continue to drift as we are, we should arrive perhaps by late tomorrow."

Black looked to the deck and the men gathering there. Mala followed his gaze then noticed Beaufort coming towards them. Before the bully could speak, Black waved him away and Mala saw the dark look on Beaufort's face as he turned away.

Ignoring the brute, she looked at the men gathering on the deck and said, "I had the men come up on deck. You need to make an announcement and give them something to look forward to, Rene." Mala looked into his face once again and Black saw the impish grin on her beautiful face. "I would but I do hate to upset your authority."

Black smiled down at her and Mala was caught by the look in his dark eye. This damned curse! She thought and groaned aloud as she looked away from him. Black heard the groan and leaned close to whisper, "I know your pain, mon coeur."

Mala laughed softly as he placed a light kiss on her temple before turning to face the men. He heard her say softly, "Aye, but I can take care of your needs through this time."

"True but tis not the same for me, either." He said softly. His smile and provocative gaze lightened her heart as he stepped away from her and approached the men assembled. Looking over the sea of faces, he saw Aubrey and Willie among the throng. He gave a few more moments to allow any stragglers to join the assembly before his deep voice carried across the main deck.

"It would seem that the slow progress of our voyage has weighed heavily on all of us." Black ignored the sarcastic grunt from Beaufort as he went on, "Captain Mala has informed me of a nearby port that at our current speed should be reached possibly as early as late tomorrow afternoon. Until then keep in mind that the rules on board this ship still stands. It would be a pity to be so close to port and not enjoy the entertainment it provides." He waited as the men mumbled among themselves at the realization of what he had just said.

"As you go about your duties, remember that the leave rotation will be reviewed. Any infractions would limit your time or even perhaps prohibit your time on shore. Dismissed."

As the men dispersed, Beaufort left as well. Still leaning against the stern rail, Mala watched as the brute took the companionway nearly behind Aubrey. How nice it would be to prohibit Beaufort's time for shore leave due to a sudden case of death, Mala thought then mentally cleared her head. No sense in taking time for wishful thinking.

Black watched the men turn back to their duties seemingly in better spirits. Mala had guessed that such announcement would lighten the dark mood hovering over the ship. Why had he not thought of it? He wondered as he turned shaking his head. Because his mind was filled with Mala and he cared for nothing much beyond that. But then she was managing her ship through him and did not seem troubled with that. He looked at Timmons who was smiling at him.

"Your captain tells me that we hold to this course, Mr. Timmons." Black said to the helmsman.

"Aye sir. I will get us to that port."

Black smiled at the young man that Mala had foremost entrusted her ship to. Turning his smile to Mala, Black joined her at the stern as she said bringing a smile to his face, "You handled yourself quite well, Captain. My men are pleased that you care."

Mala had not uncrossed her arms as Black enfolded her in his arms, resting his chin on the top of her head. His voice was soft as he replied, "I am glad you care."

"And why would I not care for my men? Such a silly man you are." Mala chided playfully. She could feel the deep rumble of his chuckle as she leaned against him. His arms tightened around her as she looked up at him smiling. He bent his head to kiss her lips and Mala's passionate response to his kiss did nothing for his need to hold her close. As always, her cursed flow impeded the most amorous of moments.

Straightening, Mala turned in his arms to face out the stern. Black kept his arms around her, his chin once again on the top of her head. Minutes ticked by before Mala moved for better look at the horizon.

"Now where did that storm come from?" She mumbled almost to herself.

"Finally something to get us moving." Black said, raising his chin from her head.

Below deck, Beaufort followed Aubrey towards the galley as she and Willie talked between themselves. Robert, York and Morgan were behind them and laughed at something Willie had said. As the small group approached the galley, Robert and York continued to the lower decks while the others turned into the galley. Beaufort continued to the lower decks as well but looked into the galley to find other men from the Captain Mala's crew inside. The little bitch is well protected at the moment but soon they will be gone and she will be attending to me. Beaufort thought with a smile as he walked on behind Robert and York.

Nearly an hour later, Beaufort was returning to the upper decks when he saw Aubrey stepping out of the storeroom heading back to the galley. Hurrying his steps, he grabbed Aubrey's arm and placed his hand over her mouth. She let out a shriek before it was cut off by Beaufort's hand. Slamming her against the wall of the corridor, Beaufort used his body to lean against her as he pressed his lips to her temple while his other hand roamed the front of her body. Aubrey bucked trying to throw him off but he only chuckled evilly then groaned.

"Aye, girl, do that again and I will reward you for all your efforts."

His words stopped her cold as she realized what she was doing with her body. Trying to throw him off balance, she was only heightening his pleasure. Suddenly Aubrey was yanked away from the wall and picked up by the waist as Beaufort carried her into the storeroom. She struggled against him as he fought to maintain his hold on her and her mouth. Draping her over sacks of flour, Beaufort leaned into her again from behind. His free hand now roamed her supple backside while he still covered her mouth with his hand. Her tears streamed down her face as she tried to kick her legs back.

"Now for my pleasure, you..."

Suddenly Aubrey was dumped unceremoniously to the floor before she was freed from Beaufort's hands. She looked up through her tear-filled vision to see Mala. The dark-haired woman had grabbed the unsuspecting Beaufort and shoved him bodily out of the storeroom to crash against the wall in the corridor.

Mala had gone to the galley to warn of the impending storm that was coming up fast from behind them. When Willie mentioned that Aubrey had gone to the storeroom, Mala thought to check on her. She had a bad feeling and once again she was proven right. She stepped menacingly towards the brute in the corridor and the two faced each other ready for battle.

"What the hell is going on here?" Came Black's deep voice from the corridor. He had just left from visiting Deats to find Beaufort crashing backwards against the wall before him. Now with Mala's presence from the storeroom and the sounds of Aubrey's sobs from within, the scene was becoming all too familiar.

At the sound of his voice, Beaufort turned to face him while Mala ignored Black, glaring at Beaufort. "To your duties, Monsieur Beaufort." Black ordered.

Beaufort made to protest but thought better of it as he saw the scowl on Black's face. Glaring at Mala, he released his frustration by slamming his fist against the wall before heading down the corridor. Mala watched Beaufort for a moment before turning to Aubrey and pulling her into the corridor.

Seeing the scowl on Black's face, Aubrey turned away quickly and headed down the corridor back to the galley. He followed slowly behind the two women as his anger began to rise. Once Aubrey safely entered the galley, Black grabbed Mala's arm. Astonished at his behavior as he continued angrily to the great cabin, Mala tried to free herself from Black's firm hold. She whirled around on him the moment they reached the cabin.

"What the hell am I do with you and Beaufort? I cannot watch him every minute and yet you seem to find him..." Black started as calmly as he could.

"You dare to reprimand me over the actions of that animal! He leaves her be!"

"Irish is not your concern!" Black said angrily as he advanced on Mala.

"She is my concern! She is a guest on my ship, you black-hearted..." Black grabbed Mala by the shoulders and shook her, letting his anger vent.

"I will decide her fate, not you!"

With a savage growl, Mala threw her arms up with such force that it released Black's grip on her. "You decide? You give her to him and I will cut you to pieces, Rene! I swear I will!"

"This is no longer your ship, Mala!"

"You arrogant bastard!" Mala shrieked in anger.

She meant to give him a mighty shove but he grabbed her hands and said close to her face with such callousness that Mala felt a chill run down her spine, "I am now captain of this ship. I captured your *Enchantress* and you..."

"This is my ship! I am and will always be Captain of the *Enchantress*! You are playing your games, Rene, but by my rules! Never forget that!" She growled at him.

Angrily, Black tossed her on the bunk and stood looking down at her crossing his arms. Mala slowly sat up on the edge of the bunk, her dark eyes never leaving his. They glared at each other as each tried to control their tempers. After long moments had passed, Black turned to retrieve a bottle of rum and a tankard. Mala sat watching him as he placed the items on the table.

"Come, drink with me and let us forget this incident." He said and heard her take a deep breath, a sign of her calming down. With a smile, he added as he began to pour the rum, "Your temper seems to be the hottest when you have your flow, mon..."

Startled at the screech emitted from the bunk, Black looked up to find Mala storming out of the cabin, slamming the door behind her. He stared dumbfounded at the closed portal, bottle still poised in hand then let out a loud sigh. Since Aubrey was not given to either Beaufort or Morgan, Mala had become her protector on this ship. Her ship! He had not wanted the ship or the crew—just Mala. So why did he say those things to her? He needed to calm her and make amends but this cursed flow was going to make that difficult. He took a big swallow of the rum before he left in search of Mala.

Black found her standing with her arms crossed and staring out from the forecastle. The ship bucked slightly as the storm moved nearer. The waves were already churning angrily and spraying water over the bow. He ran up to her and pulled her to the main deck with him. "Have you lost your mind? Are you trying to be swept overboard?" Black yelled over the building tempest as he turned her to face him.

Already drenched from the spray over the bow, Black did not wait for an answer. He held her to him as she wrapped her arms around him and their mouths met in a torrent of emotions, their anger yielding to something more lasting and more infinitely greater than either knew how to control.

Suddenly the ship dipped sickeningly low and the two captains separated, looking around in apprehension. Looking to the skies, Mala had to yell over the winds, "This will be a very bad storm. I need to see to my ship, Rene."

Black stared at her before he looked to the forecastle where they had been just moments ago. The waves were tossing buckets of water on its deck and knew that she could have easily been swept away. Mala raised her hand to the side of his face and tried to say calmly over the storm, "Wait for me in the cabin. I will be there soon."

With a quick kiss, Mala hurried to the quarterdeck and to Timmons. There was another one of Mala's men with Timmons trying to guide the ship. Black hurried below but could not resist one more look at the quarterdeck. Mala was looking to the skies and talking to her men. He stepped down into the corridor and shook the wetness from his hair as well as rubbing the drops from his face. He needed to help her but he knew she would have nothing of it. Shaking the feeling of dread, Black squared his shoulders and headed for the galley to call the men to their stations.

Chapter 34

Aubrey went about her duties in the galley. The incident with Beaufort left her shaken and Mala's timely arrival did little to calm her nerves. The galley had emptied due to the upcoming storm and she helped Willie to secure the pots and pans when York came into the area to inform them that Beaufort, Boulet and LaVoie had entered the galley.

"Perhaps you should return to your cabin, lass. But wait and I will give you a signal." Willie said while he poured three mugs of ale that he knew they would call for. As he approached the three men, he cut a glance to Aubrey and nodded for her to slip out while the three men seated themselves down at a table near the doorway.

"Hey! Whoa there...where do you think you are going, little one?" Beaufort said as he caught her by the back of her shirt as she tried to slip passed. Aubrey struggled and nearly managed to get free, but the ship bucked violently and she was practically thrown into Beaufort's waiting arms.

York stepped up grabbing for her saying in a warning tone, "Leave her be, Beaufort."

In a split second, a heavy fist crashed into York's jaw and he fell backward like a rock. With a distressed cry, Aubrey felt herself being pulled downward toward the tabletop. Beaufort swept an arm swiftly to clear the table. LaVoie and Boulet had managed to save their drink, each proud at their save. Aubrey was then down face first, full upon the table, her body bent at the hips and her toes barely touching the floor. She felt the front of her shirt soak up the ale from Beaufort's drink that had spilled on the table. The memory of being in this position before came flooding back into her mind.

"Leave her be, damn ye!" Willie spat attempting to rescue her.

"Get back to your cook stove, old man." LaVoie growled as he stood up blocking Willie's approach and giving him a shove. Willie was slammed into the wall then slid limply down onto the floor.

"Now to finish what we started, sweet one." Beaufort said as he placed kisses on the side of her throat.

"Do you plan to take her here and now, Thomas?" Boulet asked, a light in his eyes over the anticipation.

"Enjoy the show, mes amis, for you may taste such sweetness when I have had my fill of this one." Beaufort said quite pleased with himself.

"And how soon will that be?" LaVoie asked somewhat disappointed that it probably would not be tonight. He put his hand out intended to slip it

297

between her and the table. The skin of her exposed chest tempted him.

Beaufort's pistol was out in a flash and his voice came in a low growl, "I said when I have had my fill!"

LaVoie chuckled after a moment and pushed at the barrel of the pistol, "Oh Thomas, you can be so testy when it comes to matters of your crotch."

Finding an ounce of courage, she blinked at Beaufort, and said in a strained voice, "Let me go, Monsieur Beaufort, or I will tell the captain."

"He does not care about you anymore, little one. He has his other whore now." Beaufort snorted as he moved her up so that her feet were totally off the floor. Boulet ran his hand over her bottom as he had that other dreadful day. Aubrey's eyes darted back as Boulet's fingers began a gentle inward glide up the back of her upper thigh. Not noticing Boulet's caress, Beaufort had Aubrey pinned down face first on the table with his hand pressed into the center of her back and adjusting his britches.

"Release her." Came the menacing tone of Morgan. As he once again stepped up from behind Beaufort just in time. Boulet removed his wandering hand as he looked up at Morgan in guarded interest. "I said, release her." Morgan reiterated through clenched teeth, his hand dropping to his pistol.

Beaufort was watching Boulet's eyes for a sign of Morgan's intention. The other man had suddenly dropped his gaze to the pistol that for the moment remained carefully tucked away, but then his eyes darted to meet with Beaufort's in warning.

With a chuckle, Beaufort pulled Aubrey to her feet by clutching a handful of the back of her shirt then gave her pull as he did so. Fear gripped every muscle in her body, and when her toes finally touched the floor, her legs would not respond with the strength to hold her up. Without grace, she fell backward onto the floor landing on her bottom.

LaVoie and Boulet erupted into laughter as she scrambled to stand and back off. Morgan cast a look at Robert who had stepped up and taken her by the arm to help her to her feet. Robert handed her over to York who was coming around.

"Like I said many times, the little Irish bitch has a taste for quartermasters. I am merely collecting what is mine." Beaufort said. With a lascivious chuckle, he took up Boulet's untouched mug and made an attempt to take a drink. Suddenly the mug was slapped away from him, the contents showering Beaufort's face and down the front of his shirt.

"Over my dead body, you bastard." Morgan hissed.

"Then I will fight you for her." Beaufort said, gracing him with an evil smile as his fist drew back for the strike.

"Come on, you bastard." Morgan challenged, taking a defensive stance. Somehow Black had managed to appear without detection. With a nod of his head, Black had motioned York to take Aubrey out of the galley. The quiet and threatening tone broke the tension as Black said, "It would seem that the determination of Miss Malone's living arrangement is continuously challenged. As I have spoken to both of you before, I will now warn you both that this behavior will no longer be tolerated on this ship. The next time you two attempt to settle this matter for me, you will both face the whip. Is that clear?" Black watched for an acknowledgment from each man. "There is a storm over us. Go about your duties to prepare for it. Captain Mala is out there now and I expect to see her relieved of securing the ship and in the great cabin by the time I return to it."

With that, Black turned away from them and found Willie groggily coming to his feet. Helping the old man, Black then followed him into the cooking area to ensure that the galley would be secured. As the two combatants shared another glare, Robert pulled at Morgan's arm, urging him to leave the galley.

In the great cabin, Willie placed the bowls of stew on the table. He looked around but did not see Captain Mala. He had heard Black's warning and now looked anxiously at the man as Black stood looking out of the quarter gallery window and the impenetrable darkness without. The ship bucked again and there was a thunderous sound as the waves crashed against her hull. At that moment, the door flew open and Mala slammed against the doorjamb, eliciting a savage curse and a glare from her as if the ship knew its meaning. Both Willie and Black silently breathed a sigh of relief that she was safe. Willie bobbed his head slightly to Mala before leaving the cabin, firmly shutting the door behind him.

Black grabbed the coverlet from the bunk and wrapped the shivering Mala within its warming folds. She glanced up at him and murmured her thanks. He saw that her lips were blue and she was shaking violently so he pulled her down with him into a chair, wrapping his arms around her. "You are freezing." He whispered.

"Aye and the d-d-damned s-s-storm took t-t-two of my m-m-men already." Mala said through chattering teeth. Black's arms tightened around her and he closed his eye as he thought that at least she was not swept away while he was below deck.

"I n-need to get out-t-t of thes-s-se wet clo-o-othes, Rene." She shivered violently at that moment as if to emphasize her point. Black released her and watched as she retrieved dry clothes from a drawer under the bunk along with items that reminded him of her cursed flow. Mala then retreated behind the dressing screen.

Tossing the wet coverlet to the floor, Black called out, "Do you have another coverlet, warmer than this one?"

"Aye, the d-d-drawer ben-n-neath the wind-d-dow l-l-ledge." Mala answered still shivering.

Black moved to the drawer under the quarter gallery window ledge. He found several thick coverlets and pulled one out. He opened it from its folds, prepared for her. The ship pitched and rolled again and Black heard Mala curse behind the screen, having lost her balance.

Finally coming out, Mala accepted Black's attentions. Throughout their quick meal, Black took note of Mala watching and listening to the sounds of her ship and the storm but said nothing. The color was slowly returning her lips as he plied her with rum to warm her from within. With the meal done, Black took her arm and led her into the bunk. Taking the coverlet from her, he draped it over the bunk on her side. Mala settled within the warm confines of the covers while Black blew out the flame in the lantern, undressed then climbed into the bunk with her, snuggling close behind her. She was still shaking though not as violently as before but Black rubbed her arms and legs to try to warm her until she began to chuckle softly.

"And what is so funny?" He asked smiling.

"You are warming me, Rene but not in a way that could be finished as I would like at the moment."

Black's deep chuckle could be heard over her head as he held her close. He smoothed the silky softness of her hair over her pillow as he whispered softly, "Then sleep, mon coeur."

He heard a soft moan as she settled within his embrace and soon heard her soft steady breathing as sleep quickly overtook her. He stared into the darkness listening to her steady breathing as he held her close. He held her away from the storm that tossed her ship about, away from Beaufort and his menacing threats, away from Deats and his continuous declarations of love for her, and away from Aubrey who unwittingly demanded protection from her. For this space in time, he held Mala who was his and his alone.

The storm raged above, tossing the *Enchantress* over and under the waves. After Morgan and Robert appeared demanding that Mala go below, another man relieved Timmons at the helm. While Timmons retired for much needed rest, the two men who relieved him were tied to the helm to keep from being swept overboard by the waves or the buck of the ship as they settled into the task of keeping the wheel steady on their course.

Robert then went below to check on the lower decks. On his way to check on the cannons, Morgan stopped in to check on Aubrey. She was sitting on the edge of her bunk in the dark, clutching a book she had given up reading for the lack of light. The lantern had been snuffed out for safety's sake.

"Bolt this door when I leave. Beaufort is walking around securing the ship and I have to check the cannon deck." He told her. The opened door to the corridor allowed little light in the room but Aubrey could see Morgan's outline silhouetted by the meager light.

"How will you get in for the night?" Aubrey asked.

Morgan shrugged and said as he turned to leave, "I will worry about that when the time comes. Now bolt this door." He stated the last sentence firmly and waited outside the door until he heard the bolt slide into place. Smiling, Morgan then headed for the cannon deck.

After all was secured, Morgan went topside to make sure all was well at the helm. As he walked across the slippery deck, he chided himself for not thinking to go across while below where it was not as slippery or to tie himself to the ship somehow. Suddenly, he slipped and was sliding towards the gunwale. Fearing for his life, Morgan tried to grab at something on the smooth surface of the main deck. His feet slammed against a gunport and, looking down at his feet, he saw that he missed the opening by mere inches. Trying to move quickly, Morgan grabbed the railing and tried to stand. His relief was short-lived as the ship dipped low then heaved upward as if in protest to his safety. Water assaulted him from behind and swept his feet out from beneath him. With a curse, Morgan found himself clinging to the railing, his feet dangling over the gunwale and over the churning waves below, while his ribs pressed painful against the gunwale and the rail. Water splashed over him, taking his breath away. His gaze shifted to the helmsmen but he could not see them in the darkness and the downpour. If he could not see them, then they could not see him.

Morgan looked around for some help while his arms shook from the exertion and the fear of being swept overboard. Suddenly boots were in his line of vision and he peered up through the downpour of rain to find Beaufort looming over him and watching without expression.

"Help me." Morgan called out but Beaufort did not move. Suddenly Morgan could hear himself say earlier to Beaufort, 'over my dead body'. In his confrontation with Beaufort, he had planted the idea in the man's mind. Now Beaufort stood over him to ensure that Aubrey would be his once Morgan was lost to the sea.

"No, Beaufort!" Morgan screamed at the man. The wind carried the words away from the helmsmen but Beaufort heard them. His reply was to smile slowly before he turned away. Morgan saw that, like the helmsmen, a rope secured Beaufort.

Realizing that Beaufort intended for him to die, to be swept away, Morgan fought harder. It was not just for him, his own life, but for Aubrey as well. She would not belong to Beaufort, could not be made to succumb to the man's brutish behavior. With the gunwale digging into his side, Morgan pulled himself up onto the deck a few more inches. The exertion cost him a great deal and Morgan could feel those few inches slipping away as gravity pulled him back over the side. Trying to catch his breath for another try, Morgan rested his head against his arms.

Suddenly hands grabbed his arms and pulled him from the watery grave. Dragged until he was sitting on one of the steps leading below decks, he looked around to find Robert untying a rope that he had used to secure himself to the ship.

"Why did you not tie a rope around yourself?" Robert was saying, reproachfully.

"Forgot." Morgan could only gasp out.

"Let me get you to your cabin." Robert said. Morgan related what had happened on deck, including Beaufort's blatant refusal to help him, as Robert supported him to his cabin.

"Christ!" Robert swore. "The man was going to let you drown?"

"Aye, he is after Aubrey." When they reached Morgan's cabin, Robert tried the door. It was bolted.

"I told her to bolt the door. Robert, do not mention what happened with Beaufort. She is scared enough as it is."

"I had not planned on it." Robert said as he knocked incessantly.

"Who is it?" Aubrey asked almost fearfully.

"Tis Robert and Morgan." Robert answered.

Aubrey hurried to open the door and was surprised at the state Morgan was in. She shut the door after Robert deposited Morgan into a chair then hurried to light the lantern.

"Dry clothes?" Robert asked and Morgan pointed in the direction of his clothes but Aubrey was already moving. She retrieved the clothes then turned her back as Morgan shed the wet ones with Robert's help. His arms were still too shaky and too weak to manage alone. Once he was in dry clothes, Aubrey helped Robert put him into his bunk then she bolted the door behind Robert when he left the cabin.

"My God, Morgan. You could have been swept away without anyone being the wiser." Aubrey fussed but realized the words fell on deaf ears as Morgan was sound asleep. She sighed in relief that he did not come to that end and remembered a time when she was nearly swept off the ship during a storm. Jean Luc had been there for her. Jean Luc! Aubrey put out the lantern and crawled into her bunk. With tears brimming in her eyes, she turned sideways letting the tears fall until sleep mercifully took her.

The next morning, the sun shone brightly as it made its rise in the eastern skies. There was no hint of the raging and perilous storm from the night before only the promise of a warm and humid day. Mala entered the galley after checking on her ship. No more men lost and her ship held together against the tempest of the storm. She also found that they had reached the port, the storm had fairly shoved them along.

As she seated herself at her table, Morgan excused himself from the others to join her. "Is Black behind you?" He asked looking to the entrance.

"No, I believe he is visiting with Deats." Mala said as she scanned the galley.

"Then I want to tell you what happened last evening." Morgan began.

Black entered the galley and saw Mala in rapt attention as Morgan spoke to her. When he approached the table, Morgan bade his farewell and left the galley. "What was that about?"

"It seems that the storm tried to take our Morgan last night." Mala stated simply as Black looked around the galley. "And your Beaufort tried to help."

That got his attention. Black turned back to look at her. "He is not my Beaufort, Mala." Black replied tersely.

At that moment, Beaufort and his friends came into the galley. Her calm demeanor as she watched them made Black instantly wary and he turned his gaze to Beaufort. The man sat down heavily with his friends while his booming voice demanded service from what he loudly referred to as the ship's personal tavern wench. Black looked around the galley and only then noticed that Aubrey was not around.

"Where is Irish?" Black asked almost to himself.

"Aubrey." Mala correctly quietly.

He saw her look at her plate with disdain then pushed it aside. "Where?" He asked again when she did not answer.

"I told her to prepare to go ashore. I am taking her to the marketplace as soon as she is ready." Mala said making a face at the food.

Black stared at her and grumbled, "Mala, just when were you going to inform me? I could have plans for us on shore."

Mala's dark eyes lifted to look at Beaufort who was bellowing, "The lazy bitch. Tell her to get to work."

Standing, Mala indicated Beaufort with a nod of her head, "I just told you. Besides, you have other problems."

Black took her hand and said quietly, "Sit with me, mon coeur."

Mala looked at him for a moment and thought of how he kept her warm, holding her throughout the night. She sat back down and squeezed his hand in hers. Her anger was not for Black who smiled at her as he raised her hand to his lips, tickling her with his kiss. She smiled as he made a ploy to get her to eat a piece of his cured ham. She made a face then shook her head refusing the food.

"You need your water." He stated as he stood up. As he seated himself again, he grumbled, "I do not know what that does for you when you really need to eat."

Mala smiled at him as he ate. "So did you have plans for us today or were you just trying to impress me?"

Black chuckled and whispered secretively, "Actually I do have plans but I think it will be a surprise." Mala sat back and crossed her arms staring at him. Black's smile broadened as he regarded her stare.

With a sigh, Mala said softly, "Well I certainly hope it will be a pleasant surprise. Not like the time when you had to leap out of the window when the troops stormed into the bordello. Quite a show you and Jean Luc provided that day."

Black's smile disappeared instantly and was replaced with a look of utter astonishment. Mala could not help but raise a hand to cover her own smile. "You were there?" He asked in disbelief.

"Who do you think sent in the troops?" Mala asked and chuckled softly as he continued to stare at her. She leaned forward and traced his jawline with her finger.

Black pushed her hand away and, stabbing at his breakfast, replied, "Sending in the troops was not funny, Mala. We could have been captured."

"Then I would have set you both free." She said as if that was the only possible reply to his absurd statement.

Black gave her a dubious look. "If you must know, mon coeur, Jean Luc and I slept nearly the entire time."

"In a bordello, Rene." Mala teased on and received a glare for her torment. She had known that he and Jean Luc had slept most of the time and that they had spent little time with a whore. There had been a storm at sea and Black needed to recruit more men, apparently having lost many of his to the storm.

"And the rest of the time?" She questioned teasingly.

"Mon Dieu, Mala. I am only a man and I thought you were lost to me." Black hissed thoroughly annoyed with her. Mala stared at him until he finally said still annoyed, "You knew."

Mala smiled at him and leaned forward, her hand inching up his thigh from under the table. "I knew." She whispered.

Black looked into her dark eyes and the soft smile. Just as she neared his crotch, she suddenly sat up straighter and said with an air of urgency, "Well I better see what is keeping Aubrey. It would not do for her to come in here just now." Mala said, casting a glance at Beaufort and his friends. She silently laughed as Black took her hand and pulled her close to him.

"You will pay for stirring my desire for you." He whispered close to her face.

A slow smile crept up on the beautiful face so close to his. "Ah, more of the surprise." She said, making Black chuckle.

"Vixen." He muttered. She smiled and tossed him a sideways glance then left the galley.

Chapter 35

A short time after the longboats pulled to shore on a small inhabited island in the Bahamas, Morgan had all that he could take from Beaufort. Knowing that Mala had taken Aubrey into town earlier, Morgan kept a watchful eye out for them. He sat with Robert and several other men from the *Enchantress* in an outdoor tavern talking idly, all the while watching for Mala and Aubrey. Nearly a half an hour later, the women came into sight of the outdoor tavern. They walked slowly past while they talked and shared an oversized sweet pastry.

As he and Robert sipped rum, Beaufort, Boulet and LaVoie came on the scene. Sitting very near to them and ordering drinks from the serving wench, Beaufort began the dialogue that would be Morgan's undoing this day.

Casting his gray eyes to look over at Mala and Aubrey who were shopping across the plaza, Beaufort chuckled as he spoke to his companions in French. Then looking at Morgan and Robert, he said in English, "I see that the captain has sent his whore to town and she brings little Irish with her." Then standing and emptying his mug, he said loudly to his friends, "Pardon me gentlemen, but I see something at one of the tables that makes my mouth water."

As Beaufort moved into the crowd of the marketplace, Morgan lowered his mug slowly, watching the man suspiciously. His blue eyes drifted to see that Aubrey had fallen behind. She was looking at the vast array of native objects on display for purchase and completely oblivious to the fact that Mala had moved on. Glancing at Mala, Morgan saw that she seemed preoccupied and did not notice the distance between her and Aubrey.

"Does the market interest you, ma petite?" Beaufort asked Aubrey.

The auburn head jerked up and the wide hazel eyes met the amused gray ones. With a small look of distress on her face, her eyes darted around looking for Mala. Spotting her ahead, Aubrey sidestepped him to move quickly toward Mala who had yet to notice them. Beaufort smiled at her escape attempt. He watched her pass, allowing her to move just a few feet toward the dark haired woman before he motioned for Boulet to step out of the crowd and block her path. Aubrey turned quickly to avoid him as well. The maneuver was successful for it had turned Aubrey further away from Mala and out into the throngs of people at the market.

Mala turned and found that Aubrey was not with her. Catching sight of Beaufort in the crowd, she cursed silently and turned to help Aubrey when suddenly she was blocked by LaVoie. "Move damn you."

"Oh, je regrette, am I in your way?" He smiled but made no attempt to move. Mala looked past him to see where Aubrey had gone and realized the wrong move the younger woman had made. With another curse, Mala gave LaVoie a mighty shove.

Aubrey was beginning to panic. She moved through the people, trying to find an escape and would cast a look behind her to check the location of Beaufort. There were too many people blocking the way and too many tables to slip through and double back. Smiling, Beaufort strode purposefully through the masses behind her, keeping his distance, yet definitely in pursuit.

Suddenly she was like a cornered deer as she dashed off to her left through a small open space in the vendors and crowd. Beaufort grunted with a sound of approval. He knew this small village well and now that she was successfully separated from the dangerous dark-haired woman, he would get her easily.

Aubrey came to a sliding halt as she rounded the corner of a wooden building and to her dismay found herself at a dead-end. Panting in fear, she spun on her heel to see Beaufort step into the open end of the alley.

"It would appear that you have run out of space. Your lovers have no clue where you have scurried off to but then they are drunk back at the tavern." He said smiling as he made a slow approach.

In a flash he was upon her, pinning her against the wall with his hand flat on her chest. Aubrey squirmed under the hand to get free to no avail. At first he smiled in amusement then his other hand came up and he dealt her an open-hand slap across the face as he hissed, "Be still."

Aubrey ceased her struggle under the blow that left her ears ringing. "Now then." He said with some finality as he leaned his head toward her.

Aubrey strained to turn from him and a movement at the end of the alley caught her eye. Beaufort caught the glance and turned to look behind him but the alley was empty. "What did you see, ma petite?" He purred as he turned back to her.

She offered no reply, but strained to look again as he buried his face into her neck, catching her skin in little nips with his teeth. Just over his lowered shoulder, Aubrey watched as Mala stepped back into the end of the alley and drew her dirk from its sheath. Her arm went back in what seemed to Aubrey to be slow motion. Mala's hand snapped forward and just before the dirk blade was released from her fingertips, a man coming into the alley hit Mala from the side, eliciting a curse as the knife was moved from her intended aim by the hit.

The curse caught Beaufort's attention. He stepped to one side just as the dirk flew by him, barely grazing the shoulder of his thick jacket. With a thud, it imbedded itself in the wooden wall just to the left of where he still held

Aubrey pinned. Glancing down at Aubrey for an instant before he turned to see who threw the dirk, he was suddenly pulled backward, releasing her from his grasp.

"I told you before..." Morgan began as he spun Beaufort to face him. His fist crashed into the Frenchman's jaw. Beaufort stumbled back with the force and he fell against Aubrey. She yelped with the pain and pushed him back toward Morgan. As Beaufort came forward, his fist connected soundly into Morgan's midsection. The blow made Morgan stumble back and fall. Beaufort turned on Aubrey again and a look of surprise crossed his face when he found her brandishing Mala's dirk in both her hands. He smiled and shook his head, drawing back his hand in preparation to slap the weapon from her grasp.

Morgan hit him again, tackling him from behind. The impact sent Beaufort lurching forward, right into the path of Aubrey's defense. With a growl, he put out his arms over her head and stopped his forward momentum with his palms flat on the wall above her. At the same time, he lunged sideways deflecting himself from the wall and her slash of the dirk. With a yelp, Morgan found that he was now careening towards the exposed blade.

"Oui ma petite, kill the bastard for me and then I will have you." Beaufort commended from behind with a laugh.

Aubrey threw down the blade in horror of what nearly happened. Beaufort grabbed Morgan by the shoulder of his jacket and spun him around quickly to lay a heavy fist to his jaw. Morgan staggered under the blow and went to the ground.

Mala was moving forward again, drawing her cutlass. Once again someone coming from behind thwarted her advance. This time the person caught her about the waist with one arm and caught her sword arm at the wrist.

"This is their fight. I told them to bring it ashore days ago." Growled Black into her ear as he dragged her back to the end of the alley.

Mala did not go willingly as she cursed and fought the entire way. "Get the hell off me and let me go." She hissed angrily.

"Non mon coeur, let them finish." He purred.

Black held her wrist in a vice grip and shook it until she was forced to drop the deadly weapon. One of the two men who had come with him picked up the weapon. Robert had arrived nearly the same time and he now stepped forward to help his friend but Mala's blade was used to deter him. Boulet and LaVoie arrived as well but held back watching the fight. The two men who arrived with Black stood guard at the end of the alley with arms folded over their chests and 'shooed' any nosy on-lookers away from the action in the alley.

"Pirates justice! To the winner goes the prize." Boulet cheered on.

Morgan and Beaufort continued to crash and fight around the alley, both bleeding from the nose and mouth. Aubrey cowered in the corner, trapped by the two fighting men. She watched in distress as Morgan took hit after staggering hit from the Frenchman.

Finally, with one last mighty strike of Beaufort's fist, Morgan went down. He laid face first in the dirt next to where Aubrey still cowered. She dropped to her knees in weakened fear as she looked from the motionless Morgan to the unsteady Beaufort.

"Well, now we have it. The argument is over and it is settled." Black said with a wave of the hand that had held Mala's wrist.

The men behind him chuckled and turned away except Robert who stood stiffly watching for signs of movement from Morgan. Beaufort tossed back his disheveled long hair with an air of finality and wiped the back of his sleeve over his bleeding lips. Turning to Aubrey, he smiled.

"No!" Her voice came in a terrified wail as he caught her up by the front of her shirt. She reached down quickly and took up the blade, striking at him with it. He let her go for an instant and cursed at the slash she made in the sleeve of his jacket. The heavy oilcloth had taken the hit and he was not injured, but her attempt made him furious.

"Do not threaten me, you little bitch. I just took a beating for you and I won. You are mine now, so come along and you will cut me no more." With a growl, he caught her up again so forcefully that she dropped the blade.

"Rene!" Mala hissed as she struggled as well. The thought of leaving Aubrey in the alley with Beaufort enraged her.

"He is right, mon coeur." Black nodded as he held her.

"When I get you back to the ship, you are going to pay me back for these bruises with some of your own." Beaufort informed Aubrey as he struggled with her.

"I think not." Came the strained, but angry voice of Morgan from behind them. Beaufort turned in surprise and Morgan's fist took up his entire line of vision. Beaufort fell like a great tree under the axe.

Mala stopped struggling immediately as she, Black, and the other men turned at the sound of Morgan's voice. With a derisive snort, Mala cast her dark eyes to Black with a light of triumph in them, "Well Rene, it seems that you need to pick up your quartermaster now. He appears to be drooling in the dirt."

Black released her with a click of his tongue and turned to leave the alley, waving a gloved hand to the men who were with him, "Pick up the bastard and bring him along."

"No! My ship will not sail with that animal aboard." Mala countered as she stepped after him and caught him by the arm.

Black spun on her angrily but she bravely stood her ground. "He is one of my crew and I command the *Enchantress* now." He growled. With a glance to his men he ordered, "Put him in the longboat, damn you."

The men rushed past to pick up the unconscious Beaufort and drag him away between them. Mala continued to face Black with flaring nostrils, the only outward sign of her seething anger. An evil smile curled across Black's lips as he reached out to pull her to him and press his lips full upon hers. She pushed at him and he released her with a chuckle. "You are truly beautiful when you are angry."

"And if you are not careful, you will truly be dead, Rene." She replied looking at him with narrowed eyes as she snatched her cutlass from the hand of the man who held it and she sheathed the weapon on her belt.

With one last baleful glare at Black, Mala turned towards Aubrey, Morgan and Robert. Black smiled as he watched her angry strides, taking in the curves of her body as she walked away. With a chuckle, he shook his head as he walked away from the alley.

Aubrey looked in desperation to Robert as he approached for she was trying to help Morgan to his feet. Robert took Morgan and pushed Aubrey away.

"You fool, I would have had him had you not pushed me out of the way." Mala scolded as she joined the trio.

"Guess I just lost my head." Morgan muttered with a weak shrug.

"Somebody has got to kill that bastard." Robert mumbled to no one in particular.

"Well, Robert my friend...I tried." Morgan said weakly.

Paying for two adjacent rooms, Mala helped Robert to carefully lay Morgan in one of the rooms. Aubrey poured water in the basin and began to clean his wounds.

"Robert, send someone out to the ship and have Willie get my herbs." Mala commanded.

"Aye Captain." Robert said and left the room.

"That room is yours, Aubrey. Enjoy the comfort without a roommate while you can. I will be back to treat those cuts." Mala said pointing to the other room before she turned to leave.

"Thank you, Captain." Morgan replied weakly. She merely smiled as she firmly closed the door to the room.

Mala stood outside of the inn and surveyed the bay. She could see the *Enchantress* moored safely away from the harbor and the longboat heading back with Boulet and LaVoie assisting the still unconscious Beaufort back to the ship. As she watched the longboat, a smile appeared slowly as she thought of the herbs she could put together to let the man sleep—forever.

"Planning the demise of my quartermaster, mon coeur." Came the deep voice of Black as he stepped behind her.

Without turning, Mala said over her shoulder, "Absolutely, Rene, and I know just the herbal tea to cure all of his ailments."

Black chuckled as he took her by the elbow and turned her to face him. She was still angry and he could see it in her eyes. "It was their fight, Mala. Your involvement..."

"I was protecting Aubrey."

"She has plenty of protectors. Even Mr. Bates came to her rescue." He said becoming angry over her insistence to protect Aubrey.

"And what of you, Rene? She bears your mark. Where was your protection?" Mala went on relentlessly.

His gaze wavered slightly and she knew that she had struck a nerve with him. It took great effort to maintain a calm and pleasant tone when he replied, "I have chosen you over her."

Black did not like the level look she bestowed him. With an equally pleasant tone, Mala said, "Hmm, something for me to look forward to then."

Without a word, Black turned and left her standing at front of the inn. He could not trust himself with her at the moment. She had hit on a very sore spot with him. Aubrey was a mistake, and would forever bear the constant reminder of his mistake. He had never had her but Mala would never believe him because of that mark. *'Something for me to look forward to.'* She had said. He was never letting Mala disappear from him again.

Now that they were in a port, he would have to stay close to her to make certain she did not try to leave him behind. He stopped suddenly and wondered, would she leave him behind? He thought back on the last weeks with her on the *Enchantress* and how wonderful it had been, until the blasted curse made an appearance. The curse of eve! Mala was always at her cruelest during the time of her flow. So much so that, in her cruelty, she would know what would hurt the most. He sighed realizing that in her anger with him for holding her back in the alley, she struck back with words.

Black turned to find Mala but she had moved from the inn. His dark eye scanned the area for her traditional red shirt and found her surrounded by five filthy-looking men. The sight gave him a disquieting feeling although he knew Mala could probably handle herself just fine. He hurried to her side as he watched her cross her arms and glare at each man who surrounded her. One man reached out and took some of her dark hair into his big hands then let the strands cascade from his fingers. Black seethed inside. No one touched her, not even a lock of her beautiful hair. As Black drew closer, he cursed aloud as he saw her draw her pistol and point it at the man before her while four other pistols were drawn and pointed to her head.

Nearly skidding to a halt, Black watched as what he thought were bystanders at first glance pulled their pistols as well. Now he recognized the men as those from her crew, Robert among them, his pistol drawn.

"Well, little one, what will you do now?" Said the man who had Mala's pistol pointing into his face. With an evil smile, Mala lowered her pistol slowly. The man smiled then grunted painfully when she jammed it into his crotch.

Black made his way through the watching crowd and heard Mala's deceivingly calm tone, "Tell them to lower their pistols or you will not be any good to any woman anymore."

Pulling his pistol, Black let it rest against the man's temple, and said in equal calmness, "I suggest you heed her warning."

The man turned slightly to look at this newcomer after noticing the wavering of his friends' pistols. He found a tall, dark-haired man with an eye patch, dressed totally in black, and a thoroughly evil and unwavering glare in the good eye.

When no one moved, Black leaned forward and said, his deep voice carrying the deadliest tone the man had ever heard, "She is my woman. Should any harm come to her, you will never see her hit the ground."

The man's gaze roamed over Mala's body until he felt the pistol shove slightly against his temple. He looked to his friends and the silent communication was understood. The four pistols moved away from Mala's direction and the five men slowly moved away.

Mala watched them walk away as the crowd dispersed. Then she looked at each of her men who had come to her aid before resting her dark eyes on Black. With a smile, she lifted her hand still holding the pistol. She presented Black a soft leather pouch entwined in her fingers. Black smiled as four other hands joined Mala's, making a small circle and revealing the same type of prize.

"Payment for the trouble they tried to cause." She said softly, eliciting laughter from her small group. Smiling, Black shook his head in disbelief and Mala turned to her men who were now gathered closer and said, "Share those among yourselves." Then looking at Black, her smile grew wider as she tossed her prize in the air carelessly. "This one is mine and Rene's."

The men laughed and gave her their hearty thanks then left the two captains where they stood. Mala nodded towards the inn, and asked Black, "What say you, mon pirate? Shall we get a room in yon inn?"

Black gave a pained grunt as his response caused Mala to laugh softly. He took her elbow and escorted her back to the inn. "Is that not where Morgan and Irish are staying?"

"Aubrey." Mala corrected in exasperation. Seeing his smile, she rolled her eyes. "Aye, they are within but we will be on another floor."

"Deliciously sweet, mon coeur." Black whispered close to her ear.

"I do believe you owe me a surprise." She said tracing the scar on his left cheek with her finger.

"Hmm, so I do." Black whispered huskily, drinking in her provocative beauty. It was late in the afternoon before Mala returned to help Aubrey tend to Morgan's wounds.

After another full day and the final rotation of shore leave, the *Enchantress* came into the harbor to pick up the last of her crew before sailing away. Though the air was still as before, the men seemed a bit lighter of step and more companionable. However, Morgan was ordered to light duties for the next several days but plain stubbornness and pride would not hold him down.

"He is supposed to be restin', captain's orders." Aubrey scolded Robert when he aided Morgan into the galley later in the afternoon.

"See I told you she cares." Morgan said brightly to Robert.

"As if I could not see that for myself." Robert retorted playfully.

"Simpleton, have your fun now. It will not be funny if Mala walked in right now and..."

"She is in the great cabin, Aubrey. She ordered Willie to prepare a bath for her. So it is safe for now." Robert informed her with a triumphant smile.

Aubrey had known about the bath because she helped heat the water but she had hoped to intimidate them with Mala's possible presence. Glaring at them, she put her hands on her hips and said, "Well now that ya were foolish enough to come here, ya may as well sit down. Sweet Mary! Why can ya not just follow orders like ya are supposed to?" She exclaimed as she went back to the cooking area. Robert and Morgan shared a smile as they watched her retreat before taking a nearby seat.

Stepping down from the quarterdeck, Black let his mind drift back to his surprise for Mala and smiled as the surprise had turned to be a pleasant one for him as well. He had taken Mala to a hill overlooking the town and the harbor. It was dark when they reached their destination and sat looking out over the moonlit bay. In the quiet companionable moments, Mala informed him that her flow had surprisingly ended. So under the stars, they made love throughout the night.

Still smiling at the memory, he entered the great cabin and was greeted with the sight of the jolly roger draped over the long table like a decorative

314

cloth. The distinguishing shapes of the skull and crossbones were clear on the flag's design as he shut the door slowly and stepped towards the table.

"Well?" Came Mala's voice from around the dressing screen. The sound of the water indicated her movement and soon her head peeked around the corner.

Black smiled at her mischievous look then looking at the flag, he asked with a chuckle, "What is this?"

"A surprise." She said smiling at him then disappeared behind the screen. The sound of the water now told of her settling back into its slippery depths.

"Oh I like surprises." He said, his deep voice sending quivers over her skin. She could hear his bootfalls as he came towards her. He was greeted with her smile and the alluring body in the ornate tub. "Oh yes, I do like surprises." He repeated making her laugh. "Where did you find such a flag?"

"I paid a woman a tidy sum to have the flag made so quickly." She replied smiling. "The flag is yours, mon cheri. Since this ship has two captains, why should it not have two flags?" He watched her smile turn radiant as she added, "Of course, your flag will fly under mine."

His gaze turned lustful as it moved over her naked body once again before he stood and moved away leaving Mala to wonder where he was going. Within minutes, he came around the screen and naked as well, he joined her in the tub. With a soft laugh, she moved to allow him into the tub with her. The sight of his nakedness thrilled her and because he was hard for her, she was almost instantly aroused.

His lips took hers as he positioned her over him. Straddling his hips, Mala lowered herself over him and sighed with pleasure as she took him deep inside her. Black's lips moved slowly over her face, her throat, and her breasts. As she began to move over him, Black was heard to say in a deep throaty whisper, "Oui, I like flying my flag under yours."

Chapter 36

Nearly a week later, the boredom settled over the ship once again as the lack of wind forced them to drift. Because Beaufort had not been able to enjoy his time for shore leave due to his injuries, he took up his torment with Aubrey as if nothing had ever been settled in the alley.

Aubrey went about her duties with helping Willie in the galley but she was left to work alone, collecting plates and mugs to be washed while Willie left to get supplies from the hold. Black looked up from toying with the food on his plate to see Aubrey passing the table where Beaufort, Boulet and LaVoie sat. Beaufort had caught her by the arm and pulled her to him. Aubrey struggled in his grasp while he held her there tormenting her.

Black's lips drew into a thin smile. It was to be a bit of entertainment today. The Frenchman had caught her about the waist now, had pulled her onto his lap and was making an attempt to kiss her. Arms flew and feet kicked as she tried to free herself amid the sounds of delight at the show from his men at Beaufort's table as well as those of the tables around. Black noted that there were a few of Mala's men in the galley, but none of them were ones he recognized as being her self-appointed guardians.

Beaufort stood catching Black's attention. The big man had pulled the fighting Aubrey up with him in the process. On her feet, she quickly drew up her knee in defense but Boulet caught the dangerous weapon before it could connect with Beaufort's unguarded crotch.

"Whoa Thomas, see how she fights dirty with you." The man chuckled as he held Aubrey by the knee.

Beaufort grinned down at her and sneered, "Want to fight dirty, eh?"

In a flash, Aubrey was picked up and thrown down onto the tabletop on her back. The impact knocked the wind out of her, stopping her struggles for a moment. That moment cost her as Beaufort caught her shirt in his hands and successfully ripped the v-neck open to her waist. Fortunately, she was wearing a camisole this time. With a desperate cry of alarm, she began her frantic kicking and fighting as he caught at the front of the cotton undergarment. Her hands now flew to catch hold of his as he prepared to rip the fabric.

Aubrey's eyes darted around her for help and saw Black at the captain's table. "Rene!" She screamed in terror.

Beaufort had succeeded in pulling her camisole down, exposing Black's mark on her breast. Boulet and LaVoie also saw the mark and turned their heads to look toward the dark haired man. Beaufort merely grunted at the

317

sight and lifted his gaze slowly to look at his captain while holding her down on the table.

Black regarded the scene for a long moment with his dark eye. Then, with the slightest wave of his long fingers as he held his fork up to his mouth, he dropped his gaze to his plate and continued to eat his meal. Aubrey's mouth dropped open in stunned surprise at the apparent permission Black had given Beaufort to continue his actions. Catching her by the chin, Beaufort turned her to face him and smiled triumphantly.

Mala had heard Aubrey's call for Black as she headed for the galley and quickened her pace. Upon entering the galley, she missed Black's permissive wave but saw Beaufort as he leaned over Aubrey.

"Morgan!" Aubrey screamed as she fought Beaufort's advance.

"He is not here to help you. No one here will help you." Beaufort laughed as he grasped the waistband of her britches and started tugging.

Suddenly, he was violently pulled back away from her and in an instant he was facing Mala in all her fury. "Leave her be!" She hissed.

His smile was more of a smirk, angering her all the more. "The captain..." He began as he gestured toward Black.

With a violent shove of her hands against Beaufort's chest, Mala said with vehemence, "I am captain."

The room went deathly silent. The moment she was released, Aubrey managed to scramble across the long table, dumping herself into LaVoie's lap. To keep from being the next target of the dark haired hellcat that stood before Beaufort, LaVoie promptly pushed Aubrey to the floor. Willie stepped into the doorway to enter the galley but upon seeing his captain in her anger, he quietly stepped back out and peeped around the doorjamb to watch the fray.

Black's fist came down on the table with a crash and his tankard rocked and tipped, spilling its contents over the flat surface and onto the floor. Mala glared across the room at him, her arm extended, but merely pointed her finger at him as he glared back at her from his seat. Black watched as Mala slowly lowered her arm and balled up her fist before it came around quickly to connect soundly with Beaufort's jaw. The man staggered under the blow and stumbled back over his own feet. He fell, striking his head on the end of the table on the way down. In a second the room fell quiet again. All eyes darted from Mala to Black, who continued to glare at one another.

Exhaling forcefully, Mala looked down to the now unconscious Beaufort who lay at her feet. With a wave of her hand, she summoned Aubrey from her place against the wall and the two women exited the galley.

Halfway down the corridor to Morgan's cabin, Aubrey ventured to say,

318

"Captain Black did nothing, Mala. He all but gave his consent to the attack." Mala stopped abruptly making Aubrey run into her. When the dark eyes looked back at her in astonishment, Aubrey hurried to add, "I do not mean to carry stories, but I thought that you should know."

Without a word, Mala turned to head for Morgan's cabin once again. Opening the door, she fairly pushed Aubrey inside. Silence filled the room as Aubrey quickly changed shirts. The two women were startled when the door snapped open abruptly and Morgan burst into the room.

"What in the hell is going on? I got word that there was trouble in the galley again." His gaze came to rest on Mala who stood just inside the small space. She does not come here without a reason, he thought. "Are you two all right?" He asked suspiciously.

Looking at Aubrey, Mala said in controlled anger as she headed for the door, "You had best tell him. He will find out through the scuttlebutt anyway."

"Tell me what? What is going on?" He questioned as he watched Mala leave. He turned on Aubrey with a look of half anger and half question on his face. She backed up a step then she saw his eye catch sight of her torn shirt on the bunk. They both scrambled for it but he won out. Holding it out of her reach, he asked, "What is this?"

"My shirt."

"Tell me." He demanded. Aubrey tried to grab the shirt but he snatched it away. "Tell me now." He growled as he held it up between them in the near two pieces that it was.

"Thomas Beaufort tore my shirt." She said quietly.

"How? Where?" Morgan pressed on in anger.

"I was working in the galley and he put me down on the table." She muttered.

"That filthy French bastard! No one came to your aid?" Morgan spat as he turned to the door.

"No one was there until Mala came in." She said quietly. Morgan turned to the door but Aubrey darted past him to wedge herself between him and the door.

"No Morgan, please! The next time you fight, he may kill you. I am not worth that sacrifice." Morgan had been glaring down at her but her remark softened his countenance. Aubrey continued to look up at him with imploring eyes. "Please Morgan, please. What if—what if he won next time?" She pleaded on as she held onto his arm and remained in place to block his way.

With a heavy sigh and, as he continued to look into the pleading hazel eyes, he smiled gently through his anger, "You are wrong, Aubrey. You are worth the sacrifice." The thought of Beaufort having his hands on her was bad enough, but the picture she painted in his mind now was even worse. "Morgan, please let it go." Aubrey said in an uncomfortable whisper. With another deep sigh, he shook his head and relaxed his stance. To her surprise, he pulled her up into his arms and held her against him, resting his chin on the top of her head. For a moment, she stood stiffly in his embrace.

"Girl, we have got to train you to fend for yourself a little bit better."

Aubrey fidgeted in his embrace now and pushed at him gently, "Morgan, let me go."

Finally he let her go and she moved away as he said easily and with a hint of torment in his tone, "You are breaking my heart."

Aubrey dropped her head and smiled at him sadly thinking to herself as she looked at him, no Morgan, you are breaking mine because you remind me so much of Jean Luc.

Mala was standing in the quarter gallery with her arms folded when Black came into the cabin. He took off his hat and flung it into a nearby chair. "There you are. I wondered where you had disappeared." He droned. She merely glanced at him as he poured himself a mug full of rum. "Will you have a drink with me, mon coeur?" He asked.

Mala glared at him. "No, I will not have a drink with you." She replied in measured anger.

Black emptied the contents of the mug and then poured another. "You embarrassed me in front of my men, mon coeur. What do you suppose I should do about that?" He asked as he sat heavily into the chair at the end of the table. Mala snorted and watched him with her dark eyes as she stood very near the chair that he had lowered himself into.

"Embarrassed you? What do you propose to try and do about it?" She finally spat. In a sudden outburst of rage that he was all too familiar with from her, Mala kicked savagely at the side of the seat of the chair he sat in with a booted foot and growled, "And get the hell out of my chair!"

Black merely chuckled deep in his throat at the outburst. He then idly wiped at the rum that she had caused him to spill over the front of his black jacket, "Mala." He began with a purr as he stood up from the chair. "Now see what you have done? You have made me spill my drink." He took a sip, and watched her over his mug. Mala's anger was causing a stirring in his loins and a smile crept over his lips.

"You never cease to amaze me, Rene. You sat right there and watched as Beaufort manhandled her in full view of all the men in the galley. Were you going to sit there and watch as he forced himself on her as well? What does that show the men? My crew does not conduct themselves in that fashion, I do not permit it. My men know the punishment for such offenses." She told him angrily.

Black removed his jacket coolly and tossed it over a nearby chair. He merely shrugged and said with an air of boredom, "They are men, Mala. While there is no doubt that you are a good captain and your men respect you—even as a woman you must realize their nature and cannot propose to change or control them in certain situations."

Mala's face went blank for an instant before she shook her head in disbelief. With a sarcastic smile, she said, "Please tell me that it is the drink that I hear talking and not you."

He looked at her and pulled open the wrap shirt he wore. His dark eye trailed down the front of her as she stood before him. He smiled at her again and stepped a bit closer to her, "Why are you so upset over this? Irish is fine. Thomas did not compromise her virtue. The incident is over except that you embarrassed me."

"I did not embarrass you, Rene. Those animals you brought on my ship have embarrassed you, namely Thomas Beaufort. It was your duty to call him down." She said through clenched teeth.

"Do not dictate to me my duties as captain. I have been a captain for many more years than..." He growled but she interrupted him.

"But, you did not do your duty, Rene, and a woman had to. This is my ship and when I have had enough of you 'playing' captain on it, I will take it back." She replied firmly.

The remarks were biting and insulting, just as she had meant them to be. Black's eye flashed with anger. He set down his mug with a thud and advanced another step on her. Mala backed off only slightly to make note of his hands and weapons.

"We will discuss this no further. Irish is on her own. Such was her fate aboard my ship." He said in his deep voice. Mala looked at him in disbelief. Apparently he had far more to drink than she had first thought.

"That was your ship! Aubrey will be safe on my ship!" She spat. Black looked at her for a moment and then exhaled hard. His eye lingered over her again as he reached for his mug. If he had any thoughts of taking her to bed, he needed to calm her down from this argument.

Mala, on the other hand, had the strong urge to slap the mug from his lips as he stood before her. Her vision of his surprised expression the action would cause was interrupted by his voice. With a feigned pouting smile he asked, "Will you not have a drink with me?"

"No, I will not have a drink with you. You have apparently had too much already." She said shaking her head.

"Then, perhaps..." He began as he reached for her arm to pull her near.

"I think not." She said moving from his reach.

"Irish is no longer my concern." His voice was beginning to show the slur of the drink he had consumed, and yet he poured more into his mug. "You are the Captain's woman—Irish is just a whore." He said as he took another drink and turned to walk away to the quarter gallery. Mala watched him in interest. The drink apparently was affecting his brain because he had turned his back on her in the heat of an argument. It was not like him at all to do so.

"You call her that because she scorned you. She took part in a ruse to deceive you and took up with Jean Luc. You cannot get rid off that embarrassment. It would appear that women seem to be getting the better of you all the time. Perhaps you should stop thinking with the brain in your britches and think with the one in your head for a change." Mala's tone was deceptively calm and soothing. Black set his mug on the sill and turned slowly to look at her with a frown. Had she and the little bitch become so close that Mala knew everything?

"It is a pity, Rene, that you let that part of you control your thoughts." Mala went on as she dropped her eyes to look pointedly at his crotch. "The result of which has also controlled the destiny of your one and only true friend." All the while, she knew full well the effect that her speech was having on his drunken brain.

Black looked at her for a few silent moments then sneered, "What happened on the *Widow Maker* is none of your concern."

"It is my business, Rene. Especially when it spills over onto the decks of the *Enchantress*." She countered.

Black exhaled hard again, "Come now mon coeur, let me hold you. You know that you are the only woman for me. It is late, let us go to bed."

"No, you have had far too much to drink and I will not be sleeping with a drunkard tonight."

"Indeed? And where will you sleep then?" He asked with a sardonic smile.

"I will find somewhere, even if I have to sleep in the crow's nest." She replied.

"Perhaps I will join you there. I recall a day long passed when we pleased one another high above the decks." He chuckled.

Mala closed her eyes and shook her head at his constant change in demeanor. Taking advantage of her inattention, Black had her in his arms and attempted to kiss her. She pushed at him with such force that he has momentarily surprised. "You would push me away?" He asked.

He caught her up with a forceful jerk of her arm but she freed herself from his grasp once more and spat, "Do not grab me like that again."

With a shrug of indifference, he reached for his mug, "Sleep where you will then." As if in second thought he added with a scowl, "Will it be with your quartermaster? His accommodations are not very suitable for a pleasant night."

Mala's hand shot up and he winced as she slapped him soundly across his left cheek, "Go to hell, Rene." She turned from him and exited the cabin, slamming the door soundly behind her.

Black rubbed at the stinging of his cheek and chuckled drunkenly. Raising the mug to the door, he muttered, "Je t'aime." Then he dropped back into the chair and poured another mug full. Staring out of the windows, he rested his head against the back of the chair and soon fell asleep with dreams filled of Mala.

The oil in the lamp was burning low and the great cabin was shrouded in faint light and shadows. Stirred from his dreaming by a knock upon the door, Black stared at it through sleep and drunken glazed eyes.

"Mala?" Came Aubrey's soft voice from the other side of the door. Black frowned and sat straighter in the chair. "Mala? Are you here?" Came the soft voice again as the door latch clicked and the door began to swing open easily. Aubrey peeped around the edge of the open door, "Mala?" Silence was her only reply.

She ventured to step further into the room and looked around. She saw a dark blur out of the corner of her eye before she was suddenly being dragged into the room. Aubrey's heart stopped when she found herself looking up into the face of Rene Black and she heard the quiet, but unmistakable click of the door as it closed and latched. She opened her mouth to scream, but his free hand clamped down over it to silence her. Pulling her up close to his bare chest, he said to her, his words still slurred from the drink, "Mala is not here, Irish, but if you wish to talk to someone, I will talk to you."

Aubrey's head shook anxiously as she stared at him in wide-eyed fear. "You do not want to talk to me?" He asked in a near-cooing tone of voice. He dragged her into the center of the room with his hand still clamped down over her mouth. "We have much to discuss, you and me. I would very much like to hear all about how you managed to carry on a love affair right under my very nose."

Aubrey struggled in the grasp of his vice-like grip on her left arm and continued to pry at his hand on her mouth. His words were slurred as he flung her from him to go sprawling into the floor. "What are you doing here in my cabin so late at night? Should you not be in your lover's bunk? That is what you are good at, n'est-ce pas? Sneaking about after hours whoring with the lesser officers of the ship."

"I—I came to see Mala. I will go back to my cabin I promise." She stammered as he stood between her and the door.

323

"Mala does not want to talk to you. She is jealous of you." He said as he crossed his arms over his chest.

"No, Mala and I are friends." She spat in sudden anger as she came to her feet to face him. In an instant, he was upon her, grabbing her by the throat.

"What has gotten into you, Irish? Where is the timid little girl that I bought over from the *Gull*?" She struggled, gagging in his grasp and prying at his long fingers as they held her tightly. He cocked his eyebrow and looked off across the room as if in thought, "Oh yes, let me see. You are no longer a little girl are you? Oui, you gave up your precious virginity to my quartermaster." With a grunt, he threw her from him like a doll. She fell against the table and before she could turn he caught her up once more. "And here you lay with the first mate and the second mate while you go on to tease the new quartermaster." He accused.

"No! I do not tease Beaufort. He has always tormented me. You know that to be true, he did it on your ship. I told you many times." She argued with tears in her eyes.

Black drew back his hand and slapped her across the mouth with the back of his hand. "You do not tell me anything—you are nothing." Aubrey cried out in pain and he shook her savagely. "Do you hear me? Nothing! God only knows what lies you have told Mala. I ought to silence you forever." He gritted out through clenched teeth.

"I have told her no lies, Rene, I swear." Aubrey continued to cry as he held her by the front of her shirt.

Growling, he threw her from him once more in a blind and drunken rage. "It is Captain Black to you! That is all you had ever called me on the *Widow Maker* and that is how you will refer to me here for as long as I allow you to live."

In her fall, she hit the floor hard on her left shoulder and searing pain ripped through her making her cry all the more. Black towered over her, swaying a bit with the effects of the liquor. With another growl, he kicked at her. His booted foot connected with her upper right thigh and she cried out as she tried to scramble away from another kick. He grabbed her by the left arm once more, invoking yet another yelp of agony.

"Stop please." She cried as he pulled her close to his face.

"You need to learn your place on my ship." He spat.

Aubrey thought that this might be the end of her as he held her there. With her last ounce of courage she looked up into his face with hazel eyes filled with hurt and fear, muttering through bloodied lips, "This is not your ship. It is Captain Mala's. Your ship is at the bottom of that cove where you should be. Just like you left Jean Luc."

Black looked at her for a moment. Her little front of courage was almost sobering to him. Twice this night he had been reminded by a woman about the card of fate he had dealt to his quartermaster. *'Your one and only true friend.'* Mala's words echoed in his ears.

Looking down into the face of the young Irish woman, he saw the reason for the decision he had made that haunted him still. With a guttural growl, he laid a heavy hand across her face, releasing his grip on her at the same time. She went sprawling onto the floor and lay motionless.

"I should take you to Thomas just as you are." He spat. Aubrey's eyes rolled open and then closed again. "Whore." He growled as he walked away from her to sit heavily in the chair once more.

He reached for the half full mug of rum and then with another growl, he slapped the mug into the floor. The contents were splashed between the table and the now motionless Aubrey. The mug rolled to a stop against her chest. The light of the lantern cast a faint glow on her and he could see his mark on her partially exposed breast. If Mala came in and saw her this way, he would have hell to pay with the raven-haired beauty.

With a snort, he got to his feet and leaned down to pull her up by the front of her shirt. Shaking her he growled, "Wake up, damn you. You will not lay senseless in here for her to find."

Aubrey's eyes rolled again as she came out of the black abyss she had slipped into momentarily. She struggled with new energy, fearing that he was about to strike her again. He dragged her to the doorway and opened it. With a heave, he threw her out into the corridor. "Lay out there, maybe the night watch will find you and cart you ass off to the hold." With that, he shut the door.

As he crossed the room back to the table, Black kicked at the mug savagely and it flew into the bulkhead with a resounding bang. With his anger ebbing away, Black threw himself upon the bunk. Mala will be back soon, he thought and, with a smile, Black fell away into a drunken sleep.

Aubrey lay motionless in the dark corridor for what seemed to be an eternity. Though she was conscious, her body would not respond to any messages sent from her brain to get up and go back to the safety of the cabin. Finally, she struggled against the pain to sit up against the bulkhead.

Chapter 37

Morgan's eyes snapped open and he sat up in his bunk. He inhaled deeply again as he ran his fingers through his hair and rubbed at his bare chest sleepily while he peered around in the dark cabin. He sat still and listened to the sounds of the ship. It had to be nearly midnight. As if to confirm his speculation, the ship's bell sounded the change of the watch.

With a shrug in the darkness, he eased back down onto his bunk and fussed with his pillow. Just as he began to relax back into sleep, there was a soft, but distinctive thump. He sat up again, this time with more purpose and a bit more alert. The cabin was too still. He cocked his head and listened for the soft breathing of Aubrey in slumber.

"Aubrey? Are you all right?" He called softly.

The thump came again. His head turned to peer into the darkness at the door. Slipping from his bunk and pulling on his britches, he began to have a bad feeling in the pit of his stomach. Reaching tentatively toward Aubrey's bunk, he lay his hands flat to feel for the body that should be there. Cold fear gripped his heart when he found himself soundly patting an empty bunk.

"Oh Christ." He moaned as he hurriedly lit the lantern. The light cast by the fire on the wick confirmed his worst fears. Aubrey's bunk was disheveled but empty.

There was the soft thump against the outside of the cabin door. Morgan moved forward and, picking up his pistol, he took the latch in his hand and carefully opened the door. Something heavy pressed against the door causing it to open much faster than he would have liked. He put the pistol up in defense as he stepped back to allow himself room to maneuver.

On first sight, the corridor seemed devoid of all life. But at the same time, something fell against his lower legs. Morgan stepped back again instinctively looking down.

"Oh Christ!" He exclaimed as he tossed his pistol onto his bunk and dropped to his knees.

Aubrey lay draped over his feet with her right side facing him. She was nearly lifeless but soft mutterings of pain emitted from her. Morgan pulled her into his lap and scooped her legs out of the doorway. With a swipe of his hand, he pushed the door closed, leaving them alone on the floor of the cabin.

"Aubrey? Aubrey, what is the matter?" He asked as he pulled her further into his lap. Painful cries of protest emitted from her.

"Go to bed, Morgan. Leave me alone." She finally mumbled.

Morgan caught her face in his hand gently and turned her to face him fully. With another curse, he saw her badly battered face. He lifted her in his arms and carried her to her bunk.

"Aubrey, who did this to you? Was it that bastard Beaufort?" He asked. His reply was only whimpers of pain. Morgan frowned as he wondered to himself, if it had been Beaufort, would she have been able to return to the cabin?

"How did you get here?" He asked as he tried to make her comfortable.

"I think …I walked." She stammered through her bloody lips.

"Aubrey, who was it?" He queried on as he pulled off her boots and surveyed her. None of her clothing appeared to be torn, only her shirt was disheveled.

"He—surprised me—out of the darkness." She muttered again in fragmented sentences as Morgan brought a basin of water and a rag to the bunk.

"Who? Who surprised you in the dark?" He asked as he set the bowl on the floor.

He took the rag to her face and watched as her eyes rolled lazily open and then closed, "Oh Morgan—do put on some clothes then—people will talk." Her outburst came in a giggle-laced drawl.

Morgan could see no humor in the situation. "You have seen me in just my britches before. Why were you out of the cabin after dark and alone?" He scolded as he wiped at the blood on her face.

"Sweet Mary, I have such a headache." She moaned.

"What happened?" He pressed on.

"All I wanted to do was talk." She mumbled.

"With who?"

"Mala." Aubrey replied softly.

Morgan sat back and looked at her in surprise. "Mala did this?" He asked slowly as he resumed cleaning the blood from her face.

"Oh no, you silly thing." She muttered.

Morgan set aside the rag and gently touched her around the seeping cut and her cheekbone with his thumbs. Aubrey cried out in pain and drew up her knee closest to him in defense. He caught it quickly, "Careful there. I am only trying to see if you have any broken bones in your face. Keep those little knees to yourself."

"Oh Morgan, I would not do that to you." Her voice was lazier now and her speech was beginning to slur. Her eyes rolled back and she drifted into semi-consciousness muttering, "My head hurts."

"Hey, wake up and talk to me. Tell me who did this." He coaxed as he went back to gently cleaning her face. "You had no business sneaking out after hours like that. I have warned you over and over how dangerous it is. Who did this?"

"To be sure it was dangerous. Why a person cannot pay a friendly visit here on your pirate ships without getting into trouble. Ouch, that hurts." She mumbled as she tried to fend off the gentle strokes of the rag.

"Be still, you have blood all over your face." He purred in comfort.

"He was drinking I could smell it." She informed thickly.

"Who was?" He queried on. Aubrey drifted back into the black abyss of unconsciousness. Morgan called her name softly several times but to no avail. He shook her gently to try and bring her around. When she came to and he asked, "He was drinking? Who was drinking, Aubrey?"

"I wish I was drinking." She muttered.

The small comment made him smile and he mimicked her Irish accent. "Oh yes, you would be a lovely sight with a few drinks!"

"I have had brandy before." Aubrey said with a lazy air of smugness.

"Really then? And when did you drink that, me darlin'?" He tormented still mocking her accent. He shifted her in his arms and held the cool rag to her bruised face.

"At dinner one time …on Captain Black's ship. I had dinner with the captain and the quartermaster." She began.

"Well then, were you not just the special one?" He smiled.

"I did not want the drink, but he told me to take it—so the captain would not get angry." She went on.

Silence enveloped them for a moment and she drifted from him into unconsciousness again. Shaking her lightly he called her name. "Wake up here." He said close to her ear.

"Was that you shakin' me, Morgan? You are making me sick. Be still then and let me sleep." She fussed.

"Well you cannot sleep right now." He said thickly. "Who did this to you?"

"You are too persistent and bossy, Mr. Alcott. You are just like Jean Luc." She muttered. The name came so faintly that he barely heard it.

Leaning his ear closer to her mouth he asked, "Who?"

"Captain Black dragged me into the cabin and he hit me." She responded.

Morgan exhaled deeply for he had the name of the man who had beaten her but looking back down at her, he frowned. Rene Black had not been the name she had muttered just a moment ago. Her eyes closed again as she fell silent and still.

"Aubrey, talk to me, love. Who was the man on the *Widow Maker* the man that you knew?" Morgan realized that this was not fair of him to question her like this in her present state, but he thought that it might keep her awake with him.

"Jean Luc is dead." She suddenly moaned tearfully.

Morgan's hand dropped from its gentle tending to her battered face. "What?"

"He found out the truth—the truth about Jean Luc and me." She whined. Morgan exhaled deeply again, he had caught the name this time—Jean Luc.

"What was his last name?" He asked carefully.

"Pierne. We were in love—Captain Black was very angry that day." She said as she drifted off again. Morgan put down the rag. He gently stroked the side of her face that was not injured.

"Aubrey." He called thickly.

"What?" She muttered as she moved uncomfortably in his arms.

"What happened to Jean Luc?"

"Captain Black had him taken below." Came the soft reply through the swollen lips. "Oh Morgan, my head hurts really bad." She replied tearfully.

He pulled her upper body closer to his chest and buried his face in her neck, "I know, love."

As Morgan sat gently rocking her in the semi-dark cabin, she drifted into the abyss of unconsciousness once more and he began to piece together all the information that he had of her past thus far. Aubrey moaned against his ear and he lifted his head to look at her. She was in need of medical attention and his meager tending would just not suffice. He wondered if she had any broken bones anywhere so he tentatively laid her back down and began to check her legs and arms first.

She gave him no quarrel as he checked her legs until he squeezed her upper left thigh. Then she cried out in mild pain.

"Sorry, love." He said softly. Once more he checked the area, with the same response. Then he checked along her arms. When he raised her left arm to check it, she very nearly shrieked in pain. Something was terribly wrong there and it would require more than he could do for her with just water and a cloth.

"Aubrey, I have to go for a minute. I will be right back, I promise." He began close to her ear as he covered her with a blanket but she did not respond.

Morgan moved quickly along the corridor toward the galley. Willie knew more of medicine than anyone on the ship with the exception of Mala. Suddenly he stopped in his tracks—Mala. Where had she been when Black had beaten Aubrey? Where was she now? That was the person he needed.

Suddenly a hand came to rest on his bare shoulder and he fairly leaped out of his skin. Whirling around and reaching for his pistol he had tucked into his britches, he found himself staring into the face of the person he had been thinking about.

"Morgan, why are you sneaking around below decks partially dressed?" Mala whispered with a grin.

"Damn it Mala...do not sneak up on me like that." He growled as he tucked away the pistol. Then taking her arm, he pulled her along with him. "Come with me."

Mala dropped to her knees beside the bunk and peeled back the blanket covering Aubrey. "What happened?"

"Black did this." Morgan said curtly.

"When?" Mala asked tightly over her shoulder.

"I do not know, maybe an hour ago. At least that was when she fell into the cabin." He told her. "I started to go to your cabin to get you but then Aubrey had said Black had been drinking and I am in no mood to deal with that right now."

"Yes, he has been drinking. I have not been in the cabin since just after nightfall." Mala reported as she checked Aubrey's bruised face.

"She said she had gone to talk to you. Black dragged her inside and did this." Morgan spat.

Mala exhaled hard and stood to reach into a pouch that she carried on her belt. "I need a cup of water." She said.

Morgan got the water and watched as she put a powdery substance into her palm and dropped some water from her fingertips into it. She mixed a paste and began to press the substance onto the wound on Aubrey's cheek.

"This should help to draw the wound as it heals, it will keep the scar small." Mala informed.

The younger woman began to come to and fuss from the pain. Morgan sat on the bunk at her head and caressed her face gently. "Be still."

"Does she have any broken bones?" Mala asked.

"I did not really check other than her legs and arms. She cried out when I moved her left arm." He reported. Morgan watched as Mala gently ran her hands over Aubrey, checking her ribs with gentle pressing motions. Aubrey caught at the hands and her eyes fluttered open to look up into Morgan's face.

"Keep your hands to yourself then, Morgan." Aubrey drawled, her voice heavily laced with her accent.

A small snort of laughter escaped him and he smiled, leaning down close to her face, "Ach, you spoil all my fun."

"No broken or fractured ribs that I can tell. Now, the arm." Mala said as she took Aubrey's left hand to raise her arm. The young Irish woman emitted the same painful cry she had when Morgan had checked her. He saw Mala frown and then check the arm further with soft kneading motions.

"Hmm, this will be a bit more difficult." She finally said as she

331

straightened to dig into the pouch again.

"What is it?" Morgan asked.

"Sit her up and make her drink all of this. It will help her with the pain. Her shoulder is dislocated and I will have to put it back into place." Mala said as she handed the cup to Morgan after she had poured another powder into the water that was left. Morgan gently pulled Aubrey back into his lap and let her rest against his chest once more.

"Here Aubrey, have a drink with me. I went down to the hold and stole this good drink." He coaxed as he put the cup to her swollen lips.

Aubrey took a sip then made a face as she pushed at the cup and nearly tipped it from his hands, "Ugh Morgan! This is terrible! You were not very selective in your theft! Go away, I want to sleep, I hurt all over."

"This will make you feel better." He coaxed on, successfully getting her to take more. As he nursed the drink into her, he looked up at Mala, "This was uncalled for. All she did was come to see you."

"When I left the cabin, Rene was well into the process of getting drunk. Unfortunately, he was not in the best of moods." Mala said grimly. Then as if in second thought, she glared at Morgan, "Why in the hell was she out of the cabin alone anyway?"

"I was asleep! Christ, Mala! I do get tired you know. She slipped out after I had gone to sleep." Morgan poured the last of the liquid into Aubrey and handed the cup to Mala, "Now what?"

"Straddle her here and hold her down while I put that shoulder back." Mala directed as she pointed to Aubrey's hips.

Morgan snorted, "She is definitely not going to like that."

"She is drugged, you may be pleasantly surprised." Mala said with a glimmer of mischief in her dark eyes.

"In that case, perhaps you should leave." Morgan parried as he positioned himself over Aubrey's hips.

Mala handed him the rag after she had twisted it, "Suffice it to say that you will never have a woman scream under you like she will in a few moments. Now, put this in her mouth to muffle her cry or she will bring the whole crew in here wondering what is going on." Mala said with a nod and Morgan did as directed.

"Are you ready?" She asked.

"Aye." He said with a nod.

"Brace her upper body." Mala directed as she pushed his upper body down towards Aubrey's.

"Stop tormenting me, Mala." He said as he was now practically lying over Aubrey's motionless body.

"Quiet, you fool." She replied as she took a firm grasp of Aubrey's arm.

"Uh oh." Morgan moaned as he looked at Aubrey's face. She was waking slightly and he felt her squirm under him, protesting against the gag. Her right hand caught at his thigh and he could feel the bite of her nails through the fabric of his britches.

With a swift move that Morgan barely detected, Mala moved Aubrey's arm at the shoulder. Aubrey arched violently under Morgan and emitted a shrill scream into the rag he held securely in her mouth. The sound chilled him to the bone while her fingers dug painfully into his thigh and he looked down into the face etched with pain.

"Just like having a baby." Mala muttered almost to herself as she straightened from the task. Morgan made a face at her and moved off of Aubrey.

Looking down at the young woman who had settled back into the drugged sleep again. "I think that you were right. No woman ever screamed like that." He said trying to make light the grimness of the maneuver but not truly succeeding.

"Aye." Mala nodded.

They stood and looked down upon Aubrey for a few moments before finally, Morgan said with an almost air of dejection, "She holds herself for Jean Luc." Mala nodded again and met his look with passive dark eyes. "You knew?" He asked as he turned to fully face her. Mala remained silent. "And when were you going to share that bit of information?" He asked with a hint of anger in his tone. She still remained silent and looking down at Aubrey now. Morgan moved restlessly, waiting for a reply of some kind.

Finally, when he thought that he might burst with the question, Mala said quietly, "We discussed many things that day on the beach, Morgan."

Mala turned toward the door and Morgan asked in mild panic, "What—what do I need to do for her?"

"Keep her warm, give her some water and let her rest. I will return shortly. I need some things from the galley."

"What about this whole issue? Are we just going to let Black get away with this?" He asked.

"Rest assured, it will not happen again." Mala said firmly as she left the cabin.

Morgan looked down on Aubrey for a few moments and pondered all the information he had received this night. With a tired sigh, he sat down on her bunk and ran his fingers through his hair.

Chapter 38

It was later than his usual early routine when Black woke the next morning and found himself alone in the cabin. He sat up in the bunk and looked around noting that he was still dressed and had slept over the bed sheets. By the looks of the cabin, it appeared that Mala had not returned. Black slowly stood up and unsteadily made his way to the cabin door. Opening the door, he looked down the corridor but found it empty as well. He turned back into the cabin and was closing the door when he stopped. Stepping back out into the corridor, Black looked again. He had a vague memory of throwing Aubrey out of the cabin after—what? His brows knitted together as he tried to remember. His mind was slow to respond from the drink but he knew something should be out here.

Turning, Black closed the door and leaned heavily against it. He needed something for the pounding of his head. Again, he unsteadily went to the washbasin and splashed water on his face. He then went to Mala's cupboard and took out a bottle of rum. He turned to place it on the table, bumping the bottle against the edge.

"Damn it!" He said and winced as his own deep voice seemed to boom in his head. He gingerly set the bottle on the table then sat heavily in the nearest chair. Resting his head against the high back of the chair and closing his eyes, he tried to steady his breathing from all the exertion. Suddenly his eyes flew open as he remembered. Aubrey was thrown out of the cabin after he had beaten her senseless. He had not wanted Mala to find her in a heap on the floor. He looked around again and still could find no sign of Mala's return. His mind flashed back to a time when Aubrey should have been in the cabin upon his return but was not. That was because she had been with his quartermaster!

Black's gaze moved to the bunk and shook his head. Mala would not lie with his quartermaster. So where was she? Then he froze as another thought struck him. Not his quartermaster, but perhaps her quartermaster. And he made the damned suggestion himself. Fool! It was not happening again. With a low animal-like growl and ignoring the pounding in his head, Black threw himself out of the chair and was out of the cabin in a flash.

Going to the hold first, the guard told Black that no one had been down except to bring Deats' meal. Black ordered the door open anyway and peered in. He found Deats chained as before. Without a word, Black left the hold. In his search, Black had checked the storeroom, galley and other areas of the ship but did not see Mala. No one seemed to have answers for him when he questioned some of the crew. In hopes of clearing his now-massively pounding head, Black went topside for some air. Timmons was on duty now but he too had not seen Captain Mala. Black looked out to sea from the stern of the ship. Where the hell was she?

It was late in the morning before Black returned to the cabin and found Mala standing near the quarter gallery windows with arms crossed, looking out. Hearing the door open, she turned slightly, looked at him, then resumed her stance. Black shut the door and leaned against it staring angrily at the raven-haired beauty. His head still ached from the drunken stupor the evening before.

"Where the hell have you been?" He growled, his voice slurring. His anger rose as he heard her inhale and exhale loudly before she replied without turning to face him.

"With the seas surrounding us and no port in sight, where the hell could I go, Rene?" She said scornfully.

"Damn it, Mala, answer me!" He bellowed. He pushed himself away from the door and started towards her then suddenly stopped. He turned to his right and found that a hammock hung in the corner. "What the hell is that?" He asked.

"That is where you will be sleeping from now on." She answered calmly still not turning to answer.

"What? The hell I will, I sleep in the bunk with you." He retorted.

"Not anymore." Came her calm reply.

His worst fears from earlier were realized for she was casting him aside for another. In angry strides, Black advanced on her. He was beyond all reasoning now. Mon Dieu, she was his! No man will touch her, have her, or feel the sweet bliss of holding her close and loving her! No man! Before he could reach her, Mala moved away to put the table between them. Black growled and quickened his steps to catch her. He tried to grab her arm but missed as she spun around a corner of the table. With his long legs, he was able to shorten some of distance between them. He reached out again and missed her once more. But this time he caught her long hair and with a jerk, Mala's head shot backwards. She let out a painful yelp that was cut off by Black's hand over her mouth.

"Do not run from me again, Mala." He hissed in her ear as his arms encircled her in a vice grip hold. She struggled against him but despite his pounding head and the exertion of the chase, Black's hold was firm and strong.

Mala was calling him every name she could think of and saying them in a mixture of her native tongue, French and English. Her struggles slammed them against the desk, knocking the logbook to the floor. They crashed backwards against the wall. When Black's grip held, Mala emitted a savage growl deep within her throat, attesting to her full fury. Hearing it, Black knew he would have hell to pay but his own jealous fury ignored it.

Suddenly the door flew open and Beaufort rushed in, a pistol in one hand and sword in the other, ready for battle. Still struggling furiously, both Mala and Black looked up to see who it was.

"Get out!" Black ordered angrily. At the sight of their struggles, Beaufort was transfixed. "Sortez!" Black repeated when he caught a glimpse of Beaufort still in the cabin.

This time, Beaufort did as he was told and left the cabin smiling evilly. The last time the captain had a battle with a woman, he had tossed her aside. Returning to his quarters and lying on his bunk, Beaufort grinned as he listened to battle in the next cabin. Tonight the dark-haired bitch would be under him and if need be, he would inflict his own beating upon her. She would know her place.

Mala slowed her struggling as she grew tired. Breathlessly, Black gritted out through clenched teeth, "You may no longer be in the hold, Mala, but you are still a prisoner."

With a contemptuous chuckle, Mala shot back, "A prisoner with access to the entire ship and the crew? A prisoner with no restrictions, no barriers? A prisoner..."

"Merde! Cela suffit!" Black roared. "You are a prisoner and you are mine!"

"You bastard." She growled as she suddenly gave a violent shove backwards and Black was slammed against the wall, the air knocked out from him in a "whoosh." His grip slackened a bit, just enough for Mala to slip out of his hold. She whirled around and backhanded him across the face. Black retaliated in kind.

Beaufort was lying calmly in his bunk with his hands behind his head, eyes closed and still grinning. Suddenly the wall seemed to explode beside him. His eyes flew open and he shot up out the bunk. "Son of a bitch!" He roared in French as he stood staring at the offending wall.

Mala's head jerked around with the force of the blow. Taking this opportunity of her unawareness, Black grabbed Mala by the throat and slammed her backwards against the wall that sided the stern of the ship. He moved in close to her body to prevent any struggles there.

"Now answer me, Mala. Where the hell have you been all night and this morning?" He growled. Her face turned red from the pressure of his fingers. Pain exploded in her head as he slammed it against the wall then tightened his grip a bit more. "Where, Mala!"

His anger was full blown now. His breathing was coming fast and his blood had warmed to the fight. He stared at her when she refused to answer. Just like the last one. She would not answer either. No, not like her! Mala was different! Mala was special and by God, no other man will have his raven-haired beauty! He could feel her hands yanking his arm for release but he only tightened yet a little more.

Through the exploding pain, Mala's mind reeled. Mon Dieu, he was going to kill her! He was really going to do it! Finally, she tried to speak. Black inclined his head when she croaked out the name for the second time. "Aubrey."

He released her and stepped back, glaring down at her. She gulped in air as she slid to the floor, coming to rest on her knees, her legs tucked under her. Laboring to breathe and her body slumped, Mala was now nearly laying on her side against the wall on the floor. Black's anger was still riding high as he bent down and took her arm to force her to her feet. Mala groaned, thinking he was about to finish what he started and she could not lift her arms to fend him off. They felt like leaden weights and she still could not catch her breath. For the first time in a very long time, Mala could not defend herself against a foe and she was frightened. He glared into her face, seeing the half-closed eyes, the parted lips as she struggled still to breathe and a look of worry on the beautiful face.

As he looked down into her face, another emotion took over him. He leaned his full form against her body and bent his forehead to hers as the two tried to catch their breath. After a long moment, he cupped her face in his hands and his lips were upon hers. The kiss was crushing and brutal yet so full of passion, Black thought he would explode. He could not seem to satisfy himself with just the kiss and the closeness of their bodies against the wall nor could he release this woman from him.

Slowly, Mala's mind registered Black's outburst. He was insanely jealous and, not knowing where she had been, had left him with far too many illusions to the imagination. With great effort, Mala lifted her heavy arms up to encircle his waist. Black responded by grinding his lips against hers, plying her mouth with his tongue. Mala continued to hold onto him but soon made sounds of distress against his assaulting kisses. She could not breathe. Finally he broke from the kiss and lifting her in his arms, he carried her to the bunk. Hastily he first undressed himself then undressed her. He looked down at her, the medallion, his mark on her left breast, the beautiful soft body as he covered her with his. Still too weak to comply to his urgings, Mala felt him part her legs and soon he was inside of her. She noticed that his lovemaking was much like his kiss, forceful and urgent. The passion in him had to be satiated even as Mala lay coughing and gasping for much needed air she had been deprived of. But she could not move, could not respond to him.

Afterwards, they both laid on the bunk panting for air. Black stared up at the ceiling and listened to the labored breathing of the woman beside him. His mind relived the battle they just fought. He had felt as though he had lost control of something so very important and had no idea how to gain it back.

Suddenly realizing what he had nearly done, Black raised himself on his elbow to stare down at Mala. Her eyes were closed and she seemed to still have difficulty breathing. He could already see the bruises forming on her cheek and around her neck. Her neck had the imprints from his fingers. He had nearly killed her! His gaze swept over her face, her hair, and her breasts. "Mala." He whispered very low.

He watched as she slowly opened her eyes to look up at him. She looked tired and haggard. Sudden feelings of regret flooded him as he gently caressed the side of her face with his fingertips. "Je regrette. Je suis desolé." Black whispered as he watched her closely. He lowered his head to kiss her forehead, her temple, her cheeks, then her lips.

When Mala heard her name, it was an effort to open her eyes. Her whole body ached and she found it hard to swallow. Once she was able to look up, she found Black's face so close to hers she could feel his breath against her cheek while his gaze searched her face. To hear him say that he was sorry, that he was so very sorry made Mala's spirits rise. He was feeling remorse, a lot of it if she were to guess from the expression on his face. It was clearly evident that the pain he had inflicted upon her during their battle made him heartsick. Then he was kissing her, tenderly, passionately.

Black lifted his head to look into her eyes. She gave him a tired smile and he felt hope from that. Once again, he laid his forehead against hers and repeated her name over and over. Without moving, Mala heard him confess, "I had not seen you since last evening when we argued. I thought you ... Mon Dieu, Mala! I thought you had gone to stay with someone else last night and this morning." Remembering the anger, he closed his eye tightly and clenched his teeth.

Black felt her fingers touch his face and he lifted his head so he could gaze into her eyes.

"Rene." Mala said hoarsely. She tried to hide the pain that talking had caused but Black saw it and winced. "I have been with no other man since you..." Mala could not finish her statement.

Her voice had gotten lower until it reached a point that she could barely be heard. Her throat just hurt too much. Mala could hear Black whispering again that he was so very sorry in her ear as his cheek laid next to hers. She turned her head in his direction and smiling into his questioning gaze, Mala offered her lips to his. His response was to gather her to him and deliver another crushing kiss. She lifted her arms to encircle his neck and hold him closer to her. This time his lovemaking was not as urgent but it was sweeter as the two captains had come to a new understanding of their inner feelings.

Later in the afternoon, Black felt Mala move from his side. He reached out and his hand ran down her arm as she stood up. She turned to caress his face with one hand and reply hoarsely since her throat was still sore, "I must tend to Aubrey."

Black lowered his gaze and seemed to slump. He understood from her confession that she was with Aubrey and, therefore, must have known of what had happened. He remembered the hammock in the corner. It was there because of her anger over what he had done to Aubrey, not because she was casting him aside. Well that was not staying in this cabin!

He watched her dress silently and winced when she did. His gaze went to her throat and he saw the dark bruise. He then saw the bruise that formed on her cheek. He did not like her tending to Aubrey. He wondered what damage he had done but whatever it was, it would be a reminder to Mala.

After she finished dressing and putting her weapons into her sash, Mala went to her quarter gallery window and surveyed the bottles on display. She stared at one bottle for a long moment, her eyes cutting slightly toward the man in the bunk before she chose a different bottle on a small ledge below it. Turning, she found him watching her. Black sat up quickly and swung his long legs over the edge as she neared him. Putting out his arm to stop her, he caught her wrist and pulled her to him.

Wrapping his arms around her waist and pulling her to him, he rested his forehead between her breasts. He closed his eye, seeing again the staggering blow he dealt her when he backhanded across her cheek. He let out a relieved sigh and his arms tightened around her when he felt her hand at the nape of his neck, playing with his hair as her other hand seemed to hold his head to her. They held each other this way for a few more moments before she moved slightly.

"I must go, Rene." She whispered hoarsely.

Black lifted his head to look up at her and she lowered hers slightly for a kiss. He tried to deepen the kiss when she moaned painfully. They separated quickly and he watched as she pulled the shirt down from her throat. She gave him a small smile as her hand touched his scarred cheek then she turned away and left the cabin. Black inhaled deeply, staring at the floor.

Morgan opened the door to the knock and found Mala on the other side. She held up the bottle she retrieved from her ledge as he opened to door wider to allow her in. Moving directly to Aubrey, Mala was opening the bottle when he exclaimed, "Christ! What the hell happened to you?" Mala looked up and knew that he noticed the bruise on her face. "The son of a bitch! Has he lost his…"

"Morgan." She replied still hoarse. Morgan quieted in an instant, his eyes moving to her throat. The dark bruises were noticeable and would only be worse in the next day or two. She could see the fury build in his blue eyes making them darken.

"He has lost his mind." He hissed through clenched teeth almost too quietly.

"Morgan." She warned but he ignored it and turned to leave the cabin. Suddenly he found himself slammed forward against the door. "No!" Mala ordered.

Morgan turned slowly to face her, the deadly gleam still his blue eyes. "You cannot be serious. I told him what would happen if you were harmed." When he saw the questioning look in her dark eyes, he explained. "Outside of Charlestowne, when he asked for my help to board this ship, I told him that if any harm came to you, I would kill him myself. He knew I meant it, Mala, and he agreed." Mala was already shaking her head disagreeing. "Captain!"

"No and that is an order." Mala said firmly yet painfully as she looked directly into his blue eyes. Taking a deep breath, she added slowly, "This was not about Aubrey."

She received a dubious look from Morgan. He did not believe her. Taking another deep breath and swallowing carefully, Mala went on, "Morgan, he did not know where I was. He was jealous."

Mala watched him as he thought that over. He raised a brow and asked slowly, "He thought you were with someone else?" Mala nodded and he rolled his eyes then in a calmer tone, he grumbled, "Like I said, he has lost his mind." He looked at his captain who was smiling at him. He took her by the chin and held her face so that he could look closer at the bruised cheek then down at her neck.

"The men cannot see you like this. There will be a mutiny." Mala nodded in agreement. "Then here is what we will do." Morgan said as Mala listened. She smiled her agreement then nodded.

It was decided that Mala would sit with Aubrey in Morgan's cabin whenever Morgan could not stay due to his watch and other duties. For the crew's benefit, the story would be that Aubrey was ill and Captain Mala was staying with her. So that no one stopped by to check on her progress, Morgan would tell the crew that there were to be no visitors by Captain Mala's orders.

341

Chapter 39

Just before the skies lightened for the dawn on the second day, Mala was up and dressed so that she could relieve Morgan and stay with Aubrey. She looked up with dread as Black returned to the cabin unexpectedly. He stopped and stared at Mala fully dressed then looked at the dawning skies out the quarter gallery window. Slowly he shut the door then leaned against it, blocking her exit. "You are not usually up this early. Where are you going?"

"To sit with Aubrey." She replied then heard him grunt in disapproval.

Mala's gaze never wavered as she watched him. He looked to the floor as he said in tone of impatience, "Mala, I am sure that the herbs you give her makes her sleep most of the day."

"It does." She replied. Her voice was still hoarse but not as painful as she took her own herbs to soothe the pain. He looked up then, his gaze full of irritation. She clicked her tongue, seeing his look.

"Oh do stop with the looks, Rene." She grumbled with a roll of her eyes.

"Mala..." He started.

She interrupted, anger etched in her tone. "With Beaufort strutting about thinking he now has your permission to take her, I will make sure that..."

Black advanced on her angrily but Mala stood her ground. Taking her by the shoulders, his grip tight, he hissed, "Damn it, you are not her protector!"

With a burst of her own anger, Mala threw her arms up and broke his hold then stepped back. Jabbing a finger into his chest, she asked heatedly, "Then who the bloody hell is, Rene? Morgan wins that fight being the one still standing while Beaufort had to be carried out of the alley and still you give her to the beast! So why the hell then did they fight? What did that prove?" When he did not answer right away, she went on, "And that scene in the galley! You allowed it to happen! Why? Were all the men going to have a turn on her? Were you planning to take your share?"

"No, damn it!" He turned away from her and saw the hammock in the corner again. "What the hell is that doing back in here? I took the damned thing down yesterday." He growled and whirled around to face her.

"I told you before that is where you will..." She gritted out.

"No, my place is beside you..." He argued.

"Not if you allow monstrous bastards like Beaufort to run amuck on my ship! He wants something to ease his baser needs then he can find a goddamned knothole. He stays the hell away from Aubrey! I damn well mean it, Rene!"

Black's next heated reply died away as what Mala had just said registered

343

in his mind. A knothole? An absurd vision came to mind and Black's anger dissolved instantly. He stared at Mala incredulously while at the same time, the corners of his mouth twitched upward. He bit his bottom lip and turned away from her. Mala was watching his reaction and now could see his shoulders shaking as he stood with his back to her. She wondered at his humor until she realized what she had said and melted into laughter.

Hearing her laughter, Black laughed aloud as well and turned to find her leaning against a high-backed chair. Pulling her into his arms, he said, "Pray that I do not have to face the choice of a raven-haired vixen or a knothole, mon coeur."

"If that should be the case, Rene, then I would surely be dead. At the moment, I have no plans in obliging the Angel of Death on that score so I guess you are just left with me." Mala said smiling.

Black gently cupped her face and said softly, "Hmm, you definitely present a more satisfying vision." He kissed her lips tenderly then smoothed her hair with gentle fingers. He gazed into her eyes and whispered, "Must you go right now?"

Mala looked at him smiling, "I really should so the men do not see me like this." Black's passionate gaze looked at her bruises and some of the heated passion died away. Then he saw her smile widen and, with a slight shrug, she added, "I really should…" His dark eye looked into her eyes as he bent to kiss her. At her lustful response, he lifted her in his arms and carried her to the bunk.

The theory of Beaufort's dare was made fact later that day while Mala still sat with Aubrey. The day had been quiet and Aubrey was sleeping peacefully. Mala had kept the herbal tea in the younger woman to ensure that she got the needed rest. It was early afternoon when the door flew open and Thomas Beaufort stepped in as though he had every right to be in the cabin.

Mala was reading a book and merely lifted her eyes from it before returning to her reading. Beaufort smiled and took a step toward Aubrey's bunk.

"You do not belong here." Mala stated casually, stopping him.

"Quiet whore, and mind your own business." He said and took another step for the bunk.

Holding the book open with one hand, Mala squeezed her hand and the book shut with a thump. Beaufort stopped to watch her as she stood up and purposefully got in his way. "You have no business here." She warned again.

His gray eyes took in the bruised cheek and the bruises on her neck. He snickered down at her then made to push her aside. Mala dropped the book and simultaneously grabbed the front of his shirt as her fist connected solidly with his nose. Beaufort stumbled backwards into the corridor, tripping over his own feet in the process. He fell against the opposite wall but did not fall down. Mala stepped up to the doorway and meeting Beaufort's eyes, she calmly shut the door.

Beaufort touched his nose and felt the blood on his fingers. He looked down as if to confirm it then glared at the closed door before him. He turned away when he heard voices and he moved along the corridor. As he started up the companionway steps, a thought struck him. Captain Black had fought with the dark-haired woman the day before and she now had bruises to show for his displeasure. He would not be pleased with her abuse of his crew. With an evil smile, Beaufort headed for the quarterdeck where he had last seen his captain.

Black was looking up at the sails and was wondering if they would have more of a breeze soon. This slow pace was irritating. Hearing footsteps approaching, he lowered his gaze to find Beaufort coming up the companionway. His nose was bleeding and some droplets had made it to his shirt.

"What happened to you?" Black asked as Beaufort came up the quarterdeck steps to stand before him.

"That dark-haired whore hit me and I demand retribution. She broke a rule -- no fighting on board the ship." Beaufort said loudly. Black noticed that many of those on deck turned to listen. Timmons had even turned to listen and Black noted the concern on his young face for his captain's welfare.

"Very well, come with me." Black said with a heavy sigh. Beaufort followed him down the companionway steps and across the deck.

As Black approached Morgan, the sandy-haired man stepped forward. "Captain?" But his plea was silenced when Black raised a gloved hand. Morgan was quiet as Black passed but turned an angry glare on Beaufort who smirked in satisfaction.

Black turned toward the great cabin as he and Beaufort stepped away from the companionway. "She is in Alcott's cabin." The gray-eyed man informed his captain.

Black stopped and turned to face Beaufort, "This happened in Morgan's cabin?"

Beaufort nodded, proud of himself for what would be a better outcome. Black would punish that dark-haired witch and he would be able to get to the younger one. His proud moment was slowly diminishing as Black continued to stand in the corridor and stare at him. The dark haired man was wondering, how does she know what someone will do before they do it? Without a word, Black suddenly turned and resumed his journey in the direction of Morgan's

345

cabin.

Standing at the door, Black raised his hand to knock but stopped as he caught sight of something on the floor. He bent down and touched at the dark spots. Examining the fingertips of his gloved hand, Beaufort looked at it and informed him, "Blood."

"Indeed." Black replied cynically as he knocked on the door.

They could hear someone coming to the door and it opened to reveal Mala with a book in hand. She looked at Black then moved her gaze behind him to Beaufort. Black saw her gaze drop to the bloodied nose then he watched the smile she was having trouble suppressing. Turning her head to cover the grin that would not stay down, she stepped aside and allowed them to enter. Black did not take his eyes off Mala as her shoulders began to shake with suppressed laughter. When Beaufort entered behind Black, choked laughter emitted from Mala as she slowly closed the door. She caught Black's stern gaze but that only fueled her amusement as the chuckles were becoming more pronounced.

"You find this funny?" Beaufort asked irritably. Black should have done something to her immediately, the gray-eyed man thought sourly. Now that she was laughing at him, Beaufort was ready to throttle her.

Mala was laughing outright now. The image of Beaufort running to Black like one child tattling on another was transfixed in her mind. The noise was penetrating Aubrey's drugged mind and she murmured unintelligently. The murmurs drew the attention of the men as Mala stepped to the door and opened it. Through barely stifled chuckles, she announced, "I think we should discuss this out here. We must not disturb her rest."

Black turned away from Aubrey but stopped short noting that Beaufort was rooted to his spot. Looking at him, Black did not care for the lewd gaze the man bestowed on the injured woman.

"Turn around, Thomas." He growled in annoyance.

Beaufort's head snapped up and only then did he turn to leave. Mala held the door as Beaufort stepped out bestowing her a hateful glare. Black lifted his gloved hand in offer for her to precede him out. Mala did so and Black followed, closing the door. It did not take long for Beaufort to begin complaining amid Mala's chuckles that she attempted to hide behind her hand.

"There you see. A blatant disrespect for another crewmember and one that happens to also be injured." Beaufort said angrily, his arm flying out in her direction for emphasis.

Black stood casually with his back against the wall, arms crossed over his chest, and ankles crossed watching Mala give into her merriment. Each time she seemed to gain control, she would look up at Black then at Beaufort and start anew with her laughing. Looking down at the floor as a smile threatened to break through, Black said in an admonishing tone, "Mala, please control yourself."

He could have just saved his breath, Black thought to himself. His reprimand had only fueled her laughter. But Black's head snapped up when he heard Beaufort's growl and the man took a step towards Mala. Black placed a gloved hand out to stop him but Beaufort seemed to ignore it as he took another step. Black straightened and placed the gloved hand on Beaufort's chest with added pressure and still, Beaufort took another step.

"Arrête!" Black hissed, finally getting the man to stop. Mala seemed to sober a bit as well with the confrontation.

"She needs to be taught respect." Beaufort growled in reply.

"Why me? You certainly demonstrated none." Mala stated calming down.

"Respect for a whore?" Beaufort asked incredulously.

"Whore, crew, or any person whoever they may be." Mala began.

Beaufort made to reply but Black halted his words, "Since these are not your quarters, Thomas, did you knock?"

"Of course." He replied.

"No." Mala said at the same time.

"You are a liar as well just like that one within." Beaufort accused. Black gave him a fierce look but not before he saw Mala stiffen at the accusation.

"I warned you twice to get out, you pauvre con." She growled as she advanced.

Black had to bodily step between the two people and put his back to Mala, which he considered was the lesser of the two evils. Facing Beaufort, Black asked, "Is this true?"

"You would believe this lying whore?" Beaufort asked in return as he glared at Mala.

"Thomas, I have known Mala for a long time and she is not a liar." Black said calmly. "And to calling her a whore, I am sure you would consider all women whores. You and most men of our profession would see a woman, for the most part, used to appease our sexual appetites. However, as I see it, you have no business in this cabin other than to abuse one or both of these women, especially given the fact that these are the quarters of the first mate, Monsieur Alcott, and I doubt that you would rape another man." Beaufort made to protest but Black raised his hand to continue, "Therefore, this incident would have been avoided if you had not overstepped your bounds and afforded the women some respect." Black did not move as he dared Beaufort to challenge his decision.

Beaufort's furious glare shifted from his captain to Mala then back to

Black. Without another word, he turned on his heel and stormed off. Grunts and bodies hitting the wall told of the eavesdroppers who stayed around the corner and did not leave quickly enough.

Black turned to face Mala and they regarded each other for a moment before he stated quietly, "You did not help matters by laughing at him. He will find some way to get even."

Mala's smile was radiant and Black found it difficult to remain indifferent. She shrugged and replied, "Well then if that is the case, I suppose you will need to find some way to protect me from him. I am the Captain's Lady, I do believe."

Black could no longer resist the smile. He bent his head for a kiss that Mala returned. It was more provocative than need be for one standing in the middle of the corridor on a ship carrying nearly a hundred men but he wrapped her in his arms and she melted into him, deepening the kiss. Lifting his head, he could see his desire reflected in her own gaze. With a loud sigh, Black disengaged himself from her. Using one hand to open the door, he shoved Mala inside the cabin and shut the door firmly with him still in the corridor. He let his head rest on the heavy wooden plank until he could regain control of his body. Mala and her wiles reeked havoc on his desires.

In a provocative voice close to crack of the door, Mala said, "Get some sleep now, Captain, for you will need your energy tonight." His deep chuckle filled the corridor and, inside the cabin, Mala heard his laugh and smiled.

A week had passed to find Aubrey recovering nicely from her other injuries. Her bruises, like Mala's, had all but disappeared now. Her only complaint was that her two 'wardens' would not allow her to be out of her bunk for more than a few hours at a time. Even Willie sided with them when she attempted to enlist his aid so that she could help in the galley.

One afternoon, the lookout spotted a ship on the horizon. Black ordered the flags changed until the ship could be identified. Robert was sent to Morgan's cabin to relieve Mala so that she could join Black in perusing this ship. Deciding on what to do, Mala glanced at Aubrey.

"Tis Robert, Mala! Ya do trust him?" Aubrey asked annoyed, a hint of her Irish brogue in her tone. Agreeing, Mala left Robert to watch over Aubrey who made a disgusted sound before muttering, "But then, now I have three wardens to abuse me."

Robert smiled and closed the door firmly behind Mala. He sat in the chair Mala vacated while Aubrey flounced down on her bunk. She watched as Robert withdrew his pistol and casually laid it across his lap. Aubrey eyed the weapon. "Oh then, ya will not be needin' that, Robert, I promise as your prisoner that I will behave."

"Aye then, I know that you will or you will have Morgan to reckon with! Lay down there and rest." He chuckled, mocking her drawl.

"Rest he says, but that is all I do but rest!" Aubrey grumbled back, crossing her legs and arms then leaned against the wall.

On her way to the main deck, Mala met Morgan who was hurrying down the corridor. He was excited and nearly bumped into her. "Sorry, Mala." He apologized. "Tis a merchant ship and Black has given the order to board it."

Mala smiled and continued to the deck as Morgan rushed to his cabin. Inside, he found Aubrey full of questions. "Is it dangerous?" She was asking.

"Of course, but that is the thrill of it all!" He answered and pulled out a gentleman's overcoat from his trunk.

"But what if something goes wrong?" She asked still concerned.

He and Robert laughed before he replied, "Nothing will go wrong."

"But what if..."

"Will you stop worrying." Morgan chuckled as he slipped into the overcoat. "We have been doing this for some time. Next time you will probably get to go with us." He said making her grunt in disapproval.

Stopping what he was doing, Morgan took Aubrey by the shoulders and said, "Look, Mala went on deck, correct?If Mala did not like what she saw, she would have been back by now to tell us that we were not going. Since she is not back, then all must be well." Morgan tried to reason with her.

Aubrey's questions stopped. When she finally nodded, Morgan smiled and slapped her lightly on her good shoulder. "Good, now I am going topside and Robert will be here to watch you. I think Mala will be going over and I know Black will. With the eye patch, there would be no doubts left as to who we are." Robert laughed at Morgan's quip.

The ruse was that Mala, wrapped in a cloak of fine material and obviously very expensive, pretended to be Morgan's sister who needed passage on the other ship since their ship was taking on water. Their journey would take a bit longer to get to their destination but he wanted his sister to go ahead so he could be sure that she was safe. When the other captain agreed to help out, Morgan turned to Black who gave Timmons a wave. The helmsman maneuvered the *Enchantress* to pull up alongside the other ship. Black, who kept his left side turned away from the other vessel so they would not see the eye patch, wore an overcoat befitting a ship's captain.

"Would you not like me to send a longboat?" The other captain of the now identified ship, *Bellringer*, yelled across the span of water between them.

"My sister hates the rope ladder." Morgan yelled back.

Standing next to Morgan while smiling at the captain of the other ship, Mala said quietly, "You can be such a liar."

"Aye, Captain Mala, but I am a very good liar." Morgan rebuked. Mala turned her smile on Morgan that the other captain mistook for sibling love.

Black chuckled lightly as he lowered his head down then away from the other ship. "Keep your mind on the ruse." He reminded them.

"Fear not, Rene. This captain will be wrapped around my finger before he even realizes he has been duped." Mala replied sweetly, earning her a lustful gaze from Black as he cut his eye up to her eyes. Black warmed a bit more when Mala returned the gaze.

"Careful Mala or I may be inclined to take you right here before your crew, my men, and the crew of yonder vessel." Black teased.

Morgan leaned close to Mala and said tormenting to the pair, "Although I would probably benefit from some new knowledge of lovemaking from the masters, I think that you, Mala, may not be able to stop with just one, …ah, suitor. Then again, Rene, you may not be allowed to finish before another unmounts you."

Mala raised a hand to cover her laughter while Black looked away chuckling. The two ships were in position and the captain of the *Bellringer* moved to the portside railing.

"May I express my pleasure, Miss, in providing assistance in your time of need."

"Thank you, Captain." Mala replied kindly and added a small incline of her head.

The captain indeed felt lucky to have the beautiful woman join him. She was more beautiful up close and without the brother, perhaps the young lady would be able to salvage yet another boring journey to the islands.

Looking at the small distance between the ships, the captain looked perplexed. "How do you propose to send your sister over to me for safe-keeping, sir?"

"Actually, sir, I will come across first." Morgan replied.

Taking a nearby line, Morgan stood on the railing then swung across so quickly, the captain of the *Bellringer* had no time to react. Pulling his pistol from within his overcoat as the outer garment dropped to the deck, Morgan held it before the captain's face. Looking over Morgan's shoulder, the captain found the 'sister' had also shed her cloak and was swinging across along with the man thought to be the captain. That one had a patch over his left eye.

As was the rule for the crew of the *Enchantress*, the moment Mala landed on the deck of the other ship, her colors were posted and her men joined her for the plunder. Pirates appeared from all areas of the *Enchantress* and were swinging across. The captain could do no more than stare as two flags now fluttered in the breeze, a solid red flag and the jolly roger.

350

"Pirates!" He breathed as he wondered how he could have been so blind. Suddenly, there was the report of a pistol nearby and many heads turned to see what had happened. The captain turned to find his first mate lying dead a short distance behind him, a pistol lying somewhat askew in the lifeless hand. Looking around to see who had shot him, the captain found the smoking pistol in the hands of the beautiful woman whose face showed no sign of mercy. Her dark eyes that had shown humor and merriment moments before were now cold and cruel. It sent chills throughout his entire body for she could have been the devil incarnate in woman form.

She took a step towards him, drawing her dirk and placing the tip at his throat. Her visage was devoid of emotion except for contempt as she said in the deadliest tone he had ever heard. "Unless you wish it to be known that you allowed your crew to die while you watched and did nothing, I suggest you tell us where the valuables are."

Cocking her head slightly to one side and allowing a smile to slowly appear on her face, she added, "It would save us all a great deal of time and trouble." Morgan and Black shared a knowing look and chuckled as they awaited the captain's reply.

Chapter 40

From the railing on the *Enchantress*, Beaufort watched as Mala, Black, and Morgan surrounded the stupid captain. He would not be so stupid when he made captain, the pirate thought as he watched them. A smile crossed his face as he looked at Mala and Morgan on the other ship. With them occupied over there, Aubrey was alone over here. Backing away from the railing while keeping his eyes on Mala and Morgan, Beaufort moved to the companionway. With one last look to the other ship, he smiled as he disappeared below.

He remembered Black's words but ignored them as he hastily headed straight for Morgan's cabin. In his mind, Beaufort justified his presence anywhere on this ship because he was the quartermaster. Just as the captain had the right to question anything and anyone on this ship, so did the quartermaster. As he rounded the final turn to the cabin, Beaufort's smile broadened. Finally, he would ease himself on the Irish bitch and teach her what it was like to be ridden by a real man.

Suddenly Beaufort stopped when he saw two men outside of the cabin—guards! Robert was sitting on an overturned crate while Jordan, another man from Mala's crew, was standing idly by as the pair talked. The two stopped their conversation when they saw Beaufort approaching.

Deciding to ignore them, Beaufort picked up his pace and walked straight up to the cabin door. As he reached out to open it, Jordan warned, "No sir."

Beaufort was amazed to hear a pistol cock then another pistol. He turned to find each man pointing their weapons at him.

"You would dare! I am the quartermaster on this ship!" He challenged.

"In all actuality sir, the quartermaster is Mr. Deats because this is Captain Mala's ship." Robert corrected as if talking to child. "And tis Captain Mala's orders that no one disturb Miss Aubrey."

"She is not my captain!" Beaufort bellowed. Then with a dismissive wave, he turned and reached for the door.

"Orders are that no one enters, sir. Especially you or we shoot." Jordan added.

"To kill." Robert put in smiling.

Beaufort whirled around to face them again. "Captain Black will hear of this!"

"Well, that is Captain Mala's concern, sir." Robert said stating the title as an afterthought.

Beaufort glared at the pair for a long moment, their pistols unwavering.

Again, he ignored them as he turned and reached for the door. A pistol shot rang out and splinters of wood chipped away above Beaufort's head. From inside the cabin, they heard a cry of alarm. Again, turning to the pair, Beaufort watched as Robert dropped the spent pistol and pulled another from his waistband.

"That was a warning. You get no others." Robert said, bestowing him with another smile.

"You would dare!" Beaufort repeated, enraged.

Robert's smile widened, showing his pleasure in performing this task for his captain, "Aye sir, I certainly would."

Beaufort stared at the two of them and knew they would indeed shoot him. If he managed to survive, Black would finish him off for he had already warned him that cabins not his own were off limits unless invited within. Cursing violently, Beaufort snarled, "Captain Black will hear of this to be sure!"

"Aye sir, Captain Mala is counting on it." Robert said calmly and with an unconcerned shrug.

Beaufort was furious! He could not take this opportunity to have his pleasure on Aubrey Malone nor could he get rid of these two. Even if he pulled his own weapon and got one of them, the other would get him before he could get inside to the girl. And this was all Captain Mala's fault. She knew somehow that he would dare. Just as she had known when everyone had been preoccupied with the British frigate disguised as a merchant ship. Captain Mala! That damnable dark-haired witch would just have to die! Turning on his heel, Beaufort stormed away.

On the deck of the other ship, Mala scanned the faces of the men there. Then she turned and scanned the *Enchantress*. As she had expected, she did not see him. Damn! She thought to herself, must I be right all the damned time?

"Riley!" One of Aubrey's appointed guardians stepped forward when he heard her call for him. "Go back and check on Robert and Jordan. They are outside of Morgan's cabin." Mala ordered as she cast furtive glances towards Black and Morgan.

Riley nodded and cast a glance at the two men over his shoulder as well before he took a rope and swung across to the *Enchantress*. Mala scanned the decks again just to be sure.

Using the other companionway, Beaufort emerged from below in a blinding rage. He stood on the main deck trying to calm himself when he caught sight of Mala with her back turned to him. Pulling his pistol, he raised it and put her head within the sights.

Coming across the deck of the *Enchantress*, Boulet had spotted Beaufort and was going to show him what treasures were found. He looked up from his prize in his hand and saw Beaufort pulling out his pistol, taking aim. Following his gaze across to the other ship, Boulet saw the target to be Captain Mala. His eyes widened at the folly of the move and he broke out into a run. If Beaufort was successful, Captain Black would surely drop the man in his tracks.

Mala turned to scan the *Enchantress* again when she found Beaufort. She stared incredulous that he was aiming his pistol at her. She stood still daring him to do so. If she somehow survived, she would kill the bastard the next opportunity and this time, regardless of what Black would do it her!

Just as Beaufort squeezed off the shot, Boulet threw his arm out and up. The pistol fired and the shot hit the mast above Mala's head. Everyone turned in surprise, some ducking heads, some drawing weapons, some just staring. Black, who stood nearest her, looked at the splintered wood over her head and then looked to the direction from which the shot must have come. Morgan's eyes quickly followed the same trail as well. Their attention was drawn to the sights and sounds of Beaufort and Boulet arguing. Beaufort still held the smoking pistol in his hand and still pointing to his intended target, which was without doubt Mala. By the look on Mala's face, Black and Morgan could tell that she had seen it coming and she was absolutely livid!

"Have you lost your mind? Black would tear you apart with his bare hands!" Boulet exclaimed wide-eyed.

"Leave me be!" Beaufort growled and shoved his friend away violently. Looking across to the other ship, Beaufort saw Mala standing as she was before. "Merde!" He yelled as he stormed off the deck.

That evening, Black was furious when he entered the cabin for dinner with Mala. She sat calmly on the quarter gallery window ledge watching the sunset. With her back against the wall, Mala had her legs stretched out before her on the ledge. She turned and watched Black slam the door then advance on her. "Where is he, Mala?"

"Rene, I have no idea where he is. I swear to you, I honestly do not know." She told him. How many times had she told him that since their return to *Enchantress*? He was in the worst rage she had ever seen yet she remembered well the events that led up to this moment.

While Black ordered some men to go back, find Beaufort, and confine him, she had covertly ordered Morgan to go back as well and gather up the men, find Beaufort first and hide him. She had further ordered that she did not want to know his whereabouts until she asked. She had simply told Morgan that she was going to kill him and Black would never find the body because there would be no body to find.

Judging by his reaction, Mala suspected that her men had found the bastard first and had him tucked away out of sight. She sighed deeply and wondered where Morgan had managed to hide the man as Black raged on.

Black fell silent and stood before her looking down at her trying to decide whether to believe her or not. Mala returned his stare and after a few moments, she said quietly, "I have never lied to you before, Rene. Do you think that I would lie to you now? You yourself attested to that fact a few days ago."

"Mala, I would expect you to want him dead now and I would not blame you for it. But I cannot pass a death sentence on you for his murder." Black told her. He sat on the edge of ledge to look levelly at her. "S'il vous plait mon coeur, do not do something that would leave me with no other choice. Promise me that." He pleaded.

She smiled at him as she traced the scar on his left cheek with her thumb. "Oui, mon cheri. Je promets." Mala promised him.

Black closed his eye in relief and bent his head. He took her hand that was caressing his cheek and placed a kiss in the palm of it. Mala then cupped his face with both of her hands and kissed him so tenderly that Black was overwhelmed with desire and love. Mon Dieu, he thought, let nothing happen to her and surely not by my hand!

"Whatever the Cap'n has planned for him you know it will be ugly." Conner told Morgan.

"What I am worried about is what Black will do when he finds out." Morgan said, the tone evident.

With a sigh, he ran his hand through his sandy-colored hair. He looked at Conner with a critical eye. The boy was young with a thin build and wide eyes ready for adventure. What had Mala been thinking when she let this one sign on as a member of the crew? Morgan wondered as he looked down to the floorboards. Young men signed on ships in hopes of finding their fortunes but this one seemed barely weaned from his mother to now be a crewmember of a pirate ship.

"Black is scouring the ship looking for him. If he gets his hands on Beaufort, the man will not get the benefit of a trial. Black will go straight to the sentencing. He will be judge, jury, and executor." Morgan replied with another tired sigh.

"No more than he deserves for tryin' to kill the Cap'n in broad daylight. Maybe she needs to teach him how to aim." Conner said chuckling.

Morgan gave a short laugh as well then clapped the man over his shoulder, "Well tis your watch."

"Is he still, ah, sleepin'?" Conner asked, chuckling over his own jest.

"Aye, he has been sleeping like a baby. A big baby!" Morgan said laughing. "Well I guess I will leave you to it. He should be asleep until morning. The Captain will bring me more of that concoction in the morning."

"Aye, Mr. Alcott. I suppose I will be seein' ya then."

After dinner, Black had gathered his men and made a search of the ship once more. Morgan and Robert entered the galley to find Mala at her table. Seeing them she waved them over.

"Rene is still looking for that bastard Beaufort." She reported as she swirled the drink in her mug.

"Aye, we know." Morgan nodded.

"He needs to be disposed of and quickly. Tell me where he is." Mala said barely moving her lips and not looking at either man. There was a long silence at the table among them as Robert and Morgan exchanged glances then looked back to their captain.

Mala's dark eyes rose to search the face of each man questioningly. "Well? Where is he?" The two continued their silence and Mala's face masked in impending anger, "What is this? You two are ignoring my orders now?"

Morgan and Robert exchanged glances again before Morgan leaned on the table on his forearms, "Mala, you know that we have never crossed you before. You also know that we have never disobeyed an order, even if we might not have agreed with you."

"Aye." Robert nodded in agreement. Mala looked from one man to the other and sat back slowly in her chair as Morgan went on, "But this time, we must stand against you."

"Stand against me?" She echoed in disbelief. The two men caught the menacing undertone as she repeated the words.

"Aye, we are not going to tell you where we have hidden Beaufort. We intend to take care of him in our own way. You are not to be implemented in this at all." Morgan nodded.

"As far as anyone is concerned, Black included, you never even gave the initial order to make the man disappear." Robert added.

Mala looked at them in silence for a moment. She had already told Black that she did not know of Beaufort's whereabouts. "Rene will kill the pair of you." She warned.

"Aye, if he finds out." Morgan nodded.

"Which will not happen." Robert added.

"We have always covered your back. It is our job to do so. We were careless earlier today. Beaufort could have very easily made his shot true and you would not be sitting here with us now to argue this issue. By some grace from God and, for whatever reason, Boulet intervened." Morgan began again.

"What Morgan and I are tryin' to say, Captain, is that you need to just go about your business as usual. Because we were so careless and you were almost killed, and because it is our duty to protect you, we have to set the wrong to rights." Robert told her with a look in his eye that Mala had never seen directed to her.

She opened her mouth to speak but with a decisive snort Morgan interrupted, "Consider him gone, and you know nothing save that he made an attempt on your life."

With her anger boiling over, she slowly leaned forward and hissed, "Now you two listen to me, do not dare sit here and propose to tell me what to do!"

Her furious retort was cut short as she caught sight of Black in the doorway of the galley engaged in conversation with one of his crew. Morgan and Robert took the break in their conversation as an opportunity to stand and leave the table. Mala's head shot up to look at them, gracing them with a venomous glare. Morgan looked down on her knowingly and pointed to himself. She understood—Morgan was taking charge in this issue and that was final.

Robert caught the brim of his hat with pinched fingers and nodded to her respectfully, "Good evening, Captain." Mala's anger grew by leaps and bounds as she watched her officers leave the galley. They did not look back at her as they stepped past Black with a nod of greeting.

Chapter 41

Beaufort woke by slow degrees. He was drifting in the fine abyss between the herb-induced sleep and waking. He heard the voices but he recognized only one of them.

"Make certain that you get this into his water as he takes his meal." Morgan said in a hushed tone.

"I thought that you said that you would be here early this morning?" Conner questioned.

"Black took me on a search of the ship. I could not get out of it and had a hell of a time steering him away from here. I am sure now that Black will kill Beaufort on sight if given the chance. Fortunately, Captain Mala came along and led him off in another direction. The look in his eye changes completely when he catches sight of her." Morgan replied with a smile.

"Or wind of her!" Conner chuckled.

Morgan pursed his lips and looked at the younger man, "And what would you know of the scent of a woman?" Morgan saw Conner's face crimson a bit and the boy quickly changed the subject.

"Aye well, I heard ya out there and I was glad this one here kept sleepin.' He has been makin' some noise the past few minutes, like he is tryin' to wake up." The two looked down at the sleeping man. "What are we to do with his weapons?" Conner asked as he nodded to the pistol and dirk set aside, well out of reach.

"Leave them here. When we finally dispose of him, we will put them back on his body, if he should be found, it would not look suspicious. For now, he is still too groggy to know any better or to argue about it. When he comes to just a bit, offer him this. The herb has no taste, so none will be the wiser. He will be interested only in getting something to drink since it makes him very thirsty. He will take this mug willingly if nothing else. After he drinks, he will go back to sleep." Morgan said just as Mala had explained it to him.

From the shadowed corner where he sat slumped and tied up, Beaufort was more alert than he appeared. He heard and understood the directive. Through bleary eyes, he saw Morgan give the young man the tankard and tap the keg of water nearby. A moan escaped him but in his mind he was growling in anger. He was cognitive enough to respond to the well-laid plan to keep him sedated but he would thwart that plan.

"Aye sir, I will." Conner replied with an eager nod of his head.

Morgan stepped from behind the façade of the bulkhead and glanced around to make certain that no one had seen his exit from the secret area. Then he made his way with an air of purpose back up through the hold and up to the main decks. He smiled as he thought of Mala's ship. Her carpenters had been expert engineers as well as craftsmen when they had refitted the ship for her business. In many areas of the lower hold, there were places such as these. Innocent and yet deceiving areas the walls and bulkheads hid storage areas for smuggled goods. Black had found some of the storage places for stolen items because Deats was being held in one of them. But he did not know them all and given time, Mala would find Beaufort here. Luckily she had no time to search all the secret spots without her movements being suspected and reported by Black's men.

Beaufort moaned again and moved against his bonds slightly. He wondered where they had put him. As he had heard Morgan predict, his mouth was dry. Water—what he would give for a good long drink of it. He moaned again and moved more purposefully.

The young man stepped closer and leaned down to look at him. "What is your problem, Mr. Beaufort?" Conner asked.

"Water." Beaufort croaked through parched lips.

Conner was young and inexperienced, barely ten and seven years of age. He took the tankard that Morgan had prepared and went to the man on the floor with it, "Here is some water."

Trying to feed the trussed up man proved to be awkward. Beaufort did not make matters any easier by feigning to have difficulty in getting his mouth on the lip of the tankard to drink properly.

"Let my hands free, so I can hold the mug." He slurred.

Conner obliged and loosened the knots on the ropes that bound Beaufort's wrists. It would prove to be the last thing the boy ever did in his life, good or bad. The moment his hands were free, Beaufort shoved the boy back and away savagely. Conner sprawled onto his back across the floor and Beaufort was upon him at once with a growl, his hands around the boy's slender throat in a crushing grip. Conner emitted a startled and choking croak as he thrashed under the Frenchman. Within moments, Beaufort felt the boy's windpipe collapse under the pressure of his strong hands. Conner's body jerked once more then was still and lifeless.

Beaufort looked around the small dimly area with bleary eyes. His throat was even drier than before. He spied the tankard on the floor. It had been tipped in the struggle and the water within now pooled on the floor. Beaufort remembered that it was drugged as he looked around for something else to drink. Staggering to his feet against the lingering grogginess of the drug, he saw his weapons stashed away in a corner. He picked them up, sheathing the dirk and tucking the pistol into the front of his sash.

He then found his way out of the secret place and into the main hold. He knew where the water stores were kept and headed there. On the way, he passed a small cache of rum kegs. With a grunt of approval, he looked around for a mug. With a shrug, he knelt down, put his mouth under the tap and greedily guzzled the rum. It washed over his lower face and his shirt.

With his thirst quenched for the moment, he slipped down to sit against the wall, wiping the rum from his face on the back of his sleeve. Inhaling deeply, he began to recall the conversation between Morgan and the stupid boy. Scent of a woman—why did that comment stick in his mind? Why then of course! It was the want for a woman that had driven him to attempt to kill another woman. The dark haired bitch always seemed to know his moves—what made her so astute? Black should have killed her the day they fought in the great cabin. He apparently had done well of beating her judging by the bruises on her throat.

Mala's throat. Beaufort looked at his hands and turned them as if inspecting them. Let him get his hands on her throat—she would not come up to survive. Then he would ravage her lifeless body and curse her for the bitch that she was. He let his hands drop into his lap and in his mind's eye, saw Aubrey lying in the bunk in Morgan's cabin. Apparently Black had given her a sound beating too. Her face had appeared bruised and there was a cut healing on her cheek.

Black would kill him for certain if he made another attempt on Mala. Then another part of the conversation came to mind. Black was going to kill him on sight? Beaufort shook his head. Since boarding this ship, Black was a changed man. Beaufort had to admit that he had been foolish in his threats and advances on the dark-haired woman. He had seen that in Black's dark eye, even if the words had not been spoken until recently.

He was thirsty again. He took more large gulps from the keg and settled back again with a smile. No matter—to hell with the bitch Mala, let Black have her. But—Irish—that was the one that made his mouth water. With a low growl, Beaufort pushed himself to his feet and staggered under the combination of leftover drug and the rum. Wiping his hand across his beard-stubble face, he made his way along the bulkhead toward the galley.

Aubrey was glad to finally be out of the cabin. She had even reveled in helping Willie put things away after the evening meal. He had fussed with her continually, worried that she was doing too much too soon after her recent infirmary.

As she picked up a partial bag of flour, he waved a hand at her, "Leave that lass, I will get it. You get back to your bunk now, you have just about overspent yourself."

"I can put it away for you. It will not take long then I will go straight to the cabin afterwards." She told him.

"Well, thank ye lass." He said, a smile breaking his wizened face and he stroked a gentle hand over her cheek. Aubrey smiled back at him and left the galley.

The storage area was further along in the hold. A room tucked back among extra barrels of water and sacks of supplies. The lantern that dimly lit the corridor would soon be extinguished by the night watch as he made his way through his appointed area. Aubrey approached the room, watching her footing in the shadowed area.

From the other end of the corridor, someone moving along toward him caught Beaufort's eye. He stopped and ducked back into the shadows, thinking that it might be Morgan or Black. Fingering his pistol, he watched before a slow and lustful smile crossed his lips. Aubrey Malone carrying a bag and headed to the storeroom no doubt. The very sight of her made Beaufort's loins burn and respond with desire. He became hard almost immediately. Despite the effects of the drug and liquor, he judged the distance then with the swiftness of a cat slipped into the storeroom.

Aubrey set the bag down just inside the storeroom door and struck fire to the wick of the lantern nearby, throwing a soft glow on the stores that were carefully and neatly placed therein. Picking up the sack again, she turned to spot out the area where she knew Willie kept the flour. With a little bounce in her step at the joy of being out and busy now, she moved across the floor to the area. She set down the bag with a soft grunt, having to bend over to put it in its place. The sound of thunder could be heard overhead and Aubrey smiled as she looked up. When she was done, she would see if Morgan would take her on deck to watch the light show.

The bending made her sore muscles ache and her grunt was the reply to their protest. From his hiding place, Beaufort watched her bending and the very sight of her upturned bottom made him feel as if he would explode. As Aubrey straightened and started her turn toward the door to leave the area, she heard the unmistakable scraping of boots on the wooden floor. Continuing her turn slowly, her blood ran cold to see Beaufort standing a few feet behind her in the dimly lit area.

"Well, out and all alone, are we? Where is Monsieur Alcott now? Where is your Captain Mala?" He drawled in his monotonous voice.

"Where did you come from? They said that you had disappeared." She breathed as she stared at him with eyes widened with fear. He laughed at her, a slow lazy laugh that made her skin crawl.

"Oui, I was tucked away for a time but now I am out. We have a great deal to discuss, you and me. Some lost time to make up, ma petite."

Aubrey's eyes flashed to the doorway and she made to escape but he quickly stepped in front of her and she hit him with a grunt. He grabbed for her but she managed to get out of his reach as she screamed out for Morgan.

A loud rumble of thunder overhead covered the call for help as Beaufort succeeded in lunging at her and capturing her, clamping his hand down over her mouth. Aubrey felt stifled for his hand reeked of rum. He pulled her up to him, pressing her back against the front of his body. Lifting her slightly, he carried her thrashing body further back into the storeroom while she kicked at his legs with booted feet to no avail.

Leaning his head towards her, he hissed in her ear, "Where are you going, ma petite?" Aubrey continued to struggle as Beaufort attempted to put her down on the floor saying, "Oh, I know where you are going. You are going to lay down here and enjoy what I am about to give you."

She clawed and scratched with all her might, kicking her legs, whipping her head to and fro trying to break away from under his hand. Finally her mouth was partially uncovered and she screamed for Morgan again. Once more, as if her beloved thunderstorm was taking Beaufort's side, the rumble covered the cry for help. With a new fervor, she kicked furiously at Beaufort's legs and connected soundly with his thigh. He dropped to the floor on one knee with her. With a grunt and a curse, he let go of her for an instant. Taking the moment, she turned and scrambled away on her hands and knees.

He lunged for her and caught the back waistband of her britches in his fingers. He dragged her backwards toward him again and he stood with her. With a hold on her britches, he put his other arm about her waist and raised his hand to cup a breast through the fabric of her shirt, purring in her ear.

"Hmm, you feel good. If I cannot have you on the floor, then I will find another way."

"No!" She cried out as she grabbed at the groping hand and tried to pry herself free. Beaufort spun her to face him quickly and slammed her bodily against sacks of flour that were stacked nearly as high as she was tall. The impact took the wind from her and she went limp for a moment. Beaufort took the advantage of her weakness and he picked her up again to slam her down upon a slightly lower stack of sacks so that her upper body was now bent backwards. He pinned her lower body against the bags with his as he clutched the bottom of her shirt in one hand and caught her by the back of the neck with his other hand. He delivered a brutal kiss to her gasping mouth. Aubrey renewed her fight from the assault.

"I will break your neck bitch and think nothing of it." Aubrey looked into his gray eyes fearfully. His tight grip on the back of her neck and his growling statement made her wince and she stilled instantly.

"I should have had you that day on the *Gull*, ma petite, but that idiot Gibbs brought you up and the Captain set his sights on you."

"Do not call me that." Aubrey said thickly as Beaufort leaned on her.

"What do you want me to call you?"

"Leave me alone Thomas, Morgan will kill you if you do this." She warned.

"Morgan—that bastard does not frighten me. His time here is over, now this is mine." He said as he reached his free hand down to stroke her inner thighs. She pushed his hand away and opened her mouth to scream. He clamped his mouth down on her mouth again, delivering another brutal kiss. She could taste the rum on his lips. It seemed his whole body permeated with the smell.

"Non ma petite, there will be no screaming and no more fighting." He drawled in the monotone voice as he broke from the kiss.

Aubrey continued struggling in vain against him as he began to tear her shirt out from where it was tucked into her britches. He lowered his head to her throat, kissing her greedily. She felt him catching the skin of her throat in his lips, sucking and nipping at her with his teeth as if he were some animal feeding on a piece of meat. She was so tightly pinned now that she was not able to use her knees against him and she pushed feverishly at his stomach to try and get him off her. Her hand struck the butt of his pistol that was tucked in his sash he wore about his waist.

Raising his head, he stared into her terror-filled hazel eyes. His free hand clutched and pulled at the shirt tucked into the back of her britches now. Then his hand slipped inside the shirt to caress her left breast.

"The captain put his mark here thinking that it will frighten any man from touching you. It does not frighten me. He has his dark-haired whore now and does not have any concern for you at all, especially since you wronged him by laying with the quartermaster on the *Widow Maker*." He went on to say to her. Aubrey was too terrified now and at the mention of the quartermaster of the *Widow Maker*, grief and distress struck her heart.

"But he met with an unfortunate accident. That took him off the list of men in line to have you." Beaufort said as his hand roughly caressed her breast.

Aubrey suddenly remembered Jean Luc's warnings about how Beaufort fed on her fear. Mustering all the courage she possessed, she tried to calm herself. Feeling this response, he smiled down on her and he lowered his head to her, "Hmm, giving in to me now, ma petite? Just like you did to Jean Luc?"

"No." She whispered hoarsely. Jean Luc? Why did he keep bringing up Jean Luc? What did he know? Aubrey wondered. Suddenly, her eyes widened and she breathed, "It was you. You told Captain Black?"

"Oui, I did tell the Captain that you were whoring around. I knew Pierne was interested in you as much as he tried to hide it but I could tell. Things were going along well for the two of you, your little love affair right under the nose of the captain. I must tell you ma petite, that I did not truly know who it was at first. You were friendly with Jean Luc and with Jojoba so I suspected them both." Beaufort gave a gruff chuckle deep in his throat and continued, "You should have kept your secret in the captain's bed when he was off ship, ma petite. At least there, it was less likely to be discovered by him. A man would have the sense to leave in good time before he was discovered. But you were careless in your ways. I saw you creeping out in the corridor that morning. I saw you go back to Black's cabin after he and Jean Luc had gone topside but I did not see where you came from." Beaufort seemed pleased and proud with his narrative of the discovery.

Aubrey was sick. It was yet another reminder, nay, a confirmation, that she had been the cause of Jean Luc's demise. Perhaps he could tell her what had truly happened to Jean Luc. He could answer some long burning questions for her, even though something in the back of her mind told her that she really did not want to know.

"Do not hurt me please, Thomas." She whispered. His laughter and the thunder sounded as one when he moved his hand to knead her other breast.

"Do you want me to be gentle—like Jean Luc was?" He purred.

"What happened to Jean Luc, Thomas?" She asked stiffly ignoring his question.

His hand moved down the front of her and he cupped her between her legs. She caught at his hand and he slapped her hand away, "It is too late to play the innocent now, ma petite. You are not the little virgin any more. A man has touched you here before. But you have not been had by a man until you have been had by me." Gray eyes bored into her as he stroked her.

"Tell me, Thomas, tell me what happened to Jean Luc." She said stiffly as she continued to try and move his hand away. He leaned his face closer to hers but she drew back from him cringing.

"A kiss first, ma petite." He bargained. Aubrey thought that she would wretch just at the thought of his lips on hers again. With a shrug, he said, "I will take it anyway."

The force of his kiss bumped her head against the hard bags of grains and flour. The white shards of pain in her head seemed to explode and mix with the thunder overhead. She pushed at him feverishly and he broke from the kiss as she struggled to keep from gagging.

"Tell me Thomas." She repeated as she clutched at his lapels and tried to hold him back.

365

"I told you, he met with an unfortunate accident." He said as he moved his hand to the buttons that fastened her britches.

"When did you see him last?" She pressed on, her voice fairly squeaking in her throat, and her hands catching at his.

"Let us not talk about him now." He cooed as he extracted his hand from hers and stroked it down her throat while lowering his head in an attempt to kiss her again. She quickly turned her head but he caught her roughly by the face. "You cannot resist me for long, ma petite."

"Stop calling me that!" She spat at him, tears welling in her eyes despite her attempt to be strong and brave.

"Why? Because that is what that black bastard called you? Did you bed him too?" Beaufort asked as his hand cupped her bare breast under the material once again.

"No, Jojoba was my friend." She replied, trying to push his hand down. Beaufort grunted in reply.

"Then only the Captain and Jean Luc, eh?" He questioned on.

"No." She whispered hoarsely.

"What a little liar you are." He chuckled.

"What happened to him?" She pressed on, ignoring his comment.

"Who?"

"Jean Luc." She breathed.

"Jean Luc, Jean Luc, always Jean Luc. Forget him! He is dead, shriveled up and rotting." He droned at her.

She pushed at him angrily again, her hand striking the pistol in her action. "Non Beaufort! Tell me! Before you do this, I must know!"

He raised an eyebrow at her, his tone was smug, "Are you going to give up? No little Irish temper? Are you going to give it to Thomas now? Now that your lover is gone and your captain no longer wants you? What about Monsieur Alcott?"

"I must know." She whispered at him, still pushing against him, her hand coming to rest against the pistol once more.

"Very well, ma petite, I will tell you some now and more afterward, if, you make me feel as good as I think you will. The last time I spoke to your Jean Luc, he was in the hold in chains." Beaufort laughed and then his face turned serious, "He was just hanging there, puking up his guts after I slammed his head against the wall."

Aubrey closed her eyes and swallowed hard, trying not to see the images that Beaufort painted for her. The storm overhead seemed to enhance the terrible images in her mind. His voice startled her out of her thoughts as he said brightly and apparently to himself.

"Now, shall I enjoy you here or should I take you further into the hold where we can stretch out and not be bothered by anyone passing by? Perhaps I should put out that lantern then we would not be discovered or bothered by the night watch before we are finished. But then, I could knock you out so that you will not make noise and I could take you anywhere I please, here or in the hold. Hmm, perhaps both. That would be nice, n'est-ce pas? Once the quartermaster's, always the quartermaster's, eh ma petite?"

"Thomas please, please do not do this." She whispered. This was not happening, this could not happen. She could not allow it without a fight. Her mind was racing as he continued to speak seemingly to himself.

"There have been far too many times that my pleasure with you has been interrupted. You know, I think that I would rather have you stretched out, that way I can touch all of you." Aubrey nearly shivered at the thought. "Regardless of where we are, I cannot promise that I will not hurt you though, ma petite. You are so little and I am..."

She began to struggle against him again as he pressed himself against her. Feeling something painfully hard jab into her ribs, she dropped her eyes down the front of his body. He was suddenly surprised when Aubrey relaxed a bit in his hold and he smiled at her, "See there, this will make it much better. I know that you are high-spirited and I like a lively woman, but tonight I am not in the mood for that. Tonight, ma petite, I want to have you just the way Jean Luc did."

She took a deep breath, mustering all of her courage as she looked pointedly up into his gray eyes. At this stage, there was only one thing on his mind and one thing that he would understand. She would have to lower herself to his base level of thinking. Her whole body shook with the fear and tears streamed from the frightened eyes. Taking a deep breath she said in as calm a voice as she could muster, "Well, Thomas. If you want me the way Jean Luc had me, then you should not be so strong. As you said, I am so little and well..."

A half smile spread across his face and he backed up a step, pulling his hand from under her shirt, "Aye then, be a good girl and let ol' Thomas have it." With one hand clutching the front of her shirt, he pulled her to her feet.

"Why certainly I will let you have it." She replied thickly with an odd smile of her own.

In his lust filled mind, he was already envisioning her beneath him. She stared into his gray eyes with an expression that made him cock his head to one side in puzzlement.

In a fleeting glance, she dropped her gaze to the weapon and then back up to stare into his eyes. Beaufort's gaze followed hers as he heard the unmistakable click of the weapon being cocked. He had been completely unaware that she had closed her hand around the butt of his pistol while he held her down on the sacks. When he stepped back from her, she was able to pull the weapon smoothly from his sash and apparently without his notice. In a split second, his eyes locked with hers and, for first time, she saw fear in the gray eyes that had tormented her for so long. Before Beaufort could move or make a sound of protest, Aubrey smoothly pulled the trigger.

With the barrel pressed against his belly, the force of the close blast threw Beaufort back and away from her. Blood spurted from his mouth and she felt the warm liquid spray over her face and neck. Gasping, she clamped her eyes shut to the onslaught. With a crash, he landed on the floor. Aubrey opened her eyes and looked down at him.

There was no sound of the shot from the small storeroom. The loud report was covered by a loud clap of thunder from above at the very instant that Aubrey had pulled the trigger. No one would have heard. The only testament to the act was a very dead Thomas Beaufort lying on his back in the floor before her. His sightless gray eyes stared up to the ceiling.

Chapter 42

Looking down at herself, Aubrey realized that she still held the smoking pistol and she dropped it as if it burned her hand. The front of her shirt was splattered with his blood and powder burns. She swiped her sleeve across her face to wipe off the blood. She gagged violently and grabbed at her churning stomach, the bitter taste of bile rising in her throat.

Staring down at him in wonder of what she had done, a tremor of fear came over her. Choosing her footing carefully as not to step in the blood that pooled around the body, Aubrey left the storeroom quickly. She made her way to the cabin praying that Morgan would not be in there yet as she looked back down at her shirt in the dimly lit corridor. Her prayers were not answered this time. When she opened the door, she saw that he was sitting on his bunk, shirtless and cleaning his pistol.

Aubrey turned quickly away from him to shut the door as he glanced up at her, "Hello love."

"Hello Morgan." She replied trying to keep her voice steady. Exhaustion from her ordeal was taking over as was the reality of what she had done. Uncontrollably, she was began to shake. To try and calm herself, she leaned on the door with her back still to him, resting her head against the planks.

"What is wrong?" He asked in concern as she heard him rise from the bunk.

"Nothing Morgan, I am just tired. Do not fuss over me." She said weakly.

"You are lookin' a bit disheveled there." He commented as he eyed her. She looked down on herself again. Biting her lip she looked at the blood on the front of the white shirt.

"I guess I got this way when Willie and I cleaned the galley. Morgan, I am really tired and I want to wash up and go to my bunk. Would you be a darlin' and put out the lantern now?"

"All right love, just let me put this away. You need to get to sleep, you worked pretty late tonight, and this is your first day up and about. Mala will skin you alive for working so hard." He yawned as he laid his pistol aside and blew out the flame in the lantern.

"Thank you, Morgan. I will just clean up here a bit and then I will get in my bunk, I promise." She said breathing an inaudible sigh of relief.

"How can you see to do what you do in the dark?" He asked as he could be heard settling himself in his bunk.

"Practice." She answered as she moved to the washbasin, feeling her way along. She poured water into the basin and dipped the rag.

"Did you eat dinner tonight?" Morgan asked.

"I had some stew, stop worrying about me. I can take care of myself." She said, still trying to remain calm.

She finally cleaned every inch of her face and neck. Then she slipped out of the shirt and balled it up tightly. She moved to her bunk in the darkness and stuffed the shirt under her mattress before she picked up her nightshift. She scrubbed her bare chest in an attempt to wash away the touch of Beaufort from her skin, shivering all the while. She wished she could take a bath as hot as her skin would allow.

"Are you done yet? You sure are takin' a long time tonight. Did you get that dirty today?" Morgan teased from the darkness.

"Will ya behave." She scolded as she took the rag that she had used and left it in the bowl. He chuckled at her scolding. "Ah Morgan." She began sweetly as she slipped on the nightshirt.

"What do you want me to do?" He asked with feigned annoyance in his tone.

"I am not allowed on deck after dark. This water is very dirty. You would not want to use it in the morning nor would we want it in the cabin all night long. Would you please go dump it out for me?" She playfully pouted.

"Christ, what a pain you are!" He scoffed as he could be heard rising from his bunk. In the darkness, on his way to get the bowl, he ran against her. He put his hands on her shoulders to steady her. "Pardon me."

"That is all right." She said stiffly as she moved to her own bunk. "Thank you, Morgan." She called softly as he opened the door to take out the bowl of water.

There was light in the corridor, but it was dim. Aubrey hoped that he would not look down into the bowl as he passed under the lantern. She knew that the water had to be tinted with the blood that she had washed off. Where was that night watch? Black called for lights out at two bells on this ship as well. It had to be close to that time.

The door closed behind him and she laid back in her bunk. Alone at last, she had a chance to think over what had happened. She had murdered Thomas Beaufort, the quartermaster. Her thoughts quickly turned to what Beaufort had said about Jean Luc, he was dead. Tears began to fall as she realized that his beating and death had been her fault. Aubrey buried her face in her pillow. She had loved Jean Luc. She would have died for him but she never had intended for him to die for her. Fear and exhaustion overtook her and she fell asleep. Her sleep was plagued with dreams of Jean Luc chained and beaten and of Beaufort hovering over her in the hold.

Black stirred in the bunk and rolled onto his back away from the sleeping Mala. He inhaled deeply and frowned, wondering at what woke him. Then he heard the unmistakable tap at the door again. He sat up easily and pulled on his britches. There was the soft knock again as he moved across the darkened cabin fastening the britches. He opened the door to find Robert standing there with a lantern in his hand.

"What is it, Monsieur Bates?" Black asked sleepily and in a low voice as not to wake Mala.

"I must talk with you." Robert said in the same low voice, knowing that his captain most certainly was asleep inside.

Black clicked his tongue and stepped out into the corridor rubbing his bare chest sleepily. He pulled the door closed, but did not allow it to latch all the way shut, "What is it?"

"One of my men was making the rounds of the lower hold area…" Robert began in hushed tones then paused uneasily. He noticed the small cuts on Black's arm, collarbone, and a small nick on the chin. Captain Mala's fingernails are not so long or sharp to scratch the man in the heat of passion, were they? The second mate wondered to himself.

"And this is cause to disturb me from my bed?" Black asked in an annoyed fashion, breaking into the man's thoughts.

"He, ah, made a rather grim discovery in the storeroom." Robert said evenly. Black's brows knitted in annoyance.

"Thomas Beaufort is dead and his body is lying in the storeroom. He has been shot at close range…" Robert reported.

Black frowned in a mixture of question and disbelief. Beaufort had been missing for nearly two days and now he suddenly appeared. Black raised a finger for the man to wait then he re-entered the cabin and picked up his boots. Stepping back out into the corridor, quietly pulling the door shut and stooping to pull the boots on, Black then looked at Robert and said, "Take me to him." Robert nodded and lifted the lantern to lead the way.

Mala had awakened as Black got out of the bunk and was now alert to the sound of the men's voices outside the door even though they had spoken quietly. Raising up on one elbow and holding the sheets to cover her naked breasts, she cocked her head to listen to the exchange. As Black came back in the darkened cabin to retrieve his boots, she quickly laid back down and feigned sleep. She was still as she listened to him get the boots and leave again. Mala stared into the darkness of the cabin and wondered why Beaufort was dead in the storeroom. Did they kill him and leave him there? If so, that was a stupid place to leave him. There was not supposed to be a body to find!

371

Black looked down upon the body that stared hauntingly up at the ceiling with its dead eyes. There was a gaping hole in Beaufort's midsection. Robert raised the lantern to cast more light around the storage area,
"Christ, I did not look at it this close before." He breathed. Black looked up and saw blood everywhere.
"All of this will have to be discarded. It is contaminated." Black reported grimly.
"What in the hell did he do? Commit suicide in here?" Robert asked in amazement.
Black stooped down to get a closer look, being careful not to touch the blood that seemed to cover everything. "I do not know." He muttered.
"He had to have heard that you were after him, maybe he got scared of what you might do to him, so he decided to save you the trouble." Robert suggested carefully.
It appeared to Robert that Black was not listening as his head swung to look about the area, but then he growled, "He should have been afraid." Black's thoughts were turned to the attempt on Mala's life the day before. With a frown, he stood up still looking around.
"Shine that light here." Black directed as pointed in an area a short distance the body. Robert did as he was told and Black bent over to pick up a pistol from the floor.
"This is his weapon." The dark-haired man said as he turned the pistol in his hands. He stood looking at it in deep thought for a moment and then he looked from the body to Robert, "Thomas did not do this to himself."
Robert looked on as Black waved a hand to indicate the area and continued with his hypothesis. "The weapon was over there…a ways from the body. Had Thomas shot himself, it would have fallen closer to him. Shine the light on his hands." He further directed. Robert leaned down to display Beaufort's hands. "There are no powder burns on his hands. The weapon was to his left…Beaufort was right-handed. Look at the wound, it is in the center of his belly. How could a man turn a gun so neatly on himself to fire straight in, point blank? A self-inflicted wound to the belly would be off to an angle." Black went on to investigate.
"Beaufort would not let someone take his pistol and shoot him—unless there was a struggle." Robert added, now realizing that this was most certainly a murder and not a suicide. Black and Robert scanned the area, there were no apparent signs of a struggle of any kind, and everything seemed to be in its place although hopelessly ruined by the splattered blood.
"I heard no report of the pistol." Robert said thoughtfully.
At that moment thunder clapped overhead and both men looked to the

ceiling. "It could have been covered by that." Black offered.

"It has been doing that for hours, threatening to rain." Robert said with a nod.

"Call the crew awake—call all of them to the deck." Black ordered as he handed Robert the spent pistol and left the storeroom in long strides that denoted anger.

Mala did not know how long she had pondered the questions in her mind, but her thoughts were suddenly interrupted by the sound of the door coming open. She heard Black cross the still dark room toward the bunk. He cursed under his breath in French and then struck fire to the wick of the lantern.

"Where have you been?" Mala asked quietly as the lantern slowly illuminated the cabin. Black turned and when she saw the dark scowl, she asked, "What is it?" She asked in a voice that was quieter than before as she feigned alarm at his expression.

"I have called everyone to the deck for a meeting." He said as he grabbed for his shirt.

"A meeting? In the middle of the night? What are you talking about, Rene?"

"Get up and get dressed." He commanded as he pulled on his shirt.

"Very well, I will be there directly." She said with a perturbed look on her face as she sat up at the side of the bunk, still clutching the sheets against her nakedness.

"But do not delay, we have important matters to discuss." He growled as he went out the door with his open shirt fluttering behind him like a short cape.

"Could this not wait until morning?" Mala called as he pulled the door closed.

"Non!" He growled loudly from the corridor.

Staring at the closed portal for a moment, she wondered at his behavior. Throwing the sheets aside, she stood and slowly dressed, all the while wondering how Morgan and Robert managed to leave a body behind.

Aubrey's fitful sleep was interrupted by the urgent sound of Morgan's voice. She opened her eyes in alarm. "Wake up. We have to go topside." He was saying.

She frowned at him, her mind fogged with sleep, "What? What is wrong?"

"Get up, get dressed, quickly." He ordered as he moved away from her, striking a flint to the lantern. She looked toward the doorway as she heard the sounds of men moving along the corridor.

373

"Are we being pursued?" She asked as she pulled her britches up under her nightshift.

"No, come on." Morgan growled.

"I cannot very well go out half dressed, turn around." She grumbled.

"Oh, I am not looking at you so get dressed. There is no time." He grumbled in reply with a wave of his hand.

Aubrey made a face at him and turned her back, taking a fresh shirt from the little shelf beside her bunk. Quickly she pulled the chemise over her head and threw it onto her bunk. She knew very well that he was watching her. She could almost feel his eyes on her bare back as she pulled her shirt over her head even more quickly.

"Something has happened among the crew, Black has called us all to the deck." Morgan was saying as she dressed.

Aubrey made another face as he took her by the arm and very nearly pulled her from the cabin in her bare feet.

The deck was lit with torches that flickered in the wind. Black mounted the quarterdeck steps and turned to look down upon the gathered masses below him on the main deck. He waited impatiently as the men gathered in all manners of dress and varying degrees of wakefulness. He watched as Mala emerged from the companionway and moved up the steps.

The dark-haired woman leaned against the starboard railing with her arms folded over her chest to ward off the chill of the night air. The tails of Black's white shirt fluttered in the stiff breeze that buffeted them. Aubrey could see that she too, appeared to have been wrenched from sleep. Mala put her hand over her mouth to cover a yawn as if to confirm Aubrey's thought. Suddenly, Aubrey was reminded of the night that Black and his men had boarded the *Enchantress* and had brought them all on deck. He had ousted them all from bed that night too. Aubrey's thoughts were broken into by Black's deep voice as he began to speak.

"Tonight, as the night watch made his rounds, a very dismal discovery was made." He began. A cold chill ran through Aubrey's body and she shivered. Morgan glanced down at her, thinking the air brought on her shiver and stepped up to shield her with his body from the wind.

"It would seem that Thomas Beaufort has met with a terrible accident." Black droned on. A wave of muttering washed over the crowd. Black leaned his hands on the railing, his own open shirt fluttering in the breeze, "Monsieur Beaufort was murdered this evening, and apparently with his own weapon, at close range."

The muttering turned to louder remarks in English and French as Black's information was translated to those of his crew that did not speak English.

"Oh Christ." Morgan breathed as he looked over at Mala.

Aubrey stole a glance up at him then followed his stare. She wondered why Mala and Morgan looked at each other for a moment and he had a worried look on his face. For some reason, the report seemed to upset him. But Morgan's mind raced. Did Mala manage to sneak away and find Beaufort? But she said that no one would find a body.

"What is it, Morgan? What happens now? What does this mean?" Aubrey asked as calmly as her inner fear would allow.

Morgan glanced down at her and answered, "Bad news, love. The death of a crewmember means severe punishment to the person who committed the crime." God, do not let that person be Mala! He thought looking up and finding Robert. He noticed his friend had the same worried expression when their eyes met.

"Punishment?" She echoed as she looked back at Black who was still speaking.

"Shh!" Morgan scolded as he waved her to silence.

"The murderer will be found and when he is, he will be dealt with accordingly. In addition, the murder was committed in the storeroom. Much of our food stores has been contaminated and will have to be thrown overboard. We will begin rationing at once, until we can replenish our supplies. The murderer will not only pay for the life of Monsieur Beaufort, but he will also pay from his pocket for the replacement of the stores, unless we are fortunate enough to come upon prey that fills our larders. If anyone on board knows anything of this crime, let him come forward and speak now. To hold your tongue on such an offence will mean certain punishment for that man as well." Black was saying.

Aubrey shivered again and Morgan looked down on her once more. "I want to go back to the cabin." She whispered.

"We cannot go back until he dismisses us, love. Be still and quiet now." Morgan whispered close to her ear.

Aubrey looked up at Mala who was holding her long hair out of her face with one hand as the wind whipped around her. The dark eyes drifted down to meet with Aubrey's hazel ones. Even in the light of the torches, Aubrey could tell that Mala was glad the man was finally gone. Mala's eyes wandered back to look at the dark-haired captain, and muttered only loud enough for him to hear, "No great loss."

He turned his gaze upon her momentarily then announced to the crew below, "Return to your bunks. This mystery will be solved, one way or another. Rest assured, when the murderer is found, he will spend time with the 'captain's daughter.'"

Aubrey tugged at Morgan's sleeve, gaining his attention. "Who is the

375

captain's daughter?"

A chuckle emitted from York who stood close by. Leaning close to Aubrey's ear, and before Morgan could reply, York said, "The 'captain's daughter' is the whip, Miss Aubrey."

Aubrey gasped and York moved on to return to his bunk like the rest of the men assembled. Morgan took Aubrey's hand and was a bit surprised when she let him clasp her hand and tow her easily toward the companionway.

As they reached the doorway, Mala and Black preceded them. In a gesture of respect for the captain and his lady, the sandy-haired man held back. Black glanced at Morgan before they went down the steps.

"It would seem that tomorrow we will be voting in a new quartermaster." Black said then cast a condescending eye on Aubrey who followed Morgan closely. Remaining silent, Morgan followed Black's gaze to Aubrey as the captain continued in torment, "Sleep well Irish with your first mate for tomorrow night you might very well be sleeping with the quartermaster again. If Monsieur Alcott is lucky enough to be voted in."

She stared tightlipped at Black as he chuckled lightly. Mala clicked her tongue at the comment and muttered something in her own language as she went down the steps, purposefully slowing so that Black bumped against her near the bottom step.

Chapter 43

In the cabin, Morgan took off his shirt again and settled himself on his bunk. Aubrey pulled herself up into the corner, drawing up her knees and draping her blanket around herself. Morgan had re-lit the lantern and now sat looking at her for she had not changed into her nightshift.

"What is the matter? Get ready for bed. It is too early to stay up and you have not had nearly enough rest."

"I am, ah, just cold." She replied.

"Well, get out of your clothes and get to sleep." He told her as he pulled off his boots. Aubrey merely stared at him blankly.

"Goodnight then." He said flatly as he put out the lantern then laid down. Lying on his back with his hands behind his head, he wondered how Beaufort had gotten out of his prison. Morgan's mind fretted over the boy, Conner. He had a bad feeling about the lad and wished that he had stayed with the Frenchman himself.

"Morgan?" Aubrey's voice was small from her side of the cabin, breaking into his thoughts.

"What?" He grumbled as he turned his back to her.

She made her way in the darkness to sit on the edge of his bunk. "I need to talk to you."

A slight frown crossed his brow and he wondered what was happening. She had come in the darkness to his bunk? He was further puzzled when he felt her fingertips touch carefully to the back of his bare shoulder.

"Morgan, I was in the storage area tonight. He cornered me there." Her voice was quiet, almost a whisper.

Morgan turned his upper body slowly toward her, "What? What are you saying?"

"Beaufort. He trapped me in there. He was putting his hands all over me—and kissing me." She stammered nervously wringing her hands. Morgan moved away quickly and got up to light the lantern. Turning, he saw her face drained of color and looking very worried.

"I …he …Morgan, I had no choice. He was going to rape me." She finally spat out, tears bursting forth with the confession.

"Oh Christ." Morgan gasped as he pulled her up into his comforting arms. "Are you all right? I mean, did he…"

"No, only what I said. I got his pistol and I shot him before he could…"

"God Aubrey, when Black finds out." He began.

"He will not find out, there is no way he can." She said firmly as she

377

grasped frantically at his arms.

"Tomorrow he will scour this ship from stem to stern, he will find out." Morgan said.

"No, he will not." Aubrey began to argue then suddenly straightened in alarm. "Oh my God." She exclaimed as she remembered the shirt.

"What?" He asked tensely. She extracted herself from his grasp and dug under the mattress, producing the shirt. He took it from her and asked, "What is this?"

"My shirt, the one I had on earlier."

Morgan held up the shirt in the dimly lit cabin, "What is this all over it? Oh Christ!" He rolled his eyes at his own question.

"Blood. His blood." She answered weakly.

Morgan wiped his free hand down over his handsome face, "Oh Christ, we must get rid of this."

She snatched the shirt from him when he stood up, "No, I will get rid of it. You are not to be implicated in this." Morgan inhaled deeply through his teeth thinking about his part in making the man disappear the day before as Aubrey was saying, "I have already been the cause for one man's death, I will not be the cause of yours as well."

He watched her head for the door and he lunged forward to grab her by the arm, "Where in the hell do you think you are going?"

"To get rid of this." She said curtly as she opened the door and slipped out, closing it quietly behind her. He could not go after her, knowing the commotion that would draw attention. So he waited and rubbed his face worriedly. He hoped that she would not be seen outside the cabin. He prayed that Black had gone back to the great cabin with Mala and stayed there.

Aubrey crept up the companionway steps and looked out on the main deck. The torches had been extinguished and the deck carried shadows in the darkness. She was thankful that the storm clouds darkened the night sky as she stealthily moved along the hold to the starboard side of the ship. Holding the shirt balled tightly in her hand, she leaned far out over the railing, stretching her arm out as far as she could. She let the shirt go in the wind and it fluttered out of her sight. Breathing a sigh of relief she stood and turned to go back to the cabin.

Her heart skipped a beat as a man confronted her in the darkness. A small cry of alarm broke from her throat.

"Miss Aubrey? What are you doin' up here after dark?" Came the familiar voice of Robert and she breathed a sigh of relief. "You know Captain Black would have a fit if he found out you were out here. Get below to your bunk."

"I was not feeling well." She lied.

"Are you all right?" He asked in concern.

"Yes, I am better now. Thank you, Robert." She nodded.

"Well, come on then, I will see you back to the cabin. You know better than to move around the ship after dark. One of Black's men could snatch you right up." He scolded quietly as he moved her along.

"I am sorry." She said quietly in return. As he took her gently by the arm she gave an involuntary shiver, thinking about his comment. *'One of Black's men could snatch you right up.'* No truer words had ever been spoken…and the worse of the fright was that Beaufort now lay dead in the storeroom—dead by her hand.

"Now we have someone on board who has taken to killing crew members. It is not safe for you, Miss Aubrey, get in there now." He went on to say as he opened the door for her and gently pushed her in.

Morgan met her on the other side, his face masked in anxiety, and seeing Robert behind her, he scolded at her for his benefit, "Where have you been? I thought you were right behind me. Black would go off like an over-powdered cannon if he knew you were out there wandering around on the ship alone. Christ! For that matter, Mala would have my hide."

"She said she was not feeling well, must be the excitement of the night." Robert reported to his friend. Aubrey shivered and Morgan took her gently by the arm and pulled her further into the cabin, nodding. The two men exchanged worried glances that went undetected by Aubrey in her own worry.

"Thank you, Robert." Morgan said as he shut the door.

Aubrey lowered herself onto her bunk with a deep sigh and Morgan sat beside her. "Are you all right?"

"Oh certainly Morgan, I am just fine. I just murdered a man, but then, I will just add him to the list I have begun. Let me see, that makes four now." She moaned as she put her face in her hands. He put an arm around her shoulders and she did not resist his embrace, but buried her head in his chest, breaking into tears, "Oh God Morgan, I had to do it. It was in self defense—just like the others."

"I know, love. It will be fine." He said as he stroked her hair and rocked her gently. Morgan's eyes locked on the flame in the lantern as he leaned back against the bulkhead, still holding her.

Black had been sitting at the desk and had not returned to the bunk since being awakened by Robert. He pondered the news of the death of his quartermaster. His eye drifted up from staring at the desktop to look at the dark-haired woman who slept peacefully. Mala turned silently, snuggling down deeper in the covers to ward off the dampness of the cabin. Turned now, as she was facing the desk, she seemed to frown at the light cast by the lantern.

She could be dead right now. Killed right before his very eyes, he thought to himself as he watched her beautiful face in slumber. Beaufort had deliberately tried to kill her two days before. Even with that knowledge, Black wondered why he was still angry over the murder of the man. Because he had meant to kill him, he wanted to kill Beaufort. Perhaps that was it. Someone had stolen the glory from him…taken the prize. To kill Beaufort for the attempt on Mala's life would have been a grand reward for Black. To try and right all wrongs against her was his goal but he had waited too long.

Mala stirred again and opened her eyes sleepily, "Are you coming to bed, Rene?"

"Non, mon coeur. I have the log to put down, and there are things to be tended to." He said quietly as he rose from the desk and approached the bunk. Mala moved again in her place along the wall-side of the bunk. Black sat on the outer edge and leaned down to her, brushing her rumpled hair from her face.

"Go back to sleep." He said as he touched his lips to her cheek. Then he brushed his thumb over the spot almost as if he were rubbing the kiss into her skin as he said in a near whisper, "Sommeil, mon amour."

"I would sleep better with you beside me." She murmured, her eyelids drooping.

"Shh." He smiled and tucked the covers around her shoulders gently as he stood and returned to the desk. He glanced out the quarter gallery window to find that the horizon showed signs of the impending breaking of the dawn. His gaze shifted to Mala to find she had fallen back to sleep. He smiled sadly thinking again of how close he had come to losing her. Suddenly he wanted to gather her up in his arms and make love to her, glad she was still alive and with him. Instead he inhaled deeply then he gathered the logbook, the quill and the inkwell. There was much to be done today and he had yet to finish writing his entry into the log. He went to the lantern and as he put out the flame, his gaze drank in the sleeping beauty of Mala in the bunk. Quietly he left the cabin for the galley so he did not disturb her further.

On deck, the watches had changed. The dawn was trying to break through the heavy gray clouds and the weather threatened to match the mood of the ship. The events of last evening had set a mood of unease among the crew that moved about in their various morning duties.

Boulet and his deck crew had the watch now. The Frenchman strode to the starboard side of the deck with his hands clasped behind his back, brooding. Of late, he had begun to mirror the obnoxious and bullying behavior of his friend, Beaufort. Leaning against the railing with his back to the dark sea, he scanned the faces of the crewmen as they moved about the deck. For a fleeing moment he fretted if someone, the killer perhaps, would hold the same feelings for him as they had for Beaufort.

Turning from the deck to lean on the rails and stare out at the sun as it tried to peer through the heavy clouds, Boulet's mind continued to tumble. He reached into his pocket to take out his pipe thinking that a smoke would help to calm his nervousness. His fingers struck against his leather pouch of coins. Taking it out, he smiled around the stem of the pipe and tossed the pouch lightly. It jingled in the quiet of the morning. How he would much rather be at a table in the dry galley gaming today then out here on the deck to certainly be drenched by the oncoming rains.

Tucking the pouch safely away, he reached to take the candle from a nearby lantern and light his pipe. The smoke encircled his head for a second before it was whisked away with a gust of wind that blew out the candle as well. No matter, he thought, it was time to extinguish that anyway. It would be daylight soon. He shrugged as he put the candle back into its place in the lantern and shut the door. Something caught his eye in the sporadic rays of the rising morning sun. Leaning over the railing, he looked down to the spot. Wind whipped again, whistling in the lines over his head and he saw a flash of something light against the dark water, something caught along the hull.

It was too far out of reach, but whatever it was, it flapped in the winds like a flag and it flashed as an occasional ray of sun caught on it. Boulet looked for something to catch it with and found a rave hook lying nearby. Taking up the tool used for working on the decks, Boulet reached out to snare it. He heard the sound of ripping fabric as he caught it and jerked the rave hook to pull the item in. The wind threatened to whisk it away and he quickly twisted the hook to wrap the piece securely.

Boulet drew it in and took it off the hook. With a frown, he laid aside the hook and inspected the article closer. In the early morning light, he could see that it was a shirt with stains on the front of it. He looked around the ship to see if anyone had noted his discovery but no one had. With his lips drawn in a tight line around the stem of his pipe, he crushed the shirt in one hand and moved toward the companionway.

Black was in the galley, sitting at the back table. The logbook was open before him with the ink and quill nearby. He poked idly at the plate of food Willie had set before him, still brooding. He glanced at the logbook and the entry he had made there. It recounted the discovery of the body and his proclamation to the crew.

"Capitaine." Came the voice of Boulet, interrupting his thoughts.

381

Black raised his eye to look at the man, tiredly rubbing his hand down over his face. "Oui?"

"I have something here that I think you should see." Boulet began in French as he laid the shirt on the table before Black.

Frowning at him, Black reached out to look at it. "What is it?"

"I found it caught on the starboard hull. It appears that someone tried to throw it overboard to hide it." Boulet reported as Black looked at the garment without opening it fully and not wanting to attract the attention of the few men moving about in the galley.

"Tis a shirt, a stained shirt and it looks like blood." Boulet went on to report in low tones. Black easily balled it up and set it in the seat next to him. The conversation carried on in quiet French between the two men.

"Beaufort had his shirt on when they found him, Capitaine. This must belong to the killer."

"Oui." Black agreed. The two men sat in silence for a moment then Black said quietly, "Secure Beaufort's quarters. No one is to enter there except me." He picked up the wadded fabric, handing it back to Boulet. "Put this in the room. Tell no one of your discovery. To broadcast this would send the killer further into hiding. Justice must be delivered."

"Oui." Boulet nodded as he stood.

"Have Beaufort's body prepared for burial. I will perform the burial ceremony at sunset. In the meantime, have some men clean out all the contaminated stores from the storeroom and cast them over. I want a full inventory of all discarded items." Black went on to order. Boulet nodded and left the area to carry out his task. Sitting back in the chair and resting his chin in his hand, Black pondered this new piece of information.

Chapter 44

In his cabin, Morgan stirred in his sleep and grimaced. His back and neck hurt. Drawing a deep breath, he opened his eyes and looked around, discovering why he was uncomfortable. He found himself tucked into the corner of Aubrey's bunk and she lay sleeping against his chest in a semi-reclining position. He remembered holding her in comfort the night before—or rather, the wee hours of the morning. Must have fallen asleep too, he thought ruefully as he felt more aches.

Moving gently, he slowly began to lower her upper body down upon the bunk. She started awake with a sharp cry of alarm, clutching at him. "No! Stop!"

"Shh Aubrey, you are all right. It is me, Morgan." He soothed.

Drawing a ragged breath, she pushed herself from his gentle grasp and sat up. "Oh God Morgan, what are you doin' in my bunk? I had the worst dream—I dreamed that I shot Thomas Beaufort—the blood, it was everywhere—but I had to do it—he was trying to..." Her distressed account of her dream faded out as she caught the look on his face. "It was not a dream, was it?" She asked in a small voice.

"No love, it really happened." He replied with concern in his blue eyes.

Aubrey brushed back her hair nervously as Morgan got up from the bunk. "You slept on my bunk?"

"Well, I guess we both fell asleep." He smiled sheepishly as he lit the lantern to cast light in the room. The smile faded as he turned to look down upon her.

"What?" She asked in near alarm as she looked over herself, thinking that she still had Beaufort's blood on her. Morgan dropped to one knee and caught her chin in his hand, turning her face away from him.

"What is this? You were scrubbing like a demon last night, did you miss this?"

"What?" She asked again in alarm.

Morgan rubbed his thumb over her neck. "Christ, look how the bastard marked you up." He growled as he found that he was looking at bruises and not missed blood. Aubrey sat motionless in his hand, her eyes cast downward. Seeing her look of misery, he said, "It will be fine. It could have been worse."

"Could have been worse? My God Morgan, I murdered the man!" She whispered.

"You did not murder him. You killed him in self defense." He tried to

C. C. Colee

soothe.

"I have been the cause of so many deaths." Aubrey breathed in distress.

"All of them only to protect yourself." He reminded.

"No, not all of them."

Taking her face into his hand, he made her look at him, "You listen to me, you cannot blame yourself for his death. He cared for you, Aubrey. So much so that he died for you. You did not kill him." Morgan stated firmly. Aubrey stared into his blue eyes, mouth agape. How could he know? It was not possible!

Morgan smiled at the astonished look on her face. He knew that would get her attention. He stood up and backed up to sit on his own bunk as she watched him.

"Aubrey, there is something I need to tell you. But you have to understand that until recently I had no idea who he was." Taking a deep breath, Morgan wondered how angry she would be later. Aubrey made to speak but he held up a hand to silence her, "Please let me say this before you speak or maybe never speak to me again, or yell at me, or even try to hit me. I just want to let you know that whatever your reaction will be, I understand and hope you get over the shock."

"Morgan…" She began shakily but he held up his hand again and gave her a stern look.

"Aubrey, I have to tell you that I know who he was. The one you mourn for, the one you hold yourself for even in his death."

Aubrey stared and her mouth dropped open again. Morgan had the urge to reach out and, with gentle fingers under her chin, close her mouth. Taking another deep breath instead, he went on, "You know that I was on the *Widow Maker* some time before. My half-brother helped me to be a seaman. But my only problem was that I could not speak French and Black insisted on it. So I stayed near my brother and Black who was tolerate of my ineptness. But they taught me a lot of things and one was my favorite duty, manning the cannons during raids and battles. So I was one of the crew when Mala was found. God, she was a sight! She was your age then but so badly abused from her beating that I was sure she would die. But I was told to find Black and bring him to the hold. Well you know the rest about that."

Aubrey nodded as she recalled Mala telling her about Black's tender care and how they came to be the lovers they were today. Morgan took another deep breath before he continued, "Well, the man who found her was my half-brother. Only he was the first mate, not the quartermaster then. I am not sure when he made quartermaster." He paused to let Aubrey think this over in her mind. Her head bent as he spoke the last few statements and now he waited. Aubrey's mind raced as she remembered Mala saying that Jean Luc had

384

found her that day in the hold and had someone find Black. Half-brothers? She slowly raised her head and looked at Morgan. No wonder he reminded her so much of Jean Luc. The eyes were the same, the facial expressions, even the way he would turn to look at her sometimes.

"Jean Luc." She breathed aloud, then asked quietly, "But how did you know?"

"When you returned to the cabin after Black had beaten you, you were talking about all kinds of things. You kept saying you were sorry to him but I did not know it was Jean Luc until then. I only knew that you had a tormentor and you had a protector." He paused to smile at her and fidgeted slightly on his bunk.

"It was not long after we left Mala that I had a chance to go out on my own. Jean Luc was not pleased but I was stubborn and insisted on it. Finally, he helped me to leave when the *Widow Maker* was moored near the mouth of the Chesapeake. I headed further inland but it was not long before I needed money and I did well for a while. I was caught trying to steal from this ...ah, well, it was actually the struggle that caused the fire and she lost everything except the nightclothes she wore." He was saying with a sheepish smile.

"She?" Aubrey questioned with a raised brow.

"Shh, let me finish." He admonished lightly, not wanting to dwell on the fact that the woman was recently widowed and he was helping out as her handyman for a time.

"I was tried and sentenced to hang. Just as the townspeople gathered for the hanging, the guard brought in visitors. Imagine my surprise to recognize Jean Luc as an elegantly dressed man and a crying woman in lavender claiming to be my wife."

"Wife?" Aubrey repeated in shock. She sat in rapt attention as Morgan related his tale.

"Here ya go, ma'am." The guard was saying. "I can only give you a few minutes with your husband but I must carry out the sentence. Sorry, ma'am." The guard looked apologetically at Jean Luc. The woman's sobs grew louder at the mention of the carrying out of the sentence, while Morgan's eyes grew wider at the mention of the word 'husband.' Morgan looked questioningly at Jean Luc as the guard turned to leave seemingly uncomfortable at hearing the woman's crying.

"Oh Morgan, what could you have been thinking? I told you we could manage somehow." The woman wailed.

The guard nodded to Jean Luc who was attempting to comfort the woman. As the guard walked away, he said apologetically, "I will leave you alone for a while."

"Now, I am sure everything will be just fine." Jean Luc cooed as he patted the woman's shoulders while he watched the guard close the door.

Looking perplexed over the entire scene, Morgan asked Jean Luc, "What are you doing here?" As soon as they were all alone, Jean Luc gave a firm pat on the woman's back and she straightened lifting the veil from her face. When he saw the grinning visage of the woman, Morgan's eyes grew wider still, "Mala! My God!"

"Hello, Morgan. Let us see what we can do about getting you out of this predicament." Mala replied as she reached within the bodice of her dress and pulled out a thin stiletto. Jean Luc reached inside his boot and pulled out a dirk and handed it Morgan. He then reached inside the other boot and pulled another dirk, which he kept for himself.

Mala moved to the window and peered out. Using the hilt of the stiletto, she tapped on the bar. Apparently she gained the attention of someone for she nodded her head and stepped away.

"I do not think I have ever seen you in a dress before." Morgan said to Mala.

She stopped and smiled at him, "And you probably will not again, so get your fill now, Morgan Alcott."

Jean Luc laughed softly and elbowed his brother. "You would think he had not had a woman in sometime. You know, little brother, with that smile of yours, I was sure you would never be left wanting."

Morgan grinned at his brother's quip. The sound of the door opening stopped all action. Mala quickly covered her face once again and sat on the cot. Jean Luc pushed Morgan to sit next to her as he stood on the other side of the now weeping woman.

"You could have been on the stage." Morgan whispered.

"Quiet, you fool and play out the ruse." Mala growled then began her crying again.

The guard peered in to see the three together. Jean Luc looked up to see the guard and shrugged, "She is still a bit upset."

"I am afraid it is near time and you must leave." The guard stated still apologetically as he pulled out his keys.

Mala stood up followed by Morgan as he said forlornly, "I am sorry, I wish now that I was a better man for you, my dear."

The guard had to look away as the woman seemed to choke at the words of endearment. Seizing the opportunity, the woman brought up the stiletto in a quick, fluid motion and cut the guard's throat. Pushing the man aside, she turned to the men and motioned with her arm to follow her.

Reaching the door leading out of the holding area and ensuring that all was clear, Mala turned to Jean Luc and nodded. Stepping into the front office of the jailhouse, they found one man standing at the door. He turned as Mala stepped up to him and asked, "Any problems?"

"Took care of the only problem." He answered, nodding toward the boots lying behind the desk. The desk concealed the rest of the body.

Seeing the boots, Jean Luc reminded him, "No traces, remember?" He dragged the body so that nothing was visible upon entering the room from the front door.

"Quickly to the ship!" Mala urged quietly as she opened the door.

Mala and Jean Luc stepped out first and mounted the horses held by another man. Morgan and the assisting two men mounted the remaining horses. Swinging around, the group raced out of town.

Someone shouted the alarm from the crowd and the sounds of confusion, shock, and running could be heard behind them but no one looked back. The only thing the crowd was left with was a veiled hat floating to the ground.

The group spurred their horses on for a while until another group of men on horses met them. Mala slowed her horse down as they approached the new group. Another horse from the opposite direction was racing towards them.

"They are coming!" The rider informed.

"Now Deats, take your men and go that way. We will meet you back at the ship."

"Aye, aye Captain." Deats answered.

Morgan looked at Jean Luc in surprise, "Captain?"

"Not now, mon frère. Come on." Jean Luc replied as he followed Mala.

Once again, they rode their horses hard. Mala raised her arm and the two men accompanying them turned off into another direction. Morgan looked at his brother who was grinning then at Mala who seemed to be in charge. At the edge of a clearing, the three stopped and dismounted. Jean Luc shooed the horses to run wild as Morgan looked around and saw nothing but open fields.

"What are we supposed to do now?"

"You do remember how to climb trees?" Jean Luc answered with a smile.

Morgan looked at him with his mouth open, speechless, making Mala chuckle, "Now there is a moment for all time." Then she turned to a tree and began to climb. Morgan watched as Jean Luc and Mala started their climb on different trees.

Swinging himself up on a tree, he called out as quietly as he could, "I remember but I cannot climb like her." Then under his breath, he added, "God! And in a dress."

"Nobody can! Just move it, little brother, or your neck will stretch still!" Jean Luc urged. The three were some distance up the trees when they heard

387

horses coming.

"Not a sound!" Mala reminded.

The three froze on their branches and watched below. The pursuing riders had split up as Mala had expected because of the various fresh tracks. They halted at the edge of the clearing and looked around. Hearing the horses that Jean Luc frightened away in the distance, the riders took off in that direction. The three continued to watch even after the group was out of sight. Morgan and Jean Luc looked at one another then at Mala who had not moved and was listening intently for any movement below. She looked up at them just as they heard another sound. The two men, who had split from them, appeared below, looking around the clearing. They were startled when they heard movement from above. Mala reached the bottom first and jumped from her dangling position as the two men dismounted.

"Are you certain you two want to stay here?" She asked the two men as Morgan and Jean Luc reached the bottom.

"Aye Captain. We are grateful that you will let us depart from the crew." One man answered.

"My life is the sea but that does not mean that you have to live your life on the sea as well. You both have been good companions and I will miss you." Each man was given a firm handshake and pat on the shoulder by their captain. "Take care." She said and nodded as they said their farewells.

"And thank you for letting us join in this final adventure." Said the other man. Mala smiled at them as they departed on foot, leaving the two horses for the three of them. Jean Luc mounted one and Mala on the other. Morgan looked up at each as they looked down at him with smiles.

"And what am I supposed to do, wish for a horse to appear?" Morgan asked somewhat miffed that they would just grin at him. As he suspected, their smiles only grew. Morgan rolled his eyes and let out an exasperated sigh as Jean Luc softly chuckled.

"If you promise to behave, I will let you ride behind me." Mala offered. Morgan looked at Jean Luc who was just sitting on his horse with a stupid grin on his face and apparently was not offering.

"Well, if it saves me from walking to this ship of yours, then I guess I could be good for a little while." He replied with devilish grin as he accepted Mala's hand and mounted behind her. He settled in behind her and said softly, "You know you really look good in a dress."

"Do be quiet, Morgan. And just be careful with those hands of yours. I would hate to relieve you of them and I am sure somewhere there is a woman who would hate that as well." Mala replied over her shoulder.

Jean Luc burst into laughter as Morgan smiled and asked, "Just a woman?"

It was a while later, when the trio came upon a twin-masted brigantine. At the sight of her ship, Morgan exclaimed, "What a beauty!" They heard the watch call out the captain's arrival and several men looked over the railing. The ship had apparently just finished a careening and was preparing for departure. Entering her cabin, followed by Jean Luc and Morgan, Mala pulled out a couple of tankards and opened a cupboard bearing bottles of rum and wine.

"Help yourself as I see to the preparations." She told them as she turned to leave.

Aubrey stared at Morgan as he took a deep breath then let it out slowly while running his fingers through his hair. Meeting her gaze, he shrugged and said in a tone that was laced with contempt, "I also met Deats that day and hated him from the start. I could tell he was not pleased with Mala helping Jean Luc to rescue me. His whole demeanor was the same then as it is now. Stupid, jealous and untrustworthy." Morgan squared his shoulders then went back telling the rest of his tale.

"Are we all comfortable, gentlemen?" Deats asked tightly and with an odd emphasis to the word 'gentlemen.' He looked at Jean Luc who sat at the table in the captain's chair, his feet propped up in the chair usually found at the desk and a drink in his hand. Morgan was standing near the quarter gallery window also with a drink in his hand.

"Absolutely." Jean Luc replied with a smile.

Deats walked further into the room and Morgan watched him warily over the rim of his tankard as he sipped his drink. Deats did not seem very friendly despite Jean Luc's light-hearted banter.

Before any more could be said, which Morgan felt was not going to be pleasant, Mala stepped into the cabin. He noticed that somewhere she managed to get out the dress and into a red silk shirt, black britches, and cuffed knee-high black boots. In a gold sash waistband, she had tucked a pistol, a knife in its sheath, and rapier hanging at her side. Her long dark hair hung loosely down her back. She was dressed very much like the other pirates of her crew.

"Good, you are back. Any problems?" She asked Deats with a brief glance in his direction.

Deats seemed to straighten when she entered the cabin and his Scottish accent seemed to be pronounced. "Nay, Captain, no' a one."

"Good, let us hope that the fools are lost in countryside somewhere. We will be ready to leave within the hour, correct?"

"That is the plan, Captain." He answered absentmindedly turning his attention to Jean Luc who had not moved.

"I know what the plan is, Deats." Mala stated sternly regaining the Scotsman's attention. "I want to know if we will still leave here as planned." Deats looked into her dark eyes and could feel Jean Luc watching. "Aye, Captain. All will be ready."

"Then make sure everyone is accounted for before we sail. I do not want to leave anyone behind that does not want to be here." Then turning her back on him as if to dismiss him, she added with a shake of her head, "Why anyone would want to stay here is beyond me."

Morgan smiled at this because he knew Mala could never settle down like any normal woman. Christ, she was not even like normal women anyway! But something about her was different now, definitely different.

At that moment, two men brought in food and Mala turned at the sound at her door. "Wonderful, I am starved!" She exclaimed when they entered and started setting the table for four.

Mala went to her desk and pulled out her logbook. She reached behind her to sit down and pull the chair up but there was no chair. She glanced around and found Jean Luc using it. He had been watching her and his grin grew when he gained her attention. He made to move his legs but she waved it away.

Deats gave Jean Luc a look of pure disdain and when he turned that look to Morgan, the Scotsman found the younger man watching him. Without a word, Morgan moved to take a chair at the table to Mala's left. As the food was placed on the table, Jean Luc stood up and moved to the stand behind the chair.

"Mon Capitaine." He stated in his most debonair manner, offering the seat to Mala.

"Merci, mon ami." She replied as the two smiled at each other like children playing a game.

Deats took the seat to Mala's right and Jean Luc took the seat next to Morgan.

"Thank you, Mala, for helping me with Morgan. I was not sure how I would have pulled this off." Jean Luc stated after a mouthful of venison stew then rolled his blue eyes to the ceiling, "Hmmm, this is good!"

"Willie can just about make a feast from scraps. Oh, and you are welcome." Mala replied with a smile. She turned to Morgan who was tearing off a chunk of the bread, "What exactly did you do to nearly end up at the gallows?"

"I am sure there is a woman in the story somewhere." Jean Luc interjected before Morgan could open his mouth.

"Of course there is, you big oaf. When is there not a woman where your brother is concerned? Now be quiet and let him tell the story." Mala said with a smile.

"You think you know me that well, do you?" Morgan asked feigning insult.

"Aye!" Both Mala and Jean Luc answered in unison.

Morgan smiled because that they did know him very well. He told his tale then said, "…and to see you all dressed up. You looked like a real lady! I liked that."

"You would!" Jean Luc laughed looking at Mala who was smiling and shaking her head. "Well, he does have a point. You did look good in..." Jean Luc began with a raised brow.

"Oh, you both stop! Next you will have me planting and tending to a garden. Mon Dieu! What the hell are you two trying to do to me?" Mala chided playfully.

"Trying to make a respectable lady out of you." Morgan answered but could not hold the straight face. Mala rolled her eyes and threw her piece of bread at him. "Why thank you, I was about to get more but this saves me the trouble." Morgan said with a smile.

"Well here let me refresh your drink as well." Mala replied taking his tankard and standing.

Jean Luc threw his head back in laughter and dropped his fist on the table. Smiling, Morgan grabbed his tankard from Mala's hand and stood as well. "No thank you, I can manage!" He said.

Mala released her hold and sat down, smiling. Morgan did not fill his tankard as he sat back down but he moved the tankard further down the table from Mala's reach. She watched and smiled when she caught Morgan's eye.

"That was not a very wifely thing to do." Morgan feigned a pout.

"Ah, Morgan! 'A better man for me.' I nearly ruined the whole thing by laughing. You have no idea how hard it was to remember what we were there to do. I nearly missed my opportunity to make my move, you idiot!" Tears began to fill her eyes as they were laughing to near hysterics now.

"Well you could imagine my surprise to find that I am a husband! For you, Mala, I would give up the world." Morgan chuckled. With the last statement, he had placed his hand over his heart as if to make a promise.

"Mon Dieu, save me from foolish dreamers..." She began looking upward. After a very brief pause, she cut her dark eyes to Jean Luc and added with a smile, "…and their brothers."

When Morgan finished his tale to Aubrey who was still wiping away the tears of laughter from the banter between three friends. "And that was how I became a part of the crew. Later, I was voted in as first mate, with a lot of influence from Mala. Jean Luc returned to the *Widow Maker* which Mala refused to go near though we could see the ship in the distance."

Morgan was thoughtful then and said as if speaking to himself, "Sometime during those few days, she and Jean Luc must have had an argument because everyone seemed to feel the tension between the two of them." Morgan looked up at Aubrey, who was hanging on every word, he shrugged and smiled, "But Mala could never stay angry with Jean Luc for long. So you see, I know my brother. If he told you that he loved you, then he did. He cared for you. He would not lie about something like that. He would have taken a ball, or a blade, anything for you because he loved you, he wanted to protect you. He would take great pains to protect those he loved. But you are not the cause of his death." Morgan's tone was firm and yet gentle.

"Oh Morgan." Aubrey said with a sad smile. They sat quietly not looking at the other while engrossed in their own thoughts. After a few moments, Morgan stood up with a slap to his knees, "Well I better report to work before a search party is sent out for me."

Aubrey stood up as well and said, "Me too, Willie is probably wondering where I am."

Chapter 45

Aubrey could not think of much else all day except Morgan's tale. He had never told so much of himself before and she felt closer to him for it. But she also dwelled on the fact that she killed a man the night before, even though he was an evil man. She watched numbly as the contaminated food was carried to the main deck after Boulet made an accounting of the item before it was tossed overboard. She felt so guilty over the loss of so much food.

The mood on the ship seemed to reflect the gloom that an unsolved murder carried with it. Even Black brooded at the captain's table as he wrote in the logbook but Aubrey made a point to stay clear of that table as much as possible. When Black finally left the galley, she breathed a sigh of relief.

At midday, Willie gave her a tray of food to take to the great cabin while he took a second tray. No one was in the cabin at the time and the trays were left on the long table. She also noticed that Mala had not been seen in the galley or in the cabin. She shrugged thinking that perhaps she was on deck helping Black and Boulet.

Finished with the log by late morning, Black checked the progress in the storeroom. His presence in the storeroom unnerved Boulet at times when Black seemed impatient or irritated over the efforts of the men to clear the area of the wasted supplies. Boulet was relieved when Mala appeared and took Black away with her for the noon meal. Looking around, Boulet realized that many of the men also seemed to sigh in relief at Black's absence.

It was late afternoon when Boulet knocked on the door of the great cabin. Mala opened the door and took the list of the ruined stores from him. Handing the list to Black, she watched him as he documented the findings. With legs stretched out on the window ledge, she sat and watched the man at her desk. His mood had not lifted much since she found him in the storeroom with his men. She did not see the reason for his mood. Beaufort had been bothersome and now he was gone. She grimaced as she thought with much regret that she could not have finished him off.

The slamming of the book brought Mala out of her musing and turned her attention back to the darkly clad man at her desk. "I will be up on deck for the committing of Beaufort's body to the sea." Black told her curtly. Mala said nothing to him as she watched him leave the cabin.

Black found his men awaiting him with Beaufort's wrapped body laying within the half circle the men had formed. Looking over the deck, he was not surprised to see only his own boarding crew among the men to pay their respects. Any other time, he would have insisted that all the crew gather for the proceedings, but he decided not to press the issue. As Black took his place among the proceedings, he caught sight of Mala coming from the companionway and heading for the quarterdeck.

In the drizzling rain, Mala watched from the quarterdeck with her arms crossed over her chest. Had it been up to her, she would have just dumped the bastard into the ocean unceremoniously. As Beaufort's body fell to the sea, Black's gaze moved to the quarterdeck. He smiled to himself for Mala did not bother to conceal her disgust over the proceedings. With a grunt, Mala turned and went down the steps to the companionway as Black followed closely behind her.

When they neared the quartermaster's cabin, Black fell back slightly. Mala glanced at him over her shoulder as he took the door latch of the cabin in hand.

"What are you doing?" She asked.

"I will be there shortly." He replied curtly and slipped into the cabin, shutting the door behind him.

Mala rolled her eyes and went into her own cabin. Striding to the quarter gallery, she crossed her arms again and stood staring out at the rain, her mind tumbling with her thoughts. She would be hard-pressed to defend Morgan or Robert if either or both of them had killed Beaufort.

Black looked around Deats' quarters that Beaufort had occupied. Most of Scotsman's belongings were piled in a corner but some things were still as Deats had left them. Black found the shirt laying on a small table by the wall. He picked it up and in the private confines of the room, he was afforded the opportunity to open the shirt up fully to look over it. It was stained with blood and powder to be certain, but underlying that part, the garment looked far too clean and well kept to belong to one of the men on board.

His dark eye drifted up to look at the wall that separated this cabin from Mala's then back to the shirt. His brows knitted into a frown. In all the time that he had been on board, he had never seen Mala wear any colors other than black and red. He was certain Mala did not even own a white shirt. The only white shirt he had seen on her was his so this could not be her shirt.

With another glance at the wall he recalled how the two of them had been sleeping when Robert came to announce the finding of Beaufort's body. He replayed the previous evening in his mind. Mala had been with him most of the afternoon and all evening. They had been arguing again because he had taunted Aubrey on her first day out of the cabin and while she was on duty in the galley. Within minutes of leaving the younger woman, Mala had found out. Thinking he was going to have an enjoyable evening with her when she led him back to the cabin, she lashed out instead with a small dirk, leaving thin marks on his arms and collarbone. The last one she inflicted was on his chin. It had taken some time before he was able to calm her down.

He turned the shirt in his hands again and an odd stain on the inside of the collar caught his eye. He stepped closer to the bunk where there was a small window over the head of it. Although it was cloudy outside and the evening was drawing nigh, the light was better here. Black's head slowly rose from bending over the garment in inspection. Exhaling slowly, he crushed the shirt in his hand and turned to leave the room. "Ame damne." He breathed.

It was late afternoon and Aubrey felt tired from her ordeal of the day before and the guilt of this day's events. Willie patted her hand as she stood with him while there were only a few men in the galley.

"Why not go on with ye now, lass. I can take of things here. Besides ye worked hard yesterday and that being yer first day after ailin', Cap'n Mala would tan me hide if ye got sick all over 'gain." With a jerk of his head towards the corridor, he smiled.

Aubrey smiled in return and left for the cabin. Alone in the cabin, she threw herself onto her bunk and stared up at the ceiling. Her thoughts drifted to what Beaufort had said about Jean Luc. Beaten and chained in the hold of *Widow Maker*, Jean Luc died for her and for her foolishness. He had told her to go back to the great cabin, but she fell back to sleep instead. Because of that, she was not there when Black returned. Somehow, Beaufort saw her in the corridor as she hurried to sneak back into the cabin. That all led to their discovery. Shutting her eyes tight to hold back the tears, but to no avail, Aubrey drifted into twilight sleep.

It seemed like seconds later that she jolted awake as the cabin door snapped open. Sitting upright with a frightened yelp, she turned to find Morgan entering the cabin. He looked up when he heard the sound and stopped. "What are you doing in here? I thought you were helping in the galley."

"I was but Willie told me that I worked too hard yesterday and let me leave early today. He is afraid that I would fall ill again and Mala would blame him." She answered as Morgan walked further into the cabin.

He grinned when he replied, "Well you did work too hard yesterday."

"Oh stop it, Morgan. Is it raining?" His clothes were damp and his hair was coated with a misty wetness.

"Not anymore." He smiled as he pulled his shirt from the waistband of his britches. Aubrey turned her back to him as she laid back on the bunk while he changed into dry clothes. After a few moments, she heard Morgan say with a hint of laughter, "It is now safe to look."

"Are you sure?" She asked making him chuckle lightly.

Aubrey laid on her back and stared at the ceiling again while Morgan sat on his bunk and watched her. He took a deep breath and asked, "Did you eat already?"

"Aye, Willie kept me full all day with his venison stew."

Morgan was quiet for a moment before asking, "You did not do too much today, did you?"

Aubrey looked at him and knitted her brows together. "No I did not do too much." Still looking at him, she sat up and swung her legs over the edge of the bunk. She stared at the floor as she said quietly, "They threw out so much food, Morgan. I did not even…"

Morgan got up and sat beside her on her bunk. He took her chin in his fingers and lifted her head until her gaze met his. "Do not worry about that."

"But it was such a waste…"

"I said do not worry about that. It had to be done. You had no other choice. I am just sorry I was not there to help you." Morgan said softly.

Aubrey looked into his eyes, the same blue eyes of her beloved Jean Luc, and she released a slow yet deep breath. After a moment of silence she whispered, "Why do you continually worry about me, Morgan?"

It was his turn to exhale deeply and shook his head at her difficulty in understanding the feelings that were growing every day in him for her. His blue eyes searched her hazel ones and then followed the line of her delicate nose and over her lips as he held her chin. He drew her face nearer to his gently and bent his head towards hers.

"Because…" He began as his lips were nearly close enough to touch hers.

A loud knocking at the door interrupted the obvious kiss he was about to deliver. The sound startled them and the two separated immediately. The knock came again and Morgan moved to open the door. A grim-faced and wet Gibbs stepped into the room looking around. His eyes came to rest on Aubrey.

"So it is raining again." Morgan said as he stepped past Gibbs and stood near Aubrey.

"The Cap'n wants to see you." Gibbs stated trying put an ominous tone in his voice and ignoring the remark.

"Why me?" Morgan asked with raised eyebrows.

"Not you. Her." Gibbs corrected and stabbed his finger towards Aubrey, still staring at her.

"Captain Mala?" Aubrey asked trying not to sound hopeful.

"Non, Cap'n Black." Gibbs answered with a smile showing his yellowed teeth.

"But why?" Aubrey asked trying very hard to keep back the squeak she felt rising in her voice.

"He did not say and I did not ask." Gibbs answered trying to sound gruff. There were a few moments of silence as the three stood in uncertainty. Gibbs was not sure how Morgan would react if he attempted to force the woman, but he had his orders and Morgan should know the importance of following orders. He eyed the blue-eyed man and noted that he was unarmed at the present.

"Well, let us not keep him waiting." Morgan said taking Aubrey's elbow. She did not object but Gibbs stepped forward and puffed out his chest, thinking this duty very important indeed.

"He did not mention you, Monsieur Alcott." Aubrey looked at Morgan with apprehension as Morgan squeezed her arm in reassurance. She knew she had no choice but to follow Gibbs.

Aubrey was led to Mala's cabin. She felt herself tense as Gibbs knocked on the door and she heard Black's response to enter. Opening the door, Gibbs stepped aside to let her in. She felt a sudden sense of relief as she noticed Mala sitting on the ledge of the quarter gallery gazing out the window. Black sat at the head of the table, in Mala's chair, pouring himself a drink. Gibbs closed the door as Aubrey inhaled deeply, mustering up bravery she did not feel, and wondered what Black could possibly want from her. She realized that Black was watching her with a look that was not at all friendly. The look reminded her of the days after Black discovered her affair with Jean Luc.

Mala had turned to see who entered and then looked to Black who had his back to her. She could sense the younger woman's uncertainty for having to face him. After all, it had just been a week since the beating, the bruises had faded and the cut on Aubrey's cheek was healing well. Mala herself had no idea why Aubrey had been summoned and looked to Black with mild irritation for having disturbed the rest Aubrey very much needed.

Black sat back slowly, watching Aubrey as she stepped into the cabin. He noticed that she seemed to be recovering well from the beating and that added to his irritation. He was fully aware that with Mala in the room, he needed to be careful with this one. Mon Dieu, the last thing he needed was for Mala to lose her temper again nor did he want an argument to escalate into one like the night before.

He mentally shook his mind clear but he unknowingly rubbed his chin where she nicked him with the small dirk. He had another matter to settle with the Irish woman as he felt the slight twinge of pain from the cuts on his arms and collarbone Mala inflicted upon him for his torment.

"You look well." He stated indifferently.

Aubrey and Mala glanced at one another, both thinking that he could have been speaking to the wall for all the warmth he had put in the statement.

Mala rolled her eyes then turned to gaze out the window, shaking her head in annoyance.

"Merci Captain." Aubrey replied trying to put in the same tone of indifference.

There was a long pause of silence as Black only stared at Aubrey. His silence and dark-eyed stare played havoc on Aubrey's nerves as she felt the small dregs of bravery ebbing away. Since it was nearly dusk and she could see well enough in the window's reflection, Mala turned once again to watch the proceedings. She noticed that Aubrey was beginning to fidget by standing on one foot then the other then back again.

"Mon Dieu, Rene! What the hell is this all about?" Mala asked as she came to the aid of her friend and showing a little of her own irritation.

"I merely wish to inquire of Miss Malone what she remembered doing last evening?" Black asked, his gaze never leaving Aubrey's face. Neither of the women missed his reference to Aubrey. Miss Malone?

Aubrey schooled her face to show nothing of the sudden fear she felt inside. She looked to Mala and found her watching as well. Shrugging in a show of unimportance, Aubrey answered calmly, "I helped in the galley, you saw me there."

Black shot a look towards Mala. Mon Dieu, do not get her temper flared up again, he thought as he rubbed his collarbone near the cut Mala had inflicted.

"Then, I helped Willie by putting away some of the supplies for him on my way out and back to my quarters." Aubrey was saying.

"You were supposed to be resting, Aubrey. You were in the galley far too late. Morgan had his orders." Mala chided lightly.

"I know, do not blame him. He came for me and fussed once but I turned him away. Willie still needed me and I could not let him down. Besides, I was not willing to go back to confinement so early, I am tired of being in the cabin all the time." Aubrey defended with a slight pout.

"But you need your rest." Mala scolded on.

Black cleared his throat to stop the prattling. When he realized that this method had worked, he continued, "Where did you put these supplies?"

"In the storeroom, of course." Aubrey answered him.

Black paused not taking his gaze from the auburn haired woman, "Did you see anyone on your way to the storeroom?"

"Non." Aubrey answered truthfully.

"What about on your way out of the storeroom?"

"Oui, Thomas Beaufort." She replied truthfully once more. There was no way he could implicate her in the man's murder. Black's question had been vague and she was on her way out of the storeroom when she saw the man.

The fact that he was quite dead at the time she left did not really matter.

Aubrey looked questioningly at Mala as she heard the dark-haired woman speak in her language and in what seemed to be with a great deal of annoyance. Mala rolled her eyes and turned back to gaze out the window, still muttering but in quieter voice. Aubrey looked back to Black who had ignored Mala's remarks and sat calmly waiting for Aubrey's attention once again.

"Did he speak with you?" He asked. A pang of fear struck her heart, how could she effectively lie this question away?

"Of course he did. The man has the most insufferable habit of..." Aubrey started trying to sound annoyed that Beaufort was bothering her but Black cut her short.

"Did he try to detain you in any way?"

"He stood in my way, if that is what you mean." Aubrey answered.

Black recalled how Beaufort had stepped in Mala's way while she was on the forecastle that morning after he had taken the *Enchantress*. Cocking his head, he asked, "What did you do?"

Aubrey dropped her gaze to his boots as she hesitated a moment to choose her words carefully. Her mind was racing. Somehow he knew! Somehow he had found out! Now, what was she to do? Mala turned to await her answer. Aubrey felt their eyes on her but she could not think of what to say that would be nonchalant.

"I tried to get around him but he was just too big and I asked him to move." She answered lamely.

Black looked at her, reminded once again of Mala's encounter with the man and how she could not get around him at first either. "Did anyone else know you were there?" He questioned on.

"Willie knew I was..." Aubrey answered thoughtfully.

"I meant, did anyone come by that may have offered assistance?" Black asked.

"No." She replied slowly. Black paused again, watching her closely. It appeared to her that he was looking into her very soul.

"Really, Captain, what does this have to do with me?" Aubrey asked trying very hard to sound brave and added a shrug to emphasize her words.

Another few moments of silence passed as Black and Aubrey faced one another. Mala exhaled loudly to emphasize her boredom of the subject and moved to land her booted feet loudly on the floor. Black cast her a sideways glance then raised his dark eye upon Aubrey once more. With a thin knowing smile, he said with a sigh, "You ask me, what does Monsieur Beaufort have to do with you? Well, I am thinking that he has a great deal to do with you. Can you explain this?" He asked as he lifted the white shirt from his lap for

Aubrey to see.

With a great deal of effort, Aubrey had to fight off the urge to gasp as he presented her the shirt she knew she had thrown overboard the night before. How on earth did he get it? Mala could see nothing but a white shirt and could not understand where this line of questioning was going nor could she understand the look of surprise Aubrey had in her eyes for just a fleeting moment.

Aubrey made a face and tried to sound nonchalant, "What is all over it?"

Black turned it so that he could see the front and looked at it objectively in the light. From behind him, Mala had a better view of the shirt as well. Black heard the island woman mutter something in her own tongue. Aubrey watched as Mala slowly closed her eyes to the sight and slowly shook her dark head. Seeing Mala's reaction, rampant panic coursed through Aubrey.

"It appears to me to be a great deal of blood. But my question is…whose shirt is it?" Black replied.

Before Aubrey could even formulate a reply, Black turned the shirt slightly to show her the collar and Aubrey realized the folly of trying to fool him. Presented to her very clearly were her own initials that she had painstakingly embroidered on all of her clothes so she would finally have something of her own.

"Now I will ask you again, can you explain this?" Black repeated in measured anger as he leaned forward.

Aubrey took a step back as she stammered, "H-he was in my way as I had said before. He thought to finish what he started that evening in the galley."

"How do you know this?" Black asked, his anger evident in his deep voice.

"H-h-he told me, of course. H-h-he would not move out of my way and kept coming towards me until he cornered me. He had me pressed down on the sacks. His hands—his hands." Aubrey answered taking another step back and wringing her own hands in desperation as she looked from Black to Mala. The dark-haired woman was speaking again in the strange language.

"And how do you explain this?" Black asked pointing to the blood.

Aubrey held her head up in sudden defiance as she replied suddenly and curtly, "Just as I took your pistol that day and shot that man when he came into your cabin, I managed to get Beaufort's pistol and I shot him." This time Mala's remarks in this other language caught both Black's and Aubrey's attention.

"Mon coeur, if you must speak, please do so in a language that I can understand." Black replied over his shoulder, somewhat annoyed at her continued distractions.

Even though Aubrey still could not understand what was said, she could tell that Mala's next comment was in French. Some of the words she understood, but most she did not. Mala's command of the language was far greater than hers was. Black turned slightly to face the dark-haired woman with a look of incredulity.

"Did you understand that, Rene?" Mala asked, her dark eyes flashing with anger.

"Mala, you will go too far one day." Black stated in a tired voice as he faced Aubrey once again.

Mala muttered under her breath in the strange language making Black shake his head. Despite the fact that she was irritating him with her continued interruptions, she was managing to entertain him as well. He gave Mala a sideways glance before turning his questioning back to Aubrey. "Do you understand the penalties of killing..."

"Ame damne, Rene, she knows little to nothing of the pirate's ways!" Mala stated angrily as she stood up and faced him.

Aubrey felt herself jump at Mala's outburst and then took several steps back as Black, too, got to his feet, the chair nearly toppling over backwards. Suddenly he was no longer amused and took Mala's arm roughly, heading for the door.

"Mala, I will not have you come to her aid any longer! This is between Irish and me!" He growled as he pulled the dark haired woman along.

Mala tried to yank her arm from his grasp but he anticipated the move and tightened his grip. She spoke angrily in her language but Black ignored her as he opened the door and, without looking back, told Aubrey, "Stay here."

Aubrey stood as if frozen in place. She could not believe that Mala would allow him to handle her in such a way but then she did not want to be around when Mala reprimanded him in whatever fashion she decided. Nor did Aubrey want to be here alone with Black if he somehow managed to leave Mala somewhere. Until last evening when she had learned of the penalties, she really did not know what would happen to someone who committed murder on board a ship. In the past, when she had acted out in self defense on the *Widow Maker* and when Jean Luc had shot the man DeFoe in her honor, there had been no punishment delivered.

Aubrey knew that she would not be able to feign ignorance to the penalty and was grateful for Mala's timely interruption. Suddenly she felt that she could not stand any longer and sank into one of the chairs at the table.

Chapter 46

On deck with the rain beating down on them, Mala and Black faced each other. She was furious that he would intimidate Aubrey when the younger woman should be resting. Black was furious that he could not deal with Aubrey as he would like because of the friendship between her and Mala. He knew that Mala would never – ever – forgive him for that! Yet he had lost one of his crew and Aubrey had to be punished somehow. It was happening again, Aubrey was embarrassing him in front of his crew—especially if he let her get away with this without suffering some sort of punishment.

"Why, you bast..." Mala began but Black had managed to turn her back to him and pressed her against him, covering her mouth with his hand. Mala could not swing back at him even though she could feel him against her back but her arms were locked in his hold.

"She killed one of my men and she must pay the consequences for her action." He hissed in her ear. He had to uncover her mouth and hold her with both arms as Mala began to struggle violently, nearly knocking them both onto the deck.

"Merde, Mala!" He swore then tightened his grip. "Hold still so we can talk."

"You could have talked to me first!" Mala shouted in anger and continued to struggle in his death grip. "Let me go!"

"Not until we can talk about this calmly!"

"You let me go now, Rene!"

"Or you will do what? Kill me? My men will not hesitate to avenge me, my love, and I, for one, do not want to see you dead!" Black said firmly.

"What the hell do you care? You will be dead!" Mala replied in equal firmness.

Black closed his eye and inhaled deeply as he held tight to the spitting hellcat in his arms. He knew that Mala's fury was explosive and she would not hesitate to run him through if he let go of her. It took every bit of his strength and willpower to hold on to this dark-haired hellion and Black could feel himself tiring from the grip. He tried again in a calmer voice hoping that would placid her. "Mala, dead or not. I do not want you to die and..."

"You did not give a damn before!" She hissed.

"Before? Before when?" Black exploded, caught by surprise with the venomous tone of her statement. "For nearly two years, I thought you were dead!"

"Liar!" Mala shouted. She would not hold still and Black would not

403

release her. The rain poured down on them and they silently tried to will the other to relent but neither would give in.

After what seemed like an eternity to Black, Mala abruptly stopped fighting. She stood against him breathing hard from her exertion. Black continued to hold her against him as his mind went back to a time when he thought he would never hold her again. His head fell forward slightly to rest against hers and he closed his eye as he held her tight.

"You cannot hold her responsible for protecting herself, Rene." Mala stated calmly. "I only let Beaufort go that day because he was one of your men. If that brute continued to behave that way with me, he would have died by my hand."

"Oui, je connais." Black replied quietly. He refrained to say that he would have killed Beaufort himself had he tried to accost Mala. They stood in the same position for a time as the rain continued to fall, neither wanting to move.

"Very well, I will just have her confined." He said quietly.

Mala nodded her agreement. At least Aubrey would not have to go through the torturous ordeal of a flogging or worse, she thought. She never wanted anyone to feel the bite of the cat-o-nine and she knew Aubrey would never be able to withstand its sting.

With great reluctance, Black released her. He watched as Mala stood where she was, expecting her to vent out one last time because of his rough treatment of her. He was surprised when she did not and continued to stand as she was.

Black looked around to find a few men on deck who quickly went back to work when they met his gaze. He recognized one of his men and called for him. He stepped away from Mala as he spoke to the man. Seeing them talking, Mala turned without a word and went back to her cabin. Black watched her go and wondered at her silence. Although she had yelled him while they fought in the rain, he knew her well enough to know that this was not yet over. Her silence and easy agreement did not rest well in his mind and he could not place a finger on what was wrong.

Aubrey jumped to her feet when the door opened and she was relieved when she saw Mala. The island woman was drenched from being on deck and felt exhausted from her ordeal with Black but she managed a smile for the younger woman. Aubrey's relief was short lived as Black stepped in almost at Mala's heels and with one of his men accompanying him. Both men were drenched as well and Black did not look pleased.

Aubrey's attention was drawn to Black as he informed her in a tired voice, "You must be punished for your misdeed." He stated with a quick glance to Mala. "You will be confined until further notice." He looked to the man who stepped forward. Aubrey looked over at Mala who stood with arms crossed watching the proceedings from the quarter galley. With no word from Mala, Aubrey accepted this confinement and followed the man.

In the corridor, she turned to ask Black's man where she was being taken but gasped when she confronted Black behind her. He took her arm so tightly that she winced and she had to practically run to keep up with his angry pace.

"You said I was to be confined." She said worriedly and wondered if Black was going to disregard his own order.

"And so you shall be." He answered as he stopped suddenly and, taking her other arm, turned her to face him. "I would rather kill you for killing one of my men but that is not to be." He hissed close to her face.

"But..." She began with the fear visible on her face but he released one arm and continued quickly through the corridors down into the bowels of the ship. It was so reminiscent to her of their journey on the *Widow Maker* when he had her tattooed. He opened a door and the other man lit a lantern.

As the man began to tie her wrists, Black told him, "Make sure it is tight. I do not want to have to find her later. If I do, I may have to kill her and if that happens, then I will kill you."

"Aye, Cap'n." The man replied shakily.

Black gave her one last malevolent glare then left. Aubrey looked around as her wrists were bound with a rope. The room was small and filled with shadows from the lantern. She could see barrels but could not tell what else was in the room from her position on the floor. She was allowed to sit against the wall once her arms where bound and now watched as her feet were bound. The man looked down on her with almost a sorrowful look on his face.

When the man left, he took the lantern that lit the small area with him and Aubrey was enveloped by darkness. Thinking back on Black's statement to her, Aubrey realized that Mala had apparently won the battle since he admitted that he would rather have killed her than confine her. She was alive and she was very grateful for Mala's intervention. She tried to get as comfortable as she could and tried to not think of what Morgan would do when she did not return.

Black strode along the darkened corridor towards the great cabin. When he passed Morgan's cabin, the door flew open behind him. Black continued his pace and did not hesitate until he heard the angry growl of Morgan. "Black."

The dark-haired man stopped and turned slowly to regard Morgan with an air of annoyance, "Are you forgetting my title, Mr. Alcott?"

Morgan's eyes narrowed as he advanced on him belligerently but Black stood his ground. "Where is she?" Morgan demanded to know.

"Who?" Black questioned, feigning ignorance.

"You know damn good and well who I am talking about. You sent your lackey for her a long time ago. Why?" Morgan ground out in reply.

"Oh, you mean Irish. Well she and I had an issue to discuss." Black said flatly then turned on his heel to move on towards the great cabin.

Morgan caught his arm with another growl, "Where is she, you son of a bitch? She is mine remember."

Black looked down at the hand that gripped his arm with anger then looked into Morgan's blue eyes in the lantern light. "I gave her to you...remember?" Black rumbled in reply. He looked down at Morgan's hand again, but the latter still made no move to let go of his arm. Suddenly he shot out with his other hand and shoved Morgan. It broke his hold and sent him stumbling back a few paces. "Irish is tucked away for now. You will know the results of our discussion later."

An enraged growl emitted from Morgan once more as he came to his full height and rushed at Black in the semi-darkened corridor. The blue-eyed man came to a sliding halt as he now found himself looking into the barrel of Black's pistol.

"Pray do not make me lessen the number of crewmen by one more, Mr. Alcott. I value your expertise on the guns and suffice it to say that Captain Mala would be very upset at your loss. I did not know at first who it was that made Thomas disappear into thin air, but now it is becoming all to clear to me." Morgan met his gaze without flinching at the accusation.

Black's suspicions were confirmed with the mere look in the other man's eye. In secret, Black would have wished to thank him for the service, but that was not to be nor was it practical, given the present circumstances. It amazed him that Beaufort had lasted long enough to somehow escape confinement only to confront the young Irish woman and be killed by her.

Looking into Morgan's eyes, he saw a haunting reflection of his quartermaster on the *Widow Maker* the day he had stepped forward to defend Aubrey. Black's jaw muscles clenched and he exhaled deeply, "Return to your cabin and know this, Miss Malone is safe and unharmed."

"Tell me where she is. She will be frightened out of her wits. She probably already is." Morgan said thickly.

Black could not contain the laugh that built in his chest at the comment. "I would say Mr. Alcott, that after last evening, there is probably very little that will ever frighten her now. I will not tell you where she is and you are not to go roaming about the ship looking for her. My men are on watch and they have their orders. Return to your cabin or I will have you tucked away as well."

Morgan drew a deep breath to try and calm himself. He would be no good to Aubrey dead and he backed away from the pistol. Black lowered the weapon and slipped it back into his sash, continuing to watch Morgan closely.

"Go back to your cabin. If you try anything, such as searching for her or if you cause any trouble, she will pay for your insubordinate behavior." Black warned. Morgan opened his mouth to retort of the unfairness of the warning, but the look in Black's dark eye stopped him.

With an exasperated sigh, he asked instead, "When will I see her again?"

"I told you, all will be discussed when I am ready to discuss it." Black said firmly.

Morgan watched Black turn and go to the great cabin. He stood rooted to his spot for a long time, mulling over what Black had said. The soft call of one of the men behind him made him turn suddenly.

"Morgan, I think that Miss Aubrey will be all right—just like he said. So long as ye obey his commands that is." York said, stepping out of the shadows.

"What? Were you eavesdropping?" Morgan spat at the man in anger.

"No, I just was comin' along. I saw Black draw his pistol on ye and I heard his words." York shrugged. "I heard his words on deck too." He spoke almost too quietly for Morgan to hear. The blue-eyed man leaned toward him and caught him by the front of his shirt.

"You heard his words? To whom?" Morgan growled.

"Cap'n Mala. They were scrappin' like a couple of cats in an alley up there in the rain a while ago."

"About what?" Morgan pressed on.

"Cap'n Mala was defendin' her against Cap'n Black, defendin' Miss Aubrey. Black had his hackles up over Miss Aubrey killin' that worthless bastard Beaufort. Cap'n Mala was arguin' that it was in self-defense. What happened, Morgan? Why did Miss Aubrey kill the Frenchman?" York said in a low tone of voice.

Morgan shook the man violently, "Who said that Aubrey did it anyway? There is no proof."

"I heard Cap'n Mala, I tell ye." The man said in alarm at the force with which Morgan held him.

"You keep that rumor to yourself, do you hear me?" Morgan snarled.

"But Cap'n Mala..." York began.

"I said keep your mouth shut, damn you!" Morgan hissed close to the man's face.

"All right Morgan, Christ, as if I cared that she might have killed the man.

407

We know how he tormented and stalked her. I was one of the ones who protected her, remember?" York finally said as he made a face and pried Morgan's hand from his arm.

Morgan pursed his lips and rolled his eyes, "Aye, I know York. I am sorry."

"I know Morgan, ye are worried about her. But I tell ye, she will be all right." York said easily. Morgan ran his fingers through his hair with one hand and gave York a light shove with his other as he nodded.

York was about to go about his duties when Morgan stopped him, "Has Robert taken care of disposing Conner's body?"

"Aye, while Cap'n Mala had Cap'n Black in their cabin and his men were busy with the cleanin' of the storeroom." Morgan nodded, suddenly tired of the whole ordeal.

York moved along and Morgan went back into his cabin, slamming the door closed behind him in disgruntlement. He stood staring at Aubrey's empty bunk then threw himself on his bunk. He had meant to kiss her until Gibbs appeared. But now where was she? What had Black done with or to her now? Morgan slapped at his pillow in anger then stared up at the ceiling. It was apparent that Black knew something of what had happened between Aubrey and Beaufort the night before. Morgan's mind was put to ease a bit in knowing that Mala knew of Aubrey's situation and she had intervened in some way. Aubrey would be safe or Black and his cronies would have hell to pay to Mala for it.

Black entered the cabin to find Mala had taken off her boots to put on dry britches and was now putting on a dry shirt. With her back to him and her long dark hair pulled to the front over one side, he caught a glimpse of the scars on her back from a flogging she endured two years before. Her time on the *Dodger*, he thought and in an instant his anger dissolved. Now he understood why she fought him on deck. She would have never allowed him to have Aubrey flogged and he knew that Aubrey would never have survived it as Mala had. Of course, Mala had survived just out of spite, much like everything else she did and the thought made him smile.

Mala turned as she began tucking her shirt into the waistband and caught his smile. She stopped and the two watched each other from across the room. Black watched as Mala slowly walked towards him and he raised a brow when he noticed she lifted her shirt over her head and then let it fall to the floor.

Black's gaze feasted on the beauty before him, looking at his mark and the medallion. He watched her as she seemed to float the last few steps towards him. He took in every inch of her face when she raised a hand to lovingly wipe away a few drops of wetness from his forehead as the wet strands of hair around his face still dripped from the rain.

Mala felt herself being lifted in his arms and carried to the bunk. His mouth covered hers as he gently lowered her down. He realized her mouth tasted of rum as his kiss deepened then his kisses moved around her face and neck. He heard her gasp as he took one nipple in his mouth and felt her hands hold him to her. The sound flashed fire through his loins. He moved to kiss the valley between her breasts then took the other nipple into his mouth. Mala moaned with delight as Black devoted delicious time to her breasts. She wanted him now but she also wanted him to continue with his kisses, it was like a sweet torture.

Black's kisses moved up to her face as he pressed light kisses over her eyes, cheeks, and lips. Mala caught his mouth on hers and held him tightly to her in a deep passionate kiss. He lifted his head to look down on her beautiful face as if to etch it in his memory forever.

"Mala, I cannot ever seem to stop wanting you." Black whispered breathlessly, his thumb rubbing against her cheek as he gazed down at her.

She smiled up at him and, with a quickness that always caught him off guard, Black found himself beneath her as she straddled his hips. Taking hold of his shirt, the sound of renting material seemed to echo in the cabin as Mala ripped it open. Black seemed to hold his breath as he watched her gaze roam over him. She touched the cut on his collarbone and he winced.

Black took each breast in his hands as she leaned forward to kiss him, her hands on either side of his head. Mala could feel his need for her as she raised back up to sitting position. Black's brows knitted together when Mala made no other moves. With a smile, he asked, "Do we go further or are you now content?"

Mala only smiled and still made no moves. He now noticed that her smile did not reach her eyes and this made him very wary. Black's smile slowly died as he remembered his earlier thought on deck of Mala's quick agreement. She definitely had him in a position that he would grant her anything and he knew that she knew this. Her smile was like a confirmation.

"Mala..." He started but she put a finger to his lips to quiet him.

"You are a devil, Captain." She said softly almost cooing. "So many times I have thought of you as we are now." Her voice seemed to lull him and he could not help but smile in reply. "But then the vision changes as I lay open your throat." She added as she watched him closely.

His smile faded and he began to worry again, "Mala, if this is about Irish, er, Aubrey..."

"Actually, it is partly about Aubrey."

Black made to move as a sign for Mala to rise off of him. Suddenly he felt a sharp point at his throat and was surprised that Mala now held a dirk.

"Under the pillow. How clever, m'amour." Black replied trying to sound flippant at the discovery.

Mala leaned forward slightly and the movement caused him some discomfort as she was still very intimately close. Her breath smelled of rum and he could still taste it in his mouth from their kisses.

"I know she is not confined to quarters as you had hoped that I would have understood you to say. Wherever you have placed her, Rene, she had better not be harmed. Beaufort is dead, this much is true, but what she did was in self-defense, having been confronted by the bastard myself. Under normal circumstances, Monsieur Beaufort would have died by my hand that morning he tried to detain me. Aubrey would not have had to face him last evening and your entire interrogation with her need not ever have taken place." Mala's voice was even and soft the whole time she spoke but Black caught her underlying tone of menace. She was a woman who was never to be taken lightly and he had seen many a man make that mistake since he had known her.

Black looked into her dark eyes and he knew what she had just said was true. Had Mala been true to character that morning, Thomas Beaufort would have died then. Of course, Black would have had to punish her somehow. Since he took over the ship as its captain and Beaufort had two close companions with him, Black would have had to order the punishment. And since Mala was a pirate captain, she above all others knew the penalty for killing another crewmember. It surely would have been a more serious situation if that had happened and he was not sure if he could have given the order to punish Mala as the penalties allowed.

The fact that Aubrey killed Beaufort and everyone knew that she was very new to this world of piracy was actually a saving grace for him as well as Mala and Aubrey. He knew that his argument with Aubrey stemmed from her refusal of him and her choice of Jean Luc while on the *Widow Maker*. Now that he had Mala back in his life, why the bloody hell did he care about Aubrey? Looking up at Mala as she leaned over him, he made up his mind once and for all.

Black felt a sense of relief with his mind made up about Aubrey. He also realized that Mala was the only woman who ever mattered to him and the emptiness he had felt for nearly two years thinking that she was dead had lifted. But when had the emptiness lifted? The tavern! Seeing Mala that day in the old tavern at Bimini and hearing her voice, even in controlled anger, was like finding the siren that sang her song to the wind. It was wonderful and beautiful even with the imminent danger he had found himself in.

Having found her alive and still very desirable, Black had wanted Mala badly. Even though he was angry that she forbade Yvette to 'comfort' him, Yvette was not the woman he wanted. Jean Luc's theory of Mala's jealousy warmed him and he had hoped that he could find her again. But when the British boarded his ship and took him and his men prisoners, Black had thought that he would most certainly die and lose Mala forever. Fate had a way of meddling in his life but he was not going to complain this time of its meddling. Fate had placed Mala in Charlestowne just as he and some of his men had managed an escape. Now he was here—in her bunk.

With the dirk at his throat, Black smiled up at Mala and slowly lifted his arms. She moved the point slightly but he ignored it. His hands cupped her face then one hand moved to smooth the long dark hair that was like a curtain around their heads.

"True, my love. Had you been the true Mala that morning, Beaufort would not have seen the finish of the sunrise. I will release Irish in the morning. You have my word on that." He told her.

Mala did not move but only watched him as if trying to read what was really on his mind. His smile stayed as he held her face, his thumb once again gently rubbing her cheek. She took a deep breath and tossed the dirk over her shoulder. They heard it clatter on the floor as she lowered her face to his for a kiss.

The kiss was deep, passionate, and full of the need they both knew would consume them within seconds. The two strong-willed captains won their individual battles and were soon caught up in the web woven from love that neither one would probably ever voice aloud. The oil from the lantern finally burned out in the wee hours of the morning but the fading light found the lovers still very much absorbed with each other.

Chapter 47

The dawn's rays broke over the horizon and streamed through the quarter gallery. Black could feel the warmth of the rays on his bare back as he supported his reclining body over Mala's. He smiled down into her relaxed and dozing countenance. Brushing back some strands of her hair from her cheek, he said softly, "I must go, mon coeur. There is business to tend to with the men this morning."

Mala opened her eyes and searched his face. She smoothed the hair on his brow then gently stroked his moustache with her thumb, "They will not be pleased, Rene."

"I know." He smiled gently then got up from the bunk and began to dress.

"I will be up directly." Mala said as she watched him. He cast his dark eye over her. Although she was covered, he knew the beauty of her nakedness beneath. Mala stretched languidly, deliberately tormenting him. With a lustful grunt, he smiled and left the cabin. She sat up and a mischievous smile spread across her face at her torment.

Black decided to visit with Deats before seeing to Aubrey and the upcoming events of the day. "Are you awake, Scotsman?" He asked loudly.

Aubrey's head snapped up when she heard the deep voice of Rene Black through a sleepy fog. Then the angry Scottish accented-voice brought her to full wakefulness. She was held near Deats!

"Aye, ye blackguard pirate. I demand ta see my captain. God knows what manner of condition ye have left her with the anger you displayed last eve." Aubrey and Black realized that Deats heard the commotion of Aubrey's confinement and the Scotsman thought the person was Mala. Why would he think it was Mala down here? Aubrey and Black unknowingly thought the same thing.

"My anger last evening? Ah yes, but what makes you think it was Mala?" Black asked with a smile.

"I heard ye tell the man that ye may have ta kill her if she got away, then ye was gonna kill him. I demand ta see my captain and know that she is foin!" Deats stated angrily. Black smiled as he listened. So the Scotsman thought that he had Mala taken down here for punishment.

"I see that you are under the assumption that I would cater to your requests. Well you cannot see her." Black replied amused that the Scotsman was looking daggers at him. If looks could kill... Black thought with a smile. Aubrey wondered at his good mood. Black was far too cheery for this early hour of the morning. Mala was not cheerful last evening during the questioning and Aubrey was certain that if Mala had been angry throughout the night, Black would not have found peace. What had happened to cause his cheerfulness now?

"Ye bastard! She demanded my release and ye have punished her for her insistence!"

"Punish Mala? Mais oui, Monsieur Deats I punish her each night as I take her into my arms. I punish her each time she smiles at me in a way that makes a man forget everything in the world except for the body beneath him giving him pleasure. Oui, Monsieur Deats, I punish Mala every opportunity I can."

Aubrey's eyes grew wide over Black's description of his relationship with Mala. He made it sound as if he forced himself on her. Black smiled at Deats' fury as the Scotsman's face turned red with the rage.

"Aye, tis her lot ta have ye pawin' her and destroyin' the perfect woman that she was. Ye dinna kin aboot her and Mala showed ye her hatred of ye for leaving her behind while ye continued with yer old pursuits."

Before Deats could taunt him more, Black snarled, "She knew I was coming back for her! But you came along and took her away!" The memory of her log entry and the mention of her hatred burned in Black's mind.

"Aye, but how long were ye gone, Captain? Are ye sure she knew ye would come back for her? But I do agree with one point, I did take her away."

"And would have taken more from her if given the chance." Black said through clenched teeth, angry at the thought of the Scotsman trying to coax Mala into his bunk.

"Ye only stand before me because she had a change in plans in Bimini. She does want ye dead, Captain, that much is true. What her plans are for ye now, only she knows for I canna talk ta her and give her my counsel. But her hatred for ye is beyond all ye can imagine." Deats taunted.

Black was seething over the man's words. Then he remembered Morgan telling him as they talked outside of Charlestowne that Deats could not be trusted. Even Mala had requested that Deats remain imprisoned while the other men were released. Feeling the heat of his anger subside, Black faced the Scotsman using another tactic. With a smile on his face, Black asked, "Her hatred? Perhaps her hatred is not for me but for you and your loyalty to her."

"My captain knows I am true and loyal ta her!"

"Would that have been a sample of such loyalty you displayed for your captain in Charlestowne? She did not seem too pleased with you then, Monsieur Deats."

The Scotsman fumed as he recalled how his anger and jealousy for this man had gotten the better of him that day. He knew that given the opportunity, Mala would have fallen into this pirate's arms and displayed mercy yet again just as she had done in that old tavern in Bimini. That she allowed Alcott to escort him to safety was beyond all reason.

Black stepped closer to the Scotsman and said pleasantly, "Actually I have not taken Mala by force, Scotsman. She has been a willing party to our sweet interludes. I assure you, Quartermaster, that last eve your captain and I enjoyed one of the most captivating and satisfying nights I can remember. If that was hate, then I shall see to it that she continues to hate me in that fashion and strive to enhance that feeling!"

Deats said nothing. His heart sank knowing that it could be very true. As hard as he had tried to erase Black from her memory and her life, she had never let Rene Black go from her mind or her heart. For his silence, Deats was graced with another smug smile from Black as he turned to leave the Scotsman.

"Aye, I must see what I can do to enhance her feelings of hatred for me." Black repeated as if to give the matter a great deal of thought.

"Do and think as ye will, Captain. But she will never forgive ye for leaving her behind. Something terrible happened in that village, something that left her the sole survivor. It is something she never speaks of, no' ta me or ta Morgan Alcott whom she trusts more than myself. Try ta speak of it and she will show that hatred she harbors for ye. It is there, Captain. She finds sport with ye now but she will tire of ye. That ye can be assured of because ye left her there. There, she was alone ta face whatever happened. Alone, Captain. She will never forgive ye for that!"

Deats was now smiling smugly as Black stared at him. He had heard and listened to every word the Scotsman had said. Deats hoped that it would make the man question every move Mala made as though she had planned it to be as it was.

Without another word, Black stormed from the small area and the door shut solidly behind him. Left alone again, Deats smiled. He would still be able to drive that wedge between Mala and Black by using the man's own guilt for having left her behind that day. The Scotsman once again thanked Jean Luc for the information. It had been most helpful in driving the wedge between him and Mala before Jean Luc parted company from them. Now he could do the same between Mala and Black.

Aubrey was startled that Black was suddenly at her side. He was cutting her bonds in angry jerking motions. "Rene, do not listen to Deats." She whispered.

"Chut, Irish." Black growled as he pulled her roughly to her feet.

415

"Please listen to me. Deats is only..." Aubrey stopped when she saw the menacing look in his dark eye.

Taking her roughly by the wrist, Black pulled her along with him down the corridor, heading for the upper decks. Suddenly he stopped in his fast angry pace and faced her. Aubrey took an involuntary step back for the look on his face was savage.

"Why the hell should I listen to you?" He hissed close to her face.

"Because he lies, Rene! Ask Morgan! Better still, ask Mala!" Aubrey exclaimed, trying to get him to understand.

Black stared at her for a moment before looking in the direction of Deats' confinement. Morgan had said that Mala knew of the mark on Aubrey and still brought her on board. That was not like her. Did Mala see something with that powerful sixth sense of hers, those feelings she gets? Mala had asked for her men to be released and leave Deats. She knew that Deats could not be trusted

Aubrey watched him as he stared down the corridor. When his dark eye turned on her once again, she held her breath knowing that he would retaliate in some way for her outburst.

"You say nothing to Mala of what you have heard. You say nothing to Alcott or anyone else, do you understand?" Aubrey stared at him as he glared down at her. The moment she nodded, he was dragging her along once again.

The crew was assembled in the early morning light when Black mounted the quarterdeck and stood at the railing to look down upon them, just as he had the night of the discovery of Beaufort's body.

"An investigation was performed into the murder of Monsieur Beaufort. I have called you all together to announce that the murderer has been discovered." He began. A rumble of murmuring traveled through the men and Black raised a gloved hand to silence them. Morgan slowly mounted the quarterdeck steps, watching Black with suspicious blue eyes.

"Yesterday morning, Monsieur Boulet found this." Morgan stopped as the man produced the bloodstained white shirt. Black let the shirt cascade out to its full length in his gloved hands.

"A seemingly ordinary white shirt but obviously blood-stained and identifiable to the owner." Black began.

Muttering rippled through the crew. Black turned the collar toward the men as if they could all see the markings therein and announced, "Three embroidered initials—AEM—Aubrey Erin Malone." He put down the shirt and leaned on it with one hand on the railing. His other hand rested on his hip.

"Bring out the accused." He called toward the companionway.

Morgan's eyes were now trained on the opening to the decks below. One man emerged into the sunlight with Aubrey in tow. Her wrists were tied with a rope and the man pulled her along almost forcefully. There was a look of sheer terror on her face as she looked at the men of the crew while she was being pulled along. Morgan drew a deep breath and glared at Black who watched the scene calmly.

"What are you going to do?" Morgan asked in a low voice very near the man. Black merely cast him a sideward glance and waited until Aubrey was brought to stand at the base of the bulkhead beneath him.

"The other night, when we discovered the unfortunate death of Monsieur Beaufort, I decreed what punishment would be given." Black began.

Morgan took another step forward in protest hissing, "You cannot do this to her, Captain! She cannot take it."

"Silence!" Black hissed in reply over his shoulder then turned back to the assembled crew, "A lashing and the replacement of the stores that were ruined." He reminded them.

"I will not let you whip her." Morgan warned quietly. The men below did not see the confrontation that was taking place on the deck above as they trained their attention on the young woman who stood before them in bonds. Black waved his hand and another of his men stepped forward to turn Aubrey with her back to the crew, holding a cat-o-nine in his hand.

"Captain!" Morgan hissed again.

Black glared at him, his tone was low and cold, "Shall I have you removed to join your quartermaster in the hold?"

"She is a woman. She killed him in self defense." Morgan dared to argue. Black ignored the blue-eyed man as he nodded to his man with the whip.

Aubrey was forced to her knees and her captor caught the tail of her shirt that hung loosely over her hips. She squirmed in her bondage and cried out in fear for what was about to happen. A muttering washed over the men again, most of them of Mala's crew as the man pulled up the back of her shirt. Black's crew stood with arms folded over their chests, waiting for justice to be done. It did not matter to them that it was a woman about to receive the bite of the whip.

Morgan's throat constricted as he saw the sunlight glow on the pristine skin and he thought about the whip coming down on her, laying the delicate white skin open to bleed. Aubrey struggled below and in trying to keep her in place, the man was forced to let go of her shirt.

"Captain, please." He pleaded in a mixture of anger and concern. Black continued to ignore him. Morgan exhaled in angry determination and turned away but Black caught him by the arm and held him there. As Black and Morgan glared at one another, the entire assemblage watched in tense interest.

"You cannot do this." Morgan growled in the man's face.

A movement from below caught their attention. Mala emerged from the companionway and came up the steps. A sigh of relief escaped Morgan. He knew that she would not allow this to happen because she had experienced it herself and she hated the whip.

Mala came up the quarterdeck steps and passed behind Black and Morgan to lean with her back against the port side railing. Black batted a dark eye at Morgan and released his arm with a shove. Morgan met Mala's gaze as Black turned back to the railing. Mala crossed her arms over her chest and set her gaze upon the back of the dark-haired man's head.

With a subtle nod of his head, Black commanded the man with the whip to begin. Aubrey's back was bared once more as the other man's arm swung in a large circle over his head. The tails of the whip whistled through the air. With a snap of his wrist, the whip made a 'cracking' sound in the hushed silence of the deck making Aubrey scream in fright at the sound.

"Christ." Morgan breathed from beside Black. He could not believe that this was happening. The whip whistled again and once more there was a resounding crack in the air as the man snapped the whip forward just above Aubrey. She cried out again at the frightening sound and struggled like a person possessed against the man who held her. Not expecting her to resist with such strength, the man very nearly lost his hold on her and she started to scramble away from him. The man with the whip cursed her in French and Aubrey's captor caught her back up then bared her back yet again.

Morgan's blue eyes searched the assembled crowd. Several of Mala's men closed their eyes or turned away from the sight. Mala's face was a mask of the painful remembrance at the sound. Black blinked at the sound as well, casting a fleeting glance upon the island woman who had come to stand on the other side of him. Black could barely hear the ragged intake of breath from Mala as if she felt the bite of the whip again. It took every ounce of his strength at that moment to keep silent. Cold chills ran down Black's spine as he vividly recalled the feel of the scars on Mala's soft skin just that morning. Then a memory flashed through his mind of Mala lying on her stomach in his bunk on *Widow Maker* while he tended to the raw wounds on her back from a lashing she had to endure.

"Mala." Morgan pleaded softly as the man snapped the whip in the air again. He saw she was transfixed by the sounds that had taken her back to another time.

At the sound of the whip again, Aubrey responded with a loud audible sob as she proclaimed, "Please! I had to kill him! He was going to hurt me."

The whip snapped again and the man chuckled at her, "The next one you

418

will feel."

"Please!" She screamed in tears now as she struggled against the man that held her and held up the back of her shirt. "He cornered me in the storeroom—he was going to rape me—I had to kill him! It was self defense!" She continued to confess before them. Morgan was on the move, heading down the steps toward them.

"Arrête!" Black called loudly. The man with the whip dropped his arm and looked up at his captain stunned at the order. Morgan came to a halt and looked up as well. He did not know what the word meant but the commanding tone caught his attention. Mala's men breathed a collective sigh of relief upon hearing the true reason for the murder and some understood the call to stop the forthcoming punishment.

Morgan stood rigid as he looked down upon Aubrey. She cowered on the deck with her back still bared to the crew as the other man still held her. She was sobbing uncontrollably now but amid the sobs, she still pleaded and confessed, "I am sorry but what was I to do? Let him have his way? Please! I had no choice!"

Black waved the man with the whip to step back. A grumbling could be heard from his small boarding crew as his deep voice boomed over the voices below, "We have a confession. As the captain, I have the authority to change the sentence of punishment." Morgan closed his eyes with relief as Black went on in his droning voice. "Mademoiselle Malone will be confined to quarters for one month..." He began but was interrupted.

"Where is the justice in that? She has murdered the quartermaster—no matter that he tried to take her. She has tormented him since she was on the *Widow Maker!*" LaVoie yelled in anger.

"Non!" Aubrey sobbed in retort from her cowering position on the deck. "Non! I never tormented him! He tormented me."

A wave of grumbling and arguing washed over the crew. Mala's men defended her, while Black's men complained of the great injustice of the young woman getting away with the murder of one of their own.

Morgan looked up to watch Black's face as the dark-haired man watched and listened to the grumbling on deck. Going back up the steps quickly to stand beside Black, he bargained in a quiet voice, "She can be confined there in the quarters alone—I will move out if I must, take a hammock on the gun deck just do not let him whip her."

"That will not be necessary Mr. Alcott, she will need you after this experience." Black said softly, his lips barely moving. Morgan's head tilted slightly and he looked at Black questioningly. The captain's dark eye shifted to Mala who stood with her arms crossed over her chest, watching and listening to the commotion on the main deck. Her body language spoke volumes to him as he looked at her staring below at the scene. A flood of memories, painful memories were assaulting her and Black could almost read them even from this distance.

Black continued to look at Mala as he spoke to Morgan, "Even I know how the man stalked Aubrey, he did so on my ship. Before my very eyes, when she was…" He paused in his quiet narrative and his gaze met her dark eyes as he finished, "…mine." Seemingly tearing his gaze from Mala, Black looked at Morgan, "It was your brother who first coached her to be brave before Thomas. But only now, since she has acquired a new friend, has she learned how to truly defend herself and be a brave woman against a formidable foe."

Looking back to the activity on deck, Black called, "Release her to the first mate."

Morgan fairly sprinted for the main deck. Aubrey was released amid growling protests from her guard and the man who held the whip. Morgan pushed them aside and Aubrey collapsed onto the deck. Terrified and relieved sobs wracked her body as Morgan knelt beside her. She clawed her way up into his embrace when he pulled her to her feet. The stress and aftershock of the incident came over her and she shakily pushed her shirt back down into place. Morgan swept her up into his arms, purring, "You are all right."

Turning with her to go down the companionway, he cast a look up to Black. The two men met eyes and Morgan nodded curtly in thanks.

"Return to your posts—it is over." Black called down on the crew with an indifferent wave of his hand. More grumbling coursed through his small boarding party. "J'ai dis, il a fini!" He growled menacingly. Finally, they disbursed, still disgruntled.

As the last of the men left the main deck for various parts of the ship, Mala said softly as she continued to stand with her back against the railing and her arms folded. "Well done, Rene. I have to admit, you had me worried there for a moment."

"Had I made any other decision, I fear that I would have felt the cold hard steel of your pistol against the base of my skull instead of the soft warmth of the front of your body against the front of mine." He replied as he watched her slowly walk behind him.

"Indeed, he can be made to see." She purred from close behind him. He felt her brush her body against the back of him, her hand running across his backside as she moved to leave the quarterdeck. Black could not help but chuckle low in his throat as he kicked idly at the bottom of the railing and looked down at his boots. With a sigh, he looked down at the shirt in his hand once more. He walked to the port railing and threw it to the wind. He watched as the wind swept it up and it floated behind them to land in the wake of the *Enchantress*.

Chapter 48

The sun shone bright for the early morning hours, promising a hot and sticky day for the crew of the *Enchantress*. Since his proclamation a few days before to change Aubrey's punishment for the murder of Thomas Beaufort from the flogging to confinement, both Black and Mala had to intervene in several arguments between his few men and her abundant crew.

Black finished his breakfast wondering why Mala had not joined him. As he pushed his plate aside, the loud bantering from several of Mala's men preceded their entrance into the galley. Black had not caught the words but when they noticed him, they became conspicuously silent. Black sighed and stood up to leave.

As he passed the table where the men had just seated themselves, one of the men stood up, "Cap'n Black?"

He stopped and gave the man his attention. "I jus' wanna say 'at I, ah, we all 'ppreciate yer understandin' 'bout Miss Aubrey. If'n it 'ad been any o' us, 'en 'at whippin' would 'ave been right."

Black stared at him for a moment, it took that long to digest what the man was saying, before his dark eye passed over his friends. The faces he recognized but the names escaped him. With a nod of his dark head, Black turned and left the galley.

Stepping into the daylight, the smell of the sea wafted around him. The sails were down again to catch what little wind blew but at least the ship was moving through the water instead of drifting with the current. Black's head was bent as he slowly climbed the steps to the quarterdeck and only then did he notice Mala standing and staring out from the stern of the ship. Giving Timmons a nod to acknowledge his presence, Black smiled as his eye roamed over her lithe form. Her usual red shirt, black britches, knee-high cuffed black boots, and the gold sash about her slim waist adorning all her weaponry made every man look at her twice when seeing her for the first time. The ends of her long dark hair drifted on the breeze.

He smiled as he remembered the confrontation in front of the inn when she faced those five burly men, unafraid and very put out. He chuckled softly as he remembered the words she told the 'leader' of that small band. *'Tell them to lower their pistols or you will not be any good, to any woman, anymore.'* And this was his woman!

As he neared her, he noticed the arms crossed over her chest, the slow tapping of her booted foot, and the look on her face. She looked around and absentmindedly smiled at him as he neared then returned to her thoughts.

423

"Does something trouble you, mon coeur?" He asked softly. Her hair seemed to demand attention so he reached up, let his finger touch her temple, then followed the strands until the breeze caught them and swept them away from his touch. His dark eye followed the path of his finger before he looked at her profile and realized that she had not answered him. "What is it?" He asked firmly.

The toe stopped its tapping as Mala glanced up at him and replied, "I have had to break up three confrontations already this morning. Something needs to be done, Rene. I am not going to cast blame on who started what first because I know how my men can taunt but I have pulled Morgan, Robert, York and Riley aside to pass the word on to my crew that this prattling will cease or I will start handing out punishment." She told him.

She was shaking her head and bent her head to gaze down at the quarterdeck. Black's dark gaze roamed over the top of her head then lowered until he too was looking at the deck. She was tapping her foot again.

"Perhaps with a ship carrying over a hundred men and two stubborn women, we should..." He began with a smile.

She rolled her eyes and scolded lightly, "Be serious, Rene." Black was trying to be serious but whenever she was around, he could barely think at all. No, that was not true, he could think but it was always the same thing and she knew it!

Before they could speak anymore of it, there was a clearing of throats. The captains turned to find Black's boarding crew around the quarterdeck steps. Some stood on the steps while others waited along the rail but all eyes were on the captains. So engrossed were Black and Mala in their conversation, they did not hear or see the men approaching. Black turned to face them while Mala remained as she was. She recognized Boulet and LaVoie among the men then counted heads to find that there were seven. Her eyes darted up to the crow's nest. The man in the crow's nest made eight. All of the Black's men accounted for, she thought then raised a brow in wonder.

"Oui?" Black asked taking a step towards them.

"We were wondering if we could speak with you, Captain?" LaVoie asked, seemingly the spokesman. His eyes shifted back and forth from Black to Mala.

She caught the hint and with a smile walked away to stand next to Timmons, away from the group. Black watched her leave for an instant then turned his gaze back to his men. He found them watching her as well, their eyes following the graceful sway of her hips as she walked away. When their eyes slowly returned to their captain, they found his look of irritation for they had tread upon what was his.

LaVoie cleared his throat again as the men drew closer around Black and when he spoke, it was in French, "Captain, we do not want to earn your wrath over what you decreed, but we feel an injustice over the punishment."

Before Black could speak, Boulet spoke up in quiet tones, "Aye Captain. It is not fair that the wench got nothing for what she done. She should have felt the bite of the lash."

Black waited for any other comments before speaking. When none came, he said calmly, "My punishment for her stays, gentlemen. She does not understand our ways..." He raised his hand to silence them as they began to protest all at once and continued, "Would you have me flog one of you had you been thrust into this unknown world of strange rules? Where is the justice in correctly defending yourself only to face another punishment by someone else's hand? Gentlemen, that is why the British have their courts and trials of which we have scoffed, n'est-ce pas?"

"But we face our due when we break a rule." Boulet stated, arguing his point.

Black nodded patiently then replied calmly, "Then consider Thomas' actions, his attempt to take what did not belong to him. In this case, Irish's claim to self-defense is without a doubt quite obvious. There are many things that Irish needs to learn about the ways of pirates if she is to live among us. She is still too proper of a young lady to grasp our world. Although she has managed to survive thus far, she is still learning how to survive and more importantly, how to fight back."

Black noticed their eyes shift in Mala's direction. Glancing over his shoulder, he found that she was talking with Timmons and easily ignoring them. Facing his men once again and gaining their attention, he said smiling, "That one was born with a mean streak. I think she was a pirate from birth and only needed a ship and crew." His statement brought out laughter among his men.

"Aye, she is a mean one." LaVoie said, remembering how he and Boulet had tried to make Beaufort understand that. Black merely smiled at the statement and thought that there were many other words much stronger than 'mean' to describe Mala's temperament.

Still laughing, his men slowly dispersed. He watched as they filed away slowly, still smiling himself. When he turned to join Mala with Timmons, he saw that she was looking up. Following her gaze, he saw his man looking down at them from his perch on the crow's nest. Black knew that he was the only one not in attendance of the recent gathering. Decidedly, Black would leave the telling of what had transpired to one of those who had just left.

It was early afternoon when Mala slipped away to visit Aubrey. The younger woman smiled at her as she allowed Mala into the cabin. "Bored yet?" Mala asked a hint of laughter in her voice.

"Not yet but I will be soon. I am finishing this book I bought while we were in port. After that, I will be really bored." Aubrey answered.

"Well, I will be sure to bring you a book from my cabin later today so that it will be here when you finish that one." Mala said pointing the book on Aubrey's bunk.

"Thank you." Aubrey said brightly. She watched as Mala looked around the cabin. Sitting in the chair, Mala settled herself for the visit while Aubrey sat on her bunk.

"It is truly a shame though." Mala began.

"What is?" Aubrey asked confused.

"Now that Beaufort is gone and you no longer have to dread walking alone, you are confined to your quarters for one month." Mala said. Aubrey giggled for Mala had said the last few words in a deeper voice to imitate Rene Black. The dark-haired woman smiled at her own jest.

"Well whenever Rene lifts this confinement, it will be closer to how it was before he came aboard." Aubrey said with a shrug.

"Somewhat." Mala said softly.

"You really do love him?" Aubrey asked quietly.

"Aye, more so now that he is here with me." Mala said then let out a deep sigh.

"You were right, Mala. It is lonely." Aubrey said sadly, thinking of Jean Luc.

Mala watched her face as Aubrey stared at the floor. She could tell her that Jean Luc was not on the *Widow Maker* when she went down. But no, the alternative was worse, she thought, and Black had to have been furious with the deception and the embarrassment to send away his best friend like that. Marooned!

"How were you able to hold yourself from other men for so long?" Aubrey asked breaking the ominous silence that had filled the room.

"My case was little different than yours. At least, until the sinking of the *Widow*." Mala stated simply. She did not want to mention that Black was alive and that she trailed behind him until that fateful day when it was believed he went down with his ship. The loneliness set its claws deep into Mala's heart then. Unfortunately it was only then that Mala realized how much she wanted Black back. With sadness in her voice, Mala added, "Someday you may release him, Aubrey, then you can start anew. Just do not let it be too very long."

"You can say that because you got the man you wanted back." Aubrey said, a tear dropping to the floor.

"That is true. All I can say is that do not let anyone pressure you. When you are ready, you will know. Besides, look at how often Deats tried."

Aubrey sniffed and gave a small choked laugh. Trying to bring her spirits up, she asked, "Did you really cut him?"

Mala laughed softly, saying, "Aye, he sports a scar right about here." Mala's drawn out 'right' made Aubrey look up. She watched as Mala put a finger at the base of her throat and made a small line across to the hollow of her throat. Aubrey erupted into laughter. How she wished she had seen that!

"And he still did not stop?" Aubrey asked amid her laughter. She tried to calm herself and return to seriousness.

"No, that thick-headed Scotsman. But I have to admit, sometimes, he provided good entertainment." Mala said leaning close to Aubrey. The younger woman clamped her hand over her mouth but the air of laughter escaped through her nose in a loud snort. Mala laughed with her as Aubrey doubled over.

"No wonder Morgan thinks it was so funny." Aubrey said haltingly as she gasped for air.

"That fool would think it was funny. If it happened to Deats, then it was funny." Mala said causing Aubrey to laugh harder.

"Stop it, Mala." Aubrey implored as the dark-haired woman smiled at her.

After a few moments of calming down, Mala asked Aubrey, "You do know that I had planned on killing Beaufort myself?" Her answer was a wide-eyed stare from Aubrey. My God, if Black was going to flog her but changed his mind because she did not understand the pirate rules, Aubrey thought, then what would have happened to Mala?

As if reading her thoughts, Mala nodded and said, "But there would not have been a body to find." Aubrey stared at her still dumbfounded as Mala leaned forward, "Do you know how many different ways there are to dispose of a body without anyone ever knowing?" Aubrey shook her head negatively. She had to remind herself that this friend was also a pirate, a damned good and very deadly pirate! Mala smiled seemingly reading her thoughts again. Aubrey felt a chill in the room and shivered.

Settling back in the chair again, the island woman added thoughtfully, "I knew Rene would kill him if he got to him first. Probably with his bare hands for he was in such a rage. But the bastard took a shot at me." She jabbed a thumb to her chest for emphasis. "I watched him. I watched him take aim and I saw the smoke when he pulled off the shot. It happened so fast, Aubrey, all too fast."

Aubrey listened in speechless amazement as Mala shrugged. "I had my men search him out. Orders were to find him first but not tell me where he was until I asked. I knew Rene would ask me when Beaufort could not be found and I wanted to be truthful to him when he did ask. Then when I was ready, I would ask my men where he was and it would have been done within minutes."

When Mala paused and stared reflectively at the floor, Aubrey asked, "How did he stay hidden all that time? And how did he find me?"

"I gave his guards some of my herbal powders for sleeping to be put in his drink. I am not really sure what happened. Somehow Beaufort realized what was happening …no, I doubt that, not enough time for that. If I were to guess though, I think not enough powder was given to him. I do not know, but he managed to kill my man on watch and eventually found you." Aubrey saw what might have been a look of regret on Mala's face as she looked at the younger woman but it was gone so quickly. "Without a body, how does one punish another with so many other suspects to chose from and no evidence to point to any one person." Mala added softly.

"I tried to throw that shirt overboard. Actually I thought I did. I have no idea how Rene was able to get it. There was no one around on deck then, I was sure of it, I still am." Aubrey said still confused.

"I do not know but at least Rene conceded my point on your lack of pirate ways. When you know better, nothing I do or say is going sway anyone's opinion. But we have to work on your defenses. With your lessons lacking, you are going to forget what little we have taught you so far."

"I will not!" Aubrey said quickly but knew the folly of that. Mala's smile told her that she knew better. Aubrey sighed still watching Mala. "I hate to think what would have happened if you had been caught. I do not think Rene could do it, put you under the lash." Aubrey said.

Mala smiled sadly and said, "You would be surprised what one would do to maintain an effective command of the ship." With a shrug, Mala looked directly into Aubrey's eyes and in a voice barely above a whisper, "He would have had no choice."

Aubrey's mouth opened slightly in surprise for Mala took that possibility calmly, albeit sadly. Yet she still doubted that Black could give the order. He cared for Mala too much to do that to her by his own hand.

Mala took a deep breath and said with finality, "Which was why he would have never found a body. Rene could have torn this ship apart and rebuilt her but Beaufort would not have been found within." Mala's eyes had scanned the room then gave another shrug. Silence engulfed the room for a moment before Mala stood to leave, "Well I better see what is going on topside. As long as I am not around to distract him, Rene can be quite observant of his surroundings." Mala smiled at Aubrey who squelched a giggle.

"I will be back later with another book." The dark-haired woman said as she opened the door to leave, then added with an impish grin, "Buck up, mon amie. Confinement does have its advantages. No personal tavern wench in the galley means that the men must fend for themselves...and as it should be." Mala said as they laughed softly. Beaufort's referral of Aubrey's status when Black assigned her to work in the galley would be the women's own personal joke now.

Chapter 49

Later that afternoon, Mala was bringing Aubrey another book when she heard Black's voice ahead. Why would he be down here? She mused that he had not seemed interested in Aubrey's plight whenever it was mentioned. She slowed her pace to listen then glanced around the corner to see Black leaning against the open doorway with his shoulder against the doorjamb, his arms crossed over his chest, and his legs crossed at the ankles. He was smiling at Aubrey who was obviously inside the room.

"...seem no worse for wear, Irish. I would think that this confinement agreed with you." Black was saying.

"It has been boring but I try to find ways to entertain myself." Aubrey replied.

Black chuckled and said as he looked down at the floor, "Entertaining yourself."

"I have books to read and Mala is bringing me more." Came Aubrey's reply again.

"There are other ways to entertain, Irish. Has Morgan not..." He tormented her.

"We do not have that kind of relationship, Captain." She reminded him.

"Ah, I see." He said with a smile. Mala peeked around the corner again, saw his smile and clicked her tongue. Now why was he tormenting her like that, the fool. She thought. Deciding to save Aubrey from more of his torments, Mala took a few paces back then made her presence known before she came around the corner. Black had straightened and a stern look on his face replaced the smile from seconds ago.

"Rene, what are you doing here?" Mala asked innocently.

"You have been badgering me about Irish's, ah, Aubrey's welfare that I came to see for myself." He told her. Mala glanced into the cabin and found Aubrey standing near her bunk. She looked back up at Black who was reaching out to sweep her dark hair from the front of her shoulders to the back. With a last look at Aubrey, he said, "Well I leave you ladies to talk about me." Then he looked at Mala and added softly, "Be kind with your words, mon coeur."

"Never, you pirate." Mala said laughing as she stepped into the cabin. Leaving the door open for the little bit of cool air that wafted down the corridor, Black turned with a chuckle and headed for the main deck.

"What did Rene want?" Mala asked as she sat down and handed over the book.

431

Aubrey looked over the title and answered absentmindedly, "I have no idea."

Mala smiled as she glanced at the empty doorway. The man surprised her every now and then. Although he would never admit it, when he did nice things like this, Mala was challenged to find some way of rewarding him. He seemed to enjoy one thing in particular and no matter how hard Mala tried to reward him in other ways, making love always seemed to be the final outcome.

That evening, the full moon lit the darkened cabin brightly. Its light reflected off the tops of waves while in a far off distance, heat lightning intermittently flashed in the sky. After making love, Mala had moved from Black's side and now stood before the quarter gallery window looking out at the sea. He knew how she loved to look at the waves during the full moon.

He gazed at her naked slender body as she seemed to radiant in the moonlight and thought of the two years they had been apart. Never could he go through that again, he decided. Since boarding her ship and having her by his side where he could touch her, hold her and make love to her, Black knew Mala meant everything to him. He was not going to lose her again. He could not lose her again. He loved her beyond words. He had never said the words to her, but she knew—she had to know how he felt for her. His every touch for her, every kiss, every look had to tell her that. Mala noticed so much more around her than most people. How many times had he seen and experienced that she noticed everything and missed nothing? Her perception was so keen, so sharp so she had to know how he felt for her.

Getting up from the bunk, Black joined Mala at the window. He encircled his arms around her as she leaned back against him still watching the sea. Brushing his lips on her temple, he moved to sit on the ledge and pulled her down to sit with him. Mala leaned her back against him and his arms encircled her again. Her arms entwined with his as he held her, his thumb rubbing her upper arm. For sometime, they sat looking out at the sea and the sporadic flashes of lightning.

"Rene?" Mala whispered.

"Oui."

"You are not still tormenting Aubrey, are you?" She asked softly.

He took a deep breath and pressed his lips to her hair then whispered, "Let us not talk of her tonight, mon coeur."

He felt her silent laugh but she pressed on. "Rene." She whispered again the laughter quivering in her voice.

"Must we, Mala?" He asked but the laughter was in his voice as well.

"She has been confined for over a week…"

"I ordered one month. Let the subject drop." He reminded her.

"Rene, you had changed your order from the flogging to the confinement. Change it again." She insisted softly.

"If I had her flogged, I would have been shot and thrown overboard without a proper burial along with the last few of my men." He said feigning irritation. Mala caught his attempt and laughed. "I cannot change my orders so often. You know what that would do to my command."

Mala turned to face him. Her naked beauty was too tempting to resist and Black reached up to cup a breast, his thumb rubbing the darkened nipple.

"All is well then, I will just take over command." She stated with an air of nonchalance.

Black stopped his caressing and laughed heartily. His gaze took in Mala's feigned surprise as if she had been insulted. He reached for her and she melted into him. He played with her long dark hair as she laid against him, her cheek on his chest. He could feel the soft mounds of her breasts pressed against him as his desire for her became obvious.

Slowly, she lifted her head to look at him. Leaning forward to press a kiss to his lips, his arms tightened around her and he felt the overwhelming love for her take hold of him again. As she kissed his scarred cheek, Black could feel her body rise up and move over his as she straddled his hips. With one leg bent at the knee on the ledge and standing on the other, Mala lowered herself onto him as her lips found his once again. His hands guided her hips as she deepened the kiss and soon they moved rhythmically. As she kissed his face, he whispered her name over and over until he heard her moan of pleasure. Black found her lips with his and soon his own moan of pleasure was muffled within the kiss.

The next morning upon hearing a knock at the cabin door, Aubrey opened the door and found Rene Black standing outside. He smiled pleasantly at her stunned expression and asked, "May I come in?"

Surprised at his pleasant demeanor, she stepped aside without thinking. She felt apprehension when he shut the door behind him. Standing near the door, Black and Aubrey faced each other for a few long moments.

"Do not look so skittish, Irish, I do not bite." Aubrey giggled at his comment as she remembered her conversation with Mala on the beach outside of Charlestowne about how Black did not bite to make his mark.

"I am releasing you from your confinement." Black informed her as he moved further into the cabin.

"I wonder what Mala would say to your change in punishment for me." Aubrey said.

"It was Mala who convinced me that you have spent long enough in this cabin. You may resume your duties as of now." Black replied with a smile.

Aubrey caught his meaning and giggled again. "Merci, Rene and to Mala."

"Well as Mala and her crew had been so adamant the other night about your lack of knowledge to our ways, I suppose your time here has been sufficient. Besides, Thomas was going to die anyway."

"Because of what happened on the *Bellringer*." Aubrey stated quietly.

"I know Mala had her men hide him from me. I only dread the deed being done by her hand because she would have had to have been punished accordingly."

"She did give the order to find him first but she did not know where he was hidden, Rene. That much I know."

Black stared at her for a moment before asking, "You have been confined to quarters, so who told you all this? Alcott?"

Aubrey hesitated then shook her head negatively, "No, not Morgan." She hesitated again and Black waited patiently. She swallowed then said quietly, "Mala told me."

Black looked at the floor as Aubrey went on hurriedly, "Please do not be mad at her, Captain. She ordered him hidden but also ordered them that she was not to be told where he was so she could be truthful to you. You know that is her way. Besides, this is her ship and she is the captain." Aubrey cringed at her own bravery before this man. She wondered if she should have been so bold as he stared at her. Then he smiled pleasantly at her and, for the first time, Aubrey could see the handsomeness that Mala saw in him.

"I know, Irish. It would not have been like her to not take matters into her own hands. It was just fortunate that I was with Mala that night and she could not complete what she started."

Black and Aubrey stared at each other for another moment before he turned from her and said, "I think we could forego the formalities of calling me Captain. After all, you do not address Mala as Captain." As he opened the door and stepped out, he faced her again, "I think Willie has missed your company."

"Merci Rene." She said softly. He glanced at her and then he was gone. Aubrey shut the door in astonishment. What had just happened between them? He had actually been kind to her. Shrugging, she smiled as she tidied the cabin then left for the galley.

Since Black was visiting Deats, Mala had decided to see Aubrey earlier than usual. On her way to Morgan's cabin, she passed York. "Mornin', Cap'n." York greeted.

"Good morning, Mr. York." She greeted in return

434

"I was listening to some of Cap'n Black's men talking in French. I think it sounds really pretty but I ain't never been one for other languages."

"I could teach you a few phrases for the women at port. They would think you quite worldly having mastered the language with only a few words." Mala told him.

York's eyes lit up for a moment before he replied, "Thank ye, Cap'n, but I do good with what I speak now." Mala smiled at his reply as he turned to leave, "Guess I better be gettin' to my duties."

Still smiling, Mala shook her head and moved along the corridor. When she reached Morgan's cabin and prepared to knock, she froze. She heard voices within and one of them sounded deep like Black's.

"Do not look so skiddish, Irish, I do not bite." Mala heard him say then heard Aubrey giggling.

Suddenly Mala felt as though she could not breathe nor could she move. She could not make out any other words but their tones were friendly and pleasant. There was not the usual fear or hesitation in Aubrey's tone. Mala looked to the floor and felt a chill wash over her. The deep voice spoke again and there was another giggle from Aubrey. Mon Dieu! How could this be? Mala thought. He could not be left wanting! Unable to stand there any longer, Mala headed for the main deck.

Going directly to the railing, Mala placed her hands on it and leaned forward. She closed her eyes as she felt everything crashing into her at once. Her head was pounding and she could not catch her breath. It was as if her chest had a weight resting there. Her mind drifted back to that night on the *Widow Maker* when she gave herself to Rene Black, the first and only man to make love to her.

He carried her to the bunk when he realized her intentions. Apprehension and fear of the unknown gripped her but she wanted this and with him. With infinite care, Black touched her everywhere, making her aware of her own womanhood. Then he was there, lying over her, and gently caressing her as she opened for him. The initial pain as he took her virginity made her flinch with a gasp. Because she had been so bold with him, he was surprised to find she had not been with a man before and he was all the more gentle with her. When they had finished, his mouth took her left nipple and he teased it with his tongue. Then just above the nipple, he sucked on the skin until it made a reddened circle.

"What are you doing?" She had asked him.

He smiled and kissed the spot before answering, "Do not be frightened, ma petite, I do not bite."

Opening her eyes, Mala looked out at the sea. Surely she was imagining things. She tried to reason but her thoughts betrayed her. Black rose every

C. C. Colee

morning before sunrise and would leave the cabin. He told her that he was visiting Deats, but was that true? Morgan was on the early morning watch and that left Aubrey alone in the cabin. Pounding a fist on the railing, Mala fumed, he would not dare! Mon Dieu, he would not! Not on my ship and under my very nose!

Her gaze drifted to the companionway she just exited then bit her lip to keep from screaming out. Mala decided to go back to the cabin and think …and drink. She stepped away from the railing and headed for the aft companionway. She gave into the urge to take one last look at the opening for the companionway steps that led to Morgan's cabin. At that moment, Black appeared, adjusting the cuff on his sleeve. He stood on the deck and looked out at sea, breathing in the sea air and he smiled. His smile broadened as he looked at the deck, seemingly quite pleased with himself. Fury overwhelmed her as she watched him. Spinning around, Mala stormed to the companionway steps and fairly flew down them.

Black had slowly stepped from the companionway onto the main deck. He adjusted his sleeve idly as he thought of Mala's reaction to releasing Aubrey. His island beauty had been wonderful last evening and tonight the pleasure would be all the better. He imagined Mala's surprise as he would take her to the galley for the noon meal and she would find Aubrey there. He smiled, quite pleased with himself as he breathed deep the sea air to wash away the wanting he felt at that moment. He wanted to see her reaction to that surprise then have the noon meal taken to the great cabin. His gaze shifted to the deck and his smile widened as he thought of the meal growing cold and untouched.

A flutter of red caught the corner of his eye and Black glanced up to see Mala rushing down the aft companionway. He frowned wondering what her hurry was about and headed in that direction. She was not found in the great cabin nor was she in the galley.

As he turned to leave, Aubrey came around the corner into the galley. She smiled at Black as he asked, "Have you seen Mala?"

"Not from the direction I came." Aubrey replied.

Black stepped back allowing her to enter the galley and walked away as the crew announced their surprise of Aubrey's appearance. He went back to the main deck but still did not see Mala. Deciding that he would find her soon enough and hopefully before she saw Aubrey in the galley, Black turned back towards the lower decks.

His visits with Deats had been entertaining though at times exasperating. The Scotsman would talk of Mala's anger but not state more than that. It could be possible that Deats did not know anymore than Morgan did as to why Mala was angry as she wrote in her logbook. But the Scotsman's

436

wanting of Mala irritated Black. So he would visit the man each day only to gloat over his triumph for Mala's attentions. Whenever the night was unexpectedly pleasant, like last evening, Black would give the man more to think about and he would leave Deats angry. That pleased Black as well.

Mala was in the darkened storeroom so she could think. This would be one place he would not think to look for her. She decided not to go to the great cabin even though she would have dearly loved to pull down a bottle of her rum. She wanted to think but Black would have appeared and she did not want any interruptions. Sitting on the floor with her back against a stack of sacks, Mala stared at the entrance to the storeroom and let her mind race. What a fool she had been, she thought angrily. Damn, or even so blind! He had told Morgan when he put her in the hold with Aubrey that morning he boarded her ship, not to accost both his women. He would ply her with tender words and appear to scoff at Aubrey whenever she was near. He even called her Irish. Had that been his pet name for her when they were on the *Widow*?

Mala's head pounded with all the thoughts crashing together at once. Suddenly, Black walked past the storeroom and she remembered Morgan saying that Deats was held in the smuggler's hold. So was he finally going to pay Deats a visit? Standing, Mala made her way out of the storeroom. Seeing no one else in the corridor, she headed in the direction Black took.

Following Black, she realized that they neared where they had made love that first night he had released her from the hold. She neared the smuggling hold and now knew why they could not find Deats. She remembered how rope and other items were scattered about the corridor as if discarded and of no use to Black or his men. Now the area was cleared and the door was more visible than it was that night.

Mala watched as Black and the guard conversed quietly before the guard stepped to the corner as Black entered the small area. She peeked around the corner again to find the guard standing in the doorway watching the goings on inside. It took several minutes of Black's goading before Deats' voice could be heard.

"Ye filth!" Deats was saying, his Scottish accent giving away his true anger. "Mala was mine! It wouldna been long before she gave up on ye!"

"Really, Mr. Deats. That is becoming rather boring, saying the same thing each day. Since you had not had Mala in your bed all this time, why would you believe otherwise?"

"Because of your Irish whore, Aubrey Malone!"

"Ah, Irish. She is rather pretty, n'est-ce pas?" Black asked then added as if in retrospect, "She was quite a handful on the *Widow Maker*. But I must admit that she was definitely entertaining." Mala's mouth dropped open and her eyes widened in surprise at his word 'entertaining.'

"I dinna kin. My interest was and always is with Mala." Deats said.

"Well, Mala is mine." Black answered arrogantly.

"Just take the Irish wench and leave me with Mala. We were happy before Morgan came along and reminded her of ye and the past."

"Happy?" Black bellowed. Turning away from the Scotsman, Black raged on, "Happy? Did Mala caress you until you fairly screamed for release? Did she rub her soft body against you until you thought you would burn up from the heat of desire? You call what you had happy? I am happy, mon ami. But there too is the agony for Mala knows how to torment you with desire until you were sure that nothing else in the world mattered. You would promise her anything to get to that final release." It was quiet for a few moments before Black added the rub, "But then you could not get Mala into your bed, n'est-ce pas?"

Again, it was quiet until Mala heard Deats ask, "And Aubrey could not match Mala's passion?"

"Not even close!" Black barked out. "There were times when Aubrey would be just as soft and alluring then suddenly, I knew this was a different woman in my arms."

Deats looked at his nemesis and wished that Mala could hear him and his boasting. "Aye and she bears your mark."

Black looked at him as he remembered that fateful day. He had taken no other woman to his cabin since Mala and why he had chosen Aubrey still was not clear. But Deats believed that the mark was Black's sign of ownership in many ways. Why not let the man think what he wants, Black thought maliciously.

"Aye, the mark is as it has always been. I took from them then leave the mark for others to know as well. In many instances, I am their first and they learn well under me." Black boasted with a smile.

Had Aubrey seen that smile, she would have been reminded yet again that she was surrounded by pirates and would remember how cruel Rene Black could be. Had Mala seen that smile, she would have known that Black was playing another one of his tormenting games. But Mala could not and did not see the smile. She only heard the words and the words tore painfully deep into her heart. So Deats had been right all along! Aubrey had lied to her! Mala thought with long mournful sigh. And what was worse, Aubrey had gotten Morgan to believe in her lies wholeheartedly. The poor man really needed to get ashore before his befuddled mind was totally lost.

Their voices intruded upon Mala's thoughts as Deats said, "And Miss Malone learned well I suppose."

"You mean that you did not partake upon the Irish flower, either? I am sure many of the crew have done so."

"Only Morgan Alcott has had the Irish wench." Deats stated flatly.

"Oui, your sights were set on your captain." Black said with a slight rise to his brow and a shrug. The thought of this Scotsman's hands on Mala's soft body angered Black. It was with great effort for him to remain calm. He truly wanted to rip the Scotsman's heart out of his chest.

"You truly missed out, mon ami. Irish can be quite true to her nature, especially in the bed. Her nails are sharp and could cut you to pieces if not careful." Black said as he was reminded of Aubrey's fight to be released when he was trying to see how much she would assert herself against a man who tried to attack her. Black unconsciously rubbed his upper chest as if he could feel the sting of Aubrey's nails when she had raked him.

Mala closed her eyes to the exploding pain in her heart. She leaned against the wall to steady herself as a wave of nausea threatened to overtake her. Having bit her bottom lip so hard to keep the savage growl from being released, she could taste the blood. They had been caught together under her very nose and on her ship! Mala could barely breathe. Aubrey had lied! She had befriended her and told her things that Mala had never told another soul. And now, Aubrey and Black were laughing at her for they had tricked the feared Captain Mala!

With her mind reeling of ideas all at once, Mala whirled around and headed for the upper decks. She had to clear her head and think. But first things first—she was taking back her ship and now!

Chapter 50

Within the hour, Mala had regained the command of her ship. With a few of her men, she released Deats from his confinement then gathered her men together and captured all of those who boarded with Black. While Mala was below decks with her men, Deats rushed topside in search of his rival for Mala's heart. He wanted to take advantage of her preoccupation and knew what must be done. He also knew that it had to be done before she was even aware of it. Having stopped in his cabin to retrieve the one item he needed, Deats stepped up the companionway with purposeful strides.

On the main deck, he found Black, Boulet, LaVoie and Gibbs being held by a group of Mala's crew, among them was Aubrey and Morgan.

"String him up!" He ordered. Deats grabbed Black roughly from the group and shoved him towards the forecastle. The men hesitated, uncertain to the order and surprised to see him with his face red and contorted with rage.

"But Cap'n Mala says that..." One of the men began.

Deats pointed a finger at him and growled out, "Do as I say, damn ye!"

Morgan stepped forward and calmly started, "May I remind you..." Deats waved him off but Morgan ignored the gesture and continued louder, "Mr. Deats, Mala gave an order that..."

"Keep clear, ye traitorous bastard!" Tossing the rope to one of the men, Deats added, "Besides, she is in the process of takin' back her ship."

Watching Deats, Morgan was reminded of the attempt to do away with Black in the old tavern on Bimini. With a calm tone that Aubrey and Black recognized, Morgan said, "Deats, what you quest for will not sit well with Captain Mala. You will only bring disaster down upon yourself. You must..."

Ignoring Morgan, Deats yelled to the man, "I said, string him up." Stepping up to Black whose own anger was showing in the one-eyed glare, Deats felt a momentary pang of doubt as the captain stated calmly and, much conviction, "She will kill you for this."

Casting furtive glances at Morgan and Aubrey, a couple of the men did as Deats ordered. Black's hands were tied together in front of his body then hoisted over his head. As his arms were raised, Deats turned Black so that his back faced him. Taking the dirk from his waistband, the Scotsman cut a slit in the shirt then rent it in two.

"No, Mr. Deats." Aubrey cried out.

"Deats, you go too far!" Morgan added in outrage.

441

Ignoring them and the murmurs of the men present, Deats backed away and took the cat-o-nine that hung from his dagger sheath. He shook it out and with a snap of his wrist, the cat-o-nine cut into the air with a wicked sounding crack.

Black felt his blood run cold at the sound and forced himself to remain undaunted. Mala had faced this, endured the pain, and survived, he reminded himself. With the second crack, Black looked to Aubrey who let out a strangled sound from deep within her throat. Her eyes were filled with unshed tears as she looked between him and Deats, helpless to do anything. His attempt to reassure her with a small smile only made her bite her bottom lip as she fought to keep control.

All the while Morgan's rage took on new bounds. He had stormed towards Deats only to have the cat-o-nine turned in his direction. Quickly Morgan twisted his body away from the wicked instrument. "You crazy Scottish bastard!" He yelled.

Deats ignored the rest of the obscenities from Morgan as he drew back his arm for the next intimating crack. He felt his blood warm to the kill as well as to the anger that Black refused to flinch at the sounds of the cat-o-nine. He would feel it now, Deats thought with a smile as he drew back his arm for the first strike on bared skin.

Aubrey nearly jumped out of her skin each time the whip cracked the air. Each crack made her blink making the tears she fought so hard to keep back fall down her cheeks. She looked from the hatred on Deats' face to the blank expression on Black's face.

"Oh God!" She whispered as she saw the smile on Deats' face when the arm moved back for another swipe. She knew that this time Deats planned to hit Black with the cat-o-nine and she closed her eyes tight from the approaching strike. Black saw her reaction and prepared himself for the first blow.

"No!" Came a firm feminine voice from behind them all. Morgan quieted instantly as Aubrey's eyes flew open at the voice and Black closed his eye in relief. The men from both her crew and Black's turned and showed visible signs of relief at her appearance. Deats whirled around to face Mala who was walking slowly towards him.

"M-Mala! Ca-ca-captain!" Deats stammered. His face still red with anger, he tried to speak in calm tones, "I was takin' care of this prisoner."

"My order was that no one be harmed, Deats." Mala replied calmly as her eyes looked upon the quiet crowd on the deck. She noted the tears that Aubrey was frantically trying to wipe away, the uncommon reddening of Morgan's face, and the bared back of Rene Black. The close proximity of Aubrey to Black further angered Mala and the tears Aubrey shed for him was like a dagger that twisted in Mala's heart. Her dark eyes then returned to Deats.

While her eyes scanned the crowd, Deats spoke with the heavy accent that bespoke his inner rage, "Captain! This mon is responsible for ye and Miss Malone bein' in irons. He held yer men with ye as ransom, he took over yer ship...!"

"I know what happened, Deats, I was here." Mala stated calmly.

Black smiled knowing that tone of voice. Mala was not pleased that her order was ignored and that her calm outward appearance was not what she felt within.

"Captain! Such behavior must be made an example of..." Deats started.

"Not with that, Mr. Deats." Mala interrupted pointing to the cat-o-nine still dangling from the Scotsman's hand.

"But he must be punished for what he had doon ta ye and..." Deats pressed on as he pointed to Black with his empty hand.

"Not by the lash!" Mala shouted in the face of his obstinance, each word spoken slowly and distinctly as the air fairly crackled with her rage.

Deats retreated a step in the face of Mala's fury. He remembered too late that Mala hated, nay abhorred, the lash and would not use that type of punishment unless no other, absolutely no other, was available.

Mala's dark eyes fell on the crowd as she ordered in barely controlled anger, "Cut him down!"

There was much shuffling of feet as hands and knives went to the ropes. She watched as Black lowered his arms and turned to face her, rubbing his wrists from the ache. His eye met hers for a second before she turned her cold dark eyes on Deats. "Put him in chains below with the others." She ordered as Deats nodded.

As the Scotsman started to move away, she grabbed him by the front of his shirt and yanked him close to her face. Through clenched teeth as she still tried hard to control her temper, Mala added softly to Deats, "And he better not have a mark on him when I check on them later. Do you understand me, Mr. Deats?"

Deats nodded and she fairly tossed him away from her as she waited for her orders to be carried out. The seas seemed to calm and even the winds died down at the moment she spoke those words so that all on deck could hear. Somewhat stunned by her order that the prisoners were still to go unharmed, no one had moved. Her next outburst got all to move at once, "Now, damn it!"

Men scurried to their duties and escorted the prisoners past Mala to the hold below. Black kept his eye on her as he was taken away. He twisted oddly around as he tried to catch her eye. He knew that anger and, for some unknown reason, Mala was livid with rage and shaking from it. So livid that she had suddenly taken back her ship.

Mala had ignored Black as he was taken away. She stared angrily at Deats who watched Black's departure and did not bother to hide his small contemptuous smile. The smile quickly disappeared when the Scotsman glanced at Mala and found her watching him. He gave her a quick nod then followed Black to the hold, feeling her eyes on him until he disappeared below.

Sensing a movement beside her, Mala saw Morgan and Aubrey walking towards her. Morgan reached her side first and opened his mouth to speak, but Mala lifted a finger and spoke in a tone that stopped both of them in their tracks.

"Not a word from you!" Mala stated firmly, her anger still riding high. Turning her finger to point at Aubrey, she added, "And take her below. I do not want to look at her or see her roaming about my ship!" Morgan started to protest but Mala cut him off, "Morgan, it is either that or she is put in chains as well! Do you understand?" Both Morgan and Aubrey stared at Mala in disbelief. They cast a stunned look at each other then looked at the waiting woman pirate.

In a subdued voice, Morgan replied, "Aye Captain."

With that Mala stormed off toward the quarterdeck where Timmons watched her approach with apprehension. Morgan put a hand to Aubrey's elbow as he guided her away, "Come on, love. Tis best to humor her right now."

"But Morgan, I do not understand. What did I do?" Aubrey asked in disbelief.

With a shrug, he replied, "I do not know yet. I will find out what happened then make amends." Then with an exasperated sigh, he added, "Christ, making amends may be the easy part. Finding out what is wrong could be the hard part. In the meantime, tis best we humor her or she will put you in irons."

Morgan watched Mala that evening during the meal in the galley. She was not just angry, she was absolutely furious. Anyone who neared the table to engage her in conversation received only curt replies and knew quickly to leave her alone. As Mala finished her second bottle of rum, he moved to her table quickly and caught her hand as she raised the bottle to throw it at him. He took it from her forcefully and tossed it over his shoulder with a force that bespoke of his own anger. The galley grew quiet as Mala responded by standing and tossing the remains of her tankard in his face. He sputtered and coughed as he had opened his mouth to speak at the very moment the rum hit him. Recovering from that, the wind was knocked out of him when she punched him in the midsection.

Hunched over, Morgan was shoved away and he heard her growl, "Leave me the hell alone, Alcott!"

Still gasping for air, Morgan croaked, "What has happened to you, Mala?" Ignoring him, she looked around the galley to find all eyes on them. "You are not eating! Get back to your duties!" She bellowed out. The outburst, while in her present state of drunkenness, caused her to sit down rather quickly.

The men, however, took no chances and within minutes the galley was empty. Morgan had seated himself nearby still recovering from the blow. He eyed his captain angrily as she looked into her tankard expectantly before she set it down hard. "Willie, get another bottle!"

Even the old cook emerged from the cooking area hesitantly. As he neared Mala, Morgan grabbed the bottle from the old man. "Get yourself back to your cookstove." He ordered and the old man bid a hasty retreat beneath Mala's glare.

"You tempt me to shoot you, Alcott?" Mala asked quietly.

"No, of course not. But I..."

"Then give me the damn bottle!" Mala interrupted through clenched teeth.

The two glared at each other for a long moment. Finally, Morgan slammed the bottle down and said, "Fine! Drink yourself to oblivion, Mala! The only reason I know for this behavior is that it has something to do with Rene Black and..."

"And dear sweet Aubrey Malone." Mala sneered. "The 'poor lass,' as Willie would say, duped you, you besotted idiot!" Then with a laugh, the sound of which Morgan did not like, Mala added, "You have been trying to coax her into your bed and all the time she duped you with that sweet innocence."

Mala opened the bottle and filled her tankard as Morgan watched in disbelief. She lifted her tankard in a mocking toast to him then said with so much loathing that it surprised him, "You could have had her all this time, Mr. Alcott." After taking a long swallow of the rum, Mala added with a short laugh, "You men are no better than some rutting dog after a bitch in heat."

Aubrey took that most inopportune time to appear in the galley. Morgan followed Mala's drunken glare and decided to spare her from the captain's insults. He got up and quickly whisked Aubrey from the galley.

"Was Mala drunk?" She asked incredulously.

"Aye, and out of her mind." He grumbled. Aubrey sensed his anger and waited until they reached the deck and let the cool breeze calm Morgan.

After some time had passed, she asked him, "Did you find out anything?"

"Only that she is definitely angry with you for some reason but she was talking nonsense."

"About what?" She asked.

Morgan shook his head and impatiently waved his hand. "She is drunk and her mind is so disorientated, she is not making any sense."

Aubrey stared at him and could not think of anything to say. She was confused at her friend's reaction and why she was being for blamed for something. Morgan sensed her despair and took her hand in his. Giving a slight squeeze, he smiled as she looked at him. It was upon this scene that Deats appeared on deck behind Aubrey. Glancing over her shoulder, Morgan saw the Scotsman's smug smile.

Abruptly leaving Aubrey, Morgan stormed up to Deats as the Scotsman's smiled broadened. "What have you done?" He accused Deats.

"Morgan! Stop, Morgan!" Aubrey shrieked as she ran after him.

When Morgan approached, his fist struck Deats squarely on the chin. The Scotsman reeled back but regained his footing quickly and returned a blow to Morgan. Robert grabbed Aubrey before she was hit in the fray. The other men rallied around their champion as the two fought.

"Morgan! Deats! Stop this!" Aubrey screamed, stomping her small foot in anger. "Mala will kill you both for fighting!"

No one paid attention to her. She turned on Robert then, "Do something!"

"Miss Aubrey, this is..."

Aubrey grabbed his pistol from his waistband and, pointing it in the air, fired the round. That stopped the two in mid-blows as well as all eyes on deck looking at her in surprise. Some men ducked thinking that Captain Mala had appeared to intervene. Tossing the empty weapon aside, she grabbed the next man's pistol before anyone knew her move. She pointed the weapon, shifting it back and forth between Deats and Morgan.

Lowering his arm, Morgan said sternly to her, "Aubrey, put that down before someone gets hurt!"

"Step back, Morgan! or you will be the one who gets hurt!" Aubrey replied as she turned the weapon on him.

"Miss Malone..." Deats started but quieted when the pistol turned back on him.

"Miss Aubrey..." Robert tried but she ran away from the lot of them then turned and aimed the weapon at them all.

"Mr. Deats, you move to the quarterdeck now!" She ordered.

"I dinna take orders from ye!" The Scotsman retorted.

"Fine, then this ball will be for you. Either way this absurdity will end!" The crew held back since many of them had witnessed her training of weapons from Morgan and Captain Mala.

446

Morgan stepped away and slowly approached her. "You win, Aubrey. Take me below and help me with these bruises."

Aubrey stared at him and made no move to help him as he walked past her. He took a couple of steps and turned back to her, "I really need some help here."

Clicking her tongue, Aubrey dropped the pistol on the deck then put Morgan's arm over her shoulders so that he could lean on her. It took only a step for Aubrey to wonder why she thought she could support Morgan. She very nearly tripped as she reached the companionway and the two almost tumbled as they maneuvered down the steps.

"We will not make it back to the cabin, Morgan. I cannot support you." Aubrey wheezed. She was out of breath from the short distance already. The moment they were out of sight from the main deck, Morgan straightened and walked ahead a few paces perfectly fine.

Aubrey stood frozen in her spot as she stared open-mouthed at him. "Why you lousy..." She started angrily.

Morgan put his hand over her mouth but the momentum of the move knocked Aubrey against the wall. "Forgive me, Aubrey, I did not mean to do that." Morgan whispered.

She clawed his hand away from her mouth and hissed, "Then why did you?"

"I meant hitting the wall. But the bruises were just a ruse so I could leave the deck. I want to get to the galley and to Mala first."

He grabbed her hand and they hurried down the corridor to the galley. All the while, Aubrey called out his name. Finally reaching the galley, she yanked her hand from his grasp and said in a voice full of her Irish accent, "Now ya will be explainin' that silly ruse of yours, if ya please."

Morgan looked at her and smiled. The accent was evident and he knew that each step since he pulled her along only allowed time for that accent to become more pronounced.

"Aubrey, I just want to get my side of the story to Mala before Deats gets his version to her."

Aubrey thought back on how Deats lied to Black. There would be no telling what lies he managed to get Mala to believe. Her anger quickly disappeared and in a quieter, more controlled voice, she said, "Well, I can understand that."

Chapter 51

Mala was at her table, her head resting on an arm lying out on the table and other hand still holding her tankard.

"Good, she passed out." Morgan said as he went to Mala.

"Good?" Aubrey asked in surprise.

Willie stepped out from his cooking area and said, "I thought I heard voices. She has been that way only a few moments."

Morgan looked at his captain, her long dark hair trailing over edge of the table and some covering her face. He shook his head and looked at Aubrey.

"What could have been so terrible that she would drink herself like this?" Aubrey asked in disbelief.

Willie shrugged and replied, "Not sure, Miss Aubrey. She got like this when she returned from Bimini right, Mr. Alcott? Ye was with her. Boy, she was madder than a hornet then too. She was drunk all the way to Santiago de Cuba. Daft thing is she then makes us go back to Bimini."

It took Aubrey a few moments to realize the significance of what Willie had just said. Bimini! The last time they were at Bimini, the *Widow Maker* sank. But before that, Mala had told Aubrey about her encounter with Black in the old tavern. This did have something to do with Rene Black! And her?

Morgan was watching Aubrey and the various expressions that appeared on her face. Was it possible that Mala had confided in Aubrey the details of that trip in Bimini and why they went back to Bimini before reaching Santiago de Cuba? Shrugging and getting back to the matter at hand, Morgan said, "Well, we better get her to her cabin. I do not want the crew to see her this way." Carefully, he moved the tankard from Mala's hand. "Aubrey, you walk ahead of me and open the door to her cabin."

She nodded then watched as Morgan took Mala by the shoulder and leaned her back in her chair. He scooped her up in his arms and, as directed, Aubrey walked ahead as they left the galley.

Willie went back to his cooking, shaking his head, "Wonder what is botherin' the Cap'n this time."

In Mala's cabin, Morgan laid his captain down gently on her bunk and started taking off her boots but Aubrey pushed him away, "Let me do that."

Morgan smiled but said as he moved to a nearly chair and allowed Aubrey do the task, "She hardly weighs a feather."

Morgan saw a smile peep through Aubrey's concentration when suddenly Mala's arm came up and nearly hit Aubrey. Morgan jumped up but before he could reach her, Mala swung with her other arm. This time it connected and

449

knocked Aubrey onto her backside. The momentum of the blow pulled the drunken Mala from her bunk and onto the floor beside Aubrey, unconscious again.

"Sweet Mary!" Aubrey said as she covered her sore cheek and looked down at the besotted Mala.

"Damn!" Morgan exclaimed as he reached Aubrey. "Are you all right?"

"Aye, for someone who is drunk, she certainly has strength." Aubrey grumbled. Morgan chuckled and helped Aubrey to her feet then guided her to the chair he just vacated.

"I guess I should be taking off her boots." He said as he looked at her cheek. He then went to the washbasin to dampen a cloth with the cool water. Returning to Aubrey, he pressed the wet cloth to her cheek. Flinching from pain as he applied the wet cloth, she decided to take the cloth from him. He chuckled as she glared at him holding the cloth to her sore cheek.

Morgan turned to lift Mala back up into her bunk and took off her boots in quick order. He took the covering from the far corner and draped it over his captain. When he returned to Aubrey, he took her hand and said as they rose to leave, "She will sleep for now."

At that moment there was a knock and the door opened simultaneously. Deats was surprised to find Aubrey and Morgan in the captain's cabin. "What the hell are ye doin' in here?" He asked angrily.

"Be quiet! The Captain is resting." Morgan hissed. Deats moved to the bunk and found Mala within, fully clothed.

"She is drunk again." He said as if to himself.

Morgan did not like the look on the Scotsman's face as his gaze roamed over the unconscious Mala.

"I suggest we leave her be. Her mood will be sour enough when she awakens." Morgan said as he waited for Deats to leave.

"Aye, then leave. I will make an entry in the log."

Morgan looked to Mala's desk and found the logbook sitting on top. The logbook! That would explain her mood. The events would be in her logbook! Not wanting Deats to read the logbook or leave him alone with Mala, Morgan said, "You have never made an entry in there before. She will not like it that you..."

"Do not presume ta dictate my status on this ship, Mr. Alcott." Deats said in heavy Scottish accent that bespoke of his irritation. "What I decide ta do as quartermaster is none of yer concern."

"It is my concern when your decisions jeopardize the smooth running of this ship." Morgan countered.

"Ye are out of line, Mr. Alcott. I will be speakin' ta the Captain of yer behavior. Ye may leave."

The two glared at each other as Aubrey continued to watch and listen. Seeing that Morgan was reluctant to leave Deats in the cabin, Aubrey had an idea.

"Well, ya both will be leavin' now. The Captain will wake up from all the ruckus the two of ya are makin' and that would definitely set her mood to foul." She told them.

"Ye are no position ta give orders, Miss Malone..."

As Aubrey predicted, the voices were penetrating Mala's drunken state as she stirred and murmured incoherently. Deats moved away from the desk quickly as he watched the woman in the bunk. He knew how fiercely protective she was of her logbooks and the information written within.

"Now if ya gentlemen will please not shut the door as loud as your voices have carried, I know Captain Mala would greatly appreciate it." Aubrey stated as she indicated the door with her outstretched arm.

Deats glared at her for a long time before he stormed from the cabin. He stopped just outside the door and waited for Morgan who stepped up to her with a smile.

"The logbook will tell us what happened. Check for information in the last few days." He whispered while he leaned close as if to kiss her cheek.

Aubrey looked at him then to Deats who had a strange smile on his face. She whispered back, "I will." Then more loudly for Deats to hear and with a sweet smile to play out the ruse of lovers, she said, "Now go with ya, Mr. Alcott."

After the men left, Aubrey eyed the desk and the logbook that sat on top of it. There was the key to the mystery of Mala's anger. She sat at the long table and stared at her friend as so many things ran through her mind. She remembered how Mala had taught her to climb the ratlines and reach the crow's nest. The height on the swaying ship was stomach-retching but Mala had managed to get Aubrey to see the beauty of the vast ocean that was laid out before them while Morgan could not get Aubrey to look over the point during the last careening.

Aubrey also remembered how Mala and Morgan taught her to throw daggers, shoot a pistol and sword fight against two opponents. Mala had joined in the swordplay one day and was pleased with Aubrey's defensive tactics against two. She had learned so much from Morgan and Mala in such a short time and could well understand now the thrill of adventure pirating carried.

Mala stirred bringing Aubrey back to the present. She watched as Mala drifted back into sleep for a few moments before moving to the desk and opening the logbook. She remembered another time when she opened a logbook to learn French. She could hear Jean Luc's voice as he told her later

451

not to read the books anymore. *'Do not let the captain know that you have been in the logs. He is very protective of his logbooks and his privacy.'*

Aubrey's heart grew heavy hearing his voice in her mind. She closed her eyes tight and she saw Jean Luc smiling at her. A sob escaped as she covered her face with her hands. I miss you, Jean Luc, her mind screamed out.

Opening her eyes, Aubrey's vision was blurred with tears. Quickly she wiped them away and focused on the entries in the book. Going to the last entry, Aubrey scanned it backwards as quickly as she could. Finally she found an entry in which Mala noted the retaking of her ship. Turning the page back one, she found the entry she was looking for. With a gasp, she straightened and looked up at the sleeping Mala. With wide eyes, Aubrey read the entry again.

He lied to me as he laid with me. She lied to me all the while trying to be my friend. The mark is true! She was and still is his whore. He had her. They were lovers on the Widow. Lovers! Mon Dieu, but I am a fool! Well damn them both for their deception. I will never trust them or anyone again. No more lies! Yet, tis no more than I deserve for allowing myself to be her friend and allowing Rene back into my life. I heard Rene bragging to Deats this morning about his time with her on the Widow. And the two of them together on my ship. My ship! He had gone to her in secret. I am such a fool! A fool! But no more.

Aubrey looked up at the woman in the bunk. Shaking her head in disbelief as she stared at the words once again, she muttered, "It is all wrong, Mala. This is all wrong!"

Aubrey read the remaining passages in order this time. She read Mala's account of the retaking of her ship and the capture of Black and his men. There was a small note of Deats' attempt to have Black flogged:

Deats cannot be trusted either. Against my order that no one was to be harmed while retaking my ship, Deats was about to have Rene flogged. The Scottish bastard is uncontrollable especially where Rene is concerned. I will have to watch Deats and his treatment of the prisoners.

Aubrey was amazed that Mala would be concerned for Black's welfare even though she was angry earlier. Then she remembered their conversation the day before when Mala told of her feelings for him, *'Aye, more so now that he is here with me.'* Aubrey wondered on the fact that no matter how angry

Mala may be with Black, her love for him would not allow him to be harmed by her hand or by anyone else's.

Mala stirred again and murmured in a language Aubrey could not understand however, she recognized a name—Baccus. Aubrey felt the tears again at the thought of Mala dreaming of her child. She moved away from the desk and sat at the table. Crossing her arms on the table, Aubrey rested her head on her arms while looking at the sleeping Mala. Could she have survived all that Mala had suffered through if it happened to her? Aubrey wondered.

A sound from the bunk startled Aubrey awake. Her head shot up expecting to find Mala awake and glaring at her but Mala was still asleep though the covers were tossed off. She glanced out the quarter gallery window and found that it was nearly dawn. The sky was beginning to lighten in soft pink and purple hues.

"Sweet Mary, have I slept all night?" Aubrey asked aloud. She quietly stood up then made her way back to her own quarters.

Morgan jolted awake with a sound. He listened as a foot scraped along the floor and Aubrey whispered to herself, "Where is my bunk?"

She nearly jumped out of her skin when she heard the reply, "Where you left it, silly."

"Sweet Mary!" She fairly squeaked. "Ya gave me such a fright, Morgan Alcott!"

Aubrey could almost see his smile as he replied, "I could have remained quiet and you may have mistaken my bunk for yours, me darlin.'"

She followed the voice then swung her arm out, backhanding him in the ribs. She smiled in satisfaction as Morgan suddenly let out a soft yelp, saying, "How come you hit me but cannot manage to find your bunk?"

"Because you talk too much."

He chuckled as he heard her settle on her bunk. He stood up then and moved to lantern. Aubrey heard the strike of the flint and let out an exaggerated sigh of annoyance. She flounced onto her side and Morgan moved to stand over her.

"What is it, Morgan? I want to sleep."

"Tis time I wake up anyway."

"Fine you wake up, I am sleeping." Morgan chuckled again as he sat on the edge of her bunk. Aubrey let out another sigh as she turned.

"Morgan, I am trying to sleep." Aubrey saw Morgan's smile quickly disappear. "What is it?" She asked as he took her by the chin and made her face him.

"What the hell happened to your eye?" Morgan asked in deep concern.

Carefully touching her right eye, she winced. She and Morgan replied in unison, "Mala."

"Does it look that bad?" Aubrey asked as she rose to look in the mirror. "I cannot be seen looking like this!" She fairly wailed. She remembered the times her abusive uncle struck out and she had to remain hidden in her room for days.

Morgan wet a cloth and after squeezing the excess water, he handed it to Aubrey, "I will check with Willie for another remedy. In the meantime, use this."

"That will not do a bit of good, Morgan." Aubrey said looking at the cloth.

Morgan took her hand and placed the cloth in it. "Just take the damned thing." He said tormenting her further in her Irish accent. "Lie down while I find Willie."

Aubrey moved to her bunk and did as he stated. As she got comfortable with Morgan's help, she looked up at him with her good eye, and said, "I found the answers in logbook like you suspected." Morgan stopped tucking the blankets around her as she held the cloth to her eye. "She thinks Rene and I lied about the mark on me and that Deats was telling the truth all along. She thinks that Rene and I have been together on the *Widow Maker*."

Morgan sat slowly on her bunk, surprise etched on his face. "Why would she believe that now? Deats has been held prisoner since Black came on board."

Aubrey looked at Morgan and said in a small voice, "She overheard Rene bragging to Deats this morning, ah, rather, yesterday morning."

Morgan straightened up, shocked at her words, asked, "What?"

"That was what she wrote, Morgan. Rene was bragging. Why would he do that?"

There was silence in the cabin as Aubrey watched Morgan who was staring into space. After a few moments, Morgan faced her saying, "It just does not make sense, Aubrey. Why would Black say things like that when Mala could overhear—them—talking." The last three words were spoken slowly as a thought struck him.

"Mala did not even care where Deats was held. But she wrote that she had overheard them talking?" He asked trying to keep things straight in his mind. Aubrey nodded but her face showed confusion. Morgan smiled down at her, "She followed Black without him knowing. Deats has wanted Mala as long as I have been on this ship and most of the crew knows it. Many times, he nearly succeeded in talking Mala into killing Black. She very nearly did in Bimini. I am sure that Deats has let the fact be known that he also desires his captain. Knowing Rene Black as I do, he would torment Deats with his closeness to Mala."

Following his thought, Aubrey's eyes lit up and she added, "So whatever Deats thought about my role on the *Widow Maker*, Black tormented him by letting him think he had any woman he wanted while Deats could not even get one certain woman into his bed."

Morgan smiled and nodded in agreement. Aubrey nodded also as she said, "Only Black did not know that Mala could hear them."

"Precisely." Morgan said smiling.

Aubrey hesitated a bit making Morgan ask, "There is more?"

She nodded and said quietly, "Somehow Mala thinks that Rene and I are still lovers."

"What?" Morgan exclaimed.

"I do not how or why she would think that!" Aubrey exclaimed.

"Black has taken no interest in you since coming on board for Christ's sake. Mala was all he wanted!" He paused to think then looked at her. "Was there a time when Black was with you that would have looked...intimate?"

"No! He has avoided me!"

Suddenly she frowned and he leaned closer to her, "What? What do you remember?"

"Well, yesterday morning he came here to tell me that he was releasing me."

"Did you see Mala?" Morgan asked, prompting her.

"No, Rene came in here and closed the door. I remember being afraid that he might hurt me again. However, he was just telling me that..."

"That is it then!" Morgan exclaimed as he began to pace in the small cabin. Aubrey fell silent as she watched him think his thought through. Turning suddenly to face her, Morgan said excitedly, "Mala must have come by then. She must have overheard your voices in here and with the closed door..." He ended with a shrug.

"Oh my God!" Aubrey said in horror.

Morgan took her by the shoulders and said in a calm voice that he did not feel, "Now do not worry. Somehow I will fix this."

"Morgan, please. She must be made to see, to understand!" Aubrey pleaded.

"I know, but for now I need to get Willie."

Then in a swift motion that caught Aubrey by surprise, Morgan placed his hands on each side of her face and placed a kiss on her lips. With a quick smile, glad to know what was bothering his captain, he straightened and left the cabin.

When Morgan left, Aubrey tried not to dwell on the kiss and turned her thoughts to the stories Deats had told Mala for her to believe him now. She began to pace as Morgan had done just moments before while her mind raced.

What could Black have bragged to Deats that would make Mala believe all of Deats' lies? How would Morgan convince Mala that her thinking was wrong and to trust in Black again?

Chapter 52

It did not take long to tend to Aubrey's eye and with a firm order from both men to sleep for as long as she liked, Morgan and Willie left the cabin.

"I have the brew ready for the captain. Would you take it her?" Willie asked of Morgan as they headed for the galley.

"She hates that stuff." Morgan said with a smile.

"Aye, and when she stops her drinkin,' the brew stops brewin.'" Willie replied.

A few moments later, Morgan was leaving the galley with a mug of hot liquid and headed for the captain's cabin. He met Mala as she unsteadily made her way in direction of the galley.

"I have this with Willie's compliments." Morgan said brightly. He noticed her wince and nearly smiled but thought better of it. "The galley is too loud this morning, Captain." He added when Mala took another step in that direction.

At the moment, boisterous laughter erupted from that area of the corridor and Mala winced again. Morgan was hard pressed not to laugh or even smile. Thankfully, he did not have to give other reasons as the ruckus was enough to change Mala's mind and she turned to go back to her cabin. Morgan smiled as he thought of how she would do this to herself each time Black crossed her path. She could not stay angry with the man for long even with Deats' best attempts and since Black boarded the *Enchantress*, Mala had changed to the woman he once knew.

Finally reaching her cabin, Mala sank into the first seat she could reach. Morgan closed the door as softly as he could then placed the mug on the table before her. He purposely pushed the mug under her nose as she rubbed her temples once again.

"Drink this. It will help the headache."

Mala looked at it and made a face of disdain. "You know, I hate this brew."

"Be a good girl and take your medicine. If you did not drink so much, then you would not have to take this brew so often." Morgan said with a pleasant smile.

She glared at him for the reminder of her penchant to drink her problems away. His smile never wavered as she looked down into the steaming mug. After several moments, Morgan placed her hands around the mug and she graced him with another glare.

"Drink it, Mala. You know you will feel better afterwards." He watched her as she took a sip. She made another face as she lowered the mug to the table. They were both startled at the loud knock on her door. Morgan looked at Mala who had her eyes painfully shut and let out a slow groan.

Standing, Morgan opened the door to find Deats with a smile frozen on his face. Pushing the door further making Morgan step back, the Scotsman entered the cabin. Dressed in his usual attire of late, which was in total black, he greeted Mala, "Good mornin', Captain."

To Mala, his Scottish accent was more boisterous than usual. He took the seat Morgan had just vacated and looked at his captain. She was once again rubbing her temples as Deats saw the mug, and with disgust underlying in his voice, he said, "Christ, Mala, not again. Must ye do this each time ye..."

"Be quiet, Deats!" She growled. Holding her head in her hands, she poised her face over the rising steam of the brew and grunted quietly in pain.

"He is no' worth this punishment ye do ta yerself!" Deats scolded.

Morgan saw Mala slowly raise her head to look at Deats incredulously for his outburst. Realizing that the man had no concern for Mala's ailment, Morgan stepped forward and took the Scotsman roughly by the arm.

"Mr. Alcott!" He bellowed, stunned at Morgan's total disregard for him and his position as quartermaster.

Ignoring him, Morgan opened the door and unceremoniously shoved the Scotsman into the corridor. Deats turned around only to have the door slammed in his face. His hand reached for the latch just as the bolt slid into place on the other side. Deats was furious. The insolent cur, he thought as he glared at the door. He had the urge to slam his fist against the wooden plank but thought better of it. Mala was not well and she would retaliate. Instead the Scotsman stormed down the corridor then up the companionway towards the deck.

Resuming his seat, Mala grinned at him and said, "Thank you, Morgan." He smiled and whispered, "Aye, it did feel good."

Mala took another sip from the mug then another before lowering back onto the table. "I really do hate this brew." She grumbled.

Morgan was quiet for a moment before he ventured to say, "Will you tell me what has happened this time?"

Mala crossed her arms on the table then rested her head on them. Morgan waited patiently, hoping she would talk to him. He could not let her know that he already knew what was wrong as he cast a glance to the logbook on her desk. It was closed and looked like it was undisturbed. His attention was drawn back to Mala as she informed him, her voice muffled, "You and Deats are right. I should not do this to myself." She raised her head slowly and gazed into Morgan's caring blue eyes. "But Morgan..." She started, her gaze moved to the window. "I do not know who to trust or what to believe anymore."

Morgan waited a few moments but she said nothing more. "I would not trust Deats, Mala. He cares only for himself." She looked at him as he continued, "Deats is always watching you and the desire is so evident on his face that any idiot would know what the man wants from you. But then what happens? He would have his fill and toss you aside. But Black was always very..."

Mala turned away from him in disgust at the mention of the name. Morgan's voice grew louder as he tried to keep her attention, "No, you have to see this from Black's side, Mala. He..."

He was surprised when Mala turned on him, "See this from Rene's side? Morgan, I was supposed to be his last one! The last one he marked, or so he had me to believe! Then we pluck from the ocean another woman who was my age when Rene marked me! So what am I to believe? Tell me for I have no clue!"

Morgan sat back against the high-backed chair as she went on her tirade. When it was quiet, he looked down at the table and began to trace imaginary circles. Without looking up, he asked, "So this is about Black? Why now, Mala?"

"No, this is not about him." Mala growled then corrected herself. "Yes, it is about him."

He traced more circles still not meeting her gaze as he went on, "So this is about Aubrey? She was never touched by..." Looking up at Mala as she snorted derisively, Morgan stopped making circles and leaned forward, "So what are you telling me? The two of them are lovers? Who is saying they have been together?"

She gave him a look of pure venom as she hissed, "Rene."

He stared at her then asked, "He told you this?"

Mala flew back against her chair and looked at Morgan as if he had grown horns. "No, you ass! He wants me to believe that he never bedded her!"

"So you no longer believe him? Who would he confide such a secret?" Mala was silent as she closed her eyes against the intense pounding in her head. When she let out a slow exhale, Morgan pushed the mug slightly towards her, a subtle reminder of her medicine. She grimaced but picked up the mug and drank down the entire contents.

"Come and lie down." Morgan suggested as he stood up. When Mala did not move, Morgan sat down again and stated, "I believe you are being duped. But I do not think that it is Black or Aubrey. She pines for Jean Luc and you have seen for yourself that she is afraid of Black since he boarded this ship."

Mala looked at him hard and Morgan let out a loud sigh. "You should have heard him that day in Charlestowne, Mala. He was firm about his intent to board this ship. I swear to you, Rene Black boarded this ship for you and only you. He was not going to let you leave Charlestowne without him. I think that he intended to kill Deats in the attack but had apparently changed his mind. You know that there is no love lost between Deats and myself. But as your friend, Mala, and we have known each other for some time, I would not believe a damned thing that Scotsman had to say. If he insisted that the sky was blue, I would still argue with him."

Mala showed a small smile for she knew full well that the two men totally disliked the other. But Morgan went on, "You also know Jean Luc. If he cared for Aubrey as she claims, does it not sound like him to do as she described in order to save her from being taken by Black? I think so. We are brothers and, true, we are very different in many ways, but when we care for someone, we will make every effort to protect that person from any harm." Morgan leaned forward and said meaningfully, "Or die trying."

"You have made your point, Morgan."

He sighed in relief. "Then please talk with Aubrey. If Deats is in some way involved in your anger towards Black or Aubrey or both, I would reconsider everything very carefully. You are very good at thinking something through and seeing something we missed—which is quite often, I might add." Morgan finished with a smile.

Mala smiled at him then nodded. "Very well, Morgan. I will ponder on this but with a clear head. If you will see to the ship while I rest, I would appreciate it. Also, you may need to be careful around Deats. You were not gentle in your diplomacy earlier. He is not likely to forget it and you can be sure that you will not be forgiven."

Standing as he was being dismissed, Morgan flashed her his most winning smile, "I am never forgiven anyway. So what have I lost?"

Mala chuckled then winced as her head reminded her of the drink from the night before. Morgan left the cabin after seeing that Mala was comfortable in her bunk. That made twice this morning he put a woman he cared deeply for to bed.

Entering the galley, Riley informed Morgan that Deats was looking for him. Smiling, Morgan sat down catching Aubrey's eye and, with a dismissive wave, he replied, "He can wait. I am hungry." Riley chuckled and joined him for breakfast.

An hour later, Morgan emerged to the main deck. He looked over the vast ocean and found clear waters all around. He looked up and found little wind in the sails. Suddenly he was grabbed from behind and whirled around to face an angry Deats.

"Yer attitude will no longer be tolerated, Mr. Alcott. Ye are relieved as First Mate and confined ta quarters." Deats waved his hand, summoning two men forward. "Escort Mr. Alcott ta his cabin and stand guard. He canna leave his cabin unless I give the order."

Morgan smiled at the Scotsman's indignation and without a word, allowed himself to be escorted off the deck. Below deck, one of his guards, a man named Green, said apologetically, "Sorry, Morgan, but he was bitin' at the bit waitin' on ye to come up on deck."

Morgan laughed lightly and replied, "Not to worry. I am considering this as a day off. I will relax and sleep all day, if I can."

The other guard, Hudson, chuckled, "If Mr. Deats really wanted to punish ye, he shoulda had ye confined to his side. Havin' to listen to him all day would drive any man to madness. Tis a wonder the Captain ain't shot Mr. Deats for his attitude."

"Aye and tryin' to whip Cap'n Black 'gainst the Cap'n's orders like that. If ye asked me, Deats shoulda been drawn and quartered." Green added. Morgan laughed in merriment as they reached his cabin.

"Thank you so much, gentlemen. Now if you would ward off any undesirables from my door so I could rest, you would not only receive the full appreciation of the former First Mate and Master Gunner, but you would be following orders." Morgan smiled then shut the door from any further intrusion. Mala would have him out of here soon enough, he thought. She will sleep a while then hear what has happened, and, poof, he would be released for good behavior.

Hours later, Aubrey came into the cabin and stood over Morgan as he laid on his bunk with his hands clasped behind his head as he stared up to the ceiling. She literally dropped his plate of the noon meal on his chest.

"Proud of yourself, I see." She said, her accent riding high. "And what have ya done this time to allow ya to be laggin' about like this?"

Morgan smiled and replied, "I tossed Deats from Mala's cabin and it felt good." Aubrey giggled over the manner of Morgan's reply. He was definitely proud of himself.

"Well Deats is struttin' about like some new rooster in a hen house."

Morgan laughed aloud and rose up on one elbow, "Where in the world have you heard something like that?"

"Willie said that earlier." She giggled again then wrinkling her nose, she added, "Sounds rather..."

"Silly." Morgan finished for her.

Aubrey squeaked through another giggle before she turned to leave. "Well I better go back. I stayed below decks so that Deats would not see me. He also wants you to starve to death."

"Aubrey, make sure the prisoners are getting fed." Morgan said as she headed for the door.

461

"They have already." She replied.

Morgan smiled knowing that at least no other harm affected the prisoners. When Mala calmed down, they would be released as well. He sat up and ate his meal before relaxing again.

Sometime later, Morgan was about to doze off when the closing of the door brought him to full wakefulness. He lifted his head and turned to see who had entered. It was Deats leaning against the door. Morgan eyed him and said, "I do not remember hearing a knock. Even Mala will knock."

Deats shrugged and said as he gazed about the cabin, "I guess ye were dozin' and dinna hear it."

"You cannot even lie very good." Morgan sneered as he stood up.

Deats' head snapped around to Morgan and he advanced on him until he was fairly nose to nose with the sandy-haired man, "I have spoken ta the Captain aboot yer recent behavior. Ye are ta join the other prisoners for yer traitorous part in the boarding of the *Enchantress*." Deats watched Morgan's eyes for any sign of trepidation or any emotion. "Perhaps ye will enjoy the small space I called home these long weeks while ye made plans with yer traitor crewmen and that..."

Morgan smiled at him and asked, cutting him short, "You talked with the Captain? Captain Mala?"

"Of course Mala. I recognize no other captain on board this ship. Ye fools may follow the half-blinded madman but I..."

"Deats, what is going on here?" Mala asked from behind him.

Deats whirled around to face a sober Captain Mala. He was sure she would be in her cabin for the rest of the day but instead she was up and around, no doubt by some informant.

"It dawned on me, Captain, that Mr. Alcott should be with the other prisoners for his part in allowin' escaped criminals aboard yer ship." Deats did not see the smile on Morgan's face at being caught in a lie. Apparently the Scotsman had not talked with Mala, Morgan thought.

Mala stepped in to the cabin, stopping only when she reached Deats and looked up into his eyes. "By what right do you make such decisions, Mr. Deats?"

"As quartermaster of the *Enchantress*, it is my duty ta protect the crew as well as my captain."

Mala stared at him for a long time before she ordered, "Return to your post, Mr. Deats. Green, Hudson, you may go as well." The two men left immediately but Deats was slow in leaving. "Do you have a question, Mr. Deats?"

"Nay, Captain. I just..."

"Then get out." Mala said quietly.

Without another word, Deats stormed from the cabin. He had hoped to take Morgan to his prison and beat him senseless then blame it on the other prisoners when Morgan appeared within their midst.

Mala turned to Morgan and asked, "How long have you been confined to quarters?"

"Since breakfast this morning. I thought you would be, ah, resting all day. How did you …never mind, you would not tell me even if I asked." Morgan said with a shake of his head.

Mala smiled and said, "Return to your post, Mr. Alcott."

"Aye Captain."

Several hours later, Mala stood in her cabin and was looking out of the quarter gallery window, thinking. The darkening skies went unnoticed as she thought of the day's events. Deats was becoming obsessive with his madness over Morgan and Black. What should she do to bring the Scotsman back in line? Her mind reeled with possibilities and most of them would likely suit the crew as well. She was still pondering her problem when there was a knock at the door.

When she bade entry, Mala turned from the window and moved to her chair at the table. She watched as Morgan held the door open for Aubrey to enter first. Noticing her apprehension, he escorted her to the chair at Mala's right and held it out for her to sit but Aubrey only stood beside it and would not sit down as she looked at Mala. Morgan also noticed what she was doing and looked to Mala to see her smile before taking her seat. Aubrey then followed suit before Morgan took the seat beside her.

Sitting in her chair with one hand dangling over the arm while resting her chin in her other hand, Mala studied Aubrey's black eye. She had heard the story from Morgan although she was still skeptical. Morgan smiled as he watched his captain then decided to start the conversation, "You seem in better spirits now after you have rested." Mala shifted her eyes from Aubrey to Morgan who smiled at her. She did not comment as her gaze returned to the silent and fidgeting Aubrey.

"Morgan tells me that I should talk to you." Mala began. Aubrey looked at Morgan accusingly but he only smiled at her. "That tale you told on the beach that day, how much of it was true?"

"All of it is true. I hate Rene Black for all that has happened to me and especially for this mark I must bear for all eternity." Aubrey stated indignantly.

"The intent of the mark is to tell other men that he had you first. Yet you want me to believe differently?" Mala questioned with a raised brow.

"Yes, Mala." Aubrey nearly whined.

"Jean Luc was your lover and not Rene?" Mala asked.

463

Aubrey blushed at the reference of lover and nodded. "I have never been with Rene Black in that way—ever." Aubrey said emphatically.

"Then you may want to explain how Rene would know that your nails would cut him into pieces if he was not careful with you in bed? That would give credence to his statement that the mark means what it has always meant." Aubrey's mouth dropped open as she stared incredulously at Mala who stared back at her unsmiling. Morgan was even looking at Aubrey in surprise.

Caught off guard with the remark, Aubrey blurted out, "Well then he was lyin', Mala! My nails accidentally scratched him when he tormented me one day. He held me down and feigned an attacker to see how I would react." She stared at the dark-haired woman willing her to believe what she was saying. Then her brows knitted together as a thought hit her. Aubrey began slowly as she tried to explain her thinking,

"What if Rene spoke the truth but not really?"

"Aubrey you cannot lie and tell the truth in the same sentence." Morgan said.

"No wait listen to me. If you think of what Rene said and not what it was supposed to mean…"

Morgan chuckled and admonished her, "Aubrey, that does not make sense."

"I did scratch him but not in the way he meant. Umm, I can say…" Aubrey tried to think of an example.

Morgan opened his mouth to speak but Mala held up her hand and said softly, "Let her speak, Morgan."

The two sat quietly for a few moments when finally, Aubrey became excited as she thought of an example that made sense, "Here listen to this, I can say, I bunk with Morgan. But that does not mean, I—bunk—with—Morgan."

Mala stared at Aubrey who sat patiently waiting for the dark-haired woman to understand the meaning. It did not take long for Mala to understand how the same words spoken in another tone would make a difference.

Morgan leaned forward and looking pointedly at Mala, asked, "What were Black's words exactly?"

Mala was thinking that very same question. What exactly did he say to Deats? She looked up to find two pairs of eyes waiting expectedly. Shrugging, Mala consented to Aubrey's argument. "Very well, I see your point. Rene does have a penchant of turning things around without really lying. He can be such a bastard when he does that." Morgan smiled at her comment as Aubrey sighed in relief.

"I apologize Aubrey for my behavior yesterday as well as for your eye. My anger and drinking will be my downfall, I fear."

"Mala, I could never lie to you. To tell you the truth, there were times when you scare me more than Rene Black. Those first days and weeks on the *Enchantress*, I saw you as the woman version of Rene." Aubrey confessed.

Morgan laughed aloud at the confession. Giving him a perturbed glare, Mala turned a smile to Aubrey who grinned as she realized all she had said. Suddenly she realized that Mala and Morgan had become the closest to family she had ever felt since the death of her parents.

Chapter 53

At daybreak, Black was moved to another area within the bowels of the *Enchantress*. One of the guards, Manning, had told him that it was the captain's orders and nothing more. Still in chains and his arms over his head, Black was alone in his captivity as Manning and the other guard, Porter, stood outside the open doorway.

He had spent nearly two days corralled with his men and was left to wonder what had happened. Why did Mala take her ship back? Why now? Black had wondered too many times to count. His men had questioned him for what seemed an eternity, though he had no answers.

"Should not have trusted a woman, Captain." Boulet had said in French. With a shrug, he added, "She had all the time in the world to take back her ship. So what the hell happened that made her finally do it?"

"I have no idea, Michele." Black had replied in the same language.

"Did you not please her, Captain, and now she be mad at you?" Someone said and brought out laughter from the others.

Black smiled thinking of his nights—and days—then most especially that last night with Mala. She had pleased him thoroughly that last night and he repaid her by waking her in the night with his kisses and caresses. Mon Dieu, he wanted to hold her, kiss her, then correct whatever misunderstanding had occurred.

"At least she saw to it that there was no bloodshed. Even saved you from a lashing, Captain." LaVoie was saying.

"I did not care much for that Scotsman." Boulet put in.

"Neither does Captain Mala." Black told them.

"Those lily-lovin' beggars that she calls a crew would not know which end of the sword was the dangerous end." Another man had sneered.

Some men had laughed at the remark but Black rebuked him saying, "Have no doubt that they not only know which end of the sword is dangerous but they would also know how to filet you without much waste." A roar of laughter had come from Black's statement, even from the one he reprimanded.

"Well it would seem that they would have been able to tame that captain of theirs a mite. Mon Dieu, she is only a woman." Yet another man ventured to say.

"Only a woman." Black mumbled almost to himself.

"Sorry Captain. I know you had her, but she is..." LaVoie added.

"A thoroughbred killer, Monsieur LaVoie. She is deadlier than all the

467

men in the British fleet." Black looked around at the slack-jawed and somewhat disbelieving faces of his men. Then, with a smile and a prayer that their guards did not understand French so that Mala would never hear of this conversation, Black added, "Which makes it quite interesting when one is alone with her."

Again a roar of laughter vibrated within their confinement. Their guards opened the door and peered within, wondering what they found so funny.

Now he was alone. Black looked about at his surroundings for the hundredth time when he heard sounds at the door. He noticed the guards were standing straighter and more alert. Then his heart skipped a beat when Mala stepped into his confinement. Looking past her, he could not see the guards.

"Dismissing your guards as you interrogate a prisoner, Mala?" Black asked trying to sound sarcastic as he took in his fill of her. She seemed to glide into the room as she leaned against the wall opposite him.

Crossing her arms, Mala smiled sweetly. "Rest assured, they are close by."

"Why would I worry?" He asked as she straightened and removed her pistol then her sword from her waistband and placed them on the floor near the wall.

"I am in no position to take the weapons from you, mon coeur." Black said softly.

Mala said nothing as she stepped closer to him. Black held his breath as she moved so close to him that he could smell the familiar scent of her as well as feel the soft touch of her body against his.

"Have you seen my, ah, your prisoners?" Black asked.

She smiled up at him and raised one brow. "They are all hale and hearty, Captain."

Her voice seemed to purr when she spoke and Black could feel the familiar stirrings in his loins. Since his gaze never left her face, Black could tell that Mala felt it as well. She smiled as her arms wrapped around his neck and she lowered his head to hers.

She was in control and he knew it. As she kissed him, Mala moved ever so slightly with her slender body that made Black moan in anguished pleasure as he too wanted to hold her tight. The heat of passion began to overtake them as Mala stepped back from him. With a swiftness that gave evidence to the building passion, Mala easily removed her shirt to reveal the breasts Black ached to caress. Before stepping back to him, Mala let her hand gently caress the hardening bulge of him before she pulled Black's shirt from the waistband. Ripping it open, she was next to him again with the kisses, the body movements, the passion, skin touching skin. Black never felt more like a prisoner than he did at that moment. Not being able to hold her was absolute torture!

Suddenly Mala had moved away and was pulling her shirt back over her head. Black stared at her, stunned that she would punish him in this way. She did not look at him as she hastily tucked in her shirt and moved to her weapons.

"Mala?" Black asked, his deep voice hoarse with the passion still riding high. When she turned to face him, he felt his jaw slacken. The look of anger on her face surprised him.

"Chut!" She hissed as she flattened herself to the wall. Black watched her in amazement as she raised her sword to the door. Then he heard it. Voices low and angry, then grunts and footsteps. He watched the door as a figure stepped in with angry strides but stopped short when he met steel.

Mala had known who it would be and placed her sword at the right height. As Deats turned into the room, the tip of the sword was at his throat. Surprise etched his face as his eyes moved from Black to the sword and then to Mala.

"You are making it a very dangerous habit of disobeying my orders, Mr. Deats." Mala said in a quiet tone. Running footsteps could be heard as the guards hastily entered the room and found Deats at the end of Mala's sword.

"Sorry, Cap'n, but he come in and ordered us out of the way." One started to explain.

"Aye, and when we told him that was your order, he banged our heads together." The other finished. The two rubbed at their heads as if to make their point.

"And rough-housing our own men." Mala seemed to add to her earlier statement.

Deats looked to Black and saw the disheveled appearance. The open shirt flared his anger once again. Looking to Mala, he saw that she appeared fine. Of course, how could her appearance be as disheveled when a man had his wrists bound over his head? Then Deats realized she had not lowered her sword yet and was still glaring at him.

Scrambling for some sort of excuse for his presence, Deats replied as calmly as he could, "I was, ah, concerned for yer safety, Captain."

"I do not need you to be concerned, Deats. I can take care of myself." She growled out through clenched teeth. Black smiled in amusement at the thought. Indeed, Mala could take damn good care of herself.

"Aye, C-Captain..." Deats stammered.

"Go away." Mala ordered in the same low tone. The two guards took that as a dismissal and each reached for Deats' arm. Yanking free, he glared at them then back to Mala who as yet had not lowered her sword. Looking at it pointedly, he nodded slightly to her almost in an insult than in respect before turning to leave.

"Disobey my orders again, Deats, I will kill you myself." Mala stated as he took a step out of the room. Deats and the two guards looked at her with a mixture of emotions. Deats was angry that she would dare accost him in front the crew who would certainly repeat every word to the rest of the crew after their watch.

Black watched her as she cut the sword through the air with a growl to vent her anger. The air hissed as she gave into her unleashed anger. Mala lowered her head and her long dark hair formed a curtain so he could not see her face. He shifted to release the ache in his wrists for he had not realized that throughout the scene, he had allowed his body to slacken and, bound as he was, he had put a great deal of pressure on his wrists.

The sound reminded Mala of her whereabouts. She raised her head slowly and found Black watching her. Her eyes met his for a long moment then they moved down to take in his appearance. Black held his breath for her perusal was just as erotic to him as her hands. Mala glanced at the door then, with a disgusted grunt, she picked up her pistol and left the room.

Not able to understand, Black stared at the doorway until a guard reappeared at his station. His dark eye then moved about the empty room. Exhaustion seemed to hit him hard as he felt himself slump again. Looking to the floor, he glimpsed his open shirt. Staring at his chest, he wondered if Mala's desire had time to cool for he was far from that himself. He glanced at the door once again but she was not there.

Nearly an hour had passed before one of the guards came forward, key in hand. "The captain wants to see ye so do not give me any trouble." The man said showing Black the key.

Black nodded and his wrists were free. The tingling came almost at once. Black rubbed his wrists to relieve the ache but knew it would take a while before the tingling stopped. Following the guard out of the holding area, the other guard met them outside the door. Two more were found as they rounded the corridor. Black smiled as he thought of how Mala was not taking any chances of him stealing her ship again. Two guards in front and two behind.

He followed the guards up to the main deck. It was nearly dark and he could see Aubrey and Morgan standing near the railing on the quarterdeck. They watched him as he was escorted across the deck, the soft sea breeze rippled through his open shirt to reveal his chest. Morgan acknowledged him by a nod of his head in greeting. Black returned the nod then glanced around to find Deats on the forecastle, also watching the procession with open hostility on his face.

To his surprise, Black was led to the captain's cabin not the galley. Since he had not eaten, he thought Mala would talk with him with other men about.

One guard opened the door and stepped aside as the other guards cleared the way for him to enter. The door was firmly shut when he stepped into the room.

Mala sat at the head of the table set for two with a candelabra illuminating the room. She had her mug in hand and was about to drink from it but stopped midway when the door opened. She waved her free hand to his seat, bidding him to sit. "I suppose you are hungry." She said sweetly.

Black could have commented to that but held his tongue. He was not sure what was going to happen and he did not want to ruin his short sense of freedom by saying something foolish. He took the offered seat and lifted the cover. Mala reached to uncover the other dishes on the table. He looked at it before lifting his gaze to Mala.

"Eat, it is not poisoned." Mala said with a smile as she scooped up some potatoes and put them on her plate.

"And my men below?" Black asked.

"Ate hours ago." Mala finished.

"Ate what?" Mala stopped piling her plate and laughed softly. The sound made Black's heart skip a beat. To cover his yearning, Black made a deep sigh as if in irritation.

"Your men were laid out with nearly the same menu, Captain. They ate well and that pleased Willie to no end." Mala replied nonplussed to his sigh.

Black looked at her plate then slowly scooped up some potatoes for himself. Mala poured out some wine in the mugs, the same ceramic mugs she had said once before that she was saving for something special. Black's brows knitted in question and he looked to Mala for answers.

She ignored him until her mug was filled with wine as well. Then lifting the mug, she toasted to him, "To you, Captain." Black showed his surprise as he lifted his mug and Mala chuckled, "That you could survive someone like me when we are alone."

Black's mug lowered slightly as he recalled his comment to his men. One of the guards must have understood French and repeated their comments to her. That was one of the remarks he hoped Mala would not hear. Yet she did not seem angry but then one could never really be sure.

Mala's smile broadened as she added, "Meaner than the entire British fleet. Interesting comparison, Rene."

Black watched her closely and could not understand why she was pleased with his remarks. Taking out of context just as she had done was humorous but if she heard of that part of the conversation, she had to have heard all of it.

"Do eat, Rene. The food is getting cold and there is much more to this evening." Her remark did nothing for his appetite for food yet it did wonders

471

for his appetite for the woman beside him but he mechanically ate his meal while Mala kept his mug filled with the wine.

"I tried this wine while in Antigua and found it so sweet tasting, I bought all there was to find. Bon, n'est-ce pas?" She asked as he took a taste.

"Very sweet." Black replied in short as he eyed her.

"Good God, Rene! The way you look, one would think I would cut you down for some wrong." She laughed.

"What is going on, Mala? Why am I here?" He finally ventured to ask.

"What is going on is that we are having dinner. Why you are here is because I intend to finish what I started earlier and without blasted interruptions. Does that satisfy your curiosity?" Mala answered with a provocative smile.

Black became intensely aware of his stirrings and wished the meal was over. The look he bestowed upon her gave her the answer and she chuckled as she lifted her mug inviting him to a silent toast. He quickly obliged and ate heartily.

"Though I do have one question to ask." Mala said nonchalantly and Black tensed instantly. He knew there was something more to this meeting than just finishing what she had begun in his holding area. He looked at her waiting for the final blow. She smiled and let the fork dangle from her fingers as she asked conversationally, "Your relationship with Aubrey while you kept her in your cabin on the *Widow* was ...what exactly?" Black relaxed a bit and smiled at her.

"Mala, I never touched her in the manner in which you are eluding. But to be honest, I thought you were lost to me forever, mon coeur and she was the first one I chose since your disappearance."

"I did not expect you to become a monk in my absence, Rene. It is that I have heard many different things about you and Aubrey and I wanted to be sure of what was the truth."

"I was not to her liking as Irish will tell you. Her preference was Jean Luc. As for me, I needed a diversion from you. I could not stop thinking of you."

"And in a jealous rage, you did away with your friend who had sailed with you for many years." Mala commented softly,

"I was not jealous, Mala, he duped me and the crew knew. What was I supposed to do?" Black retorted. "You would have done the same thing, friend or not."

She looked at him thoughtfully for a long moment for she had nearly done the same thing with Morgan and now Aubrey. For helping Black to board her ship, she wanted to kill Morgan. And now thinking that Aubrey was still Black's lover was nothing but jealousy. That jealousy clouded all rational thinking and she had Black put in chains.

Black began to squirm under her intense stare. Finally, she smiled and pointed at his meal with her fork, "Tis getting cold." She said quietly then turned her attention to her own meal.

Black let out a silent sigh of relief. Mala's jealousy was far too dangerous as he had found out first-hand in Bimini.

When the meal was over, Mala stood up and turned to retrieve another bottle of wine from her cupboard over the quarter gallery windows. Black stood as well and followed her. His arms encircled her waist as she reached up for the bottle and he heard what sounded like a purr when his lips touched her throat. She let her head fall back as she enjoyed the embrace.

"I have missed you, mon coeur." He whispered hoarsely as his hands moved up to cup each breast.

She pulled free of the embrace then taking his hand she led him to the bunk. Her hands rubbed his bared chest, no longer holding back the ache to touch him as she had watched him throughout dinner with his shirt opened.

Black's hands cupped her face to still her movements as he gently kissed her lips. Then his lips moved about her face as she pulled her shirt from her waistband. He heard her groan and her hands were once again on his chest, her thumbs teasing his nipples.

He took a half step back to remove her shirt. For the first time since entering the cabin, he realized she had no weapons on her. Suddenly she left him no more time to think as she moved and molded her body to his. She whispered his name as his mouth took hers and they both fell to the bunk, giving into their passionate frenzy.

Much later, Mala felt movement beside her and turned to see Black getting up. "Where are you going?" She asked dreamily.

"Saving on the candles, mon coeur." He replied as he blew out all the candles on the table. He returned to the bunk and enfolded Mala in his arms. Her soft body next to his aroused him almost instantly, making her chuckle softly.

"Mon pirate capitaine, you are a slave to your body's needs." She whispered.

"On the contrary, mon belle capitaine, I am a slave to your body." He replied as he moved Mala to her back and once again loved her as only he knew how.

Chapter 54

The dim light of dawn came through the gallery window as Black rolled onto his side. Lying on his back, he reached out for her. He turned to find that side of the bunk empty. He sat up and looked about the cabin but did not find Mala. How could she have gotten up without him noticing? He got out of the bunk and put on his britches. He eyed the door and, walking to it, he decided to test it. He was surprised to find it unlocked and, peering out, found no guards posted. Perplexed, he quietly closed the door and finished dressing. Just as he put on his shirt, the door opened and Mala came into the cabin. She smiled when she saw him and moved to her desk to make a quick entry in her logbook.

"You are too trusting, mon coeur." Black said as he watched her.

Mala chuckled as she made the entry but said nothing. Black finished his dressing as he continued to watch her. She moved from her desk to a cupboard where she retrieved two tankards and a bottle of rum. Putting them on the table, she told him, "Help yourself."

"Thought you would never ask." He replied as he took her in his arms just as she walked passed him. Mala smiled up at him but obliged him with a kiss that deepened when he did not release her.

"Really Rene, is that all you think about?"

"What else is more important?"

Mala thought for a moment then answered, "You do have a point." She raised her lips for another kiss and received it. After some moments, she disengaged herself from his embrace and said, "We do not have much time before Willie appears with breakfast..."

"I think I could manage it though." Black said with a smile.

Mala chuckled and shook her head as she reached into another cupboard to pull out some rolled up charts. "You are incorrigible this morning." She said with a smile.

Black watched as she placed the charts on the table and giving him a sideways glance, she added, "You have not poured the rum."

"I was preoccupied." Black said smiling as he approached the table.

He opened the bottle while still watching her as she searched her charts. He poured the rum and was handing her a tankard when Mala muttered something, apparently finding the chart she was looking for.

Looking at it upside-down, Black recognized it as the area in the Caribbean around Bimini and the surrounding islands. Mala picked up the bottle of rum and placed it so that held down one end of the rolled chart.

475

After taking a swallow of her rum, she used her tankard to hold down the other end of the chart. Then straightening up, she looked at Black and said, "I intend to find Jean Luc for Aubrey."

Black gave her a derisive snort as he put the tankard to his lips, "Tis a waste of time, Mala. It has been too long, he is no doubt dead."

"Very well then, I intend to find Jean Luc's body for Aubrey." She stated more sternly. Black looked up at her over the rim of his tankard and found her steady gaze on him. He hated that gaze. He felt as if she was seeing through him and could read his mind. She could stare without blinking for what he thought was a God-awful long time and that unnerved him.

To avoid her stare, he lowered his gaze to the chart. His dark eye fixed on the island instantly but instead of informing her, he placed a hand on the chart effectively covering it. Leaning heavily on his hand, he let a finger of the other hand move about the chart.

"Hmm, I am not really sure I remember it, mon coeur. It has been some time ago."

"By my calculations, Rene, I figure it has been about three months." Black looked up at her in question making her smile as she answered, "That was how long ago I saw the *Widow* sink and we found Aubrey washed up on shore."

"And how could you know when he was marooned?"

"From Aubrey. You stabbed her, remember? It had to be during that time of her infirmary because she thought that Jean Luc was still on the *Widow* when the *Majestic* sank your ship."

Black was silent as he eyed her. Looking at him, Mala tapped an impatient finger on the chart to bring his attention back to the matter at hand. He moved his finger to a small island far south of Bimini saying, "Perhaps there. No wait!" Changing his mind, he moved his finger far east of Bimini stating, "Could be here. Oh, now there is an interesting place." He stated as his finger moved yet again to an island between the first two he pointed.

Suddenly the point of a dagger embedded itself just above his fingertip. His head shot up as he looked at Mala in surprise. "I was only jesting, Mala." He said defensively.

"I am not." Mala said impatiently. "Here is Bimini, Rene. I know he is not far from there."

"I had someone take him away."

Mala gave him a look as though he had said the most absurd thing ever. Pulling the dagger from the table, she asked, "Unless you truly believe that I am some kind of fool..."

"That thought would never cross my mind." Black muttered almost to himself.

"Then where is he, Rene?" Mala asked becoming impatient.

Black looked down at the chart, at the island. He straightened up and crossing his arms as he looked at Mala, asked, "What happens after I show you? I go back to my own special place where I was this time yesterday?"

Mala looked at him for a long time before she sat in a nearby chair at the table. Suddenly she looked tired. Black knew it was unfair to blackmail her like that but he did not want to go back to that damned room. He watched as Mala looked at the chart, then out the gallery window where the sun had already made its rise above the horizon.

A knock at the door interrupted them. She bade entry and Willie appeared carrying a tray with two covered dishes. He placed the tray over the chart and carefully placed the dishes on an area where the table could be seen. He removed the covers and the steam rose from the hot food.

Mala looked away from Black to the steaming dishes. She noticed a slab of salted ham, biscuits, and eggs. At the sight of the eggs, she raised a brow at Willie. The wizened old man smiled and said with a shrug, "They be tame enough, Cap'n."

Picking up the tray, Willie turned to leave. He looked back at the occupants of the cabin and found both of them watching him. He nodded then closed the door firmly behind him.

"Tame?" Black asked.

"Your eggs." Mala answered and said no more as she picked up her dish and began to eat.

Black still did not know what that meant but decided it was not important since Mala thought it unimportant. He sat down in a chair away from the chart, then moved his plate before he began to eat. They ate in silence, each with their own thoughts for company.

After she finished, Mala set her dish at the end of the table closest to the door. She got up and stood looking out of the window. The water glimmered like crystals in the morning sun but at the moment they went unseen. She was contemplating Black's question. He had bounded her below decks for a day when he first boarded her ship but that was because she was angry with him and he said he needed rest. Now she had taken back her ship and had him locked up below decks for several days. She had been allowed to roam about her ship, unarmed for a time, and was able to stay in her own cabin. She had enjoyed their nights together since then. What could she do for him?

She heard the chair scrape on the floor as Black placed his dish with hers. She turned to face him and when she got his attention, she said, "Show me where he is and you stay with me. If I find out you lied to..."

"I would not lie to you, Mala my love. Come ... " He beckoned as he pointed on the chart, "He is on this island. But the chances that he..."

"Never mind that. If he is dead, then Aubrey will grieve for a time. After that, I am sure Morgan would take her."

"I thought Morgan had already..."

"I am sure not." Mala said in a matter of fact tone. Black wondered about what Deats had said. Could Deats have been lying about Morgan and little Irish? If so, what else has he lied about during his visits? His thoughts were interrupted as Mala walked to the door and opened it.

"I have to see to my ship. I do not see a reason for bolting the door unless you think I should and have a guard or two placed at the door." She said raising a brow.

Black smiled and shook his head. "I will manage to somehow keep myself company and stay out of trouble." Mala smiled at his silly look of reproach then she was gone.

Black walked around the cabin and finally came upon her desk, noting the logbook that was left opened. Looking at the door and seeing that he was still alone, he sat at her desk and read the entry she had written when she came in for breakfast.

We set sail for the isles near Bimini to search for Jean Luc.
When Rene shows me Jean Luc's whereabouts, I will have to
think of some way to reward him. What would you like, Rene?

He laughed aloud at the entry as he looked at the closed door. The little enchantress had it all planned out already. With a broad smile on his face, Black began to tidy the room as he awaited her return and his reward.

The day was cloudless and the sun shone bright. The rippling waters in the wake of the ship was a soothing sight. It was nearly midday and Black stood looking out the quarter gallery window. Where was Mala? What was she doing? He did not hear the footsteps and was jolted from his thoughts with the knock that followed. He turned with a smile as the door opened slowly but his smile froze and disappointment washed over him as Aubrey peeked in. She caught sight of him and opened the door wider as she entered carrying a tray.

"Mala was busy so I brought you the noon meal." She set the tray down and then glanced around the room. Facing him, Aubrey smiled up at him.

"What do you find so amusing, Irish?" He asked irritably.

"You perform domestic duties very well, Rene. Were you a chambermaid in France?" Aubrey asked in a mocking tone.

Black scowled at her as she continued to smile sweetly at him. Then it dawned on him that he had asked that very question when she had tidied his cabin on the *Widow Maker*, lacking anything else to do. Now he found himself having done the same to Mala's cabin.

He moved to the table and took a seat before the meal brought to him. Aubrey made to leave the cabin but Black asked, "Why have I put up with you for so long, Irish?" Aubrey turned to find that he was not looking her but at his food.

Mischievously, she answered, "I am not sure of that. I suppose it has to do with the fact that you love..." Her pause made Black look up at her, "...adventure."

The relieved look on Black's face caused her to laugh aloud as she left him in the cabin. Alone in the cabin and safely behind the closed door, Black allowed a smile. Aubrey was definitely in good spirits today. With Mala's influence, she had shown signs of actually being able to survive in this pirate world that she was reluctantly thrown into. Somehow she had managed to gain Mala's friendship and protection as well as kill a man like Thomas Beaufort. Black shook his head as he mused, Irish will be a survivor just as Mala will instruct her to be.

Just finishing his meal, the door opened and Mala stepped in. Closing the door, she leaned against it, looking at him. Black's gaze was seductive as was his smile and she looked at the logbook to find it closed. An impish grin appeared on her face as she remembered her log entry and knew he could not resist reading it especially since she had left the book opened, intentionally. Black stood up from the table and approached her.

"So what have you decided your reward to be, Captain Black?" Mala asked, her own dark eyes softening with the passion that rose up within her.

His answer was to lift her in his arms as she breathed his name. Her arms went around his neck and she pressed her lips to his. He deepened the kiss as he held her in his arms and felt her groan against his mouth. He lifted his head and looked down into her half-closed eyes. His voice was deep with the love and the need that he had for this woman, "Stay with me all afternoon. I have missed you these past few days, mon coeur." Black closed his eye as Mala pressed her lips against his throat just below his ear.

In a soft whisper, she told him in French, "Very well, I am yours for the afternoon." Black smiled down at her as she gazed up at him. "Then as captain of this ship and as you are my prisoner, I claim you until the dawn."

"Non, mon coeur, I am yours for all time." Black whispered softly as he carried her to the bunk. Mala's hand caressed his unscarred cheek as he lowered her onto the bunk and followed her down to lie full length over her.

She moaned as Black kissed her throat then her face. As his lips were pressed near hers, she whispered, "Hmm, for all time? Not long enough, Rene."

It took several days for the *Enchantress* to sail on her course to an island on a southeasterly direction from Bimini. Aubrey went topside and asked one of the men where Mala could be found. He pointed to the forecastle. She found Mala and Morgan looking to the horizon and squinting against the glare from the water, she saw land. Her heart began to race as she went to stand next to Mala and set her gaze upon the tiny island.

"Is that the island?" Aubrey fairly breathed. Neither of the other two could help but note the sound of mixed excitement and apprehension in her voice.

"If the information Rene gave me was correct, then this should be it." Mala replied without looking at her.

Aubrey could barely contain herself as she stepped closer to the bow as if this would clear the distance in seconds. "I am coming, Jean Luc." She whispered to the wind that caressed her face.

Mala heard Aubrey's words and exchanged a worried glance with Morgan. "Aubrey, it has been three months. He may..." Mala began.

"Ah now, ya will not be startin' that too!" Aubrey retorted, casting an angry frown upon Morgan as she did so. "I have to believe that he is alive!" She stubbornly replied.

Mala watched the doubt appear then disappear on her friend's face. Looking back to the island, she stated, "We should drop anchor in a few hours."

"I will be ready." Aubrey told her, then with one last look at the island she left the forecastle. Mala watched her leave without another word before glancing at Morgan who had yet to speak on the subject.

"I am going with you." He finally said. Mala nodded and turned back to watch the island as they sailed closer.

Morgan watched his captain and wondered if she thought of what Aubrey's reaction would be if they found Jean Luc's body instead of him alive. Of course, she did. Mala would have thought it all through. Staring back at the island, he vowed to himself that he would see to it that Aubrey would not be the first to find such a sight.

Aubrey laid on her back on her bunk staring up at the ceiling, her heart still racing, "You have to be alive, Jean Luc, you just have to." She said as tears began to stream sideways from her eyes.

Looking at Morgan's empty bunk, she thought about the talks he had with her the last few days. Sometimes he had sounded like he did not want them to find Jean Luc alive. Well, he will be on that island, damn it, and he will be alive and well. She thought as she glared at the bunk as if he were there. She got up, wiped her tears away and prepared herself to go ashore. Looking at her reflection in the mirror, she vowed that she would hold Jean Luc in her arms again this day.

It was nearly midday when a longboat pulled up to the shore of the tiny island. The small search party consisting of Mala, Morgan, Aubrey, and three other men from Mala's crew disembarked and stood on the beach looking around. One man remained with the boat while the rest of the party started up the beach. The island was not overly thick with trees except for some small areas. The small group circled around the thickness, trying to stay in the open as much as possible.

Deats stood on the deck without expression, watching as the longboat neared the island. Jean Luc! Surely the man could not still be alive! But what if he was alive? It would come out somehow that Jean Luc had told the truth about the repairs to Black's ship as well as Black's time in prison which was why he was delayed in returning for Mala as he had promised. With Black on board and Jean Luc to tell what really happened, it would not take long before Mala believed them and, she would know how her own quartermaster had been lying to her all these months! She would not understand that it was all done out of his own feelings for her. Deats had wanted her since he found her on that cursed island but she still held herself for Rene Black. The anger welled up within him as he tried for months to turn her away from Black's memory but all to no avail. Now, here was the possibility of another person who could tell her the truth of what really happened. Something would have to happen to Jean Luc that would keep him quiet—forever.

Deats continued to watch as Mala stepped out of the boat and into the water. She waded to shore and stood facing the woods as the boat and its occupants were settled on the beach. He saw Morgan step up to Mala and the two conversed. Aye, Deats thought, may as well get rid of the brother too. And what of Aubrey? Well, he could take her, force himself on her until he could coax Mala into his bed. Mala was worth the patience but Aubrey was nothing to him! She would be amusing but his real hunger was for the raven-haired beauty.

When the party entered the woods, Deats continued to watch the island thinking of his plan and how it could...and would work. He went over it in his mind yet again. He knew that he had to have all the answers that Mala would believe in order for everything to work out. It was nearly a half an hour before Deats turned on his heel and headed for the captain's cabin.

Black was sitting at the table with his feet propped up in a nearby chair. The guard Mala had posted sat across the table from him as the two shared a bottle of her rum. As Jordan rambled on about some adventure Mala had taken her crew on, Black's mind drifted to his adventure with Mala more than an hour ago. Her kisses and her need to be touched aroused him and when they made love, it was demanding and very satisfying.

The knock at the door broke into Black's reverie and he watched as Jordan jumped up. The door flew open before Jordan reached it and Deats stepped in, surveying the scene. It angered the Scotsman that the crew would be so stupid as to become friendly with this man. Closing the door, he bestowed the two men a look of disdain that Black found amusing.

The smile was more than Deats could bear and with a gruff edge to his Scottish-accented voice, he ordered, "I suggest, Mr. Jordan, that ye return ta yer post."

"I am at my post, sir. Cap'n Mala's orders were that no one see the prisoner. She named you in particular." Jordan replied, standing his ground.

"I see." Deats said with a nod then turned to leave. Suddenly he whirled around full circle and stabbed Jordan with a dagger. As he fell, Deats pushed him to the floor towards Black.

Taken aback by the move, Black stood up quickly ready to fight this foe. When Deats made no other move but to stand glaring at him, Black stated as calmly as he could, "Killing Mala's men, Monsieur Deats?"

"Nay, Mala will hear that ye killed him." When Black raised a brow, Deats added, "In an attempt ta reclaim her ship, of course, and leave her behind on an island again."

Black became suspicious now. Watching the Scotsman closely, he asked, "Now why would I do that?"

"Because ye steal. First her ship, then Mala. She should be mine." Deats ground out through clenched teeth. "She should have been mine long ago but she always had the soft heart where ye were concerned. Ye were supposed ta have died by her hand in Bimini. That would have been a wondrous sight ta watch. Ye see I never bothered ta tell her the truth that ye did go back for her as a reliable person had told me and begged me ta get her ta understand. It was so much easier ta let her believe ye no longer cared. I even embellished yer nights in bed with other women. But she had a change of heart when she faced ye."

"She thought I never came back for her? That was her anger towards me?" Black asked, his own anger rising. His mind raced, the two years apart, nearly a year away from her and then another year thinking she was dead because he found the village destroyed and no sign of her. That was her anger! Because this Scotsman let her believe that he no longer wanted her!

Black came out of his thoughts as Deats took a step closer and snarled, "It was that damned kiss!" Deats felt again the sense of betrayal during that episode in the old tavern. He could have torn them apart if he was sure Mala would not have killed him for doing so.

When Deats made no other comments or move, Black said slowly through clenched teeth. "So I take her ship and leave her behind?"

Deats gave him a smug smile and answered, "Aye, and give me the reason I need ta kill ye."

"I have no weapon, Monsieur Deats." Black replied still trying to remain calm. Right now, he would welcome the chance for a fight and to rid himself—and Mala—of this Scotsman.

Deats pulled out a pistol and motioned toward the closet. "In there ye will find swords. Get them and let us be done with this."

Black obliged and stepped up to the closet door. Keeping an eye on Deats, he quickly retrieved two of the swords kept there. He remembered watching Mala clean and sharpen them after the last raid. Suddenly Black felt a pang of remorse that he may not live to see her again. Because he refused to leave her to this arrogant bastard, Black mentally shook the thought away and faced Deats with the swords, tossing him one of them. The Scotsman then tossed the pistol where it landed near Jordan's body. The men faced one another and, with a savage growl, Deats made the first lunge.

Chapter 55

Resting in the shade against a tree, Jean Luc mused on how many times he had thought about how curious this situation was. Had it been three months on this tiny island? He checked his makeshift calendar, a piece of driftwood that he had been making notches in for each day he was there. Oui, it had been three months to the day. Black had left him with more food than was normally left for a man marooned. Even though he had been strenuously rationing it, it was nearly gone. Water was no problem for there was a fresh water stream nearby. He had made a few attempts at fishing in the ocean, but those attempts did not yield much. There were some edible indigenous fruits on the island as well and he had made use of them to sustain him.

It was also curious that Black had left him on this island that was within sight of the trade lines. Many times in the past three months he had watched longingly and forlornly as ships of all sizes and flying all matter of flags sailed by. He would have tried to gain their attention with a fire, but Black had not been generous with the black powder. He had only one shot for his pistol and he looked at it in his hand. He was a stouthearted man but he was not ready to take his own life and tucked the pistol into his sash.

Even with all of his fortune and bounty here on his tropical prison, he knew that he would not last another three months. Maybe he would succumb to the elements first, just easily drift off to sleep one day and not wake up.

He leaned back against the fallen tree that was his resting place in the shade and closed his eyes to the unrelenting glare of the sun on the sand and water. His thoughts drifted to her—it was the one thing that had kept him going all this time. He did not want to remember her as he had last seen her, lying on the deck behind Black with her life's blood spreading over her shirt. He willed that she had survived the wound the captain had dealt her. Instead he remembered her in the marketplace in London, the first day he had laid eyes on her. She was looking at the things on the tables while her hair was ablaze in the late afternoon sun. He remembered her searching for her lost bracelet among the shrubs beneath her bedroom window. Jean Luc slipped his fingers into his pocket and pulled out the small treasure. He wondered when she had put it back in there and why. He opened his eyes narrowly against the glare reflecting from the water and turned the bracelet so the light filtering through the trees would catch on the chain.

"It glows like her hair in the sun." He said aloud to the wind and smiled. Closing his hand over the treasure and closing his eyes, he remembered her on the day he had easily pulled her to him for that first real kiss. He could still taste her lips. How he wished he could feel them against his now. He remembered with a smile the times that they had *'chosen to disagree'* as she had called their times of indifference. He sighed deeply and readjusted his position against the tree.

Mala glanced up at the trees and touched various plant life as they made their journey around the perimeter of the island. "Mon Dieu, it is so much like home." She said softly.

Aubrey tried to get between Morgan and Mala as they walked along the beach. Morgan would not have it and was continuously pushing her gently, yet insistently behind them then closed the distance between him and Mala. With a knowing glance, Mala smiled sadly because she knew he was just trying to save Aubrey from certain horrendous disappointment. After a while, Aubrey grew exasperated with his 'shoving.' Mala looked back again when she heard Morgan grunt with the sudden pain of Aubrey hitting his arm forcefully.

"How do you expect to find him if we walk around so quietly? We have to call out for him so he knows we are here." She finally complained. Mala and Morgan sighed.

"Jean Luc!" Aubrey yelled at the top of her lungs. The other two exchanged pained glances...no man had ever survived a marooning this long.

"Jean Luc!" A frown crossed his brow. A sign of madness for he could hear her calling him, he thought to himself. He slipped the bracelet back into his pocket and sighed again. In his mind, he saw her beneath him the night he had made gentle love to her in Black's bunk. He had relived the scene and the memories of her in his bunk the next night many times since he had been left here.

"Jean Luc!" Aubrey cried out again. She shoved at Morgan again as he pushed her back.

"Stop it Aubrey..." He complained.

"Children..." Mala scolded. She wanted to get this over with and get back to the ship. She was getting a bad feeling deep in the pit of her stomach and turned to look in the direction from which they came but the ship could not be seen through the trees.

"Help me call for him, Morgan...please. Ya must care! He is your brother for God's sake." Aubrey persisted.

"Jean Luc!" There was her voice again—on the wind. Perhaps he had already succumbed to the sun for his brain surely must be on fire.

"Jean Luc!" Morgan finally yelled to try and appease her. She smiled at him with innocent eyes filled with heartfelt thanks. He smiled back as Mala glanced at them and quickened her pace.

"Jean Luc!" His eyes shot open. Why would he be dreaming of a man calling him? Moreover, that had sounded just like Morgan! Straightening up slightly and squinting against the sun, he looked toward the sound. "Aye, I may be insane, so where is the harm?" He muttered aloud. With a shrug, he called to the wind, "Hello!"

Suddenly Mala stopped, pulled out her pistol, and listened. The lead man in the party had also stopped and stood with cutlass drawn, looking around warily. Seeing them, Morgan drew his pistol and Aubrey pulled her dagger from her boot.

Jean Luc raised himself wearily from the shady sand and squinted down the beach in the direction from which the wind blew. What he saw made his heart skip a beat. Five people had stepped out on the beach and stood looking around. He took a few hesitant steps forward, peering against the sun, praying that he was not hallucinating.

Aubrey let out a choked sound then suddenly broke out into a run, pushing past Morgan forcefully.
"No wait!" Mala and Morgan yelled in unison, trying to stop her. Then they saw the man standing on the edge of the beach, just out from the tree line. In their walking and searching, they had reached the other side of the island. Mala and Morgan exchanged questioning glances...could it be possible?

Jean Luc watched with bated breath as one person broke from the group and was running up the beach towards him. He was not dreaming. The person, this group of people, were all real. He stumbled further out into the sunlight and a tear sprung from his eyes as the person drew nearer and he recognized her...Aubrey. His breath now came in excited gasps as she came nearer, her hair streaming around her head in the winds.
"Dieu merci!" He gasped as she flew into his arms. He dropped to his knees pulling her down to her knees as well. Falling onto his back in the sand, he pulled her over him. "Merci." He said again through happy tears as she peppered his face with kisses.
He laughed aloud at her excitement then they were both crying. He finally

487

caught her face in his hands and held her there just looking at her for a moment as she lay draped over him. Then he slowly lowered her face to his and pressed his lips against hers firmly. She responded hungrily to the embrace. After the kiss, Aubrey cupped his bearded face in her hands. She made a face then giggled happily as he smiled up at her.

Mala and the rest of the party stayed at the edge of the beach, allowing the two reunited lovers a few private moments. She glanced at Morgan who was looking up to the sky. "Sorry, Morgan." She said quietly. Morgan looked at his captain and shrugged.

After a time one of the men turned to Mala saying, "Here they come, Cap'n."

Mala and Morgan turned to see Jean Luc and Aubrey arm in arm coming closer. Aubrey's face radiated with pleasure at finding him. Jean Luc smiled, stretching out his hand to Mala in thanks. The island woman looked at the hand briefly then slapped it away with a smile before she drew him in for a fierce hug, "Tis good to see you well, mon ami."

Jean Luc returned the embrace then looked at his brother. "Morgan, mon frère." He said thickly as he embraced him.

"Hello big brother. You look no worse for wear, considering the circumstances." Morgan answered with a smile.

"Shall we leave this place and get you back to the sea where you belong?" Mala asked with a smile.

"With immense pleasure." Jean Luc answered.

As they made their way back up the beach toward the longboat, Jean Luc looked at Aubrey and asked almost carefully, "Where is Rene?"

"On my ship." Mala replied. No one except Morgan noticed the slight emphasis on the word, 'my.'

"So, you are together again?" Jean Luc asked with a gentle smile towards her.

Mala gave him a small nod and smile in reply. She quickened her pace and pulled just a bit ahead of the rest of them. Aubrey beamed up at Jean Luc as they walked along hand in hand. Morgan reached out to grasp his brother by the back of his neck and he smiled in response at having the man back and alive with them as well.

Suddenly without looking back at Jean Luc, Mala asked, "Did the *Widow Maker* come back for me?" When he did not answer right away, she stopped and faced him, "Jean Luc, did Rene come back for me?"

"We did go back for you, Mala, but we found a burned village and a lot of graves. Rene and I thought that you were among the dead. That was why I was surprised to see you when I went for Morgan. Did Deats not explain this to you?"

Mala looked surprised and Jean Luc continued with a frown, "After we saved Morgan, I tried to explain everything but you refused to talk about it. Deats promised me that he would make sure you understood what happened. Remember I tried to tell you that…" Jean Luc broke off his narrative when he heard Morgan's contemptuous snort and glanced at his brother. When the blue eyes shifted to Mala he realized that she was not listening anymore.

Everyone grew uneasy as Mala stared at the ground, but saw nothing as she remembered things that Deats had said over time to her, *'Remember Mala, he left ye behind.' 'He has had other women while ye waited for him.' 'Look Mala, Aubrey bears the mark of Black's affection now.' 'Ye never rally meant anything ta him, except as his latest conquest.'*

There were so many other words that had hurt her. That was why she had been so angry with Black at Bimini and why she had made the threat to Yvette. That was also why she had wanted nothing to do with Aubrey at first, until she learned the truth about the other young woman's association with Black. Mala knew that Deats wanted her but she had been and still was in love with Rene Black. Deats knew that she would not have another man while Black was around raiding the high seas. It was Deats who suggested that she should kill Black for having left her on that island where she could have been killed like the others. But Deats knew the truth all this time!

As if Morgan could read Mala's thoughts, he said quietly, "You left Deats in charge."

Mala's face changed. She did leave Deats in charge and she left Black in her cabin, defenseless on the *Enchantress*. Looking up at Morgan, Jean Luc and then to Aubrey, she could do nothing more than breathe, "Rene…"

Turning from them and heading down the beach for the longboat again, Mala began to walk faster. As she remembered the other hurtful words from Deats, she broke out into a full run. On the beach where the boat waited, the man turned with a look of excitement as she ran up to him, "Cap'n, I hear the clash of swords on the *Enchantress*."

Mala looked to her ship and could hear the swords too. "Damn it, Deats! No!" She yelled in the direction of her ship. Her words were carried away by wind, heard only by those on the island. Sensing their captain's urgency, the men pushed the boat back into the water and Mala jumped in, turning to face the ship that rocked gently just beyond the breakers.

Deats slashed out with his dagger he held in his left hand then followed with his sword in his other hand. Black easily stepped back from his reach with the dagger then brought up his arm to cross swords. With a growl of frustration that this fight had lasted longer than he had intended, Deats slashed out again with the dagger but Black had moved behind the main mast then reappeared on the other side. Not reading the move until it was too late, Deats' hand hit the thick wooden mast. Pain shot through his fingers and he dropped the dagger from his numbed grasp.

Black maneuvered the Scotsman away from the dagger lying on the deck. With vicious swipes to be rid of this foe, Deats lurched forward raining blow after blow while Black seemed tireless in his defenses. In Black's mind, this fight was more than for his life. It was for Mala and the lies that she believed from this Scottish bastard. It was for the past year of thinking Mala was dead and forever lost to him. It was for loneliness both he and Mala had to endure.

Robert had been watching for his captain's return and dropped the rope ladder. He turned to his companions nearby saying, "The Captain will finish this."

Mala barely had a hold of the ladder before swinging herself up. Morgan went up behind her quickly and could hear her already yelling for Deats to stop. Robert heard her orders as she climbed then helped her as she fairly threw herself over the railing, "Deats, I said stand down!"

Black heard her but could only glance her way as Deats ignored the order and continued to thrust with his sword. Deats' concentration faltered only slightly but he refused to stop. With Black's attention momentarily diverted, Deats reached into his coat and pulled out his Sgian Dhu from its sheath under his armpit. The small knife caught the light of the sun and winked wickedly at Black. The flash from the blade drew Black's attention to the Scotsman.

"Deats, that is an order!" Mala growled as she broke into run.

Morgan staggered a bit as he landed on the deck. He saw Mala running to the fighting men and yelled, "No, Mala!"

He knew she would have never stopped at his command and he ran after her. Before he could reach her, Mala had reached Deats. Grabbing the Scotsman by the back of his coat, she swung him around to face her. Morgan saw the flash of light reflect off the blade then saw Mala's body jolt. He slid to a complete stop unable to believe what had just happened.

"No!" Black breathed as he stared in disbelief at Mala.

With a stunned look at the Sgian Dhu that was embedded in her left upper chest, her vision blurred and she looked up at Deats who was staring wide-eyed at her. With a glare so intense with hatred and a snarl laced with malice, she told him, "You are a dead man, Deats." Then her world darkened and she felt herself falling.

Black dropped his sword and slid on his knees to catch Mala before she hit the deck. His gaze swept over her limp body, the small knife and the blood-soaked shirt that surrounded the weapon. He felt the familiar ache of losing her all over again, only now it was an overwhelming pain. His hand gently brushed back the hair from her ashen face as he whispered her name. Her eyes remained closed and she gave no response.

Seeing Black's unguarded back, Deats raised his sword for the fatal blow. "No!" Morgan yelled as he tackled Deats and the two fell backward on the deck. Jumping to his feet, Morgan ordered, "Hold him! He just attacked our captain!"

"Nay, it was an accident! I dinna mean ta hurt her." Deats cried out. Then pointing to Black who was startled from the confrontation and was watching him, Deats yelled aloud, "He was tryin' ta take back her ship!"

"Liar!" Morgan spat out as he advanced on the man and backhanded him across the face. He turned from Deats when he heard a gasp and saw Aubrey run forward to kneel beside Mala.

She and Black locked gazes and saw the pain etched on the other's face. Jean Luc pulled Aubrey to her feet and she buried her face in his chest. He suddenly felt Aubrey stiffen and she raised her head to look at Deats who was still loudly proclaiming his innocence. Jean Luc turned his attention to Black as he held the limp form of Mala in his lap.

Aubrey took the advantage of Jean Luc's attention being drawn away and pushed herself from his embrace. Without warning, she lunged at Deats, her dirk drawn from her boot and now in her hand. Her arm arched as she threw herself at the Scotsman but Morgan had seen her remove her dirk and guessed her intentions. He caught the striking arm with one hand and, with his other arm, he encircled her waist to draw her to him and away from the Scotsman.

"You killed her! You murderer! You killed her!" She screamed as she angrily fought to be released from Morgan's grasp.

Deats glared at her and said firmly, "I dinna hear her comin.' Twas an accident!"

Jean Luc gently took the now sobbing Aubrey from Morgan as one of the men asked, "Mr. Alcott, what do we do with Mr. Deats?"

Tearing his gaze from his fallen captain and giving Deats an icy stare, he announced loudly, "Mr. Deats, you are charged with disobeying a direct order..."

"Nay!" Deats interrupted struggling against the hold of his arms.

"You are charged with the escape of a prisoner..." Morgan continued without pause.

"Nay, I am innocent!" Deats yelled but Morgan ignored him.

So that his voice carried above the Scotsman's, Morgan nearly shouted, "You are also charged with the attack on and the possible mortal wounding of your captain."

"Nay! Twas an accident!" Deats yelled in defense.

The men looked at one another in uncertainty. Their captain always made the decisions. She always knew what to do. Now, they had to decide on one of their own.

"Therefore, your punishment is..." Morgan began.

"Death." Black interjected loud enough for Morgan and those nearby to hear him. When all eyes turned to him, Black said calmly, "By her own orders and many of you heard her. She said, *'You are a dead man, Deats.'* It was her sentence for his disobedience and betrayal." Then turning to Mala and brushing his thumb over her pale cheek, Black added, "Hang him."

No one moved, stunned by the order. Morgan exchanged looks with Jean Luc who was trying to comfort a sobbing Aubrey. Black's head shot up and he barked angrily, "Hang him!"

Some men ran for a rope. Jean Luc, still holding Aubrey, bent as low as he could to Black, but he held his warning when Black carefully picked up Mala and carried her off the deck.

"Robert, prepare the sentencing, but wait for me!" Morgan ordered as he hurried to follow Jean Luc and Aubrey who had followed Black.

Robert turned as a man appeared with rope. "Up there and make sure it holds. We would not want it to slip through the knot." He told the men coldly.

"Mr. Bates, ye must listen ta me. Twas an accident. I never meant ta..." Deats pleaded.

"Quiet, Mr. Deats!" Robert broke in angrily. "We could hear her ordering you to stop as she boarded."

"But..." Deats tried to interject.

"But nothing! I saw you! You reacted when she called out your name and ordered you to stop!" Robert snarled. The men stopped what they were doing to listen. Some nodded in agreement.

"Nay, he was escapin'! He was goin' ta steal her ship and leave the captain here!" Deats tried to explain.

Robert pointed into the Scotsman's face and growled, "No, Mr. Deats! Captain Black would never leave her behind. I know that and these men know that. If you had seen them together, you would know that too." Taking a step closer to Deats, Robert added through clenched teeth, "You can try to lie to us, Mr. Deats, even now as the rope is being prepared for you. She ordered you to stop and you ignored your captain's orders."

Shaking his head vigorously, Deats opened his mouth to retort but Robert's next words froze the words in his throat. "Save your denials, Mr. Deats. No one will help you now!"

The two men stared at one another and, for a moment, Robert thought he saw fear creep into Deats' eyes.

Chapter 56

In the cabin, Black gently laid Mala on the bunk. He sat beside her, his eye closed to the pain that tore at his heart as the tear slipped through and down his cheek. He gently swept her forehead with his thumb as he lowered his head to press a kiss on her slightly parted lips.

Then he felt it. The soft air of her breath. She was alive! He straightened slowly and looked at her chest again. The slow rise and fall of her chest was almost undetectable but now he saw it. "Stay with me, Mala. Please, mon coeur, please do not leave me, not now!" He whispered as he stared into her pale face.

Stepping into the cabin, Aubrey's sobs could still be heard even though she tried to silence them. Jean Luc and Morgan shared a worried look before Jean Luc whispered in the quietness of the cabin. "God, I cannot believe this is happening. I thought she would cheat Death forever."

"She is not dead." Black said quietly, turning to face them.

He found three stunned faces staring back at him. Morgan was the first to break the silence as he looked to Jean Luc and Aubrey. "Be damned."

"Well she is not dead now, but I do not know what to do. I do not know her medicines." Black said helplessly as he looked back at Mala.

Aubrey stared at him, seeing a side of him she had never noticed before. She glanced at Mala then back at him. Rene Black was a different man! Never before had she seen him looking so vulnerable, so unsure of himself. A knock at the door broke into the stunned silence. "What is it?" Black growled angrily.

Slowly the door opened and Willie's head peered in cautiously. "Sorry, Cap'n. But I was wantin' to pay me respects. Even though she was me captain, the lass was like a daughter to me." He said slowly.

"Only if you know about her herbs and medicines." Black told him gruffly.

"Rene." Jean Luc cautioned.

"Actually, I do, Cap'n, but..." Willie said not sure what that had to do with paying his respects to his captain.

"Of course, you do." Morgan said as it registered through the shock that Willie could help.

Suddenly the old man found himself yanked into the room by Morgan grabbing his arm as Jean Luc glanced out the door before shutting it quickly. Aubrey stood shocked at the suddenness of the brothers' actions as Morgan was all but pushing the old man to the bunk.

493

Willie gazed down at Mala as tears welled up. Sniffing, he said, "She was always good to me old bones."

"She is not dead." Black whispered.

Willie turned to him, stunned. Then he looked at the others waiting for the denials. When none came, he looked back at Mala and the small knife. "Sweet merciful heavens!" He muttered. Then dropping on his knees beside Mala, he said to her, "Well, I guess you showed 'em, eh Cap'n! Heart of stone, they be sayin'! Now you have gone and proved 'em right!" Everyone smiled not able to contain the sense of relief. What Willie had said was probably being said among the taverns and wharves.

"Aye, she is alive but I do not know what she knows." Black said.

Willie looked up and was helped to stand by Black as he said, "Well Cap'n, she taught me in case she was wounded. Once she was grazed across the middle in a battle. 'Tis time you learn this, Willie.' She says to me. 'Who knows when I will be the one bleedin' and I cannot very well do it myself,' she says. I had hoped never to use what she taught me on her, but I guess she had another one of 'em feelings of hers."

Morgan snorted and said, "God, when does she not!"

"Aye Mr. Alcott, gives me hairs to stand on end sometimes!" Willie mumbled.

Black nodded and felt a chill run through him as he exchanged looks with Jean Luc and Aubrey. They had all experienced one of those times and they knew exactly how eerie the feeling had been to see that she was right.

"What do you need?" Black asked getting back to the seriousness of the situation.

Willie looked down at Mala, assessing the wound and her condition. "I will need plenty of thick cloths. When that knife comes out, she will bleed plenty and it will have to be stopped by pressin' it with cloths."

"I think I know what we could use." Aubrey said as she went to a cabinet where Mala kept cloths and towels for a bath. "Will those do, Willie?"

"Aye, they sure will, lass. But we will need to fold them just right."

Aubrey nodded and gathered the cloths. Black followed Willie to the quarter gallery window where Mala kept her jars of herbs and medicines. The old man handed a few jars to Black who placed them carefully on the table. Then Willie showed Aubrey and Morgan how to fold the thick cloths. He showed Jean Luc how to tear the long towels into strips.

"We will need to cut away her shirt so we can get to the wound." Willie said as he concocted a thick paste in shallow bowl. Looking at Black, he added, "You will need to pull out the knife."

Black nodded solemnly. Jean Luc and Morgan looked at one another then Jean Luc said, "We will wait topside, Captain."

As they headed for the door, Black ordered, "Irish stays." Seeing Aubrey's hesitation, he added, "You can be ready with the cloths when that knife is pulled out."

At their nods, Aubrey stepped closer to the bunk. As Jean Luc and Morgan were closing the door, Black yelled out, "And if they have not finished with Deats, hold him until I get there."

"Aye, we will wait, Captain." Morgan told him as he closed the door. In the corridor, Morgan turned to Jean Luc saying quietly, "He would not blame her if something goes wrong, would he?"

"Of course not." Jean Luc replied firmly, though he had wondered the same thing just seconds ago. He had better not or there would be another fallen captain on this ship today, Jean Luc told himself.

Topside, they found Deats lying unconscious on the deck with hands bound behind him and a man tying his ankles together while Robert and several men held their pistols on him.

Seeing Jean Luc and Morgan approaching, Robert told them, "He put up a fight." Turning away from the other men, Robert added to Jean Luc and Morgan in a low voice, "I was also told that Jordan was found dead in the great cabin, stabbed as well. York and Riley moved the body before Captain Mala found him."

"Deats has been busy." Morgan said solemnly as he looked down at the Scotsman.

Willie looked about him and found all in readiness. Aubrey stood nearby with several cloths in hand. Black sat on the edge of the bunk, cutting Mala's shirt. Watching as Black laid the shirt open, Aubrey could see the line across Mala's midsection, the scar from the wound Willie had just mentioned. She did not remember seeing it when she and Mala swam in the pond at the mill but then she had looked away in embarrassment. She also noticed now Black's mark over Mala's left breast and a gold medallion on a gold chain.

Frowning slightly, Aubrey noted that Mala's mark was different from her own. It was more than just the initials. The initials were within a circle and even the RB was slightly different. The medallion had the same design as the mark. Aubrey noticed that the gold chain looked similar to the one she had received and had cast away. She wondered if the medallion would have been another 'gift' from Black. Looking at him, she decided that it would not have been. He was very particular with the jewelry in the small casket that day Jojoba was helping her to chose a trinket. The medallion was something special and only between him and Mala.

Black picked up the medallion and noticed that it was strangely bent and chipped. He glanced up at Willie as the old man mumbled absentmindedly,

"She was always wearin' that."

"It must have slipped to the side as she came aboard and ran to help me." Black said almost to himself.

With an air of certainty, Willie said, "Good thing, too. By the looks of it, it turned the direction of that knife and missed her heart. Just may have saved her life. But the wound is deep and it will bleed."

There was a silence in the room as the words said sank in. Black gently laid the necklace on the bunk over Mala's left shoulder so that it would be out of the way, but still around her neck. He hoped to share a good laugh with Mala over her good fortune of retaining his gift. His hand caressed her cheek as his gaze traveled over her pale face and he prayed hard that he would be able to laugh with her later.

"Ready, Cap'n? Miss Aubrey?" Willie asked setting the basin on the other side of Mala. Seeing their nods, he said, "Cap'n, tis time to remove what does not belong."

Black nodded and, taking a deep breath, took hold of the black-handled blade.

"This is wrong! I am telling ye, twas an accident!" Deats yelled out. The moment he had regained consciousness, three men pulled him roughly to his feet and now a fourth was placing the rope around his neck.

He looked around at the faces of the men he had sailed with for months, even years but found no sympathy. His gaze fell on Robert and knew from it that no one would believe him. They had heard Robert earlier and believed him.

Suddenly the deck grew quiet and heads turned towards the stern of the ship. Deats had to struggle to see and a chill gripped him as Black appeared in his line of vision. The wetness on the front of his black shirt was obviously blood. The look on Black's face made Deats tense for it was worse than any foreboding look from Mala. The thought of Mala and the blood on Black's shirt gave Deats a sick feeling in the pit of his stomach. He had loved her as he had never loved anything or anyone before and now she was dead, by his own hand.

Black stood before the Scotsman then made a circle around him, looking him over like a prized goose hanging on display in a store window. "Take off his boots." Black ordered coldly.

Several men leaped forward. One cut the bounds around Deats' ankles as the others struggled with the boots. Deats paid no attention as Black was again looking at him with that same cold intensity. When they started to bind his ankles again, Black waved them away. No one dared to make a sound or even move until Black spoke and every man seemed to breathe at once.

"Do you recall my warning to you that day in Charlestowne?" Black asked quietly. Deats did not answer though he recalled it all too well. "I told you that I would hold you responsible should anything happen to Mala." He reminded still in a calm tone as Deats remained stubbornly silent. "Little did I know that by your own hand..."

"I would never harm her!" Deats defended.

"Never harm her!" Black bellowed, giving into his rage. The men looked around at one another.

Stepped up close so that he was nearly nose to nose with the Scotsman, the movement caught Deats by surprise and he never thought to use his unbound legs and feet. Suddenly his Sgian Dhu was before him as Black seemed to produce it from thin air.

"Never harm her!" Black snarled. "This is yours, n'est-ce pas? This was meant for me but now she lies in her cabin from this! This gift of yours!" Shaking the small black handled knife in Deats' face, Black growled, "Meant for me, not her!"

Deats remained silent but looked at the bloodstained blade before him. The man's silence infuriated Black all the more and he whirled around as if he could no longer face the man. All eyes were pinned on him but Black could only see in his mind's eye Mala and this damned knife. Mala who was always strong and vibrant, who never backed down from a fight, who never surrendered easily or at times gracefully, and who was now barely alive! God, how he wanted to kill Deats a thousand times over.

Turning and walking back to Deats once again, Black growled, "I promised you a slow and painful death, and so you shall have it." Holding up the knife, Black added, "At your feet is your gift to Mala. She no longer cares for it."

Realizing what Black intended to do, Jean Luc took Morgan's pistol from his brother's waistband and held it against Deats' temple. The Scotsman could also see several other men follow the gesture as they pulled out their pistols and pointed at him.

Black glanced at Jean Luc then back to Deats before bending to place the knife on the deck. Looking to the men holding the other end of the rope, he ordered, "Raise him until his feet are just off the deck."

Deats jerked and felt his throat constrict as the rope tightened when he was lifted. He swung slightly and felt the tip of his toe touch the small blade every few seconds. Finally, Deats was gripped with a fear he never known before as he faced Death. His eyes met Black's and through clenched teeth, he hissed, "She hated you!"

Black's look became even colder as he tried to control the urge to break the man's neck with his bare hands.

"But she loved you more." Deats said quietly. With the constriction of the rope, he choked out, "She would not ...let anyone near ...until you came back."

Black was surprised at this. Was he making a confession? But Deats said no more. The weight of his body was pulling him down and, in doing so, the rope tightened. He began to cough as his face changed color. He looked up as high as he could to the tops of the masts on the ship he had grown to love and said hoarsely to the skies, "Mala, forgive me!"

Robert looked away as did many of the crew. Black turned away as well but in anger. Staring out across the lagoon to the island that had been Jean Luc's home for many months, Black's anger subsided a bit. After what he had done to his friend and quartermaster, Jean Luc had protected him just moments ago by putting a pistol to Deats' head as a warning of no sudden moves. Black's only thought was revenge for Mala and the two years they had missed being together.

Turning slightly and catching Jean Luc's eye, Black motioned him over. When Jean Luc was beside him, Black said quietly, "Get the crew together, even the prisoners below. Morgan will show you." Jean Luc nodded and moved away but hesitated when Black added, "But leave Aubrey and the cook with Mala."

Jean Luc looked at Deats and nodded. Aubrey was not going to see this and Black had thought of that as well. He wondered at Black's concern for Aubrey. Had he changed somehow where Aubrey was concerned? How long had he and Mala been on this ship together? There was much that he and Aubrey needed to talk about. As he left Black, Jean Luc motioned for Morgan and Robert to aid in gathering the men.

Within minutes, the men were assembled, most having been on deck for the execution. From the quarterdeck, Black looked around at the men then at Deats. His eyes were closed, either unconscious from the lack of oxygen or dead. Looking at the men assembled, Black began, "What has happened here was as you have heard. The charge of disobeying a direct order today was punishable by death. Many of you heard your captain order him to cease his fight against me. Even I heard her but Mr. Deats chose to ignore the order and there he is because of his choice." Black paused knowing that what he would say next would shock them.

"I, for one, have always admired your captain for many things and not the least of all was her courage and daring. Never has she backed down from a challenge or a fight. This man, your quartermaster betrayed her and tried to kill her." Taking a deep breath and seeing some men look around, he added, "But I must tell you this, Captain Mala is alive, but barely."

He remained silent as that bit of news sank in by various degrees.

Shocked faces, murmurs, and shouts of glee ran through the crowd. "Oui, she is not dead. Your cook, Willie, and Iri …Miss Aubrey are with her now and working hard to save her. But we need to get to a doctor and the nearest port is Bimini."

"The *Enchantress* is a fast ship, Captain." Robert proclaimed proudly.

"Oui, she is at that. But to sail through the seas at her fastest pace may do more harm than good for your captain." Black interjected through the chatter. "Therefore, we will sail to Bimini at a fast pace that would not hinder any healing process."

Turning to Timmons at the helm, Black ordered, "Set sail for Bimini, Mr. Timmons. Mr. Alcott, I leave you with the speed of her ship. You know the *Enchantress* better than I."

"Aye, Captain." Morgan acknowledged in a tone that momentarily took Black and Jean Luc by surprise. Morgan's emphasis on Black's title brook no disobedience and every man there seemed to notice it.

Men began to go about their duties with spirits lifted a bit higher at the news of their captain's condition. Robert stepped to the companionway and asked Black, "What about him?" With a thumb toward Deats, Robert awaited as Black contemplated the Scotsman.

"Cut him down and toss him overboard." Then looking at Jean Luc, Black said, "I do not ever plan to return to this island." Jean Luc nodded in agreement.

Robert nodded and headed for Deats' body as another man readied to lower the rope. Black called for Boulet and LaVoie as the two were walking away. With a brief nod of greeting to Jean Luc, they turned their attention back to their captain.

"You are to inform my men that there will be no tolerance given for confrontations with Mala's crew. I am putting you both in charge of maintaining order where my men are concerned until a new quartermaster is voted on." Black told them.

Boulet and LaVoie looked at one another then nodded in agreement. As Black spoke to them, Morgan and Jean Luc exchanged glances. Morgan made a mental note to gather Mala's crew together and pass on the same directive.

In the meantime, Robert stood before Deats, pausing to look up at his former quartermaster. Suddenly, he found himself in a leg lock around his neck.

"I dinna kill her. Ye lied!" Deats croaked hoarsely.

Robert had let out a yelp of surprise but had been cut off by Deats' legs tightening around his neck. The men nearby also let out an alarm. Suddenly the air roared as a pistol shot rang out through the chaos and Robert found himself freed as Deats' legs went limp. Looking up, Robert saw a portion of the Scotsman's head gone then turned to find the source of the pistol shot. He saw Black with arm still extended and a smoking pistol in hand.

"Thank you, Captain." Robert croaked out through the silence. Black nodded then left the quarterdeck towards Mala's cabin.

"So much for slow and painful." Morgan whispered to Jean Luc.

Jabbing his younger brother in the ribs, he said admonishingly, "Now is not the time, Morgan." But Jean Luc could not hide his smile and Morgan grinned knowingly.

Chapter 57

In the cabin, Aubrey and Willie turned when the door opened and found an angry Black storming inside.

"Was that a pistol shot we heard?" Aubrey asked in concern.

"It was." Black answered curtly.

"I thought it was a hanging." She ventured to say.

"Deats decided to play games but I was not in the mood." Black replied cryptically.

Aubrey and Willie exchanged glances as Black tossed the now-empty pistol on the table. He glanced at Aubrey and Willie before approaching the bunk. Mala was covered by the sheets and seemed paler.

"She is restin' now, Cap'n, and she is doin' fine." Willie said answering the unspoken questions.

Black nodded then sat at the table to begin loading his pistol, "We sail for Bimini. There will be a doctor to tend to her."

"Well, if it is all right with you, Cap'n, I will be gettin' about me duties. I got me a ship full of men to cook for. But I will come back later to tend to her."

Black nodded the dismissal and said, "You may go as well, Irish. I will sit with her."

Aubrey hesitated then moved the cloths closer to him. "Here is cool water for her. Willie says that her fever will get higher soon. I will come back with Willie to help." Black looked at the water in the basin and the cloths while nodding again. Aubrey stopped at the door and looked back. He sat at the table just staring at the pistol.

Jean Luc stood on the bottom step leading up to the quarterdeck and stared at the island that had been his prison for three long months.

"So, you are the man she pined for all that time?" Came the voice of Robert from behind him. Jean Luc turned slightly to look at him as Robert smiled and went on, "Every morning when she could since the day we plucked her from the waters off Bimini where the *Widow Maker* sank, Miss Aubrey would sit right on that very step and stare out to sea." Jean Luc's piercing blue eyes searched his face as Robert paused and looked up at the sails. "I saw many a tear fall from those pretty eyes those mornings."

Jean Luc glanced around the deck and Robert watched him, noticing the look in the blue eyes. "She has been with no one on board this ship. Your brother, Morgan, took her in. She stays in his cabin but they each have their own bunk. Like Cap'n Mala, Miss Aubrey has kept herself for only one man. The way I figure it, you and Captain Black are damn fortunate men to have two strong-willed women like..."

"Morgan's cabin?" Jean Luc echoed, cutting Robert off.

Nodding, Robert was struck with the thought that Jean Luc had not heard of this. "Aye, and Morgan says that she sleeps in your old bunk too."

"Merci." Jean Luc finally managed to say.

"Just thought you might like to know." Robert said with a shrug.

Jean Luc watched the man walk away. The second mate seemed to know quite a bit about Aubrey and her business. Frowning uneasily, Jean Luc turned and crossed the deck to the companionway. Morgan was coming up from below as Jean Luc started down the steps.

"How is Mala?" Jean Luc asked tightly as he stopped his brother on the steps.

"I just saw Willie in the galley. He said that she is resting better now, but she has not awakened." Morgan replied.

Jean Luc nodded and as Morgan started up, Jean Luc took him by the arm and said firmly, "We need to talk."

Morgan caught the look in his older brother's eye immediately as he followed Jean Luc to the stern railing. Many long and tense quiet moments hung between them when suddenly they were speaking in unison. They chuckled at one another, somewhat nervously. It had been almost a year since they had been together and a great deal had happened in that time.

Taking a deep breath, Morgan smiled and said, "You go first, you have been gone a long time from civilization—there must be a great deal on your mind."

Jean Luc nodded and sighed as he looked out to sea. "Oui, three months is a long time, especially to be alone." The two brothers fell silent for a moment before Jean Luc put his hand on Morgan's shoulder, "I thank you for your confidence in the recent vote but the position of quartermaster should rightfully go to you."

Morgan shrugged and gave a lazy smile as he said, "I was quartermaster for a while before Deats reclaimed his position." Looking down at the deck, he added with a sigh, "Ah hell, Jean Luc, you are more qualified for that position than I am."

"But these men know you." Jean Luc said shaking his head.

"Aye, and that is why they agreed to select you." Morgan replied firmly. He glanced over the deck beyond Jean Luc and nodded toward the men who worked about at their daily duties. "Besides, who would keep that gun crew in shape? No one else on board is as good at it as I am."

Jean Luc had to laugh at the braggart remark. "Oh ho, and I thought that

I was the egotistical son of our mother!" Morgan smiled charmingly in reply and shrugged his shoulders. With another smile, Jean Luc said, "Have you seen Michele Boulet aim a cannon? I would wager that the two of you would have much in common."

Morgan shrugged again as the tension seemed to have lifted for a fleeting moment and before an uncomfortable silence fell over them as the two pairs of blue eyes met once more, Jean Luc asked quietly, "What is your association with Aubrey?"

Morgan folded his arms over his chest and looked up at the sails. "Oh, I was waiting for that question. I wondered how long it would take you to ask." He began with a slight smile. Then he sighed deeply and looked his brother straight in the eye, "She is my friend, Jean Luc. I gave her a place to stay, offered her friendship, gave her protection..."

"Protection." Jean Luc echoed. Given their profession, they both knew all too well what the word implied.

Morgan let out a long sigh and said firmly, "You know Mala runs a tight ship, Jean Luc. Aubrey was as safe with us as a babe in its mother's arms. The protection became necessary only after Black and his men boarded the *Enchantress*." Jean Luc continued to stare at his brother as Morgan looked out at the sea.

"I offered her comfort when she would allow it. So much had happened since she was pulled from the waters near Bimini. She had ugly nightmares about her awful life with that ass of an uncle of hers. Did you know that the old bastard beat her? Beat her for no reason at all but for having been born? He sent her to confinement in her room with no food..."

"Oui Morgan, I know that." Jean Luc nodded.

Morgan looked down at the deck and sighed. "She had bad nightmares about the day you challenged Black for her." Jean Luc clenched his jaw and looked away for a few seconds.

Morgan cleared his throat and added carefully, "I was and still am just her friend, Jean Luc. I have to admit though, any man would have to be a fool or blind to want less of her—she is beautiful. I will also admit to you that I would gladly have given her my love on more intimate terms. I would be lying to you if I said that I would not. Nevertheless, I am only her friend. It is the only way that she would let me love her."

A heavy quiet fell over the pair of them when Morgan paused. "I have been one of her teachers in the ways of seamanship. I have taught her how to defend herself and how to use some weapons. I have been her confidant in times when she would open up to me and talk. I knew that she had fallen in love with a man on the *Widow Maker* and she was devastated when she was separated from him. She kept that secret very close, but she made it very clear that she had no feelings at all for Black and that he had never had her. It was not until just recently before we came here to find you did I know that my own brother was the man she loved."

Jean Luc sat perched on the railing and stroked his bearded chin, looking down at the deck and listening. At the last remark his eyes raised up to meet Morgan's. Once again, he found himself looking into eyes that were as blue as his own—a trait they had both acquired from their mother.

Jean Luc's mind tumbled as his gaze dropped to the deck at his feet once again. Aubrey was a beautiful young woman, starved for friendship and love. She had not seen any manner of affection since the death of her parents until he came along. Then, just as their love began to blossom even in light of their situation, he was gone, cruelly torn from her. How could he blame her if she had accepted the affections of another man after all this time alone? It would have been unfair and selfish for him to wish something like that upon a young woman that he had come to love so deeply. It was a relief to think that she had the good fortune to meet Morgan. Jean Luc mentally shuddered at the realization of who or what she could have fallen victim to instead. After the promises of Thomas Beaufort that day in the hold of the *Widow Maker*, Jean Luc had fretted and had nightmares of his own about that as well.

Morgan waited patiently while Jean Luc sorted through his thoughts. When his brother looked up, he informed him with a hint of anger, "Deats hated Aubrey. He hated her because of her friendship with Mala. Deats did not want anyone close to Mala, man or woman. He figured that Mala would get rid of Aubrey because of her being on the *Widow Maker* with Black. Deats had very often referred to Aubrey as 'Black's whore' because of the mark."

Morgan hesitated in his narrative. Admitting to his knowledge of the mark probably had not been a good decision. He watched his brother's eyes narrow. "You have seen the mark, Morgan?"

There was only one way that a man could have seen that mark and Morgan dared to stand before him proclaiming that he had not been intimate with her and yet he knew of the mark. Jean Luc glared at his brother but before he could say anything, Morgan threw up his hands in defense and explained how he came to know of the mark.

"Later, she told me about the ruse the two of you played on Black." Morgan was saying.

Jean Luc nodded but Morgan had the feeling that he still did not completely believe him. In an effort to smooth ruffled feathers, Morgan smiled with mischief, "Would you like my bunk for the night?"

Slowly Jean Luc rolled his eyes at him. With a grunt, he was forced to smile as he said, "Hell no! If I slept in there tonight, do you actually think that I would sleep in your bunk? Moreover, do you actually think that I will be sleeping? It has been three long and lonely months. We were just getting to know one another when—I was put off the ship."

The two men looked at one another for an extended moment before Jean Luc said firmly, "I will be moving her to my quarters, the quarters that Monsieur Deats has generously vacated to me." Then he clapped Morgan on the shoulder and the two brothers embraced once again. "Merci Morgan for taking care of her." Jean Luc said as he clapped Morgan's back.

"Well, let me give you one piece of advice, big brother." Morgan began in a confidential voice after the brotherly hug. Jean Luc raised a brow as Morgan winked then said, "Aubrey is very clean and fussy. I do not think she will like the beard."

Jean Luc glanced at Robert who stood talking with the helmsman then looked at his younger brother, "You and the second mate seem to know a great deal about my woman—for men who are assumed to be 'just her friends.'"

"Robert is my best friend. He watches out for her too." Morgan replied.

Jean Luc nodded in understanding then said with a small mischievous smile, "I do not care for the beard either, and I intend to get rid of it soon. I most certainly would not want to keep anything that might come between Aubrey and me! Now, if you will excuse me, I have to go move a certain young woman into her new quarters."

Aubrey had gone to her bunk after being dismissed by Black from Mala's side. The cabin was empty and she was glad because she was exhausted. It had been a day filled with emotions and she had run the whole gauntlet of them, from anxiety and anticipation during the search for Jean Luc to the elation when they had found him alive. Then when she was at her height in joy, she was struck with the scene and the horror of the attack on Mala. She thought about that for a moment, running the scene over and over in her mind. The blood—there was so much blood.

Her hands were clean, but she still could feel the wet stickiness of it. It had seemed to quite literally gush all over her hands when she had pressed the rags to the wound Black had left after he had pulled the blade out. She remembered how she had feared that she would faint right there beside him as she pressed the rags. Aubrey pulled herself into the corner of her bunk, drawing her knees up tight to her chest. Unconsciously she began a slow repetitious movement of wiping her palms on the knees of her britches. "God, the blood." She breathed.

For the moment, Jean Luc was far from her tired and tormented mind. His rescue was like a dream to her. With all the commotion of the day, she wondered if finding him had been real. Aubrey had not seen or heard from him since the incident with Deats upon their return. She closed her eyes, scenes of the day flashing through her mind, until she finally slipped off into twilight sleep.

Jean Luc easily opened the door and stepped into the small quarters when there had been no answer to his soft calls and knocks. The room was dimly lit by a lantern with the wick turned down low. He found her tucked in the corner of the bunk with her arms draped loosely about her knees. Her head was leaning back into the corner and her face was relaxed in sleep, her lips slightly parted.

"Aubrey." He called softly again as he moved closer. When she did not respond, he eased his lean frame down onto the bunk. "Aubrey, ma cherie."

Her eyes came open slowly, she stared at him as if she were looking at something unreal. Her voice came timidly, "Jean Luc?"

"Oui, ma cherie." He smiled.

She scrambled out of the corner and literally flew into his arms, "Oh my God, I was afraid that this was all just another torturing dream!"

He stood and pulled her to her feet so that he could better put his arms around her and hold her. He took her upturned face gently in his hands and touched his lips to hers ever so slightly. Then his kisses became more purposeful and feverish as he pressed his mouth on hers firmly. She finally gasped to be released and pushed against him, "Jean Luc, please."

"Mon Dieu, I am so glad to see you—so glad to hold you." He breathed, hugging her tightly and burying his face into her neck.

She clung to him, unable to cry or laugh, "This is real, I am not dreaming now." She breathed into the hollow of his shoulder.

"Oui m'amour, you are not dreaming." He replied as he raised his head and smiled down on her.

"And Mala is..." She began sadly.

He nodded and pressed her head to his chest, "That part is sadly true." Cradling her there, he looked around the tiny cabin through tear-blurred eyes. Jean Luc felt Aubrey emit a great sigh and she pushed lightly back to look up at him as he smiled down on her.

In a vain attempt at joviality as she stroked her fingers over his face, "You need a shave."

"Hmm, Morgan told me that you would not approve. Well, believe me when I say that a dirk is a poor substitute for a razor!" He chuckled. Jean Luc released her and turned toward her bunk. A rush of urgency coursed through him as he looked at her little place. With another smile, he said over his shoulder, "Been sleeping in my bunk, have you?"

"What? But, how did you know where I was?" She asked with a small frown.

"Morgan told me that you have been sharing this cabin with him, did he not tell you that he and I once shared this cabin? And that this was once my bunk?"

"Yes, he told me about that." She said then frowned at him when he picked up the neat pile of her clothing that was stacked on the little shelf at the foot of her bunk.

"What are you doing?" She asked.

"Moving you. Gather the rest of your things." He replied firmly.

Aubrey looked at him in alarm. "Moving me where? Why?"

"You will be staying in quarters with me from now on." Jean Luc replied.

"But…" She began. He took up her chemise that was neatly folded at the foot of her bunk, but she snatched it from his hands, "Leave that alone. Ya will not touchin' my nightgown!"

Jean Luc looked down at her and chuckled at her tone. It had risen a few octaves and fire flashed in the hazel eyes. A flood of old arguments came to mind. On the *Widow Maker*, her angry retorts had been just slightly laced with the brogue, but now it was thick and dripped with her temper.

Leaning close to her face that caused her to back up a step, he nearly burst into laughter at the expression on her face. "My order could be that you leave it here since you will not be needing it at any rate. For you to sleep without a stitch on would be my command." Then tucking her clothes under one arm, he caught her free hand in his and they went out of the cabin.

"Why would I not need it? Why are you taking my things? Where are we going?" She asked as he pulled her along behind him by her hand.

"You are full of questions." He scolded playfully as they passed the galley and moved toward the captain's quarters.

Just before they reached the doorway to the great cabin, he stopped and opened a door. She pulled back in alarm, "Ah now, I will not be settin' foot in there. Those are Mr. Deats' quarters!"

"No Aubrey, they were his quarters. Now they are mine since he has no need for them." Jean Luc replied firmly.

Aubrey recalled the death sentence Black had put upon Deats and the sound of the pistol shot. The sounds alone had painted the picture of his execution in her mind. Taking advantage of her distraction, Jean Luc pushed her gently inside and, following her, he closed the door behind them. They were cast into semi darkness, save for the light of the now rising moon that shone into the window in the bulkhead over the bunk.

Aubrey clicked her tongue and threw her hands onto her slim hips, "That Scottish bastard had a damned window! I been wantin' a window since the one in Captain Black's…" Her voice trailed off and she looked at Jean Luc worriedly.

He turned up the wick then glanced at her. Smiling as he indicated the window with his free hand, he said, "It is not a quarter gallery window, but it is a window nonetheless…and it is yours."

She looked around the quarters noting that they were much larger than Morgan's cabin though not nearly as large as Mala's. With an exasperated sigh she looked at her clothing Jean Luc had merely tossed on the floor. "Jean Luc, my clothes." She fussed as she bent to retrieve them.

Suddenly she found herself caught up in his arms again and he planted his lips firmly on hers. Kissing down her throat, he looked past her at the bunk. The desire to put her down right now was nearly too much to resist. Aubrey pulled back with a look of mild disdain.

"What is the matter, ma cherie?" He asked.

She made an apologetic face and said gently as she extracted herself from his arms, "Jean Luc, you do not smell very good."

With a concerned look on his face, he quickly released her. It had been at least the day before when he had washed up at the stream on the island. As he had told Morgan, the last thing he wanted right now was to thwart his own plans because he was offensive to her! "Now, you make yourself comfortable in your new home while I clean up." He said as he pushed her gently away and he moved to the washstand.

Chapter 58

Aubrey looked around the room again. Reaching down once more to retrieve her belongings from the floor she noted that there was a set of bagpipes in the corner. She recalled the nights when Deats had sat on the deck and played tunes for the crew in addition to the musicians among them.

Jean Luc chuckled at the look on her face as he watched her in the mirror and poured water into the basin, "Do not fret, you will become used to this cabin soon enough." With vigorous scrubbing motions, he set to work washing up.

Nearly a half an hour later, he was his old self again—somewhat leaner, but clean and freshened up. Now he was ready and eager to get to the business of re-consummating their relationship. He turned down the wick in the lantern to create a soft glow. Then he moved to the bunk and turned down the covers neatly. He bowed at her and smiled handsomely, offering the bunk with open hands, "Your bed, mademoiselle."

She stared at the bunk in surprise before stammering, "I have to sleep in his bunk?"

"Not his bunk. My bunk." Jean Luc corrected.

"Jean Luc, I—well I am not very tired right now. I was sleeping before. Perhaps I should just go and see if Willie needs me." She stammered as she made a move toward the door.

A frown crossed Jean Luc's face. "What is it, Aubrey? Why are you so shy? Ainsi timide?" He asked in a mixture of English and French. He moved closer to her, pulling her into his arms, kissing her mouth, then touching his lips to her eyes. She remained still as he moved his kisses down her throat. He pulled the neatly tucked shirt loose from her britches and encircled her slim waist with his hands.

"Oh ma cherie, we have been apart for so long, and now we are back together again. There is no need to hide now. There is no one between us. It is just as we wished for it to be before, do you not remember?" He purred against her skin.

She caught his face as he lowered it into the front of her shirt and bringing it up to look at her, she said pleadingly, "Well, yes, I remember but can we not just talk for awhile?"

"Talk?" He asked sharply as a frown crossed his brow again. With a low chuckle that rumbled deep from his chest, he caressed her back and the front of her lower rib cage gently with long sun-bronzed fingers. "Non ma cherie, there will be plenty of time to talk later."

He looked down to watch his own fingers caress her. It had been three months since he had held her but she felt painfully thin to him. Pulling her up to him, he rested his chin on the top of her head. "Tu es encore maigre. Have they not been feeding you? You are skin and bones. Please do not tell me that Rene has mistreated you."

"No, Jean Luc. As always, I eat when and what I want, unless Willie and Morgan badger me to do so and I take some food just to quiet them." She smiled easily.

"Morgan." He echoed tightly.

Aubrey caught the tone of his voice and pushed away, saying, "Morgan protected me, Jean Luc."

"Hmm, so I have been told and protection by more than one man." He replied putting his hands on his hips when she wandered away from him. Looking up she caught his frown in the mirror's reflection.

With abrupt movements, she tucked in her shirt and said angrily, "Morgan is my friend. I am sorry that ya think or suspect otherwise."

Jean Luc recognized the tantrum all too well and was amused at how he had actually missed them. With a frown, he realized that the passion in him was beginning to ebb away as his mind drifted to the thought of her sharing space with his brother again.

"Sweet Mary! I would never have dreamed that our reunion would reek of such jealousy. I will leave ya to rest in the comfort of your new home, Monsieur Pierne. I will be needed soon to help Willie tend to the captain." He stepped forward, his mouth dropping open in retort as she glared at him. "Close your mouth then. Mala would say that ya look like some great codfish!"

She cursed under her breath as she angrily snatched the clothing from the floor then straightened to head for the door. He stepped in her path, putting his hands on her shoulders to stay her. "Wait, now you act like Mala with your temper."

"Well thank you sir, I will take that as a compliment." She said sharply as she jerked free of his gentle grasp.

"Where are you going?" He asked in quiet concern.

"I will be returnin' to my bunk." She replied firmly.

"Aubrey, ma cherie." He breathed. Reaching out, he caught at her arms again and despite her struggle against him, he pulled her up to his chest. Aubrey pushed at his chest and he smiled gently to her method of rebuttal that he recalled all too well. Catching her chin in his long fingers, he made her look up at him, commanding her to be still. Ever so gently, he administered a soft kiss upon her lips, the passion for her rising in him again. "You dreamed of our reunion?" His voice was barely audible.

She looked down and a sudden remorse enveloped her, "I had nightmares of your battle with Black and the sinking of the *Widow Maker*. I thought that you were in her hold. After we had discovered that Black had marooned you, my daydreams—my day thoughts were full of the hopes of finding you alive. I drove them all crazy with the certainty that you were still alive. I would not let it rest until today when we came upon the island where he left you. Morgan and Mala tried to keep me back, but I would not have it. I knew you were still alive."

He gently plucked the clothing from her arms and tossed them aside once more. "Oh, Jean Luc." She moaned, looking over the mess.

He scooped her up into his arms and carried her to the bunk, easily laying her down. Kneeling on the bunk to hover over her, he was reminded of their last night together in his cabin. Now, with some degree of balking from her, Jean Luc pulled her shirt from her britches. There was one thing on his mind now, and nothing would deter him in his mission, not even her little temper tantrums. He wanted to make sweet love to her in their newfound freedom.

The small yet well-formed breasts he had remembered were exposed in the soft lantern light before him. He laid his hand on her chest and lovingly caressed the outline of each soft mound with gentle fingertips. Aubrey squirmed nervously and caught at his hand but he gently and insistently shook his hand free from hers. "Be still, ma cherie, and let me love you." With undaunted determination, he lowered his face, letting his tongue and his lips caress her breasts until the nipples stood erect.

When he moved to unbutton her britches, she grabbed his hand quickly and her voice was apologetic. "Jean Luc, slow down please."

Drawing back from her, he searched her face. "Pourqoui? Slow down? You tell me of your dreams. You imply that you wanted me to be back into your life, and now you ask me to slow down? You act as if making love was something completely new to you."

She looked away from him, staring at the lantern, a blush spreading over her cheeks. "It has been a long time. Jean Luc, I cannot go into this so quickly. This is all still very new to me. I am afraid that I would not remember how—afraid that I will disappoint you."

He was still and stared at her for a moment before he smiled down at her and, trying to relieve her fears, said, "Aubrey, ma cherie, it has been three very long months. Mon Dieu, I have done nothing less than dream and think about you all this time—it was all that kept me alive. You have not forgotten, I promise you. If you have, I will teach anew. You will not disappoint me, you could never disappoint me. But I cannot wait another moment." She looked up at him as his hand went back to the buttons.

"Take them off, s'il vous plait. I want to see you." He cooed quietly.

Aubrey finally relented and with naked bodies against one another, Jean Luc's hands wandered lovingly over her just as he had imagined in his mind all those long days on the island.

"It is as our first time, but tonight there is no need to hide, no fear of being discovered. We do not need to hurry, no one will stop us." He whispered against her ear, easing himself over her.

Even after such a brief encounter on the *Widow Maker*, and after such a long time of abstinence, Aubrey could remember the feel of him. The scent of him was etched in her memory and it surfaced now to ease her in her relaxation. Jean Luc could not help but emit a low moan of pleasure as he slowly entered her, feeling her surround him.

The delicious sensation brought chill bumps to the tanned skin of his back, chest and arms. Aubrey closed her eyes as Jean Luc kissed her throat, speaking to her in hushed tones of French and English, just as he had the first time they had been together. She submitted to his will, but her body still trembled with apprehension. Jean Luc's passion began to ride high and he covered her mouth with his as he held her face framed in his hands. Then he dipped his head down to seek her breasts. Aubrey emitted a small moan and she gasped quietly.

"What is it? What is the matter?" Jean Luc asked thickly in concern as he raised his head to look into her face.

Aubrey reached up to frame his face in her hands this time, and she replied in her own throaty tone of building passion, "Three months seems like a lifetime now."

Jean Luc chuckled deeply and replied, "Oui, three months is a lifetime."

Aubrey responded to his movements, opening wider now as he buried himself deeply into her. Her shyness suddenly changed as she began to meet his thrusts with a vigor of her own. Her responsiveness both surprised and delighted Jean Luc. She seemed to hold her breath as the passion within her began to swell. With a soft cry, she felt that same wonderful sensation she had felt the other times with Jean Luc. He felt her climax as her body arched for him and within seconds Jean Luc finally let loose his rampant desires.

Afterwards he held her close to him and his mind drifted as she dozed. How much longer would she have held out? He could not be angry with Morgan. As he had stated earlier, she was beautiful and very desirable. He could, however, envy his brother those three months that he had been privileged to see her, to hear her and to take care of her. Aubrey was his and now he knew that she, like Mala, had truly held herself for one man. With a contented sigh, he hugged her closer and kissed her ruffled auburn hair. Jean Luc's eyes closed and soon slipped into blissful sleep.

A knock at the door broke into Jean Luc's slumber. He inhaled deeply and opened his eyes. Aubrey lay nestled against his chest, sleeping peacefully. He eased from under her gentle embrace and got out of the bunk. After donning his britches, he went to the door and opened it just a crack to see the wizened face of Willie in the corridor by the light of the lantern on the wall. "Oui?"

"Mr. Pierne, beggin' yer pardon sir, but I need Miss Aubrey. Cap'n' Mala needs to be tended to." The older man said apologetically.

"I am coming, Willie." Aubrey called from the bunk.

Jean Luc shut the door as he looked over his shoulder to watch her rise and reach for her shirt that lay nearby. When she was dressed, he approached her and pulled her to him for a kiss.

After a moment, she pushed herself away from him, blushing lightly, "Rest now, it has been a long time since you have slept in a real bed." He nodded with a small understanding smile. He slipped out of his britches and got back into the bunk. With a contented sigh, he buried his tousled head down deeper into the pillows and closed his eyes.

Cool night air wafted down the companionway steps from the above deck. "What time is it?" She asked as she followed Willie to the captain's door.

He turned a wizened smile on her, "Ye lost track of time, have ye luv? Been busy sayin' hello to that lucky man of yers. Tis nearly midnight and ol' Willie sees a glow in them eyes, yer happy now. It pleases me old heart to see ye happy. Yep now that yer man…" She smiled at his rattling on. He stopped his chattering as the door came open before them.

Black's face was gaunt and tired-looking as he let them in and he whispered worriedly, "She is burning up with fever."

"Aye Cap'n I knew she would be by now, but do not fret, she will be fine." Willie told him.

Aubrey laid a gentle hand against his chest and said softly, "You should get some rest, Rene. We will take care of her."

"I cannot rest." He grumbled and moved from under her touch. She sighed and moved past him to help Willie. Mala was drenched in sweat and mumbling incoherently.

"Let us change this bandage and these wet bed linens. We cannot have her layin' in dampness. Take care ye do not move her too much." Willie directed.

Aubrey nodded and set to work. Once the dressing had been changed and the bed linens replaced with dry ones, Willie wet a rag with clean fresh water then showed Aubrey how to give Mala water without choking her. As she set to her new task, Willie gathered up the old bandages and bed linens then, much to Aubrey's distress, he left the room.

513

Black approached the bunk when Willie left. Aubrey cast a worried glance to him, but continued her duty. He stood over her, raising his mug to his lips. He longed to take Mala up into his arms and press his lips on hers. He set the mug aside and leaned past Aubrey to brush his fingertips across Mala's sweat covered brow, whispering in French to her. Aubrey drew back from her task, allowing him a moment with her.

"You have been with him tonight?" He asked suddenly.

"I have." Aubrey whispered bravely but did not look up at him.

He drew back away from Mala and picked up the mug again. "Do you love him?"

Her reply caught in her throat at first and she wondered what his reaction would be. Finally, she said quietly, "Aye, I love him—just as she loves you."

After a few silent moments, she looked up at him. He regarded her for another long moment before he nodded and moved away. She returned to her task of feeding Mala drops of water. Black set the mug on the long table and literally threw his lean frame into the ornate chair at its head, watching the young Irish woman as she administered care to the love of his life. Willie returned with fresh water, bandages and linens. He commended Aubrey quietly on her job well done.

"Do not leave me alone with him anymore, please." Aubrey breathed as Willie leaned over her shoulder.

The old man patted her shoulder, whispering in her ear, "You were fine, luv. He ain't interested in you. What he wants lies here and that is why we need to get her back on her feet."

"Go on now." Black finally growled standing from the chair.

"Aye Cap'n, try and get some more water into her. We will come back later in the mornin' to change them dressins." Willie told the captain then took Aubrey by the arm and pulled her up from the bunk.

As the two neared the door, Black called her back. Willie dropped his hold on her arm and left, closing the door almost in her face. Left alone with Black again, she turned bravely to find him slowly approaching her.

"Here." He said as he put out his hand. She frowned and looked at his closed fist. He nodded to his hand and she put an open palm under it.

Looking into her palm after he dropped something, she nearly gasped, "Mama's ring." She breathed turning it in her hand. Looking up at him, she smiled, "Merci, Rene."

Black merely nodded then turned to ease himself down on the edge of the bunk. She watched for a few moments as he carefully resumed the task of feeding Mala drops of water just as she had been doing. The strong urge to break into tears almost overtook her as she heard him speaking to the dark haired woman ever so quietly in his native tongue and Aubrey understood the soft loving words of encouragement and endearment.

As Aubrey turned to leave the cabin, she heard him say quietly, "Irish, the mark was made out of anger. Je regrette."

The room was so deathly still that he raised his head to look to see if she was still there. Aubrey stood staring at him with her mouth agape. In a voice so small that he barely heard it, she repeated, "Merci, Rene."

Jean Luc was sleeping soundly when she entered the room quietly. The room still unnerved her as she picked through her strewn clothing on the floor where Jean Luc had left them for the second time. She retrieved her chemise and, as she undressed, she looked around the room with a shiver. She felt as if Deats was there watching her. Putting out the lantern, she used the moonlight streaming through the window to see her way to the bunk.

Getting in proved to be a task, Jean Luc was sprawled quite literally across the entire surface. She smiled, hating to disturb him. He looked so peaceful, resting so well after his long ordeal.

"Jean Luc." She whispered as she pushed at his arm. He stirred slightly, mumbling in French. She rolled her eyes, "Jean Luc, Englase, s'il vous plait. Move over—unless you want me to go back to my bunk in Morgan's cabin." She coaxed. He stirred again and opened his eyes, looking at her in puzzlement. Was he dreaming again? Dreaming that he was in a warm comfortable bed and was that Aubrey hovering over him?

"Move." She said firmly as she pushed at him again.

"I thought that I was dreaming just now." He said sleepily. He caught her about the waist with one arm and pulled her down beside him. "This is a dream come true." He sighed as he pulled her in tighter, her back against his chest.

"Oh ma cherie, why are you wearing that cavernous nightgown? Take it off, let me feel you against me." He purred sleepily against the back of her head.

"No, go to sleep." She scolded lightly. Aubrey settled herself in and sighed in exhaustion. The realization and memory of the day's events came slowly back to him as he snuggled his face into the side of her neck.

"How is Mala?" He asked, his voice was low and sleepy.

"She has a fever. We redressed her wound, changed her sheets and gave her some water." She reported. She fingered the ring on her hand, glancing over her shoulder at him as he held her. "Rene gave me back Mama's ring—the one he took from me the day I was brought onto the *Widow Maker*."

"Bon." Jean Luc mumbled in her ear as he drifted back into deep sleep. Aubrey smiled in the darkness. She supposed that the ring did not matter much to him, nor the return of it. But it meant a great deal to her. For Black to give back the tiny treasure meant the world to her. A tear slipped from each eye and she sighed deeply, feeling herself drift off into a peaceful sleep.

A short time later, Jean Luc was snoring lightly in her ear. Opening her eyes, she stared into the darkness and listened for a time. Then she smiled and nudged him easily, "I cannot sleep with that noise in my ear."

Aubrey laughed lightly when he mumbled but continued to snore. Raising up on one elbow, she looked down at him as he laid on his back, one hand resting on his stomach and his other hand flung up over his head.

"You sound like your brother!" She whispered to his sleeping face as she kissed his cheek lightly. A fleeting smile stole across his lips and Aubrey settled herself back down onto her own side of the bunk.

Chapter 59

Aubrey turned in her sleep, brushing up against another person and her eyes flew open. How could Morgan be so close that she could touch against him when she was in her bunk? What was that strange light that illuminated the room? There was far too much light for a candle. Her head snapped about to look up at the portal, a frown crossed her brow. She and Morgan did not have a window in their cabin.

In the semi darkness, she noted that someone did lay close beside her in the bunk, and was between her and the door. The broad bare back and slim waist looked dark against the whiteness of the linens.

"Sweet Mary, where am I?" She whined in a terrified whisper as she looked to the door. In the faint light of the dawn, she saw a kilt and sporran as they hung on a hook. Sweet Mary Mother of Jesus—she was in Deats' cabin! She sat bolt upright grasping at herself, fearful that she would most certainly be naked. Had the delicious session of lovemaking she recalled from the night before not been with Jean Luc but with the Scotsman? Had she imagined Deats to be Jean Luc and given herself freely to him?

Aubrey felt suddenly ill and scrambled to get out of the bunk but her legs were trapped in the long chemise and the sheets. Her mind was fogged with terror and her stomach rolled with her mounting fear. The man beside her groaned in his sleep at her frantic tugging on the sheets and turned on his back, his head rolling to face her.

Aubrey froze and looked down into the peacefully sleeping countenance. With a small nervous giggle at her own foolishness, she realized that the man beside her was Jean Luc and the recollection of the night before came back to her. Jean Luc slept soundly, completely unaware of her fit of near hysteria. She looked back at the window overhead a bit more calmly now. It was nearly dawn. Suddenly she remembered Mala. Why had Willie not come for her? Surely he had gone to check on the captain by now? Willie was always up before the dawn. Aubrey looked back at Jean Luc, what if Willie had come for her and she had slept through his summons?

She heard the ship's bell toll four times for 6am. Thinking that Willie may well be in the captain's cabin right now, she slipped from the bunk and picked up the closest thing to cover her nightshift that she could find in the strewn mess in the cabin. It proved to be a shirt that Morgan had loaned Jean Luc. There was no time to dress just yet, Willie needed her. She ran her fingers through her hair as she quietly opened the door.

The corridor was quiet, but she heard the voices of the men in the galley.

517

Frowning, she went to the door of Mala's cabin. She turned the latch easily, calling softly as she opened the door, "Willie? Why did you not call me?" She swung the door open wider. A brief flash of memory ran through her as she remembered another time that she had come unannounced to this cabin.

"He is not here. He has finished and gone." Black replied softly. He was sitting in a chair beside the bunk holding Mala's hand in his.

"But he should have called on me for my help. I shall go then." She said, turning to leave the room.

"Irish." He called softly. "You may as well stay for a while."

Aubrey hesitated for a moment before moving to stand beside him and look down at her friend in the light of the rising sun. "How is she?" She whispered.

"The same. The fever broke, but now it is slowly returning." He told her.

Aubrey could hear the tone of helplessness in his voice. She laid a comforting hand on his shoulder and said, "She is strong, Rene. She will be fine."

With utmost care and gentleness, Aubrey's hand reached out and hesitantly smoothed his dark hair at the back of his head. With a forceful exhale, he bowed his head and reached out to encircle her waist with his free arm. He gave her the briefest of hugs then dropped his arm.

Dropping her hand, she turned to leave him in private with Mala. She was surprised when he caught her by the sleeve and held her there. "Will you pray with me?" He asked, his voice gentle and pleading.

She looked on him almost incredulously but he had not taken his eyes off the woman on the bunk. A lump caught in her throat, "Oui Rene." Aubrey dropped easily to her knees next to him, and crossed herself. She noticed that Black did not as they began to pray.

Jean Luc awoke with a start, wondering where he was. Glancing around he wondered where Aubrey was. He pulled on his britches and boots then left the cabin. The door to Mala's cabin stood slightly ajar and the morning sun could be seen through the quarter gallery window beyond. Thinking she must be there with Willie, tending to Mala, he easily ducked his head in. The sight before him made his jaw drop slightly in surprise.

There on the floor, on bent knees beside the bunk, in the broad rays of the sun, were Aubrey and Black. Jean Luc noticed that next to Black she looked small in the shirt she wore over her chemise, her bare legs and feet exposed. The rising sun through the quarter gallery window made her hair glow. On the bunk, he could see a portion of Mala covered by the sheets.

He felt a tightness in his chest. Although he had prayed for Aubrey's safety while he was on the island, he had never been one much for—real prayer. He smiled sadly for here before him were three of the very few people he had ever cared about in the world—in his life. Quietly he stepped out and closed the door so that they never knew he had been there.

Black raised his head from prayer almost at the same time as Aubrey. "Merci." He said quietly.

With a deep sigh and a nod, Aubrey stood or attempted to do so. The hem of her chemise caught on a loose nail in the floor and there was the unmistakable sound of tearing fabric. She looked up at Black in alarm as he gave her a sideways glance in amusement. Aubrey giggled nervously, the solemn tension in the room lifting for a few moments. She bent down to try and release herself from the nail, fussing for several moments.

"Shall I help you with that?" He finally asked quietly, his deep voice hinting of a smile.

"No, I can get it." She replied in nervous embarrassment. He heard the sound of ripping material again then she straightened up.

"You will be hard-pressed to explain that." He commented, shaking his head. He offered his hand as she started to rise to her feet. Still on his knees, he glanced down at her feet and asked, "Where are your boots, Irish?"

"In the cabin. I was afraid that Willie had called me and I had not heard. I just wanted to get here to help Willie." She explained softly.

"He did not want to disturb you and take you from your bed—Jean Luc's bed. Run along now and get some clothes on before you cause trouble. Have we taught you nothing in all the time that you have been with us?" Black said smiling as he stood.

"I have learned a great deal." She replied with an arrogant lift of her chin.

As she turned to the door, Black said behind her, "By the by, Mala would have loved the entertainment just now. You quite literally lit up the room with your blush." Aubrey rolled her eyes and reached to the door.

At that moment, Mala stirred restlessly in the bunk and emitted a heart-wrenching sob, "Rene?" The heartrending call sent a chill through both Black and Aubrey.

Moving quickly to her, Black sat on the bunk beside her saying softly, "Je suis ici mon coeur, I am here." His thumb caressed Mala's warm cheek lovingly.

"Rene?" Mala whined again. Aubrey shivered at the helpless sound from a woman she had known to be so strong and brave.

"C'est moi, Mala." Black soothed again in reply as he brushed at her fevered brow.

"Pourquoi?" Mala asked quietly in her fevered sleep. "Pourquoi, Rene?" She repeated in the same helpless voice.

"Pourquoi?" Black echoed as his brows knitted into a frown. Why? He wondered, why what?

Aubrey clapped her hand over her mouth to squelch the audible sob that threatened to escape. With quiet swiftness, she did not hesitate another second to leave the cabin.

Throughout the day, Jean Luc spent a great deal of his time on the quarterdeck assuming the command while Black sat by Mala's side. The feel of the sea breeze in his face as he looked up at the sails made him feel alive again. He missed the sea, missed the gentle rocking of the ship beneath his feet.

"Let us keep a sharp eye out on our horizons. We do not have the time to play with any of the British today." Jean Luc told Morgan and Boulet who stood with him on the quarterdeck.

"I have a man on the fighting top as well as the crow's nest to ensure no encounters." Morgan told him.

"Aye and, with Timmons at the wheel, we should be on a direct course to Bimini." Boulet added.

Jean Luc looked at Boulet and wondered at his change in demeanor. Did Mala change his attitude once he boarded her ship or was it the absence of Thomas Beaufort? He remembered seeing LaVoie as well as several other men from the *Widow Maker*. He had been told of the sinking of the *Widow Maker* and wondered if Jojoba, Beaufort, young Henri had all perished from the battle. Although Morgan had related bits of information of how he had helped Black and his men board the *Enchantress* and Aubrey told of how Morgan and Mala taught her many skills for combat, Jean Luc knew there was much more to tell of the three months since he was marooned.

Deciding that all would be told in time, Jean Luc allowed Morgan and Boulet to show him around Mala's ship. He was surprised at her ingenuity for making smuggling holds within the cargo hold. After a brief report of the watches and other details of the ship, Jean Luc headed for the galley. There he was surprised to see Aubrey not only helping Willie but she was also making sure that rum and ale flowed easily as the men moved in and out of the galley. Once, he joined her when she took a tray to the great cabin but the two of them could not get Black to leave Mala's side, even for a quick trip to the deck for some air.

It was nearly dawn the next morning when Jean Luc knocked softly at the door of the great cabin. Hearing Black call out, he entered to find the cabin dimly lit by a candle on Mala's desk. Jean Luc found him sitting at the head of the long table, the chair turned to face the bunk but he was gazing out the window. Black turned slightly and nodded for him to come in.

Closing the door quietly, Jean Luc stepped to the bunk to look down at Mala and said softly, "We are nearing Bimini, Rene." Black nodded but said nothing. Jean Luc looked closely at him then back at Mala. "Is all well?"

After a few moments, Black said, "With her fever, she talks in her delirium. She talks about our days on the *Widow Maker*. But when she becomes upset, she speaks in her language and I cannot understand her." Turning to face Jean Luc, he emphasized, "I want to know why she gets so upset."

"Tis frustrating, Rene, I know. For nearly two years, you were not there."

"So much happened since I left her on that island. Mon Dieu, I should never have left her behind, mon ami."

"It was better that you did. Remember, you were in jail for over two weeks before we could get you out. Before that, there was that battle with the British frigate. We lost so many of our crew and we had to spend a great of time on repairs."

Black nodded as he remembered his arrest for being drunk. After the delay with the repairs to his ship, he still had the trading to finish but he wanted to go back to Mala. Stopping in a tavern and ignoring the whores that seemed to hover over him, he drank a great deal. When an officer tried to get him to a warm bed to sleep off the drink, Black hit him. It was while he slept it off in jail that a captain named Fulton recognized him as the pirate from various postings. Fulton pressed charges on the attack and had the younger officer demoted for not recognizing the criminal. Because of Fulton and the setback he created, Black blamed him for the delay in returning to Mala. Instead of reuniting with his island beauty, he found a burned village and graves.

Black looked to Mala but said to Jean Luc, "All that time, mon ami, I thought she was dead." Jean Luc remained quiet and looked at his friend. This was the Rene Black who had been distant and exhausted when they could not find Mala. "But why did she never look for me? Why did she want me dead? I had not known the answers until Deats boasted of it that day you were found." Glancing at Jean Luc, and seeing that he was listening, Black said, looking at Mala, "She thought I never returned for her. She blamed me for leaving her on that island."

Jean Luc looked down at Mala and understood now why she would not go near the *Widow Maker* after rescuing Morgan and why she made him make that promise. He sat in a chair near Black and asked, "Did Morgan not talk to Mala about what happened? He had been with us during the battle."

"Non, on different occasions, Deats and Morgan had told me that Mala refused to talk about it."

Jean Luc sighed as he remembered how she refused to talk about the

Widow Maker or going back to Black.

"Since I boarded her ship, Mala and I have been together almost constantly." Black said almost to himself as he looked around the large room until his gaze came back to Mala lying in the bunk.

Jean Luc looked at Mala as well and said unbelievingly, "I cannot understand why she would not talk to you about it. After telling her of how you had felt when we could not find her and telling her of your love for her, surely she relented in her vendetta."

Black was quiet for a long moment before letting out a sigh and said quietly, "I have never spoken the words to her, mon ami. I have never told Mala how I felt for her."

Jean Luc looked at him incredulously. "Why not?"

"They are just words, Jean Luc. I show her my love with every action I make with her. Mala has always been so wise and there were her 'feelings' that ought to have told her how I felt for her. Besides she never said them either." Black refrained from saying that he had read the words in her log. He knew she loved him and her actions told him more than the words ever would.

"Rene, you know that women want to hear the words. They like to hear them. And as to Mala not saying the words, it was probably because she was not sure about your feelings for her."

"They are just words." Black said again, shaking his head.

"Then do this, Rene. When she is well and you are holding her close again, say the words. You will be pleasantly surprised at her reaction."

There was silence between them as they looked at the pale Mala who began murmuring in French. "She cannot die, Jean Luc. I cannot go through that again and knowing that this time she was truly dead."

"She will not die, Rene. She will not leave you behind, not now, because she knows you did go back for her."

Black closed his eye against the pain of losing Mala and whispered, "I do love her, Jean Luc, far beyond the words."

"Oui, I know, mon ami. And she will soon be well for you to tell her yourself." Jean Luc looked at his friend and knew the pain. Could he endure such pain a second time around if something happened to Aubrey?

Jean Luc remained silent. How could he tell Black that he had known Mala was alive? He had made a promise to her in return for rescuing Morgan. Even when Black took Aubrey, Jean Luc had kept Mala's secret. Even as Black thought he imagined seeing her in Jamaica, Jean Luc kept silent. How many times had he wanted to tell Black about her? Thankfully, Aubrey was able to hold her own before and more so after that night they duped Black into thinking he had her. Suddenly Jean Luc had a thought

What if Black really had not wanted Aubrey then? Did Aubrey just happen to be there when Black chose that time to try and forget Mala, by trying to go back to the way he had lived before Mala came into his life?

Jean Luc realized that Black was speaking of plans for Bimini, " ...do not want to alert the authorities by intimidating the doctor."

"I quite agree." Jean Luc said with a nod.

"I am sure the doctor will need to see her several times over a few days. He will need to come here for I will not have her moved. It is a wonder we did not lose her when I carried her from the deck."

"She is too stubborn, Rene." Jean Luc said trying to boost his friend's spirit.

"Aye, that she is. But usually to spite me." Black replied with a sad smile.

Jean Luc nodded with a knowing smile on his face. For a few moments, the men were quiet as they listened to soft creaking noises of the ship amid Mala's quiet murmurs.

"I actually came in for something else." Jean Luc said breaking the silence. "I had the flags taken down. I will check with Morgan about a ruse and make sure everything is ready when the dawn breaks."

Black nodded and said smiling, "Good idea. Not many would think of a pirate ship named the *Enchantress* as dangerous. I wonder if she named her ship for that purpose."

At that moment, their attention was drawn to the bunk as Mala muttered something and gave a sorrowful moan. Jean Luc looked to Black whose smile was gone instantly.

"You do not remember her native language? Mon Dieu, but I wish I knew what she was saying." Black said as he stood up and knelt beside the bunk. He caressed her forehead and took her hand in his.

Jean Luc left quietly, not wanting to intrude as he heard Black whispering her name.

Chapter 60

The *Enchantress* was moored in the harbor off the island of Bimini. Morgan stepped on deck and looked around. Everyone was dressed accordingly to the ruse of a merchant ship. The men were cleaned up and dressed as merchant seamen and the Union Jack flew high and proud in the breeze. Since Mala's men were familiar with the ruse, Black ordered his men to stay below until permission for shore leave was given.

Morgan noticed that the *Enchantress* was moored between two British warships. Looking at the ships' names, the *Iron Prince* and the *Lightning Jack*, he was thankful that his brother had the foresight to change from pirates to just plain sailors. The rest of the harbor held various British frigates, foreign trading ships, and other merchant ships.

Aubrey stepped up looking every bit the cabin boy. Her hair was tucked under a tricorn hat, which she fidgeted with every few minutes.

"I hate this hat." She muttered in disgust. Pulling at her clothes, she added, "I hate these clothes. I hate the idea of being a cabin boy. I hate..."

Morgan broke in, "The list would probably be shorter if you just said what you did like about this ruse." That earned him a disgusted glare and he only chuckled all the more.

"Leave her alone, Morgan." Jean Luc said approaching them with Black trailing behind him.

"You know me, I could not resist." Morgan said grinning.

"Try anyway." Jean Luc said with a sigh, then turning to Aubrey, he said sternly, "And stop fidgeting."

"I hate this hat..." She began.

"Here we go again." Morgan said to the heavens and successfully avoided a jab to his ribs from his brother.

"Between you and Jean Luc, tis a wonder I am not black and blue." Morgan grumbled, looking at Aubrey and Jean Luc.

"It is a wonder you are still alive knowing Mala's patience or lack of it." Black muttered in good humor as he looked to the town across the harbor. There, a doctor would be found for Mala.

"I know how to stay out of trouble when Mala is around." Morgan replied.

Throwing her arms in defeat over Morgan's behavior, Aubrey said to sky in a heavy Irish brogue, "Saints preserve us!" The three men smiled but all smiles quickly disappeared when Aubrey faced them again. "Ya know, if Mala knew how close we are to those ships, she would have strung ya up."

She said looking at Black.

With a disgusted snort as he walked away, Black said over his shoulder, "Do not look at me, I am not the navigator."

"Indeed then, just blame me." Jean Luc said following him.

"Indeed, I did." Black said over his shoulder. Morgan smiled at Aubrey then slapped at her hands as she fidgeted with her hat again.

"Stop that!" He scolded.

"Oh! You are absolutely incorrigible today, you scamp!" She growled then stuck her tongue out at him.

Bowing to her as she turned away, Morgan said in his best Irish accent, "Why, I do try, me darlin'."

"No truer words were ever spoken, Morgan. You are trying our patience and our sanity." Aubrey replied as she walked away from his grinning face.

Black was talking with Robert as the others joined him. " ...and give as many men shore leave as possible. But I want the ship and Mala guarded."

"Aye sir, I am planning to stay on board myself and see to the care of Captain Mala. Willie is, too, sir." Robert told him.

"Good, we may be here a few days, so make sure to rotate and have plenty of men..."

"Rene, he knows what to do." Jean Luc replied placing an arm around Black's shoulders.

Robert smiled and replied, "Aye sir, all will be well. Good luck in finding the doctor."

Black nodded and moved to the rope ladder.

The small group boarded the *Witch* and was taken to shore. Their journey across the bay was observed by many of the sailors from the various ships. However, one man was watching with great interest.

He recognized Black immediately then looked the others over carefully before an evil smile crept up. His gaze shifted to the ship from which they just disembarked and he muttered, "Perhaps a surprise visit is in order, old friend." He moved to lean against the bulkhead and covertly watched the movements of the newest ship in the harbor.

It took nearly a half an hour to locate where the doctor's house had been. Black vaguely remembered his last visit with the good doctor. He did, however, remember well how he got there. Since that visit, the doctor had married and now lived outside of town in a quaint cottage home that was surrounded by a low stonewall. It took nearly another hour to locate the cottage.

Jean Luc knocked as the others rested on the stonewall. Black sat with his back to the house so that his one eye did not cause undue stress upon the doctor. Morgan watched Jean Luc and idly spoke with Aubrey as she too sat with her back to the house.

"I suppose that would be his wife." Morgan reported as a woman answered Jean Luc's knock. "Uh oh, she is shaking her head. Perhaps the doctor is not at home."

"Damn." Black grumbled, rolling his eye to the sky.

Jean Luc bowed his head slightly to the woman as she closed the door and rejoined the others. "The doctor had to leave well before dawn. Apparently he has been called away to deliver a baby."

"A baby! Mon Dieu, that could take hours! Days!" Black said impatiently and then added, "Does she know where he is?"

"Probably but I did not ask." Jean Luc replied. Black looked at him as if he should have. "No, Rene, we are not taking him away from delivering a baby." Jean Luc defended. Black stood up and began pacing. Jean Luc added with mild amusement, "You did say not to alert the authorities."

"Well, that would definitely do it." Aubrey said mimicking Morgan's flare for sarcasm.

Black turned on them and growled, "I know what I said but we are running out of time."

"Rene, we are not kidnaping a doctor." Aubrey told him amazed that he would actually consider the thought.

Jean Luc noticed a curtain move within the cottage and told the others, "Perhaps we should wait for the doctor down the lane."

Nearly two hours later, the four spied a one-horse buggy slowly bouncing down the lane. Black threw up his arms and muttered to himself in French.

"Rene, please." Aubrey said trying not to laugh.

Their efforts to control his impatience had been a test of combined strength if not entertaining. Aubrey thought back at how Black had paced, growled and devised various kidnaping schemes only to have Jean Luc remind him of his own order to not alert the authorities. At one point, Black snapped at him, "Do not repeat my own words, Monsieur Pierne."

Jean Luc shrugged and said unperturbed at Black's menacing tone, "As you wish, Captain. However, tis only the welfare of one Captain Mala I would like to see recover from her wounds instead of a doctor putting her to a quick end."

Black had stopped his pacing to stare incredulously at Jean Luc. Aubrey and Morgan looked from one to the other. Aubrey thought that this was Jean Luc's end while Morgan wondered how his brother had managed to stay alive with someone like Black and his temperament.

They had been about to draw straws to see who would go back to the ship and check on Mala but now that the doctor was finally on his way, everyone breathed easier. Black leaned against a tree and pulled his hat down further to cover his face as he bent his head. Although he was clean-shaven and well dressed, his eye patch still caused others to be wary.

The doctor slowed the buggy to a halt as he neared the small group. Jean Luc approached him with his most winning smile. Giving a mischievous look in Aubrey's direction, he greeted the man in a heavy Irish brogue, "Top of the mornin' to ya."

Aubrey's head shot up as Morgan stifled a chuckle and Black growled with impatience.

"May I help you, sir?" The doctor asked looking over the others.

"Yes Doctor, we are in need of your skills."

"I was on my way home, sir. I have been out very early and am rather tired."

Jean Luc pulled out a pouch and dangled it so that the coins within jingled, "You will be paid well for your services, Doctor. Our friend cannot wait any longer. We would greatly appreciate it if you just took a look."

The doctor looked over the other three again warily but Jean Luc replied softly, "You will come to no harm, sir. We are here to personally guarantee your safety. You see, our friend is important to us."

"What ails your friend?" The doctor asked.

"A stab wound. Tried to stop a fight and got caught in the fray."

The doctor pondered this for a few minutes then nodded, "Very well, lead the way."

The doctor began to wonder his good judgment as he neared the ship that loomed over him. Jacobs expertly lined the longboat alongside the ship as Jean Luc assisted Aubrey to the rope ladder. Black motioned for Jean Luc to follow then he stepped up, leaving Morgan to assist the doctor.

As Jean Luc stepped over the railing, Aubrey leaned close and whispered, "There is no one around and it is too quiet."

Jean Luc's gaze swept the deck and found no one around as she had said. He turned as Black stepped onto the deck. The captain caught his wariness immediately and put a hand on the butt of his pistol. At that moment, Robert appeared from the companionway at the stern of the ship and he stopped when he saw the small group. From his face, Aubrey could tell something was definitely wrong. As he walked towards them, she also saw that he did not seem sure of his step. A knot began to tighten in the pit of her stomach.

"Surely, not everyone is on shore leave." Jean Luc asked incredulously.

"Ah, no sir." Before Robert could say more, another man appeared his head wrapped in bandages.

Aubrey looked back at Robert in alarm and noticed for the first time the rag in his hand that he was trying to hide. "Whose blood is that?" She asked hoping it was not Mala's.

Robert swallowed hard before answering quietly, "Mine."

Black, Jean Luc, and Morgan were already scanning the ship. Morgan noticed chips cut into the masts while Black and Jean Luc saw areas of blood on the deck. "What happened?" Black asked apprehensively.

"We were attacked, sir. The British..." Robert stopped and watched as Black ran towards Mala's cabin. As the others made to follow, Robert grabbed Morgan's arm and said quickly, "She is gone."

"Dead?" Morgan asked wide-eyed as Aubrey gasped.

"No, they took her." Came the quiet reply. Robert watched as Aubrey ran below deck.

Jean Luc turned to Morgan, "Get the men back to the ship. We must go find her!" Suddenly thinking the same thing, both Morgan and Jean Luc looked to where the warships had been. "Find out the names of the ships and their destinations. She must be on one of them." Jean Luc added.

Morgan nodded but a small tingle at the back of his head made him pause as he tried to remember the names of the ships before he barked out orders to Jacobs. Jean Luc turned to the doctor and said, "I am afraid you have more patients than we had intended for you, sir. Robert here will show you to the wounded." Turning to Robert, Jean Luc asked, "Any dead?"

Robert nodded, "Three."

"Where is Timmons?" Morgan asked Robert.

"On shore leave."

"Thank God! Get him back first if you can." Morgan told Jacobs.

Leaving the doctor with Robert, Jean Luc and Morgan headed for Mala's cabin. They found Black staring out the quarter gallery window and Aubrey was tending to Willie's head.

"Always said I had a hard head, Mr. Alcott. Guess ye be right." Willie said when he saw Morgan. The latter smiled weakly as he and Jean Luc saw the empty bunk. Sheets and Mala were gone. Only a small patch of blood could be seen near the edge of the bunk.

Following their gaze, Willie said unhappily, "I tried to stop 'em but there was just too many."

"Shh, you did fine, Willie. We will find her." Aubrey said soothingly, casting a worried glance to Black's rigid form.

Willie was shaking his head, his voice choked with emotion, "I will ne'er forgot the look on their captain's face when he saw her. His smile was too evil like he was the Devil himself coming for her."

Aubrey patted his shoulder and tried to soothe him. But Willie continued looking at Black's back, "When he told his men to take her, I tried to stop 'em. One of 'em must have hit me from behind and that was how Mr. Bates found me."

"Who would know who we are? I mean, Mala named this ship the *Enchantress* because no one would think she was a pirate ship." Aubrey asked, not realizing that she had said the same thing Jean Luc and Black had discussed earlier in the day.

Black turned and looked at the empty bunk. Before he could speak, Willie spoke up, "Well, I heard them say, 'We have one in here, Cap'n Alexander.' That was when the Devil himself appeared."

Willie looked at Aubrey as she dropped everything in her hands and sat down suddenly. "Not him." She said in horror.

At the same time, Morgan hit his fist against the wall of the cabin with a resounding bang, "Damn! We must get her back and fast." He exploded.

Black took their reactions in with keen interest. Aubrey was definitely upset while Morgan was blustering about Alexander killing Mala and something about vengeance. Trying to calm the situation down, Jean Luc turned to his brother, "See if you can help Willie to the doctor, Morgan."

Morgan nodded and helped Willie up. Once they had left, Jean Luc asked Black, "If he knew we were pirates, why not take the ship and wait for us?"

"He wants to play a game of hide and seek." Black answered as he extended one hand out to them. In it was a crumpled piece of paper. Unfolding it, Black said with disgust, "He asked how well are we at the hunt. To find her we need to find him." Looking at Aubrey, Black added, "He says to 'tell the little girl hello.'"

Aubrey's mouth dropped open and eyes opened with in surprise. "How did he know I was on this ship?" She asked.

"Bermuda, remember?" Morgan answered, having returned to the cabin. Then saying to Black and Jean Luc, "We ran into him while in a marketplace in Bermuda. It was all quite civil until one of his men demanded an apology from our cabin boy here. In the scuffle that followed, Aubrey lost her hat and when he took one look at that fiery mane of hers, …well." Morgan shrugged and gave them a rueful smile. "But he has reasons of his own for taking Mala. She gave the order for me to blow his ship, the *Majestic*, out of the water as we left Bermuda."

Black and Jean Luc both swore under their breath at that small bit of news. Alexander would have a very good reason to take and torture Mala. But Black knew another reason as he remembered his encounter with Alexander after the trial. He knew Mala's name then. Was that episode in Bermuda as innocent as Morgan believed or did Alexander manage to figure out who Mala was and know her by sight? The cabin was quiet for a few minutes while each dealt with their own thoughts about Alexander and Mala's fate in his hands.

Suddenly, Jean Luc went to Mala's cabinets, found her charts and began plying through them. "We need a plan."

As the men began talking, Aubrey slipped unnoticed into the corridor. Leaning against the wall, she closed her eyes and let out a deep sigh. Somehow Alexander had recognized her. Well, she was dressed much like she had when they were in Bermuda. But when did he see her? Was it going to shore or while they searched for the doctor? Well, somehow he did see her and knew that Mala had to be close. Instead of looking for them, he decided to wait on the ship and behold, he had found Mala.

With her head bent and tears falling, Aubrey whispered in the empty corridor, "Oh God, Mala. I am so sorry. It is my fault. It is all my fault!"

Chapter 61

"Well yer quieter than usual." Willie said as he sat in the galley watching Aubrey prepare the trays of dishes for the captain's cabin.

It had been hours since Black and his small group returned to the *Enchantress* with the doctor. Aubrey could not be still and decided to help Willie in the galley. The guilt of being recognized had built up within her that now her head ached unmercifully.

"And you should be in bed resting." She replied curtly.

He waved off her admonishment. "This is me room and no one gives me the boot from me own room." Aubrey gave him a small smile and Willie gave her stern look, "Tell old Willie what has ye so quiet."

She merely shrugged hoping he would leave it alone but his persistent stare and occasional nods caused her to smile. "Willie, it is really nothing."

"I will be the judge of that."

"Nothing." She insisted.

Having arranged the various dishes on the trays, she picked up one but Willie made a grab for it, "I will help ye with that."

"No, you are not!" Aubrey said sternly as she slapped his hands away.

Willie smiled and took the tray of goblets. "Ye have only so many hands, lass."

Aubrey rolled her eyes and clicked her tongue but allowed Willie to follow her.

In the great cabin, Jean Luc and Morgan had various charts out on the table and were going over several routes while Robert looked on. They had found out that Alexander was in command of the warship named the *Iron Prince*. Morgan was saying, " ...the *Iron Prince* was headed for Jamaica. One of the men was heard saying that they had to drop off their prisoners."

"We could stop there first..." Jean Luc started.

"Gentlemen, he does not intend to let her hang." Black stated casually as he sipped his wine. Aubrey placed the tray down which caught their attentions.

"Food." She said simply. "If you want more, send someone..."

"Are you not eating?" Jean Luc asked.

"No, I am not hungry at the moment." The men shared looks that prompted her to say quickly, "It is just that I have been cooking and the smell in the galley does not appeal to me."

"And you want us to eat this?" Morgan joked.

"I meant that I got my fill from sampling while I cooked." She retorted as she headed for the door. "Like I said, send someone if you want more." The door closed before anyone could say more.

Aubrey hurried back to the galley and sat where Willie had been earlier. Only then did she realize that Willie was not with her. Before she could wonder further, Robert appeared.

"The Captain wants to see you." He told her.

"There is no way he could have finished his meal that fast and want more already!" She grumbled.

"No, Miss Aubrey, he and the others have not yet started."

Aubrey's brows knitted together in aggravation. "I told them I would eat later." She stated angrily and waved him away. But Robert stood his ground and waited patiently for her attention. When he had gained it again, he smiled at her.

"What is it?" Her accent pronounced.

"The Captain wants to see you." He repeated.

"Sweet Mary!" She muttered as she stormed past Robert and out of the galley.

The few men in the galley glanced up at Aubrey's display of anger and watched her leave. When Robert caught their gazes, he smiled and shrugged but continued out of the galley. He caught up with her just as she neared the captain's cabin. He took the latch first, which earned him a glare, but he merely smiled and opened the door.

"You did not knock first." Aubrey said testily.

"He is expecting you." Robert said allowing her to step in.

Aubrey noticed that the charts had been moved to the empty bunk. At the reminder, her gaze fell to the floor and she felt another pang of guilt.

"We hear that you have been rather quiet. More quiet than usual." Black told her gaining her attention. Her eyes flew to Willie who just smiled at her and she pursed her lips to show her irritation at him. "Have a seat, Irish. We need to talk." The captain said.

Aubrey looked over her shoulder at the door and found Robert standing there with arms crossed and big smile on his face. Letting out an unladylike exhale, she grudgingly took a seat. Jean Luc and Morgan exchanged amused glances as Black covered a grin behind his hand. Aubrey saw only Black's reaction and felt an enormous urge to hit him. For a few long moments, the cabin was quiet save for the sounds of the ship.

"Aubrey, is there something you wish to discuss with us?" Jean Luc cajoled. Lips tightened stubbornly as she shook her head. "Are you sure?" He asked leaning forward and giving her a sweet smile. She nodded.

Black and Morgan were both finding the scene too comical and Morgan knew he would lose control soon. Black interjected, "If you are worried that he would harm Mala..."

Aubrey released a loud exhale of disgust. "Well of course, I am worried!" She snapped.

"Not eating will not help Mala either. When we find her, and we will, you will need your strength. You know there will be a battle. You do plan on going with us?" Black said slowly.

"Indeed I do!" She snapped.

The five men watched her quietly. After a few moments of uneasy silence, Aubrey could no longer stand the attention and broke down into tears. Jean Luc got up and knelt beside her. "What is it, paramour?"

Trying to control her voice, she replied, "It is my fault! It is all my fault she is gone!" She looked at them through watery eyes, "He recognized me! I was supposed to be a cabin boy but he saw me and knew me from before!"

"Actually..." Black was saying as he stood and went over to the desk. "He recognized me." He opened the logbook and picked up the crumpled note, they had seen earlier.

"But he left me that message!" Aubrey retorted.

"No, Aubrey." Black said gently as if speaking to a child. Morgan and Jean Luc noticed his use of her first name instead of the usual nickname. "He addressed this to me."

He waited allowing Aubrey time to gather herself and understand what he was saying. When he could see that she had understood what that meant, he held up the note in his hand as he stated, "Somehow he saw me and recognized me. This reads:

Captain Rene Black
It appears that the pirate Captain Mala has met with a
foul end. More is the pity, though I must certainly agree
in her present state of dress, or rather, undress. She is
certainly a beauty.

I am, however, going to relieve you of such a burden and
leave you her medallion as a reminder of who now possesses
the sweet Captain Mala. I will show her all the nice things a
beautiful woman should surround herself with—and that would
not be a ship full of men.

How are you in the hunt, my good pirate captain? Shall we say
the prize is the charming Captain Mala? Once she is well, she
would be the 'Enchantress,' do you not think so? What a sweet

535

*prize! So I leave you this ship—obviously hers. I believe yours
is off the coast not far from here. When you find me, should you
find me, Captain, you will find her. Do hurry, Captain. My appetite
to taste such sweetness grows as I gaze upon her. You may want
to consider that should you find us, she may no longer find you such
a catch!*

Captain John Alexander
Post Script
*Please express my sincerest greetings to the "cabin boy." Tell the
little girl hello for me.*
JA

Black held up Mala's misshapen necklace and said menacingly, "We all
know that Mala is currently in no condition to defend herself from his or
anyone's advances."

"She will kill him if he tried." Morgan said.

"She will kill him anyway. At the first opportunity to be sure." Aubrey
replied. Then under her breath, she said to herself, "Dear God, if he only
knew."

"Knew what?" Robert asked from behind her. She turned to find that he
had moved from the door sometime during the reading of the note and was
now so close to her that he had heard her.

"If only he knew what, Miss Aubrey?" He repeated. When she did not
reply, he said firmly, "I owe the Captain my life. In a fight, she saved me
from a sailor who came up from behind. I was already badly wounded and
she took care of me with her medicines. I had hoped to help her this time."
Aubrey looked at him then at Morgan and Willie.

Morgan said thoughtfully, "She really never told anyone about her battles
with British and why the *Majestic* was so important to her. I only know that
she wanted the *Majestic* and Captain Alexander at the bottom of the sea."

"I only know that her fight with the British was for revenge." Robert
answered then looked at Aubrey and said, "But she spoke with you for a long
time on that beach before we went into Charlestowne. She even cried and I
have never seen a tear in her eye, until that day Miss Aubrey."

Aubrey looked around the room and found everyone quite interested.
Black in particular was staring at her intently, "What did you talk about, Irish,
that would bring tears from Mala's eyes?"

With Robert back at the door, she could not escape this time. "I promised
her that I would never tell a soul. She made me swear." She told them.

Jean Luc still kneeling beside her and taking her hand into both of his said softly, "Aubrey, I know of promises and secrets but her life is in danger now, more so than from that knife the Scotsman had. There may be something in what she has told you that might help us find her."

"I do not think so." She said quietly.

"Perhaps it may mean nothing to you, but it could mean the world to us. There is so much more for you to learn about our ways. So tell us, Aubrey. What is it?" Morgan interjected.

"Irish, please." Black said quietly, his deep voice reverberating in the stillness of the room.

Aubrey stood up and turned away from them. She needed to think and could not do that with their pleading. If she were to tell, she obviously could not tell all of it. She could leave out the part about Baccus and no one would know she had left it out. That was something that had to be told by Mala herself to Black, if that was something to be known. On the other hand, Mala herself did not know the whole truth until that day they found Jean Luc, the day Deats stabbed her.

Deats! That Scotsman had fueled Mala's anger and built that wall between her and the man she loved by dwelling on her misconception of what had happened. Never did he allow her to find out the truth. Somehow he had even managed to drive a wedge between Mala and Jean Luc. Aubrey remembered Morgan's story about how they were at odds on the journey south after saving him from the hanging before Jean Luc rejoined Black on *Widow Maker*.

Perhaps Deats did not …No, Mala's fury towards him as they were in the longboat and could hear the swords was definitely livid. She fairly flew up the rope ladder to stop Deats from killing Black. Aubrey could hear Mala's voice once again as they sat on the beach talking about Rene Black, *'I hated him, Aubrey. But I loved him more, I still do.'*

Aubrey turned to find five men somewhat patiently awaiting her decision. That they had managed to remain quiet as she carried on with her inner battle surprised her. But they seemed to know and understand how she felt.

"What I am about to tell you now does not leave this room. Is that understood?" Aubrey looked to each man for confirmation. "Especially from you." She said to Black. He looked at her for a long time before he nodded in agreement. "God, I hope she does not kill me for this." She muttered as she took her seat again.

Motioning to a chair, she bade Robert to take the seat. When he was seated and all eyes were riveted to her, she began her tale from the time Mala was left on the island and the role Alexander played in her hatred for the British.

At the end of her tale, the room remained silent as each man mulled over those events and their memories of Mala. To Black, Jean Luc and Morgan, it was painfully clear why Mala had turned so deadly.

"It all makes sense." Morgan said as he and his brother exchanged looks.

"I thought she just wanted to tweak the nose of Death." Robert said.

"Actually she did, she was." Aubrey replied. Then looking pointedly at Black who was watching her, she added, "To Mala, she had lost much and felt there was nothing left. When she was made captain, it gave her a new purpose—taking care of a ship and a crew. But then it also gave her the means she needed for revenge." As Aubrey looked at Morgan and Robert, she missed the look of concern between Black and Jean Luc.

"And she did so well at all of them." Robert said softly.

"Aye, and as our captain, she gave us adventure." Morgan said.

"And treasures." Willie added with a smile.

"You remember the ship carrying the doubloons?" Morgan asked with a chuckle.

Robert nodded smiling, "It was the first time we played the ghost ship."

"I remember the stupid navigator telling the helmsman how to come alongside a ship." Morgan piped in. Willie and Robert gave a derisive snort of disgust.

"Nearly ruined a good meal." Willie said.

"Damned near rammed us and put a hole in our hull." Robert put in.

The men were smiling as they remembered that day. Jean Luc asked, "Dare I ask what became of the...navigator?"

Willie choked on a chuckle as Robert and Morgan laughed. Through his laughter, Morgan replied, "Mala decided he needed a swimming lesson. Told him that since he could not tell fathoms from leagues, then he should measure the distance from the ship to shore as practice."

"The lad then found himself in the water." Robert finished.

Black shook his head and with a smile, said, "Sounds just like Mala. She has little to no patience at times."

When the laughter died down, Willie stood up saying to Aubrey, "I will bring you a plate then I will clean up the galley."

Aubrey glanced at him then nodded. No sense in arguing about it. She was not hungry but she did not want to hear any of them scold her either. Robert decided to leave as well and followed behind Willie.

Chapter 62

When all was quiet, Jean Luc noticed Black was sitting quietly watching Aubrey. "Is something wrong, Rene?"

"As part of her revenge, I would suppose that was why she wanted me dead in Bimini?" Black said to Aubrey.

She shrugged and said, "I do not know. She mentioned that too but she could not follow through with the original plan as she had said. She had wanted you dead but did not really want to do it so she avoided you."

"Actually, I believe what happened in Bimini was Deats' plan." Morgan put in. "Deats and I were standing in the shadows behind you and he was impatient to see Mala strike you down. When she did not, Deats contemplated finishing you off himself."

Black sighed and Aubrey went on, "You must remember, Rene, at the time she believed that you had never returned for her. Deats reinforced those thoughts almost daily and I am sure added to them. The man was evil and had no thought for the pain he was putting her through. Remember the day I told you not to believe him?"

Black nodded as he remembered Aubrey's warning when he had tied her up in hold after Beaufort's murder. His attention was brought back as Aubrey continued, "Well, he lied to you about that, imagine what lies he told Mala. He wanted her for himself and resented your memory that she never would let go."

After a few moments, Black turned to Morgan, "When did you become a member of her crew?" He asked and wondered why he had never thought to ask before now.

"Sometime after Jean Luc helped me in the Colonies." He said simply. He knew of Jean Luc's promise to Mala that he would not tell Black she was alive and Jean Luc had obviously kept that promise.

Black nodded, saying absentmindedly, "Oui, your hanging." Then he looked at the crumpled note before him and was lost in his own thoughts. Aubrey caught the look exchanged between the brothers. She knew Mala had helped save Morgan as well. She looked closer at Jean Luc and thought he seemed uncomfortable. She would have to ask them about that.

After a few moments, Black's voice broke the silence again as he looked at Morgan and asked, "In Bermuda, did Alexander engage Mala in conversation..." He trailed off seeing that Morgan was shaking his head.

"Never spoke to the man. When they found out Aubrey's true gender, Mala decided to end the quarrel. All I remember was Alexander watching the

539

fight a short distance away. She recognized him just as we made a run for the ship. In the harbor, she saw his ship and ordered me to ready the cannons. She had been after the *Majestic* for a while and the only time we were close enough to it to take action, the *Majestic* had just sunk your ship."

The cabin grew quiet as Black digested this information. But Morgan added more, "You may as well know, Captain, Mala trailed you often. She spotted you as you raided that ship, possibly the one Aubrey was taken from. She would consider facing you but I managed to talk her out of it. I knew that to face you, only one ship would sail away. I guess that too would be due to Deats and his treachery. I never liked him from the start."

"If she trailed me often, then why did she let them take me off my ship and then sink the *Widow Maker*?" Black asked.

Morgan knitted his brows as he tried to remember what happened, all the while shaking his head in a negative fashion. His face lit up when he finally remembered the chain of events, "Mala was so angry with you and your time with Yvette that she ordered us to head for Santiago de Cuba even though you had not left yet." Smiling ruefully, Morgan confided, "She was so drunk most of the way there, she did not even realize that you were not behind us until we were almost to Santiago de Cuba. She ordered us to go back all the while keeping an eye out for you."

Black and Jean Luc exchanged glances as Morgan continued, "By the time we moored in the cove on the other side of the island so Willie could gather whatever it is he gathers for our meals, there were two warships flanking the *Widow Maker*. When the battle ensued, we went after Willie who had by then discovered Aubrey on the beach."

The men looked at her and she felt compelled to reply, "Jojoba threw me overboard to save my life."

"To save your life!" Jean Luc exclaimed nearly coming out of his chair. Black cast him a perturbed glance at the outburst. "You cannot swim! How the hell did that lunatic Jamaican expect you to survive that?" Jean Luc went on.

"Well, he did not know that I could not swim." Aubrey rebutted back. Jean Luc snorted in disgust at the thought of the man.

"You should have told him Aubrey, just as you told me." He said in growing anger. Black leaned back languidly in his chair and propped his booted feet up on the empty chair between him and Morgan. He had rested his chin in his hand and appeared to be watching the scene with amusement.

"I did. Just before he dropped me." Aubrey replied stiffly.

"See how you trusted him? He knew you could not swim, yet he tossed you overboard anyway."

Aubrey clicked her tongue at him, saying flippantly, "He did not toss me

Jean Luc, he dropped me, he was wounded."

"Wounded? Be damned, cowardly he was, putting a defenseless woman overboard during a battle." Jean Luc snorted again.

"I would not call Aubrey defenseless." Morgan ventured to interject ever so quietly. The three others in the room all turned their eyes upon him and he very nearly melted back into his chair.

"You could have drowned!" Jean Luc exploded again.

"Well, I did not. I am no ghost that is sittin' before ya!" Aubrey shot back, her tone heavily accented.

Black finally straightened in his chair, setting his feet back upon the floor and reaching for his tankard. He hid a smile as he took a sip. Jean Luc still could not forgive the man for accidentally leaving him behind. Setting the mug down easily he said calmly in a tone that stayed the pair of them, "Jean Luc, the man is dead. Let him rest in peace. He saved your woman's life. Had she remained aboard the ship, she would have drowned anyway." Jean Luc turned his attention full upon the man as Black added thickly, "Or worse! She could have fallen into John Alexander's hands."

Aubrey looked at Black as he spoke. Looking back to Jean Luc she nodded and said with a thickness in her voice, "That is exactly what he told me Jean Luc, when he put me over. He told me that he was doing it to keep the British from getting me." Jean Luc's blue eyes were cast down and he settled himself back into his chair.

Morgan suddenly asked, "Jojoba! Why are you angry with him, Jean Luc?"

The question brought back the memories of being left behind, half-dead and in much pain. Jean Luc growled deep in his throat as he glared at his brother, "He left me for dead when I was only injured."

"Well, you looked dead, big brother." Morgan said in defense of the Jamaican man he had known from his time on the *Widow Maker*. Both Black and Jean Luc stared at Morgan in disbelief.

Leaning forward suspiciously, Jean Luc asked in a quiet voice that Aubrey knew was bordering on unleashed anger, "And what do you know of that day?"

"It was not long after I joined Mala's crew. We were watching this fight from a hill when Mala and I recognized you and Jojoba fighting the British. She ordered us to fire upon the British and leave Black's men unharmed. The British thought it was reinforcements or such and retreated. When we checked for any wounded, Mala found you."

"She was the island woman who took care of me?" Jean Luc asked incredulously.

"You did not recognize her?" Black asked Jean Luc.

"Non, I was always so sleepy that I could barely open my eyes to see at all." Jean Luc replied as Black continued to stare at him.

Morgan came to his brother's aid, "True, Captain. Mala kept him drugged so that he would not recognize her. When he was well enough, she ordered a couple of the men to make sure Jean Luc made it back to your ship safely. I could not go in case someone recognized me."

"Mon Dieu!" Jean Luc said.

Black said at the same time, "She was so close again."

The cabin grew quiet as each thought of what had just been said. Black remembered Mala telling him about sending those troops into the bordello where he and Jean Luc had slept most of the time. He looked at Jean Luc then to Aubrey. No, now was not the time to mention of that day when Mala was close, Black thought as he cleared his throat.

"Morgan, you had said that Mala trailed us. Actually, the lookout spotted the *Enchantress* several times. Her solid red flag was a mystery. We had no idea if that was friend or foe." Black idly toyed with his tankard on the table and not looking at anyone. He again missed a quick exchange between the two brothers.

A thought struck Black as he looked at Jean Luc then faced Morgan again. "It was Mala that day I thought I saw her in Jamaica. But I thought she was dead, so I had put that to wishful thinking."

Morgan smiled and replied, "Aye that was her. She was rounding the corner when she spotted you. She turned so fast, I nearly collided with her in her effort to get away."

Black stared at him for a moment and then said with a mischievous smile, "Following her a bit close that day, Mr. Alcott?"

Morgan returned the smile, "If you had gone all the way down that alley, you would have found us out. A tall fence that separated the back areas of the buildings trapped us. Mala got drunk that night too. She kept saying that it had been too close for comfort."

"Mon Dieu, she was that angry with me that she could not trust herself to face me." Black said, shaking his head.

"She saved your life that day, Rene." Morgan chuckled. Then looking at Aubrey, Morgan said, "Until now, I did not understand why. I remember the days on the *Widow Maker* and your last night together on that island." Morgan winked at Aubrey and with a devilish grin added, "He made us late leaving the next morning."

Black gave Morgan an exasperated look, then asked, "Who had engaged Mala in that battle near Jamaica?"

Morgan looked at him perplexed and Black added, "We heard the battle but the watch was the only one to see. I remember the ship with the solid red flag and another ship firing cannons at each other. Then a British frigate appeared but the larger ship did away with it in short order. But during that short time, Mala escaped."

Morgan shook his head thoughtfully, "I remember a battle but I had been in the town gathering our men. Mala had some trouble the night before while looking for Deats and got one of those feelings of hers. Before dawn, she ordered me to find the rest of the men and meet her at the rendezvous point. I saw her fighting back and when she picked us up, I asked her about it. All she said was the captain was a crazy Frenchman who fancied himself the world's gift to women."

Seeing the confused faces around him, Morgan shrugged and added, "I have no idea. She refused to talk about it anymore."

Jean Luc glanced at Aubrey who was looking at the cupboards. Remembering where Black had kept his logbooks, Jean Luc caught her eye and shook his head slightly. Aubrey was puzzled at his reaction. Mala's logbooks may have some information on that.

After a few moments, Morgan spoke up again, "You may as well know too that Mala did away with the *Lady Elizabeth*. Since that ship was with the *Majestic* when they sank yours, Mala assumed that it was the command ship."

"It was the command ship and I was on board her. It would seem that the Lord Admiral was suspicious of Captain Alexander's actions because of his hatred towards me. The man actually struck me in front of the Lord Admiral." Black said in reflection.

"According to Timmons and Robert, the Lord Admiral was on board the *Lady Elizabeth*. Timmons told me that when Deats saw him on the deck issuing commands, Mala just walked to the rail and shot the man."

Aubrey was confused then about the attack on the *Lady Elizabeth* and now she was confused at Mala's deliberate act of murdering the Lord Admiral. "I still do not understand why we pretended to be a ghost ship before Mala fired on them if that ship did not fire on the *Widow Maker*."

Morgan smiled and replied looking at Black, "To Mala, the *Lady Elizabeth* was just as guilty as the *Majestic* for our good captain's death even though she was already hunting for the *Majestic*. She was avenging Captain Black here since she could do nothing for him or the *Widow Maker* during the battle."

Black remembered accusing Mala in Charlestowne for not helping him after she admitted seeing the battle. She was right, it would have been suicidal then but she had found a way to avenge him. Before he could dwell too long on her actions all on his behalf, Aubrey looked at Black and asked, "Why was Captain Alexander looking for you? Mala mentioned that he was demanding the chief to turn you over to them but, of course, you were not

543

there."

All eyes turned to Black who gazed at the wooden tabletop. His reply was thick with remembered emotions, "It appears that Captain Alexander had an uncle once. This uncle was influential enough to have aided his nephew through his military career. Somehow Alexander managed to find out that I was responsible for the man's death. You see, Irish, his uncle was the captain of a ship named the *Dodger*. We found Mala on that ship, beaten, starved and almost dead."

Aubrey remembered reading in Black's logbooks that Mala's name was tied to the ship, the *Dodger*, but Mala never knew the name of the ship.

"So it comes full circle." Jean Luc said absentmindedly. "Mala was taken from her home by the uncle and now she is taken from you by the nephew."

Aubrey watched the dark scowl come over Black's face as he looked into Jean Luc's eyes and said, his deep voice in anger, "Aye so it does. Fate placed Mala into my hands that day and this time I will take great pleasure in taking back what is mine."

There was silence for a time before Morgan said quietly, smiling, "You and Mala are so much alike, Captain. In her angrier moments, I would swear I was back on the *Widow Maker*. You taught her well." Black did not smile at the younger man's humor as Morgan continued, "But when she thought you were dead and had on board whom she thought was your latest conquest, she drank. Willie told me after the sinking of your ship, Mala was in the galley before the change of the early morning watch. She was drunk and staring at a necklace. Willie said he never seen her that bad before. If I were a bettin' man, and I am, I would wager that she was mourning for you."

Black looked into his tankard thoughtfully then asked Morgan, "Did she get drunk often?"

Morgan chuckled and came to his feet. Passing Black's chair, he slapped Black on the shoulder as he replied, "Only when you were around and were with other women."

Black looked at Aubrey and once again felt relief that he never was intimate with her. "What about Deats?" He asked.

Morgan gave a disdainful snort as he took another bottle of Mala's rum from the cupboard, "What about him? Mala told me once that he tried to get very familiar with her but she put an end to that quick enough. He had a scar to remind him how much closer that knife could have been."

"I saw it." Black said.

"She held herself to you and your memory until you boarded her ship. Though I swear the man acted like a male dog after a bitch in heat in the meantime."

Aubrey was taking a sip of water at the moment Morgan spoke. Hi blatant comment made her choke and the men laughed as she dabbed her wet chin. Morgan handed Black the rum and the bottle was passed around the small group while Aubrey still declined the drink.

"No slur meant for Mala, Irish. Only that the man was adamant in his pursuit for someone who did not want him in return. You better get used to that kind of talk if you are to remain with us and not be embarrassed every moment of the day." Black said with a chuckle.

Although it angered him to think that another man would desire her in such a way, Black remembered the first night he had made love to Mala on the *Enchantress*. So much time had passed since then yet their joining was as always, all consuming as if it was that first time. He let out a sigh and looked to the bunk, willing Mala to be there. But it was empty and the sadness of her disappearance—no, kidnaping—weighed heavily on his heart.

The newly found friends sat at the table, drinking and talking. Aubrey sat and watched Black became less of an ogre and more of a man in pain. She remembered his sadness on the *Widow Maker* and now understood it. They would play this silly game of Alexander's and they would find Mala. She just hoped the game would not last a long time.

To Be Continued……..
(Coming soon, RB: The Game)